WINTER GODS & SERPENTS

THE AURAN CHRONICLES

WENDY HEISS

Second edition. ISBN: 9781739169657

Heiss Publishing

Book over Illustrator: Fantastical Ink

Original line editing: proofreadebook.com/ **Roxana** Coumans

Map illustrator: BMR Williams

Interior formatter: Lizzy Heiss

Re-proofread (March 2023) by Bree & Jessica (Blue press editor)

www.wendyheissauthor.com

This is for you, for those that feel too much, those that feel nothing and those that want to feel something.

PS: Mother, I am twenty four and do know about birds and bees, but I am sorry you had to find out like this.

Note from author
Content Warnings

Gore, death, murder, vulgar language, torture, self-harm, violence, emotional and physical abuse, loss of loved one, depiction of panic attack and PTSD, mention of slavery, flogging, scars, mention of rape (no scene or explicit description).

THE AURA

Thousands of years ago, eight prime gods of Ithicea descended on the realm of Numen. Taken a like on the human lands, they bestowed the realm with gifts and blessings of their own powers. Amongst their blessed were the Aura—humans veiled in god alike magic, true believers and humans of true hearts deemed pure by the gods.

THE ELEMENTALS

Order of the Sun

Aura blessed by goddess Cyra of sun and healing

Glare

Medi healer

Magi healer

Bruma Caste

Aura blessed by god Krig of winter, war and wisdom.

Verglaser

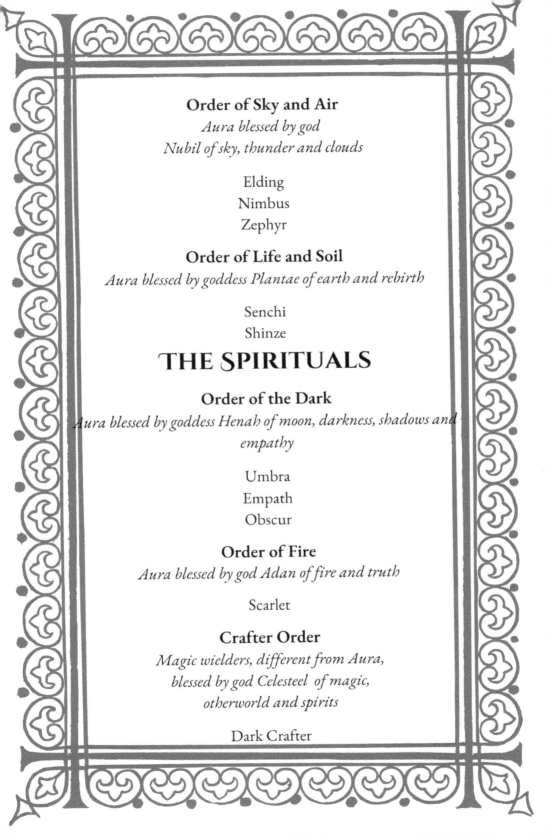

Order of Sky and Air

Aura blessed by god
Nubil of sky, thunder and clouds

Elding

Nimbus

Zephyr

Order of Life and Soil

Aura blessed by goddess Plantae of earth and rebirth

Senchi

Shinze

THE SPIRITUALS

Order of the Dark

Aura blessed by goddess Henah of moon, darkness, shadows and
empathy

Umbra

Empath

Obscur

Order of Fire

Aura blessed by god Adan of fire and truth

Scarlet

Crafter Order

Magic wielders, different from Aura,
blessed by god Celesteel of magic,
otherworld and spirits

Dark Crafter

SOLARYA

Theros

SERAPHIM

Heyes

Hollow Sea

OLYMPIA

My

Moor Sea

N

NW   NE

W   E

SW   SE

S

Comnhall

VRAMMETHEN

GAR✝H

DARDANES

Casmere

Brogmere

Isline

Seer Sea

ISJORD

Venzor

Tenebrose

Koy

Modr

Grasmere

HANAI

ernfoss
Village

Sable Abyss

Brisk

Aru

Kirkwall

HIGHWALL

Arynth

lmarnock Forest

Asra

River Nyx

ELDMOOR

Sitara

Heca

ADRIATA

*Sea of the
Dark*

yra

Sidra

Part I
Nightmare

1

Nightmares and Kingdoms

Snowlin

Patience was the virtue of the dead. My pulse thumped frustrated in my temples, proving I was indeed alive, and that this quest was not suited for me.

I tapped my foot impatiently on the broken wooden floor of the empty room, the sound following the pace of my bored breaths. Something echoed. I could not make out whether it was my foot or heartbeat, but it was loud enough that I could not concentrate. How could you break someone? I had learned the way of blood and steel, but some ran on venom and dressed in scales.

The hollow dark room lit only by small cracks between the old broken walls filled with ragged breaths and gold dust that shimmered between the odd rays of light filtering in. Smell of autumn penetrated inside, the air tasted of chestnuts and chimney smoke—melancholic.

Do not kill him. My friend's order had been clear, but was I one to usually obey?

The man in front of me had dropped his body forward, too fatigued to hold upright. He sat tied on a half broken wooden chair, his short yellow hair matted in blood and grime, blue eyes covered in a blanket of fear and surrounded by violet bruises. His blue uniform had almost turned black from the dry crimson blood he leaked so generously, no trace of the wolf crest of Isjord anymore on the rich wools he wore.

He'd only stared at me in insatiable anger ever since I'd tied him down. Unwavering, as if I were his prisoner. His features tightened, he turned red and let out a groan of struggle while he shifted his bound hands again trying to conjure magic.

"It won't work," I said pointing to the craft halo around the room—the dark magic binding him powerless. "Your magic is nullified within these walls by a Crafter." The man was an Aura. A human veiled in godlike magic. This particular one was an ice Aura, an elemental magic wielder. A Verglaser.

I took a seat afront him. "Pretty far from your borders, haven't you heard of the monsters in the mountains?"

He spat in front of me, mouth twisted into a snarl. "The only monster we found there was you, princess. Wait till your father learns of you, he shall be most satisfied."

He would be. Greatly. It was what he'd made me to be after all.

I shook my head. "He won't ever find out. All your comrades are dead and dying some scorching deaths. Living proof that you are not stiffs of ice, it happens you melt, pleasantly even. And please, no one with this face could be a monster," I said, leaning in and fluttering my lashes.

He shook in his chair, tugging on his bindings. "You're a psychopath."

"I consider it an attribution not a fault, but I am one with very thin patience. What were you doing in Myrdur?" I asked sternly at the loss of will to spin in circles.

Isjordian soldiers had not been this far into the fallen kingdom of Olympian for decades. Not since they had been the wielding hand of their destruction. The night of *Draugr*. Like eudemons, Isjordians had crept inside Olympia between the curtains of night and shadows, through the autumn wind of November and the silence of peace, armed to their teeth. They'd burnt and massacred the lands while Olympians rested unprepared under the impression of the protection treaty that had been established earlier that day when they had finally settled an agreement of peace sealed by the marriage of the Isjordian King to their princess, my mother.

"We were looking for you," the soldier revealed.

"That, dear, is a poor piss lie. Father knows where I would be and that is certainly not under the caves of the Volant mountains or the ruins of Myrdur. I am no blind bat to nest there." He knew, more than knew—father had chosen where I would live my exile, right where I had been for the past twelve years.

The soldier remained silent after my words, his jaw ticked from anger while his eyes dug daggers onto me. In his head I probably bled, but there was no blood in my veins anymore, just rage and hate. I would leak black. Or perhaps not at all.

I cocked my head back, surveying him. "He wishes to occupy the lands? Finally gathering the courage to face the souls of those he tarnished?"

He only laughed, shaking his head without answering me.

I clicked my fingers and leaned forward. "Has Isjord ran out of gold? Coming to mine it here?"

"We need no gold. Gold comes to us."

Ah yes, the famous tagline. "You're looking for something," I stated, and his attention dropped to the floor, turning expressionless. "Interesting, what did you lose in the mountains, soldier? Aren't you aware the spirits haunt those that chase and search on these lands? Are you that desperate as to tempt their fury?" Myrdur was cursed, roaming with restless spirits that preyed on anyone who dared disturb their resting place, no one had a remedy for it. Neither had my father, who had not touched these lands after he destroyed them.

"They cower before us—their demise, they still cower to our greatness."

Standing, I unsheathed the dagger from my thigh. Being rude to me was one thing, being rude to my ancestors who were dead because of them, quite the unforgivable other. The soldier's eyes widened, and he began shifting nervously on the chair. His feet wiggled trying to break free while he leaned back to meet my tall stare. My blade licked at his skin, digging into the hollow flesh of his face and he began shivering.

"If you are this scared, might as well give up your secrets," I taunted, flipping the cold decorated steel through my fingers.

His features tightened in challenge. "You will not spare me anyway, so I will carry them with my death."

My brow rose. "So, there is a secret." I dug the dagger cutting a line through his cheek and he let out screams of agony and pain. A stream of red leaked from his face, pooling beneath my feet. "There are two deaths in this realm. One that will hurt and one that will really, really hurt. Pick wisely. Though I'd be partial to number two, for optimal entertainment," I said, digging the blade once more tracing another wound.

The door behind me opened loudly, interrupting. "Snow, gods and heavens. Alive, we need him alive. You cannot get handsy with him just yet.," the strong, frustrated voice of my friend called behind me.

I turned to the tall, buffed figure that approached to grab the dagger out of my hand and sheathed it back to my thigh. "Only a little."

He scoffed. "I know your little—your little dead is a lot dead."

"And we only need him a little alive."

"A lot actually." He pulled me outside, the bright light fogged my sight making me slightly dizzy. I had been in that dark room for far too long.

Tension tightened every muscle in his face and body, his emerald stare darkened with concern. "We found the rest of his squadron by the ruins, very eager to protect what they knew. They slit their own throats before I could even capture one. If we want to find anything out, it will have to be through him." Cai was not prone to displays of frustration, he was known for his calm demeanour, but I read it there along with devastation. They'd come again, to soil the lands of the mightiest people that had existed in this realm. The lands of his people—our people.

I huffed a sigh and turned to him. "Isjordians will never speak, their blessings are to thank." They were people of war, tactics, wits, and schemes, but most importantly, they were people of god gifted honour. To them, death was better than betrayal.

"They could be here for you," he stated half-heartedly, blatantly avoiding meeting my gaze.

"He knows exactly where I am, he would have come for me, formally. I am still a royal." By title. In armour I was still a monster. In truth, a human woman, and in my father's eyes still a pawn.

Cai threw a puzzled look behind the Volant mountains, behind Myrdur, the fallen lands. Staring into the dark clouds gathered atop and the thick mist surrounding them, letting nothing show in sight. A blanket of omens and elder magic. "There is nothing left for him to barge into here again. These are no-man's lands, graveyards. No one has claimed them. Not even him who destroyed them."

The small hair on my neck rose and I threw a wary glance over the tall giants of rock. My guardian called it a sixth sense, Cai called it paranoia, but this time he'd given into it. The mist dressing the old Olympian mountains called to me, a warning whispering my name. And I saw it stare back at me—the dark cloud of terror that had enveloped the air, land, and sea. It had a scent. Bitter and tangy like poison, metal, and fear.

"There are no lands he cannot have, it is power he is looking for. Whatever he thinks he can find here, I want to find out. He can harvest power even from the dead, let's not lower our guards," I warned.

Upon both our heavy sighs, bitter memories and fears creeped in my thoughts causing blood to pulse and thrust in my temples in a drumming beat, and slowly, air began meeting my lungs with difficulty. Before I would be sent begging for air, before my eyes would cloud black, before I would see my whole world spin and shift onto the void, before I would tremble and drop to the ground clutching my chest in pain—I moved. Unconsciously, striding in quick paces toward the forest.

"I will come with," Cai called, following steps behind.

I swallowed a clog in my throat. "No, I just need a few moments." Maybe more than just a few. My day nightmares were clocking longer than they usually would. It was terrifying to confess that they were no longer containable. Now, I felt my head warp so deep in my thoughts that once it had taken me a day to gather myself fully.

"Return quick or Nia will hunt you down," he called again, his voice fading in the distance.

The moment trees had surrounded me I took a deep breath and with their own volition, my feet took off in a sprint through the brick coloured forest floor. The gusting sharpness and friction of the air almost scraped my skin, it moved the towering trees like wandering spirits and pulled my hair against its current. The moment my feet carried me to a pace, my eyes fogged as my surroundings engulfed in dark black flames, creeping through branches, leaves and air, crawling towards me, hungry for my taste, to burn and devour me. The smell of burnt flesh and screams tore the heavy air, retching, pleading and fearsome as my face twisted in a cry. I shook my head to rid the drowning thoughts and plaguing memories. But I felt it then, in how my limbs trembled, the oily shame and fear that hit me as my chest clutched in disgust from my own actions. Again and again, I would experience it—having left everyone behind to save myself. It was my punishment for the past twelve years, and I had accepted it with open arms.

Strange dark shadows began following me from all sides, their mouths hungry and dark steel claws itching for blood, my blood. A shudder went through my spine when I felt their heavy presence nearing me, their flesh leaking a darkness of a void, pooling all around them like tar. My heart caged not from bones, but from fear and frustration, a hot emotion that I had felt without halt for the past twelve years, since the night my mother, sister and brother were killed by the same monsters chasing me, led by him, the Adriatian King. The famed *Obscur Asteri*, ruler of night and my hunter.

The edge of the forest became visible, it laid ahead like a painting in a dark corridor. Trees cleared out and two blue landscapes crashing onto each other came into sight. The marbling sea water and floating sky blended in a marvellous painting, and I halted before the cliff, my breath catching and my chest bursting with fire. Reality began shifting, it warped in gusts of black smoke and mist. I breathed in jagged pants taking in what laid in front of me as the monsters approached. Pushing my shoulders back, I forced myself to look at them like I always did before they disappeared.

One moment they stared pure darkness into my soul, the next they started turning to nothing. There were no ghastly wicked creatures chasing and hunting me, the monsters staring back were those of flesh and blood, they were men, one of the worst kind. Since the night twelve years ago, I've tried to outrun these creatures who once haunted me and hungered for my death—twelve years had passed since the feeling of guilt and mourning corrupted my whole being. Once physical, these monsters were now just remnants of nightmares. A cursed prison of thoughts.

The smell of burnt flesh was now taken over by that of chestnuts and salt, the screaming now turned to only rustling leaves and crashing waves. The brief momentum of returning to my reality was accompanied by a razor-sharp pain dulling across my palms and up my arms. Metallic taste and the smell of blood creeped in my lungs and my gaze dropped down to my hands now leaking of blood and smearing the paled leaves under me a crimson colour.

Pain—the wrong cure for panic, but a temporary remedy to forget it. It was wrong, but there were so many other wrongs with me.

He would come for me. My father would soon come for me. My curse for being born in a castle of darkness was to always be surrounded by nightmares. He was the largest darkness in my life, and he had cast all my nightmares. Because of him, all evil had followed in a chain motion. The fall of Olympia, the continent's fear and uproar, the attack, my mother's and my sibling's death, my exile. A mourning child sent away to another foreign land only days after the people she loved most died seemed the perfect plan for my father.

The useless one survived? Gone till she can serve me something, away from danger, away from bringing any to us, were his exact words. Exactly what any daughter craves, such affection for his orphan. Almost ridiculously funny. I would have laughed had those words not gnawed at me for months when I was a child. My uselessness was what I had thanked the heavens every day, it would be his sweet torture. My uselessness was his failure, but it was also mine.

"I do not like you doing this anymore, not when there are soldiers of all kinds hovering around Fernfoss, and it is not Isjordians I am fearing," Alaric's voice startled me from behind. He was right, I had been so endorsed into my own head that I didn't even hear him approach.

Alaric was my guardian, my mother's closest friend. An Olympian. He had accompanied her to Isjord after her marriage and stayed as her guard. He had become my family since the moment I was born, and after the attack my father had sent me with him into hiding. He was the only one I would ever recognize as a father. Alaric did not have big shoes to fill, but he was exceptional at being more than just a father figure. Even though the stern bastard willed my nerves out of my brains sometimes, I loved him more than anything or anyone.

"That is exactly why I need to be here," I said, approaching him.

He let out a heavy sigh, rubbing his paled grey beard. "I need you to be scared, Snow, you become reckless when you have no fear."

Fear was a lie, the shackle of submission. I submitted to no one. "I am reckless however. My father thrives in the fear of others, I will never give him the pleasure of feasting on mine and as for the Adriatians," I said, a grin drawing wide in my features. "Of them I truly am not afraid, their courage will soon be their fear."

"You're determined to return to Isjord then?"

He was coming for me. My father would soon end my exile and I'd soon end my hibernating vengeance. "I don't have a choice."

Distress shadowed his black irises. "I know this feels like it's your responsibility, to deal with him and guard Myrdur, but it truly is not. The soldiers could be after what everyone is after in these lands. Relics, bones, gold, glory—"

I shook my head. "Not him. And I owe these lands, Alaric. We cannot run and hide forever. What I can do is chase him down and what better way to do it then inside his castle as his daughter and right so close to Adriata, too."

His expression soured. "Isjord is filled with worse than your father, Kill him and you will leave that throne open to them. Do you really even think you can kill him?"

"No, but there are worse things than death, old man. I will not kill my father, I will kill Isjord. What is a king without a crown but breakable?"

"Isjord—"

"Is powerful," I interrupted. "And I am very keen in learning all about that power, every nook of every battalion, fleet, exit, entry, and passage and then I will gift it all to those who wish to be more powerful. Solarya, Hanai, Eldmoor, perhaps even Vrammethen. Aren't I generous?" Twelve long years I had to simmer, sift, and stew my rage, hide my vengeance, and plan my move. I had no place in his game of chess, and a princess was not a piece in that play, but it was a start.

"Some will not appreciate that generosity."

He was right. Not many had the courage to face Isjord, but they had the spite.

"I only need one. With a fleet, an army and courage to take my father, and I already know more than one." I'd spend those years studying every kingdom and every ounce of their resentment to Isjord. Solarya craved the status that Isjord occupied with their power over the continent. Hanai longed for unagitated peace that Isjord denied with their hunger for more power. Eldmoor coveted the vast lands of Isjord with desire to unfurl and feed their magic. And Vrammethen, the unblessed lands, those barren from like and touch of gods, demanded recognition, if not from the heavenly, from their blessed.

"And Adriata?" he asked, knowing who rested first on those that had wronged me.

"For them something sweeter." For them I had patience. With them I'd waltz.

He sighed. "You are no longer a child to be lectured, but as someone who has raised you I have the right to say that this vendetta will not heal your wounds, Snow. Even the mightiest wielder of a sword has bruises and calluses from the weight of steel."

Nice words old man, falling onto bouncing eardrums. Unlike him, leaving the past behind was not something I was able to do, and forgetting didn't come easy even if I wished for it. "You could be right, but I will find that answer myself. If it only mends parts of what they broke I am willing to bear new scars. And those wounds don't hurt nearly as much as the ones they gave me," I said pointing to my chest. "Not to mention my pride when they gave me this," I added, pointing to the scar running from the middle of my cheek down to my neck.

He held a moment of silence before letting out a laugh that surely didn't meet his eyes. "Your beauty is uninjured, though it might soon be. Nia has been growling around looking for you. That girl is vicious."

Shit. Nia. "Fuck. Shit," I blurted, closing my eyes at what I had forgotten.

"I didn't teach you that."

I scowled at his scolding. "I am twenty-three, you old man."

"You never grow in my eyes."

I cringed. Sentimentalists, the epitome of 'I might make myself sick' thoughts. I planted a kiss on his stubbly cheek. "With Nubil's blessing, to Caelum heavens," I greeted, two fingers in my forehead, two in my heart. Mind and soul, the holy greet.

"With Nubil's blessings, might it welcome us. Be careful," he warned as I sprinted down the forest to Fernfoss village to find Nia.

Tonight was the autumn festival, the blessed celebration and its outdated traditions annoyed the life out of me, but Nia enjoyed them severely. And as a fool, I had given her my promise over a very drunken state. For someone as righteous as Nia, I was surprised she held onto that semi-unconscious promise very tightly.

The village was buzzing with excitement and preparations for the celebration. I barely managed to dive through the crowd of people that had gathered, but made out Nia's figure from afar, along with the drawn in angry expression.

"You promised, I even convinced that idiot to come just so you would," she sneered.

"I am here, aren't I? And Cai will be very disappointed you called him an idiot."

She rolled her eyes and pulled me inside the seamstress house. "He knows what he is."

2

PINS AND NEEDLES

SNOWLIN

THERE WAS A NOISE—LIKE a hive of bees or a silent tempest of thunder. My hearing gurgled with it as I stared through the large pane of the seamstress shop overseeing the heights of the Volants dressed in fog. Words, sounds, screams and noise. Maybe all of them together, but I could never make out what it meant or said, I only knew my skin prickled and all my senses vibrated in warning. It had never happened before—to be called by it. Two years now, endlessly, it drew my attention.

"Does it still call to you?" Nia asked, and I dragged my attention from the Volants to the floor before the mirror I'd been propped afront.

"Sometimes," I said, taking a deep breath. A lot of times. It felt like part of me, part of my thoughts. Sometimes it brought me out of sleep, out of nightmares even.

I yelped. A pin pierced my skin. "Do not speak of spirits and mist, girl, one might hear," the elderly seamstress whispered the warning, looking panicked.

"One does not care if one might hear."

She scowled. "One should fear if the Olympian souls call to you and I am not talking about the spirits." Her eyes hovered around the room as she leaned in to whisper, "Isjordian soldiers are here."

I leaned in close to her and whispered back, "So?"

She frowned, her greyed brows pinching in. "There is a price on Olympian heads, Aura or din-Aura."

All those of Olympian blood will be banished from the world of living, those had been my father's orders. It had been the first time I'd read an ounce of fear from my father. He'd been afraid they'd rise and come for him, claim the head of the famed killer king.

"I am not an Olympian."

"But the mist calls to you," she stated, confused.

"I am half Olympian," I explained, adjusting myself slightly under the dress, afraid the pins would poke me again. "Half Isjordian."

She stumbled back, her mouth parting open in somewhat of realisation. There were no half of this or that in Dardanes. There were only normal people and then me. Most would never believe me if I muttered such words. At times I'd amuse myself by telling this story to everyone just to see if there was recognition of fear amongst their reactions. Fear, I was taught to feed on it.

Her clear blue eyes drew wide. "You are Alaric's child."

I dismissed the reaction and smiled at her words. "Yes, I am Alaric's child."

She bowed her head, lowering to a curtsy before studying me in a stunned stare—a stare I knew too well. "But you are beautiful."

"Well," I said with a shrug. "*Ybrises* are still human." An *ybris*, hybrid, that was what most called me. Child of two Aura.

She avoided my gaze and began adjusting my waist. "That is not what I meant," she said, tucking in the fabric. "That man is everything but able to raise a girl. How has he not made you grow a beard or shave your head and swear like a huntsman?"

"The latter I should not hold on too hopeful," Nia muttered, fiddling with some lace behind me.

"How do you know Alaric?" I asked.

"Signe wleg rroz gha." We all know him, she answered in Calgnan—Olympian tongue. She took a deep breath and folded my sleeves. "He helped my family settle over Whitebridge in Solarya when Isjordian soldiers were looking for survivors. I only returned a couple years ago when my husband died. I figured I'd like for my bones to rest where they were born. Myrdur was my home."

I swallowed, remembrance filling me with guilt. "It was of many."

Her finger went under my chin, lifting my gaze to hers. "To many it will again become, grandchild of Jonah, greatest king of Olympia. Have faith, Eldingchild, your bloodline rose from where no light ever saw the dark, between clouds and sky, from earth of rock, and from there one day might it once more rise." She offered me a smile and patted my cheek before crutching to fix my hem. "The *zgahna* awakens to you. It is a sign from your ancestors, one of warning."

My eyes met Nia's in the mirror only to be interrupted by the loud bang on the door. All thought of the magic mist flew away in the presence of the smug fool.

"She did it," Cai said, leaning in the door, enveloping the whole frame with his stature, a victorious expression painted on. "Made you look like a maiden."

Nia snorted. "I don't do the work even gods failed to do, but she is a decent version of that. If she keeps her mouth closed for longer than two seconds."

"The 'scowl don't voice the offence' doesn't really do it for me."

"*Mlla malaght, Lena,*" Cai saluted good day to the seamstress, and took a seat by Nia on the sofa by the wall.

I blinked rapidly. "You know one another?"

Lena sighed and wore an irked expression. "He dallied with my son a few times. *Mlla malaght, rrahgan.*"

Nia and I blasted in howling laughter and Cai crossed his arms bewildered at Lena. Rake—that would not be the best word to call him, but it came somewhat close. He was a free spirit, the realm was his canvas and he enjoyed colours. Who could blame him for that? But I could blame him for the nonchalance he showed to those erased from his canvas. And he did grow out of like for a colour quickly.

Lena clicked her tongue at him. "Broke his heart that one."

Nia patted his shoulder. "Growing a following with your promiscuous behaviour."

Nonchalant and unbothered, he crossed his ankle over a knee. "Your son is a grown man, Lena. He knew he was 'dallying' with a...*rrahgan.* He also seemed to enjoy my *rrahgan* ways."

She huffed in annoyance and went to her work table, noting down where to take in the measurements.

"What did she bargain to have you convinced to attend the festival?" I asked, striking a stiff pose when a pin dug on my back.

He gradually smirked, throwing an arm over Nia's neck. "The pleasure of seeing you being taken measurements for a dress."

I swung round with a sneer, and then yelped at the prickle of pins on my skin. Nia sunk on the sofa, her mouth tight, suppressing a laugh.

Cai waited for Lena to leave out back before he revealed, "There were soldiers seen close to crossing our border, they will rest by the village, probably attending the festival. I will follow them towards the ruins."

"Nia," I almost shouted. "When I told you not to fade into Isjord it was an order not a suggestion." Nia had grown a penchant for pushing the tolerable limits of safety and I did not enjoy it. She was Adriatian born and an Aura, she could take herself places even kingdoms apart with a thought, but before she'd never tried even crossing Fernfoss. Cai was probably feeding her the unnecessarily dangerous courage she'd grown lately.

"It was only for a minute," she grumbled as though it justified sense to her reckless-ness. "I needed some frost thorn and winter cress. The village herbalist is closing. Not that he had much there anyway."

"Her salad trips are useful, too," Cai added.

She frowned at him. "They are herbs, you fool, not lettuce."

He fluffed the crown of her head, her dark coils springing free from the bun atop her head. "Grass is grass."

She didn't laugh or reiterate. Cai was the master of word games and she knew not to enter that unending trap.

I blew a long exasperated breath, refusing to meet eyes with myself in the mirror. I wanted to laugh, too.

Nia stood, her hand on my shoulder, a reassurance she had felt what I did through whatever bond she'd magically tied between us some odd day by mistake. "I know you hate this, but I don't. And it might be the last one you attend. You know he will come for you eventually, his soldiers are already looking around in bunches."

End of my exile approached yet there was no sign of it. "I'm beginning to doubt that. Apparently, mountains spirits and ruin stones are more to his liking than I have ever been."

"The Crafter said in her visions you were in Isjord."

Dark Crafters were magical humans, different from Aura, their gifts were bestowed by a spiritual god, Celesteel, of magic, underworld, and spirits. They were able to summon another type of magic from the elementals, drawing power from the realm of their god—the terrifying realm Caligo also known as the Otherworld, land of the dead. Dark Crafters were able to manipulate and influence extraordinary magic—strange magic. Such powerful people were now growing rare century by century, their god had grown angry from the immense power being drawn from his realm that he had only let his true followers to be able to do so. A couple weeks ago, one had shown us her visions of my return to Isjord—the end of my exile.

"She said between snow, blood and a dark castle." Did I mention that they were very vague in their wording?

"Sounds about the Isjord you have described," said Nia.

"The witchling could have been wrong," Cai meekly threw out there, but I knew there was hopefulness in those words that I would not return, that he wouldn't have to accompany me back to his own land of nightmares.

"Could have been, but they never are," Nia said, straightening a pleat on my dress with some scrutiny. "Maybe you return without him sending for you."

I shook my head. "He has to ask for my return and end my exile, the only way he will not doubt my intentions—the only way I won't end up in a dungeon. Before I was a child with a grudge and now a woman with revenge. He will not underestimate me, not unless he thinks of me as a child with a grudge still, and for that, he has to invite me in himself." My eyes went to Cai who had fallen silent, staring a hole onto the ground. "Then we begin—then we ruin Isjord."

His stare rose to mine, and I offered him a smile. He stood and ruffled my hair. "Be on time," he said to me and then turned to Nia. "Don't let her run before or she will make you very late."

Laying back on my bed half ready, I could hear Nia shuffling around in her dress and fluffing the skirts. I propped on my elbows, too tired to stand and my breath halted at the sight of my pretty friend. Her beauty shone like moonlight through a cloudy night sky, easily the most beautiful woman I'd ever seen. The white short sleeved gown hugged her waist, accentuating her generous bust and soft curves, the ones I still was very jealous of. Pleats dropped in layers to the ground, the pearlescent white made her beautiful dark skin radiate. Her curls propped up to the back of her head with various beady pins giving onto her soft gentle features, and a long red sash tied loosely around her waist.

It was then my smile fell again.

The sash was a tradition of the autumn festival. Maidens that wore it were chased around by the unmarried men to court them for the rest of the festival night. A tradition I detested, but would never outgrow the satisfaction of outrunning all the men that would chase me.

I rolled to my feet, my white dress draped over my legs and fell barely touching the ground. Different from Nia's, the dress I wore had long sleeves and a neckline that came close to my neck. I was used to my scar, but it often made me easily recognizable. Not only attracting danger, but curious attention which to me was worse than that. My hair was loose, almost touching the end of my back. I thoroughly disliked having my hair tied or trapped in pins and contraptions, it made me feel restrained. It made me feel as if the hands of that man from the night of the attack still had hold of me. Nia did not know that, but I could feel her stare poking a hole in my head.

"Only one pin, Nia, no more."

She could not hide her smile when she started rampaging through her pins to find one to use on my hair. She loosely braided two thin pieces of hair on each side of my head and pulled them together at the back with a pin dangled in loose pearls and emeralds.

"There, have a look."

I turned to the object a moment too late as she was already guiding me to the mirror. Caught by surprise by my own reflection, my eyebrows drew in. I looked too much like her, my mother. My own reflection mirrored a painful memory. My hair was the darkest shade of black falling in waves just below my waist, just like hers. My features were slightly softer but everything else was a side-by-side copy. My eyes on the other hand, the colour of honey, a bright deep yellow. I hated them, they were so unnatural and they made me look like him, my blessed father. Everything on my face served as a reminder of someone I lost and the cause of that loss. Nor my eyes or my face bore a reminder of as much as the scar stretching from the middle of my cheek to my jaw and towards my collarbone and shoulder. A flesh carved reminder of what I had survived. I could almost feel it leaking blood as if fresh. Five counts, five breaths and one look, that's all it took for what stared back at me to warp into something of nightmares. My reflection resembled a black shadow, a floating lifeless creature of mist. Darkness and wrath. What I saw staring back at me...I hated it, like I had always.

Sensing I was lost in a deep perusal, Nia pulled me face to face with her. "Do not allow anyone to cloud your view of yourself, Snow. You know you are more than what they made you be and done to you." She let out a deep sigh, frowned and went on, "Even though that person staring back at you is terribly beautiful. Now let's go, you might not be worried about finding a lover, but I am starting to."

I pulled a smile saved only for her and kissed her cheek. "Now let's not go and frown for pity reassurance, not when you wear a face like yours. And since when is miss 'I hate all people' looking for a lover?"

"Since now," she almost squealed. She had always found it hard to lie, she was too sincere for her own good.

I traced a line above her brows. "Nia, your forehead literally folds in half when you lie."

"I didn't lie and I don't hate all people."

"Mhm."

"Fine," she sulkily admitted. "There is a writer from Asra travelling the continent. Jeremiah from the village council said she is coming tonight to witness the Autumn festival for her travel diary. I wanted to meet her, she has written some of my favourite books."

"You know there is romance outside books, too?"

"I don't care for that, not when it is so beautifully done in writing."

"Alright my hopeless romantic who doesn't like romance, shall we be any more late?"

"Says 'the lust is romance' woman who is the reason we are late." I had gone for a run before meeting with her, and she would hold a grudge about it forever.

"That is because just like you, I know men only love you back in those books. Pretty words fade, the caress lessens, there is no fluttering heartbeat when you look at their faces and no desire to have their heart, only what stands between their legs."

She frowned. "That only means you have never been in love."

"I'd think I would have found one by now, the moment they open their mouths is the moment it reminds me it might never even exist." The dizziest a man had made me was when they stared at my breasts long enough to have my eyes roll so far back my head they had forgotten to return.

"It exists, one who has never been in love can never write books like the ones I've read. Speak like that and never have not experienced it, even if for a short moment."

"It is hard to find it, not imagine it. Now let's not make you late. I bet you're dying to be lied to by that author."

Nia slapped my shoulders viciously. "You cynic, some faith wouldn't kill you."

Faith kills a lot of people, I had no desire to end up a martyr.

3

AUTUMN AND FIRE

SNOWLIN

THE FESTIVAL TOOK PLACE at the edge of Soren Forest, just above Fernfoss village, where it had taken place for the past few years. A foreign tradition brought by nomads and travellers of other lands that had settled here fearlessly after Olympia had perished. All around Fernfoss, the only habitable location in Old Olympia, was surrounded by people from every corner of the continent, even some from the continent of the unblessed lands, Vrammethen.

Your grandfather would cry tears the size of glass shards, Alaric had said once we'd arrived in Fernfoss. *If he saw who resided in his solemn lands, we'd see him cry for the first time in history.*

The forest appeared grimmer at night, it had gone deadly quiet. The only noise and light omitted were from the festival that grew between a scarce patch of trees. Crowds gathered towards the food and game stalls. Several men and maiden were sitting in tree logs in front of the hot crackling autumn bonfire, toasting on ale and chatting their way to each other's hearts. Tavern maids had relocated into small tables, serving food and drinks to the festival goers. Flushed red from work, they boomed with energy as they circled around the busiest day of the year.

Just outside the perimeter of the celebrations, I could spot Cai's dark brown head hunched over on a log, drinking. His mother's emerald stone pendant left to him after she'd died in childbirth dangled by the brush of wind. Different from Nia and I, Cai was born and raised in the lands of Old Olympia, to him this was home. He never got to see Myrdur, at least not to remember, but he often sat amongst the ruins and ran his hands over their silhouettes, imagining what it would have been. He'd walk around there for hours, picturing himself amongst his people that had perished while he'd been barely two—held by his grandmother in a deep cave in the Volants while his father had been killed fighting back in the attack.

Alaric liked to call him lucky, one of the very few that had made it out, but Cai had different words for it: gods' sour sense of humour.

Nia pulled my arm, dragging my attention to her. "I will get us food and drinks. If you even think of tricking me and going into hiding I will hunt you down myself. Remember, fun can be found outside the bedroom and away from bloodied knives, too."

"Never found it anywhere else," I murmured to myself, overtaken with an itching rash I got when surrounded by people.

She shook her head and left, approaching a group of people into conversation. Cai hadn't yet noticed we'd arrived, probably credit to the white face veil that all women young and old were wearing as tradition. Men were to follow us in the chase without knowing who we were. Archaic, just like the idea of women wanting to be chased by men only. I'd like to be chased by a woman—I'd like to be chased by many beautiful women. Why would we be chased in the first place? We were not elk to be made venison.

I shook my head from thoughts and headed towards the edge of the celebrations, taking a seat next to Cai. Noticing he was startled, I threw an elbow to his stomach. "Who else besides me and Nia would approach a lone loser like yourself?" Snatching his goblet, I lifted the veil and took a sip. The sour taste hit my mouth, throat and then stomach, causing me to wince.

He chuckled silently. "All those brave words yet your body betrays you."

I dared take another sip. Some numbness would help tonight go quicker. "Just why are you sitting out here, you look happier when I make you chase me through the woods."

He turned to me, emerald eyes piercing through mine while he took a big gulp from his goblet. Once, that stare had made my stomach flutter. "I could ask the same or are none of these gentlemen worthy of your royal arse?" A smirk lifted on the corner of his mouth all tease he wanted me to fall for. He and I have been friends for the past twelve years, at one point we tried our luck at being more than friends, but it never felt right. The flirting had always left us with a cringe. We kissed the night of my seventeenth birthday while on our way home from our run in the forest. We were both confused and agreed to never speak of what had happened, not that I particularly wanted to recall embarrassing moments.

"Certainly they are not, you better than anyone would know that," I said quietly, taking the goblet from his hand and gulping down the remaining ale. A wash of dizziness hitting me.

He turned the empty cup over. "Nia will kill me if she knows I let you drink."

"You will die a solemn death. She will bury you pretty to honour that face you love staring in the mirror for twenty-three hours of a day. Her wraths of daisies are unmatched."

He raised a brow at me. "What about the other hour?"

"The body of course, any new dents of muscle in these past twenty-four hours?"

He wrapped his arm around my neck tight and rubbed his fist on the crown of my head making me yelp from the burn. "I'll let you know tomorrow if that exercise worked."

"You fool," I accused, straightening my hair. "Nia will really kill you for ruining her work."

He brushed his fingers through my hair in an attempt to help. "You tell her I did that, I tell Alaric you broke his precious ebony cane while play pretending to be him in front of a whole tavern."

My mouth twitched into a grimace. "You have yourself a deal," I said, extending my hand and he shook it in agreement.

"The Isjordian man," I asked cautiously. "Did he give anything away?"

He shook his head. "No. As you said, torturing an Isjordian is pointless. Alaric is there trying his feat now."

I knew it would have been fruitless, but I was ruining the mood already. Today was a celebration, one that could help drag our heads out of my father's mess. Standing, I extended my hand to him. "Now, shall we see how we can entertain you for the rest of this miserable night? Men and women are lining up for you as per usual and all the staring is starting to annoy me. I don't get the simple mind of man." The side prying eyes were really beginning to irk me. Men and women equally fancied Cai all around, no one could blame them, but he fancied no one except himself. Great at self-love, terrible and very unintuitive with the love of others.

He puffed his shoulders back. "Simple, just have one look at me. It was enough for you."

"Caiden—" I called sternly at the joking fool.

Standing, he towered over me with a smirk full of tease. "And the full name returns."

I groaned, annoyed at having brought this up again. "I was seventeen, you were a teenage girl's dream and now you are a grown woman's cringy memory. Might I remind you since we are calling old days that you kissed me back? Several times?"

"Yes, moment of weakness," he said in an insouciant shrug. "You never look much in the mirror, have you forgotten your face can make a man weak in the knees?"

I snorted. "So much for weak, not a day later you went out with that forger's daughter and then the barmaid. The cherry on top was that merchling boy from Comnhall." That seventeen-year-old girl had been upset, not heartbroken, but upset. The twenty-three-year-old woman was understanding. I, for one, could not hold a flower alive let alone a romantic relationship. Nia and Cai were my family, if they had not become that, we would have not become anything else.

"I am not good with matters of the heart, Cakes."

"I have noted. Could have made the point by telling, not showing me."

"It will be a good story to tell your poor future husband and my nieces and nephews."

"Yeah, yeah."

He threw an arm over my neck and we headed toward the crowd. The fire was crackling loudly, only drowned by the laughter of the festival goers. The forest surrounding us was growing eerie from the shadows of the trees dancing along with the flicker of the flames from the bonfire and the noise echoing through its air corridors.

Nia spotted us by the game stalls and headed towards us. We both tensed to her reaction when she noticed what we were doing. This girl was indeed vicious. "You are not seriously going to play that?" she asked in disbelief, looking down at the knife I was holding preparing to throw at the red tree log target. "You do that every day, I brought you here to do something new."

We *did* do this every day. Alaric trained all three of us religiously everyday as if we were to head to battle the next, but not very oddly I enjoyed it, and for me this was pure entertainment. Concentrating on something else besides my own head was sanctuary—safe, calming sanctuary.

"As?" Cai asked, hitting a target.

"Eat, sit by the fire, converse."

I shook my head. "The more I talk to these people, the more my love for animals grows. This is fun." I threw the knife hitting the sweet spot of my target. "Look, fun," I added, facing her again with a full-on grin. I could use a dagger better than a spoon.

She shook her head and looked over to Cai who was doing the same as I, his face pulled in a tight smile stretched almost ear to ear.

"I have to take her now, the chase is about to begin," she said in one breath, grabbing my hand and dragging me towards the crowd of girls waiting for the signal to rush through the forest.

I turned back, shooting a pleading look to Cai, but he only laughed and leaned to the stall, crossing his arms and probably enjoying this more than he should. "Good luck, Cakes, you know even I can't save you from her."

He was right, Nia was sweet and gentle at the same time fierce and demanding. She was determined to learn the normal way of living, that she'd never had before, and I'd promised to help her till the day of our last breaths. We had sealed the promise with the still lingering cut on my thumb and then mud, which had infected it, earning both us a mouthful from no one else, of course, but the very delightful Alaric. Having to go through this was way easier than having to fight her head-to-head. That would waste me a whole good week from having to use all my mana to hold her off from killing me. Nia was terrifying in sparring, the blade was never of concern, she could rip your organs out with her hands and then lay them down to build you up again. Alaric originally sent her to train as a healer thinking she had a faint heart for blades, but she'd shortly come back a fighter with intense detail on how to carefully pluck a heart out between the ribs without hurting yourself. So, there were three people I truly feared: Cai, Alaric, and Nia. To my luck, all three were on my side.

We made our way to the forest edge. The autumn wind brushed my neck and I shuddered. Maybe it was just revulsion. Women wore beaming white gowns and floated above the juniper floor that started the forest. Red sashes loosely tied around their waists and in a similar fashion, a white cloth was covering half their faces, only leaving eyes and forehead exposed.

Nia quickly wrapped a red sash around my waist and threw me a look that told me not to object. So I expressed my dislike the best I was allowed. I rolled my eyes, sighed, and let her continue. The drum sounded and all the maidens ran ahead, laughing and chatting through the thick of the dark whistling forest. Nia grabbed my hand, pulling me to a run till we faced and stood alone with the branched giant alders of Soren surrounding all our sides and our shadows.

She let go of my hand and warned, "Don't kick anyone too hard or Alaric will have to go down to the village mayor to apologise again. For the one hundredth time this week."

"You have my word."

"Then I have nothing, gods spare us all," she said, and disappeared away from my sight, enveloped by darkness.

My eyes cast heavenward, the single moon no longer shying between clouds, it had cast a halo on the tree crowns and darkness to our shadows. Glittering, tiny flower and moon folk jumped around in jigs, celebrating the night as they passed old grumbling enchanted oaks who demanded peace of rest. Like little children, they tickled and teased the ancient creatures restless and I could help but laugh. Shy forest spirits sprinted past trees, rustling leaves and chattered truths of those they brushed against. They said one could speak to one's soul. A trail of gold specks travelling the air was the only proof they even existed.

Love, they whispered and giggled. *Oh, so much of it, young love.* Gasps of their small voices shrieked in the air and I knew they had sensed me. *Frost, sour frost, and...death.*

I scoffed. They never had anything else to say about me but that very sentence. "Good to see you, too, little busybodies." I heard the swift wind bellowing escape they made away from me and I was left to the silence of the forest. Between cooing and the rustling of leaves, I heard steps approach me, and within seconds a massive black cat nailed me to the ground, licking, growling, and purring.

"I missed you too, Memphis," I said. stroking her fluffy pitch-black mane. My most trusted companion was a morph from the lands of Aita. A creature that took the shape of various animals, blessed by Dyurin, the god of all animals, with gifts before ascending to the heaven of Neith. She was a gift from my mother on my tenth birthday, one that I have cherished more than anything. My companion since the days in my father's kingdom.

I managed to stand and stroked her head, her eyes a piercing pale yellow, often reminding me of my own. "Ready girl?" I urged, before taking off in a sprint with her shortly after me.

I ran, wind whistling in my ear, the forest grew thicker, my arm brushing branch after branch, my thighs burning and my feet tingling at the excitement of touching the ground. I felt free but caged at the same time by the oddly familiar emotion. Even if I was untouchable, unreachable, even if I was stronger and powerful, fear crept in every broken fragment of my being.

Strange arms wrapped around my waist from behind pulling me from my thoughts, grabbing me mid-air and thrusting to the ground along with them. We rolled on the ground from the impact, my head throbbing and my hands flat on a man's chest.

I lifted my head to meet his gaze and an angry scowl framed my eyes.

"Are you alright?" he said in an oddly quiet voice that angered me further.

Alright? My luck with idiots was grand, they popped in front of me like wild mushrooms. "I was. Before a boar toppled me to the ground." Removing my hands from his chest, I managed to dig a knee on the ground and hoisted myself up.

A rough laugh left his chest and he propped himself on his elbows, eyeing me from top to bottom before meeting my glaring gaze. I almost unsheathed the dagger hidden in my boot offended by the audacity to look this calm after plunging someone to the ground with no obvious reason.

"Surely better being toppled by a boar than eaten by that beast that was chasing you," he said, all severe and worried.

Confused, I looked around, and when realisation hit me I turned to him. "Not every maiden is assumed to be in need of saving, dear. Surely, you do not think I would not be able to handle a beast on my own?" I said, straightening my skirt, hoping he would give me an answer as smug as him, reason enough to plunge my knife inch deep in his throat.

He stood, almost two heads taller than me, the silver moonlight paled the long golden hair that was pulled back from his head, his black eyes shone a flickering black fire and a few day's stubble adorned his face. He bowed his head slightly. "My apologies, miss. That vile creature had me assuming the worst."

My eyes widened in offence. "That vile creature also belongs to me, so you now owe both me and her another apology for jumping on your own rushed conclusions."

A roar erupted the silence of night and tree branches rustled in our direction till gracefully Memphis came into view, growling in his direction. She stalked past him and nestled around my back, her head just under my arm as I stroked the top of it.

He looked at me confused, shooting glances between myself and my morph back and forth. Before he could speak, screams and laughter surrounded the air and our attention shot towards the two women running from behind bushes, giggling and chatting amongst themselves as two large men hoisted them up to their shoulders and pulled their sashes off as part of the tradition. That meant the women were theirs to court for the rest of the festival night. Both waved towards the man who had just tackled me, clearly familiar with each other despite never seeing either of their faces in Fernfoss before.

"Do you think we have spotted her yet? We don't even know how she looks exactly, not that it would help, they all look the same tonight," one of them asked the man in front of me.

"Simply bad timing, we will continue in the morning, tonight we rest. Stay away from the ruins, I don't wish to take back a halfwit dazed by spirits," he responded.

"I don't know if I even want to find her at night. They say she grows claws and her teeth extend like those of a wolf," the other man said with a shudder. "I have not the slightest idea why the king wants to bring that demon back. What did the Adriatians call her?" he frowned, trying to remember. "*Ybris*, yes, the hybrid."

"Enough," the man in front of me called sternly. "Call a royal such words one more time and I'll toss you to a real demon."

Demon. *Ybris*. I was both of those, yet I was not.

The man assessed his words in a revolted and repulsed manner and begun to insist, "But—"

"Would you like to sleep by the ruins?" The man before me snarled and the other two bowed their heads lightly and dispersed. Soldiers, bounty hunters?

My sash felt loose, and I turned to find the man in front of me holding it between his fingers. "Do I have to hold you up my shoulder?" His head pointed to the men walking towards the forest. "Or will you kindly walk on your two feet along me? You are mine for the evening," he exclaimed gleefully, making it more a statement than an offer.

This man would already be choking on his blood if not for my ill-timed moment of panic. I turned towards the men who had the women still up on their shoulders, looking to prove what was chasing me. My prisoners or my killers? They had their scabbards still fastened at their hips, facing the same direction, and dressed in an almost similar fashion. As I neared them closer, the man stepped behind me, followed by Memphis who most certainly had detected my thoughts through our bond. My eyes rested heavy over their attires and the familiar insignia they were carrying. A blue crest adorned the shoulder of their shirt. A wolf at its centre, two arrows crossing behind it and draped at the sides with golden vines. Isjord crest, my father's kingdom crest. They were soldiers, Isjord patrol guards, and they were here for me. The Crafter had been correct, I would return to Isjord after all.

A hand wrapped around my wrist. "If you are going to run from me, at least let me have your name. I am Elias," he introduced.

And I would be his gravestone would he not let go of me. My eyes darted to his shoulder, the same crest resting there. Had he noticed who I was? Surely not, I had left that kingdom barely eleven years of age, I had outgrown that child years ago and my face was covered, my scar was covered. No recognition had lit his eyes either. I was sure he thought of me as no other than one of the village women. Ignoring his question, I whistled at Memphis who shifted into a black mare and jumped onto her back, riding towards the festival gathering. As soon as the first flickers of the bonfire lit into sight, I noticed Cai's figure shifting around uncomfortably.

I lowered down from Memphis and ran in his direction, his eyebrows pinched in worry similarly as mine were, all our fears had now come for us, it could no longer be avoided.

"Cai," I called breathlessly, reaching him.

He flickered his hand up, a navy envelope between his fingers with the red arrow seal of Isjord. "Noted their saddles, a wolf crest carved in the leather and found the letter of permit for your return."

"They came." Realisation had just hit me.

4

ICE AND COIN

SNOWLIN

NIA HAD SPENT THE past half an hour tracing countless maps for our journey. She was fastidious, meticulous, and dizzying at best. It bothered her, being unprepared or caught at odds that could have been prevented by planning. She counted our moves step by step, over and over till Cai dozed off beside me. Then repeatedly rearranged her satchel as if there was a proper way to arrange one. The paradox within our friend group were Cai and Nia. While she'd prepared herself almost for battle, he sharpened his blades leisurely, fiddled with a loose bunch of hair atop his forehead and then proceeded to complain of a headache that the concertation to fix it had given him. And there was me, the referee. I'd sat silently between them, my head going back and forth between the two poles. I'd yawned, laughed, concentrated, and then gone for a last run around the village.

We had to avoid the main roads. Nia was Adriatian and Cai Olympian, both without proper identification tags. If tested by a Magi-healer, a Solaryan magic healer Aura, they would both be revealed.

Cai approached the table, fastening his scabbards, ready for the long journey ahead. His brows drew in and he cringed down at the map atop the table. "Who drew this violation of ink on that poor paper?"

Nia's head popped up like a hen. "I did."

He picked the map up and blithely nodded. "Immaculate detail, remarkable tracing, the shading close to spot on, are we using this perfect example as our map?"

Nia frowned. "You are holding it upside down."

He blinked rapidly and turned the paper around carefully. "Cartographers like to view their maps upside down as well."

Nia rolled her eyes. "You are still holding it the wrong way round."

"And sideways, did I mention?" he said, turning it once more. He threw a glance at me, noting that I'd bit down on my lip to suppress amusement. Warm tears were ready to sprout at the exchange as I motioned my finger round in the air. He quickly glanced down at the map and made another turn to the correct way round.

"All nine cities have been traced," Nia said, blowing a tired exhale. "Exits, tunnels, secret chambers, and streets. Alaric has noted all of them for us. Once we reach Venzor, I will replicate them for you two."

What we had planned was beyond dangerous, and if we were to get caught, what Nia was reserving would not even be used. We were to infiltrate perhaps the toughest and most strict court in Dardanes, there were no odds to our favour and no escaping if we were found, my father would execute me with his own hands.

"How will we know to direct ourselves with these?" he murmured in my ear.

"They are for her, not for us. Since when have you and I held onto a map? Let her have it."

He nodded. "Agree, agree."

Nia clapped her hands together and the both of us startled to attention. "Shall we go over everything again?"

Cai sunk in his chair, rubbing a hand over his tired eyes. "Hot air of summer, spare me."

Once Nia was satisfied with her work and Alaric resumed his blabbering cautions and advice, we left Fernfoss. We were on the road only a few hours after the festival, giving us enough time to ride at least a day ahead from my father's soldiers. By the time they would receive word from Alaric that I was already gone we would be in Venzor.

We crossed Old Olympia's border before sunrise. Our familiarity with the forests made it easier to navigate through the night, but the moment we stepped on the cold and snow-deep land of Isjord we grew weary. The meek sun had met its match against the pristine blinding ash of frost. Isjord was the land of eternal winter. God Krig blessed its lands and bestowed people with his gifts, having taken like for these lands before ascending to the heaven of Hodr. The lands were not the only that had received this said blessing, but their people as well. Verglasers, ice Aura, who with ease controlled, created and wielded the element. Gifted was an understatement. Verglasers were viciously powerful, and my father had battalions of them. Along with their impeccable art of war, their army of skilled fighters and ice Aura, my father had earned great leverage when he marched all them together to the doom of Olympia. The kingdom who he had feared, loathed, and envied all together, the one who he had thought stronger than himself, the danger he had to eliminate. Those whose power he had wanted for his own, the power he had wanted to mix with his own to create beings of unseen power, hybrid Aura—me. Yet he had failed, miserably. That was his weakness. The insatiable greed for power.

To someone who despised the cold with all might, this was not a blessing, winter was a damn curse. Miles ahead laid only stark scenery, barren fields, white mountain ranges and towering coniferous forests all covered in dense blinding white snow and ice. The road ahead wavered like a mirage from the white infinite landscape painted ahead like a blank canvas. I was born in Isjord, but twelve years away had made me forget my dislike for its frozen bristling air that was razor sharp against my cheeks, for the prickly and numb feel of my cold fingers and toes, and the damp flakes that coated my hair and eyelashes already heavy with sleep and weariness.

Cai rose a hand above my head and shook away the snow coating atop. "What will they think when they see their princess looking like a scruffy village boy?" he teased, breaking the deafening silence. "You know Isjordians are known to be pompous bastards."

I flicked a bunch of half wet hair back. "You will find the better side of the coin when you see my father's face at this sight."

Isjord was a powerful country, even its smallest cities had riches far more than any bigger city in the continent of Dardanes. Its people were known for lavish lifestyles and polished governing systems that made sure this was maintained. My mother had never been fond of such extravagances and had not particularly encouraged us to participate in its glories, greatly displeasing my father who was perhaps the most pompous bastard of them all. If I got to see my father the least displeased, it would bring me great satisfaction, one which I have tended to indulge since I was a child.

"That is absolutely not how this is going to go," Nia jumped, bewildered at the thought that I might be tempted to actually do just that. "We are heading to Venzor first, bless the heavens, and will fix that. You are their princess, Snow, you need to be seen as one."

"What do you think he wants?" Cai asked absently.

To use me, kill me, torture me again. The list could go on and on. I could well be leading myself to a trap. Problem was that to find out, I'd have to fall for it first. "Whatever it is, it will be nothing I will like. I am worth nothing to him. If he wants my return, he must have found use for me after all."

"You are still the crown princess, the heir to the throne."

His words made me laugh. "He will outlive gods before he passes that title to me. My brother was different, father adored him, raised and treated him like a future king," I explained. "He despised me—a powerless disobedient child. He'd rather pass it to his bastards than me."

"What if he still hopes you have magic?" he asked wearily. "To want and torture them out of you again?"

"He knows what he will find. Nothing." What he'd failed to find through years of torturing me.

Venzor laid only merely miles away when we noticed the unending city walls that stretched for miles ahead. A terrifying giant of stone, steel, magic, and frost. The grey stone walls towered the landscape for miles, breaking the ghostly white scenery. Sentries were heavily armed and dispensed all over the wall and gates, the blue coats hovered around ready for any unwanted visitors. We showed a letter of passage stolen from the Isjordian soldiers, necessary if anyone wished to enter any city in the kingdom. Since the night of the Adriatian attack twelve years ago, my father seemed to have raised security measures around his cities. More than occasionally on our journey, we'd spotted sentries patrolling the main roads, forests, and city outside parameters.

Nothing had changed from my last visit to Venzor from when I was a child. Wooden cottages and buildings with onyx stoned roofs spread and heaved like wild mushrooms beyond the city walls. The air was warmer within them and filled with the smell of cinnamon baked goods and burning wood. People paced hurriedly in their furs around the streets, attending their business, moving as puppets, their attention heavily concentrated on their work. Only dogs rose their heads and noses at us, but even they did not bother paying any more attention than that. People of Isjord were grown used to visitors, these lands were the main connection between the six blessed kingdoms, no one could enter the other without stepping in Isjordian soil first. The kingdom had profited richly from these circumstances. Venzor was even more surprising visited on feet, the cobblestone was warm beneath my soles. Magic cursing through it to keep the city warm. Isjordians were not affected by the cold, but it made Isjord suitable to foreigners who loathed the freezing temperatures. A large proportion of Isjord was foreigners, manual labourers, and many more skilled artisans. The population had been in decline for hundreds of years bringing the decision to open borders to other kingdoms.

After having our fill of food in a small tavern and locating ourselves in an inn for the night, we headed for the city. Halting afront a printing house, Nia and Cai dispersed to their business, leaving me alone. A bell chimed as I pushed the door open, and a white head popped up from beneath the dusty oak counter.

The old man adjusted his specks. "With Krig's blessings, how could I be of assistance?"

My eyes hovered around the walls filled with news pamphlets, the shop completely ordinary. "I am told you can fake letters. Trina sent me to you."

His eyes shot wide and he moved quickly, hovering around the windows before shutting the door tightly. "Hells, no one told you that business is not to be said out loud for patrols to hear?"

"Apologies," I said, narrowing my eyes on the many newsletters spread all over the tables.

"What letter?" he asked nervously, lowering his specs down to rub the bridge of his nose.

"An identification letter."

He pursed his lips and shook his head. "Letters, pumpkin, not the impossible. I do not fiddle with allowing criminals from wherever you sort are onto Isjord."

"Patriotism is a poor substitute for coin."

"And coin is not worth a hanging. I forge simple letters, if you have nothing of the sort, the door is behind you." He pointed, putting his specs on and shuffling through pamphlets.

"Your wife did not say so. She bragged to my friend vastly about your skills. Ten years she said, you've been forging the unblessed as Isjordians. She was very proud of you. Didn't she have lovely red hair? She also offered to read my friend's hand. A Crafter in Isjord, how impossible. How illegal," I provoked. Nia had oiled the barmaid for information, but she'd spilled beyond extent and very happily, it had made her so dizzy she'd complained of a headache all the way here.

He smacked the papers down in frustration. "Mad woman, she'll be the death of us both. How many and for whom?"

I gave him all the instructions to work on Nia's and Cai's documentation. My father would not allow a soul in his castle that he did not feel safe having there.

I drummed my finger on the glass counter. "Could you recall forging a birth certificate for a lady called Helga Larsen about eighteen years or so ago?"

He blinked confused at my request. "I would not remember; memory is rusty you see, with all the words I put down every day."

I threw ten pieces of gold dar on the table and he smiled.

"Any other detail?" he asked, chucking the coin in his pocket.

"A brothel owner, here in Venzor, called Iris Meadows. The bastard children are of someone high up in the king's court."

"A general," he recalled, cleaning his specs with the edge of his shirt. "That woman could not keep her mouth shut for the heavens. Yes, I do remember."

Well, well. "Do you happen to have a copy?"

His expression pinched in concentration and he raised a finger at me before heading around the back. Moments and rustling sounds later he returned, blowing dust atop a document before handing it to me. "I always keep a copy if they decide to return for another. May I ask what you need it for?"

I eyed the document with relish. "A good luck charm in befriending the general. I will pick the documentation in the evening. Good day to you."

He laughed and nodded. "I know who you are."

"I know who you are too. *Signe oşh feh erycht.*"

"We will see again," he repeated back in Calgnan.

5

SERPENTS AND DENS
SNOWLIN

WE CROSSED THE CASTLE walls and gates followed by my father's soldiers. Everything around gave me a feeling of unease. Nothing had changed. It was almost as if I had never left.

The castle grew in sight, a dark grey stoned giant between century old conifers that barely allowed light to enter the premises. The grey walls of the castle were dull, several high towers spiked towards the sky, highlighted by the large rounded red tinted glass windows that stood out like spilled blood amongst the blank snow, probably that was the desired effect knowing father. Adorned around the front terraces by countless statues of all gods, with Krig at its centre and several of his heavenly guardians all in the same dark grey stone covered scarcely by the glistening white snow surrounding all corners of sight. The ghastly objects still send shivers down my spine as they did when I was a child. They were things of fear not of belief, but then belief was all fear.

The castle was surrounded with winter gardens only intercepted by wide black stone walkways leading to entrances of the castle, all heavily guarded and patrolled.

I pulled the hood down, brushed my hair back and removed the cloak covering me. The closer we neared the castle, the more attention we drew. Soldiers in blue and Verglasers dressed in white lined the entrances turned and kneeled as we passed. I could hear them chatting amongst and faint whispers from all corners. *Hybrid. Demon child. Blood cursed.* There were many words to describe me. What I was and what they thought I was.

Magic meant honour in Numengarth, it meant being blessed, a chosen—god chosen. To me it was a curse, the hand of evil. And when I showed no sign of possession, it became my brand of uselessness. A title of dishonour and a badge of mistreatment. It gave liberty to my creator to discard and mistreat me. But my title remained and I was still hunted as one. A monster only in skin, the flesh more human than a human could be and my presence a sully of the living.

Dark castle corridors welcomed us, red hue wavering shadows, faltering candlelight, red drapes, and grey stone. They spun, warping us as if in a nightmare, unable to run from it. Nia and Cai stationed leaning into a window and nodded as I turned to approach the wooden door. A soldier announced my presence, and the large door flew open as did all old flutters of memory of fear.

I marched inside the winter court. Old, wrinkled faces and vain new ones lined the walls, some wavering in shock, others in disgust and disregard. All stood from their chairs gesturing an empty bow, respectless. I chased the aisle towards where my father perched enthroned in his gilded dais, dwelling in power, tyranny, and much testosterone. He was the same, barely looked over his thirties. Bastard was over his eighties. Aura could channel their magic back through the course of mana, just how they allowed mana to fly through the course of magic. Once a certain age, they were able to at best slow their ageing, but powerful ones like my father could actually stop it altogether. His yellow hair had turned just slightly paler and so had his dense beard, a gold circle crown rested on his head. Not that a snake needs to bear fangs to know it was one. That drop of revulsion returned in my stomach when I met his eyes, still shining an unnatural yellow. Dressed in all black attire with a thick grey fur around his neck, he looked every bit the tyrant I'd left him twelve years ago.

After all these years, merely steps away, I was in front of him again. It brought back that rush of emotion again. Before I would let it take over, I got on one knee and grounded myself still.

"My child, your return pleases me greatly. Welcome back home, Snowlin," his voice cold and laced with a vileness that made me wince.

My chest burned to plunge toward him. It probably really did please him greatly to have me back under his cage, his favourite to torture had always been me.

Slowly raising my head, I meet his slithering stare once again. My hands gathered in fists at my sides, nails digging in my palms, almost shaking in anger at his sight. The pain somewhat soothed the ire flow of my blood. "Home?"

He stood and made down the steps of his dais to me. "Yes, home, my rose." He threw his arms open approaching me. "We have not seen one another in twelve years, let me have a look at you."

He reached for an embrace, stopping short before touching me and glanced down between us at the little blade I held right to his gut. "Try, father, touch this rose, see if the thorn prickles," I whispered, pushing it just slightly deeper in his thick coat.

He chuckled, deep and dark and vile. "I see you still hold grudges, daughter. No matter how much you would like to think that what happened was my fault, it wasn't," he responded too quietly, unbothered, taking a step back from me and I sheathed the little knife back to my belt.

"Fault?" My brows rose in question. "Oh no, father, no one said anything about fault. You were the cause, the fault on the other hand was my mother's incapability to end you in your sleep."

He tilted his head in warning. "Enough, child," he gritted out sharply between his teeth, attempting to keep composure in front of this court.

I could hear gasps and muttering behind my back, so I continued, "Hopefully your new companion is one the wiser. Moreen has always had a thing for dead husbands. Has she not been widowed twice before marrying you?" At his drop of reaction to sternness my smile grew gleefully.

Father's gaze broke from holding mine, throwing a threatening stare towards the lords who held up his court. "The meeting has ended, everyone see yourselves out," he ordered sharply and in a flash they all stood to exit.

"But why father?" I asked, turning to his court. "Don't they miss their princess?"

Almost in command they halted their feet and half turned back to us before dropping to a kneel.

I laughed. "Do your solstice candy still taste sweet, you irrevocably incapable old farts?"

"Snowlin Krigborn—" my father warned.

One of the lords stepped forward. He bowed, offering me a smile. "This irrevocably incapable old fart is pleased you have returned safely, Your Highness." Albius Arynth, one of the eldest in the court since my grandfather's early time in the throne.

"Where were you Albius Arynth, Kirkwall, Modr, Brisk, Venzor, Casmere, Grasmere, Brogmere? Where were all of you when your heir, my sister and my mother fought for their safety?" Few dropped their heads in guilt and others chose to wear their apathy. I held my breath from shivering as I said, "That is right, not keeping them safe." They'd fled, most of them had run for their pathetic lives and hid.

I turned around to him. "Where were you father when she," I broke myself to take a breath. "When she called your name, when she died and bled before me with your name on her lips." Everywhere and nowhere—no one knew where he'd been.

He turned round, making for his dais. "I need to speak with my daughter, everyone continue and excuse yourselves out."

"However charming that idea is," I said. "I am in need of rest. All the journey to this piss hole truly wore my will to argue off." I turned past the lords, clicked the wooden door open and exited slamming it back.

"Snowlin Krigborn, return here immediately!" he shouted my name in an order.

I scoffed at the use of his ridiculous surname. What Krigborn? I was bloody mud curse born.

Coming up the corridor, two large figures approached. Shape of a familiar face took form, terror of a blue eye and brassy long hair. He wore the marred features of another nightmare, one wearing an eye patch.

I deviated, avoiding his stare. There was no energy left to fend off another serpent. Nia and Cai leaned against the corridor walls waiting for me. She held out my brother's sword and scabbard, helping attach it to my back, anxious to know what had happened.

"Irrevocably incapable old farts?" Nia whispered, almost agitated.

"If you had a better one, you should have told me."

Cai's attention suddenly turned behind my back to where the footsteps had now stopped.

"Twelve years is a long time but not enough to forget your uncle's face. We wouldn't want others to think you are ignoring me, would we? It is simply impolite."

My jaw tightened at the pretentious voice filling the corridor. Calmly putting my gloves on, I went down past him, ignoring him altogether. He had worn that same amused face with no issue when my mother had died. *They missed the little pest.* He had clicked his tongue as he had expressed his disappointment at my survival to my father's consort. If one had enjoyed what happened that night the most, it was him.

"Impolite?" I asked calmly, making my way down the corridor. "I was going for discourteous." From dirty tricks to have me punished, to straight up abuse and not the mental kind, this man had done it all to me. I had never endured them, always lashed out and clawed him marks that I could bet a good dagger he still could not heal. But I had not always been successful in protecting Thora from his hands. My little sister had slept in my chambers for months from fear of him, refusing to leave my side even when I had to use the bathroom. We had only had each other, everyone else was either spun in cyclops by my father or too busy to even pay mind to us, including our mother.

"Do not start thinking your importance is of value now, everyone is a soldier in your fathers army and you, merely a stone in our walkway," he shouted from behind, his words biting with distaste. Nothing I had not already known, to my father we were all game pieces to his grand scheme. I was no more to my father than he was and obviously he was already aware of that but hoped to find comfort in my reactions.

I halted my step and slightly turned to him again. "He wanted me back, didn't he?" His face went rigid at my words. "If I am, as you say, merely a stone in your walkway, why insist on stepping on me, and hurting your poor, poor fragile self. Merely avoid me, it is not all so difficult." Before I turned to make my leave, the corner of my eyes caught a familiar face standing on my uncle's right. My gaze shifted to his direction only to meet the same dark stare I had met days ago at the autumn festival. The man in the forest, Elias, stood beside him. It appeared he was not just a patrol soldier, he wore the navy army reefer jacked with my father's crest on each side of his shoulder, two gold buttons adorning the top of his breast pocket. He was a captain, probably the captain of the team sent by my father to escort me back. Probably on his way to report to his king how I had slipped before he got to me. I would almost feel apologetic, if only I didn't remember his smug behaviour from that night.

"One should mind their own business, or they might catch the early death, dearest uncle. This slithering den can kill you, but I can do it most efficiently," I warned, the second in command serpent.

He scoffed in disbelief. "You threaten me?"

"A simple warning, if that had been a threat you would already be painted in these walls. The last threat I made had you missing an eye, the next will have you missing your heart." Opening the corridor doors, I made my exit. The first time I'd seen that much blood leak out of a person, the gelatinous sphere had made me gag in my sleep several weeks after. He'd bruised Thora's, so I took his out. An eye for an eye. Earned me a beating, each bruise worth it.

"Always this affectionate with your relatives?" Cai teased with a lupine smile, throwing his arm around me.

"You are in for a treat, wait till you see the rest of this den then I will show my real loving."

"I believe you have been a tad sweet in their description," Nia said, almost nervously, rubbing her arms.

"My heart is generous like that."

She turned frowning and shaking her head at me. "You are spending too much time with him again, he is rubbing on you."

Cai threw his other arm around her and said, "I am rubbing on no one, not for a while now, sweet Nia."

She violently spun and hit his back a few times, making him shake in laughter.

We headed to my old quarters, hoping they had not been removed. My feet remembered the way before my head willed them to move, but my rush was interrupted. A small girl no more than in her adolescent years shot toward us, startling more herself than anyone. Her double braided hair was the colour of autumn, eyes glazed in green, dressed in a beige dress coming to her ankles with a black apron tied to her waist and neck.

She dropped in a shaky curtsey. "Your Highness, my name is Penelope. I am to attend you and your guests and show you to your rooms," she said before I had a chance to walk past her. Her eyes tracing all of me in curiosity, lingering longer on my scar. I could feel it—her pity—and I frowned.

"Your Highness?" Penelope queried softly and cautiously after my silence.

"Snowlin. Not Your Highness and certainly not princess. Now lead away, if you must," I responded.

Her eyes shot wide open and she threw a glance at Nia and Cai before nodding. "Of course."

We followed her through the all too familiar stony corridors, the marbled floor shone reflecting the light from the grand crystal chandeliers adorning the ceiling, sinister paintings occupied one side and wide arched stained-glass windows the other. The huge corridors that had once made me feel trapped when I was younger oddly still made me feel the same. This place has always had an odd affect on me, like I have never belonged here.

"His Majesty had this unit sealed after you left." The young servant pointed toward my old chambers, lowering her head, she added, "And a few others as well."

Was my father afraid their spirits would chase him, had he burnt sage and cast craft on them, too? "Where are they buried, Penelope?"

She swallowed in hesitation. "In her garden, the rose bush maze, in its centre, but no one is allowed there—"

"Show my friends to their rooms." I interrupted. "I need no permission to see my family."

"I will come with you, Nia will go rest," Cai offered, stepping forward.

I nodded in agreement, it was pointless to fight it from this point, he'd probably attach himself with glue to me. Cai was distrusting, but that distrust elevated when it came to Isjord and its people.

We walked past the vast corridors and halls of the castle. Soldiers, servants, and officials stopped and bowed at my sight. Word must have flown quickly of my return. Then again, I was easily recognizable. Most Isjordians had distinct blue eyes and yellow locks, and I was a far cry from that, not the most convenient when you try to be discreet.

What did they think, seeing the princess who never felt as theirs march back down these corridors, scarred and orphaned? I had never managed to grow close or even make friends with a single Isjordian, all those around me had been foreigners, but then I suppose so was I.

Just as we were about to reach the doors that lead towards the back gardens of the castle, a man's chest blocked my view. I tilted my head up in anger at the abrupt gesture. Elias was blocking my way with a hand stretched on the door frame and a smile forming on his lips. I heard Cai unsheathe his blade and I motioned towards him to draw back. Had this one recognized me, or had his smug personality gotten the best of him and was trying to hit on the princess.

"You know, a voice is easily forgotten, but those eyes, I would never forget those eyes." I sneered in distaste at his attempt of flirting flattery. "Ah, and that sharp mouth," he shook his head and finished, "definitely difficult to forget."

I would give him something not to forget in a minute. "You on the other hand definitely take more than a shake of memory to remember, remind me of your name again?" I asked lazily, hoping to wound at least a bit of his arrogance.

He removed his hand from the door frame and drew closer to me, my head tilted back to meet his tall gaze.

"Elias, Elias Venzor. I was sent to escort you back here, but I see you had no trouble in doing that and I might even congratulate you for getting the king to reprimand me and my men," he said with an almost playful tone. "Your Highness."

My brows rose as I traced him and asked, "Venzor?"

He tilted his head to the side, swivelling his gaze to study all of me before lifting his eyes back to mine, "Yes, my father is Lord of Venzor and I am his son," he answered proudly.

Ivar Venzor, a very important member of the Winter court, his city was the richest and the lord's greed still famished. He was my father's biggest contender yet his most trusted ally, one who has had eyes on the Isjordian throne for years. My grandmother was Venzorian and they somehow had expected for the tradition to hold—for my father to marry there as well so their ties to the crown deepened. However, not only had my father greatly displeased them by marrying an Olympian princess, but had attempted to push their position in court down multiple times. My father knew where their eyes were set, so he had moved the largest fleet by two other port cities, Grasmere and Brogmere, where two of his close allies ruled and then had reduced Venzor to a fishing port and turned half of it to a forgery. Krig blessed indeed, Ivar had not fallen for the trap, he had used all of that to his leverage, making fishing the tightest trade deal and bringing forgers all around the kingdom to produce only the best steel, sold all over the continent. A silent battle which surely my father would win ultimately, but I liked when he was put under pressure, challenged—he hated being challenged.

I chuckled, turning to my friend. "Another pompous bastard, Cai, this must be your day," I teased, yet he did not laugh, only glowered at the spoiled heir of Venzor.

Elias's eyes darted between me and my friend before he flashed me a sharp grin. "At least I was not called an irrevocably incapable old fart."

"I meant it to be equally as offensive. Now, if you will just move, I might make my exit, Captain. Though I enjoy the entertainment, I am as they would say, too occupied to care," I added lastly. He stepped aside and bowed, but amusement was still hitched in his lips.

"You know the idiot?" Cai asked, walking beside me as we trailed down the snowy grounds of the winter garden.

"He is the one I saw in Soren forest the night of the festival, along with his soldiers."

"I don't like him."

"You don't like no one, with the size of that ego one can only fit so many in his life."

"Pot meet kettle."

"Fitted you, for that I have to get some credit." Halting, I turned facing him. "I have meant to talk to you about this, but you keep avoiding me like a sickness when I do."

His brows furrowed in concern. "Don't get all serious with me, Cakes, I don't need to tell you again that there is nothing to discuss."

"Surely there is, my father killed your family down to the roots, he didn't leave a distant cousin of yours alive to call a relative. Does it really not bother you, who I am, what I remind you of?" I'd hate to think that it did, but I wanted to hear it, for him to let it out, unmask his real feelings. It bothered me that he would have to play pretend around me.

"Never has, never will. You are not what he has done, and you are not him. You are nothing of his either."

I shook my head. "I don't believe it."

"Has it ever bothered you what Nia is?"

"No, but what was done to you—"

"You cannot compare misfortune, Snow, we will always be on the losing end of someone else's, especially not when you play no part." His hand fell on my shoulder and I felt the warm support it offered. "Let us go, they have waited twelve years for you and I will have you for a lifetime to discuss all matters."

We managed to make our way down the back gardens, the dark evening and new vegetation had sprouted everywhere, dangling my memory and making my navigation difficult. Several lost turns later and a green maze grew more than ten feet tall, higher than I remembered, but I knew where I was.

"I will wait here," Cai said, offering a smile of support though his eyes flashed with worry.

The maze was devouring and confusing, a few corridors past and I found myself at its centre. My eyes fell upon three graves bearing the names of my mother, brother, and sister. They were buried in my mother's favourite place in the kingdom, a garden bearing her name. Serene. I had left with no last farewell. They had not allowed me. After twelve years, this was how I would see them again. Being away, I dared bare hope— hope that everything was a lie. The thought kept me alive of a sort, thinking that they would be here, roaming corridors, filling them with their laughter and sounds. My throat swallowed a cry, but my eyes welled up and a hot tear rolled down my cheek. Longing, pain and anger burned my chest.

I fell to my knees, the thorns from the roses picked from the garden dug on my skin and drew blood that pooled to taint the white snow crimson. Grief coated my senses. The sound of the blood dripping heightened, each drop reminded me of the heavy marching steps of the Adriatian soldiers who attacked that night. The sharp wind mimicked the hiss of the swords drawn and each drop of snow made me relive those memories once again. In this very garden my mother had been killed, on the very walls of this castle my siblings had burnt while I ran—while I left everyone to die.

Barely managing to stand, I approached their resting places to remove the snow that coated them. My chest hurt, it felt like it wanted to burst.

Heartache, my snowflake, my mother had once said. *When you long so dearly for someone you love that it becomes painful, you learn that the worst emotion you could feel is yearning, that is called heartache.*

I wore a terrible heartache.

Placing each rose in them I sent a prayer, "Gods and heavens bear my witness, I will kill them all, and with their blood I will paint the sky red."

Not a prayer, a promise—a vow.

6

THORNS AND ROSES

SNOWLIN

PENELOPE HAD FLUFFED RELENTLESSLY about my room for the past hour, trying to sort my attire. Father had ordered that I eat with them. Ordered, not suggested, that is what she had repeated several times. She was young and bubbling with energy, and did not stop speaking my name as if it was the only one she knew.

Tired from all her clattering and pacing, I hopped out of bed.

"What—who—in Krig's heaven did that to you?" she exclaimed in disbelief, her viridian eyes livid at my wounded hands.

"You surely do not think me weak enough to let someone hurt me." I smiled and fluffed her red hair before sliding towards the bathing chambers.

"I've heard stories," she shyly murmured, pulling my nightgown down before I made to slip through the burning hot water in the tub. "From my father."

"Such as?"

She stood silent for too long, so I turned to her. She'd gone still, gaze fixed in silent shock at me. "Those ones," she said warily, pointing to my back.

I reached a hand over my shoulder, feeling the dents of raised flesh. "They are signs that show just how long it took them to realise they could not break me." Maybe at a point I thought they had, maybe if they had kept going they might have, but now each slash and welt reminded me of a head that was to be parted from their body—my revenge. "They are never a weakness."

The hot water enveloped my body in warmth, completely relaxing onto the lavender mist. Penelope on my toes, grabbing soap and a cloth approached me, sat on a stool starting to lather my arms. I had not been given a bath since I was a child and was certainly not one now so I grabbed the soap from her hand, startling her.

I noted her stiff pose and awkward mannerisms. "Are you afraid of me?"

She stood abruptly looking somewhat offended. "I am not, it's just...I've never served a royal before."

"Did the other servants beg not to serve me? Did they bully you into becoming my servant?"

She shook her head. "Some did, others were already on the consort's service and few gave up after they heard what you said to your uncle. They say you eat hearts to keep your magic satiated."

I laughed, sinking further in the bath. "And you?"

"I volunteered," she shyly revealed. "I actually begged the head mistress to let me tend you. Claire, a friend of mine from school, said our hearts would be too small for your liking, we would be safe. It worried me not."

"Why? You must have been merely a toddler when I left Isjord, you do not know me. Do not think many perks will come from serving me. I am not the most popular around here."

She fiddled with the towel she held, her attention lost absently. "My father," she answered in a half voice. "He died two years ago, he was one of Queen Serene's guards. Actually, he was your guard. The night of the attack he said you saved his life, but he wouldn't say how."

Remembrance hit me, I could see it now in her green eyes, the same eyes that had pulled me away from the attack when we were running for shelter, the same ones that had held soldiers back while I made my run away from the castle. Lysander, one of my mother's trusted guards who had been with us since I was an infant.

"Lysander," I said quietly, memory surging through me.

A smile grew wide on her face and she jumped up from her seat. "Do you remember him? I did not think—" Interrupting herself from the excitement, she sat down quietly.

"Whatever you think you owe me, you don't." I truly meant it. He had done more for me and my mother than I had done for him that night. "Your father was more than a guard to me, if anything I owe you."

She smiled and took the soap from my hand once more, washing my back. "I just want to, please let me."

Too tired to argue, I leaned onto the bath, relaxing to its comfort. "So it shall be, Lysander's child."

After the bath Penelope directed me to the dressing chamber. Massive and fit for a princess, just not for this one. I'd never seen so much colour even on rainbows. I spun on my toes without being able to hide the cringe of colour sickness.

"Absolutely not," I said, throwing what she'd picked for me to wear to the ground. A washed-out green dress with layers and layers of ruffles, a high neck bodice in some strange lace and long bell sleeves with a yellow ribbon around the waist.

Pen cradled the sickly cloth as if I'd injured a child. "The consort chose them for you."

I cringed. They did look her taste for sure. "I will not look like a solstice tart, a jacket and breeches will do." My thoughts grew horrid at the image of me parading in that absolutely ridiculous pile of ruffles.

"That will not happen, you are a royal not a soldier," Nia's voice filled the chamber. Leaning against the door, her arms crossed over her chest, she was dressed head to toe in a navy jacket, tight breeches and black boots, a guard's uniform.

"That, I will wear the same," I pointed hurriedly to Nia's attire.

My friends shook her head. "You will stand out like a nose wart if you parade around ordinarily in this attire."

"What?" I asked, bewildered. "And that green pile of horse shit won't?" My words seemed to have been harsh for Penelope's soft ears since she gawked at me in horror.

"I am not saying it won't, but it will be the right type of attention. You are a princess here after all, aren't you?" Nia asked, raising an eyebrow and my mouth gaped open in disappointment. She really expected me to be dressed like a peacock. Knowing Nia, this probably amused her.

Along with Penelope, they both hovered over a chest loaded with different dresses. All I saw was ruffles, icky colour, and more ruffles which I absolutely refused to wear, unless I joined a circus.

"Penelope, are all my mother's belongings sealed in her room?" I asked, nervously biting my lip. My mother had never worn the typical pompous gowns of Isjord, she was always dressed comfortably in silky flowy dresses that flew around her like clouds. I had always adored how she looked and floated in them like a spring dove. She and I were now similarly the same body.

She nodded and hastily left the room, almost jumping and tripping on her way out.

Nia pointed towards the green dress. "I would eat my limbs to see you in that one."

I grabbed a pillow and threw it with force toward her.

She extended a palm stopping the pillow floating mid-air. Nia was an Adriatian Aura, she could materialise and transport herself places within seconds and freeze shadows along with their owners. She was what they called an Umbra, shadow wielders. Adriatian Aura were able to do much more, but Nia had left for Olympia when she was no more than nine years of age. Her powers never developed fully and always took a toll on her when she used them for extensive time. Not that she particularly enjoyed using them anyhow—her identity was what she strayed furthest away from. She had denied that part of herself for a long time, and still continued to do so.

Footsteps approached from my bedroom and Nia pulled her hand back making the floating pillow drop to the floor. Penelope looked between us in confusion and laid down several of my mother's gowns. My chest rose in excitement. My skin turned electric at the feel of them. I remembered—remembered how my mother walked wearing them, how she sat, how she floated around in her gracious smile. A piece of her, that is all I had left now, only pieces of them.

"They are mostly in good condition, except a very few. I can have them brought here, all of your mothers belongings if you wish?" she asked carefully, looking at me.

I cupped her cheeks, planting a kiss on her forehead. "Thank you."

I headed toward the dinning chambers wearing a silky long sleeved emerald silk gown that came tight to my waist and flowed swiftly touching the floor, its neckline hid my neck scar, my hair loose on my back and two of my mother's silver beaded pearl pins on each side of my head. The first servant that saw me covered her mouth to hide her gaping. Was it the dress, my scar or my bare feet peeking from under my dress when I took a step? An old habit of mine, I liked feeling the ground beneath my feet, it calmed me down.

When we reached the dining chamber doors my feet hesitated, and I spoke over my shoulder to Nia, "Do I have to?"

She rolled her eyes and pushed me forward. "Try not to offend too much, keep death threats to your head, curses out of your mouth and if you can't be respectful, just glare at them not voice the disrespect," she warned. "We don't wish to be banished to some dungeon on your first day back."

Soldiers announced my presence and the doors opened, revealing the happy family of Krigborn.

"My kingdom for the dungeons. The dungeons have my vote."

"Unless you can enchant a mouse with your sass to get you inside your father's court, I suggest you move," she murmured, before giving me a shove inside.

My stomach rolled and I tried to calm myself while moving inside the massive dining chambers. The table and chairs were painted gold, dozens of lavish dishes laid ahead, fruit, meat, fish and all sorts of luxuries even fresh flowers stood in the middle. What idiot fetched my father flowers across the kingdom? I almost laughed at the thought of a poor boy having to travel that far only to get this flowery tyrant some peonies. The ceiling adorned with grand gilded chandeliers, walls draped in red curtains adorned in the Isjordian royal insignia, the same ghastly paintings as those on the corridors were positioned between them. Bet they startled a guest or two before. Had my father ordered them to be positioned there on purpose, to choke some poor emissary mid-chew? My eyes landed on the faces sitting across the long table and I sneered involuntarily. The royal consort Moreen and her two children, Reuben and Fren sat on one side, my father at the top, my uncle opposite them.

What a sight.

Father stood abruptly, his eyes drawn wide while tracing me top to bottom, flashing with some form of wild astonishment. He took a few absent moments just staring at me before silently sitting back down.

The old consort stood and approached me. Moreen always played pretend kind to me for whatever reason I still wouldn't care. She was my father's consort for years before he married my mother, even having Reuben a few years before Eren. She was not of royal or highborn blood, born to an unblessed merchant in Grasmere, therefore she could never marry my father. Of course, in any other circumstance, both would have been hung, blessed and unblessed were oil and water, to laws and realm we stood above them in every form or way. To marry one was to sully the choice of gods in leaving them in their nature of unexpected and unworthiness. However, my father had broken worse rules. Moreen was a shadow in his court, a wicked one at that, just as all unblesses were described as. Rangy and veiled in human age, her blonde hair gripped and pinned in colourful beads at the top of her head like a peacock, nothing impressive compared to other kingdoms' idea of a king's mistress.

She cupped my cheeks with her svelte long fingers to study me for a moment. Her thin lips twisted in an unpleasant half-moon curve. "With Krig's blessing, to Hodr heaven. Welcome back, Snowlin," she greeted with an eerie calm voice. Didn't she tire from the play-pretend? It was one thing for an unblessed Vrammetheni to play a blessed, but to pose as a caring mother figure was another form of depraved. She gripped my chin, tilting my head up to meet her almost hollow washed-out blue irises demanding for a polite answer.

Once I had let her, but once I had been a scared child. I wrapped my hands around her wrists and her smile dropped, turning into a wince from the force of my hold. "With his blessing, might the burning hells welcome you back, Moreen. I see you have withered like the old crone you are," I said, giving her a tight-lipped smile. Slipping by her gawking expression, I headed to greet her spoiled produce.

"Dearest uncle," I nodded, and continued past him after he warily returned the greeting.

Reuben and Fren studied me cautiously, their white pearly heads shone under the candle flames, their features thin like their mother's, eyes a washed blue and they were so pearly white like snow spirits, pampered like wooden dolls in their ruffles, beads, feathers and diamonds.

"Half breeds, I see you have grown to be just the trolls you are. Your mother has always liked a good joke, now she has two."

My uncle spat his water and was coughing and chuckling under his breath. Their noses flared and their lips curved down in distaste. Reuben rose to replicate, but his mother approached to put a hand on his shoulder, prompting him to sit down.

Well, my father got his trained lap dogs from them at least.

Father still continued staring at me like he had just seen a dead spirit. Bowing my head again, I took the seat next to his. His vile eyes lingered for a few moments and then turned to his food. That look, the same one he would once give my mother, it felt as skin creeping as when I had caught it towards her.

Moreen interrupted the silence, "The children and I are finished, we will let you continue as we have duties to attend."

My father nodded and waved a hand at them. Fren stood and planted a kiss on his cheek and I could swear bile rose in my throat. Father's little pet that one. Little lamb had always tried so hard as if anyone cared for the affection of my father. Fren prided herself as his favourite child—my father's favourite child was his throne.

"So soon? But I have missed you dearly, dear, and it is not every day I get to see snow spirits in the castle," I purred, taking a sip from my water cup. "Surely, cattle can be milked by someone else?"

My father tensed and waved them away again before turning to face me. "Your rudeness is appalling."

"So is their audacity."

"Let it pass, you are no longer a child, but a royal and one in my court."

"What, will you flog me?" I asked, pushing a grape in my mouth and giving him a sweet smile.

He flared in frustration and the knife he cut his egg with almost broke the porcelain. "I will not do no such a thing to my child."

Funny this one. "You mean your heir."

He gave me a scalding look. "I have not chosen my heir."

"Of course, given the pool of choice you have, it must be so daunting." I feigned a gasp and turned to him. "Letting the northern barbarians have their roulette?"

Burning tension leaked in the air, turning into a sizzling frost. My father's biggest fear and the daunting contender for his throne—the other Krigborn line. The second oldest Krigborn bloodline that camped by the Islines in centuries. The two sons of the first king of Isjord, Edric, had battled for the throne. Tenebrose, the prince that won, took the crown while Isline was exiled in the heights of the sharpest, tallest mountains of the kingdom along with his avid followers. Generation after generation, they had grown and formed their own villages without contacting the rest of the world. They lived, ate, breathed, fucked, and ruled as barbarians, but they were still next in line if my father had no heirs or if all of us died, they had a blood right to the throne.

"There is rudeness," he said, whilst ice grew from under his fists, spreading a map over the table, freezing all in sight. "And there is tempting my fury."

I pouted at him. "What will you do, father, freeze me?

Blisters of ice vibrated ready to erupt, but the doors opened, and Elias entered, dropping to one knee for my father.

My eyes rolled at the theatrics and father shot me another pointed look.

"Sit, Elias." My father cleared his throat and motioned to the chair facing mine, still red with rage.

The Venzor heir was not only a captain I noted, it also appeared he had taken my father's like. He'd been trusted enough to escort me from Fernfoss to here. Was it due to his Venzorian roots? Under Silas's claws along his army of the wicked, or father's son and a spy—what was his position?

He sat facing me, looking like he had every other meeting, like an arrogant prick. He bowed smugly and threw me a wink. Before I could reply in a not so polite gesture back to him, father interrupted, "This is Elias, son of Ivar Venzor, Captain of my fifth guard and your sister's betrothed," he introduced.

I snorted, confusing myself at which part, the betrothed or the casual use of the word *sister* for someone I detested wholeheartedly. "You are marrying the snow spirit?" I asked, half laughing and lifting my goblet to salute him. "Good for you."

He looked as amused as I was at my remark and nodded. "Thank you, Your Highness."

A political arrangement. Father feared the Lord of Venzor. Interesting.

"Snowlin!" father's brisk warning erupted in the chill air.

And that was my mark to make my exit. I took a toasted bread in my hand, plopping loads of jam in it and stood. "Well, this has been the most fun family reunion, let's do it again some other time. Congratulations to you, Elias, may the gods bless your poor soul," I said, having sent myself in giggles while on my way to exit the room.

I heard a loud sigh behind me that could only belong to father dearest. "Meet me in the winter garden before noon, I have to speak to you," he said calmly.

I turned, holding the toast in my mouth, stretching my arms wide before bowing deep. "As you wish, Your Majesty."

Nia joined my side as I made my exit, shaking her head, possibly having witnessed my gesture towards my father. "Was that necessary?"

"Yes, you said it, I am their princess. That makes me the most pompous princess of them all." I took a big bite from my toast. "Just playing my part."

She shook crumbs from the collar of my dress. "Let us not upstage main leads."
I frowned. "How can I be supporting with this face?"

I circled around the castle bored to bits and headed towards the soldier's training courts.
I had always liked to observe them since I was a child. I'd sit there memorising their
moves and imitate them when training with Alaric who had always been impressed at
my ability to reproduce them with exact sharpness.

The training courts were at the back of the castle grounds, only a few minutes' walk
away. Nia tried her best to persuade me this was a bad idea, but she came to make peace
with it after the second round of our argument that I'd instead tour the city.

When we approached, the soldiers took a halt, studying and looking in wonder
towards us, most of them half naked and all sweaty. This would be my best preferred
landscape in all Isjord.

Letting out a low whistle, I waved at them to continue. "Finally, some change in
scenery."

"Isjordian soldiers? You call that a change in scenery?" Nia asked with an expression
of disbelief.

"Half naked Isjordian soldiers, Nia." She shook her head, but I let my eyes ponder
around the muscled flesh around me.

"Your Highness," a strong familiar voice called behind my back. A voice I had heard
often argue with my father, and a voice that had been gentle to my mother. A voice that
had caught me spying the soldiers training, one that had scolded me for lifting blades
twice my weight, one that had nursed my leg when I had tripped on the muddy courts.

"Samuel." Before he could respond, I threw myself at him and wrapped my hands
around his neck, hugging him tight. He was one of the three Isjordian Generals serving
my father, extremely skilled and loyal. One very dear to me, he'd probably seen the most
of my torture here and never backed down in defending me, even if it got him punished.

"You have grown well, a spitting image of her. I never had the chance to express my
condolences," he said, bowing his head. My father had hidden me in his chambers for
days after the attack, closed from everyone, going as far as not letting me attend my
mother's and siblings' funerals. Immediately after, I was banished to Fernfoss.

"How is Alaric?" he asked, bringing me out of my thoughts. They had both grown
close to each other during Alaric's time in Isjord as my mother's sentry, often they
had trained and lounged around taverns together, enjoying one another's presence.
Well, more than just enjoyed. A few instances where I had joined them on their leisure,
I'd noted their undisguisable like for each other. Never understood what happened
between them, why they had broken up and distanced from one another. Not when
they looked at one another as if they only ever wanted to look at one another.

"Grumpy, demanding and growing bald."

He laughed hard at my remark. "Sounds the same as the one I remember."

The training courts snaked and expanded for long miles into sight, mud splattering around as half naked bodies duelled hand to hand and steel to steel. Sheer force, different from what Alaric had taught us. They relied on muscle mass and bruteness of force, but applied with Isjordian technique, they made for fearsome soldiers.

"No Verglasers?" I noted, examining the empty courts that used to blister with ice from all sides from the Aura learning their craft. Elementals had it easy to call upon their gifts, the art of learning to wield it adjustable within little time, but the Bruma Order only harvested the finest most outstanding talent for their battalions, their training just as rough. I'd seen countless of them bleed to death from exhausting all mana to the brim of it just so they could please their king.

Sam pointed his head north. "Their station was moved to the north side of the castle. We have had a good batch of them lately so your father decided to move them in a separate court. Bruma Halls. The Commander still takes great pride in his students, but he's particularly triumphant at the new elevated state the Verglaser school has given him. No offence to the late king, but your father knows what to utilise best. With him it was sheer strength, your father is all about careful tactics."

Renick Salazar, the Bruma Commander. The man who flashed in my nightmares before I even knew what they were.

"I see Renick is still fondling my father's balls," I said, wearing the disappointment that he'd not dropped dead somewhere up the northern mountains where he was from.

He halted and turned to me wide eyed.

"My pardon," I said with an apologetic bow. "I meant...licking his boots?"

Sam laughed jollily and gently patted my cheek, the dark rough sound was somewhat sweet and gentle. "Alaric always wanted a daughter after you were born, flushing with envy at your mother. He must have been so happy to raise you."

"We have had our moments. I might have made him lose his wits about a dozen thousand times, but he's managed."

He swallowed, throwing his gaze somewhere far. "He didn't wish to come with you?"

I shook my head. "He is better needed where he is."

"I see." His voice was full of disappointment and a spec of hurt flashed through his umber irises.

"Why did you not leave with us, Sam? I know Alaric asked you."

All woe, he dropped his lost attention to the ground. "This is my life, all I ever knew. Alaric wanted peace, a family to the brim with children, a nice house by a meadow. And I was this, a soldier. I will be till the day I die."

"He misses you," I offered. "I did, too."

His hand fell on my shoulder and he offered a short smile. "I suppose it's my time to have you for a while then."

"I suppose so."

We parted moments later to head for the Winter garden to meet with father. The wide bushes hid their green under frost, the only colour was that of buds peeking from the blanket of white. Red for miles ahead, only red and white. Once Isjord knew clear skies and visible greenery, but now everything was buried under the thick cold blessing of their Winter God.

Nia stood back and warned, "Behave."

"If I have to do something I don't like, the least I can be allowed is an attitude." Annoyed, I flicked the snow from my shoulders. How I disliked the blessed thing.

"I wish it was the attitude I worried about." She held out her hand. "Your daggers, please."

I frowned. "But...they come with my attitude." She didn't back down, so given up, I handed them to her. "You are getting like Alaric. One cranky old man is enough in this family."

"Your attitude seems fine without them, now go before I confiscate your tongue."

He was already waiting for me, tall against the snow coated rose bushes, the dark attire he wore contrasting the white of all.

He noticed my presence and turned, bearing a strange expression. "With Krig's blessings, to Hodr heaven, my child."

To Caligo's burning hells, you wicked bastard, might they welcome you. Simply, I bowed without returning the greeting, taking Nia's advice not to end up in a dungeon. Stomach twisting that was, the pretend belief of his. With belief came fear of the divine, all which he had none.

He smiled stiffly, planting his hands on either side of my arms. The false exaggerated affection made me wince and I tried to shake his hands, but the grip was firm. "For a moment I thought Serene walked through that door this morning, you look very much like her," he said without hesitation. Mention of my mother's name made me freeze. I hated hearing her name from his mouth. He did not deserve to speak her name or of her, not to mention everything he had done after she had birthed useless children, and the unforgettable pain she carried when he had massacred her family along with the rest of her kingdom. It had sent her in crying fits at least once a few days. She never had a chance to mourn them, give her last goodbyes or even bury them. My mother held so much guilt along with the pain, she had always felt fault for what had happened.

"Though for this behaviour I hold Alaric responsible for and he will answer for it," he spat in a threat. "Nothing we cannot fix."

His condescending words made my blood boil and my eyes rose to meet his, every gaze onto them made me want to scoop my own out. He had mentioned my mother's name, my precious mother's name casually as though he had not been the cause of her pain and demise, insulted and threatened the only person I ever considered my father and now he was treating me like a broken doll in his playhouse.

Thunder echoed loudly in the horizon and he tilted his head towards the skies just as lightning landed mere feet away from us.

"Unhand me, father," I ordered composedly. His attention switched to me and his hands dropped, but before he could step away, I inched closer. My nails dug in my palms, drawing blood from the wounds from last night, a shudder of pain cursed all over my body—my grounding was pain, it kept me still.

I flicked my hand over where he'd touched me, brushing the faint feel away. "Spare me the theatrics, if you want something from me I advise you to speak away before you bore my wits to death."

He cocked his head back. "You will never let this go, will you? But that matters very little to me and you know that," he said flatly, a vile smile snaking across his face making him look amused almost.

"Expecting nothing less. I have been raised to always expect the worst from you, given your love for a dramatic scale of actions." Actions that sent an entire kingdom to extinction, my mother to a painfully dreadful marriage, her and my siblings to their deaths and two kingdoms to hostility.

He studied me before turning to survey the garden, the calmness in his stature sent chills of anxiousness down my limbs. "I have promised a deal with the king of Adriata."

"What of it involves me?" I queried, shocked at the mention of my family's killer.

"Twelve years is a long time for two kingdoms to remain hostile, with war expectant at any moment," his voice grew dark as he reached to pluck out a red rose. "For our kingdoms to join unity once more, establishment of peace and our people to freely live amongst both, your hand in marriage."

My eyes widened as I faced him, too horrified and stunned to even believe what my ears just heard. This was the reason for my return? To sell me to the Night King? It couldn't be? My father bargaining agreements with Adriata? My father bargaining *me*?

"What?" I shouted and thunder grew louder, pulling his attention towards the skies once more as though he had not heard my question.

"Isjord is not what it once was," he said all mellow. "Winters are growing wilder, my lands colder, my people impatient, their beliefs weaker. The Ianuris agreement will soon change that. You are a sacrifice I will make to solve it."

I laughed gutturally from years of resentment, disdain and pain that had coated my existence. My purpose had returned once more. No, I'd never stopped being his pawn. "Such a difficult sacrifice for you, your black heart must be leaking tar. Should have sired more daughters, could have had the whole of Numengarth in your hands had you sold us off like cattle to everyone you intended to butter their arse in exchange for silks and spices."

A smirk rose on his lips and he slowly plucked the thorns out of the rose he held in his hands. "You're a diamond I found out was only coal, but even coal can burn to become useful."

"If I refuse? Where is the threat, you should have already spent it?" He could not have expected me to accept this madness. I would not. Not for a thousand lifetimes would I wed that monster.

A wicked grin spread wide, my resistance amusing him. "Myrdur. The precious land that you adore. Vrammethen has offered an interesting sum for it, it is still mine after all."

Was this why he had sent his men in my lands? "Isjord has not claimed those lands, it cannot," I insisted.

He peeled his sleeve back, revealing a braceleted tattoo around his wrists. The old blood oath engraved in black runes spelling Myrdur. "Not Isjord, I have. *My* lands. By oath of marriage."

What? He had tricked my mother out of a blood oath? The *zgahna*, the restlessness of the lands, all was because of him, because all laid under the name of their killer?

I sneered, my hands searching for my absent daggers. I would cut that hand off. "Those were to remain free lands, Olympians rest restless, the soil leaks of blood and the air cursed. You made a blood promise to my mother, you would not do such a thing. You promised to be satisfied with your war and lay no claim on those lands." How had he tricked her? It was impossible to trick a blood oath, it could claim your life.

He rose a brow all unbothered. "Serene is dead and so is that one oath I made to her, but I can make one with you if you will quietly agree to this."

I froze. Not a blood oath. The law of the other half. After my mother died, anything belonging to her had gone to him. He was her other half. Hells.

"You make deals with me now?" I grit out, holding onto my flaring calm.

"I'm a politician not a brute, my child."

"Politicians don't have morals, politicians are brutes."

He reached and tucked the thornless rose behind my ear before quietly threatening, "Agree to this or I will have Alaric's head on a pike, his guts latched as flags for your dowry, you dragged to Adriata in chains and Myrdur levelled to sea."

Another laugh escaped from me while his own satisfaction leathered down. "There we go, now you have a deal. Should have started with that killer line for your pitch."

Stolidly he asked, "Why provoke me? I can have you do all that I want and keep Myrdur, too."

I took the rose he stuck in my hair and brought it under my nose. Odourless. A rose with no scent, austere decoration—a red decorative lie, just like his threats. "You know what you have raised. Also aware of the fight I would put up and from what I see, you really, really want this agreement. Threats and punishment, you know those petty tricks have no leverage against me. Do you know why I never truly became your weapon?" He remained fixed and expressionless. "Because, father, you could never shackle or tame me no matter your attempts. Had you done that, even human, I would have been your mightiest sword. So, here you have me, shackled by one ankle. Praise, it only took you twenty-three years and a desperate agreement, but you have done it." It was not the threat that had made him desperate, it was the bargain. I wanted to hear the threat to know the severity of his desperation.

"You have my eyes, young rose," he finally spoke again after stark silence. "The only one who has my eyes. Eren and Thora had your mother's emerald ones, Reuben and Fren, Moreen's. Had you not had that one trait, I'd never think you were mine."

"We can only dream of such delights, unfortunately." I said, putting the rose back behind my ear and flashing him a smile.

He levelled a doubtful stare on me. "What do you plan to do with Myrdur since it was enough to convince you to wed the night king?"

"What do you plan to do with Adriata since it took a whole land to convince me to wed the night king?" I bit back.

"Do you have to fight me on every occasion?"

"Yes," I said, fluttering my lashes at him. "It pleases me greatly. So, are you trying to annihilate the spirituals, too, or just weaponizing their ignorance for something greater?"

He flicked snow from my shoulders before gathering a bunch of my locks between his fingers. "It is now past me, child, humans are foible and breakable, untethering to command only to their brittle emotion. You cannot weaponize something that feels."

"Then what are you getting from that deal? What was so precious that you had to seek and sell me out after twelve years for, especially when you knew my reaction exactly?"

He smiled, too terribly entertained. "For someone who has no desire in royal affairs, you do want to know more than you should. I have to admit, this was not the same reaction I expected. I thought you would be happy to have your mother's murderer under your clutches."

"But I already do, father. I already have my mother's murderer under my clutches. He is in front of me right now," I spat with years and years long of spite.

His smile faltered, wearing the face of a slighted beast. He had said enough and I had heard plenty.

Seeing him distracted, I turned to leave, all that talking to him had tired me enough that my eyes felt heavy. A buzzing sound thumped the sides of my head and my body numb enough to not feel my own. Getting stabbed felt better and less painful than having to speak to the venomous serpent that was my father.

"You were not dismissed, I was not finished," he called from behind.

"Yet here I am, leaving. What will you do?"

"Snowlin," he shouted, interrupting me.

"Exactly, father, you will do nothing," I shouted back, waving a hand over my shoulder. "You have me by one shackle, I have you by two."

I jolted awake in the middle of the night, panting, sweat beads stinging my eyes. My demons refused to let me go even in my dreams despite having just faced the very real ones. That night played through and through every time I shut my eyes to sleep. By now, each name, sound, face, every smell and every smear of blood that covered my face, all were memorised to haunting detail. The feel of the black metal that had pierced my skin, the hands of blood hungry Adriatians that had pulled my hair and hit me, the sword that had gone through my mother's chest. Her screams and my own, the blur of the black smoke and the heat of flame eating air. Every sense of my body refused to forget that night. I tasted the metallic sting of blood as if the wound in my cheek still leaked fresh.

Bile rose to my throat, rushing me to my feet. Halfway, knees betrayed my weight and before I hit the hard ground, strong arms wrapped around me and lifted me up.

Cai.

He lowered me down in the bathroom, letting me retch my stomach open on the sink till breath could not meet my lungs and tears stung my eyes. Pleasantly, all memory fled as pain grew.

"All is fine, do not make that face," I said to the stern features behind my back while I lowered to wash my mouth. It didn't suit him, I needed his comforting face, the one that had always managed to soothe me out of my nightmares with teases and jokes.

"You intend to keep what happened in the winter gardens a secret?"

"No." I slouched down on the cold bathroom floor, surrendered. How could I tell him that I had just accepted to be pawned off to Adriata for Myrdur? How do I lay out the new plan I'd concocted the moment my father revealed the reason for my return? "Do you remember what I promised you that night, when you took me to the bakers to get cake for my sixteenth birthday?"

One day, let us make the land ours once more. Let us make a promise that we will make Myrdur Olympia once again.

His anger began flickering to surface, twisting his features. "Snow—"

"I promised that Myrdur would be safe, that I'd get it from my father and that the souls of Olympians would finally be put to rest. The promise will be fulfilled sooner than I thought, he will give me Myrdur."

He kneeled down to face me, his brows pinched together. "What? Why?"

"Because I agreed to marry the Adriatian king for it. He promised a blood oath, the lands will be mine and I...the Adriatian king's."

He stood fast and barked, "Get up, we leave this hell hole now."

"I intend to keep my promise."

"I don't give a damn about that promise."

"I do."

He lowered down to me again. "We came to figure out why his soldiers were in Myrdur and sell him out, we did not come to juggle this along. It changes too much, Snow, we will retreat." Plea and something resembling fear flashed his emerald eyes as he repeated, "We will retreat."

"Myrdur is under his name, it will never be free for how long he lives."

He was stunned for a moment in realisation, but it was all the reaction he gave even though I'd just stabbed a nail in his heart. "Then we kill him."

I shook my head. "Then his land will inherit whatever he owns and our chance at grasping Myrdur from Isjord's rule will be gone forever. Our lands will turn to winter. My father doesn't realise, but he has granted me a bargain where the wind favours me."

"You will have to marry him, Cakes, that oath won't be sealed unless you marry him. Whatever plan you weave, whatever you think you can use to get out of, it won't work. It will take your life as a prize."

"It won't happen, because I will marry him and enter Adriata at the front gates," I revealed and he paled. "They will seat me on the throne, close to him, close to them, close to my revenge, with their own two hands. My father has granted me the greatest bargain of all."

"Or he has put you right on the mouth of the shark."

"The *Obscur Asteri* is no shark, he is just a man with breakable bones and four canines that probably have a hard time chewing on lamb."

"Snowlin!" he shouted, his jaw set tight.

I gave him a smile though my face had slumbered to fatigue. "You haven't called me that since that day."

I don't like your name. Those were his first ever words to me, then he'd proceeded to make up other ways to call me. Every day he'd dropped by to see me when I'd arrived in Fernfoss I was called by a different name, never Snowlin. He'd always been odd to me, how he found ways to make you feel as if you'd known him for countless lifetimes. Maybe that was why I had liked him—maybe that was why he had been the first boy to somehow rattle me. My lids began giving up, swirling me to utter darkness when I felt him gently lift me up from the floor and onto the soft bed.

"It never suited you, Snow, you were always warm to me. Like the sun. Too close, burning. From far, yearnful. From where I stand, soft, like autumn rays, perfectly delightful."

"Yeah, yeah." I murmured half asleep and I heard him laugh.

"You are telling Nia about this, her ire is yours to deal with."

7

PEACE AND QUIET
KILIAN

I WAS ONLY FIFTEEN when the council of Adriata unanimously voted in majority to attack Isjord. Twelve years had gone by since we'd received news that our soldiers had successfully infiltrated Tenebrose city walls and attacked the castle, leaving thousands in mourning. The innocents murdered that night were an accessory to their planning to distract Isjordian soldiers away from their castle grounds to assassinate their queen and the royal children.

Adriata relied on the spiritual magic of goddess Henah, who had graced our lands with her gifts. We were people who studied the heavens and the spiritual, also the most connected to it. To us, the union of the Olympian Princess and the Isjordian King was viewed not only as defiance of laws, but a terrible foreshadowing omen. The moon had been red for months straight, there had been no shadows following us and it had hailed and rained red leading to their wedding. Gods had already sealed disapproval.

When the union was being discussed between their kingdoms, Adriata had reacted hostile towards Isjord, considering it an act of war and defiance to the natural laws older than time. Queen Serene was a Zephyr, she had come from an Auran bloodline and not just a normal bloodline, but the strongest one, the royal one, those that commanded lightning—Elding Aura.

The Kingdom of Solarya and Hanai, more from fear than like, maintained neutrality to his decisions. But Adriata and Eldmoor shut their connections with Isjord and took a cold position to their plans, fearing the intentions of King Silas. When he had then attacked Olympia after his union with their princess, massacring all its people and their royals at their most vulnerable time, fear had grown twofold. His intentions had come in the clean. He was looking to produce an heir, a weapon only his to wield and toward whom was very clear to all.

For generations, Aura diluted their powers by mating with din-Aura—humans. Even the union of two identical gifted magic wielders often amounted dangerous for their children due to the power they would channel. To mix two Auran bloodlines was cursed, forbidden by god given laws.

Astrum liber, our sacred book, spoke of very few hybrid Aura. They were described as powerful monstrous creatures that drowned in their powers unable to control them. They had raged war and destruction upon our lands. *Ybrises*, creatures of doom.

Olympians were powerful, if not the most powerful of the elementals, their people blessed by one of the most divine gods. Legends spoke of beings powerful enough to command skies, winged beings able to fly that had descended from his realm Caelum and those that could crack clouds, air and land with lighting. Silas had gone rabid to seek what heavens punished.

Fifteen years later from the union, he and Queen Serene had three children, and to their fathers' displeasure none displayed any signs of either of their parents' gifts. They had inherited humanity. Had gods and heavens taken the living side, was everyone's question.

However, twelve years ago, the council and the whole of Adriata had suddenly received news anonymously that all of king Silas's children had in fact displayed great powers from both their parents and were being trained like soldiers readying for war, hidden away from everyone's eye. Unease and fear grew strong amongst the spiritual lands. The council had gathered for a decision and attacked merely days after the news. In their rashness, they had not only failed to kill all the heirs, but found out the truth that none had in fact possessed magic, instigating conflict between our two kingdoms and killed thousands of innocents and three innocent royals.

Scorching sun heated the earth and my air. It was warm, too warm, while our south was about to drown in frost our lands had never before and the west constantly under the eyes of storms and thunder. It was too quiet, while our east was clouded and crawled by monsters from the Sea of the Dark and while our north was under constant need for attention to honour the agreement of the Highwall, a physical border built to separate our kingdom with Isjord. Not only made of rock and steel, but laced with magic and protected, an impenetrable fortress which had left our kingdom stranded. Before we were isolated, now we were imprisoned by cursed waves of natural and unnatural disasters that for almost two years straight had relentlessly cost us hard work, attention, tens of villages and even lives.

The hay dug on my hands, scratched the surface of my calloused palms, the weight of the large pellets almost weightless as I moved them around the stables. Besides the swish of loose hay on the ground being stepped on by me, the neigh of horses and the summer breeze, there was nothing but silent peace.

A low whistle came from the gates disrupting the strike of calm. My brother leaned against a wooden wall all smug, observing me. "If you are looking to charm a stable girl, I'd take the trousers off, too."

So much for my peace. "I don't have the nerves for you, Mal."

"I'd feel bad for poor you if you were not the biggest prick." He pushed from where he leaned and stalked to me. "She is back."

Her. The only one whose name felt forbidden to speak out loud—the Winter Princess. She was back and soon she'd be here, in Adriata. Married to the king.

I halted, dropping a pallet and turned to him. "When?"

"A few days ago. Moon Court has called for a meeting."

I picked up the last pallet and said, "I will be there."

He did not budge despite my words of dismissal. "You know we do have stable people who look after them. Will I be finding you in the kitchens next?"

"If it keeps my ears with blessed silence, you might even find me with the sewage workers."

He cringed. "There are other hobbies you could acquire. Like drinking."

I scoffed. "You will not get your delicate nose near any of those places, and you will keep away from me. I thought the stables were good enough, but apparently I'll have to rethink my hiding spots." It had taken him exactly a week to figure out where I'd chosen to spend my time of rest.

"Gaining a sense of humour in your old age? Get your funny arse to the meeting, I will not sit there on my own and hear the old bats grumble."

I threw him a withering glare and he backed away in a small jig. How was this man-child my brother? How many times had I asked myself that per day?

I faded to my room. The magic used to bring guts to my throat, but now it was as swift as the click of fingers. Sometimes I'd thought of fading myself to the bottom of the ocean or the top of a mountain, but I'd been taught not to run from my troubles and somehow each time I tried, I ended up being reeled back in the place—that thought had stuck like the worst glue.

Tearing my clothes off, I dipped under the cold-water surface of the bath and pulled all shadows around me, clouding the room in total darkness.

Quiet. Silent quiet.

A knock sounded at my door and I let out a long breath of frustration. I knew quiet, the quiet did not know me.

"Kilian," Driada's voice called, moving about my room. "Are you decent, son?"

Barely pulling my body out of the water, I wrapped the robe around me. "Is there something the matter, Driada?" Mal's mother, my stepmother.

She shook her greying head, her hands nervously lacing on one another. "I heard the princess is back. I wanted to hear from you if she was alright."

"I heard from Mal also," I explained, offering her to sit down. "Also, not sure if she was *alright*. To us, if she is alive she is alright."

A frown gathered between her brows, more worried than perturbed. "She is to be queen of Adriata. How is that not a concern of yours? It is a concern for everyone."

It was my concern, just not how it was for the rest. I ran a hand through my soaked hair. "In title, Driada, only in title. That creature will not be anyone's queen."

"Creature?" she asked, standing up from where she sat, holding onto the table to balance herself. "She is only human, son. You cannot think of her like that. Not you."

I took a deep breath, leaning back on the chair. "Why not me? Was I raised with different beliefs from everyone else, am I not a Henah blessed, do I have no wits to know whose product it is?"

"It?" she asked, her expression aghast and hurt as if I'd offended a god. "Please have the decency and call the poor girl who suffered from our people as what she is."

"There was no poor girl, we hunted an *ybris* and you know that."

"Who is just a human."

"Who can still well be the *ybris*." I sighed, arguing was not something I enjoyed, especially with her. "Driada, I have a meeting to attend in a few short moments. The princess is well and hopefully will remain so till the agreement. If there is nothing else."

Disappointment wore over her face. "No, son, attend your meeting."

The council room buzzed, my ears filled with the noise of a busy street. This room did not know quiet—this very room was the antonym of quiet. Moon and Night court formed my council. Despite the harmony of the moon and night, these two were similar sides of a magnet. Arguing a song of lyrical offences at every meeting. Young criticised old, old offended the young.

"Do not tell me we are still heading with this madness," Stregor, one of the eldest councillors, jumped without hesitation.

The head councillor rubbed her temples, frustrated. "The agreement is sealed, signed and in work. The madness has already gone through, Stregor."

He huffed curses under his breath, all offended. "We are not bargaining for her to be our prisoner, she will be our queen. Do you understand that we have won nothing from this agreement?" Yet he'd voted for the agreement, then surprised himself when it had gone through and realised the court and king intended to truly make the Winter Princess our queen.

"We have won our people's freedom," I interrupted. "And what have you brought us so far, Stregor? I mean, beside their imprisonment." Stregor, also a general at the time, had led one hundred of our Aura towards Isjord, toward the attack. The one who'd pushed the decision of attack, the one who'd carried the massacre of thousands.

He snarled. "We rose for this kingdom."

"And this kingdom is falling because you rose." Larg, General of the Highwall argued.

Stregor flinched upward in his seat. "Silas was going to use those creatures."

"Those creatures were human," Mal interrupted, entering the meeting. His hair dishevelled, shirt buttoned wrong, belt off. This fool would be the death of me. "What were they going to do, yell for surrender at our gates? Heavens forbid they learned to spar. We might have had to battle all three of them with our very minute, hundred thousand men army." He sat and raised a snide brow at the councillor. "Tis not so?"

Stregor leaned forward, a poor attempt to intimidate my brother who only snickered. "It is what they symbolise. Just because gods were in our favour, doesn't take away what they were or *are*."

Mal leaned forward like him. "This *ybris* propaganda is exhausting. Getting subtle by the day, too. One moment she is a monster, the other our salvation?" He grinned at the cascading silence of the room. "Funny how it spins, isn't it?"

The councillor bared his teeth at my brother. "A worm is still a worm though it helps the soil breathe. A monster is still a monster even inside prison bars."

"Humans," Mal said, nodding to himself while his eyes hovered over everyone in the meeting room. "So many of them in this very room, yet so very little humanity. Who gave you the scale, Stregor, to measure what one calls a monster? With a list of kills thrice of any beast in this realm, what have you weighed yourself against? A plague?"

"Enough, Malik," I warned, and he gave me a wink before backing down, victorious knowing he'd gotten his point across.

"Why was this meeting called Adriane, we don't have all day. Our squadrons are waiting for dispatch to aid the cities on our borders being swarmed with eudemons crawling out of the dark waters all of a sudden," Triad, Commander of Umbra Order asked the head councillor, tired of the arguing. The elderly Aura had no desire in politics, little less on what people called a monster. He'd seen truer ones.

"If Silas, that sneaky bastard, asked for a single line to be changed or revoked on that agreement, I will pull my vote out," Relgan, the eldest council member, threatened.

The head councillor flagged her hand down. "Not to worry, councillor Relgan, it is not of that sort."

"It's the after sort," Mal pushed. "What happens after."

She nodded. "Yes."

He laughed, unamused. "Of course, which tower will you propose to lock her in? Which tower do you need the king to agree where to lock her?"

I leaned close to him. "It is but the last time I warn you, brother."

He raised his hands in surrender and leaned back on his seat. "But how else would it be, you and these bastards are joined at the hip. You have a proposal of your own? Northern tower? Bridge bay tower?"

I ignored his incitements. One grows warm even to the sound of a thud once heard long enough.

"It is not of the sort, Commander," head councillor clarified. "There has been a proposal of the demotion of her power over the court. As we know, she is the *ybris*, but she is also Silas's daughter. It would give the Winter King more leverage than we thought at the start of the agreement. We have proposed her role at court to be reduced. For our subjects' peace of mind, too. Do we have your votes, Generals, Commander, to pursue this new rule of demotion?"

"No," Mal said, crossing his arms. "I want her at this very table and see you tremble every time you dare speak to her." His vote had weight, he was the commander of the deadliest squadron in Adriata, if not the whole of Dardanes. A team of Empaths, Aura that didn't need even touch to harm their enemy.

Larg scoffed and shook his head. "I am with the Eldritch Commander on this one."

"Not mine either," Triad spoke and stood to leave undismissed. "Call me when you have a real beast to slay, not some girl you probably already killed once."

The head councillor sighed and turned to me. "I trust we have yours, Kilian."

My brother glared and shook his head, expecting the worst from me.

"No, you don't." I spoke. "Do you think Silas is an idiot? That would make the whole lot of you idiots, too. We will not take such a risk. Even if it plays to nothing with him, no such demotion will happen. Kings have married worse for politics. Are we this scared of Silas as to be the first kingdom to deduct the most respected woman in this kingdom. What will happen next, husbands demoting women on their right to breathe, sleep and eat? Is this the example we are setting for our people? Is this short sightedness blinding the repercussion, or is fear as corrupting as they say it is?"

She cleared her throat, her gaze jumping between several councillors who were probably the ones to propose the ridiculous thing in the first place. "No, of course not. If none is in disagreement with the head general, we will pass the proposal as dismissed."

"Do raise a hand, Stregor, for dramatic effect," my brother said, standing and patting the wrathful councillor's shoulder before leaving. But even he remained silent and partially agreed to its dismissal.

I sat by the roof of a hill in Amaris Bay, overlooking the Moor sea. The tender waves of high tides rose and fell, slowly enveloping the shore that once laid for miles down, white sand and shells now dark sea and rage. The waned moon shone a pale silver, bright and full of glow. To us Adriatians, it brought more light than the sun. The wind was not kind as it once had been, now it drew chills on the spine and made you require a mantle of heat. Once the kingdom of summer, Adriata had become the kingdom of the unexpected rage of seasons. Once the favoured land of gods, had now become a beacon of their fury. Adriata was poisoned, and the antidote had become her.

I sighed, dropping my head forward, surrendered. "How did you find me?"

Mal seated beside me on the cool white stone. "Asked every child if they'd seen a moody statue and they all pointed here." He handed me a paper cone filled with corn sweets of all colours. I could taste the colouring dye on my tongue just by looking at them.

"We are not twelve anymore, brother."

He frowned. "I know you still like them, save the brooding for the council."

I took them from his hand, the candy crackling in my mouth, the taste of nothing but sugar. He was right, I still liked them.

"You know, he beat me once," Mal said, taking a candy from my cone. "When he caught me eating them. He said they are for children. I did not understand what he meant because I was a child, but to him we were men the moment we took our first step."

"Father beat you," I said, putting two red coloured ones in my mouth, a faint taste of strawberries between sugar. "Because you snuck out, stole them, wrecked a tent while running away from the seller, then flashed your behind to him before calling him a twit with three tits because of that mole between his eyes." Mal's list of foolhardy moments deemed no case of victory, there was always room to top with another. Our father was nothing short of authoritative, it was his way or no way and Mal grew a penchant for his frustration.

He chuckled silently. "I am definitely writing my autobiography under a pen name."

"What do you want, brother?"

"Where do you think she was?"

It was always her. The only person he wished to talk about was her and the only person I never wished to remember was her. "Does it matter?"

"Will she come to kill her betrothed?"

I turned to him. "That would please you, would it not?"

He leaned back, facing heavenward. "Would you not be pleased, too? The man is a prick."

"The man is a king. All kings are pricks."

"You should have said no, Kil," he said quietly. "You should have disagreed the same as I did when the Ianuris agreement was proposed. They will use her, asking for her was a trick. One way or another, they will find a way to get rid of her, or to keep her from her father, but she is being used nonetheless. Don't you feel we owed it to her to have stood up and said no to the condition in the agreement? Her sister would have done fine, we are already drowning in our misfortune, we needed the agreement and could have done without dragging her back into this."

"Mal," I interrupted. "The council would have let Adriata drown before accepting the Ianuris agreement with Silas. She is the one that saved it, and I only agreed to save our kingdom."

8

GALLEYS AND OARS

SNOWLIN

NIA HOVERED AROUND MY room like a fly. Restlessly tapping her finger to her temples, attempting to come up with the next reason why my father was tying an agreement with Adriata. She halted. "Adriatian steel, if his armies had that they would most certainly gain the upper hand above just anyone," she said half-heartedly, replaying that thought through a fearful expression.

I rubbed my scar in remembrance of the black steel on my skin. She could be right, but he would not remove a whole wall to just get that.

"Produce?" Cai asked, leaning onto his knees, tired from having stayed up all night and then taken hostage by Nia at dawn when I'd told her about the agreement. "These lands are dead, for just how long could you eat fish and pine seeds?"

"I doubt it," I said, knowing my father and his flashy actions.

Nia narrowed her eyes on me. "What? Say it, what do you think he needs from them?"

I hesitated, nibbling on my thumb unconsciously. "A military agreement, to join forces against the continent. Could you imagine their Aura together?" A shudder went through my body at the thought that I would be used to invade the continent, perhaps even beyond.

Nia shook her head. "The scale is too grand. We cannot think like that and Adriatians are sick fanatics, but not foolish to indulge in such plans. To history they are a peaceful kingdom, never started any war beyond their borders."

"The attack twelve years ago seemed pretty close to one," Cai chimed in.

"Exactly that attack makes me think otherwise. Totally not defending them, but they were trying to prevent one by that, remember?" she pointed.

Kind of right, if we were bred and raised to kill, it didn't leave much to think about my father's plans for us and Adriata would have been first where he would test his weapons.

I sighed. "What else beyond power does my father wish to have I don't understand. I know his tactics, believe me. War is his pleasure, he could be tricking the spiritual into something, they were easy to trick a decade ago."

"How would this be connected to his soldiers in Myrdur?" Cai asked.

"Is it even?" Nia questioned. "It makes no sense even if he were to rage war, why would his soldiers be in Myrdur?"

"We will postpone entering Winter court," I announced.

Cai strung still in shock. "We don't have much time, Cakes, four moons would probably not suffice to gather all we need to have other kingdoms attack Isjord. We cannot rely on petty battalion numbers and exits. We must figure out their reserves, spies, his main weapons, weak points of every city, detailed map of Sable Abyss, all nooks and hiding spots and veering pathways. That will take us too long if you are not on duty. We need someone on the inside and we need distraction. That was you."

"I understand," I said, feeling his devastation fill the air. "But that plan is in halt, till further notice. If what I fear is true, no kingdom will take their chance with Isjord now that they are tying an agreement with Adriata, no matter what we give them. Solarya has one fear and that is Adriatians, they are their nemesis since gods created disputes. Eldmoor will pull away if they know another spiritual is siding with my father, and Hanai, if they even decide to go forth with it on their own, will no longer do so. Their queen does not rely on numbers because she doesn't have numbers, and now she will be dealing with exactly that."

"Comnhall might step forth," Nia offered, seeing Cai's disappointment.

"Which blessed do the unblessed fear the most?" I asked.

Cai rubbed his eyes and answered almost distraught, "Adriatians." He stood and fluffed the top of my head. "I trust you. If it is at halt, then so be it. Do I retract from the training courts?"

No one beside me would know how difficult the thought that we'd step down from destroying Isjord was to Cai. It was his comfort knowing we were on the path to take Isjord down. "No, keep your contacts close. We might still need weaknesses and numbers. I'd like to keep store for mistakes. If father plans to make Adriata another of his prey then we might get to use them still." He nodded and made to leave. I grabbed onto his arm and quickly retracted my hand awkwardly. "I will kill him, Cai, and I will kill this land, even if it is the last thing I do."

He offered me a smile, half-moons that wrinkled to hide that mole just under his eye. "A simple I love you suffices."

"You hate those words."

"I hate those that don't mean it." He gave me a wink and left.

A whimsical whistle ringed about the room and I turned annoyed at Nia who conducted two fingers in the air. "I will kill him, Cai," she mocked, and then screeched as I ran, chasing her.

Penelope had been silent all morning, stealing glances toward me till she finally approached to sit at the corner of my bed, checking on my bandaged hands. Unwrapping and wiping them gently before applying an ointment that stung and made me wince.

"It will help them heal," she said, seeing my reaction. "Though I am starting to think...you might not want them healed."

"You ponder upon such philosophical thoughts at your age. Don't you have dolls to play with?"

"Don't be insufferable," she huffed before ordering me to the baths.

She draped me in an emerald flowy chiffon dress with several layers, long sleeves with a square neckline showing a peak of my bust and an inch of the scar on my shoulder. My hair was loosely braided down my back and large emerald adorned earrings hung from my ears. She placed a small square mirror in front of me, my own reflection startling me. I looked regal, there was no sign of the village boy from days ago and as if reading my mind,

Cai marched inside the room, smiling ear to ear and crossing his arms while eying me head to toe. "Now that is some royal arse, right there," he said, earning the well-deserved vulgar hand gesture that I gave him.

"What is the matter, Pen? Is she already wearing you out?" he asked the little red head sulking in the corner who had argued with me all morning.

She scowled at me before turning to him. "She keeps humming that horrible song all the time. I am starting to see things because it's so creeping. Yesterday at the market I had a shivering fit when I saw children, so tell her to stop, please."

Cai threw a not very amused look at me. "Cakes, that creeps me as well, enough of it."

I spun on my toes singing the lines, "For three burning suns and moons, the dark blight celebrated all afternoons. Their plague corrupting with stink of death, of little white lambs beloveds' last breath."

Pen covered her ears and Cai began chasing me about the room. I loved that song, it had brought me more comfort than anyone would know.

"I shall hate forests, flowers, night and children all together after this." Pen sighed, "How can they sing those verses? Those little children saw their families slaughtered, they were starved, watched the invaders celebrate with their parents' heads on pikes, throwing them around like balls and then poisoned an entire army before poisoning themselves. How on Hodr is that supposed to be sung in a happy tune?" she asked and shuddered.

"They got justice. It was a happy ending."

She twisted in disbelief. "Couldn't they live to witness it?"

"What they saw marked them body and soul, you would rather die than crumble. Death is death, but a quick death is salvation."

She shook her head. "I will never understand it."

I pinched her cheek. "I hope you never have to be in the crossroads of having to understand it."

She scowled and swatted my hand. "You ponder upon such philosophical thought at your fragile old age, Your Highness. Don't you have someone to be rude to?" she asked, before blowing a raspberry at me.

Cai cackled. "She is my favourite."

I pointed a finger at him. "I'll have her head, just wait for it."

We made our way to the dining chambers again, this time wearier and troubled.

Thoughts dimmed all sight.

"If they make you eat with them every day you will starve to death," he sighed, before taking his position by the wall.

I scoffed. "I wish, but the Night King probably prefers his bride alive to unalive me himself." And I wish this was a joke.

Cai only sunk further onto his stern expression. It was not a good not-a-joke apparently.

Today Elias sat with them next to my uncle. Ignoring the others, I strode toward my father and bowed again before taking the first seat next to his left.

"You are late, child," father said lazily, taking a sip from his goblet.

"Oh, my deepest apologies. I had forgotten bread and milk took off from the table at a certain time," I replied, lowering myself in a mocking bow. To my displeasure, he did not react.

Leaning back, he seized all of me, narrowing his vile eyes on my attire, hair and face. Then it rested on my hands, studying my gloves before he tapped his finger atop one of them. "Why the gloves?" he asked, tilting his head.

Putting a grape in my mouth, I looked at him and pointed a finger above my head. "Why the crown?"

He wavered in anger and I threw him a wink. I heard both uncle and Elias choke on their food, coughing before they returned to their conversation. My father on the other hand seemed to be growing used to my remarks. He only pursed his lips and went back to his plate.

Moreen cleared her throat and leaned forward. "We are meeting with the ladies of Casmere this afternoon, for the winter solstice silks. Should I order the same costume as last year for you, Silas?"

At the mention of the winter solstice, I froze. Did Isjord continue to celebrate the day I mourned, the day Adriata attacked, the day of their deaths?

Father lazily and disinterestedly leaned back, assessing her before nodding. "Order something for Snowlin, she will attend along with us."

The fork in my grasp almost snapped in half. "Attend?"

"Yes," he answered, continuing to cut his breakfast. "It is not your first one, child. You know your duties as royal involve participating in the glorious day of our ancestors."

"Glorious day of our ancestors?" I grit between my teeth.

At my withered reaction his smile grew gleefully, he knew which wound he poured salt into. "Yes, you heard me."

The reaction between the consort and her children had grown cold while following our conversation. Before they had never been allowed to attend the event, now it seemed they thought themselves the main stars. Moreen nodded. "I will get her something similar to Fren's."

"Blessed heavens don't, spare me crone, spare me father," I begged mockingly, and he strangely smiled.

"Pick it yourself then. Why don't you attend the tea afternoon with the ladies of Rose court? You never debuted in the society you were born to belong to, make yourself scarce, too."

Fren gasped loudly. "But she will scare everyone."

I dropped my goblet and clapped my hands together making her flinch. "You know, father, that is the greatest idea you have ever had. Moreen dearest, you will be there, along with the sea urchin, right?"

The consort swallowed looking between my father and I, and nodded.

"The guard outside, is he a friend?" father asked, peeking through the doors while his half breeds left. I knew he'd asked around, knew he kept a close eye on them, and knew who they were, too. He was testing me and my reactions. He was lurking for weakness like he always did.

I shook my head. "Medius's son, the guard you sent with Alaric. The girl is Drian's daughter."

Father had sent me off with the two Isjordians and Alaric into exile. Drian and Medius were legends among soldiers in the Winter court, but they both had very unheroic ends.

He gave me a confused look. "Where are my soldiers?"

"Medius died four years ago and Drian is half paralyzed after an Adriatian trailed us for a couple of weeks. Their children took their place." The best lie is the one with bits of truth in them. Medius was indeed dead and Drian paralyzed, but their children were far from here and far from being Adriatian and Olympian.

"And no one bothered to notify me?"

"Why for, so two new faces suddenly trailed me about the village? Alaric thought it best like that."

He dropped his cutlery all fury. "Alaric this and Alaric that. I am your king and your father, it should be up to me what is best for you."

"Ah," I said, loading up fruit in my arms, before standing to leave. "Aren't you father of the year. Applause. Applause."

Rose hall was the ladies court in the castle. Designed to welcome pathetic gatherings where puffed peacocks like Moreen spent their useless trophy lives in gossip, tea and knitting. The latter I could do with, Alaric had forced the both of us to take knitting classes for years. The burly man had sat each Wednesday by my side pulling yarns through needles and sticks. The old fool thought it a calming activity to soothe my quick temper, but the precision of the task brought immense stress to my attempts at not missing a single stitch. I'd thrown more tantrums and broken more objects at missing a loop than anything else, but at least I could knit myself a scarf now.

Fren and Moreen sat puffed up by a tattling table that could not shut up or make it less obvious that I was the target of gossip. I stood, taking the lilac yarn with me, it was mine now, I'd taken fancy at the colour.

"You have something here, dear," I said, wiping my fingers next to my mouth to the woman sitting next to Moreen.

She blinked stunned and then wiped her mouth with the corner of a handkerchief. "Gone?"

"Still there. All the shit that you speak is staining." Throwing her a handkerchief, I went and sat next to the only person who stood on her own. She was young but beaten by life, dark circles accompanied her seafoam blue-green eyes. Her delicate features and thin lips had paled the colour of a corpse and the almost white blonde hair, lustreless, washed her out completely.

"Snowlin Krigborn," I introduced, extending a hand to her.

"I know who you are, Your Highness." She gave me a shy smile and shook my hand. "Freja Olsen Modr."

Not afraid of me, I noted. A smile crept up on my face at the pleasant surprise. "The Lord's daughter," I said, taking her in. "That makes you a candidate for a gossiper, why are you not joining the hells dominion over there?"

She threw her head back laughing and the crones took turns shaking their heads at us, full of lush judgement. "More like a candidate for good gossip, I'm married to general Gabriel Olsen, the arse-wipe of whore houses here in Tenebrose and further away."

I spat my tea, coughing my lungs out, and she rubbed a hand behind my back. "Don't choke, Your Highness, they will think I tried to kill you. Next thing you know, they have me hung at the murder attempt of a royal, that if I am not caught at the murder attempt of my husband," she said with a nervous giggle before letting out a sigh and straightening herself as if she had slipped out of an act.

Alaric had told me about her, the only child of Kalius Modr. If she was not married, she would also be the direct successor of the northern city. Her father was rough as winters up his city's mountains. A strict maintainer of old tradition and avid supporter of my father's—all in all, a rotten piece of dog crap. He'd married late and only sired a daughter whom he had been most eager to hand off to general Gabriel Olsen, who just funnily enough was someone I intended to make myself associated with.

"He sounds like a delightful man."

She suppressed a giggle and snidely added, "Oh, most definitely a gentleman of the finest."

Her embroidery hoop had flawless needlework from corner to corner, intricate patterns of flowers and colourful threads delightfully enhancing her precision. Her posture unstirred, not a crease in her modest navy gown, hair propped up not a single stand out of place.

"I might need to take a lesson or two from you on how to handle myself," I said, unfolding my legs that had creased my dress and straightening the loose hair falling madly over my shoulder.

"You have the most beautiful hair, it would be a shame to not flaunt it." Her knitting needles stopped and her lips pursed back as she gently touched the surface of her head. "Three servants check my bearings before I leave the house, at fathers orders. Not to bring shame to the Modr house. It is a shame already that he was blessed with only a daughter."

Isjord and their politics, views, restriction, and dislike of women, never ceased to draw a reaction from me. Once, I'd witnessed a father bring his daughter in audience with the Lord of Kirkwall asking to have her flogged for rejecting a marriage offer herself and losing him the lucrative bride price the elder merchant had offered for her hand. From what Alaric had told me regarding Kalius Modr, he was at the top of the list in ranks of small-minded bigots here in Isjord.

I studied her for a moment, the bravery of her dislike without feel of fear, and dared to ask, "What is your biggest wish, Freja?"

She blinked surprised at my question, pursing for a few seconds in thought. "Living my barren life, one has so many. Run...run far away," she answered, lost in pondering. "Or some way to buy my freedom, be where I want, with whom I want as far away from here. Uhm—"

"Your husband," I said, moving a teaspoon over my neck.

Her eyes shot wide, bright with sparkles of eagerness making them shine, and she grinned before adding, "My father, too."

Be careful what you wish for. Should gods not listen, a princess with a dagger certainly might.

A smirk rose on my lips. "Isjordians don't make for the best paternal figures, do they? From one with a crap father to another, don't we all have the same wish." Complete sincerity coming from the one pawned by her own father to her family's killer for an agreement.

"Your problem is worse than mine. Your father," she said looking around before leaning in and whispering, "is the king."

I leaned in close to her whispering back, "He is also made of flesh and bones, dear."

She blinked blankly before leaning back in her chair taking a deep breath. "Wishes, right?"

I gave her a smile. "Good thing they belong in a well or a fountain."

"Good thing they do," she said, raising her teacup in a toast.

I toasted my cup to her. "I believe you and I will be great friends." I had a ship to take down and mine happened to be a galley. Heavy timber was heard to sink, but this ship already had holes.

Light had faded, the greyish corridors were dimly lit by the reflecting crystal chandeliers that swayed just lightly when the current circulating hit them. Eerie as the rest of the castle, they resembled spirits. Pay enough mind and you could convince your thoughts that they actually were spirits. Pay enough mind and the whole of Isjord would convince a saint they were resting in one of the seven hells.

"What are you gloating about in your head, sparks are almost flying out of your mischievous eyes," Nia said walking in step beside me.

I let my face wear the amusement of my thoughts and she scornfully clicked her tongue at me.

"Nia, how many heads does Winter court have?"

She halted, brows pinched in confusion. "Well, eight lords, three generals and the Bruma commander. Twelve?"

"What is wrong with a galley ship?"

She then blinked, lost. "I have a feeling you will soon tell me."

"It needs oars to sail," I said, doing a rowing motion which she followed with a cringe. "If one oar isn't working or compromised the chain link is broken. Now imagine if several oars don't work or are compromised." Emphasis on compromised.

"I am being tested now on... ships? At least make the lecture a bit longer or understandable, or use a less horrible metaphor for another horrible plan of yours."

I grabbed onto her fluffy cheeks with both hands and she struggled away from me. "The fate of the ship would be left to the wind, drown or worse, to the compromised."

"How can they be compromised?" she muttered between pinched cheeks.

"An oar already despises my father, a possible one already likes me and another soon will be persuaded into liking me."

"So...compromise the ship?"

"Much easier than drowning it all together, with the ship at hand we can sail to distant seas. Imagine a whole ship in our control, how many others can we drown. Imagine how much better it would be to drown it ourselves instead of having another do it for us."

She shook her head hard. "Let us drop the metaphor, all this sailor talk is drowning my head."

"Get Cai, I will enter Winter court."

"I thought—"

"Plans have changed again. Well...somehow."

"It scares me when you get those eyes," she murmured between the pinched cheeks. "The 'I am itching to cause some damage' eyes."

"Well, I am itching," I said, scratching my back. "I should not be getting so close to dogs."

She scowled. "You are not allergic to dogs."

"To Isjordian foul mouthed bitches I am."

She glances sideways onto the corridor, before turning to slap my back. "You crude, vulgar woman."

"Hello, little princess," Elias said, startling Nia upward. I knew sooner or later he would approach me, but I was yet to decide if I wished to explore my chances with Venzor with him or his father.

"Hello," I said, tracing a look over him. "Big dog?"

Nia nudged my side in warning.

He laughed though my words were meant to offend. "I never seem to get a moment alone with you."

"I am allergic. To dogs, that is." Nia pinched my under arm enough that I almost squirmed in pain. Ignoring the shooting pain, I stretched my shoulders to relieve some of the tension. "How can I help, Elias?"

"Have a walk with me?"

Nia reached close to me and murmured, "Have a walk with him."

"You have a walk with him," I murmured back, rubbing my arm.

She pinched me again. "He is in your father's court. Do it."

Ouch, her pinch was inhuman.

Elias blinked confused between the two of us. "Is there something the matter?"

I blew out a tired breath and went to hook my arm to his. "That walk, are we having it or not?"

We made rounds over the massive winter gardens, but he'd not said a word. "Elias, you're running us out of laps to run."

"Do you remember much from back then? When you were younger?" he finally spoke.

What? I took a few minutes of silence to grasp the sort of trick he was trying to play with me. "No, not much."

He brought us to a halt. "Then I suppose I will have to take you on more walks till you remember."

What the hells was he on about? "Let me know prior, next time I'll bring my leash. Shouldn't Fren be taking you round? You're her poodle."

He laughed and ran a hand over his long blonde hair. "She is my leash, not my owner."

I stuck my bottom lip out. "Is your own father dearest forcing you to marry the snow spirit?"

"You don't need to get the answer out of me, you know that is the truth."

He felt familiar and strangely sincere. *It is the eyes,* Alaric always says, *if they go soft and mellow, if they stare with force of cotton, the window of sincerity is open, it will just pour out.* Alaric was into his riddles and wise words, but this one I'd always relied on. I felt bad for a moment, or perhaps I was reminded of my own situation.

"Another time, Elias, truly let me know why you wish for these moments alone. With your permission," I said, turning to leave.

"Is this permission to ask for more of your time?"

I waved a hand over my shoulder. "Yes, but don't waste your luck with me. The Goddess of Luck is not my friend, I owe that bitch many favours already, you will get on her bad side, too." I wanted to know if he was looking at me as prey, ally or enemy.

Oars and galleys, kingdoms, kings, and pawns. Less than four moons I'd be married to the king of Adriata. My plans ran on borrowed time and it began counting down now.

I stalked along the corridors in my most elegant blush rose dress and entered the large meeting room in the northern tower. Empty, except a long table in its middle with maps, books and papers scattered atop. The red tinted glass ceiling casted a red shadow in the room and dropped a hopelessness atmosphere of doom. Lords, the three generals, captains and the Bruma Commander of the Verglaser legions all sat around the large wooden table, deep in discussion.

Winter court was weaved by King Edric, the first king of old Isea, and held to this day. Isjord was rough land, mountain, and snow whilst the largest kingdom. He'd dissected the land in nine cities and appointed a lord for each to rule as viceroy in his stead and under his rule. Despite the land being all bloodlines and ancestry, a lord was carefully selected to duty; scholars, merchants, generals, captains, priests and even healers sat on that post. Once appointed, it would take death or scandal to dethrone you from such a position, the king had no power over it. A rule that Edric carefully planned to prevent his successors from bringing ruin to the land and it had worked. Lord Albius Arynth once was a captain in my great-grandfather's army, after the previous lord had died, he'd been promoted to the role. But Albius had no heir and that meant that Arynth would go to someone appointed by my father. Those with a male heir or an unmarried daughter would automatically be able to pass it through to their child. Though any had yet to inherit their city to their children, many still held onto their post since my grandfather's rule.

All stood and bowed though still exchanging surprised glances and confused murmurs amongst each other. I stifled at Renick's sight—he had been the one training Aura out of myself and siblings. My head filled with all the lashing and beating I had received from him when I could not even bear the cold let alone produce it. *Olympian scum*, he used to call us. His favourite torture always remained the simplest yet cruellest—leaving us out in the cold for hours to days after he had found out we didn't have the tolerance towards the cold like all other Isjordians. I suppose we were not all other Isjordians. My blood boiled at the thought, but a few coils twisted and knotted in my stomach at the remembrance of old fear. Everyone turned at my approach and bowed their heads surprised at my presence, except for him.

As if he could sense my thoughts and panic, he gave me a vile smile.

"Snow?" Sam called from a corner of the room almost startling me. "Your father will not be happy about this, you know that?"

I cleared my throat of all bitter memories. "Well, he is a miserable man, Sam, and his emotional affairs have never been of my concern," I said, throwing my hand in the air in disregard. Not a single lie spoken, my sincerity was applaudable.

"Alaric would kill me if he knew I let you do this."

I leaned close to his ear and whispered. "It was his idea." I straightened and threw glances at the half full room. "So much sandalwood, sweat, loose balls and unfathomable ego all in one place. Where is that horned eudemon, Lady of Grasmere? She is the one missing the loose balls and the only one with loose tits." The hellhound of winter hells, one worse than all of those gathered in this room.

Sam suppressed a laugh beside me and shook silently in amusement. "The sealine cities gather on a different day."

"I imagine on a Sunday. They bring my father the most riches. I bet he picks Sunday to be his happy day."

He stilled, eyes wide in surprise. "How did you know?"

"No one knows that tyrant you call your king better than I, unfortunately."

We took seats next to one another and moments later my father marched in, lost in deep thoughts to take notice of me. It wasn't till he sat in his seat when his head flew once and then twice in surprise in my direction.

"Was it the dress? Definitely the dress gave me away," I said, giving him my most saccharine smile.

My father leaned back in his seat and nodded. "Very well then, you will join us. After all, you are a royal."

I scoffed for a better reaction. He did like spinning the tales to his favour.

The four eastern city lords reported their weekly incomes, taxes, and latest produce to be shipped out to Grasmere and Brisk for trade to the other kingdoms. Lord of Kirkwall was particularly mouthy, expressing his displeasure and concern for the shippings not being received in timely manners from Eldmoor. Sanctimonious bastards surely had been outside their borders to see how the rest of the continent lived compared to these stuffed turkeys sat across me.

"Come now," I interrupted, all attention falling towards me. "You need not ruffle your feathers for a mere day's delay, not every traveller is accustomed to travel through your lands snow knee thick and deep. Such delays are to be expected and we are nearing winter season, I hope you are aware, dear Lord?" I asked, batting my eyelashes and leaning back in my chair. The generals, captains and the other officials chuckled under their breath and few gasped before my father interrupted by clearing his throat.

"You're so versed in running a city, maybe you should take our position," Kalius Modr said snidely, flinging his papers to the table and crossing his arms in an indignant expression.

He was just like Freja had said: the first to be riled by my presence and mouth.

"Maybe, but it's too minuscule of a position for me, your small head could do a fine job had your pride not grasped your balls tight enough you've gone red. Oh wait, that must be the whiskey."

"You're not careful in your offences, young lady."

"No, I'm not Lord, but I did lower to your standards. If you didn't wish me to offend you maybe you should have not offended me. Remember, it is still *Your Highness* to you, not young lady. Offending a royal, what is that, father, twenty lashes?" I asked, cocking an eyebrow at him.

The lord swallowed and bowed just slightly. "Apologies, Your Highness, I meant no offence." Not an ounce of apology but tight irritated features.

"I limit myself to one good deed a day, call it already spent," I warned, souring down to irked.

"Careful now," Sam murmured. "You know what these people hate the most, don't gather a crowd of enemies so soon."

"Chickens that coo too loud have their necks snapped first, Sam, I worry not."

The generals proceeded next, reporting on their numbers and weaponry as though war was nearing. Not surprised at the updates, Isjordians had won their riches and status for their tactics, war theories and wise military decisions, being prepared was their best front. Except the night they let Adriata march in their homes killing thousands including its queen and heirs they were not.

The captains then reported on rising petty crimes and the condition of their respective city borders. Kirkwall and Arynth had more to report, their borders were the ones surrounded by the Highwall. If you were to ask me, it was one of my father's least stupid decisions from his thirty years as a king. One that came too late, but it gave me a small satisfaction to know those barbaric creatures were locked with themselves and their spirituality.

Sam and the other two generals chatted amongst each other regarding vandals that had raided the northern villages and a two-day expedition towards another village that sat by the edge of the Islines, close to where my father's lands broke from the old Krigborn ones.

"Could I join you?" I asked and the two generals were sent onto laughing fits. Sam, on the other hand, was looking at me full of worry.

"Meaning no offence, Your Highness. A princess is surely to be out of place amongst soldiers and most out of place amongst vandals," Clar, the white haired younger one said, still laughing and I certainly took offence in what he said.

Gabriel, the other general, looked me up and down before saying, "You are certainly no soldier, Your Highness, and we do not take decorations in our expeditions. We are faced with a lot of bad people."

Such condescending mocking tones would usually send my fist flying on someone's face, but this one grew flutters of anticipation in my stomach. I leaned onto my seat assessing the satisfied general. "Well, they allow hogs," I said, pointing to him. "Certainly, I shan't be an issue. You see, I am much nibbler and can see behind me without having to make a full spin to see my tail," I teased, gesturing my finger in a circle.

The general paled and straightened his uniform, almost offended. His features turned irate at my disrespect but he would not speak, throwing glances between myself and others who had now turned and carefully listened to our conversation. Father was well aware that I was no decorative princess by any means, but I knew he did not want me to prove that to anyone. To him that was an invitation to defy.

Defying was my purpose, however. "How about we test a theory tomorrow, that of my decorative purposes. Training court? The hog spars the decoration?" I asked the general.

The room grew loud from the laughter, but it was not at my remark, my courage even to challenge him was hilarious to them. They often found hilarity in those that dared.

Gabriel flashed me a crooked grin. "That attitude, princess, will not take you far. You expect me to believe your sparring is as good as your banter?"

"Yes, your fragile ego is at stake."

His mouth pursed, nostrils flaring in offence that he'd taken too much at heart. "Let's say we indulge in this bravado of yours and I win, you will have to get rid of your presence from these meetings and your nose out of this kingdom's business."

Isjordians dislike for me had always been noticeable, but what surprised me was his nerve to speak with such spitefulness and disrespect to a royal with their king in attendance, at that. But then, my father did like for me to be disregarded like that, for me to be put in my place, for me to be disliked. He did not have to try at all for that part, I would do those honours myself. He was a general well trained and massive and I was smaller, softer and a woman, untrained in his eyes. His odds appeared to be in his favour by this point, but I nodded in acceptance.

"And if I win, you will hand your post to me, along with those lovely circlets," I said, pointing to the top of his breast pocket where the three gold brooches were lined.

He rumbled with uproarious laughter all mirth from the prognosis of my failure. He cast a confirming glance to his king and then nodded. "A deal that is."

I nodded. "Pleasure to have dealt with you."

He stood like many did and murmured for only me to hear, "I will give you another scar to match."

I flashed him a smile. "My vanity is hard to injure. Yours is impossible."

After the meeting ended, father asked for me to stay behind. He waited for everyone to exit and stared at me in silence for a few very long moments.

"Words, father, I do not read minds," I said, rolling my eyes. He was clearly very, very angry at me.

"You are aware you entered a bargain you will not win. Gabriel is one of my generals, therefore if not one of my best soldiers. Not very smart on your behalf to offend him either. He will take retribution for the disrespect," he said, folding his hands on top of the table leaning forward.

And he would let him. That was how he intended to end that sentence.

"And I, father, your daughter, if not your best one." I stood and made for the doors. "You shall know I don't make unfavourable bargains or promises."

9

RAVENS AND OMENS

SNOWLIN

WINTER COURT: EIGHT LORDS, an Auran commander, three generals. Anything regarding all matter crosses there first. If it is done in secret, any position from any of the twelve will have you close enough to it. Gabriel Olsen. His past is foible. He is your way into the Winter court, Alaric's voice reverberated inside my head while I marched towards the training grounds.

Despite the many participants, the air shifted silently and almost cautiously. A small crowd gathered by the far ledges of the pits and in the balconies of the castle overlooking the courts. A few officials, Samuel, Elias, my uncle, and Reuben among them. Cai was positioned beside them, ready for any unwanted move, whilst Nia had taken the opportunity of the distraction to visit the Bruma halls, her most recent obsession.

The general, Gabriel, sat in a stool laughing in all his arrogance and confidence, surrounded by other soldiers. "I thought you had changed your mind, princess," he said, peeking a glance towards the balconies where my father now graced us with his presence.

"No, but you still have time to change yours. Awfully embarrassing, wouldn't that be? Losing to me?"

A sneer took the place of his crooked smile. "I remember when you were young, how many times they would flog you right in these courts for that character."

My mood now faltered. Flashes of memory send waves of trembles down my body. They would clap—the soldiers would clap and laugh as Renick's whip hit and marked my skin, as he marked my soul with it, too. My attention diverted to where he was standing in the balcony, still the posture of someone who owed me.

"You could never tame an Olympian beast, let alone one of their whores. Their cunts had mouths of their own. Shame they rest in bones, might have tried to tame one myself," Gabriel bit out, wearing an oily grin.

The last words returned my breath and fury, snapping me to reality. I unbuttoned my jacket and hung it neatly to a pole. I unsheathed my brother's sword, the sound of magic quivered in my ear, and again, Eren's presence danced around it, feather weight in my hands while I swung it back and forth a few couple of times.

When my brother was born, the heir to the throne of Isjord, people around the kingdom had brought presents and gifts in his honour, one of the eldest forgers in Isjord had gifted him the silver hilted sword, an elegant beauty carved in vines and intricate designs with a deep blue sapphire at the centre of the hilt. The sword outmatched any jewellery or decoration of kings and queens, but its sharpness and craftiness was one of the deadliest—it could cut and slice air itself. The forger had been an Aura himself. He'd claimed no magic laced the weapon, but I could feel the tangy remnants every time I unsheathed it, the ring of the metal heavily unnatural. After the attack, Alaric had brought it to me, it was now mine and it made me feel as if Eren was protecting me himself. I could have sworn every time I wielded it, a hand laid on top of mine giving my swings more strength. A piece of him—a piece of my brother. It always went with me.

"First to draw blood," father called from the balcony. If blood is what he wanted to see, blood I would give him.

Incite him, Alaric's words rang again. *He must put up a fight, you have to look like you struggled otherwise your father will stop the challenge.*

"Never tamed an Isjordian hog before either," I said, stretching my neck. "Always thought they had thick brains and writhed under pressure, but it happens they have a piss mouth and poor wits."

His face wrinkled from heated tension and disdain at my words, and he unsheathed his own sword. Gabriel was tall, and three times my weight. To him, I was easy prey, but traps did not have to be big to catch a plump mouse.

First attack was his, rough like a grizzly bear and just as wild. He swung his sword powerfully, cutting air itself and making it whistle. Yet his blade did not meet mine, not even once. My lightness of foot and nimbleness came to my advantage as his steel repeatedly met nothing but air. He was indeed the grand general my father spoke of. His mastery of the steel was impeccable, he was well trained, but relied heavily on his size and weight, something not very smart in the art of fighting.

Duck, evade, incite.

Alaric words made me laugh as I ducked under his hit and said, "Not much in courts, too much in taverns, I see. The White Spade, was it not? Every other day you start with brandy." I finally halted and caught his blade with mine, getting close so only he could hear me. "Then ale, goat stew, but the goat must be of Modr, you say the flesh of mountain goats tastes sweeter. After, you have one last glass of whiskey and go to Iris House for a dive with Miss Helga, the madame of the brothel, your personal favourite."

His expression turned wide and ghastly, and mine amused.

Nia had not missed a single detail in her research, and neither had Alaric when he suggested my way into Winter court. Alaric had made me aware Gabriel was the easiest pride to wound in Winter court. He had the most hate for foul mouthiness, irked by women who didn't know their place and the general with most flaws to use in my leverage. He was my way in. Everyday since our arrival, Nia had kept close watch, following him in and out of taverns, brothels, shops, and all sorts. By today, I knew him from his oily yellow hair to his spiral tail.

He wavered, face completely red, sweat coating his clothing thickly, his eyes lost and dazed while he struggled to stand straight.

"Is there something wrong, Gabriel?" The answer was yes, something was wrong. Nia had also meticulously placed frost thorn in his food and drinks to weaken him. She slipped through the shadows, her magic aiding to poison him for days. Nia was not only gifted in magic, but in wits, too. The generals had weekly health checks from Medi and Magi healers who might have detected it in his system easily, but frost thorn had an alcohol toxin. And considering the amount of alcohol the general consumed, it would slip by as a glass of salt water in a well. I was not a fool to head onto a duel without armour and with an Isjordian at that, no matter my skills.

I twirled around as if dancing with him, avoiding all his blows till he panted breathless and probably dizzy, too. Right where I wanted him. His eyes narrowed in confusion—he finally seemed to have stopped underestimating me. An applause to the hog.

Once he has put all his might, threaten.

"Does your wife know of Miss Helga and your two bastards in Venzor?" I finally said, and he staggered back in bewilderment.

His nostrils flaring while he charged forward, and I caught his heavy blow this time. Swiftly sliding my blade down his, sending sparks flying at the friction. And in a quick motion, I spun around and slammed the back of his knee with my heel, causing him to half kneel on the ground.

Gasps filled the air, but the show had yet to end.

Provocation causes distraction. Status wins above all in Isjord—harm his position and you have threatened his life.

"You bitch, how dare you play dirty with me?" he groaned, holding his knee.

He turned, and I waved my sword up, motioning him to stand. I had just started and was yet to spend my fun from this game. "All is fair between hogs and pretty decorations."

He stood confused and struck again, meeting my blade, his blows softer. He halted a moment for air, measuring me and my intentions before striking again. "Let's hope the Adriatians won't mind another scar on that face, for I'll carve it out myself."

"Hope your wife likes hog ball soup, I shall deliver her some myself as a victory gift. Or she might do that herself when my friend reaches her door along with the news. Aren't you married to the daughter of Kalius Modr, the lovely Freja? What will he have to say to that? You lose your position or your life. Decide. End this quickly and you might get home before she does."

His eyes shot wide. "Relying on petty tricks to have your win?"

"Tick tock," was all I said. Taking the opportunity from the distraction, I took a few steps back, making him stumble forward. I jumped up before landing on top of the flat of his blade, his hand twisting against the ground.

He screamed in pain and muttered a chain of curses, but did not resist or fight back.

"I hope you use your left to pick your nose," I teased, kicking his hand and picking up his sword, throwing it out of the pit. He was in front of me on the ground, disarmed, the tip of my sword at this neck.

"First blood, right?" I asked playfully, and then I grazed his skin, causing blood to gush out. I dropped to my heels to face him, still not removing my sword despite Alaric's words ringing on my ears.

Do not kill. Living with shame is worse than death, your father enjoys that. It is his punishment for someone who has failed him.

My knuckles turned white from the tightness of my grip around the sword's hilt—I'd been trained all my life to fight till death, to hand it to the person I fought against. One would think that twelve years would make me forget how much of my days as Silas's monster had ingrained in me. "The ale stomach and lungs don't help, neither do your tendencies of a piece of horse dung. I could offer you a few training sessions had you not the tongue of swine."

"You whore."

I gave him a wink. "Die knowing a whore gifted you your gravestone."

The tip of my sword moved to his face and I dug it deep enough that I was shaking, holding myself from sending his wife brain soup.

"Forgive me," he said breathlessly, putting both his hands up in the air. "Don't kill me."

Fear before death writhed my appetite. I disliked beggars. I waved my sword in the air for him to scatter and he immediately took off running out of the training courts. He could run, but he was running right into a trap. Freja had already been informed days ago about all the details of my plan by myself. Phase two of my new plan, I now needed him dead, too, just not from my hand.

I stood, turning to face the balconies filled with spectators whose expressions had turned grim. Delicately putting my jacket on, I met all their gazes one after the other. Few of those who had once seen me wither in pain and the one who had made me scream in agony lowered theirs down. Father had turned a pale angry—his face no longer a solemn mask. Alaric was owed some thanks, it appears I had not just angered my father, but impressed him as well.

I was up and ready before Penelope came in this morning, jittery to face my father for the new position I'd obtained, one that would not last long hence the agreement with the King of Adriata, but a position I planned on using and abusing till it was time to do so.

I made my way to the dinner chambers in a burgundy short sleeved silk dress with beaded embroidery at the hem that swished heavy when I took steps, this one clung to every curve of my body almost as a second skin. A memory of my mother's youth, a dress she'd once worn when at my age, before marrying father—after, she'd never been allowed to. The healing wounds of my palms concealed by deep burgundy gloves, they probably had to be sown to my skin at this point, I even slept with them on. My hair was in a loose braid hanging above my shoulder, concealing part of my scar, and flaunting two massive golden earrings with rubies, a gift from father to my mother on one of their anniversaries. The tyrant had taste. But just as beautiful, they were also Alaric's plan.

Distract. Anything that will have him angry will draw him out of questioning.

Father sighed deeply at my sight when I bowed delicately, a hand over my very exposed chest. My uncle was strangely missing so I sat next to Elias, who did not hide his staring from others. Fren, too, stared between the two of us with confusion. Her face did that thing when she got envious—splotched red in places. It made her look entirely too much like her mother.

Father had not spoken a single word to anyone, only casually peeking at the jewellery dangling from my ears, so I broke the silence first, "I am now a soldier in your army, like you always wanted just not how you wanted." He had worn us loose for years trying to beat and train Aura out of me and my siblings, to bring out the hybrid Aura he had intended to create, to wield us at his desire towards more wars he was trying to rage. Eren had been his biggest prey, my brother had never spent a day in his short life out of training courts or his examinations. He had never said anything and abided by our father's words without question. We never had a life here and now they are gone without even experiencing living.

He cast a short glance over my gloved hands. "Very well, if that is what you desire." Crossing his arms on top of the table, he leaned forward. "Since you're convinced in dallying and offending just about anyone, I would indeed prefer you away from the castle anyway, but you are to be a captain, not general. That is a duty too grand and filled with much bigger responsibilities you could handle, and I will not put a kingdom in jeopardy for your games. You might pick your team, for which I will have a perfect assignment."

Once you have beaten Gabriel, you have entered your trap. He will impel you out of it. Entering is not the difficulty, staying there is.

Alaric had been right once again.

I rolled my eyes, but it would have been too good to be true. Half-heartedly I nodded, accepting his terms. My initial plan had gone to waste, but at least now I was inside his court. It was his perfect assignment that had me clutching my hands. I'd defied my father therefore I was to be punished. He always had the perfect punishments for me. Once he'd made me kill every living stock that came into the castle when I refused to eat meat knowing animals had to die. I was only seven. Everyday along with the servants, I slashed and gutted animal after animal while his bastards leisurely enjoyed the luxuries that should have been mine, that of a royal. The two radishes paraded around learning etiquette, stuffing their hollow heads with how to drink tea and use forks, yet he was the most surprised when it came to my behaviour, which he had shamelessly labelled *wild*. I had tried to be strong for Thora more than myself, I wanted to teach her to be strong yet every night I had silently cried myself to sleep from the horrors of the day that kept flashing in my nightmares as well. I always failed them, till the day they died.

If need comes, use Highwall as a reason. He knows your anger, he will buy into that.

"I would like to tend to the trials of the Adriatians caught at our borders and tending Highwall. I might as well make myself familiar with them. I am, after all, marrying their king," I interrupted before he could finish. However, this was no longer a lie. With both kingdoms close to my watch I could use this opportunity to seek information on the Adriatian side as well. If my fears of a military union were true, they had to be preparing along. I doubted Adriata kept their secrets as guarded as my father.

"She is what, Silas?" Moreen called from her seat. Had he not told anyone about his arrangement? There was no reason to keep it a secret, and definitely not from his consort who he had shared all his vast plans with prior to anyone else, even my mother.

Father explained his plans to the table. The agreement with Adriata and how that would benefit both kingdoms, as if he cared about anyone besides his own nose.

Once he was done, his attention returned to me. "Seems a well thought plan, why are you insistent on that?" he asked, studying me with scrutiny at the doubtfulness of my query. It felt as if he could read through my thoughts, was he beginning to doubt my true intentions?

Lifting my chin, I cocked an eyebrow at him. "Would you not be insistent if you had few of their kind to torture to your like and under the veil of law at that?" Not entirely a lie, just a very twisted truth.

His lips curled wickedly. "Revenge on petty peasants?"

"Anything better than nothing, considering they will probably lock me in a cage when I get there."

He blew a raucous laugh, eyes flashing eagerly, no denial on my claim, it was probably what he wanted. "If that is your wish, you have my permission. No. A gift. A wedding gift from me," he added, toasting his goblet in the air.

He bought it after all.

I could see the contempt in Fren and Reuben's features, the idea of my demise seems to still satisfy them, so I leaned toward Elias. "When are you going to ask for that other moment alone?"

His gaze eagerly followed me, too distracted to notice everyone had turned to our attention. "If I ask for a small one tonight?"

"Tonight you shall have it."

He ran the tip of his tongue over his lip and nodded.

"How did my general get beaten almost to death and then thrown to the dungeons for hanging right after you fought him?" my father snapped in distaste, throwing glances between myself and Elias.

Questions, they come after, once you are comfortable in your win. He will make you think you have won, then dispel any trust he made you think you formed before catching you unprepared.

"You expect me to know how?" I taunted, continuing to chew on fruit.

He narrowed his eyes, like a hunter at his prey. "Strange coincidence, don't you think so? Strange that his wife had found out he had committed adultery, and she is not just an ordinary woman, her father is Kalius Modr."

"Is she?" I asked, raising my brows. "Strange indeed. So, what do you expect to hear from me, father?"

"How did you find out?" he snapped, impatiently.

"Find out what?"

Ice crawled from his fingertips and over the table. "Do not play with me, Snowlin." *Servants.*

"Servants," I lied, throwing a few grapes in my mouth. "They told me all sorts of stories about him. He particularly angered me during our fight, called me a whore, you see, and I decided his wife should hear how much of a whore he was."

If he finds your threats, tell him servants spoke, place doubt about loose words around the castle, it will bring him out of the thought of your win.

"And who was this servant?"

I snorted. "You can barely remember your children's names and you expect me to remember servants? What is the matter, you think I have a spy in your court?"

"Do you? Do you have a spy in my court?"

He will think you have your spy.

I smiled, remembering Alaric's words, everything had gone to his advice. "I don't need to, here even walls talk. Your expression is very giving, too, which means you had no idea about the general and have doubts about a particular servant serving as someone's spy. Venzor? Oh, the Islines?" I jumped jollily in question.

He blanched. "That is enough."

My mouth was stuffed from corner to corner when I shrugged and said, "You started it."

Bring up the Venzors and the Isline Krigborn, and you have a checkmate.

No one knew my father better than Alaric did. He had spent years in Isjord, knew his very rotten core and every habit and dislike of his.

Samuel stood positioned between two training pits, instructing and training his men. His moves were more precise than any other soldier I had seen in Isjord. Sam was of Solaryan origin, a Glare Aura. Handpicked by my late grandfather himself, and served under the crown of Isjord for more than six decades. He was an orphan from Whitebridge sent to a special regiment when he was barely a toddler. Trained, bred to kill and fight. A tool of regimes, bargained back and forth armies. His worth was one of the highest. If a human could be bought, no one could afford him. Samuel had seen poverty, destruction and lived in war—one of the worst as well, the Ater battles. The longest war between the elementals and the spirituals, the roughest and hardest ever fought in the last two centuries. The continent had fought Eldmoor for three years, united against the plague they brought. Dark Crafters had been at their most greedy, their numbers had not only been large, but powerful. The 97th Grand Maiden, their leader, a Potioner, had experimented with more than any had dared before, more than their god allowed. She created mutant creatures of human flesh and blood drawn from monsters in Celesteel's realm that had no control and fed on human flesh. Adriata had fought against their fellow spirituals along with the other elemental kingdoms, Isjord included, to sustain and survive. The gods had listened. Well, Celesteel had. He had drawn his power back from the Grand Maiden and all Dark Crafters who had not been true believers. I always doubted that had been where my father got his idea to sire hybrid Aura. Sam had faced real beasts and seen true horrors, if there was one general that I did not wish to fight, it would be him.

His soldiers halted and bowed. His attention now turned to me, a smile wore his face when he noted my presence. "Have you come to take me down as well?" he asked playfully, catching a glance of me from where he had twisted around a young man.

Soldiers laughed in unison and then dispersed at his order.

"I only deal with those who run their mouths as if it is their bottom. You are safe, Sam," I said, pulling him in a hug.

We both sat down on the bench just outside the training pits. Grunts, heavy thunder, and restless neighs from the stables nearby drowned our conversation.

Sam sighed heavily. "A dozen men, all my own, trained from my hands since they were barely old enough to hold a wooden sword," he said, looking around the pits before handing me a list of his chosen team that was to be my own. "Be careful, Snow, your father is not happy about this, he is aware you played unfair and he doesn't like to be tricked. Others will soon know you have returned, to be travelling the kingdom as a captain could put you in the line of danger." His eyes darted down to the ground. "They have looked for you before, a few times, not giving up on what they had thought back then. They still hunt you as if you truly are that monster," he added somewhat distressed, but I was already aware.

I grabbed his hand between mine. "Maybe I am. I ran from danger once and it became my biggest regret. I am no longer that eleven-year-old of that night. To their misfortune, they will have to try really hard to get rid of me this time." I wanted them to come to me so I could unleash the pent-up vengefulness that circled my flesh and bones, the more to hurt the merrier.

"What stance have the Venzors taken on the agreement with Adriata?" I asked.

He narrowed his eyes at my question. "The usual. Against it. Whatever your father requests they are usually on the wrong end of his scale. They think the deal will be useless and too much is being put at stake. Remember, Venzor is the city that lost the most that night, they attacked there first, drawing our guards to them. Half the city was in flames before we could come to aid. If someone would disagree with the deal, it would be them and for a good reason."

So I might be right, Elias could well be a distraction from Lord of Venzor, he would profit greatly from having the deal fail. It would be a good opportunity to use it against my father as well.

"Are his eyes still on the throne?" I wanted to know if he might also make this an opportunity to gather somewhat of an opposing group to overthrow my father.

Sam huffed a laugh. "Ever since your grandfather was on the throne they have been open about their greed." He interrupted himself to assess me and my oddness. "What is going on, Snow? Are you thinking about what my conclusions are bringing?"

I shook my head to deny his thoughts. "Believe me, I would rather have my father than those thorny asses on the throne, at least I know what type of serpent my father is. I cannot wrap my head around another unfamiliar one, who from what I have heard could be as bad as lovely Silas." What I wanted to know was whether that oar was already loose, compromisable, or loyal to my father.

"Ah, so this is about Elias then?" he asked, and my eyes widened. How did he know?

He laughed and put a hand on my shoulder. "Words spread fast when a thousand servants and walls have ears. Elias is a good boy, but just as you are fearing he is still his father's son. And worse, your father's soldier. I know you will be careful, but you are what my daughter would have been, so I have to warn you. He is one ladies' man," he added, lightly patting my cheek.

"Worry not, I am a mens' lady as well," I reassured, greeting him goodbye with another hug.

He shut his eyes, shaking his head at my words. "Exactly what a father wants to hear."

I rubbed my palms together for warmth. "If you wished to kill me without anyone knowing, I would have given you better choices than this," I said to Elias, dismounting from Memphis in gods knows where he'd brought us. It was freezing cold, I couldn't see anything without squeezing my eyes and there was a trailing howl behind us since we'd left the castle. Perhaps I'd been rash to think I could use Elias. Perhaps he wished to use me. For murder practice.

"The castle has you all agitated. The further away, perhaps the nicer you will behave to me," he said, tying his horse to a tree.

Elias had dragged the two of us somewhere in the outskirts of Tenebrose borders, by a small village outside the city walls. Scarce wooden houses scattered nearby each other, thick smoke coming out of their chimneys and in its middle stood a little tavern filled with heat and laughter.

"You should have not worried about me being nice when you brought a royal in the midst of wolves." I said, pulling the hood of my coat over my head and covering my scar with a scarf. "Your king will have your head."

Elias took notice and pulled my hood down. "There is no need to hide, princess. They take very little interest in new faces, northern passersby stop here everyday on their way home."

Surely no northern passerby had a black head and a long scar in the middle of their face, but I raised my brows and nodded—I was freezing.

Elias was right, no one turned their attention to us as we took a seat in front of each other at a corner. I was looking around, uncomfortably shifting in my seat, when Elias's hand flew before my face to drag my scarf away.

My jaw tightened as I bit in threat, "You really wish to provoke your death out of me?"

"Relax, princess. Plus I do not wish to lose precious time having you so near me and not seeing your face," he said just as a young barmaid approached us.

Her eyes lit in recognition and she planted a fist in her hip facing him. "Look what the snowstorm brought my way. We haven't seen you here in months and here you are all frilly with a girl in front of you, who I dearly hope it's the one you are to marry," she said, turning to face me when I snorted.

It didn't surprise me that they knew each other. He was a captain and a player by looks and reputation. Wouldn't shock me if they had been more than acquainted and they were close enough to know he was betrothed. Had he come here to cry when he had been arranged to the snow spirit? A thought that made me burst in giggles.

I shook my head to deny her claims and she clicked her tongue at Elias.

"Trust me," I said between chuckles, "you would not be able to mistake me for her."

"I have missed you too, Lori, this is Snowlin," he introduced. He then instructed Lori to bring us warm drinks and food for which I was impatiently waiting for—I was starved.

Music sounded around the tavern and several old and young stood and danced to the cheery jig.

I caught Elias staring at me. "Speak, Captain," I spat, annoyed at his face.

"Captain?"

"You insist on calling me princess even though you know my name."

He laughed and leaned closer to me over the table, he smelled of pines and mint, insatiably delicious. "You might not remember, but once you threatened me with my life when we were younger. I called you a raven and you insisted you were a princess and made me promise to call you that for eternity."

Confused, it took me moments to part together what he meant. "What?"

When Lori came to lay down our ales and food, it hit me. I had been called a raven once in my life, at a solstice celebration when I was no more than eight. I remembered the blonde boy who had run around the food tables laughing at my hair and the tears drenching my eyes as I was chasing after him. I had cornered him when he had reached the stairs to leave and plunged toward him, screaming, shouting and hitting—telling him I was a princess and that he should not call me a raven. He had stopped laughing and lowered to his knees, apologising and wiping my tears away.

Promise to never call me a raven but a princess for all eternity, I had told him, and he had obeyed seeing how upset I had been.

I looked up at the man in front of me and that boy took his features. "You," I said quietly.

He took a deep sip from his mug before sighing. "Me," he replied, dropping farther back in his chair.

"Well, you have certainly outgrown the bad teeth and you are released from that promise, Elias." I took a sip from my hot ale. My stomach warmed and I let out a groan of relief.

"Well, raven," he teased, "you did not outgrow your love for violence, but everything else is absolutely beautiful."

I leaned closer. "What is it that you want, Elias, certainly you did not kind-heartedly bring me to see a few snow spirits, and most surely not reminisce about the past."

His eyes hardened at my words and he leaned further back in his chair, putting distance between us again. "I thought it was obvious what I wanted."

Another answer that was not an answer. "What is it that you want, Elias?" I questioned firmly this time.

He crossed his arms. "You. I want you."

A laugh left my throat but not longer than two heartbeats. Was this the game he was playing? Me, he wanted me? I was not a fool, but somehow I still could not blame him if it was true. He was to marry a wretchedly spoiled snow spirit whose veins ran on venom not on blood, but his betrothal was not what concerned me. It was mine. I cared very little how fair I stood to the agreement, even little less to respect it, but I knew this could indeed be thought of as a way to object to it. Despite all that came with the deal, they still despised the spiritual kingdom. Venzor and the rest of Isjord had never understood why the Moon Goddess taken so much like in Adriata and offered so many more blessings and kindness than what Krieg had offered Isjord. Bet Isjord had been more than happy to establish the Highwall.

"Elias, Elias, you play a little dangerous game, my dear. Is this your father's attempt to find a way out of my marriage to the King of Adriata or an initiative of your own doing?" I asked, distaste inking every word of mine.

He turned rigid and he looked at me as if I had told him I had killed his horse. "What has made you think that?"

"Well, this interest of yours given the circumstance seems idiotic, if you wanted someone to fool around I would have suggested others, much easier to chase and to convince to do so. Though you do look as if you might enjoy a challenge. But I assure you, there is very little time to convince me into that." I would not have averted a distraction, especially a delicious one, but this one seems to involve too much, one I would not allow when I was already being thrown between kingdoms like a game piece.

He nodded, but not in agreement to what I had said.

I motioned to stand, it was getting too late and if I didn't return before midnight Cai was going to hunt me down like a dog. I'd barely convinced him to leave me alone with Elias in the first place.

He took my scarf and threw it behind my back, tugging on either end of it, he pulled me to him, my palms landing flat on his chest. Leaning over, he murmured in my ear, "You are wrong, and you have no idea how much."

Releasing me, he tied the rest of my scarf around and marched to the horses.

10

TRIALS AND DEBTS

SNOWLIN

PEN BRUSHED AND BRAIDED my hair loosely down my back. My new uniform had arrived, the navy blue coat came down mid-thigh, gold buttons afront, two circlets above the chest pocket, the sign of my position. Captain.

"Are you going to keep frowning at me all day again?" I asked the red head.

"Mother says it's terrible to dally with married men, or those to be married, and you are soon to be a married woman yourself."

"Mother is right, but Pen is wrong. I am not dallying with Elias." I was playing with Elias.

"Are you certain Elias is not dallying with you?"

"That is on him."

She exhaled annoyed. "Will you not have a look?" she asked, pointing to the mirror.

I pinched her cheek. "Only when it stops showing me a dark shadow instead of my pretty face."

Her eyes widened and she glanced shortly at the large mirror. "What dark shadow?"

"You will soon see it too, little carrot."

She flinched and took small steps back from me. "Ominous aubergine."

The dining chambers had turned gloomy in expression, everyone stared at me for a long while till I sat next to father, who surprisingly looked quite pleased at my attire. It was probably a little less scandalous than the dresses I had been wearing.

"A soldier indeed," he interrupted, my attention snapping to him. "But you will break your prisoners with your beauty before your sword touches them. You have your mother's looks," he said, slowly chewing his breakfast.

I did not know what to feel about such absent words I was hearing for the first time. From his mouth they were venom coated in sugar. "Well, she unfortunately did not break you, so I shall think my prisoners will be well acquainted with my blade."

He laughed a deep dark laugh, like thorns rippling through my ears. Moreen and her half breeds had stopped eating as though they had just heard a bird bark.

Fren stared between her father and me all green in envy before saying, "Don't give yourself too bitter of an impression to the Adriatians. Us we hold back because we are family, but what will they do to you if you speak to their king as if you speak to father? I heard their old king lashed his second wife for speaking to the crown prince. Father, aren't they barbarous?" She fluttered her yellow lashes all innocence at him as if expecting a good job pat or a belly rub.

"Worry not about me, Fren dear. I heard the last Lord of Venzor stuffed salt up his consort's arse so she could taste like fish. Maybe this one can stuff your mouth as well and spare us from the misery of hearing your squeaks."

Elias coughed his water and turned wide eyed at my words. *Come now, laugh, it was meant to be funny.* Frozen icicles, Isjordians were.

"Elias sweetness, don't mind her. We will be left in peace soon," Fren said, offering him a smile.

I turned to Elias. "Can't say the same about you, poor dear. You will be honoured a fallen soldier, brave of you for taking one for the kingdom," I consoled, patting his hand. Jokes aside, I felt bad for him, bless his heart.

Father loudly thumped the table with his palm, pulling our attention to him. "Respect."

I pursed my lips and nodded. "An adequate heir."

He frowned, confused. "What?"

I shrugged. "I thought we were naming things this kingdom does not have."

He sighed, frustratingly rubbing his eyes but said nothing more.

I gathered all various foods my arms could carry, and made to leave, only brought to halt from Elias's hold.

"A moment, alone," he demanded quietly, but loud enough that surely everyone heard.

I was past being cautious and Fren was right there, so I seized the moment. "You have been asking for one too many lately, dear."

He let go of my arm and his eyes went a shade of mellow as though I had hurt him. "Please," he grit out without an ounce of pleading in it.

I sighed and nodded. "Fine, one you should have. Just not now, at the library before evening." I was curious what he would stir up for me now.

A team of a dozen soldiers in my service awaited ready by the stables, all recommended by Samuel himself. He was particularly cautious who I was to take with me, sadly not everyone was a big admirer of mine. Besides them, my second in command appointed by myself were Nia and Cai, both dressed similarly to me only with a gold circlet atop their breast pocket instead of two. A hilarious sight given that both were as good, if not better than me.

Our first orders were to attend a trial in Arynth for a crosser and to investigate their part of the wall due to several crossings in the same area within a short period of time.

It was early morning, but through the official passage, Sable Abyss, it was only a few hours' ride to Arynth. Hours that passed like minutes from anticipation. We knew city walls were near when the air grew warmer and sweeter. Grass strangely peeked through the snowy ground. Arynth shared its own borders with Hanai, the kingdom of harvest and eternal autumn—therefore sharing some warmth with their neighbours, too. Or perhaps it was the fact that much of east Isjord had once been Hanai and the earth remembered its origin even if the air did not.

Arynth city walls rose similarly in fashion to Venzor and Tenebrose. Though smaller in size, the city still grew grand.

Directed by the guards who had been expecting us, we headed to Highwall. Memphis turned to a raven and sat on my shoulder while we followed the guards toward a buffer zone where the two sides met to conduct trials. Astonishing, the wall stood like a mountain, tall and strong, it looked impenetrable. I had not the slightest idea how anyone could cross through it. Magic laced the rock, too, with a barrier spell conducted by a Dark Crafter to prevent Adriatian Aura from fading in and out of it.

We stood inside an open ceiling tower called a Zone of Peace, it joined both lands under open sky and an agreement of peace. We were surrounded by hard stone, shadows and shy rays of sunlight that barely made their way in. Empty of objects and empty of sound, but filled with the presence of spirits, enough that the hair on my neck rose—instigating that their presence was more than just a figment of my imagination.

A young man stood kneeling on the ground, his hands tied back while two Isjordian guards stood next to him.

Mere moments later, the Adriatian side gates opened, and a tall, beautiful honey skinned woman, rounded head to toe like a sausage in black leather, came in view, bowing slightly towards us.

An Adriatian.

At the sight and sound of her, tight panic and anger crawled all through my skin. Faces of the men from that night flashing, crawling, and charging for me. Blood roared through my ears, my skin burned feeling their hungering touches once again and my eyes drew tightly shut.

You are safe, my snowflake.

My eyes flew open at the sound of my mother's voice and a chill travelled my limbs. Was I finally losing it?

"I am Captain Nesrin, here to plead on his behalf," she spoke almost arrogantly.

I relaxed, letting out a light laugh. "Plead?" No one pled for my life when her people came to kill me.

The guards had informed us that the boy was caught stealing from a jewel shop, not a fish or produce or fabric shop. He had loaded the biggest ones in his pockets before being caught making an escape towards the Highwall. The boy was round faced, his body well fed. He did not dress as a poor one either, so he was not stealing to feed but to profit. Not that stealing was justifiable, but in certain circumstances, understandable.

She skimmed me with a bored gaze and in a deep dislike she did not even try to hide. "Yes, that's what the trial is for," she looked down at my circlets and continued. "Captain?"

"Oh no, dear, there will be no pleading on today's trial," I said, and she crossed her arms, confused.

Bringing my hand forward I began counting all his offences. "The boy was caught crossing the Highwall, trespassing an Isjordian city, impersonating an Isjordian, stealing from a jewel shop, and attempting to smuggle stolen goods to your kingdom." I waved my fingers towards her, titling my head in question. "A full hand of mistakes for such a young boy."

Her brows furrowed and she carefully assessed me as if she had just heard the oddest words. "It is his first offence, he has no previous account of doing such acts before. He is a good boy and we have gotten his father to vouch for him not to repeat today's actions."

One could almost laugh at her words—words she threw so easily. I waved my hand in the air. "No need, he will most definitely not repeat today's actions." Turning to Cai, I grabbed his bigger sword. "A hand for a handful of mistakes," I said nearing the boy.

Nesrin stepped forward, eyes wide in shock. "He is just a boy, he did not harm or hurt anyone. This is too much, Captain, think again," she shouted in panic, loud enough to echo through the walls.

No he didn't, but he might as well just have.

Within seconds, my soldiers grabbed the boy's hand, and I swung the large sword, impaling his hand. Blood splattered my face, the touch of the forbidding liquid sent a shiver down my spine and I heard my breathing grow loud in my ears. His screaming and the Adriatian soldier's shouts sounded like thunder through the forest, birds flew away and air rippled through the tower, drawing me awake.

I threw Cai his sword. "Make sure the boy is marked before returning him to the Adriatians, and without the hand. I want that on a pike at the top of Highwall."

He peaked a glance at the severed hand. "Your like for odd limbs really turns my stomach."

"Undeserving even ones turn mine," I said, turning to leave.

"Your Highness," Lord of Arynth called, coming towards the direction of Highwall. "I trust the trial went well. Stay tonight, see the city. We will try to be most accommodating, we have not had you in Arynth since you were growing teeth."

I remembered some, but not most. I knew I spent time here with Eren. It was warmer, I liked Arynth. Besides that, only fog and distant flashes of bad memory remained.

I pursed my lips in apology and bowed slightly. "I will have to reject your offer. Father's orders to return immediately to Tenebrose after trial."

"Young Silas still doubts my welcome?"

"Young Silas doubts his daughter."

"It is odd," he said, giving me a smile. "If I could turn a whole court around in mere days of return, dethrone a general and make all quiver with only words, I'd be cautious, too."

"If I didn't know better, I'd say you sound impressed."

"You are an impressive character, but you are Silas's daughter, I expect nothing but that."

I grimaced a little. "That deeply offended me, Lord."

He laughed. "Please, call me Albius. Only Eren insisted on calling me Lord. The boy was always too polite."

All expression cleared from my face. "You remember my brother?"

Something in his stare turned mournful. "Of course I do. He was tasked under me to learn the ways of court. He became the son I never had. I see you have his sword," Albius said, pointing to my back. "I took him to a forger to inscribe your name in it." He approached and planted a hand on my shoulder. "Arynth is your home, visit whenever you wish."

I was envious of him. To remember and have spent time with Eren, the memories and time I could not recall myself. "I will."

We returned to Tenebrose just before evening. I sat in the servant dinner with Penelope, devouring the mushroom stew Ken, the cook, had thrown for me. Hunger made me anxious and remindful of times I wanted to forget.

"Aren't you meeting mister sharp smile?" Pen teased, dunking bread in her pot.

I coughed, almost choking on food. "Shit. You could have reminded me long ago, Pen."

She shrugged. "Not particularly fond of him, nor you partake in adultery. Had you cared enough to meet him, you would have not forgotten."

I ruffled the top of her hair till she was left resembling a running hen. "I will deal with you once I return," I said, throwing her a glare.

How did I forget? I was late, but I did not rush. If he left, he would have wasted his last opportunity for a moment alone, and I knew he would wait.

The massive library flocked with librarians in their long hooded robes, the odd mapmaker, healers, and no frilly captain. Dim candles shone above the reading tables, everyone draped in their chairs reading and writing, paying no means of attention to me. The smell of musk and dust enveloped me while I passed through the mahogany shelves lining in long corridors.

Elias rested by a shelf, a book in his hand and devoured by concentration.

I reached and grabbed the book out of his hand, startling him to attention. "Your moment alone, Elias, use it well," I said, shutting the book and placing it back on the shelf before leaning against it.

He swiftly trapped me between his arms, his hands tightly clasping the shelves behind, knuckles white from the force. "Last night, what you said about my father planning to sabotage your arrangement, I thought you had heard or known something I hadn't. After returning I asked my informants if any of what you said was true and then confronted my father, both of whom denied any claims as such. And then I came to realise those had been your assumptions." His eyes narrowed, his voice raspy and deep, "Wrong assumptions."

I approached, inches close to his face. "You think I believe a single word of yours? He is your father after all, it is expected that you protect him and that is without considering your deep loyalty to Isjord." Was this why he had wanted to see me?

He inched closer, his body touching mine pushing me back to the shelf, and my hand slid down to the dagger sheathed in my thigh. "My father might be who you think he is, and one selfish, greedy bastard. but he does not keep word from me, and I do not make up empty lies. For that I give you my word. If it even means something to you."

"Not really."

He drew even closer, and I finally unsheathed my dagger. "Do you think I asked for this? To like you, to not be able to think of anything else day and night?"

I swallowed, the smell of pine and mint strong in my throat. "It seems to be your problem, not mine, Elias."

He pulled away, leaning back on the shelf opposite me. "It seems it is," he said, his voice soft. He rubbed his eyes with a hand and turned to leave.

I do not know what took over me, my limbs moved at its own volition and grabbed his arm. As he turned towards me once again, I grabbed the collar of his coat and lifted myself to my toes, planting a kiss on his lips for a few seconds before pulling away. Just before I let go of his collar, his hand went around my waist, pulling me close to him and he kissed me back long and hard.

Steps sounded approaching our direction, forcing us apart. Something that annoyed and made me thankful at the same time.

"I guess today is not your day after all," I said, patting his chest. So much for a test through the waters between my father and the lords. A damned fool, what was I thinking?

"It appears not, my raven," he said, before pulling away and fixing his jacket.

"It is odd, Elias. My senses never betray me, but this once they might have. I do trust you, somehow."

"Good to know, but to me it sounds like regret."

"If it was?"

"I would ask why?"

You're the son of my father's enemy, and I've possibly entered your game.

But there was something else that bothered me more. "Usually, I do not let men speak this much to me before bedding me, it is afterwards they confess. But you have confessed before which troubles me because that leads me to think you might have feelings and I have a strict rule of not messing with what I cannot understand and certainly not respond to."

His face drew in disappointment as he said, "You are too sure."

"Because I know myself too well."

"Am I getting rejected?" he asked playfully.

"Just sparing you and myself a messy parting when I head to marry my nightmare."

He swallowed, eyes darted lost about the room. "If I said that I have no wish to give up?"

"I'd say that is ridiculous, but if you will bear the consequences of disappointment silently, I have no issue."

He chuckled shortly, cocking his head back on the shelf and intently staring at me.

"This is why I like you, raven, you're not afraid to nail a dagger in a man's heart," he said, grinning wide. "I've never met someone like you, so charming, feisty, fearless and beautiful."

I sighed, annoyed. These types of confessions usually marked the moment I fled from someone. "You have known me for three seconds."

He shook his head. "Just because you have only seen me now doesn't mean I have not seen you before. You caught my eye since you were a girl, not a woman, and that is what I can say differently from all the other men. You have not changed at all, truly."

I crossed my arms and cocked a brow up at him. "Should I be offended?"

He pointed to his head. "Do you know Renick still rubs that bald patch in his head that you tore from his scalp during that Yule dinner every time your name gets mentioned?"

At the mention of that writhing memory, my gaze dropped to the ground. "I should have torn his head for what he said, and stuffed it up his arse so all shit could be in one place." My body still shivered at the memory of the words he had uttered in my ear that night.

Once your sister is plump enough, I'll make the bitch a woman.

His smile faltered, eyes lingering softly over me. "You should have. I should have, for all that beast has done to you."

"I suppose you are in my debt."

"For all my life," he swore and I felt the sincerity in his hardened features.

"Good to know, Elias Venzor, heir of Venzor. Good to know you are in my debt." I reached up, planting a kiss on his cheek before leaving.

Father had laughed himself to tears when he read the report on the trial I directed in Arynth. For a short fluttering moment I thought I saw a splint of pride there.

You will go again, come back with something entertaining, he had said, and handed me orders to attend six more trials and plenty of time to study Adriata.

We travelled to Arynth once more, the city walls were safer than a mountain range and there clearly was no war coming their way for the amount of guarding my father had assigned his squadrons to partake in. Which I suppose had come in fear of what had happened twelve years ago.

This time an Isjordian had been caught crossing their borders. If I could not stand something, it was treacherous vermin. For whatever reason he had done such a thing, it was still more than unacceptable according to my rule book.

Nia had chosen to still stay back, neither I or Cai had protested. She was more needed in Tenebrose than with me anyway. I did have a spy within my father's servants. No, I had many and Nia overlooked all of them. Isjordians' tie with coin was not exactly tight, but there was better payment and threatening means—secrets. Isjordians had heaps of them, and none too far from sight for Nia's abilities to dig them out.

Lord of Arynth waited for us this time, I had taken a liking to him since our last visit. He took upon himself to explain why the man had crossed their border, which left me infuriated and murderous.

The Zone of Peace stood eerie as usual, the same woman soldier as last time, Nesrin, was present, but this time accompanied by a tall dark-haired giant. He was a scary sight to behold, he had the face of a troll, body of a rock and the halo of an ancient oak.

The Isjordian crosser sat kneeling on the ground, hands tied to his front, refusing to lift his head to meet our gaze.

The Adriatians bowed their heads, greeting us. "This time it is one of your own," Nesrin proudly spat out without hesitation, as though she had me wrapped around her hand.

My brows rose. "My own? Oh no, dear, his blood might be Isjordian, but his soul is certainly Adriatian."

The troll next to her let out a low laugh. "I like her," he murmured joyfully to Nesrin who only glowered at me.

Couldn't blame him, I was charming like that.

She motioned to the man to cross to our side. "He was trespassing for shelter, your soldiers informed us he was a criminal, but we do not kill or mutilate our captives. I believe that is your expertise. Whatever he has done, he must have feared your punishments to make the decision to flee into our lands. Certainly could not blame him as I expect them to be nothing less than monstrous. We still cannot offer to keep him in our lands, unfortunately, our law refuses to facilitate Isjordians. He is free to go by our decree."

"You are right," I said, approaching the man now in our reach. "We do not have your generous hearts. Typically for rapists we mutilate their genitalia, but for child rapists we are, as you say, monstrous?"

Both the Adriatians shared a look of shock.

The man now shook with horror and wiggled furiously out of the soldier's hands, screaming not to let us take him toward the Adriatians. Attempt evil and you should expect evil, yet many wicked feared wickedness. Make yourself a bed of embers and expect not to burn?

"But," I said, examining the human filth afront me. "I bet you are so used to the wrongs of your sort that this might seem petty. Genocide does par petty over this, doesn't it?"

The troll leaned over to Nesrin. "I really *do* like her."

"Cai," my voice was a hard order. "The man is to be stripped and properly mutilated, hanged by the Highwall and drained out of blood. Invite all those above sixteen to witness if they wish to do so." Lowering in front of the man, I dug the tip of my dagger on his neck. For vermin like him, I would go to hells myself to drag and kill him a thousand times, over and over. "A beautiful ending, you will go down in history," I exclaimed spitefully. "But buried with dung, right amongst your like."

The two Adriatians had now gone silent. Nesrin rested her pensive and guilty gaze on the ground, and the other one only blankly stared at me in a haze as if struck by the sight of a ghost.

"Shame this will come to an end, I very much enjoy these trials," I said, and the two very silent guests blinked to reality.

The troll laughed. "I have a godson who might like you."

I stuck my bottom lip out. "I'm promised, to his unfortunate luck."

"Your promised one is a lucky lad."

I turned on my heels to leave the haunted tower. "Oh, he has not the slightest idea."

We stayed in Arynth for the night for a few other prisoners since our journey took most of the daylight, they were to be dealt with tomorrow.

Cai had done just what I instructed. A massive crowd gathered by the draining man. Women and men threw rocks and slabs at the body, but he had been dead not long after being slashed. Such a shame.

We dined with Albius who had told us several decade old stories. He was much older than he looked, given that he was a Verglaser, probably even much more than I'd guessed. He knew my mother, spoke to her a few times, and told me how he had thought her wise and gentle amongst many other traits. He offered his condolence once more after noting I had gone silent from his stories.

When I took my leave for the night, Cai was on my heels. "So?" I asked nervously, halting mid-corridor.

He spent most of the time here questioning the trespassers, the wall guards, and people in Arynth. He shook his head. "It seems all far from what you thought. The Adriatians say this agreement is mainly about lowering the Highwall, permission to move through Isjord for trade deals with the other kingdoms. Apparently they are already in negotiations with Hanai and Eldmoor for trade."

"And for my father?"

"Produce given monthly. Rental land for Isjordian workers and more produce free of taxation, spices, fabrics, medicine, passage through Moor sea for expedition purposes, and lastly—you. The final seal to prove their safety, that you don't turn into an Auran beast. It seems just like that, truly. Both kingdoms are profiting plenty from one another."

Laughable, all this was extremely entertaining. How was Numengarth filled with idiots who utterly underestimated my father. Poor, empty brained fools everywhere. Father was spinning everyone in circles. This deal was his new plaything, but what I didn't get was how could the spirituals fall for it.

"Do you know what is one thing that is just as heard, easy as made and simple as thought?"

"Cakes—" Cai's voice filled with worry as did his face.

"A plain lie, that's what is." I tried not to sound paranoid about being paranoid, but it all came out the same. "Do you think I buy into any of this bullshit?" I felt my breath grow rapid while I paced back and forth the narrow corridors of the lord's house. My chest clenched tight, restraining me out of breath, my sight already clouding in specks of black.

His hands rested on my shoulders, bringing me to a halt. "Remember that time you followed that girl everyday back to her home, Jess was it not?"

No air. I couldn't breathe. "Jasmine," I said, almost panting, my world still spinning.

"You thought her father was beating her. No, you were determined, even though her father could not kill a hen without flinching. Everyday for months you harassed that poor man, threatening and glaring whenever you passed by him," he said, chuckling from remembrance. "The girl was a farm worker, you could not possibly believe one got so beaten during farm work, so you went and tortured yourself dry with work in her farm and earned as many bruises as she had, if not twice as many. And when you realised the truth, you simply said: *oh*. Did or didn't Alaric make you apologise in front of his house on your knees for a full day and night for that behaviour?"

"Yes, but that has nothing—"

"Three years ago, in the first month of summer, a few weeks before your birthday," he said, interrupting me. "Berry was his name?"

"Bernie," I clarified, knowing another mistake of mine he was about to point out next.

"Yes, Bernie, you were convinced that other lad, which I surely don't remember his name."

"Clarence."

"Yes, him, you had him tied, gagged and hanged upwards at that tavern in front of everyone and beat him to teach him a lesson for bullying poor Bernie in secret. Not only did you hurt him enough that he remained pale for months at your sight, but you forced Bernie to profess his secret of fancying him to make you stop. In front of everyone at that, his family had not even known."

"In my ultimate defence, as I explained to Alaric," I began defending my questionable actions. "Clarence was thrice Bernie's size, spoke like a grizzly, looked feral when he pulled Bernie toward the forest and what about that ridiculous expression on Bernie when he saw him. He looked terrified."

"He was in love, Cakes, and my point was that you have a head made of rock and a heart of burning lava. I know it is hard to admit to something and so easy to fall into that panic of assuming, but take a step back each time that happens, look things from a bit further back, see the wider picture."

"You're right," I admitted. "I should have caught Clarence in the forest instead, it's wider there."

"Silly girl," he said, fluffing my hair. "You did well today, we will deal with it tomorrow, you need rest."

It had stopped. The clutching panic.

I reached for his hand when he made to leave. "Thank you."

"Always."

I awoke twice that night panting and sweating, and by the third time I decided not to go back to sleep. Foreign environments were a trigger for nightmares. Well, everything triggered them, who was I lying to?

After breakfast with the lord, we headed once more for the Zone of Peace and dealt with five more cases of trespassers. All Adriatian to my luck, and I had been the most generous all five times. Nesrin and the troll, Larg, had only sighed and shaken their heads, and by the last one, they had given up altogether to persuade me otherwise.

After, I had gone straight to my room without dinner, to scrub the retching and the prisoners' blood out of my skin till I left it raw, swollen and red. But I could not scrub or claw away the screams, the scent of souls I'd punished. Revenge was meant to feel heart filling and satisfactory, but nothing could seem to fill the emptiness. None of the lives I'd taken ever compensated what was taken from me, but I was determined to look for that fulfilment till the day I died. Killing was not difficult, it was what I knew best—what I was raised to do.

Midway to Tenebrose, somewhat happy to return, a messenger guard reached our group, riding furiously towards us.

"Captain," he greeted. "His Majesty has sent an order for you to head to Kirkwall. There is a new trial to be attended. The Kirkwall Lord is out of town on business and there are no other Captains nearby, many have been sent north to deal with the vandals."

Sleep and fatigue had begun setting over my every limb and my body slightly trembled, but I straightened and asked, "How many?"

"Five. We believe one of them is a smuggler, he was caught with maps and pathways out of the wall."

"Maps?" Cai asked surprised, throwing a glance at me that dug straight through my worries.

"Pieces of it, he tore most of them before we captured him," the soldier explained.

Cai still took careful glances at me as he continued to ask, "How can there be maps?"

The soldier cleared his throat and leaned in to say, "There are venting tunnels, sewage and sentry passages throughout Highwall, except for sentries and captains, no one should be aware of their location, but they seemed to be aware."

"There is a mole in Highwall?"

The soldier shook his head at my friend's claim. "Adriata might monitor entry, but Isjord is mounted on exit, there is no possibility for crossing."

I laughed at his conviction, coin could buy a soul in Numengarth. For the right price, your life. "What do you think of it then?"

"Dark craft?" He answered unsurely, he had not the slightest idea either.

Our squadron turned round to Kirkwall. There were five captives, a pregnant woman amongst them. How such a big group was able to cross remained in my head the whole journey there. Maps? How had they maps for crossing this impenetrable looking wall? Gods, how many others had managed to cross just the same? How many of them had crossed for me? The last question settled rough on my thoughts until it became the only one.

Cai and two soldiers went ahead towards the city to investigate since he had been as curious as myself at the probability of a mole.

When I expressed my concerns toward the messenger, he had informed me that trespassing was extremely common in Kirkwall, and that only the past week four groups had been caught. When we approached the city gates, an unexpected figure waited for us. Finally, I found out how my father had alerted Kirkwall so quickly of my presence nearby.

I dismounted Memphis and hugged Nia tightly. "He sent you?" Shit. I should...I should have made sure she remained far from these borders.

She shook her head. "I volunteered. Barely convinced your father that you would hate to miss this one." She handed me an envelope with the king's seal. "There is now an order of first sight kill, no more trials. I am inclined to think it's because of you. There is something strange about this batch, the soldiers mentioned something along the lines of a meeting tunnel through the Zone of Peace with access only to one person."

"Whom?"

She handed me a map of Highwall detailing a small exit by the far west of the wall. "I found this, well...stole it from the archive tower. I will put it back later."

"Nia," I bit out. "There is a craft veil around the castle walls, if the Crafter detects any magic inside it, my father will begin to search, and guess where he will look first?"

"I believe you will want to hear this before you reprimand me any further."

She handed me an order of use which she had also stolen.

One name. Esbern Kirkwall

PART II
FEVER DREAM

11

OBSIDIAN AND GOLD

KILIAN

THIS WAS THE FOURTH time in a week that Isjord had caught my people crossing Highwall towards their winter lands. Both kingdoms were not to cross each other's, a rule that apparently had not done much to prevent that despite the repercussions being many—one of which even death. Larg usually dealt with Highwall, but the old man demanded two days a week of rest claiming his old age had weakened him. The only thing that had weakened him was his lover who lived all the way across Adriata in Lyra.

"They have caught five of ours, one of them a woman," Mal said, as we dismounted our horses by the Highwall stables. "And pregnant."

I took a deep breath and shook my head. "We will plead for her, whatever they ask, whatever it takes."

"I trust you Kil, it's them I don't trust."

The Zone of Peace was distinguishable from the flat large wall, established in a round tower in the middle of the Highwall. One general and two captains were responsible for maintaining the efficiency and preventing people from crossing either side. Clearly, they had room for improvement since a pregnant woman had easily slipped through it and three others along with her.

"General," one of the guards approached and saluted my team. "They are here, waiting for their captain." He threw an uneasy glance towards the tower. "They are insisting our presence is unnecessary, our people were caught miles into their lands, therefore the law fully sides with them."

"It is what they always say, yet how many have we saved," I said as we reached the massive black metallic gates that separated our side of the Zone of Peace.

Mal was always uneasy during these trials, but I could tell this one had really gotten to him.

Nesrin and Grey, two of my captains and my most trusted soldiers, were a step behind us, both shifting nervously.

My brother shared some hard glances in my direction and finally managed to pull my attention. "If you insist on being obvious that you have something to say, just say it in the first place."

"I thought you and Nesrin ended things?"

Sigh. Was this what all of that was about? "There was nothing to end."

"She doesn't think so, her shadows should be of a broken heart or at least some resent.

She has liked you since we were children, yet I see, well...that," he pointed with his head and I turned to Nesrin who gave me a smile.

How was he right? I'd spoken to her a few days ago, she'd seemed convinced when I told her that I was not interested in her at all. I scratched my head confused. Had I been too vague in my wording?

"She is not an Empath, this time you might need to actually tell her, especially if she is still warming your bed," my brother added.

"You are too invested in this, it's concerning."

"Your love life, however grim, has always been entertaining. Thank Henah you're an Aura or you might have never understood a woman."

"Have I been lenient on your duties that you have this much time to fluff around?"

"Good sir, I take back my words," he said, raising his hands in surrender. "Do not send me to Sitara, I cannot rub off the stench of those creatures from the Sea of the Dark for days. Just like you can't rub off your arrogance and that stiff spine."

I exhaled a frustrated breath. "Grey might need help there after all, you leave after this trial. Maybe you will not need to face them, you might just annoy them away."

He shook his head in disbelief. "Very low of you, brother, so very low."

It was low, but Mal provoked all sorts of low from me. "And she is not warming my bed."

"Then who is? I swear I saw someone by your quarters the other day," he pushed, eager for an answer.

"She is not the only woman in Adriata, and you think your brother is a fool to bed the daughter of a councillor? There was no one, not for a while." Not the daughter of the one who had the most spite for me, anyway. Not anyone for that matter, even if I forced myself. "It was a healer, from Asra. For...your mother. She came to discuss a new treatment she'd been working on for Driada's sickness." Several days a week, the healer came after she'd tested medication for Driada's lung disease and then each time she'd broken the news that it had not worked. This time was different, there was progress, but I could not build Mal's hope only to crush it again. It was all he had—hope.

"Poor Nesrin," he chuckled. "And thank you."

The gates opened, revealing a tower that stood as large as an arena, it had no ceiling and the walls ran feet high creating deep shadows in the room. Three men, two barely above their teens and another who looked like their father were on their knees, hands tied behind. Backed by the tower wall, four soldiers in Isjordian blue uniform stood solemn with their hands on the hilts of their swords. At the other side, a young man and woman were positioned the same, her stomach was large, meaning she had not far to go till birth. So there were five not four caught. Another life to beg for. My eyes closed at the frustrating thought.

Behind them stood two figures dressed both in the Isjordian uniform, but theirs was darker, a navy blue and a golden circlet on top of their chest pocket. Their faces were austere and without expressions.

My eyes veiled black, magic floated freely through my body and clouds of colourful mist rose around each person in the room. I had been partly gifted with blessings of an Empath, one who could read emotion through colour almost as words.

Deep burgundy surrounded the girl and a familiar feel crept upon me. She dressed in old pain and anger muted with creeping panicking fear she hid terrifyingly well, but the man next to her only had a pale grey shadow circling his head—he was merely bored.

When they both turned to look at us, distaste crept in their eyes and their shadows turned green.

"Are we waiting for something?" Mal asked, unsure why everyone was so still.

The girl cast a swivelling glare at him before she replied, "She will be here any moment, your eagerness shall fade soon enough."

"So hostile and joyless," my brother murmured beside me.

"Not the moment, Mal," I said, examining the fearful Adriatians in their hold. The heavy shadows framed by the lack of light in the tower were almost cowering for shelter. Even remnant shadows of the dead that roamed the space swirled around in distress before fleeing.

There was something wrong. So very wrong.

Within seconds later, the gates on the Isjordian side of the wall flung open and a form walked to us. Tall, with long obsidian hair that floated like a dark sky of silk, eyes that glistened gold chips of amber fire, her features soft and full, crafted gracefully to fit together, and at the right side of her face, a scar stretched down her jaw to her neck. Beautiful. Her presence radiated something otherworldly, her movement almost unnatural—predatory even. It felt as if we had stepped in her hunting ground. I'd never seen her before and still the hair on my neck rose with each step she took forward.

The four Isjordian guards clicked their feet and bowed in unison to her. Few steps away, a massive black cat-like creature followed her, growling in our direction before nestling near the tower gate, monitoring the captain's every move. At every flicker of noise, morph's muscles shifted, ready to pounce.

"Well, well, well," she sighed, examining the Adriatians kneeling on the floor. "The trap must have been big. I have five large plump mice in my hold."

"Hells, not her," Nesrin murmured beside me.

Her golden eyes flickered towards us and she innocently tilted her head to my captain. "I see you have grown fond of me, Nesrin, but your presence again is most unnecessary. Surely wasting your precious time, they were caught on Isjordian soil. The decision is ours to make."

My captain only swallowed repeatedly with unease, her gaze drifting to the ground. Why had Nesrin grown so uneasy at her sight?

"We will stay," I answered for my party.

She scoffed and nodded, her gaze lingering on me. "Fine on my behalf." She went to kneel in front of the young couple in their hold, looking back and forth at the two terrified souls. "Were there not enough Isjordian whores to fuck that you crossed a whole wall to get an Adriatian one? Is there something special between their legs that I am not aware of?"

Mal's gaze as all of ours turned to the captain and her biting words that settled rough on our ears. So the young man was Isjordian.

Her cold stare pierced into his frightened one, but he dared to speak, "We are in love, we did not mean any harm to anyone, just to be together." His breath was trembling and his face turned pleading while holding his weeping partner tight.

The Isjordian captain did not drop her smirk, as if amused, she cocked her head to the side. "Ah, you are in love. That ought to do it, right?" She turned slightly towards us and took a deep bored breath, her brows raising in question. "Would Adriata allow an Isjordian to live on your lands, would you accept the man if I were to give him to you?"

Her question took me aback, she did not sound as a lenient one, didn't feel like that either considering the horror from Nesrin's shadows and reaction toward her. Was this a test if we would break our laws for them?

"Yes, we would," I answered flatly. We would if it meant sparing a life.

"It is all settled then," she said and turned to order her subordinates, "Nia, untie him. He is free to live in your borders, but if he is as much as to breathe near ours he will be killed at first sight. No trial."

As soon as she untied him, the guards handed him to our side. Grey barely held his fearful limping body up while he struggled to reach a hand to his partner. "My wife?" he demanded, taking ragged breaths and I turned to the captain once again.

Her lips twitched. "She will stay in Isjord. Looked after and cared for. Both her and the creature she is growing."

Ire flared through my veins like never before. I dug my heels on the ground to stop myself from committing to any dangerous thoughts flying through my head. "What?" I demanded.

Pleased from our reaction, her smirk grew to a wicked smile. The punishment for them was to separate them. This was unusual, Isjordians were rough on their prisoners, but not in this manner. Flogging, banishment to the unblessed isles, imprisonment to hanging. Isjordians didn't get creative, not with their prisoners.

The young man sobbed and pleaded towards her, Nesrin and Grey holding him from both arms to stop him from crossing, and I could hear Mal muttering curses to the gods behind my back. She was breaking her kingdom's laws. too. A captain making such a decision was unusual, unless her plans afterward were different. Unless she'd done it to tempt the Isjordian man to his death.

I felt sweat beads coat my temples, my body stiff from tension. "She is Adriatian, as much as I would like to rely on your word, I don't rely on your people. She is expecting his child, one who should not be raised without a father. Hand her to us, banish her with a criminal record, I do not care, just hand her back, she is of no use to you."

She knelt in front of the pregnant woman. "We should have thought of that to start with, shouldn't we?"

The young woman shook from anger and fear, tightening her arms around her stomach. "You are a monster, gods and heavens will curse you this day for leaving my child without a father in your waste lands," she shouted and spat in front of her.

The captain reached over her shoulder and murmured in her ear, "No one thought about leaving me without a mother when your kind drew a sword through her chest, and that, my dear, was when the gods and heavens cursed me."

She rose and motioned toward Nia to drag the woman outside the tower premises. Her shouting and screaming grew harrowing and chilling as they disappeared behind the tower gates.

I felt a stab at her words. My people had killed her mother. My magic floated through me again to read her and I went still at what I faced. No emotion, nothing, she had no shadows. I narrowed my eyes, confused. This had never happened to me before. Everything had shadows—humans, blessed and unblessed, even animals, even beasts from the Sea of the Dark. What was she?

"Bored, so soon?" she asked playfully, studying my confused sight.

The three men grew uneasy on the other side when she motioned her soldiers toward one of the boys kneeling on the ground to position him next to her. Putting a hand on his shoulder, she then turned to face the older one. "I hear you know the best ways out of the wall, even some sweet maps, care to share how that came to be?"

He laughed rough and angry at her, and shook his head. "Not to an Isjordian bitch I won't."

In a flash, she unsheathed a dagger and pierced the young man's shoulder who screamed in pain and fell to the ground forward.

My feet shot forward, but Nesrin gripped my arm pulling me back. "You cannot save them, not from her. Six trials I have witnessed with her, and none have escaped unscathed. They are dead by her decree," she explained, her eyes glued on the Isjordian captain with surrender.

Ruthless. Abnormally ruthless, this felt no longer as a trial for the crossings—a trial for her justice, vengefulness.

The captain lowered on her heels, pulling the young man's head back by gripping his hair, her hand swinging the dagger playfully and full of threat. Isjordians were known to be cruel, but this one was a monster of our doing. My breath tightened from pure anger—didn't know to whom exactly it was directed. Her or Adriata for creating the mess in the first place.

Tilting her head to the side, she seized the old man again. His lips pursed back, refusing to back down to her. "It appears I was unclear. It was not a question intended not to be answered."

Seeing she was not about to get an answer, she flipped the dagger to her grip and pierced the young man again on his back.

Shrieking in pain, he collapsed to the floor and I shut the gates of my magic that intensified at the feel of life seeping away. Taste of acid immediately coated my mouth.

Blood pooled around her feet and specks splattered on her face. The painting of evil. Remorseless, there was no grain of emotion on her features either.

Soldiers lowered the second boy to her, ready to be used, leveraged, and then killed.

Her hand dug on the young boy's hair, turning him to face the older man again. "I could do this all day, you know. You would not believe it, but it gives me immense satisfaction."

Personal—this was personal to her and I could do nothing that would not start a war.

The gates on their side of the border flew open suddenly. A tall man in black official militia uniform entered. Lord of Kirkwall whom I had seen on numerous occasions during crosser trials. Marching inside along with a dozen other soldiers, he seized the whole scene and then her, half knelt in front of the old man. His eyes flew wide open at the sight laid in front of him.

The soldiers, including the lord, all dropped to one knee. "Your Highness, Princess Snowlin."

Deadly quiet fell inside the tower.

All halted. Shadows, darkness and spirits stood still.

What?

Princess—Princess Snowlin?

Nesrin and Grey immediately stepped forward, and Mal pushed from where he leaned, resting a hand at my shoulder. His brows pinched together and we both shared a look. Disbelief coated me completely. She was her, the half Olympian princess, the mixed blood Aura, the one Henah's prophecies and telling's painted with blood and wrote about in ash—the *Ybris*. The entitlement, the anger and pure hatred. She is the one that the King of Adriata would marry barely three moons from now. King Silas's hybrid child. The one who Adriata owed the lives of her loved ones.

She rose to her feet, sighing deeply and facing the lord. "Why is it that this is the fourth time in a week Adriatians were caught in your city?"

Confused, the lord opened his arms, calmly gave her a wry smile and said, "Kirkwall is a fine city, Your Highness, deeply envied by many, it is expected even Adriatians would take like in it."

The princess clicked her tongue, a displeased glare framed her golden irises. "Not my answer, dear Lord." With no warning, her dagger fled from her grip and landed straight in his chest.

His soldiers and all of us were left gaping and gasping in horror at the dead lord sprawled and leaking of blood in the cold ground.

The princess looked rather bored at the whole situation. "Cai, pick one of our finest soldiers to be put in charge temporarily till we root out all the rot in Kirkwall," she said, stretching her neck.

He nodded, and left to obey her order.

One of the lord's soldiers stepped forward, still wide eyed at the scene. "Your Highness, he was a Lord. One cannot simply kill a Lord. The council, your father—"

"Do you think me daft, soldier?"

He shook his head and swallowed a hard lump of fear. "Of course not."

"Then you must know exactly why I have killed Esbern."

He nodded, almost shaking. Shadows of fear circled him as he cautiously backed away from her, his gaze still latched on the dead lord.

Mal chuckled under his breath. "Our future queen, Kil. This will be fun after all."

This was a disaster. She wasn't what I'd thought her to be.

My attention snapped toward her again, to the words that drew flame out of me.

"Kill the men, hang their heads in the city walls and burn the bodies, feed the ashes to swine for all I care."

"You cannot do that," I said loudly, bringing all her side to a halt and to my attention.

She slowly cleaned her bloodied dagger with a white cloth. "Well, as you see, I am."

Adriatians carry a celestial spirit, a gift from our goddess Henah, to be sent to the sky, to return among stars. We bury our dead and guide their celestial spirit to rest. Those not guided to the sky were to wander lost in this realm, fading away without joining heavens. A custom well known even amongst the elemental kingdoms, spoken in their holy sacraments and written in their history books, one I was convinced that she, a royal, was aware of.

I stepped forward. "We carry tradition as we carry our lives, let us have their bodies. They are worth nothing to you."

She walked towards us, not averting my gaze, her eyes burning a freezing golden flame, cold and deadly beautiful. She'd reached close enough that I could see every detail of those eyes, of her features and of that scar. How...how had she gotten that one?

"Bold assumption that I care, but you can have the bodies since I am feeling particularly kind today." Mal scoffed, interrupting her and the princess's head turned to him. "Tell your king to strengthen his guard or I might just disembowel all of Adriata at this rate without even crossing the wall. A gift, a warning, call it whatever. This is the last trial to be held, all my soldiers have now been ordered to kill at first sight of trespassers, and then I will do as I please. Burn, bury, drown, all the good stuff."

I could not understand how someone could be so unwavering and unafraid, if not of gods at least of their humanity.

"Why did you have to go this far?" I asked. Why did I ask? Did I not know who she was and what she was?

Her tongue swept over her top lip and she smiled. "Catharsis? It appears to be achieved one scream at a time." She threw me a wink and then the bloodied handkerchief before backing away, turning to leave.

I stared a long while at the white square of cloth marred red with blood before turning around to Nesrin. "You knew her?"

She'd paled, clutching a hand over her chest. "Yes, but I never knew she was the princess."

"That was the spawn of all evil? She is just as vile as they have made her, the sick bitch," Grey spat looking towards the Isjordian gates.

I saw the nerve jump in Mal's temple and I prayed to gods no one ended with a broken nose. "That sick bitch caught four Adriatians trespassers, and Captain, your skills might not be as great as mine, but we all saw the shadows on that man," he spat as predicted.

"They only crossed the wall, they did not murder younglings," Grey countered with a disgusted expression at my brother's reaction.

"No, but we did, and for that this wall rose and they became criminals and then dead. Do you need to be sent to preparation school again? Is this who you appoint Captain, Kil?" He reached an inch away from Grey's face who also seemed on edge—except that it happened to be the other edge.

"Calm down, Malik," Nesrin interfered, getting between them. "We can see there is no right in this situation, but she chose to show too much evil for us to take this lightly."

Mal laughed imperceptibly. "I am calm, Nes, but if I had been her," he sneered, pointing towards the gates. "I'd fucking lose it, too. So how about you stick to doting on my brother and stop playing saint. Was Stregor not in the attack twelve years ago? Maybe your father is the one who killed her mother, too. We'd never know that, but we do know he had such a fond heart for torturing the weak."

Nesrin stepped back in disbelief, her eyes dropping to the ground, her shadows embarrassed and angry, but not guilty.

Mal laughed all distaste when he noticed the shamelessness, the disregard many had for what was done to her—to the princess.

"Enough, Mal," I interfered.

He raised his brows in challenge. "Why, brother, did I say something wrong?"

I tilted my head in warning, but he had no intention of backing down, so I said, "Maybe Sitara will make you figure it out." He was not a child to be punished, but he was also a grown up to be behaving so hot blooded.

He started backing away. "Maybe. Maybe not. I am surrounded by enough beasts here. It won't be much change in scenery, they stink as foul as your attitudes," he added before turning to leave.

Grey's eyes followed him intently with a glare till he left. "He always has a soft spot for the oddest creatures, didn't expect him to caress the emotions of that *Ybris* too, as if one can have any."

I pocketed the bloodied handkerchief. "That is because he understands people better, not just as an Empath."

He was particularly sensitive when it came to the attack twelve years ago, never resting to point out the consequences we suffered from it and because of whom. It satisfied him when the council would go silent at the mention of their mistake.

"Are you saying he is right?"

"No," I responded, planting a hand on his shoulder. "But it's in his nature to be compassionate and with that I cannot argue. He will aid you in Sitara till the villagers have returned to their houses."

At the mention of the sealine city Grey blanched. "It might take us a while. It was a colony of basilisks and they'd laid eggs a few villages west as well."

"I don't understand, are gods mad at us?" Nesrin said, her voice soft with worry. "Eudemons have never left their underwater sanctuaries, they hate land and they're sick at the taste of human flesh. Why are these creatures washing up on our shores?" She scowled in concern. "We have been plagued, our lands sick for months and now this—the last thing we needed was her."

I clutched the handkerchief in my pocket tightly. "She is to bring our salvation, the last misfortune is not Adriata's to carry. It is the king's."

12

Prices and Payments

Snowlin

The pregnant woman kicked, screamed, and cursed almost all of the way to Tenebrose. I did not know how the Winter court would react to me bringing an Adriatian back to their lands, but that did not worry me as much as my father's reaction to killing Esbern Kirkwall.

The evening had grown cold, our horses tired and having a pregnant woman slowing us down did not help. We stopped and camped for the night as hours awaited ahead in our journey back. We wasted most of the afternoon rampaging through Kirkwall for evidence related to the crossings and helping Sebastian, the soldier we left in charge, adjust to his newly appointed duties.

We deviated onto Fernby forest, out of the main road, and established a fire, camping around it. Isjord at night made a fearsome scenery for a horror book. Wolves howled around us endlessly, we'd faced two wild almost rabid boars, and now the tall shadows of conifers cosplayed monsters of tales.

Nia and two other soldiers agreed to take first guard while the rest of us finished our meals that Albius had packed for us before leaving his city. I sat by the fire along with the rest until I noticed the pregnant Adriatian attempting to gather herself tight for warmth. Dressed lightly and shaking from the cold, she had turned a pale shade of violet.

Sighing in anger, I pushed up and stood towards her. The moment she noted my approach, she backed further with very readable fear. "If you insist on dying, you should have just said so at the trial. I would have spared you the torturous part of freezing by killing you there," I said, a cold bite on every word.

Grabbing her arm, I pulled her towards warmth. She resisted but eventually gave in and sat with the rest of us near the fire, extending her hands and breathing in relief as her face began to warm up.

"Be gentle, Cakes, she is pregnant," Cai warned, throwing a blanket over her shoulders and I narrowed my eyes in judgement towards him.

If she had cared for her child, she would not be here and under my mercy.

"How far along are you?" he asked, handing her something to eat.

She glanced toward me for a few moments, and then turned to him, pulling the bread and cheese shyly in her hand. "Almost due," her voice was no more than a whisper. "What are you going to do with me?"

"Exactly what I promised," I responded, lazily stretching my legs and leaning back on Memphis who had nestled behind me.

The woman looked at me full of questions. "Why did you have to do that, why did you have to bring me to live alone in a wasteland of people who hate my kind?" she cried out, eyes welling with tears.

I didn't have to do or not to do anything, I just wanted to. I did it to make her feel an inch of what I have felt the past twelve years. Was I wrong to do so? For that I cared very little. "You committed a crime and therefore you are receiving its punishment. You chose to get involved with an Isjordian." My eyes rested on her pregnant stomach before continuing, "Who just like the rest, is from this wasteland who hates your kind."

Tears streamed down her cheeks and she lifted her hands to wipe them away. Her eyes rested wondrous and fearful on the fire for a long while. "I heard you are to marry our king," she said, pulling my attention back to her. "The Lord called you princess Snowlin. It is against your wish, is it not?"

My eyes were half coated with sleep, but I forced myself forward from Memphis to face her. "Would you marry the killer of your dearest with your own volition?"

She hesitated at first as if my question even needed that much assessing, before she shook her head. "He has done well by his name. A good man, right, fair and caring, he will treat you well," she offered quietly, and I almost laughed had I the energy.

Treat me well? Good, fair, and caring? All these descriptions for the man who took light away from me.

She yawned. "The people thought you were powerful and extremely dangerous, just how the prophecies and omens had predicted it. Not entirely a lie, but not in the way they thought."

The others and Cai included had gone silent and were taking in the conversation. Not how my father had thought either, to his misfortune and many others' good fortune, their attempt had been entirely useless with a very grand loss.

"Their assumptions, my dear, cost me and now you greatly. To you they still could charge more, remember what you are carrying. They didn't think twice when they aimed to kill me even though I had no magic."

Leaning onto Memphis and pulling my blanket over, I slumbered in a most needed sleep. The rattle of my morph soothing me.

Breathless, I awoke to everyone gone. The embers were fading and it was silent—deadly silent. I stood, examining the snow on the trees and the ground soaked with ruby red blood. The snow had sullied crimson for miles, a sin to the cold pure beauty. The blood looked like poison against it. My lungs gasped for air at the sight, my eyes felt heavy and my face wet, but not from tears.

I ran a trembling finger over my scar and blood met my touch. I spun around and ran looking for Nia and Cai only to be faced with their lifeless bodies hanging from the trees, branches piercing through their chests.

Screams erupted from my throat, tears sprawling from my eyes as I ran toward them. Each step the snow sank me deeper, blood choking my throat.

"Snow," a voice called again and again. The sound grew clearer in my ears and drew me awake. "Snow!"

My lids were assaulted with light, fluttering open to recognise a panicking Nia. I lifted my upper body to stand and she wiped my wet face with her hands. Everyone had turned looking at me in shock, including the pregnant Adriatian.

Cai pulled them away, throwing a worried glance towards me.

My eyes and throat burned. "I am fine," I said, my voice raspy. Memphis nestled around me, weeping in her sleep. I wanted to claw our bond away at times like this.

"You are not fine, you were screaming," she stuttered, still breathing hard with panic. "I thought you stopped having these nightmares, that Dark Crafter said they would stop."

I let out a breathless laugh and rose to wipe the blood from my palms. After several unsuccessful doses of horror elixirs and nightmare catchers, Alaric had finally paid one handsomely to go inside my head and lock them away when I wouldn't stop shaking the whole Isliot peninsula awake from my screams every night after I left Isjord.

I wrapped cloth over my hands and said, "They never stopped, just grew less vivid, and I guess whatever she did stopped working months ago now."

She scowled, probably upset at how I had kept that from her. "Since when do you keep things from me?"

"I'm not keeping nothing from you, Nia, but that one time you told Alaric I'd missed my cycle did do some damage," I teased to lighten the grave mood.

She slapped my shoulder viciously and repeatedly as I laughed myself to tears. "So not funny."

"Indeed, it was not," I said, feigning a frown. "Imagine having to tell Alaric all the men I'd slept with, to hunt them down because he thought I was with child."

Nia was very close to Alaric, too close. Never sparing him any secrets, including mine.

She loosened a giggle at the memory. "I still can't believe he punched Lazarus right across his arrogant jaw."

I cupped her cheeks and gave them a playful tug. "Don't mock his jaw, he knows how to use it well."

"Ugh, away thoughts or I'll be sick," she cringed, shaking her head and hands.

"You held something from me, too, Nia."

Her mouth parted slightly open, and I saw the slight shiver her limbs enveloped. "I felt her...I felt their presence, my sister and my father. I think...I could be wrong or maybe it's just my imagination." She froze, her breathing shallow. "Or just remembrance." Nia's own nightmares, though hers were quiet, they were even more hunting than mine.

"It's that place, Nia, just how Isjord reminds me of mine. They can never hurt you. Spirits of the past are just there to haunt your memory, I gave that promise to you."

I assured her several times I was fine and that she would be fine, too, before we mounted and rode back to Isjord. The journey was in utter silence, soldiers kept stealing glances my way, but the pregnant woman was flatly staring at me. Even when I caught her, she did not turn away, making me laugh. To my surprise she gave me a short sad smile.

Cai had tried to assure me that no one would speak of what they had seen, but I told him I had little care if they did. My status as the orphaned broken little Isjordian princess was not going to receive any further damage.

When we neared Tenebrose, we greeted goodbye to Amerie, the pregnant Adriatian girl, who was taken by my soldiers to a safehouse they knew and assured me would keep her safe till I procured other arrangements.

My feet begged for me to halt and turn around, but my head anticipated my father's reaction to what I had done in Kirkwall.

The meeting room sounded only of his restless paces. He was alone with uncle and Renick. His eyes had drawn in with madness, ready to bestow it upon me. The other two wore a more amused expression—one that would be fully achieved when they would see me punished by father.

"I sent you for one thing and you come with a Lord's blood on your hands? You disobedient, vile child." he shouted, voice travelling through the doors down to the corridors. "Care to explain how you just managed to commit such a crime and take responsibility for the revolt of the other Lords upon hearing of your actions?"

I laughed hard and loud till my father hit the table with his fist, a trail of ice shards heading towards me, the sharp edge stopping short right before it reached the space between my eyes.

Going round the anger sculpture he intended to kill me with, I sat across them. "You act so grand though you know your people very little, dear father, especially the ones so close to the crown."

Confusion began coating his face instead of rage so I threw towards him a pile of documents. The other two stared at them doubtfully before grabbing and skimming through the pages of guilt and crime. Looks of perturbed surprise were thrown back and forth at me.

"What does this mean, child, explain!" father shouted again, rubbing his eyes.

"It means, King Silas," my tone an inch away from mocking. "Your kind Lord, was smuggling goods from Adriata in exchange of free passing to your land, hosting rebels to his city and assuring them free passage through Isjord in exchange of Adriatian steel, rubies, emeralds and all sorts of that jingle, helping them escape trials by conducting them himself and even bestowing little to no punishment on them. Kirkwall has had more than one hundred trespassers in the past month according to those notes, just a little shy from the group that attacked twelve years ago." I had tapped my point when his features leathered down to a taken aback shape. "Now, how do we say all this to the other Lords, they are all so upset from my actions," I pouted, fluttering my lashes.

He didn't answer or even react to my incitement. Seeing I had managed to achieve the exact reaction I was expecting, I stood to leave. Uncle and Renick began to discuss amongst themselves, amusement wiped away completely from their faces.

It had taken me a long while of searching thoroughly through all his properties, offices, and preferred locations to fetch those documents, almost beaten one of his guards to death for information and even almost missed the trial before I had found receipts and receipts of the lord's little crimes. When Esbern had interrupted, and seen his trusted Adriatian ally knelt in my grasp, he had dared to mock me and try my patience.

"Wait, Snowlin, how...how did you obtain all this?"

An apology would have been more ideal, but seeing him stutter was all the better. "It matters very little, father, your order of kill at first sight was passed through. Very smart on your behalf, if I must say."

His eyes dropped searching on the ground. "Yes, very well," he said, almost unsure.

"By law as a royal, I appointed Sebastian, one of your soldiers on my team in Lord of Kirkwall duty, one that would not betray you or Isjord. He is the son of a priest from Casmere. Samuel spoke highly of him."

He nodded at my words. "Good thinking," he praised absently.

"Aren't you letting her too loose, Silas?" Renick called indignantly. "She killed a Lord and appointed one herself."

"I killed a guilty Lord, Nick dear." I gave him a wink and he flared, almost ready to stand and strike me. "By power bestowed to me as your king's daughter, I can appoint any Lord to duty. Don't you have ice cream to go make, let the important ones deal with matters of court."

Just like that, one oar had been pushed to sea and substituted with another. Sebastian Kirkwall had a nice ring to it. But Snowlin's oar was a better nickname.

13

SALT AND SEA

SNOWLIN

LAST NIGHT THORA AND Eren showed up in my dreams. My siblings whose features laid almost forgotten in a corner of my memory I so rarely chose to visit.

When I awoke, I headed for their resting place, wrapped tightly in my cloak, and slept on the ground next to them. Despite the freezing ground and air, my sleep had been dreamless and sound. It reminded me of the few nights we had spent together, when Thora would crawl in my bed and when Eren's footsteps would reach to check on us after midnight, the air around him thick with fatigue and faint smell of blood after a long day at the training court.

You have grown, he would whisper. *You can protect Thora now. Well done, miss Lin.*

The words hung loose in the air and my hands reached for my brother's sword still wrapped in his essence.

Lin, I will call it so. My sword will carry your name, little sister, but it will never honour the strength you have.

"What strength, Eren?" I murmured to the open sky that melancholically shed loose flakes of soft snow. "Even the cold can hurt me."

I waited as though I would hear an answer or his warm laugh, but it was only familiar silence that greeted me.

Cai had slouched to the ground behind the maze wall, no words were said between us, just the usual silent understanding. He'd never asked, not once, what I saw, why I did what I did, what haunted me most.

"You never ask," I said, settling beside him.

He stretched his back with a groan. "Asking is not my thing and answering is not yours."

I gathered myself tight under my cloak. "You don't want to know?"

He threw an arm around me, rubbing my arm for warmth. "You don't like telling."

"Yes...I don't like telling."

He brought out a piece of paper from his pocket. "He wants you to inspect Grasmere for a delivery."

I straightened, narrowing my eyes on the confusing order. "I am to patrol Brisk tomorrow, why this?"

"The envoy said it's a direct order from your father."

I almost jumped from where I sat. "I take orders from Sam, why is he getting involved in a captain's duty?"

"This was Sam's duty now passed to you."

I flicked the envelope open. From handwriting to the red wax seal, all my fathers. "A general's duty to a captain?"

He glanced shortly over the letter, as usual unbothered to think it anything concerning. "You recon something is happening?"

"It is strange, that is all," I said, fiddling with a hangnail. Strange? It was absolutely to not be trusted as what it seemed to be. I still kept quiet though.

He shook with laughter. "You can say it, miss paranoia."

I frowned. "I will not say anything, and I am not paranoid. It is a sense, you know it."

"Ah," he said quietly. "Did you hear about that moose attack on Modr the other day? The guards could not stop talking about it."

I got on my knees, facing him. "What moose attack? You think Hanai sent them."

He snorted, eyes folding in half moons along with his smile, that small black mole under the left one disappearing again. "Oh, yes, Hanaian moose, they kept giving fluent orders in Kemeri, too. Perhaps they were Hanaian spies?"

I slowly retreated to my seat. "There is no moose attack, is there?"

He shrugged. "There could have been."

I flashed him two middle fingers and he swirled two gusts of wind that chucked a bunch of snow on my face.

Grasmere, a port city on the south of Isjord that dealt mostly with the trade between Solarya, Whitebridge Island and Isjord. It held perhaps the greatest fleet in the continent, called the *Isenhound*. Its warmer waters made it easy for ships to pass through without the difficulty of icebreakers or Verglasers on board to break ice. Grasmere had been my father's mechanism to Isliot peninsula when he attacked Olympia. The city was run by an old Lady, a true Isjordian patriot and my father's biggest supporter. A true bitch one might say. That one being *I*.

Nia had stayed back again, her obsession with Renick and Bruma halls had become concerning.

My soldiers and Cai had now grown used to our trips, they chatted the whole way through, but I had been running a fever and my whole body shook lightly, too tired to partake, their voices had gone into a void while we rode ahead to report for duty.

When we reached the city walls, I could feel the fresh sea breeze, the sound of waves thundering loudly as they crashed by the rocks and the smell of fish that made my stomach turn.

Cai extended a bottle of mud foam, an elixir for sickness that Nia had mastered better than its creator given how many times she'd prepared for me alone. I inhaled the liquid over a cloth and my stomach returned to normal in a matter of moments.

The crinkled old Lady waited for my squadron by the city gates. Thin, her hair in several braids and turned completely white, her features had sunken from age, still elegantly beautiful and her eyes two dark pearls. She stared at me all wondrous as though she had just seen the dead. A look I was getting a little too often lately.

"Fascinating how much you look like her," she said with a distasteful sneer.

"Fascinating how you are still petty after so many years, dear." I bit, dismounting Memphis, and she frowned. The wicked old fox disliked me for the strangest of reasons, because I was a half Olympian. That was her greatest peeve. Anyone not Krig blessed was Malena detested.

"You are not speaking to just anyone and however impossible it seems to appear, you are a royal," the sea spirit lectured, examining me with an irked expression. "Some respect would have been ideal."

I managed between exhaustion and dizziness to huff a mordant laugh. "Earn it, then you shall have it. Now, show me to the port or do I need to fetch a lead? You are my father's bitch, but a bitch nonetheless so I would suppose habits are hard to forget." Hilarious this woman was. Respect? What blessed respect? This woman didn't know how to spell it let alone recognize its meaning. She probably had been most happy when chosen by my father to lead the troops from here to Myrdur and kill Olympian women, men, younglings, and babies. Just imagining her grin as she slaughtered my people made me sick.

Malena's mouth twisted. Despite the resistance and berating shape of her features, she forced herself to turn and take us to the port.

I tried my hardest to focus straight ahead, though my surroundings had warped and fogged ahead of me. Loud oscillating sounds of sails and chime of bells of docking ships accompanied my ringing headache and deepened it.

I stumbled, but Cai caught me, his hand lifting to my forehead. "You are burning, Snow," he said, worryingly surveying my state.

"Don't be ridiculous. Snow melts, it does not burn." I joked, but I was really burning, and melting and my back was coated with sweat.

He flicked my forehead. "This one is giving me a brain freeze. Let's see a healer before heading down there."

I shook my head, and he lowered his gaze to me, annoyed. "If you collapse on me, I'm not carrying your fat stubborn head," he warned, yet he held a hand behind my back all the way to the port.

Dozens of sailors awaited at the port afront their ships with faces drawn in what looked like worry and distress. They greeted and guided us into one of their ships. Confused by what they had to show, I followed silently though the swaying prow along with the fever almost made me fall twice.

"We have never had this, Captain. Solaryans are cocky bastards, but they had never acted hostile towards us," said the ship captain. Gathering his hat anxiously onto his hand, he removed the top of one of the wooden crates.

I ran over the taffrail and retched my stomach raw once, and then twice.

Cai carefully gave me a hand to straighten, discreetly pumping air in and out of my blasting lungs.

I approached the crates once more, the whole dozen of them filled to the brim with rotting fish heads and insides. "Why would they send this?" I asked, disturbed, running my finger over the Tahuma engraving at the side.

Urun ryah. The sun sees.

Was this a sign of a trade deal growing cold, had they been unsatisfied with any of Isjord part of the shipment, or did they want to cut ties with Isjord? None of which made sense. Solarya was the biggest importer of Isjordian goods, they needed their part of the deal as much as Isjord did. If they were to cut their ties with Isjord, father would stop Hanai ships who used these waters to send goods to them as well. Whatever the situation, Solaryans would be the side with the most losses, and it made very little sense to bring this hostility between them and Isjord.

"I am not sure, Captain, but my men are saying that we are preparing for a deal with Adriata, and it might have not settled well for the islanders," he explained, covering the shipments and showing us out of the ship.

Solarya always attempted settling ties with Isjord. I was not the only game piece my father had used to settle an agreement. He had married my aunt Eleanor to their fourth prince with the promise of a four dozen ship fleet and deals of elk, coal and much more. My father was about to damage his ties to fix those with Adriata? Did he consider the other kingdoms were going to react this way?

"How many?" I asked the ship captain, hoping they had at least sent the rest of the produce shipments and that this was only a message. Winter almost neared and Isjordians were already scarce on food sources as it was, they were about to pay for my father's games.

"All of them, I am afraid. All the dozen ones you see in front of you," he pointed, turning towards the ships.

Solarya was not playing or trying to send a message, they were really trying to make more than a statement even—a declaration.

My soldiers began questioning the rest of the sailors for any valuable information that might point to the reason for the missing shipments. Two Solaryans that were caught travelling hidden with the sailors toward Isjord were to come with us to be questioned by my father. We searched all the other shipments carefully to check if anything had been missed, but all were filled with rotting fish heads and insides.

My eyes roamed about the large port while working out the conflict of thoughts on this new matter. "Grasmere is larger than I had thought," I said, examining the coastline stretching ahead and between for miles with sturdy large ships and berths to boast. Malena was indeed father's favourite. I wondered how much more riches and position in court his decision to move the main port here had given her.

"It's the largest port and with the sturdiest ships in the whole of Dardanes, the best timber comes from Isjord," the sailor boasted, proudly.

Cai placed a palm atop my head, pulling it straight before murmuring in my ear, "Enough with the crazy eyes. You start another lesson on galleys, ships and oars and I'll dunk your head in the Seer."

I laughed and threw an elbow between his ribs to silence him.

"How strained would you say are the ties between the two kingdoms?" I asked the sailor again.

He blew a long breath and shook his head. "Depends how the king decides to resolve this."

My brows rose in question. "War?" If so, my start plan would have worked a wonder, but if matters were hostile enough for war, my new plan would work way better.

He frowned, taken aback. "Heavens no, I hope not. We have not seen one in decades. Let's pray it stays the same. But unfriendly exchanges? Definitely."

I nodded my thanks and he headed back to his work.

"Did you hear that? Unfriendly exchanges," I said, wiggling my brows at Cai.

He cupped my head, thumbs resting atop my brows to stop their movement. "How is that in our leverage?"

"Father has the biggest fleet if not the strongest, what would happen if a few got destroyed?"

The emerald irises pinched in as he answered, "Damage, some damage. How do you intend to make that happen?"

"I will do nothing, Solarya will in the midst of this...heated agreement."

He finally moved away from me, raising a brow full of doubt. "You will get Solarya to attack your father? Did you retire the oar and galley plan so soon?"

"No, that one is still in the works," I said. "Do you know who would lose greatly in this?"

"Who?"

I pointed my head to the long white haired sea spirit conversing with the sailors. "That hells hound, the favourite viper in his court. Would it not be tragic if my father loses control over Grasmere? The fleet, trades, best voting hand in his court, all the gold and much more?"

"Let's guess, Solarya will be doing all that?" he asked, crossing his arms, throwing a snide glare in my direction.

"Correct, Solarya will."

He shook his head and threw an arm over my shoulder and lowered to murmur in my ear, "You're crazy, but I like crazy you."

After handing the direct order paperwork for the halting of the next shipments toward Solarya to the Grasmere Lady, we headed to leave before the rising snowstorm caught us.

I felt the burn of temperature steam off me at the touch of cold air brushing my skin—it almost hissed at the contact. Beads of sweat trickled down my temples and my tongue stuck dryly at the back of my throat. For a moment, my sighed fogged and the world went round just as screams and sword clanking filled the air. Was I dreaming again?

Two strong hands gripped me before I toppled from Memphis. I opened my eyes to Cai's muted face attempting to say something I could not hear.

I was not dreaming.

He lowered me to the ground, turning and catching a blade behind his back with his own and digging a dagger held on the other hand on the masked man's chest.

"Don't pass out on me, Cakes, come on now," Cai called as we began getting surrounded from all sides.

My feet turned to liquid and I fell to the soft snow coated floor. The cold travelled through my gloves to my palms sending me in a wakening jolt. It drew me to consciousness, limbs at last obliging me.

"Duck down," Cai shouted, shooting his hands forward when the rest of my soldiers obeyed his order. A slice of air shot from him all and around us, the attackers fell to the ground one after the other, sliced in half. Flurries of wind travelled furiously above us and they gathered around Cai, the tentacles of air grasped the masked prey before they swiftly cut through limbs, sending bits of flesh flying from all of our sides. Snow had lifted in the air along with branches as his hands moved in a chanting dance directing the element to its target. Cai was a Zephyr, wind Aura, a powerful wind aura. He was descender of a prime bloodline emanating from the first ever ancestors to be blessed with magic. If my father found him, he'd be dissected in pieces and then reassembled into a beast for his sick trials.

"The Solaryans," one of my soldiers called. "They are gone."

The stutter of anxiousness returned to my breaths. "They saw you, Cai."

"Snow, it won't matter—"

"Spread," I ordered my soldiers, interrupting him. "Find them."

I spun round trying to let my senses decide where they had gone and then I took off between a thick strap of forest. Wind cut my skin and branches held me back while I pushed deeper inside Fernby forest. Faint smell of fish surrounded me, one I knew well. The two Solaryans had been in that ship for days—they had to stink of it, too.

I unsheathed my daggers, spinning them to my grip while I pushed further towards the trail of scent left behind.

A branch veered in my aim and I ducked back, avoiding the hit. Footsteps of the other one crunched the snow behind me and I spun around, evading another strike. Twisting the daggers to hold them from their blade, I threw one and then the other in their directions.

Fighting between heavy breaths, I made toward their lifeless bodies lain between cold snow and attempted to retrieve my blades from their skulls. All energy suddenly drained from my limbs and I struggled to dislodge the blades, only to end up on the ground between them myself.

"One hundred and five, one hundred and six," I murmured to the nothingness of the forest and the open sky.

Not moments later, hands picked me up and steadied me to my feet.

"I couldn't let them, they'd seen you," I whispered to him while he silently shook all the snow from my clothes, like a little child being cleared from the mud of a playground. "They would have said something, sold the information and hurt you."

"They could have," he answered and guided me back to the rest of the squadron.

But they might have not. The rest of that sentence hung in the air unsaid, like many other things he was too afraid to say because they might wound me.

Memphis nestled around me protectively, shielding me from the forest while my soldiers raked through what was left of the attackers for any sort of clues.

"Snowlin," a soldier called, pulling my attention. "I suggest we head straight to Tenebrose, there could be more. This seems a well thought trap and they have had to know the area and your itinerary. This is the thickest strap of the forest we pass though Sable Abyss, a perfect hiding position."

"You think they were sent for me particularly? Could this not be thieves?" I asked tiredly, slouching to the ground.

He went and searched a dead attacker's clothing, examining their features before pulling up his sleeves. An arrow tattooed in his forearm. "Mercenaries," he said, lifting the dead man's arm up. "These are no thieves."

We immediately gathered our bearings and cautiously rode ahead through the faltering day. The magic burning lanterns along Sable Abyss made it more eerie than helpful to pass through, each shadow had us unsheathing our weapons. We had lost two soldiers and a third one was gravely injured. Father would probably throw a fit.

We had reached city gates when I awoke from Cai's arms. Soldiers came down running towards us, helping my tired soldiers covered in blood and taking the dead. Halfway to the stables, my father came riding forwards, masquerading with feigned rage.

Meeting us midway, he dismounted his horse and ran toward me. I startled when he reached and held me in his arms before walking us inside the castle.

"Let me go, I can walk myself, this false affection is turning my stomach," I said breathlessly, and I was not lying. I wiggled out of his arms and retched over the bushes, surprised I even had anything left to bring out.

Father took me into his arms again, and when I tried to move away, he only gripped me tighter. "Call a healer to my chambers, immediately," he yelled the order and soldiers went running.

I could almost laugh at the expression etched in his face. Did he think he lost his precious agreement?

He dropped me lightly on a massive golden bed in the middle of a dark walled open room draped in burgundy curtains all over, above which a massive chandelier hung and was dimly lit. It smelled of wood and deep darkness, just like him—just like I remembered. This room was often part of my nightmares. A prison of mine where he'd once locked me.

He paced about the room as the healer came, and then went outside to let him privately inspect me.

"You are running a high fever, princess, nothing that a bit of rest and good food cannot fix," the healer explained before heading out of the room to exchange words with my father.

My eyes had narrowed on my father who had now stopped in the middle of the room watching and studying me. "I will not die, your deal with Adriata is safe," I said spitefully. I had not once received the smallest care from my father, which meant I knew very well what this was. The nights I hurt, ached and spent sick were always with my brother and Alaric, both of whom I was now missing painfully.

"One of my soldiers told me you spent an entire night out in the gardens," he said, approaching my bed and ignoring what I had said.

"Good heavens, are you spying on me now?" I do not know why I was so surprised, I expected worse from him. Of course he would keep an eye on me.

"You will not resume your duties anymore, what happened today should have not taken place. Whoever attacked you was aware of your itinerary. You are to stay within safe castle grounds."

I lifted my upper body to stand, but my legs had gone numb. My heart began drumming all ire and vexation at what he had just said. That feel of chains creeped over my wrists and ankles, and I flinched at the memory. "You will not make me a prisoner again, father. I will not allow it, my duties remain and if you fear for my life then keep me safe, but not locked," I challenged, livid that he might trap me here again.

He shook his head, jaw tight and angry ready to object to my words.

I stood, barely holding myself up and came face to face with him. "I will never be you, but I am not my mother either."

He studied me for a moment, I felt the disregard there though he did not say it. "Stay, use my chambers tonight, you are not well. We will speak of this again tomorrow," he said, grabbing my arm as I went past him.

I shook myself free from him. "It smells of death in here, this is your room to rot in, not mine."

Three enemies circled me now—father, Adriatians and possibly Solaryans. I had now more on my plate that I bargained to find when I took my chance and returned to Isjord. This was no longer just about my father's plans. Or was all of it revolving around them? As per usual, the shit was his, but I was getting the stink of it.

14

LILIES AND POISON

KILIAN

THERE HAVE BEEN NO trespassers through the Highwall in the past two weeks on either side of the border. It was either the new rules to kill at first sight that had done it, or the Isjordian princess had truly found the leaks in the wall. That day played continuously in my head, every flash of remembrance ignited a sort of anger I'd rarely felt before.

Mal and the others did not mention what happened that day, but I knew they all had been affected just the same as I. She was not just a cruel captain, but the cruel princess Adriata's king was to marry. The council discussed the deal for months, but nothing out-balanced the freedom of our people to our pride, nothing but her. She'd won council over the deal the moment they'd snapped on the idea.

Adriata was a powerful kingdom, but we were always surrounded by unfavourable lands and water. The dark sea was the sanctuary of Golgotha's creatures, the Demon God whose realm had been destroyed. God of all gods, Fader, had offered him refuge in Numengarth. The Sea of the Dark was now polluted by creatures of the dark—they were peaceful but mindless. When they crawled onto our lands, it caused quite the havoc and damage. While one sort of monster riled our east, our west was crawling with unblessed pirates from Vrammethen, frequently attempting to cross to Dardanes through us. It kept our guards on a constant edge and our people under fear. With the addition of Highwall we were scarce all over. Remote villages were left empty, those who relied on crossing the border seasonally for work were living in poverty with no access to food and other living necessities. Those who had been trapped within our walls were heavily relying on our product ability with no trade deals from any of the other kingdoms. We lived on a highly productive land, our soil adaptable to all produce, our farms facilitating all living stock and our seas drowned in fish, but our population grew rapidly by day, and those lands and farms once cultivated had now become villages and our forests were growing scarce for wood that was now not enough to build new fishing boats to replace the ones that were growing old and broken.

Mal only returned yesterday from Sitara and he had been right, the stink of what he had slaughtered stuck like mud to his skin. He'd come back with the wildest stories and most shocked I'd ever seen him.

"Lilies, how can lilies grow like wild bushes everywhere destruction plagues?" he asked, scratching his stubbly jaw. "Is this something holy? What does it even mean?"

Lily of the valley had spurted everywhere these past months, all over the parts affected by this mist of misfortune that plagued Adriata endless. Gods had funny metaphorical ways to thank, mock and warn us.

"They are lilies of the valley. I believe they mean poison." Henah had planted the flower in mourning to her guardian who died by the earthly flower. Even the eternals were not immortal. It was said the flower would bloom in warning every time poison and misfortune surrounded someone.

"Our lands are poisoned? From what?"

"I don't know, Mal. I don't know." I truly did not know.

We rode out of the Adriata's capital, Amaris, towards Kilmarnock forest, now the last barrier between our kingdom and the Highwall. Before, the forest had grown hundred feet tall giants that were seen miles away. Once home to folk, animal and all magic, now new sprouts were yearly planted to preserve it from becoming an empty landscape just like most of its sister lands had become.

We were on our way for the weekly wall checks and updates on guard rotations and news from Isjord which were delivered there. Larg had called us for news, insistent on speaking it personally.

My brother sighed. "He keeps calling us to the wall for the most ridiculous reasons. Does he think we are jobless?"

"He is our godfather, Mal, and has no family. How many times do you normally visit him?"

"The normal never," he said, flashing me a grin.

Highwall was quieter than usual, solemn and gloomier from the new quiet. Soldiers sat bored along their posts, some together in front of a game board and others almost snoring out of their armour.

"The princess did not lie, she truly must have rooted out all rot from Kirkwall, no more crossings in a fortnight," Mal said all too quietly and casually as we dismounted our horses.

"Or she massacred all of Kirkwall."

He laughed at my words that were not intended to be funny. "You remember those flyers of her drawing that Amaris priests were throwing around? They had made her look like a troll with a tail, wings, and horns. The mighty *Ybris* of centuries. You have to admit, we have certainly been lied to," he added playfully.

His amusement at this whole situation truly concerned me. "Doesn't change the fact that she still is. Those horns, tail and wings of that troll are inside her, facades can be deceiving."

He scowled, staring doubtfully at me. "You never used to think like that when we were young, always objecting to others when they used to call her a monster. What's changed, brother? The old fanatics in the council telling you old tales, plaguing your head with unfulfilled prophecies of the Elding cracking our realm in half with her lightning?"

"It was to defend a life, not in objection to what she was. That day at Kirkwall did well to prove her roots. Being made into one is not the same as turning into one," I said, guiding my horse to a stall. "It's worse."

"You cannot in honesty blame her for that."

I halted and turned to him. "If everyone succumbed to their emotion whether anger, grief, hate or even love, this world would be torn apart without the need of *Ybrises* or beasts or prophecies. It would be by people, humans even. You learn to control them, not dress your sword with them."

He fell silent for a few moments before asking, "And if they are too drowning?"

"You are an Empath, tell me if you have ever seen that happen? Did you see her shadows? She feels nothing, steered by reckless thoughts. A child with a crown who doesn't realise she is no longer wielding a wooden sword but one made of steel."

He frowned at my words. "You are harsh today."

"She has killed eight of our people and exiled two in her death lands to whatever torture awaits there for them. Harsh would not even cover it. Do not argue with me on it, Mal, I am aware of your stance, however disagreeable."

He stood silent a moment, taking my words bitterly by the hues of shadows surrounding him. "We are Empaths, yet so very few of us allow ourselves to feel. When you know the impact of emotion, you become weary of it so one shuts it down. You, brother, have shut those gates and sealed those locks long before there was a gate," he said, pointing to me. "Yet you blame her for not feeling when you deny yourself of any emotion. How would you understand how she feels when you yourself don't know how to feel?" He patted my shoulder and greeted past soldiers, leaving me alone with his words.

For a few moments, my eyes had glued to the muddied ground softened by summer sprays of lone clouds. Should I feel something at his words? Reconsideration, regret for my own, sympathy? Was he right?

Climbing the long stairwells to enter the watch tower atop the wall, I took in the long miles of Isjord camouflaged by the thick snow coating its walls, roofs, trees, and land. A blinding dull blanket of blessing that I never understood. How was the cold ever a blessing?

Nesrin and Grey had arrived ahead of us and sat around the large table along with several other soldiers reading through documents and mail received from Isjord.

"With Henah's blessings, to Cynth heaven."

"With Henah's blessing, might it welcome us. Kilian, Malik, thank you for joining us for this meeting," greeted Larg. He was a large man, older than time but still as strong as any soldier in his youth. The same one who trained Mal and I since we were barely able to hold a wooden sword. A true Adriatian and a dear friend of my father's.

We sat there for hours, discussing how a few of our own were caught in Kilmarnock heading towards the wall to cross. All that were caught had spoken and confessed almost immediately after Larg threatened to send them to Kirkwall himself for the princess to deal with. The statement made the whole tower room shake with laughter. The prisoners had told him they were headed for Solarya and that the Kirkwall dead Lord had promised them safe passage through Highwall in exchange for payment. They had confessed that he had been aiding crossers for years. The princess had most definitely known, everyone could read the annoyance in her face when he had spoken, an annoyance that had not been groundless as we thought. The actions she took still felt cruel and rash, but with motive. Isjordians were known to be harsh judges of traitors and the corrupted, a gift from their god—a gift that had helped them win countless wars through many centuries.

Larg turned to me as if knowing I was deep in thought. "She's a clever girl, but brutal to her captives so it feels funny to say that I admire and fear her at the same time."

"There is nothing to admire in a beast," Grey spat.

"There is nothing to admire in a man who screams like a little girl," Mal murmured beside me and I nudged his foot.

He cried out a little and then turned to me furious. "What was that for? He did scream like a little girl. I'd never before seen a man scream so high pitched at a tornado, let alone at a two-metre long basilisk." He cocked his head back and folded his arms. "Could put little girls to shame that one."

Larg let out a sigh, looking over the tower window towards Kirkwall as he continued, "The issue is that it seems she is also preyed upon, by whom we still do not know."

My face must have shown surprise because Nesrin added, "We heard from the Isjordian wall guards that her group was attacked on her way from Grasmere to Tenebrose."

They had attacked her, had she been hurt, and attacked by whom, who wanted her and why? Had it been her people or mine? My brain fogged at the thought of Adriatians attacking her. I tilted my head back and forth to release the tension that was building down my neck. "Was she hurt?" I asked Larg.

He shook his head. "They had fended off more than four dozen soldiers, but she was well, only two of her own hurt."

My muscles relaxed at his words and I nodded. Four dozen attackers had cornered her. Four dozen. They wanted her dead. No thieves or scavengers remained in such big groups. They were there with the purpose to hurt her.

"And the attackers, have they been identified?" Mal asked.

Larg nodded in confirmation. "Paid Isjordian assassins and mercenaries, none of which were captured." Somewhat satisfied, he leaned back in his chair, grinning while he added, "All dead, just how the princess likes it."

Someone must have been really determined to gather a group of more than four dozen of such expensive and hardly attainable characters to attack the princess, and what I feared was that it could have easily been one of our own. We were three moons away from the royal matrimony and judging from her character, too long to have her running around her kingdom gaining more haters than admirers. I just hoped Silas wanted this agreement as much as Adriata did to keep her safe within his city walls till she came here.

"It does her well," Grey interrupted, snarling. "She should not be parading around her kingdom and ours killing and running that sharp mouth as if she is invincible."

Grey was the one to spew the hottest curses and hate towards her and he did not hide his hate for the future queen of Adriata. However, they were all thinking the same as him, I saw it on the soldiers who nodded and their shadows of dislike.

Larg stepped in. "You would think so, but her people said she had headed straight out the next day to deal with a vandal attack on a remote village up their north. She might not be invincible, but she surely is fearless."

I rubbed my face hard, that ridiculous idiot was probably doing it on purpose at this point. Was it to avoid the agreement or just because of her own blind stupidity, I did not understand. But something had to be done before she ruined all our plans.

Grey scoffed. "Reckless bitch."

On beat, the heat of Mal's composure leaked out of his shadows while he leaned onto the table. "Lush that coming from you. Had I not been in Sitara you would have turned into basilisk dung, and might I remind you to mind your tongue, Captain, she is to be your queen—our queen," he warned.

The two have been on the wrong odds with each other since that day at the trial. Grey came complaining to me that the whole trip in Sitara my brother had refused to utter a single word to him. For someone with that much compassion, my brother was too petty.

The room went quiet upon his warning as if they had forgotten what she truly was going to be to Adriata and them. The agreement was one thing, her becoming queen, another.

"Oh, you are thinking of something," Mal said while we rode for Amaris. "Something I won't like,"

I knew he had just read my shadows, though we usually never used it towards our own so openly. Mal however, always used it on me. When we were children he'd never been able to read the emotions on my face. He'd thought me angry only to find out I had been perfectly calm if not happy, he'd thought me sad only to find out I'd been ecstatic. From that point he'd decided to always use his magic from fear of misunderstanding.

We rode back through Kilmarnock, past river Nyx, onto Amaris and towards castle grounds where we unsaddled our horses.

Adriata was beautiful by my standard, but the late queen had made sure the castle grounds looked like goddess Henah's heavens. The large white stone castle stood several floors tall, dressed in crawling violet wisteria and located in the middle of miles and miles of colourful and fragrant rose bushes that had sprung all around it. The sound of wind brushing the evergreen leaves was an oasis itself and the sweet pollen, a perfume around my senses.

We headed to notify the council of the latest events, who would have a lot to say and argue to death till the day grew tired and dark, as per usual. The same council who was formed by those that had partaken, organised and prepared to attack Isjord. And just the same who had not given second thought or doubted their choices. However, it was the king's hands that ultimately carried the fault for the Adriatians' misery and the death of thousands of innocent Isjordians who'd lost their life that night.

"You have got that insane concentration you get when you play chess. I don't like it," Mal interrupted the silence while we made our way to the Council chambers. "Do tell, I hate surprises."

"Lies, you love them."

"Unless I am expecting a puppy to jump out of one, no, I do not."

"An *Ybris* will jump out of this one, will that satisfy you?"

He halted, annoyingly forcing me to do the same. "One with long dark hair and pretty murderous eyes?"

Pretty? "Yes."

He scowled. "No."

"It was not a question, brother. Answers don't need answers."

"If you propose to have her locked till marriage, I will piss in all your morning coffee till the day we die."

I grimaced. "I don't drink coffee. And no, I will not propose to lock her."

Before we reached the meeting room doors, I heard him murmur between his teeth, "But you do drink green tea."

Moon court sat round in stalls located by both sides of the wall, all concentrating on the documents they were shuffling through. We stood in the middle of the room and bowed to the head councillor who was also our blood relative. She was older than my father, her grey striped hair was braided around her head in a crown and her eyes were an odd grey colour, the same as mine.

"If you have come to notify us of recent events, Head General, you have wasted precious time, we are aware of what has happened," she said absently, flipping through pieces of paper in front of her.

"No, I have come to notify you of a decision, rather. One regarding recent events," I bit back in a tone same as hers. She reminded me of our father when it came to leadership, both were cold, calculative but fair, traits that had deserved her position in the King's Council.

She raised her narrowed stare at me. "A decision? I did not know we were to come to a decision for this. She is still theirs to deal with, we are to do nothing."

"I was not asking, aunt, as I said, I am only notifying," I stepped closer to her. "Send words to King Silas that we are to send two of our best men to escort, tail or guard her, whatever you like to call it, at all times till the wedding."

"Sweet crescent moon," Mal murmured behind me.

If the princess wanted to dally around carelessly, she would have to do it with two Adriatians attached to her. If not to protect her, to annoy her enough to stay put. Isjord had armies, numbers, and strategic maps, but we had better skilled soldiers, Adriatian steel weapons and our Aura were far more vicious than theirs. If Silas wanted this deal as much as we did, he would agree to it. It would not be smart to refuse it knowing his princess was now someone's target.

She laughed. "Am I to guess who these two soldiers will be?" Her tone was angry and displeased.

The two soldiers would be the two Adriatians I trusted the most in this kingdom. Myself and Mal, who was already sneering and shaking his head in disparagement.

"I understand Moon court has plenty of time to play guess the word so I will leave you at it," I said, ready to leave. "We will leave the moment we receive immunity to move through Isjord."

"What makes you think Silas will allow two Adriatians to enter his court?"

I halted. She was right. He didn't build this wall only to ensure we both kept out of each other's kingdoms, but more to keep us away from his. But now, we were to become allies, and if he could trust his daughter to live in our kingdom, it would be too hostile of him to refuse our request.

"He will." I left with Mal furiously charging behind me. I knew he was going to react this way, but he would not refuse to join me because he would not allow me to go on Isjordian lands on my own.

"This is not about protecting her, is it?"

"Imagining things at your young age?"

He laughed shortly and unamused. "So I was right."

"About what?"

He only blew a breath of frustration and remained silent.

Mal had not spoken a word as we made our way to the tavern down Amaris which we had frequented since we were old enough to keep our drinks down. The sun nearly drowned down the horizon, casting a purple shadow on the stony streets of the city. Candlelight flickered inside the square stone houses lined in a perfect symmetry with each other, children ran towards a leather ball, their screams and cheers filling the busy street—a perfect Adriatian evening. The city became livelier at night, we were worshipers of the dark, our lands grew under moonlight and the shadows got darker, bigger at night. It was the time our Aura were the strongest. The time when Empaths saw emotional shadows brighter, fading was swifter and easier on our life strength and our telepathic hold tighter. To us the air grew sweeter at night.

We made our way to our usual seat, the ground shaking from the music and dancing which our people enjoyed beyond anything.

"It seems you have truly lost it, Kil, old age is not settling well with you," he said sipping from his drink, finally breaking the silence between us. "If this is your plan to study Isjord, you are wrong. Silas would not allow us near any of his precious secrets, no matter what agreement is between us. We are still enemies to him, not to mention her."

There it was, his true concern. Her.

"We're only going to protect the agreement," I said half truthfully. I was curious about Isjord and this would be a great chance to explore its endless lands.

"You mean the princess?"

"One of the same."

His shadows dressed in suspicion and disbelief. He relaxed onto his chair and raised a toast. "Well, cheers to the princess and the suffering bastards she will make of us."

"I thought you liked her."

"I enjoy being a suffering bastard to a beautiful woman. Let alone a beautiful woman with a sword."

I scoffed. "She'd rather have your head on a pike."

He sighed all bliss and gave me a wink. "Rather exciting."

I coughed my drink. "You sicken me, brother."

Two days later, Isjord responded to our request, granting permission to escort the princess till the wedding. An answer I had expected, but strangely it struck me with surprise.

When we notified the council of our departure, they had been in disbelief more at themselves for adhering permission to us to enter Isjord, thinking Silas was going to send a rejection. They argued a whole evening, protesting we do not leave, but we left our goodbyes with them last night.

It would take a whole day's journey to arrive in Tenebrose according to the wall guards. So we left Amaris just before dawn, well rested, dressed and packed tightly. Adriata was a warm kingdom, never having experienced harsh weather, winter, snowy or icy terrain at that. To me and Mal, we were entering a whole new realm. Our father had travelled to Isjord countless times, but he had never brought me or Mal with him. Shortly after we were old enough to travel far, he passed away and then the Highwall treaty was established.

"Don't make me regret agreeing to let you two do this," Larg warned, opening the Zone of Peace gates to the winter lands.

"This is against my will, old man, the only thing missing are shackles," Mal complained. "The idiot I proudly call my brother didn't even care to ask for my opinion."

"We will be fine," I reassured, but it was not us that Mal worried about. To my dissatisfaction it was her, the princess.

"You better be, you two are my responsibility. I gave my word to your father the day both of you were born and when I swore on your blessings day. Don't make me face him up in the heavens with a scowl, he had a terribly angry expression."

"He was a terrible man."

"Mal," I called sternly.

Larg frowned at his ill tongue directed at the man he'd once called a brother.

My brother clicked his tongue, shadows of disdain swirling his head. "Sometimes I forget that *us*, people of truth, cannot bear the truth."

We greeted Larg and the guards at our side of the wall and headed out of the Zone of Peace. As instructed by Silas, a dozen soldiers dressed in the blue royal guard uniform were waiting for us just outside.

We rode through the brisk snowy terrain, my eyes hurting from the white of snow. It took a long while till they adjusted to the landscape. The Isjordian guards guided us through what they called Fernby forest to a black stoned road that curved like a black snake for miles, this was their manner of quick travel through the kingdom. I finally understood how despite the thick snow, Isjordian captains travelled down to Highwall for trials almost within hours after being notified.

After hours of travel, the captain of the Isjordian group notified us of a halt to feed and rest the horses. When we dismounted, the ground felt foreign, the snow was crunchy and satisfying when we swished past.

Mal removed his glove and touched the ground, lifting snow on his hand. He looked at me madly. "How is it that it's cold, but it burns?" he asked, shaking and wiping his hand to his clothes.

The Isjordian soldiers laughed at his comment and explained to him that because it was so cold it felt like burning his skin, to which he still looked confused after.

"Doesn't it bother you, the continuous cold?" I asked, feeling the brisk wind bite dull pain on my neck.

"We cannot feel it, to us the snow is purifying and warm. To the land it is like a blanket of life," the captain explained, fisting a bunch of the white mush. "The lands of Isjord before the gods were lifeless and dry, we might not be able to cultivate much, but now they are liveable lands. Full of life, even."

Isjordian history has always been the one to draw yawns from me, and history was one of my guilty indulgences. I drowned those books by the dozen, most of those in Amaris city library had already been read by me. I suppose with the exception of those belonging to Isjord, relatively boring just like their brooding god and their dull blessings.

The soldiers were polite but still cautious around us. I saw the shadows of their tension and distrust, their hands never left the hilts of their swords nor did they ever turn their back to us. Mal and I agreed to keep our magic hidden till we judged the right circumstances, it would not be smart to appear a threat to them.

The day started to grow dark, we had not seen the sun the whole day, tucked between grey clouds and serving only as a source of light to the land. Just as it was beginning to turn into night, torches lit automatically and revealed Tenebrose walls hidden by darkness. They rose dark grey between the empty landscape and hundreds of guards patrolled the surface above and the front black metallic gates which opened to let us in. The city stood grand, wooden buildings with black stoned roofs crowded for miles close to one another, almost as a unit. Above the city, a thick layer of soot and smoke from the burning wood leaked from chimneys, hovering almost like a second sky. Roads all laid in the same black stone, clear from snow and warm. It resembled gloom incarnate, yet it smelled lightly like baked bread and vanilla.

The castle grounds grew in sight as we left the city behind. Laying atop a large rock overlooking the city—Tenebrose castle carried the might of its owners.

"It fits the character. Dark, cold and stony. Though rather bloodless, I expected heads on pikes, crows nipping on guts and all of that," Mal said as we entered the castle stables.

"Never speak too soon," I warned. Everything was expected from Silas, one didn't just get the name kingdom slayer. This one deserved it, too.

We were led through gardens covered in snow, red roses peaked from behind the covered bushes looking like blood droplets against the white blanket. Not at all how we had imagined Isjord.

Several servants and soldiers halted to stare at us as we made our way to meet the king. Fear rounded their heads and a deep forgotten guilt churned in my stomach.

Had my people killed someone they loved as well? I wanted to kneel, apologise, and ask for their forgiveness, for they were innocents trapped and hurt for what had not been their doing or fault.

Mal planted a hand on my shoulder, dragging me out of my thoughts, he squeezed once and let go, signalling that he knew what spiralled my mind, probably his as well.

We reached a pair of massive black doors guarded by two soldiers who motioned to them, but they flew right open before they had a chance. The dark-haired princess came out, looking dead ahead, her eyes unwavering and no more the shining amber I once had witnessed them to be. Her hair flew around like raven wings, almost reflecting the ire readable on her face. She went past us as if we were not there, marching down the corridor, her hands in fists so tight her leather gloves had discoloured grey at the knuckles.

"Snowlin Krigborn, I demand you here at once, it's an order. No one turns their back when I speak!" A shout sounded from inside the chambers she'd just come out of, one so loud I could have sworn it made the doors shake.

She scoffed and then darkly laughed, enough to make crows fly away. "I am sure dear Moreen does all the time, so I suppose you will live to grace my miserable life another day, Silas Krigborn," the princess shouted back in a snide tone before turning out of the corridor and out of sight.

My brows had hiked to my hairline. Silas...she spoke to him like that?

Amusement shadows filled the corridor, the Isjordian soldiers along with Mal chuckled and coughed under their breaths, shaking their heads.

They finally cleared their throats and tightened back their cold expressions. "You will find yourself plenty entertained by the father and daughter," one of the soldiers whispered, letting us pass.

The dark princess was not an act, this was what she was and I was happy even her father had to face her wrath. Only till I remembered it was not long till us and the whole Adriata would take the turn.

Guards announced our presence before guiding us to the room. A gilded flamboyant dais sat in the middle, several golden chairs scattered in lines before it and a red carpet between them pointing towards the king, enthroned with poise of a killer ruler.

The King of Isjord sat in front of me feet away, a fist propped under his chin, brown shadows circling his head. He was furious, but he hid it well. His features were a blanket of calm, composure and that of perpetual turpitude.

"Welcome to Isjord," he greeted all languid. "We have not welcomed Adriatians—well, you know, I suppose."

He was the reason to begin with, despite what my people had done. He instigated fear and chaos amongst our realm for only his plans to fail and my people to still assume in fear that those plans had not. How he was able to throw away his daughter to her worst enemies I would never understand.

"The safety of the princess is as much a priority to us, as it is to you, King Silas. You have allowed her in the way of danger once, which is more than enough," Mal's voice erupted from my side.

The king leaned forward and nodded, lips pursing all desire to order 'off with his head'. "Very well then, she is yours to protect from this point," he added firmly, though no regard read in his shadows. He did not care.

We were guided down the large cold corridors that arched around a garden and right outside. The dark headed princess rested on a bench, her head lowered down and resting in her palms while she breathed fast, her knees shaking.

For a brief moment when she stood and turned to leave, her eyes met mine.

I looked away first, following the soldiers down to our new quarters.

God defiers, born for carnage, born a ruination and harbinger of death, the definition of *Ybrises* on the sacred liber of Caelus. She was powerless, but it didn't change what she was—the blood cursing her veins.

15

GODS AND GUARDS

SNOWLIN

PENELOPE DRAGGED ME OUT from the slumbering bath that had turned cold and pimpled my skin with gooseflesh. She draped a grey long sleeved shimmering silk dress over me, with a square neck that showed my bust and came curving around my body, dropping till it barely touched the floor. My hair fell loose, two emerald coated pins on each side to hold it back from my face. My sore palms from last night were still thumping and aching, wrapped in a white gauze under the white gloves covering the evidence. Pen said I looked beautiful, yet I still saw only grim shadows floating in the reflection on the mirror.

Nia stepped inside my room, leaning against the door just before I reached it. Her eyes jumped in hesitation about the room, avoiding mine.

"Speak Helenia," I demanded, annoyed.

"Whatever you do, do not kill anyone. Not yet at least," she asked, carefully stepping aside, letting me exit my room.

I already knew who she meant. "I'll play dice for the decision."

She scowled. "Snowlin."

I rolled my eyes. "I won't kill them," I said, pulling the door open. "Yet."

Two tall figures resembling my fears stood before my chambers. The dark-haired men bowed their heads. One had lush brown long hair to his shoulder, half pulled up in a bun, brown eyes that were darker than most, his features strong, carved but gentle somehow. The other was striking, perhaps it was his grey eyes resembling starlight, a shimmering silver, or his jaw that curved so sharp it resembled a blade I wished to prickle my finger on. Perhaps it was the resistance in his eyes and the hate he did not fear to hide. His short dark hair was almost as dark as mine, features were strong and impeccably stern, almost still and so, so cold. In his chin a dimple dipped when his jaw twitched. He looked like a carved god sculpture, the same thought that had gone through my head the first time I had seen him at the trials in Kirkwall. I remembered them. It was not difficult to forget such faces. They were both dressed in deep black leathers and contraptions, hugging every inch of their muscular limbs, looking every bit the fanatic barbarians they were.

Directly upon my return from the north trip to Islines I'd been summoned by my father. Adriata were to send two guards to accompany me till my marriage with their king, to assure my safety. He gave me a choice: accept two Adriatians to trail me, or remain still and safe inside the castle grounds. It was punishment—punishment for disobeying and leaving for the Islines, for challenging the general and entering his court, and a plan to keep me away from his business. This was a game to him, but to me, he'd gone too far and he knew it. I had chosen right when his eyes had grown as wide as an oysters egg and his nostrils wide enough to suck all the air in the room. Had he though me stupid enough to fall for his tricks? Even if a whole army of Adriatians had tried to guard me, I would have allowed it since now I knew the extent he was willing to go to keep me away from his plans. These two men were the ones sent from the Adriatian King to keep me safe, a thought that had sent me in laughing fits since last night, but now that I was facing them it didn't appear to entertain me all the same.

They bowed their heads slightly. Both studied me carefully as though they had never seen me before, their eyes falling to my dress and gradually to my face.

"Do Adriatians name their dogs or just the snakes?" I asked, scrunching my nose playfully, giving them my most saccharine smile.

The silver eyed one flared with anger, his eyes unwavering into mine, but it was the other that stepped forward before he had a chance to react. "Malik, Your Highness, and this is Kilian, my brother," he said calmly, motioning to the man next to him. Such normal names for such barbarians. "We will be your guards till your marriage with our king."

I scoffed. "And after, my undertakers?"

I found it funny, but the two guards stiffened.

"After, you are to be our queen, princess. However we or you like it. There is no joking in that matter. We are to protect you with our life from this moment and even more so after," Kilian spoke harshly, his expression dialling from furious to irked.

My jaw locked tight. "Is that so?"

His locked tighter. "Yes, that is so."

I studied his gaze, the lingering disdain behind. "It will eventually become burdensome, you know, looking at me like I am inhuman all the time."

"You are inhuman. Your whole existence is a contortion of the unnatural. This is just the look all your sort get."

Malik bumped a fist to his side in warning, but the older brother did not even budge.

"Please," I snorted, somewhat amused by all of it. "Don't try so hard to hide your disgust."

"It's not disgust."

The corridor had grown cold enough to prickle my skin with shivers. "Humour me."

"Curiosity," he replied plainly and too fearlessly to my taste.

Curiosity? "I suppose you would be curious. Don't I look similar to the beast they portrayed me to be?"

"No," his voice was so cold, colder than anything.

"Of course, I had my fangs and horns filed down, claws still retractable though so be aware."

"And your heart, what did they do to it? Toss it to the Isjordian wolves?" Kilian asked and his brother nudged his shoulder in warning again.

"Your people carved that out twelve years ago, it should be in your lands."

A tick in his jaw hammered and he averted his gaze to the floor shortly before fearlessly meeting mine again. "You intend to find it by torturing innocents?"

Innocents? "Why so surprised, darling, didn't you hunt me because I was meant to torture innocents? Now, however, will be at my bidding, not my father's."

The two brothers exchanged short glances before turning to study me again.

I clapped my hands together. "So, will you stand there all day and charm me or shall we move so I can sacrifice a virgin and drink orphan blood? You know, for my hybrid rituals of bringing doom on Numengarth," I teased, opening my arms and dropping my head back like I'd seen Dark Crafters do during summoning rituals. "Though today I would prefer a bath in goat blood. Pen, have it ready for when I return," I said to my red haired servant who had covered her mouth to suppress her giggles.

"I thought it was the flesh of new-born babes on Fridays, Your Excellency?" Pen asked, lowering down in an exaggerated curtsy and struggling to hold her laughter.

Nia slapped her behind her head before throwing me a glare. "Defiling the fifteen-year-old now, Snow?" she asked incredulously, shaking her head. "Back to work, Pen."

Malik lowered his head to hide the tight smile, but the other one blankly glared at me.

"But that is my purpose, I shall defile and soil humanity, my true *Ybris* purpose." I said and threw a wink to the wrathful silver eyed snake who wavered and bit his tongue that was ready for another reply.

"Take your *Ybris* bottom to breakfast, your father is most excited to see you after you threw a chair at him," she said, folding her arms all disappointed at me.

A chair, two vases and a painting, but small details, right?

"She did what?" Malik asked and then retreated, carefully glancing between us all.

"You," I said, pointing to him. "The tolerable one. You guard me during the day, that one at night."

The barbarians agreed. For today, Malik and Cai were to follow me around. I was happy with the arrangement, not that I could like any of them, but Malik seemed more agreeable than the other. Though I attempted to convince myself otherwise, every step I took it felt like a blade was digging on my back, making me turn my head over my shoulder several times to check that my mind was still intact. That dark emotion started to creep against me, making me jittery and anxious, my breath rapid and uncontrollable.

"A beautiful raven crossing me. Is that a bad omen or a good one?" Elias called by the dinning chamber doors and brain fog cleared all of the sudden.

I turned around, Cai and Malik blinking at me surprised. "Now, Cai, what hurts most: a knee in the crotch or a knee in your ego?" But truthfully, I was going to hurt Elias for the smug flirts and his tattle-tale mouth, I just did not know what was best.

"Crotch," Malik spoke, examining Elias. "Measured it myself. That pain almost amounts to a blade wound. Men often take little offence over words. Aim for the crotch I say."

I blinked stunned at him for a few moments before nodding. "The crotch it is."

I charged towards Elias, reached around his shoulder to wrap my arms around his neck and kneed him in the crotch like suggested.

He yelped in pain, closing his eyes as he leaned forward, clutching himself. "Glad to see your spirits remain strong," he spoke breathlessly, cringing in pain.

Leaning over to his ear I said, "One raven is sorrow. That was for telling my father about the Islines, you fink."

He groaned and attempted to straighten. "He knew, Snowlin, my soldiers reported back at him the moment they saw you up there and so had Casmere when you didn't show up for the patrol."

Of course my father was keeping a detailed eye on me.

"Tell me, Elias, what the heavens and hells is happening there? I know there are no Isjordians attacking the north." I'd veered my patrol the second I'd caught rumour of the vandal attacks. I'd done it to piss father off after his soldier had almost imprisoned me in my quarters after the attack in Grasmere, but stumbled upon a strange discovery.

He glanced nervously around the corridor and warned, "Keep it to yourself, that is all I have to say to you, do not let your father find out what you know."

"Is that why he is trying so hard to keep me away from there? Because he doesn't want me to find out?" He'd forbid me from tending anywhere near the Islines, something about a poor excuse the Isline Krigborn could target me. The mountain wolves could care more for rabbits than a royal with soiled blood that couldn't even become heir.

He straightened, diverting attention around the corridor to the sentries posted by the dining doors. "That is all I can say without betraying an oath to my king."

"Sworn to a serpent, an oath made to hells."

"It is my kingdom, my people, my lands."

"Your burden to bear then when he uses fools as yourself blinded by an empty oath to raise hells in his name. All the life that will be lost will be yours to repent for."

"He is my king," he argued as though it made sense.

"And death is our fate yet we fight every day to live."

He sighed, given up and offered politely, "If they attempt anything funny, you know where to find me."

"If you think I will waste your debt to me with requests of this sort, you're wrong," I said, sliding past him.

Throughout the whole meal, my father and the rest had just silently stared at me as I ate. I knew they, too, had grown uneasy at the arrival of the Adriatians, especially my father who had not thoroughly thought his plan through and underestimated just how much more spiteful than him I was.

"Happy with your choice?" he asked in what looked like vexation.

Flashing him a tight-lipped smile I said, "Ecstatic."

He leaned back, assessing me and the truthfulness of my words for a moment before ordering, "The men you caught up north will be handled by one of the generals, you are not to question them."

"I caught them."

"In my lands," he argued strongly. "You are not to question them, understand?"

"I ignored you just fine the first time, no need to repeat."

His eyes widened and his tone flared higher, "You have no more business up north, disobey me and you won't go unpunished."

Ah, but see now it changes. He really wanted to keep me away from there, that meant something was definitely not as seen and he was adamant on me not knowing the truth.

"As if you can stop me," I murmured, chewing on my fruit.

His fist hit the table loudly, dispersing tiny ice shards that knocked food all over, one had sent a scratch bleeding on my cheek. This over display of power was beginning to tire me out.

Fren pathetically squealed at the splashes of tea staining her dress, the rest of the table turning rigid in attention to me and my father.

"Silas, let her eat," Moreen interrupted our stare down.

"Why is the untamed beast on this table anyway," Fren huffed, trying to wipe the liquid from her sleeves.

I scoffed, a highborn speaking to a royal in that tone would earn a lashing in the olden days. She would not be sleeping under this roof let alone dine with me had this been another king. "Well, three yellow trolls are allowed, one needs a rest from all the eyesore." Leaning in, I shot her a glare. "I might tolerate you for entertainment, but talk like that about me one more time and I will gut you. Better, don't talk at all in my presence."

"I am not scared of you. You know of your purpose as we all do, so don't act so high," Fren bravely spouted out.

"I don't need you scared, half-breed, the hunt is better with a dim-witted critter and so are the screams."

Her mouth parted to retort back, but she bit on her tongue. Suddenly she began shivering and sweating, a cry trembling atop her lip.

"What is the matter?" Reuben asked his sister.

Slowly, Memphis slid around her middle and the brother screamed, dropping from his chair.

"Call it off," father ordered composedly.

"But I wanted her to scream," I said, sulking. Sooner than expected, Fren began crying from her seat and I signalled my morph to retreat. "That was even better that I expected."

"Father, she threatens us plainly, you are to do something," Reuben urged him, attempting to calm his crying sister.

"Oh, grow a spine, you balls for brains," I called out, immensely annoyed now.

Uncle and Elias both coughed under their hands, the latter turned to me and shook his head, barely withholding a smile.

Gathering a mountain of food on my plate, I made my leave, having grown annoyed at the staring and the talking. Father clattered his cutleries loudly on his plate when I left, but did not say anything.

Malik and Cai followed behind me silently while I made my way to the winter gardens, the plate in my hand and some more food in my mouth.

"Your father?" Cai asked, leaning to clean the blood coating my cheek while I sat on the snowy bench.

Malik looked around the garden as if someone were to jump behind me at any moment, pacing about and all over.

"The whole lot today." I raised my head to the damned skies. "You spiteful swell-heads."

"Are the gods at fault now?"

"When are they ever not at fault." I stuffed my face with grapes, toast, and cheese till I found it hard enough to swallow that I coughed.

Malik almost but ran towards me and I laughed, which seemed to startle him.

"I survived your kind's blades, a grape will not kill me, dear," I said, propping more food in my mouth and he pulled back.

He gritted his teeth, eyes dropping thoughtfully to the ground in front of him. I could almost swear I saw a flash of pity in that gaze. Pity, an emotion I detested wholeheartedly.

"Tell me, Malik, did they celebrate after the attack? Killing powerless children, women and men must have been such an accomplishment."

"No," his voice was flat and pensive.

"Oh, I almost forgot," I said, biting on another grape. "They didn't kill me. The disappointment, right?"

He assessed his thoughts before saying, "The king didn't allow it."

"But of course, he would be the first to mourn his failure."

He shook his head. "You don't know half of it."

"Tell me then?" I asked, leaning onto my knees. "Why did a small piece of anonymous information I was told you received take matters to that extent?"

"A prophecy."

I guffawed. "Ah yes, gods and their tales. This better be good, what did they spin now?"

He studied my amusement for a moment before saying, "A dire-wolf of war and frost, a dragon of wind and clouds, a thunderbird of lightning risen by the cold white ash. Children of two lands, the Elding children. One would spin the sky to the void, the other freeze the lands and the last would crack the realm in half with lightning. Three Aura born under the sky of Nubil and the lands of Krig, the wrath *Ybrises.*"

My gaze diverted to Cai who turned and stared at me the same. I cleared my throat, and gave Mal a smile. "Ah, but all good prophecies should rhyme, didn't that make you a bit sceptical? Are you saying a grandmother's spin tale is why my family is dead?"

"It is inked in black shadows on the moonstone of Lyra, the sacred gates of Cynth, along with five others. Gods can see our paths of future and all the possibilities along, Henah used the gates to warn us."

Was that supposed to make sense to me, more yarns of the divine? "Well, is it still there?"

He swallowed and hesitated as if preparing for my reaction. "Yes."

A dark laugh erupted from me. "An unfulfilled prophecy, either a sham or you had the wrong three. They did die for nothing. For one, I am the last remaining. Unless you expect me to be all three of them whilst not even being an Aura."

"They have never been wrong before, the last prophecy predicted the Ater battles."

They needed no predicting from what I have heard. Alaric would tell me how Eldmoor went mad appointing someone like the 97th Grand Maiden, apparently everyone sane knew the state of her lunacy. So he might as well have proven an empty point to me.

I looked up at the snow pouring skies. "There is a first for everything, shame this one was at my expense."

He didn't say anything else, only looked at me through heavy eyes.

"Your brother," I said, interrupting the silence again. "Is he always such a sweetheart?"

"He has his days."

"And you, why don't you look at me like he does?" They were rather kind russet eyes, not usually used to strangers unaffected by my presence, especially not Adriatian strangers.

He gave me a smile. "You are too pretty."

I nodded. "You are right, I am."

"Stunning."

"Indeed."

"The most beautiful woman I might have ever seen."

I smiled back, throwing a bunch of hair behind my shoulder. "Don't look any further, Malik, you have found her."

"Please, call me Mal."

A sigh of relief almost left me, maybe a layer of shivering caution left with it, too. "Well then, Mal, join Cai and quietly adore my face while I deal with some business."

Samuel eyed Mal suspiciously for a long while before I pulled him away to tell him all about the people we had caught up north and how they surprisingly were not Isjordian. Travelling that far up north was impossible to go undetected by at least one Isjordian patrol, yet Solaryans had.

I pointed to my arm. "They had trident shapes carved in their forearms, all of them. Is it some sort of cult?"

He halted, examining me in disbelief. "Tridents?" he asked, and I nodded. "Solaryan mercenaries this far above our borders? Impossible. Why would they be raiding our villages and temples at that? Why are mercenaries acting like petty thieves?"

I'd questioned the same thing. "Do you think this has anything to do with shipments? Would it be connected to the agreement? Maybe King Magnus sent them to rile my father into cutting the Ianuris agreement. Elias knew they were Solaryan, and so does my father."

Solaryans had openly shown their dissatisfaction towards Isjord these past weeks, they were becoming hostile and had withdrawn all their relationships with Isjord. Last week, they had secretly pulled all their emissaries and councillors back to their lands. No more shipments of any sort left or came from mainland Solarya.

Sam shook his head. "I served their previous king for years before your grandfather recruited me. They are not flashy in their actions. This means they are beyond displeased. It is their patterns that I don't understand."

I let out a sigh of frustration. "He forbade me from questioning the prisoners, apparently some new general is in charge of them now."

"General Moregan, she is from Modr, very skilled and vicious, stay out of her sight," he warned. "Considering what you did to the two you caught on the shipments three weeks ago, I would not let you near a breathing prisoner either, nor a dead one at that." Sam laughed jollily while I cringed at the bloodied sight of them, and the later berating from my father who intended to use them for information.

"If it only was that. I know he is trying to keep me away from something."

"I will ask around for information and get back to you," Sam assured.

"Thank you, and I am sorry at the same time for involving you in all of this."

"It is my pleasure to help you, Snow."

"I could ask Freja for some help, too."

"Her father is not one to keep his daughter near court business. He has not been happy since he was forced to kill Gabriel. His plans were never calculated for Freja to step in his position. He'd already trained a young scholar to take Lord of Modr duty after his death. Now that Freja is widowed, she is directly in position for it."

Funny enough to make a gator giggle, women were successors to their parents' duties only if they were lone children, unmarried and childless.

"He must be plucking his feathers at the thought of passing a daughter as his successor in the Winter court. The biggest woman hater succeeded by a woman." I laughed and clapped at the thought. "The first time that Isjordian ridiculous laws of women not being able to marry more than once has come to some good help."

A widowed Isjordian woman was forced into solitude. A vessel solely for the purpose of one man, while men could dally and wiggle their cocks at any woman and marry however many one could fit it into.

"I would not be too happy about it. Freja will be patronised by the old wolves. Probably forced to retire her position the minute after one of them begins addressing her as 'tits' or 'cunt'." Sam sighed and shook his head. "She is not a princess and she is not you."

"No, but she can be so much better than that, I know her." She had the wits, spirits and the perfect amount of hate for the patriarchy that had sealed her in a dark fate. She only needed encouragement to use them and a hand of support alongside.

We went through a few other details of the attacks on the villages. He asked to precisely recall and trace each one step by step. "You are a natural. You would have had a great future in Isjord," he added painfully, mouth pulled back with concern.

"There was never a future here for me, Sam. I have always known that and I think you know as well." I never fit in this place. I still had trouble feeling compassionate and relating towards its inhabitants, these people were never mine. To these lands, I will always be a foreigner, just like my mother had been.

I became numb at the thought. How my mother, Thora, Eren and I had been trapped in this ice prison like exotic animals, forced to adjust to the new caged quarters.

"Shall we stop dancing around sentiments, I know you hate them as much as I do," I said, raising a brow and extending my palm to him. "You owe me two new daggers, just as you promised."

After the attack, I had left my trusted daggers in the forest along with the bodies who had 'disappeared' after my father's soldiers had gone to retrieve them.

Sam laughed and reached toward a weapon shelf where he took two red leather scabbards sheathed with daggers. They were thin and elegant. The handles were made of silver and carved with vines, and at their centre stood a round emerald. He had tried to match them to my brother's sword.

"Use them well."

I hugged him, squealing in happiness at the pretty gift.

Still unable to resist finding out what I long doubted after Malik's revelation, I asked, "Sam, have you heard of this Eldingchild prophecy before?"

He studied me for a few seconds and his eyes diverted to the Adriatian guard behind me. "Yes," he answered with a half voice. "It is tales, Snow. Nothing but tales and false fears to ignite desire for a strong fortified army—fear prompts tight preparation, believe me. It was nothing else."

"Did my father know?"

"Yes."

I exhaled a painful, restricting breath while my insides writhed. Was this why and where he had gotten his idea? Had that prophecy pushed him to create us, so we would destroy this realm? Adriata had killed my family to prevent a prophecy my father had intended to fulfil.

It did not take me long to spin crazed thoughts in my head. Hovering about my room unsettled, sleepless and worried. I jumped from one end of the spectrum of conspiracies to the other. Two Adriatians stood at my guard, two of the sort that tried to kill me, who might as well try again, freely and at extreme ease. Had I picked wrong, had I dug my own demise? Oh gods, I had allowed my friends to be on guard with them, putting them in unpredictable danger. And Nia, she had to stand beside one of her kind, the people that had violated her in any humanly way possible, marking her with harrowing memories and heinous scars. What had I done?

I cracked my bedroom door open. Nia and...Kilian stood on either side of the corridor and away from one another.

"Snow? What's the matter?" Nia asked unsure, pushing from the wall.

Yes Snow, what was the matter?

I didn't look at the Adriatian who halted right before me like she did. "I got hungry," I said, moving down the corridor.

"You have food in your room," Nia argued, possibly wearing a scowl of confusion that I felt even with my head turned away from her.

"I meant thirsty." I moved quicker, hoping she'd stop the questioning. My bare feet slapped the ground gently.

"You have all sorts of that in there as well, remember?"

"Something warm."

"You hate warm drinks," she retorted.

I halted and groaned, turning to her. How could I tell her that it scared me to leave her alone with him, that it made me feel like a terrible person not having thought this part through? "Nia, Caelum heaven, I cannot sleep, happy?" My eyes shifted to the left and right onto the silver eyed snake's—cold and deadly like their owner. They lingered over mine and somehow my own refused to stare away. "What?"

He threw a look down at my feet. "You have no shoes."

I wiggled my toes over the cold floor. "I am aware."

"I will retrieve them."

"And if I throw a treat and rub your belly, will you spin for me? Your duty is to remain beside me as silently as your barks can be. Don't make me put you on a nuzzle, Adriatian." You play with your prey and they think the chase is a game. I wanted to enjoy the chase with both sides knowing it was a deadly one. Plus, it would be a shame to have that face covered.

He stretched his neck, jaw tightening with obvious anger before he said, "As you wish."

"Are we headed to the gardens? Please don't, you have been sick twice already with fever," Nia warned, pulling my attention to her again, cutting the conversation with the silver eyed snake.

I turned, continuing past the corridors. "Then we will be familiar with the third time, but it will not be today. I will roam about the kitchens tonight."

We entered the kitchens, only two candles were lit and formed caving shadows, the sound of our steps echoing at the silence of night. Ken the cook had sat alone on one of the tables and was quietly sipping on a drink. I'd always find him here at this time, even when I was a child.

He made to stand after seeing me. "I will have food ready in moments."

I waved my hands, stopping him. "No, I am not hungry."

He halted, blinking in surprise. "That is new."

I fell silent, standing before him, not knowing what to do with myself while he eyed me in surprise. "A drink?"

I nodded and he went to get me a cup of ale.

"Half," Nia called behind me. "She is lightweight, Ken. Make it a quarter better."

I spun fast, scowling annoyed at her. "Are you Alaric now?"

She huffed a short laugh. "If I was, I would have not let you drink at all. Remember that once you had two sips of wine and jumped on poor lanky Simon thinking he was a horse. Ken is old so you will feel bad, I don't believe you will get near this one," she said, pointing to Kilian who only blinked in shock at the revelation. "And that leaves me, and I most certainly will not be your pony for tonight."

Heat creeped up my body and I felt my cheeks and ears flush red at her revelation in front of the Adriatian snake who stared blankly between myself and Nia after her words.

"Quarter cup of ale," Ken said, sitting down with me. "Tough days or nights, pumpkin?"

All of it was tough, but did it matter? I didn't want to answer so I took a sip from the bitter drink.

He slid a small plate of apple slices to me. "You used to bring Thora down here when she couldn't sleep, now you come alone. You must miss her," he said.

I remembered this place used to be our safe haven—our latibule. We acted as if troubles unveiled us at the entrance, it still felt like it. Perhaps it was why I still liked it so much.

My head dropped and my breath lightly stuttered. This was not the moment to look weak, not the moment to panic. "You wife," I said, straightening. "She used to make us jam scones."

She did more than that, she would let us weep in her lap, wipe our wet eyes with her apron, tend to the whip scars on our backs from the Bruma commander because even healers refused to aid our wounds, tell us scary stories of mountain beast to make us forget the real ones and cuddle us till we fell asleep by the kitchen fire.

"She did," Ken replied with a short pained laugh, as if remembering alongside me. "She tried that day as well, to bring them when they found you, but the king would not let her."

My eyes drew shut and I bit my lip down from trembling. Too painful...too painful. I had heard her by the doors, begging and pleading to give the sweets to just see me.

"I will ask her to make them again," he offered.

"No, I only ate the scones because Thora liked them, now they just remind me of her. I don't want to be reminded."

Ken sighed, leaning onto the table and reaching for my hand. "Your sister was sweeter than a scone, don't make her a bitter memory."

"It wasn't her who made them bitter," I whispered harshly, trying to reign in a full breath.

At my words, Ken's eyes darted behind me, possibly towards the Adriatian guard who would have heard everything we'd said. Softly he patted my shoulder. "You are the one mixing the dough, choose how much salt and sugar, spice and fruit you add into it yourself, don't let your sweet taint by kneading in whatever they give you. Good night, little fierce one."

They gave me nothing, Ken. They threw them at me, ash, dirt, poison, flame, black steel, and darkness. I tried to shield them away, each mark on my back served as a reminder, but flake after flake made their way onto my bowl. Coated and sprinkled, dressed, and soured those memories.

Nia's steps sounded closer as she approached me, her hand falling on my shoulder. "I know what you are doing."

I turned to face her. "One word Nia, just one and I will go back to him right now."

"No, no need. This time you really got him on edge, we wouldn't want to lose the satisfaction, right?"

"It was selfish of me and very wrong. I should...should have thought about it better. Should have thought about you."

"Don't, please. It is all fine."

All is fine. If one said it is all fine, it truly meant all was fine. The three of us had come up with that, to understand each other better. It was needed, all three of our heads worked so strangely that it was impossible to know the truth, so we had settled on acknowledging it loudly.

I gave her a smile. "Now that I am seeing better, you look like the perfect pony for me, let me stroke that mane."

I stood rapidly and she took off running away from me.

We took laps around the kitchen chasing one another. I swear our laughter tore the castle silence and had woken everyone up. I had not let laughter fill my chest so mirthfully in a long while, here, at the same place where once I'd chased Thora with the same sound.

I caught her, launching us both on the floor and held her arms pinned down while she wiggled and struggled under me. "You drunk maniac."

"Shall I give you your first kiss," I teases, smacking my lips together. "I'll be your whatever charming."

"What a joke, whatever charming doesn't kiss, fuck and then run away at dawn. They stay. They wake up in each other's arms, cuddle, kiss again, have breakfast together, hold hands, embrace, and speak sweet words to one another."

"Ugh," I gagged and she rolled me over underneath her.

"You know what those are, right? I heard you have a no talking rule, too."

I giggled loudly, throwing my head back, indeed I was light weight. "When prince charming starts yapping and moaning about ten types of cheeses he likes his wine within the middle of your fun, tell me then if you would not leash a gag in their mouth."

Kilian snorted and began coughing loudly from the other side of the room and both of our attention turned to him.

Nia's eyes and smile went wide. "You can make hells turn prayers to gods. You made the poor Adriatian almost choke on air. Get up," she ordered, moving away from me. She extended a hand to help me up before carefully asking, "Did that really happen, the cheese guy?"

I laughed and nodded.

"Heavens," she said before bursting into laughter. "Do all of you do that?" she asked the Adriatian.

He glanced shortly in my direction before answering nonchalantly, "I am not particularly fond of cheese, it would be very unlikely for me to do that."

"No," I spoke, and he looked over at me again. "You would probably recite the holy Caelus liber, chapter one hundred on how to slay an *Ybris* and then jollily plunge a knife in my chest."

Could swear the shadows behind him grew darker. "Chapter forty as well, murder and the deprecations of the soul."

"Oh, yes," I purred, lowering my lids halfway. "You turn me on when you speak religion to me, Adriatian."

His eyes narrowed on me, his features twitching with revulsion and ire. So very satisfying.

I stood and sat at the table, lids heavy with sleep as I sprawled my upper body atop the table. "Sing it to me. Sing me the lines in Caelus liber where murdering my family was deemed holy."

He did not answer, not for a long time, and I slightly raised my heavy head to find him staring at me. "Aren't gods ambiguous in their ways? You do something wrong, but it might be a justifiable sort of wrong. You do something right, but it might be a dubious sort of right. Why does a right or a wrong need to be justified if it is a right and a wrong? You kill and that is wrong, you kill with the pretence of eliminating the greater evil and that is right? Isn't killing just killing, isn't it just the simple wrong? Doesn't that make you the same as I?"

His face was clean of any expression when he answered, "Yes."

"Then don't look at me like looking at me is heresy."

He stared at me and I stared at him. I hated that stare, but his silence was delightful. His head tilted to the side. "How do you wish I look at you?"

"Not at all."

"I am ordered not to leave you out of sight, it is not a request I can comply with."

"You were my punishment," I said, making my head comfortable on my arms. "At least don't behave as one. Look at me, do not stare at your beliefs of me."

16

HEIRS AND HEROES

KILIAN

A WEEK. A FULL seven days. I'd heard enough offences, snarky remarks and received enough glares that I'd grown the thickest skin. I was not one easily offended, but her insults always found a way to affect me.

Look at me, do not stare at your beliefs of me. How could I when all she did was prove them right.

She blasted out of her room, all ready for carnage. Upon the second of meeting corridor air, she frowned, sniffing around. This woman was odd in all human and inhuman sense, a human facade and inhuman force of words and presence. She rarely slept and if she did, it was in the oddest of places. She hated people, any that weren't the cook, the general or her friends—she especially hated children. Her skills in chess were terrible. She had selective eating, that is if she even ate at all. Sigh. I could count her vices to infinity.

She spun round, looking all puzzled, and then began slowly reaching toward me till she had gotten close enough I could tell apart strands of her hair. Leaning forward, she sniffed me. What was she doing?

I put two fingers on her forehead and pushed her head back.

She blinked slowly and then glanced up to where I touched her.

Retracting my fingers, I took a step back and said, "Speak from there, offend from there, ask from there."

She gradually frowned. "Are you ordering me now?"

"Setting boundaries, Your Highness."

I had said nothing entertaining, yet she smirked. "Many of your sort try to settle these...boundaries, but probably wish to wake up on the other side of my bed. Is it that hard for you, enough that you have to set boundaries?" She stuck her bottom lip out and fluttered her lashes with taunt.

A nerve jumped on my temple, but I held composure. "It must be a big bed to hold your murderous ways and my dislike of you along with us squished in there, too."

"King size," she said, flashing me a sharp smile.

What offended this one?

Caiden chuckled from the other side of the corridor. "Survive a second week, soldier."

She glanced out of the window at the meek daylight. "It's daytime."

I raised a brow. "Astute observation."

She blinked annoyed. "Why am I seeing your face now, too? Where is Mal?"

Mal? Why was she calling my brother Mal? "He has travelled this morning back to Adriata, his mother has fallen ill, but he will return soon." Driada had collapsed, again. These past months illness had overtaken her more than you could count. Mal never knew when it would be the last time, so he always stood beside her each and every instance.

"Aren't you brothers?"

"Half," I revealed, taking another step back from her. My eyes travelled down to her attire. She was in the captain's navy uniform. "Are we heading somewhere?"

"Yes," she said, tapping the golden circlets over her chest pocket. "I am Captain, remember?"

Despite almost drawing blood out of my tongue from how much I'd bit into it, the tight words escaped me. "I am inclined to ask why. Is it necessary for you to be doing that? Isn't Isjord the kingdom with the greatest number of soldiers in the whole of Dardanes? Would you be so desperately needed around danger?"

She rolled her eyes and strutted down the corridor. "Must we converse?"

I followed rapidly behind. "Must you not answer my questions?"

She brought a hand out and counted, "I want to. No, it is not necessary. And astute observation, Adriatian, Isjord indeed has the most soldiers. You want a good boy rub or a treat, hm?"

She was impossible. Sarcasm was her breakfast, lunch and dinner. Not that she ate much of anything else. Perhaps it was more than enough that she didn't need food.

All ready, her squadron rested prepared by the agitated stables circling wildly with numerous soldiers ready for patrol. Her morph croaked from the sky, batting her ever black wings down to land, dust of snow flying in the air as she descended and shifted to a mare.

"Snowlin, sister," a male voice called, coming from the distance.

The princess's features leathered down to a murderous ire with a flare of annoyance. "Reuben, half breed," she greeted back distastefully, sharpening a feigned grin.

She spoke to her sibling this sort? I rubbed my eyes and sighed. She spoke to everyone like that.

"Delightful as always," he remarked unimpressed.

"And annoyance is still your best personality trait."

He sneered and glared but she was unhurt. "Off to set father *off* again?" he asked, flicking some invisible dust from his oddly decorated navy uniform. Ruffles of a white shirt peaked from the collar and the sleeves, threaded gold vine embroidery ran down his sleeves and trousers. He had no gold circlets to state his position, but instead a golden arrow broach. They looked nothing alike. She was flamboyant in a way, but she never had to dress herself in decorations and power to know she had it. She carried it in her stance alone.

She wiggled her fingers at him. "Off to have your balls tickled by a Lord, doesn't your mother do that? You poor little precious thing, has mommy dearest been neglecting you?" she said, approaching to straighten his lace collar and he almost flinched away. She held him so tight that a red flush spread over his pale face and down his neck.

I grimaced at the image she put in my head whilst her friend shook from silent chuckles by my side.

Reuben cleared his throat, orange shadows of embarrassment setting his head almost aflame like his face. "I am travelling down to Arynth because father has asked of me to discuss the new deal with—"

"There." She raised a palm to interrupt him. "That's where you lose me."

"Jealous?" he bit back. "I, the heir of Isjord, is doing the important work?"

Was she not supposed to be the actual heir? Silas intended to put an unblessed man on the throne? Silas planning on retiring that soon from his crown, didn't humans have seventy years of living at best?

She waited a moment and then blasted in a howling laughter, holding her stomach till tears of amusement leaked from the corners of her eyes. "That would be my entertainment for weeks."

"But you are," he insisted, baring his teeth in a snarl.

"If it helps you sleep at night, half breed, I'll even play dead for you. Do you not understand that you will wither away with your pathetic mortal life while my father will live to honour that blood crown for perhaps eternity?"

He half retreated, still flaring in the heat of his anger. "Father will find a way."

To prolong life? Were the unblessed this uncultured in the sense of our abilities and way of living?

"He is many things, god it's not one. But," she stopped, raising a finger toward the sky, "even they could not help. You are unblessed for a reason. There is no god for you, no blessing, no eternalness, just small, short, wrinkly pathetic lives."

I was with her on this one, except the need for insults to state her point.

"You are human, too, blessed or unblessed."

"I didn't say I wasn't, but I am not the one playing heir, half breed." She let go of him, annoyance readable in her features as she took off.

"Why do you pretend not to want to be," he called behind her, "I know you are seething in your head."

"If I wanted to be the heir of hell, Reuben dear, I'd try my chances in Caligo. I'd rather be between fire than frost, the cold it's terrible for my skin."

That...was funny. Sigh. The cold was freezing my senses.

"Then why did you come back?"

"I was bored."

"Now you are marrying the *Obscur Asteri*, should have stayed hidden."

"Hide? But why, dearest, a crown waits for me whilst a gilded head stone awaits you."

"That should have been you twelve years ago," he shouted, shaking out of his skin. "Under earth, silent and dead along with your siblings and your bitch of a mother."

She stood still for a while. I didn't know whether that was her expression of hurt or anger, but I wished she was neither. It was a horrible thing to say to someone who'd escaped death and lived while you saw your family perish.

She turned, that feigned smile returning to her absent face. Her brother stood his ground, all high chin and glaring eyes though his shadows read of leg shaking fear that turned into horror when she approached to fix his collar once again. "Serpent patterns are strange to follow, slithering in locomotion when you can just keep straight. It must be so difficult to waddle about your life, but you would not know. You're a worm, your pace is that of others' mercy."

"Gloat in your words, Snowlin."

She leaned over his shoulder and his face froze aghast while she said, "Says the worm I am holding under my boot. I am heading to Arynth, too, you little mortal, half breed heir."

Reuben's eyes dropped between them, lurid shadows of fear swirling in gusts out of him. When she moved away, I saw what had caused the half-brother to stiffen.

She sheathed the elegant silver dagger back to her thigh and strutted towards the stables. She was a terrifying sight to behold.

"Mercy becomes you, princess." I said, mounting my horse after her.

"I prefer my feed alive, where is the fun in the dead."

A stupid comment deserved the stupid answer it got. "Why are we headed to Arynth?"

"Father has called a meeting to discuss your ilk and their proposal for the Crafter unveiling back the magic and the border control after the wall comes down. The bordering lords are concerned your little grasshoppers will pollute these grounds upon unchaining."

"Is Silas not worried his own snowhoppers might change frost for sun?"

"Why would anyone exchange one hell for another is beyond me. I am only attending for entertainment and perhaps some lovely pumpkin seed cinnamon buckwheat biscuits. Arynth is a master at them."

Was she joking?

She cracked the meeting room door wide open and searched the room all bored with her gaze.

"Snowlin, you have made it. Reuben...you, too," Lord of Arynth greeted, somewhat confused at the presence of the highborn.

Albius Arynth, I knew the man. Many did. An ancient Verglaser, a terrifying one at that. He'd fought beside many in the Ater battles, along my father, too. He cast a glance over to me and bowed his head just slightly.

Reuben puffed his chin up and stalked to a seat, still clouding with offence.

"Albius, words are for beggars, where are my treats?" she asked eagerly, extending a hand to him.

He handed her a square box wrapped in a silk navy cloth. Several biscuits lining it edge to edge, and the princess licked her lips corner to corner eyeing them.

She had not joked.

Albius shot another look at me and then Reuben. "Your brother is here? Why for?"

"Sacred heavens," the princess coughed, looking around somewhat startled. "My brother is dead, Albius, almost frightened me out of my wool."

This...was a joke? I studied her absent glances around the air and decided she had not joked about this one.

The old lord patted her back gently. "*Ghur signe mahar.*" *Later we speak*, he murmured in Calgnan close to her ear.

"*Ghur.*" *Later*, the princess responded.

Why the need for secrecy? Was it another joke...or more biscuits?

"Your Highness," a sleek old voice called from behind us in her direction. She was popular it seemed.

She turned, fashioning at what looked to be a pleasant smile. "Ivar Venzor, what tide do we owe the pleasure?"

He laughed shortly before taking her hand to plant a kiss atop her knuckles that made her mouth twist in a little grimace before she quickly reverted it to the false flattering smile.

He swivelled a slimy gaze on her. "As always, shining with the beauty of the sun."

"Stare too long, old creep, and you will get sunburn," Caiden murmured beside me, and she threw him a warning glare over her shoulder.

"Father asked for you to join?" she asked.

He straightened his collar. "Actually no, it was I who asked. You surely know I took your side in this case and voted against the agreement, this barbaric alliance with those we banished ourselves. I fought hard twelve years ago to have that wall sealed and I will fight till my last breath to keep it like that. Knowing your position, you have to plead in my cause, surely."

So there had been opposition just as I'd thought. I'd always wondered how Silas had convinced all his court with this agreement, considering they'd insisted for months on the Highwall. They must have truly needed it the same as we did.

"What is my position?" she asked, somewhat defensive to the presumption.

"Against, of course. You wouldn't willingly marry him, would you?"

"Well, father is not forcing me. I am not running away, neither kicking nor screaming," she said, leaning in before teasingly whispering, "that has to be willingly."

I had thought about this too. The reason why she had not chosen to run away at the moment of finding out about the agreement.

He frowned at her with sheer disbelief. "Might I ask why?"

She examined her gloved hand, rather bored. "I am told he is an incredible lover, tender too."

A breath passed through the wrong pipe and I erupted in a cough. This ridiculous woman.

Caiden patted a sombre hand behind my back. "The rumours must be true."

"There are no such rumours," I said, straightening.

"Your Highness," Lord of Venzor scolded, unamused.

She gave him an unimpressed look. "Ivar, I am not up to being recruited in your little resistance. The life of a partisan in that cause will be very short lived, like every attempt of every Venzor to snatch my father's crown. I will not wear a hat, sleep on dirt, lay between wolf dung and fur, so I am afraid I can only watch from afar." She inclined her head back and forth, almost deciding in thought before saying, "When it fails altogether."

There was discord in the Winter court midst?

She left the offended lord and sat all leisurely in a seat.

"You sure don't care for others' respect," I said, positioning just beside her.

She spared me a glance over her shoulder. "Respect buys you civil greetings, fear buys you submission. Polite words catch fire like lint under summer sun, but I give pretty leashes with diamonds and corruption." Rolling her lashes up at me, she smiled. "You want one? You'd look pretty on a leash."

I scoffed, lacking a better reaction. She'd starved me of surprise. Nothing seemed to shock me any longer. "Fear? That is your goal. I believe you have already achieved that the day you were born."

"Not like that, Adriatian, the sort that has children screaming at night, the one fear told around withering bonfires that have you jump and sleep with an eye open. The fear where every pattern of leaf, shape of clouds and sound of fire reminds you of my face and my presence. The fear that will be told centuries from now, and not for my power, but for my might."

She was mad, absolutely mad.

Insane.

My aunt entered along with Larg and Isjordians drew weary and stern, no longer chatting amongst, all their attention was now on my kind.

"Your Highness," Larg greeted her whilst they took a seat opposite the Isjordian side. "We meet again."

"Larg, what a pleasure," she greeted all innocence. "But I preferred it better when you had venison for me to tear."

"I am sure Isjord is keeping well up to your satisfaction."

She laughed, yet somewhat gently, not offended. "Well enough." The smile she wore snapped to tight ire in mere flashes of a second when she turned to my aunt. "Adriane Drakos, we meet at last. Alaric Drava sends his regards. Though personally, I am a little less partial to greetings, more to putting a dagger just between your little ribs."

My aunt's gaze shivered and bounced almost terrified around the faces in the room. She knew her faults and she knew her fears. Both now stood in front of her. Courage, vengeance, golden gaze and dark might.

My aunt quickly glanced at me before taking a seat. "We have come to discuss important matters."

"Oh, yes, pardon me," the princess said, leaning back on her chair, crossing a leg over the other. "We must discuss your death right after, priorities first. Still, I would not kill you without hearing you call me *Your Majesty* or *my queen*." She threw a wink and then a kiss to my aunt who almost swallowed herself within her own skin.

She knew something—the princess knew something.

"How does she know the head councillor?" I asked her friend.

He blinked all bored. "Her guardian does, along with her anti *Ybris* propaganda and the order of attack from that night issued by her and approved by your king. Her guardian found the man with the direct order when he scavenged the attacker's bodies in an attempt to find Snow after she'd fled from the attack. Your king had sent three orders, she read all three of them, memorised every name and especially that woman's," Caiden said, pointing to my aunt.

Fled. That word stuck muddy on my throat. She had fled.

The princess half turned in her seat, motioning her hand for me.

I leaned down close enough to feel the heat of her skin over mine when she reached over my ear to say, "Or shall I kill her now? What do you think?"

I tried to take it in as another joke of hers, but then I noted the empty spot just outside the large window where Memphis had previously sat. I skimmed the room nervously and noted a black slithering tail peeking over the far corner of the room and almost reaching the Adriatian side of the meeting table.

"Call the animal back," I ordered quietly.

She giggled a little. "And why should I?"

"Looking to innate a war?"

"And what will you do? Go on," she whispered, softly brushing her lips over the shell of my ear. "Charm me so I can become mercy again."

The morph grew closer and closer to my aunt. Hells. "Call your animal or I will kill it."

Her smirk grew wide and right into a grin of challenge, she was terribly amused. "Show me how you kill then."

She had no care or too much faith that I would not. "Princess!" I hissed.

"Guard?" She examined me closely, gold irises glowing with hilarity. She softly bit her lip to suppress that smile of victory and my gaze dropped there. "Yes, you and your rules not to kill. Where was this pride when you sent your hounds off to kill me?"

She played with me. From the start, all she did was play with me and I'd fallen for her every trap...and lost to all she had to prove to me. That was it. She wanted to prove my wrongs, our wrongs. And there were many.

Memphis suddenly slithered and curled onto her lap. She stroked a hand over the ghastly animal's head, all pleased. "You will find that I am more creative in my pursuits, death doesn't please me as much as demise."

I should have felt relief, but she'd put me in a perpetual state of anxiety.

The meeting began and soon filled with noise. Complaints from the Isjordian side were with continuous concern of a repeated attack like the one twelve years ago. They were in all right to their dismay. Three thousand one hundred and twenty-seven. The number of innocents who'd died from our irrationality. Stregor and my aunt had not revealed the collateral damage that their actions would follow. Blind from their fear, they'd never considered or repented for the lives lost.

"I'd prefer the wall to stay up," Lord of Venzor expressed.

"It will stay up," my aunt countered, lowering her specs to examine him. "It's a big wall."

"Ivar," Albius called, interrupting whatever venom Ivar was about to spew. "The agreement has been voted for a pass. Let us not waste time on idle opinions." He turned to my aunt. "I believe you have agreed on the Crafter seal to remain."

"Yes," she said. "And the joined guard in the borders."

"We have an identification policy within our walls as I am sure you are well aware," a young lord said, handing a handful of documentation to my aunt. "Your people will be able to travel undisturbed through our lands, but entering our cities will prove difficult if they have no identification to show."

She nodded. "We are aware, our citizens are already provided with such."

The conversation was led by Albius who carried respect above his dislike far better than any ruler. A wise man with a peaceful manner of leading. Rejection and approval, one after the other rolled over the table, but I was glad there were even such discussions. Finally, my kind's freedom was being spoken about and soon to be reality.

The princess had not said anything, not a word, not a single reaction, but silently observing. After everyone had left, she stood almost still and unbreathing without moving.

"Cakes," Caiden called after the sun had drooped and was now defeated by angry thunder clouds.

She took a deep breath and stood, stalking out of the room, hands tightly curled at her side. And I then saw it—what had been hidden under the table. Their tremble. Why was she trembling? Anger? Want to hurt? Inability to contain herself?

"What is it with you?" I called, chasing after her.

Her steps did not halt, but she flexed her fingers open, no longer trembling. "Oh mighty heroes of the realm, you made me evil, yet it surprises you when evil gives you evil back."

"To be toying with millions of lives is not a game."

She halted then, turning to me. "Who said it was a game?"

"You want war, destruction?"

She smirked. "Adriatian, don't turn me on. That would not be a game you would like."

I clicked my jaw tight and swallowed the venom my brain had gathered to spit at her. "This is serious."

She took a step forward, now head-to-head with me. "And this is your work."

I reached close enough that she had to tilt her head to meet my gaze. "Answer should not have to be death!"

She pointed a finger to my chest and shouted back, "Then the question should have not been murder!"

A sword came between the two of us. "That boundary might need to be applied right about now," Caiden said, patting the side of it to my chest.

Loud hooves halted just near us and then a panting figure approached. A familiar one.

"Nia," the princess called surprised at the sudden presence of her friend.

She breathed quickly. "He is dead, Snow. He is dead."

17

MOURNERS AND MARTYRS

SNOWLIN

LAST NIGHT, LORD OF Modr was announced dead. The court was in mourning and my father had ordered my presence at the funeral.

If you have any hand on this, child, I will cut your animal in half, he had threatened. Father wanted to doubt and blame his death on my hands, but the proof was too bewildering against it. Fishing for cod he'd caught a shark and all his long line of digested colonies of scandal and deceit. In a court of serpents, you will stumble upon a feast of skeletons, and Kalius Modr's skeletons hid in no closets but a pleasure house.

The sepulchral head stones surrounding us emitted a creep of discomfort, the fall of the snow sending muted dolent tones only drowned by the crowing song of chatter. It was gloomy, cold, weeping women, black lace, pearls, deceitful murmurs and praises of the lord's blissful living. I hated it, the talk as if they knew him, the praise for a villain made a martyr only because he was dead. That was the thing with death, it was often worn as a badge of honour even from the wicked—mostly by the wicked.

"Can you believe he ordered me to put this on? I look like a chandelier, Nia. Was his sparkly arse not bright enough for this damned funeral?" I said, adjusting the excruciatingly heavy gold and ruby studded crown atop my head.

Dress in proper Isjordian etiquette, it is not a suggestion but an order; those had been his exact words. Pen, bless her heart, had tried her best, but the tight corset and the puffed skirts of my black dress were squeezing me out of my existence. If it was left to my devices, I would have worn red, glitter and a smile.

"This bloody corset is rubbing over my breasts, itching as mad and I can barely breathe. Reach up and remove the garter, the lace is scratching my skin," I said, turning round only to find Kilian standing still, eyes fixed on me. No Nia in sight.

"Hells," I startled, almost jumping out of my skin. "Are you a mute, why can't you say it's you?" I had forgotten Mal had travelled down to Highwall to his ill mother and I was stuck with this face in daylight, too.

A dark brow rose on his absent face, always so present with defiance. "Do I have to make my presence aware out loud every time I approach you, full name, city of birth and title, too?" he coldly spoke. "I would have, but we are in the middle of a funeral. Still need me to reach for your garter, though not sure what I can do for your itching breasts."

His defiance was severely entertaining, a challenge I would not forgo, but right now, murderous thoughts were tickling my itch to hurt someone. Perhaps it was still the bloody lace.

"Your Highness," a soft voice called, approaching and pulling my attention from the bastard.

"Freja—"

Before I could speak, she threw herself over me in a hug and almost plummeted me to the ground. She wept and sobbed—a grieving daughter, a freed woman, and tears of happiness.

I patted her shoulder. What did one do in these situations? Surely I wasn't expected to cry with her. "My condolences, may his soul rest in Hodr."

She attempted to straighten despite the relentless sniffling.

Kilian handed her a handkerchief—a neatly folded, flower embroidered handkerchief. Did his lover send him here to guard me with a stash of them? I bet she knit her initials on his sleeve too. I almost laughed, but the corset barely allowed me to breathe.

"His soul rests burning in the hells, right where it should be," Freja hiccuped, blowing her nose on the unfortunate cloth. "The sodden bastard bruised me dry, then sold me to be bruised drier to my husband before killing him then bringing the old bruising back."

We both snorted at the same time and then smiled before erupting in silent giggles despite being aware of our surroundings.

Her face twisted in a cry before squeezing my hands between hers. "I'm a widow, an orphan and now a Lady, how can I be one? I could not even sit around with my father let alone with those stuffed squealing piglets who complain their wrists are heavy with gold and need a servant to wipe their arse."

I understood her worry, the only Lady in my father's court was a eudemon, even *she* had to grow claws to keep her seat, but this one was under my wing, she already had claws.

"I will be there."

She let out a loud cry and I withheld a grimace. Public show of emotion made me itch. "You're going to leave me, Snowlin."

I hooked a finger under her chin and raised her gaze to me. "And when I do, you are going to be ready to face them on your own. Remember, they are only men, the worst they can do is breathe."

She nodded and repeated my words to herself in a murmur before leaving to join the line of mourners by the casket. She was an oar on my boat, I'd make sure she became a sturdy one.

"Profound words," Kilian said from behind me.

I threw him a glare over my shoulder. "Now he speaks. Where is Nia?"

"Right behind me speaking to a sentry. You are in her sight, no need for worry."

A scowl drew in my brows. "I don't worry, you fool, I need someone to loosen my corset or your king will receive a lung collapsed corpse. Call her down unless you intend on getting handsy with me."

He blankly stared at me for a few moments as if contemplating my words to be a charming idea before he went to apprise Nia of my suffocating circumstances.

I did not wish for her to free me of lace as much as I needed her there to free me of disquiet.

She approached, looking around before reaching under my dress to loosen the ties. Her face alone banished all sense of apprehension. "Blessed heavens."

"You don't look well," she said, examining me and resting her gloved hand on my head.

A shiver suddenly sent a shudder all over me. The air—it was too suffocating. I couldn't breathe. "Do all funerals last this long? I'm starving." I moved back from her doubtful stare. "I wonder if any of these putrid ilk shed any tears for my mother, if they were this sorrowful to the young lost lives of my siblings?" As if on cue, my brain began to spin feigned images of their amusements and joy when laying my loved ones to rest. If they laughed and celebrated, if they thanked their unheeding god.

"It was private, only your father was present." Sam came from behind and put a hand on my shoulder, his eyes sorrowful. "Alaric did not tell you?"

I shook my head. "He refuses to speak about them." He would not even utter my mother's name, not even to himself. He wouldn't even tell me where they had buried them.

"He thinks he failed them."

"How did you know?"

He smiled with woe. "He was not difficult to understand. And I was there when we found you. It took him a long time to believe you were actually alive. He... he'd lost all hope," Sam said, drowned in remembrance.

"Now he berates me for skipping vegetables during meals," I joked to liven the mood and he smiled.

He pulled me away, cautious to prying eyes. "You father will know. He will soon trace a lead onto your plan to have the lords removed. It is one thing to have them take your side and quite the other having them killed."

Sam had grasped my intentions the second I had told him of my friendship with Freja. *Mad, undoable, dangerous,* the exact words he had said while pacing back and forth before me. I had told him about Myrdur, the reason for my return, my plans for Isjord, my actions on Adriata. He had not believed me for a long while till the second I killed Esbern. My plan went from destroying, to overturning, to corrupting Winter court. This ship had loyal oars, but why did I need to puff their feathers if I could just pluck them and substitute the peacocks with vultures—my vultures—who would venture on my behalf to aid my father's cease of reign.

"He won't, because she did nothing except encourage," Nia revealed, eyes glued to the wooden casket resting ready to be buried.

Sam glanced between Nia and I. "What do you mean?"

"Snow put me in his trail since her lesson about galleys and oars when she met Freja. A few days ago, Kalius met Helga to put terms to her silence regarding her relationship with the general Gabriel, to keep the scandal from erupting and having him lose the title he carried for ten generations. Apparently, Kalius knew of her and the bastard children, and had even aided them for years. Helga demanded quite the demands that got the lord heated. They got into an altercation after threats were made. The Medi-healers report I plucked from the archives showed his heart stopped from age. My expertise, however, held tobacco, grease, drinking habits and stress from all that has happened surrounding his family as the ultimate heartstopper."

He frowned with surprise. "He died on his own?"

"Why is it harder to believe that he died on his own than believing I did not kill him?" I asked, feeling somewhat offended.

"Because it perfectly matches your intentions."

I shrugged. "Gods picking the lesser evil."

"Many have proved that sinner's prayers are answered, too," Nia added slyly.

"If he had not died?" Sam countered. "Was he not one of your...oars?"

"She planned to kill him before even finding a way to corrupt him. That poor substitute of a human would never take her side. That would have left the situation in my graces," Nia said proudly. "Finally given my winter bane potion a go, it would have left Medi healers scratching their magic."

Though she'd boast about it, she'd been most thankful she had not needed to avail her skills. Nia experienced death abysmally, I'd never put her on the line of killing no matter her skill. She would never have to kill someone if I could do it for her.

"Human poison?"

Nia raised her chin proudly. "With few alterations, one deadly to Aura, too. No one better than the unblessed knows poisons, even to us Aura."

I threw an arm around her neck. "She is my little genius. Did you know she is a herbalist?"

She crossed her arms and scoffed. "Only when she needs me, other times I'm either *miss menace* or *boss in boots*."

Sam smiled widely, shaking his head. "What will you do with Freja?"

"Nothing, she is my ally."

"You trust her."

"Trust?" I laughed. A strong word for someone who would at times not trust her own senses. I peeled my sleeve back enough to make the thin bracelet tattoo curling around my arm. A blood oath. "We have a bargain. Her freedom and my support, for her trust."

Freja and I had fallen to agreement. Once Isjord was overthrown, she would be free to travel the continent how she had always wanted. We'd bonded on our dislike for the patriarchal society that had pressured our unhappiness and bruised our courage. She'd thought this was the perfect time to have it come crashing down and agreed to support me moving forward with procuring Isjord out of my father's hands. But words were good as nothing. A blood oath that claimed life as a price on the other head was quite the deal setter, and I had not needed to persuade Freja too far, she had nothing to lose.

Sam shook his head and pointed a finger in warning. "Feet on the ground, you are not out of his doubts just yet," he said, joining the line forming ahead as the rituals commenced at the sound of the seventh drum.

"Who was *miss menace* speaking to a moment ago, by the way?"

"A soldier sent from Cai, there is something odd going on Kirkwall," she revealed, glancing around us. "There is a family down there working as a bypass for trespassers."

I let out an irked sigh. "Execute them." We'd found more Adriatians in these lands after that day than one could find flames in hells. I had even been forced to spare Cai and send him on their chase.

"Miss 'off with their head' might need to hear this," she said, frowning at my rashness. "General Moregan—she rode from the Islines to visit them a couple of nights ago along with a bunch of soldiers. His informant said they left with a dozen or so Adriatians picked up from the inn. The Adriatians left willingly, unchained." I scowled and she continued, "The inn was not on the list we found from Lord of Kirkwall, even we did not know. How did Moregan know—how did your father know? Sebastian had to trace them down for days."

"Aura?"

She shrugged. "Could have been."

"They could be recruits, father has always recruited foreign Aura in his army." There was a special division years ago, I had not the slightest idea if it was still alive. I would have to ask Sam.

"That was also not what surprised me the most."

My brows rose in question and she handed me a receipt in answer. Esbern Kirkwall to Pine Inn. The ex-lord had bought supplies for the inn in his name.

"Esbern was a family friend of theirs," Nia explained.

My eyes went wide in realisation. "Heavens, he knew...my father knew about Esbern?"

She nodded. "I believe some of the Adriatians he was giving passage were for your father, or at least profiting from their passing. He also charged no easy price in crossing."

My father was still collecting Aura. "Notify Sebastian, we are to head there two days from now."

"What do you intend to tell your father?"

"A truth and some lies. Our patrol in Kirkwall is in two days, send word for Sebastian to prepare."

"And the Adriatians?"

"They have my answers. Till I get them, they remain breathing." Whatever he needed Adriatian Aura for, it would not be up for anything I would like, and there were about a thousand lines of distressing thought cursing my brain already without even considering any of the main reasons.

"This could be nothing, Snow, maybe we are just wasting time on a goose chase."

I shook my head. "No, something is up with the islanders attacking the north, Isjord, and Adriata." Whatever my father was concocting, he'd dragged Solarya's attention. And wherever Solarya's attention was, father needed Adriatians.

"Do you think this is connected to Myrdur?"

"No, but I'd like to eliminate the probable."

She nodded and backed away, slowly letting Kilian approach as I took place in line with the mourning. People began lining up, preparing for the ceremony. A grey faced old priest approached. Draped in white robes that only hollowed his expression further, a red belt with the seven guardian saints of Hodr stitched in colour across his waist. He looked every bit the god arse wipe he was. Religion in Isjord was perplexing. They directed their prayers once they needed gods, not sooner, not normally. Yet they held their belief with shameless pride. But praying in a temple did not make you a saint, as sleeping in a stable didn't make you a horse—sleeping in a stable only made you an idiot as Isjordians became when they travelled down to a temple once in their lifetimes and wore a guardian saints embellishment around their belts.

The priest laid down the sacred book of Eirlys and Caelus liber, flinging through pages of the written mania of deities. "With Krig's blessing, to Hodr heaven," he called groggily.

"With Krig's blessing, might it welcome us," everyone greeted back in holy sign.

He flipped the book open, named the seven guardians of Hodr gesturing his hand up and down in calling to the heavens. As if the heavens even bothered to welcome this sort. "Krig made his blessings on this soil, he'd seen the lands of Isea, old Isjord and he'd fallen in love with its people. We'd welcomed his gifts and he'd welcomed our prayers, from now."

"Till Hodr," everyone replied in unison.

I withheld my eyes from rolling back with no intention of return, so instead I murmured my spite, "Fuck the gods and their prayers."

"Some respect, you heathen," Kilian demanded.

I glanced back at him, half refusing to believe he called me a heathen, and then I shook from amusement. He was not very keen to hold onto his living.

"What is so funny?" he demanded harshly, already weakening in patience.

"You're not scared of me."

"Why should I be?"

"Many reasons, darling. For one, I'm attending the funeral of the man I killed myself."

His head snapped to me. Nothing readable on his face, nor anger or hate. Nor anything, actually, just pure blankness as he calmly asked, "You killed the Lord?"

"It would not be the first one and you know it. I remember your pretty face from the trial in Kirkwall."

He frowned. "Why?"

"That's it, I don't need a reason."

His features pinched while he examined me. "How could you stand here, in front of his grave, in front of his family? Even console his daughter?"

I turned to face him and opened my arms wide. "Just like this. It is not hard."

"You have no fear of gods?"

"Gods have done nothing to make me afraid. Men have, and now they pay."

He scoffed shamelessly. "This life is not eternal for you to dip your hands in murder blood this easily," he spat. "No heaven shall allow a soiled soul to step in the door of purity. Giving up on the next lives? Are you this content from this one alone? Or just keen on choosing one of the seven hells?"

"You assume I will meet a human end when you call me anything but that? I was born not to belong to any heaven, Adriatian, already violated the first rule by being born."

He measured my words. "That is not on you."

This time I laughed. Loud hard enough that my father turned halfway, throwing me a stern look over his shoulder.

"Everything is on me, you did not send your people after my father who made me, you sent them after me. I was a weapon only in the hands of the man who intended to wield me. To my mother, I was just a precious child who witnessed her life fade away right in front of her eyes while protecting me from being the said weapon, so excuse my heathen ways."

He studied me for a moment, silently. "What do you believe in, princess?"

"Retaliation."

He blew out a long exasperated breath, rubbing his eyes surely from frustration and fatigue—he'd not slept in days. "May I ask who is on that list?"

I drew closer to him, the silver eyes following me intently as I ran my fingers along the lapels of his jacket before stopping over his chest. His heart was loud below my touch, the tiny little thing that betrayed all. Hearts were a weakness. "One: front row, big crown, King of Isjord." His eyes diverted to my father before turning to me full of questions. "Two: far away, bloodied crown, King of Adriata. Three: a wretched land, wretched people, Adriata." His face drew stern lines, a tick in his jaw hammered wildly and his eyes dropped below, refusing to meet mine. "Four: handsome, very handsome, looks like he wants to choke the life out of me." Leaning in, I whispered, "You."

He grabbed my wrists, pulling them down. "Don't touch me." His hands curled at his side as though touching me burned or prickled like thorns.

A wide smile stretched across my face. "The *Ybris* disgust you, my touch creeping and repulsive, what does it remind you of? A eudemon? A serpent?"

"Enough," Nia murmured the warning from my side.

"Do you know what you remind me of?" I asked, raising a brow at him. "Being inside flames, feeling your skin peel and blood boil from the heat but never burn. Continuously for the past twelve years that is how I have felt, burning unburnt." A fever dream, that was what my life became after that night, and I'd burnt on those nightmares, a non-ending run over heated embers.

"Snow, enough," Nia repeated, putting a hand on my shoulder pulling me back. "Your father is looking, don't give him the pleasure to see you riled from your own decision."

Ignoring her, I neared closer to him. My chest had set aflame and burned with malice. "Look at me and remind yourself every moment of what I feel about your people and about you." My body vibrated, heat pouring out of every word. "Look well, Adriatian. Look well and see how I spend my retaliation."

"I will have to watch you destroy yourself," he gritted out.

A smirk rose on my lips. "Enjoy then." The path I chose bore no survivors. I had no intention of surviving.

"Snowlin," my uncle called, approaching me, and I finally pushed away from the Adriatian. "My sweet niece, you finally look somewhat Isjordian."

A sneer lifted at the corners of my mouth at that slithering tone in his voice.

He smirked, taking in the sight of me. "You come back then a general and two lords are dead."

I raised a brow at him. "Fearing for your turn? You have an 'eye' for things after all."

Nia snorted and Kilian turned, staring at me again.

Uncle's face fell and his hand rose halfway between us, almost preparing to hit me like he'd done in olden days. That remembrance almost settled in, my body almost obeying to let him strike me at the memory. "You—"

But that was all it was—remembrance. And it had built a backbone of courage in my spine. I grabbed onto his hand tightly, the dagger strapped to my side now on my hand, resting just above his wrist. "Do you know why I took only your left eye?" I asked, digging the dagger slightly in his flesh. "Because Thora's kind heart said people deserve a chance at proving you they change. But her kind heart is also dead. So, if you speak to me one more time, I'll pluck your heart string by string and knit your other eyeball a hat with it. Hm?"

He let out a stuttering laugh, his body shaking but not from amusement. I let him go and sheathed the dagger on my side as he disappeared out of my wrathful sight. Sometimes I feared that I felt so little fear.

"He is your uncle, you mannerless heathen," Kilian accused.

I snorted at his prejudiced scale that always levelled me peccable, his sight that held me reprehensible. I was accustomed to such judgement, yet I felt inclined to break it. "The very same one who broke my little sister's arm twice, bruised her six-year-old face beyond recognition and shaved her head with a pocket knife because he thought she was too pretty for an Olympian spawn. The very same bastard." Eye for an eye, it was what I'd meant to say, yet I'd just made myself pitiful.

His eyes widened just slightly before he turned to narrow them on my uncle. The most reaction I'd seen him draw. "Where was your mother, your servants, tutors, guards?"

I had stopped waiting for someone to save me long before there was something of mine to save. "Where everyone else was, cowering in fear of my father or cowering in fear of us. The demons needed taming, that was what everyone thought so they said and did nothing. I was left with a brother who was breaking down from not being able to help us and with a sister who wore those bruises as a cloth and pretended everything was alright. That left it in my graces to act, but what can a worthless child do more than claw—and you can't claw through scales, so I only ended up tearing my own nails. They were also not me, sometimes I think the best thing that had ever happened to them was die."

I bit my lip suppressing the tremble those words I'd uttered out loud had caused. Why did I have to tell him that? Why did it feel liberating to say it out loud? I had not known how heavy it had been on me—the truth.

"Snow," Nia called, wrapping her hand around mine.

I took a deep breath and straightened. "Shame they missed me. However, they have given me purpose and mannerless heathen ways."

He made to speak, but his mouth fell in a sharp line before he turned away to face the funeral crowd. After a while, between prayers, the loud storm and silence, he asked, "Did he hurt you, too?"

I contemplated, maybe for too short a while because I confessed unrestrained, unnecessarily, "First time he tried, I nailed a butter knife right in his thigh, an inch or so from his soggy treasures. The second time, he lost another sort of soggy ball, and now he wears an eye patch."

"Creative," he murmured. "Metaphorical. too."

I shrugged proudly. "I'm a poet of sorts."

"A poet who had her fair share of punishment after those actions," Nia said, clicking her tongue.

"All suffering makes for great art, sweet Nia."

She shook her head. "As you say, you maniac."

He glanced shortly at both of us, more so at me. "She is not afraid of you either."

"Oh, I am," said Nia. "I just refrain myself from calling her a contortion of the unnatural and a heathen. Also, I lack the *'in my head you bleed'* look you give her. Little do you know, it provokes her more in a terrible sort of way, the *'a challenge for someone to break'* sort of way."

"Do not warn him, Nia, I like him the way he is." I turned to him, raking my gaze over his tall figure top to bottom. I liked reading the challenge in his stare, it was attractive. "Conceited and lush in blood. I do hate a dry corpse."

He straightened, his chin raising a bit higher before he glanced sideways at my friend. "Is she always like this? Engrossed in her role."

I shrugged. "What's so wrong with capitalising rumours, fears and views of others?"

"It is a lie."

I stuck my bottom lip out. "Oh, spank me."

He rubbed a hand over his eyes. "Does the flirting come with your capitalising ventures or is it particularly directed at me?"

"It can be whatever you wish it to be."

His tongue pushed against his cheek and he nodded to himself. "Got my answer."

18

BIRDS AND CAGES

KILIAN

CASMERE WAS COLDER THAN Tenebrose, the wind sharper and filled with air of salt, smoke and fish. Twice, the princess had retched her stomach out since we'd arrived and now she was almost collapsing while her gut betrayed her a third time.

I handed her a handkerchief which she warily glanced at through tired lids before straightening and walking away from me. It was a handkerchief, not a poisoned dagger. She always reacted this sort of way to any help. My eyes followed her, hovering around restless while her soldiers finished patrolling the city walls.

She clutched her stomach once again before erupting in a dry cough—there was nothing left to bring out.

Tired, I stalked to her and reached for her arm to help her straighten. "What is this about? Why are you ill?"

She shook herself free and wore a wide fatigued smile. "Doesn't it please you?" She got close to me, tracing a finger up my chest. "Come, be happy, I won't go mad."

I flung her hand away. "You are sick in the head."

Her eyelids lowered from exhaustion and she huffed a short throaty laugh. "It's my stomach this time, Adriatian, my head is fine."

Caiden stalked over from where he was speaking to the Casmerian Lord and brought out a small flask of clear liquid from a pocket. "Your handkerchief," he demanded, and I handed it to him. He emptied a small amount of the flask content and placed it over her mouth.

She took a couple breaths and then her lids closed in relief.

"The fish smell," her friend said. "It troubles her stomach, it will pass."

I raised a brow, mostly unconsciously. She was sick because of the smell of...fish? The *Ybris* brought down by mackerel and salmon. Why did I find this entertaining?

"Did you need to tell him?" she grumbled, half muted from the piece of cloth still over her face.

"I won't swing tuna in front of your nose, rest fine." Severely tempted, however.

"How much longer?" she asked her friend.

His reaction changed to pure blankness and so did his shadows. "Soldiers should be there by now, to collect her."

The princess nodded through stern features. "Soon it will be over."

What were the two concocting? "Planning to murder some other Lord?"

She threw me a glare. "Planning on occupying his slot first?"

"I have fish, remember?"

She unsheathed a dagger and made for me, only blocked by her friend intercepting between us. "You cannot kill him, Cakes. Your father has signed a treaty of their safety."

A girl's screams broke the busy air of the city. Then another followed by a man's shouts and her attention followed them.

"You," she said to one of her soldiers. "Go check what all the noise is all about."

"Cakes," Caiden called, shaking his head at her. "Don't, we got what we wanted. It is not for us to deal with what happens to these people."

"It is not, but you see, I have not had my fun today, and if I am not allowed to kill him," she said, pointing her dagger to me. "It will have to be just anyone."

"It's all types of innocents then, no one is spared from you."

She shut her eyes tight. "Voice of reason, is that you? Have not heard from you for a while." She gave a quick snide smile before charging toward the crowd her soldiers were parting. Her revenant stance shifted somehow. I saw her head tilt to the side, the next step changed, something around her air varied, the lightness yet the force of her muscles stringing in her body almost predatory—like a lioness ready to pounce on her prey.

"Hello there," she greeted the man kneeling to the ground who held a bruised woman by the hair.

She'd been shackled by her ankles, dirt and grime clung to her half-torn remnants of a dress that barely hung to her. Bruises, blood and much had veiled the thin features of her, but the white shadows of pain were rampant and thick, almost blurring my surroundings and forcing me to shut my senses down.

The man grabbed a leather belt from the ground and said, "Nothing for you here to see, Captain, move to your business."

The passersby who had halted at the show flinched and continued about, almost fearful at the man's authoritative tone.

She laughed and then turned to us, brows raised. "Did you hear that, we have no business here, what are we doing?"

Her soldiers levelled a stare on the man, a hand over all their swords, ready to their captain's command.

She crouched to the ground to be at his eye level. "Yes, I give the orders as you see. Let go of the girl."

"She is my child, my problem, my business."

"Is she? I have some business with her, too. How did you acquire the bruising, the lice and cuts? You look like a painting," she commented casually.

The man threw his head back laughing, and she chased his laughter with a vileness of her own. An odious sound. "I am the town's bailiff," he introduced, letting go of his daughter. "I knew Isjord raised some tough women."

"Oh, yes," the princess said, tracing the movement of the girl to the safety of our side. "Tough indeed."

What was she doing? Did she really agree to this monster's way?

The girl scrambled to her feet, barely walking two steps before almost collapsing, caught only by my arms. She shivered, bled, smelled and clung to me tightly.

"You are safe," I offered, half shielding her.

"I know her," the girl whispered in a cry. "I know her. Don't let her hurt me."

Was she more afraid of her than her father?

"So, how did your fascinating work come to be this...fascinating?" the princess asked the bailiff.

Caiden blew an exasperated breath beside me. "Blessed gods, could you not just give her a hobby instead of this obsession?"

The father sneered and turned to glare at the girl I held. "She went around dallying with a lowlife, unblessed slave of one of the rich here. I caught her just before she lost her virtue, taught her a lesson and she is ready to be shipped to her buyer in Vrammethen. She wanted to taste the rank flesh of the unblessed so I'll give it to her. It's what she wanted, it's what she got."

The princess threw a scalding look to the girl who sobbed in my arms. "Did she? She wanted it, asked for it?"

She could not be serious.

"Yes," the man said proudly. "By the last beating, she went limp, almost searching for my belt to hit her again."

"Fascinating." She stood and reached a hand to help the man stand. With no notice I saw the dagger previously strapped to her thigh on her hand and etched right on the man's side. "She wanted it, just like you wanted that?" She stabbed him again. "She asked for it, just how you asked for that?"

He dropped to the ground bleeding a stream, but not dead, only careful spots hit nothing vital.

I was wrong.

"Of course," Cai murmured, annoyed and rubbing his head.

She stretched her neck and turned to us. Flipping the dagger to hold it at the blade, she pointed it to the girl. "You have choices. Nightmarish nights or nightmarish nights with the image of you nailing this dagger where his heart is asking it to be."

The girl had stilled, truly contemplating taking her offer. Though her shadows were all in denial, she raised a trembling hand to the blade. Before I could step in, the princess pulled it away. "Or you can leave this all behind and know you never sullied your soul for a bastard that never deserved it in the first place. They never leave, nightmares, no matter what you do, no matter what you do to him."

I hid my reaction and forbade myself from gaping at her. Did she know the comfort those words brought to the girl, how her shadows had thinned?

"He hurt me," the girl sobbed.

"I know."

She cried out, shaking her head. "He locked me."

The princesses eyes dropped to her still bound wrists and ankles and she swallowed thickly before repeating, "I know."

"He really, really...hurt me." Tears had chased a stream down her face. "But I don't want to kill him."

The princess nodded and walked back toward the man. Her sword drawn, and with one clean cut, she severed both of his hands before piercing his heart with it. There had been no breath left for resistance or for pleas and whimpers of pain, the man had gone painfully.

His death gave my mouth a bitter taste of charcoal, a screech of protest rang in my ears. And when that claw of death dug at the side of my head, I shut my magic down to the slim of it, the furthest down I could, where I would not feel it this intensely.

"Cai," she called to her friend while cleaning her sword. "Help the girl clean up and sort her bearings."

He warily approached the princess, already done with her behaviour. "Who will help you out of your father's wrath?"

"My handsome personality," the princess playfully whispered to him.

I scoffed only a beat after him.

She turned to her soldiers and ordered, "I want a stake through and through him, then place him at the top of his house till there is nothing for birds to pick on." She halted and turned to them again. "Ah, string his hands around his neck."

"Could you just not let it at that?" I asked, pointing to the man bleeding lifeless on the ground. Why did she have this fixation with stakes and severed limbs?

She glanced at the man, looking almost confused. "He will be grateful I have accessorised him. Once crows pick his eyes out, what will go with his smile?"

A cord of nerves strung at her appetite for jokes. This damned woman. Now I really wanted to swing tuna in front of her face. "Why remind the girl of what she went through? To see that every day till he rots away. That image will embed in her head. Didn't you tell her to forget?"

She headed toward the town stables. "The girl is not staying in this nightmare. When you free a bird you don't just open the door. You rip the bars, blow the whole thing away and take the bird to a forest. Opening the door and giving a choice to leave to someone in a cage is locking them a second time. This time inside their own head." She halted, turning to face me. "I free the bird, the bird comes with me to a forest called Modr where my friend, Lady of Modr, will look after her in a nest for birds just like her. Those who have had their cages opened and are still afraid to flee."

"Your metaphors are terrible." Her actions not half as bad.

"Ah," she said, clutching her chest, "but you wound me, Adriatian."

"Why do you care?"

She raised an amused brow. "I shouldn't care?"

"Should you?"

She pursed her lips. "No, not really."

"Why did you?"

She threw a look toward the bailiffs house. "I despise cages."

A brawl had started where the bailiff's body lay. Soldiers and what looked like a priest bickered back and forth over the dead bailiff.

She stumbled a step back and then another before I took attention of her wide expression, and then of her stifled breathing.

"Princess?"

She did not answer and she did not blink.

"You should have stayed well-hidden, you vermin of hells," an ice thin voice called, reaching us. The priest wore spite and disdain well enough in his features before I read the very same painted in his shadows. The robes of devotion he wore were somewhat soiled with pretend.

"Murdoc," she called, too meek from how I'd usually heard her. They knew one another.

"You should not be here, and you should not be doing this," he spat, making a step for her, almost wanting to strike her.

I stepped between the two and the lanky priest stumbled a few steps back almost dropping to the ground. "I'd be a bit careful how you speak to her and I'd be terribly, terribly careful when you approach her."

He laughed all slime and vile. "Adriatian. Yes, protect her then tear her to pieces. How I would have loved to have seen her shredded by you."

My grip went to my hilt at the acid taste of those words, but a light hand rested atop my own and the owner finally stepped forward. Battle rage wearing her face.

Her hand went tight around mine. I didn't think she noticed that she held me. "What is it, Murdoc, why did hells open their gates to free you today?"

His mouth twisted. "Bailiff Sander was a good man and he will receive a proper burial."

She snorted and then blasted in a euphoric laughter. "No."

"What?"

"He. Will. Not. Be. Buried." A grin spread wide on her lips, but I saw the shiver and her grip tightened around my hand. "What will you do, Murdoc? Preach me mercy? But didn't you teach me yourself that monsters need their monstrous ends?"

I studied the priest. So much hate, entitlement and unremorseful linger of malice for a person of faith. There was something wrong, but this time it was not with her.

She let go of me. "Scatter, before I scatter you over him, Murdoc."

He snarled, his lips peeled back to reveal rotten teeth. "Gods will skewer you in hells."

She gave him a wicked smirk. "This is hell and I am fire. Shouldn't you be scared, you sinning little saint?"

She knew how to make a man shiver. Murdoc's shadows of hate overlapped murky with fear. "This doesn't end here," he shouted from behind as she began walking away from him.

She waved a hand in the air. "It will never end and you cannot die for you will repent first. You owe me three souls."

What had the priest done? What had he done to her?

"Did you just let that man live?"

She flicked a bunch of hair back as she strutted forward with the grace of a true princess. "I don't like rotten flesh, darling."

That word again.

Silently, we backed toward the stables. Too silently. Silence was a bad tell, it had to be, she was rarely silent.

"Who was he?" I asked as we mounted our horses.

No reaction wore her face, almost convincing me she was fearful. She couldn't be. No, she wasn't. I didn't want her to be, not with me around.

I saw her swallow almost nervously before she answered, "One who taught me to despise cages."

A crowd of soldiers had gathered by the stables in Tenebrose castle. A luminescent angry red mist circled the vicinity, blurring the sight of her father. I never had seen someone with that much anger. When he saw her, he turned into something murderous.

"Having fun?" he shouted. "Murdering just about anyone? From Lords to Bailiffs?"

"Only catching up with you, father, you're a tough one to beat. Move, I stink of pig blood."

How did she get to speak at him like that?

"You will not run wildly about my kingdom. We have rules and punishment. You are a captain, not an executioner. You are now dismissed from all your duties. From this moment you are to do nothing. You are not to leave these walls or even cross those gates. Do not force me to lock you in some dungeon." He'd gone red and she'd gone pale with boredom.

"My fun has just begun," she said mirthlessly. "With all this free time in my hands, what will I do with it? Yes, first I will visit Rose hall, then Bruma halls, then…maybe I'll write a letter to my betrothed and tell him all sorts of fun stuff about breaching walls, fleet numbers, soldier numbers and all sorts of other delicious details. There is no secret in marriage, is it? I better begin being as honest as I can with him."

Did she not know how close Silas was to clawing her throat out?

"You would not dare," he said, carefully glancing around those that heard her.

She did dare because she said, "The Tenebrose wall is weak by the western cliff, the land below is ice, therefore it takes a little heat and some persistence." She clicked her fingers. "And you are inside your very city."

"How dare—"

"Venzor," she continued, unafraid and unbothered. "The bay between Grasmere and them has a dam, it conceals a secret that takes you right inside—"

"Enough," he shouted, almost shaking to control his ire. "Patrol only, you are to deal with no prisoners, no crimes, nothing but patrols, checks with the wall guards and documentation handling with the Lords. Are we clear?"

She had just threatened the King of Isjord and gotten him to comply with her terms.

She grinned like a feline and bowed deeply to her father. "Clear as ice."

All frosty ire, he strutted away defeated to his castle.

Caiden parted to his quarters and I settled by her door, waiting for Nia to take shift with me.

"Ice isn't clear," I said before she made it to her door.

"Astute observation, Adriatian." She halted and then leaned back on her door to face me. "When is Mal coming back?"

Why did she keep calling my brother Mal? "But you wound me, princess. I thought we had just begun getting along."

"He promised me moon treats," she said, leaving me aghast in my own sarcasm. "You know, those little crescent moons that have that gold syrup atop, they taste of apple and butter. My brother brought them once when he returned from Sidra."

"Moon...treats?" I asked, blinking confused. "You mean *loonor*?" Children sweets?

She shrugged. "I suppose."

I frowned. "Why did he promise you that?"

She unsheathed her dagger and showed me some sort of complicated trick with it. "I showed him how to do that."

She was not joking.

"You exchange bargains with my brother now?"

She tilted her head, swivelling a heavy gaze over all of me, each time she did it she'd only frustrated me further and I believed she did it with that purpose in mind. "I would have asked him for one of your king's limbs, but where would the fun be in that? I want to dissemble him myself."

"A day after," I said, retreating to the wall, tired of arguing with her and sort of bothered by the way she looked at me. "He returns the day after tomorrow."

She nodded and then halted again, turning to me, taking a few moments, looking like she wanted to say something. "H-How is your mother? I mean...his mother? Yours, too?" She blinked to herself. "Both of yours?"

Why did she care? "She will be fine."

She cleared her throat, nodded, and then abruptly halted a third time.

"Yes?" I asked, blowing a tired breath.

"You could have gone, too."

"Fine way to try and get rid of me."

"But you wound me, Adriatian. We'd begun getting along."

Funny. "I have a name, princess."

"Me too."

"Your Highness?"

"Dickhead?"

I bit my tongue. I asked for that. "Adriatian it is."

"I thought so," she said, throwing me a wink before finally entering her bedroom.

I ran my fingers through my hair in an attempt to soothe the drumming headache. This was harder than I thought.

19

Blood and Shadow

Kilian

SHE'D COME TO THE library, floating like a spirit around the dark lifeless corridors filled with rotting pages and the musky scent of ink and cellulose. I had not the slightest idea why she chose to wander at night and why particularly here. Murder needn't much research.

Her slender fingers gently traced the dark wooden shelves, the white shift she wore floated around her, luminant in the darkness lit by only odd candles, and her hair—her hair was ever black, as always waving down her back, unbound and alluring like silk of night. I followed only a few paces behind, able to take in all the details in all her silence. What she had told me at the funeral, the patrol in Casmere—they had stayed on my mind more than I'd usually like to keep thoughts. Overthinking created hesitation, doubts and fear. None of which were qualities of a good soldier, but it made me wonder what her life had been like.

She halted and turned to pull out a wine-coloured leather-bound book from one of the shelves. Her eyes travelled along the harsh ink and faded words. She had such a strange concentrated expression. She always bit the side of her lower lip and her dark brows pulled tight together that wiggled just slightly when she found what she was looking for. Unsatisfied, she abruptly slammed it shut and placed it back before turning to face me.

"I'd suggest you end the staring. It would be disastrous if you ended falling in love with me," she said, flicking a bunch of her satiny dark locks over her shoulder. "I'm bewitching, you see. All the *Ybris* charms." Moonlight peeking from the small iced windows had given her a white halo. She looked divine more than anything.

"I could," I said, approaching close enough that she leaned back, almost folding backwards in half. "If this realm turned upside down and sideways to hells." Reaching over her head, I removed the soft feather that had rested there since she'd left her room. "Revolting really, all the murderous wiles."

She glanced sideways at the feather resting in my hand and backed away, straightening herself. A winsome smile stretched innocently on her lips, looking to devour me into her tease. "They make for the most of my appeal, darling." After throwing me a wink, she continued strutting graciously onto the library corridors humming that same melody she sang at nights before bed.

That cursed word again. She knew how to play with my patience—too well. Or was I letting myself be riled by her? She was easy to dislike and I'd fallen into that trap too deep. Disliking her was a trap, I realised, she enjoyed the back talk and torturous teases.

"Doesn't she ever sleep?" I asked Nia who had sat by a reading table eyes glued on a book.

"Mostly not, but something must be bothering her if she wanted to get out of her bedroom. Usually she just lays in bed."

So, this was a common thing? "There is Medi healers that—"

"Tried."

"And Crafters?"

"Tried."

"Doesn't it worry you that she never rests or sleeps?"

She lowered her book down and finally looked up at me. "Doesn't it ever worry you that you might be the cause of why she can't sleep?" she asked, raising her brows and then shook her head at my silence.

"It doesn't, does it?" she continued. "After all, she is the *Ybris*, a vile creature of the unnatural, now a pawn who your king will most likely have mysteriously killed not hours after that agreement sets in place. I know your kind, Kilian, very, very well. It never surprises me how soulless you spirituals are, how the divine rules over every human aspect, how the living depends on the gods' graces and the fates set by them. It won't kill her, the restlessness and the fatigue, you will." She then turned back to her Kemeri written toxicology book, flicking the pages silently. "What is belief but tales and threats of gods who fear and cannot control human nature and bound it with fictitious shackles of obedience with promise of heavens. Are they not the ones that say life cannot be all sweetness and purity, and then offer the very same to entice us into belief? Hypocrisy or just spiritual salvation by means of deceit? And you fell right for it—that fear that allows submission."

Now I knew why the two of them were friends, bonding over heathen ways. "You speak too sourly for something you don't understand."

"And you sort act too rashly on the very same basis of understanding."

I almost scoffed. "Is it Adriatians or gods that have hurt you?"

"Does it matter, it always comes in circles with you sort and gods. Either could have hurt me and both would be guilty."

A book slammed down at the other side of the table. The princess threw glances between Nia and me as she sat down, suddenly cold and shivering. "Vexing my friend now? Aren't you having a blast?"

I unbuttoned my jacked and stood towards her. "Living the best days of my life, princess."

She scooted away from me and pushed my jacket away. "So soon going out of your word? Are the realms turning sideways to hells already?"

The teasing beast, I swear she could almost make me laugh sometimes. I threw my jacket over her shoulders, the skin under had pimpled and prickled from the cold. When I glanced at her feet it was then I vibrated with frustration. "What's with you and the blessed shoes?"

She removed the jacket and threw it back to me. "I didn't say I was cold, nor that I wanted your opinion on it."

I threw it around her again, tucking it tight before lowering face to face with her. "Jacket or I drag you back to your room and tuck you nicely in bed. I'll even sing 'Children of the Forest' for you, dance it too if you like, and then...then I'll quietly stand guard, unbothered and undisturbed by your face, that mouth or your freezing limbs."

She'd done it again, riled me up beyond the usual.

Her face had gone still, unblinking. "How dare you speak to me like that?"

I opened my hands just slightly and bowed my head. "Pardon me, Your Highness."

Nia snorted and then burst into laughter, drawing the princess's attention. "That was a good threat." She gave me a thumbs up. "I'd be terrified too, Snow. Imagine being tucked in bed by him. Better take the jacket."

"You know," the princess said, almost vexed, pulling her arms through the too large jacket. "I'm too tired to argue or joke with either of you two."

"Then sleep, heathen."

She laughed shortly and tiredly, pointing a sleeve covered hand to her head. "It's too loud."

"You don't have to go there tomorrow, Snow. Cai said he and Sebastian could deal with it," Nia offered, putting a hand over hers in comfort.

Both wore gloves, I'd never seen either without. No, the three of them did, all the time.

The princess shook her head, willing and forcing her features to a certainty that her friend did not buy. "I will go. I want to deal with it myself."

Confused, I looked between the two friends. "Where?"

"Where you can see just how charming my murderous wiles are, Adriatian." There was no teasing or joking in her voice. She was a scary thing to behold in this stature. "I won't let you forget, nor your king or your kingdom, that I don't let my revenge grow cold."

She stood abruptly and I followed suit. "Where are you going now?"

Her face was stern. "There is nowhere to go in hells, you just adjust to where it burns less or...most. Depends on what you crave."

I frowned at the level of her dramatism. "You're tiring me. Where is that?"

"The kitchens, I am hungry."

Nia shut her book loudly, the two friends shared the same love for dramatics apparently. "You just ate, not an hour ago, then the buns, the cinnamon rolls, even the damned fruit. Sit, I'll ask the servants to bring you some carrots to munch on. You will get your stomach upset again and I don't have enough wort raisin for your pain."

"Really, Nia, carrots?" she grumbled almost devastated. "What are next, avocados?"

"W-What is wrong with avocados?" her friend stammered with confusion.

"The vile slime most call a vegetable?" the princess asked, shivering and gagging at the mention. "If I wanted to eat soap, I'd eat soap, and I've scented better smelling soaps."

My mouth had dropped open at their antics. Was this the *Ybris*? Afraid of tuna, repulsed by avocados? Was I hallucinating?

I stood, fresh air had to get to my brain or I'd start rotting at my young age at these two pointlessly arguing. "What do you want to eat?"

She turned to me, eyeing every inch of my face like I was cream dessert. "You."

Her friend drowned a snort with her hand and sunk on her seat, covering her face under a book.

I blew a heavy breath, stretching my neck before straightening. Hells, didn't she know how to frustrate me? "I'll get the cook to prepare you something."

"Letting me out of your sight?" she gasped playfully.

Ignoring her, I headed out for the corridors, murmuring to myself, "Even hell ghouls turn to heavens in your presence. I'm more scared for them than for you."

"Heard that," she shouted. "You flatter me, Adriatian."

The princess sat by my brother on a bench, munching on the treats he'd brought her and jollyly accompanying the biscuits with riveting chatter. What did the two have to bond over, their shared hate for the Adriatian kind perhaps?

She raised her head, noting my presence, staring at me with heavy eyelids and drowsy eyes. Goddess of temptation had met her match with this one.

"What are you staring at?" I asked, approaching them.

She licked her upper lip before biting on her lower plump one, her eyes never leaving me. "Your head."

"Let me guess. It would be better parted from my body?" I'd learnt the pattern of her play with me.

She grinned and stood, nearing so close to me that I had to look down at her. Air of her might brushing my skin, close sight of her beauty tricking my senses. She was so...so—

"It would be better between my legs." She gave me a wink. "Got you." Leaning closer, she whispered, "Again."

My eyes followed her as she strode away from us all victorious and then I blew a loud breath of exasperation.

Mal chuckled silently and I gave him a stark look. He'd only returned this morning. Driada had gotten better from her disease. She was not an Aura, so her body healed slowly and sometimes not at all. At the progress of her illness, she was lucky to even recuperate back for a few days at a time.

"How did you leave Driada?"

He stood, his shadows turned all gloomy and filled with despair. "She is fine...for now."

I rested a hand on his shoulder. "She will get through it, Mal."

He took a deep breath, washing his feelings down and skilfully away from my sight. "Yes—yes she will."

Not an ounce of truth, but losing hope was losing her.

"You should have stayed a while longer."

"They actually begged me to return, my charms did not work with the healers, they seemed rather annoyed. I am glad I did though, you look like shit."

I threw a glare to the black-haired fault bouncing all energy over her soldiers. I wanted to hope it would soon be over, but I couldn't. Soon she'd continue doing this in Adriata. I was too fatigued to even sigh.

Kirkwall was blooming compared to the rest of Isjord, the cold was still present, but it had not turned its lands to empty snow pile waste. Trees were undressed and gloomy, but there was still more life to them than the evergreen conifers that donned every corner of Isjord.

The city must have grown used to the presence of soldiers as none turned to even throw a curious glance towards us. A young man dressed in the black militia uniform approached and greeted our team when we neared the viceroy quarters where the lord and his team gathered to discuss their duties.

"Snowlin, thank you for responding to my request," he said, coming to greet us. He almost did not look Isjordian. Tanned, sharp features, his dark hair half tied back, almost as dark as mine compared to the yellow heads of Isjord and his eyes were deep olive—he looked more like Caiden than any Isjordian.

"It appears I was right to put you in charge here, Sebastian, you have done my orders a great service," she offered, bowing slightly to him.

So he was the soldier she had put in charge after she killed the Lord of Kirkwall.

We followed him down the busy streets of the city, the smell of baked goods, vanilla and cinnamon had filled the frosted air.

"The family has been working here for years now, they own a tavern by the borders of the wall, Pine Inn. They have two young children," he explained, throwing a glance towards us as he pulled her closer to him and further ahead from us. His words were muted by the surroundings, but I could see it from how she walked and how amused she looked that there was something very wrong.

The inn was small, close to the Highwall, enough to make out the sentries patrolling above. Noise of cutlery clattering, and trivial conversation leaked to the outside. Almost all tables were occupied with Isjordians enjoying their lunch and casual drink.

I spotted the owners preparing meals and drinks behind the counter and two children aiding the tables. Why had the princess brought us here for?

"Everyone out, except you four," she ordered, pointing to the family.

Fear rose to their faces, they paled and pulled their children close to them. She grabbed a chair and sat in the centre facing them while the room emptied at her command. Sebastian greeted us and left as well. Mal, Caiden and the soldiers took the corners around her and blocked all exits. The only ones who seemed to be surprised were myself and my brother whose feet shifted repeatedly from the heightened mist of tension.

I took position behind the princess, surveying the surroundings.

She placed her hands in the holy greeting and bowed to the four with a wicked smile. "With Krig's blessings, to the heavens. Or shall I say Henah's?"

Adriatians, just as I had thought.

"My, my, a whole rotten nest right under our noses," she cooed. "I must give it to you, fooled just about everyone. Certainly, you did not have to try much to hide considering your connections. I heard Esbern was a good friend of yours."

Was this connected to the Lord helping with the crossings, had they been helped by him?

The father stepped forward and pushed his children to nestle around their mother's lap. He stopped short, her soldiers blocking her from him. "We are simple and hardworking people, whatever has happened between our kingdoms has nothing to do with us," he said. "We have resided in Isjord for years and my children were born here. We have not done or meant any harm to anyone, the whole city could vouch for our words."

The princess chuckled as if his answer had been a great joke. "Does the whole city know of your origins?"

She had achieved to receive the answer she wanted to hear, the father's face paled, he swallowed deep and took a slight step back. "Does it matter what we are? You cannot gather us in the same batch."

"It matters to the law and to me, for all the little that I care you might as well prove yourself to be the *same* rotten batch. A snake can shed skin, but not habits." Cocking her head back, she surveyed him. "Do you think me a fool to not see beyond this facade that you play and have created? Come now, dear, give me some credit."

To her it did not matter if you were Adriatian, you were all the same, even I knew that much but something else was brewing here.

"The Lord—"

She interrupted him with a hand. "The Lord was killed as a traitor and is no longer here. So, how do we settle this? Imprisonment is definitely not in consideration, so we just have to sort out the method of death I suppose."

The mother and children erupted in cries while soldiers surrounded them on her order.

"Please, please do not do this," the father begged on his knees, restrained by the soldiers.

I stepped in front of her. "They have done nothing to you or anyone, does it matter what they are? They bear no one's guilt, certainly not their king's," I spat, pointing around the room. It was impossible for me to hold any longer, having borne too much from her words and her overly exaggerated manners of punishment that more than anything came from personal roots. I understood—no, I couldn't even begin to know her suffering, but it was not these people's bargain to suffer. If anything, it was mine and those in the Adriatian court for allowing it.

"Proceed cautiously, Kilian," Caiden warned, almost bored. Silently followed suit by my brother who shook his head for me to stop.

"A bit of hypocrisy I smell?" Her hand slid to her dagger, flinging it around playfully. "Neither did the Isjordians your people killed, yet here we are, me and you, across a separating wall, an accessory to your acts." She smiled wickedly, eyes aflame, burning shards of amber ice. "Take your morals and bury them just like you do with your wrongs."

How could someone be so wrong and yet so in right at the same time?

Satisfied from my long silence, she took turns about the room. "Their heads?" Cocking her head to the side in question she answered herself, "No." Halting as if in realisation, she faced them again. "Ah, since you have spread your very selves around this city, tainting and staining it with your Adriatian stench, how about I wrap your insides all over the walls of the city, your heads on some lovely spikes and the rest of you, out of kindness, I gift it to your king to have and adore," she mused and my blood boiled. "Shall I do it before your younglings? They will learn a lesson for sure."

This was beyond monstrous. I moved towards her, wrapping my hand around her throat and pinning her hard to the wall, dragging her other dagger strapped to her thigh to rest on her throat.

Caiden and the soldiers charged towards us, but the princess raised her palm stopping them, a smirk playing in her face as she waved them to step away. She simpered. "It hurts then, to hear these things being done to innocents? How much do you think it hurts to see it? What about experiencing it yourself?"

"I understand your anger, but not your actions."

"I don't need you to understand anything, only to watch."

"Have you forgotten to be human, just how are you so twisted?" I spat, our gazes clashing. My eyes dug into her hypnotising ones. I held the dagger yet she had already pierced me with their stare. My knuckles had gone white gripping the dagger, holding myself back from digging it through her flesh.

"Surprised? To suffer the consequences of your own doing, to crawl through the claws of the monster of your own creation. But why?" she asked breathlessly, huffing a delicate laugh. "I find all of this so very poetic."

"Whatever you do to this family it will not bring them back, these people were not the ones to kill your family, they do not deserve this reaction, this cruelty," I said, pressing closer to her, the dagger almost digging in her flesh.

"Kilian, let her go," Mal interfered.

Her features dropped to stern lines and she rolled her cold gold gaze up to meet mine once again. "Yes, I do understand." Those eyes of hers wavered for a moment. I'd never seen them so affected before. "But you see, when you break the law it is only correct to enforce its repercussions, isn't it? How I do that is entirely up to me."

She moved closer and the dagger dug in her flesh drawing blood from her neck.

I flinched back from her.

I had hurt her.

"Go ahead, enjoy making me your evil like your kind has always done. I will give it to them, the monster that they thought they were hunting."

In a flashing moment, she grabbed my hand and drove the dagger I was holding through her shoulder. My eyes drew wide, my body paralyzed and my heartbeat loud in my ears. No one moved, only silently watched us, afraid of the princess, not afraid for her.

Blood gushed down her wound yet she didn't even blink.

"See, how much pleasure that gave you, to hurt me, to release your own thoughts, your own anger. Did it not carve your insides to be so close to the one you hate and not do that, huh? Can we all kindly agree that our methods are different and you have no right to judge or interfere with mine."

Wrapping both her hands around mine, she pulled the dagger out, causing her to wince and twist in a cringe. Gasping, she clutched her wound and then straightened as if pain was fleeting.

She had gone mad. I could see it in her face how she was losing herself to her anger, there was nothing left there, empty just like her shadows. Why did her words appear so heavy at times? I could not understand her, not a bit.

"How many?" she asked half breathlessly, walking towards the family. "How many Adriatians have gone through here to our borders? How many did you offer respite and help? I bet a good cheek you keep ledgers and detail."

It was them.

"We...we did not do such a thing," the father lied.

She blew an exasperated breath and turned to me, a scalding look etched on her bloodless face. "Did he lie?"

She was doing it on purpose. I glanced at the silently pleading father and then her before I said, "Yes. But you knew that already."

"I did, what I don't know on the other hand is whether this bunch will continue to test my kindness."

"My children," said the mother, stepping forward, "I want them to live, whatever happens to us." Lowering her head, she stepped forward. "I will tell you what you want to know."

The princess sighed. "Well, this was not as difficult as I had hoped it to be. I expected a bit more oomph of resistance."

The mother brought down five large ledgers from under the floorboard and handed them to her. Again, she had been right.

She flicked through the boasting ledgers with relish and dazzling eyes. "You keep quite the trail, Ester. Meticulous you Adriatians."

The mother cast a cautious glance at all of us, then turned to her. "I think you know why...Your Highness."

"Clever."

"Has he sent you? Was he not pleased?" Ester asked.

Who was *he*?

The princess giggled and leaned back on her chair. "Oh he is pleased. I intend to make him displeased. You might have another answer for me. Has anyone been selected or sent to Myrdur?"

The mother pursed her lips in thought and shook her head slowly. "No, not Myrdur."

What was this about? Why was Myrdur being mentioned, what did it have to do with this?

The princess's blood had soaked the jacket on her left arm completely, the navy fabric shone a metallic bright ruby, her face, too, had paled—she was losing too much blood.

"Remove your jacket, princess. I do not need you dead just yet," I ordered, turning to ask the Adriatian mother for a bandage.

"You will not touch me, ever. And you think me so weak as to die from this. You will have to try harder when time comes," she answered flatly, grabbing the bandage from my hand.

Her friend stepped forward to help.

"I can do it myself," she said, dismissing him as well.

"Stubborn woman," he murmured under his breath before taking position back on the wall.

Could have not agreed more, but I would add mad, angry, bloodthirsty, murderous, and psychopathic to that. She drove a dagger to her flesh to prove a point. She had to have known I would never hurt her—my reaction must have given her some satisfaction.

She removed her jacket, the white undershirt she wore had soaked red in blood and clung tightly to her curves, matting to her chest and left arm completely. She hurriedly wrapped her wound, around her shoulder then across her chest, tying the bandage to the front, almost as if she had done this before—wrapped wounds just like a soldier would.

"Your children," she continued quietly, "will not remain here, they will be taken under the care of your own people. You on the other hand are my prisoners till I find the Adriatians in Isjord. If any of them attempt any move in this kingdom that is not what you have told me, I will hold you two responsible, as hosting and aiding in criminal activity, accessory to their crimes. Then I will hold true to what was promised and all of that fun." She then turned to me. "I need you to take them by the borders and offer them protection in your lands, the whole city will soon find out my reason for visiting here. I might have not killed them, but I can't guarantee they won't, and a promise was given on my behalf. They are also forbidden to enter these lands from this point on, even after the agreement. I will put them on the criminal records, all four of them."

A long loud sigh left my lungs. "Is that necessary?"

"Are you still questioning me?"

My eyes deviated to the cut on her neck still streaming blood. "You are still bleeding."

She huffed a laugh. "I thought you liked me bleeding?"

"I do not like you in any type of way, especially bleeding."

She scrunched her nose with tease. "Pretty liar, I could bet a good cheek I am your favourite *Ybris*."

I retreated, rubbing my tired eyes before I would give in to her torture.

Nesrin and Larg approached the Zone of Peace, both of their expressions in shock and grimness at our sight. I explained to them both what had happened and the instructions of the princess regarding the children.

"At least she did not kill them, it would have not been beyond her. I have witnessed her judgments before and considering those, this batch has escaped completely un-scathed," Nesrin explained. "Be careful there, Kilian, she could hurt you, too. I will pray for your safe return." Nesrin left, taking the children and greeting us goodbye.

Larg studied me and my expression. "I hope that is not your blood, but for Henah's sake, please tell me it is not hers."

"She lives, but she does tempt her ways with me more than I can sometimes bear."

"Kilian, son," he shouted. "You went to protect her. However she behaves, you are not to harm her. You were the one who could not trust anyone else to go with Mal, and yet you are the first to hurt her."

Tension built in my neck at his words, but he was right. "How are the border cities holding?"

His expression turned sullen. "Sitara has gotten worse, we have evacuated more than half the city in Amaris. None of our ships can leave five miles into the Moor Sea, but the unblessed have docked tens of theirs into our lands and...Sidra, five of our battleships were destroyed, dragged by the hightide directly into the storm. This wall needs to come down, son, hold the princess safe."

The squadron had readied for return. The black morph circled the skies ahead and around. Her sight in the skies. Smart and handy.

I studied the soldiers and noted the missing two Adriatians.

I reached Caiden, the one she always left in charge. "Where are the two prisoners?"

Unbothered, he checked his horse's saddle. "Isjord has a no prisoner policy, they are Snow's prisoners. If you still hope for that agreement, I'd keep quiet."

"She intends to keep it hidden from her father?"

He laughed shortly, unamused. "No, what she intends is to forgo details of how she got rid of the Adriatians."

She planned something. This was her personal hunt, but what was she exactly hunting?

"I will ride with him," she said and I whipped my head in surprise in her direction. With a tight-lipped smile, she strode towards me and her brows rose in question surely at my expression. "What?"

"Absolutely not," Caiden said, grabbing her arm and pulling her in his direction.

In a swift movement, she shook herself free and they stared at each other through a silent battle of conversation.

At her persistence, he retreated in disbelief. "If he as much as flinches around you, I will kill him," he spat, pointing to me, and she nodded gleefully before turning to me once again. Possibly the reason why she had chosen to ride with me, considering she shuddered in disgust at the sight of me every time. She was either really wanting to test my patience with her or trying to invoke and provoke a reaction that would have me hurt her again—for her to find a reason to kill me.

"What's with the," she said, waving her hand in front of her face before pointing to mine, "angry?"

I tightened the horse saddle straps before turning to her. "You can will gods out of their holy patience and I am only man, one that can only be angry at the moment and not act like it as well."

She smiled, that inciting sly smile she always gave me. "What would you do to me, Kilian, if one could act on their anger?"

My name on her mouth reiterated around the air—such a strange sound. It was either Adriatian, dog, snake, scum or vermin, the only terms she had called me before. This was the first time she had called my name. Was this another invitation to provoke her?

"What would you have wanted me to do to you?"

Her brow rose as she said, "To act smart and dug that dagger deeper in my flesh. Now you will live knowing you could have killed me when I turn Adriata to ash."

I halted and examined her amused expression. "Surely I will get another chance, but that is if you do not poison yourself to death first."

Her smile faltered and she blinked slowly. "What?"

I pointed to her jacket. "Cherry red blood, almost luminescent. You are an *Ybris* not a eudemon. Your pupils are dilated all the time, more in the morning. In the afternoon you sway just slightly and often stare blankly in empty spaces. You hate warm drinks because few of them mask their scent. Your lips are usually a shade of violet, too. So, frost thorn, grey thistle, winter cress, gutweed, barbed clove and what else? What other poison are you micro dosing on?"

"Silkwort," she admitted blankly. "Nia says it's the one that gives me stomach pain, why I am hungry at night."

Her honesty took me back so I dared ask, "How long?"

"Twelve years this coming January."

My nerves stung. Heavens, how was she even breathing? "Why have you been ruining your body with poison since you were barely a child?"

"Because," she enunciated, sticking her bottom lip out all innocence, "I got poisoned twice after the attack, right inside my father's bedroom without seeing anyone for days. Anything else to reveal, any other examination? My left eye bigger than the other, my right foot more angled than my left?"

My eyes fell to her feet. "Your left leg, you shift more weight into that one."

She gradually smiled, a different one this time. "I am aware, it's from my training to make my left dominant as my right. Keep staring, Adriatian, you might find something you like."

I shook my head at her nonchalance and chance to turn the situation to her leverage. "Mad woman."

She moved swiftly mounting my horse and I followed suit after her. Surrounded by an echo of death, but she smelled softly of sweet flowers. She shifted herself away from me, almost at the hilt of the mount as if walking on a tightrope. It made her lose balance and made me lose my patience. "You were the one who wanted this, so I suggest you move back before we both topple to the ground," I said, gripping the reins and she did as told.

Her injured shoulder met mine and she winced in pain. I stopped my hand from reaching her wound. She would be fine, maybe she even deserved some of it.

In her odd silence, she began slightly shivering, but I was certain it was not from the cold. Then I felt her stiffen before she grabbed the reins to pull them back, almost throwing us to the ground.

Just before I was about to turn to her, I noticed a tripwire on the ground and then a black tipped arrow flying towards our side. The princess leaned forward, groaning from pain and letting the arrow fly between us.

I dismounted, bringing her down with me. She had noticed them both before I had. How?

Men one by one came from the forest, masked and in masses. Certainly such groups were usually caught and fought from sentries patrolling these roads, but twice now the princess had been targeted.

I unsheathed my sword and she stepped back, her features going wild and aghast at the sight of the black steel. She hid her trembling hands behind her back and took a small step away from me, her attention never leaving my weapon.

"Not the time for games, princess."

Two men charged toward her and two daggers flew from behind me, landing on their skulls.

"Put that away," Caiden barked at me, reaching us and handing me one of his swords. "Snow, look at me," he called to her. "Come now, Cakes, look at me. Put that thing away," he repeated, turning towards me and I sheathed my sword back.

The princess still seemed to be in a state of shock, but she tried to right herself and relax, finally managing to come out of her daze.

I pulled her behind my back when Caiden left to join the rest of the fight. I swung the sword back and forth, leaving five men injured afront us.

Another jumped from behind a tree and she ran in his direction, skidding on the snow below him and avoiding his strike. Her sword met his shin before she stabbed it on the ground to stand herself up. Swiftly, she unsheathed her thigh dagger and nailed it behind his head.

Bitter taste filled my senses.

But that was not the most intense thing I felt at that moment. Surprise was.

"What?" she panted, walking to me.

I had not realised I was gawking at her with my mouth open. She was not all talk after all, had this been how she had fended off those men before?

"Behind you," she warned.

All gates of magic opened on command and I lifted the man in the air while she threw her dagger forward, piercing his chest. Two others came and I froze their shadows in place before she swiftly slit both their throats.

"Wait," she shouted in my direction. "I want one alive, can you do what you did again?"

I nodded and the last attacker stilled on his knees on the ground.

Her soldiers gathered around us along with Mal and Caiden, panting and covered in blood.

"He is good," the latter said, pointing to my brother. "Nice to know Adriata did not send two wimps, but not so nice to know they might as well have sent two assassins in Isjord. Your father will be most glad to know that for sure."

"Good thing for those bracelets of eternal friendship we weaved," my brother joked, throwing him a wink.

Caiden grinned at him. "Mine better be thick with diamonds."

Silas did not care, castle grounds were laced in dark craft, suppressing us of spiritual mana, disabling us of wielding most of our magic. Guards, too, had doubled since the day we first came.

The princess' attention moved to the man I held under magic. "Who has sent you? Adriata?" she questioned, kneeling to face him.

Her words took me back.

She removed his face covering and he spat in front of her. "You will rot, you *Ybris* bitch."

My eyes fell shut at the thick Darsan accent he spoke in. Adriatian.

"Lovely," she mused. "Did you follow us from Kirkwall?"

He did not answer. He was terrified of her even though he would not show it.

"Tell her," I spat in order, "and I will be the one to kill you, not her." That earned me a death glare from the princess, but no gainsay, so I took that for approval.

His eyes went wide on me. "You betray and kill your kind for her, the bringer of death?" Disdain laced every word and his shadows grew a pale green of disgust.

I shook my head. He had no right for that reaction. "You betrayed and put us to great risk by doing this, the lives and freedom of millions were to be put in danger by your recklessness and old outdated ungrounded fanaticism." I neared him. "You speak and I can at least spare you your honour."

The princess murmured under her breath some sort of curse in Calgnan, still letting me hold to my word.

The man stood silent for a moment before cautiously revealing, "You caught Van and Ester, we figured we did not have long before we got discovered in your lands, before you came hunting for us."

Lies, shades and specks of lies, yet I did not tell her, and to my prayers, neither did Mal. "Why are you on Isjordian lands to begin with?" I questioned, hoping to find the reason for his lie.

"Most for work or trade, some with families to move to Hanai and Solarya, and some to hunt her since they found out she rose from wherever her father had been hiding her. They would rather have her dead than have their freedom and lives back," he lied once again.

I saw her eyes shift at his words, though her face never read of fear and her shadows were still empty. It felt wrong for me to allow her to hear those words. I had failed today to protect her—having to still hear those words from the people that once tried to kill you, from those who had hurt you, must wound your insides more than a blade.

"And you?" I asked, hoping to find a pattern pointing to their lies, but the princess interrupted before I could bring another word out.

"Whatever he is here for, is in illegality and he just attempted murder," she said, rising to her feet. "Deal with him or I will."

Was she really letting me give him the honourable death that I had promised? I stared at her half confused, half thankful and she rolled her eyes. "The men's bod—" I started.

"Will be sent with half of my soldiers back to the wall, now stop tiring me, I am hungry."

Relief fell through all my breaths, but I stood still blinking in surprise in her direction. What had just happened? Was I trying to read too much into it?

We were back on the road mere minutes after I had to kill the man, quick and painless with my magic. She then instructed half of the soldiers to separate with the dead Adriatians to head back to Highwall while we continued ahead towards Tenebrose.

Her head bobbed side to side, fighting her sleep. Every time it dropped to her left, she winced and clutched in pain.

"Lean back," I ordered.

She straightened, pretending to make herself comfortable. "I would rather die."

"Why did you let them go back? What about the burning, burying, drowning and all of that good stuff?"

I felt her tense for a moment. "Exactly to avoid discussing with any of you. As I said, I am famished, whatever got me on the road the quickest. I guess I was wrong since I am still being questioned as you can see." She narrowed her eyes at me over her shoulder displeased with my questioning.

A lie—that was most definitely a lie, but as much as she was too hungry to get into discussion with me, I was glad not to. It was not beyond her to change her mind and run to do all the good stuff she had mentioned if I annoyed her enough.

"Lean back," I repeated, pulling on her jacket.

"Again, I would rather die." She pushed my arms away and further apart not to rest on her waist as they had been. She clutched the hilt of the mount to balance herself, the force probably sending pain to her shoulder. A small whimper escaped her lips as proof.

"Since we are on the jolly topic, could I request a favour?" she asked, adjusting her shoulder.

"What favour?"

"Hypothetically, of course, if you do manage to kill me, could you make sure it is done with your magic. I'd hate to strut around the Mid-world with a bloodied attire and a dagger protruding my chest. You see, I am very partial to my chest and that image would be very inelegant of me."

I rubbed my eyes intensely. "Congratulations, Your Highness, you just added some big points to the list of most madness I've heard in this lifetime."

"You keep a list of the sort? What do you have on me?"

I could not tell anymore if she was joking or being serious. "There is only you there."

"I am one of a kind," she said, puffing her head high, almost with pride. "But the issue is, you have not spent enough time in Isjord. It shall fill in no time."

"Such praises for your people."

"They are far from being my people."

"Isn't it hard being so wary of the world all the time. No trust in gods, not in people either, nor in your family since you have just become a traitor to your father and the crown. Isn't it lonely? One woman against the world?"

"No," she blankly answered. "Also, I am not alone"

"Yes, Nia, your shadow I suppose, and Caiden. What does he do exactly besides wielding a sword on your behalf?"

"He carries my refreshments. Nuts, fruit and stuff."

I grit my jaw, biting out blood from my tongue. "I am being serious."

She turned halfway to him. "Cai, do you have almonds or cashews?"

"Cashews," he said, tossing a bag of them to her.

My mouth had dropped open when she offered the bag to me. "Want one?"

"Why do you do that?"

"Do what?"

"Prove me right, then wrong and then right again."

"I believe that is a conflict you have to solve with yourself."

"Tell me something." My voice grew cold in realisation that she was right again. "What does it cost you? A life that you take?"

"Nothing."

"That is a lie."

"Another conflict you have to solve with yourself."

I pulled the reins and brought us to a halt. "Get off."

She yawned. "Can't we do this later? I am lacking energy at the moment, it won't be as fun."

I dismounted and the rest of the squadron brought to a halt. "Get off. Now."

Caiden approached and she did not move. "I thought I warned you once."

I grabbed her arm and faded us both somewhere in the middle of the forest. Her lids lowered from dizziness and she struggled to steady herself on her feet.

"Answer me."

She chuckled tiredly. "You wish to know this badly?" she asked, her eyes gleaming with malice. "Nothing but pure, pure satisfaction. Overwhelming, like a full breath of air after a long day inside."

"Lies," I spat. "Lies and more lies."

Everyone lost something when they took a life—most lost their innocence, empathy, humanity. What did this one lose when she had either of that?

"What do you wish to know? That is so hard and my soul consumes at the sully of my hands with blood?" she asked, raising a brow. "But it is not true. What I lie on the other hand, is how much more I want, how dissatisfying and much more hungry it makes me feel. How much more I crave."

I shook my head. I was wrong, monsters could feel compassion, too, they could hurt too. How could I forget? "You are truly that—the monster we hunted."

She laughed darkly. "A ravenous one."

"They are people," I shouted. "Living, breathing people, with lives—lives that you take. They die hurting and causing others to hurt."

Something shifted in her expression. "I was not a person then, neither were my siblings or my mother? What were we? What am I, Kilian?" she shouted back, coming close to me, her breathing ragged and furious. "Am I not a person? Was I not then even if I am not anymore?"

"You—"

"I what?"

My feet tripped while I backed away from her. "You were wronged and hurt. So wronged and so hurt. I have no word for what was done to you and I cannot have a say in what you were and what you are, but I cannot help but revolt against what you are becoming."

"This is who I have always been, what it was planned for me to become. The only thing that has changed is my purpose. Bitter, isn't it, the taste of your own doing?"

Terribly right again.

"Will it make you happy, this, your revenge?"

"Happy?" She flared at the verge beyond offence. "I cannot wait all my life for my sun to start shining again for a bit of light. I can never be happy, what I can be is satisfied."

"You cannot light the world on fire for light either, princess. Everyone can be happy, you are just choosing the path of unhappiness at the expense of your soul."

She stilled, her eyes wavering slightly. Anger or hurt I could not tell yet another time. "You assume choices on my behalf as if you know me, as if you have been me. Isn't it easy? To assume? Isn't it easy to diverge all faults of your own wrongs as justifiable and then judge my own? Isn't it easy being you, the hero I waited my whole life to tear my own cage, only to put me in another?" she asked calmly, straightening herself, and it was then I felt the power of her rightness, the truth of her confession. "When you learn of forced grief let me know then, the choices you would make in my stead. Tell me then that having to sell your soul for revenge doesn't seem a bad idea, that one's soul doesn't have any worth if it is broken to begin with."

Right, so right.

"Tell me," I said, taking a deep breath. It wasn't sympathy what I'd been raised to feel for her. "What you truly feel." I didn't care for it, I just needed to hear it. I needed to. I could not feel it, I couldn't see it, I could not understand it. It hunted me, it confused me. It should not confuse me, not her. She was simple and plain, she was her—she was...she was....on heavens, what was she?

"I didn't lie."

I tensed again. "You did."

She took off towards the forest. "Take me back, now."

"My answer," I called, chasing behind her.

She unsheathed one dagger and quickly spun on her heels, throwing it to me.

I veered to the side, the blade passing half an inch away from almost meeting my head. She had good aim. "I need my head to hear your answer, princess."

She unsheathed her other dagger and before she could throw it at me, I faded in front of her and grabbed her wrist. She winced and dropped the dagger, only to catch it with her other hand and aiming at my stomach. Both her wrists were then tight on my grip.

I tsked, shaking my head. "No holes in me, I need to be solid to tell this tale around those withering bonfires you love."

She made to kick my crotch, but I caught her leg between my knees. "But my children, princess, they need to exist just to hear how I got the glorious answer I am looking for."

Her foot went under my shin, toppling the both of us to the ground. I rounded her in my embrace and rolled her over my chest to take the impact of the fall before rolling her back under me, pinning her arms crossed her chest.

She panted and wiggled furiously. "Let me go!"

"You know the way."

She suddenly halted her struggle, panting and breathless. Beads of sweat coating her temples, her eyes heavy on me—heavy with fever and surrender. She stood silent for a moment beneath me, taking jagged breaths before her body completely loosened in my grip. Surrendered, she laid on the cold snow, her eyes casting heavenward, lost.

"It doesn't feel like anything." Soft notes left her lips, yet they shook the very core of me. "Nothing feels like anything. Pain doesn't feel painful, I don't hurt anymore. A hug no longer is warm, it is just an embrace. A smile is only the work of muscles, nothing ticks to make me smile, I've just learnt the cue for it. I don't know what I feel at that moment you ask. I just know that I feel something very faint, but nothing I can recognise, nothing too grave or warm or more than a tickle. I am...so bored. Every day...to do it all over again and feel nothing. It is so boring to feel nothing. I wish I felt what you think I feel." Her head tilted forward, the golden gaze sinking into mine. "Here you have it, my truth."

Nothing.

Blood began spreading under her in veins of crimson over the white crystals. A painting—a strange painting, incomprehensible.

She shut her eyes and took a deep breath before she smiled just slightly. "It is liberating, I have to admit. Dying...feels very liberating."

And I was lost in that moment of words and heavy confessions, lost in the crookedness of that smile that bore no symbol of happiness. "You will not die. Not on my watch."

"You are right, I won't die," she said somewhat regretfully. "It never wanted me, you know. Dying knows me, it passes, ignores, and makes fun of me...all the time. It never once wanted me. It never pitied me. People are so versed in pitying me, yet the one thing I wanted to take pity on me cared so very little." She giggled mirthlessly. A drop of silver slipped out of a golden eye and down her temple. "I could bet anything, even if you tried to nail a sword in my heart right now, I would not die."

She told me a truth, yet I found it harder to understand compared to her lies.

A breeze of wind blew and rustled tree branches, snow lifting in the air as mist. It became the only sound beside our hearts at that moment. She blinked slowly up at me. "If you have no intention of trying, would you take me back? I am starving. Or try it after I've eaten." She shook her head, clutching her eyes tightly shut. "Mid-world cannot welcome me starving. I'd be such a terrible glutton. How could someone with my face be a glutton?"

She made it so easy to forget, maybe she wanted to forget what she'd just told me.

"You're terribly mad."

"You will be in so much trouble," she sighed. "Once this fever passes and I realise what I've allowed you to do, what you have made me say."

"Unless you become a glutton. I eat too healthy, you would not even sniff near me without feeling sick."

She giggled jollily. "Careful planning, well done, Adriatian."

It was dizzying, the sound of her laugh. "Your obsession with hating all green vegetables has become my salvation."

She blinked surprised. "How did you know that?"

"Not hard to notice the cringe at their sight, and your careful, tactical methods of picking out all traces of them from your dish."

"Broccoli is vile. Do not make me start on peppers and that shiny leather atop," she made a gagging sound and it almost made me laugh.

"Why green only?" I asked, letting go of her hands.

She shrugged. "When I was young I used to dislike red vegetables too, and it just seemed odd to put only that aside. I began lining the green along it so it didn't feel lonely. You know, like when you lose a slipper and you are stuck with a lone one." She shivered. "Doesn't that bother you as well? Why is a shoe lonesome, it comes in a pair?"

Shaking my head, I said, "I've never heard so much madness come from a sole mouth."

I began pushing myself from her, but she gripped my jacket tight, holding me still. "Answer me now. Truly, why do you hate me? I am sure it's not because you were raised like most to hate me. There is something else. I know I am right."

I glanced at where she held me, how she still shivered. "You are wrong, it is just because of that."

She smiled knowingly, reading through my lie. "You lie so pretty to me, Adriatian. But your lies are yours. Isn't that what your goddess says? You defy all your upbringings just to find my truths. *We read emotion, but one's' emotion is but theirs to show, hide, fear and adore'*. Astrum liber has such pretty lies, too. Unlike you, I don't care about your lies. Different from you, truths are featherweight, they lift no change to me."

"Let go of me."

She let her hands fall and then lifted them as if in surrender. "See how easy it was to let go of someone when they ask you to? Even an inhuman knows to read a situation better than you."

"Your verbal sparring is commendable."

"Once, it was all I had, Adriatian. It has become perhaps my sharpest blade."

"What happened to calling me Kilian?"

She put two fingers on my forehead and pushed my head back. "What happened with boundaries?"

I nodded, biting a strange smile back. "Sharp indeed."

"Yet you stroke it with such delight," she purred, fluttering her lashes all tease and flirt. "Haven't you been told not to play with blades?"

"Don't you tire from the metaphors?"

She tsked. "Come now, I know you like them."

"If I have to admit liking something of yours, it will have to be your silence." And perhaps...those eyes.

I helped her stand and faded us back to the squadron. I had my truth, yet it weighed heavier than all the lies. What did I expect to hear? Did I want to know that she took pleasure in her kills, to condemn my detest for her just?

Heated stares bunched from the soldiers in my direction. All loomed with desire to tear my head off.

"Head or all limbs first?" Caiden asked, unsheathing his sword.

"No one touches him," she ordered, dismissing all her battle-ready soldiers. "He is mine."

On command, everyone retreated, even Caiden who a second ago stood murderous. They all obeyed as if her words stood above the law of everything. Were they that scared? Even him, her friend?

"To kill," I added. "*Yours* to kill. Just so we are clear on that."

She bit her lip, holding in a smile. Her tired eyes tracing me top to bottom and it...frustrated me enough to have me shift on my feet.

"Yes," she said before mounting my horse. "To kill, of course."

20

WOUNDS AND HEALERS

SNOWLIN

SAMUEL ARRIVED BY THE stables at the same time we did, his eyes widened when he took in the scar on my neck, the matted blood and the bandage across my chest under my jacket.

"One of them will explain otherwise I might eat your horse, Sam," I said, trying to move past him.

"I will send a healer to your chambers." I motioned to talk back, but he interrupted me. "You will be seen by one or I will tell your father. Take your pick."

Letting out a long sigh that sent shooting pain down my whole body, I turned to narrow my eyes at him. "Your soldiers are right, you can be vile at times."

He patted my cheek. "Whatever keeps you healthy and alive."

The warmth of the castle wrapped around me like a vile hug in scorching summer, the one that left you scraping the feeling of sweat from your skin. But I savoured the smell of fresh baked bread as we went down the servant dining chambers. Sometimes the scent would fill me quicker than food, sometimes it would be all I had for breakfast, dinner and lunch.

Ken shook his head at my bloodied sight, but went right back to cook my favourite stew. My soldiers all sat hungry next to us and my three guards positioned themselves across me side by side, looking like they had plenty to say.

Ignoring their stares, I tapped my fingers impatiently on the table, shifting in my seat as my stomach roared like mountain beasts.

I glared at the silver eyed snake with the corner of my eye and as if noticing the heavy prayers for him to bleed excessively from his skull, he turned and blankly stared at me for a few moments before he laid back on his chair and raised a brow full of challenge. I held back a chain of curses. He would not get the honours of experiencing my fury just yet, so I flashed him a tight-lipped smile.

He huffed a sigh in response and shook his head. This silent conversation between us was more infuriating than when he used words, ones he spoke very sparingly anyway and full of opinions.

The second Ken placed the hot bowl in front of me, my eyes rolled back at the delicious steam laced in the smell of spices. I ate so fast that I might have coughed over a dozen times, and each instance, Cai laughed and the Adriatians stared confused.

"Your father will tear this place down if he finds out you abandon dinner with him to eat here," Nia said, leaning on the archway of the dining chamber. She must have faded back before our arrival. "But you might choke yourself to death before he gets a chance. Chew then swallow, Snow, chew then swallow," she teased and the two friendly fools in front of me shook with silent laughter, the joke of course missing mister stern.

Throwing Nia a very polite hand gesture, I resumed my eating.

"Ah, yes, one of the many manners of a princess," she said, taking a seat.

She and Cai dove deep in conversation regarding some sort of herb, all conversation my ears had turned to muffled noises of bees. I leaned on my bench, halfway fading to sleep when my head jerked to the left and made me almost jump up from the pain on my shoulder. I hissed and clutched my wound. "Shit."

Nia moved quickly, pulling my hair covering the wound on my shoulder behind my back. "W-what...is this?"

"A dagger hit me," I said, yawning.

"I believe the correct term is stabbed," Cai explained. "She helped Kilian stab her, as one does."

She turned looking at me bewildered, waiting for a longer answer, one that I was too tired to tell.

"It was what I deserved. After all I am so very twisted," I mocked, clutching my wound still radiating with pain.

Kilian crossed his arms. "Something else to say, princess?" he questioned in his stuffed ass voice of a prick.

"Please, if I did, I would most certainly not spare you my thoughts. Right now, however, rather than words, a few actions requiring a dagger do seem more appropriate."

He held his stern features and that dimple made a show. "Let's meet at the training courts sometimes, I might have to show you how to actually point the sharp end at the one you want to hurt."

I narrowed my eyes at his teasing remark. "Oh, I hurt you. I am your precious sweet little pawn, after all. You want me back in Adriata shining and polished, right?"

"You forgot to mention devious. Precious, sweet, little devious pawn."

He was in for a sweet ride, I would show him just how devious I could get pretty soon. "Miniscule detail, darling."

We were sneering and glaring at one another and the others had halted to share glances between myself and the silver eyed snake.

"They have bonded," Mal said gleefully, planting a hand atop his brother's shoulder. "A promising start to an eternal friendship."

"Shut up, Malik," both his brother and I said in unison, startling ourselves.

Mal's smirk grew. "The bond is really deep. Can you two read each other's thoughts now, is that what the glaring is about?

"Glaring?" Cai asked, not pausing as he chewed on a piece of bread. "It looks like something on the lines of love at first sight."

"Look again," Nia chimed in. "I think it's a staring competition. Five silver dar she wins."

"My bet is on her, too," Mal leaned in.

"No, no," Cai added. "Mine is on him. Two summers ago, a little girl threw a pine at her catching an eye and ever since, she keeps double blinking at times."

Kilian's attention snapped away from me to them. "Has she not had it looked at?"

Instead of answering, they brought out five silver dar handing it to Cai who jollily counted his victory before pocketing it.

I didn't understand.

"You did that on purpose," Nia accused. "She would have eaten that little girl if such a thing had happened."

Cai shrugged. "He kept asking me during the duty we shared about her paleness, the limp on her left foot, why she stretches her back after horse-riding, if she slept or ate or rested. It was a random try, I never thought it would work."

"Do you often do this?" Mal asked. "Counter bet?"

My friends nodded and Nia added, "Reverse psychology."

I glanced over at him again, still dour faced and unbothered while staring at some random wall ahead. Was he afraid I'd suddenly drop dead before the agreement?

Cai threw his coin up in the air. "What can this much Isjordian money buy me, Nia?"

"A proper haircut?"

"Hey, my hair is almost the same as his," Mal leaned in, wearing a frown of offence. "I can spare enough for your poor self, too."

I tried to laugh but everything was fogging, and I felt hot and cold and feverish. An arm wrapped around my waist, holding me up. "Come, Cakes, that was enough entertainment for today, the healer is waiting."

The Medi-healer examined my wound carefully. "Burning Hemera, you should be more careful, the dagger had nearly pierced a large blood vessel."

I knew not to do that—I drove it there particularly to avoid any major damage. I was angry, not a fool.

She raised a glowing palm over my wound. The feel of magic stitching my flesh shut sizzled like oil over heat. Solaryans were blessed by the goddess Cyra of sun, light, and healing. Medi healers were one of the three Solaryan Aura. They were the best and quickest healers in the continent. Through their magic, Medi healers mended the flesh from within, stitching all of it to the previous state. Solarya also had Aura that healed magical abilities, restored and amplified them—called Magi healers. As tempting as many found that to be, it came at an excruciating cost for the Aura. Some had turned to dust after not being trained well or enough that they had channelled and poured their own mana by mistake onto the person they were healing. Magi healers were rare, highly trained and usually went through decade long apprenticeships. Probably why many were said to be reluctant to even go through the route. Knowing my father's greed, he probably had a stash load of them hidden in a safe house for him to use.

She gave me a scalding look. "I have seen you more often in a couple of weeks than any soldier in all their service."

"You've fallen into my trap of seducing you," I said, giving her a wink.

She clicked her tongue at me. "I am married."

I leaned onto my side. "How is married life? Fancy a mistress? I will be gentle with you."

She pushed onto my wound and I winced at the burn. "Keep looking after it, you know I can't heal it completely." She placed a moist bandage over it, stinking foul of herbs and alcohol. "I will remove the scar in the next session."

"No," I said quietly. "The scar stays."

All my scars stay, they were mine. Mine to remember, forget, use.

She glanced over the marred skin, probably wondering how a princess wished to remain marked. "It stays then."

Nia laid in my bed, eyes glued to pages of a brown leather-bound book. "Cai said you went by the Bruma halls again though I told you to stay away from there. If I repeat it to you once more to keep away from unnecessary danger, I will send you back to Alaric."

More than once, she has kept putting herself in the front row of danger, one I never would normally allow.

She didn't answer, I didn't think she even heard me. "And she is gone," I said and leaned over the pages she was intensively studying. "Mirkroot, isn't that like an aphrodisiac? Nia, Nia," I teased, amused.

She frowned at me. "Mirkroot is that only for humans, it is something else completely to Aura. The plant is magic grown from Koy. To Aura it acts as an enhancer, combining with magic to heighten its flow. It doesn't add more to it, just courses a heavier concentration of your mana in one gathered moment, but only for a while. Mirkroot is deadly, Snow."

I shuffled in bed, making myself comfortable. "Why are you inquiring about this?"

"The Bruma halls stank of it every time I visited. In Fernfoss, the herbalist would keep it in the front desk so the whole place reeked of it. Imagine my surprise when Bruma halls brought me the lovely memory of lusting couples who lacked vigour. Verglasers were strange, agitated and on edge, their magic almost sizzling in the air and leaking out of control."

"What?" I scooted near her, flipping through the book pages. "You think the Verglasers are consuming it, do you think my father is giving it to them?"

"I don't know, but someone definitely is."

"Is that why Cai barely took that one by the western bay ruins?"

After each trip, each batch of Verglasers that he'd fought and caught heading toward the Volants, he'd returned even more tired and worn out. Now we knew why.

She bit on her lip. "I never believed the stories of that fool, but he said that one of the soldiers blasted ice about a mile within their radius. I'm thinking he didn't lie about it. I will have to enquire a bit more about this. Why would anyone sacrifice a perfectly capable Aura for what...maybe a year at best of exhilarated magic?"

I snatched her book and threw it across the room. "Renick is not someone I take lightly. You will not mess in his court anymore. No more of this, it's an order."

She raised her head to protest, but I threw her a glare. "I didn't come here to make sacrifices, Nia. You are to end it. If Verglasers are consuming mirkroot, damned they be, I care not. We are not going up against them, not with my plan."

"Alright," she sighed, dropping back on the bed and thankfully giving up.

"He is preparing for war, isn't he? What I can't understand are these confusing patterns he is leaving."

Father was usually simple, leaving traces here and there with an obvious result, but now I'd found him spread all over and there also was this confusing deal with Adriata.

"I am telling you, it is not your father. He is greedy, not stupid to sacrifice so many of his Aura. Alaric was right, some tutors were complaining about the lowering number of Aura in Isjord." She approached, laying by my side and fiddling with a long strand of my hair. "Why do you pick fights with him? You ignore and bear Malik just fine."

Surprised at the sudden change of conversation, I turned to face her. "He is not scared of me."

"Then he is an idiot."

"Not anymore, he found out about the poison micro dosing just by looking at my blood, eyes and lips. He could tell every single one you've been giving me."

"What?" she asked, wide eyed before biting her lip in concentration. "You think he might try and poison you with something else now that he knows?"

"He snapped a man's neck without even touching him, poisoning is the least of my troubles. There have been several chances to kill me, and he hasn't. They might truly need me."

He'd fade us in the middle of nowhere to ask for my truth, not to harm, kill, threaten or anything at that. He might have been given the opportunity a thousand times to do just that, whisk me away to kill me with no issue and without anyone even doubting, yet he didn't and hadn't.

"He is Adriatian," she whispered, throwing a look at the doors.

"And he despises me deeply, but he won't kill me, not him, not his brother either, not yet," I said, maybe a bit too assuredly. "How do I make him scared? He is used to seeing me kill. Shall I truly sacrifice a lamb, paint a Crafter's halo and chant a summoning verse in Borsich while doing a crazy dance on a full moon?"

She groaned and gradually laughed. "Let it go, would you. Drop this conquest, you won't break him."

"I don't want to break him, only....you know....stretch his mind."

"You are a maniac."

I rolled my eyes. "So you keep saying." I spread my arms wide on the mattress, rolling the ball of my feet up and down the soft sheets. "I like playing maniac with him." He fed it while many avoided it, ran away, gave away to it or even tore apart from it, that is if they didn't stroke it enough to end up dead.

Nia gave me a look of concern, almost doubting if she should say what she said next, "He reads through your lies."

How? I blink frantically at her. "How do you know?"

She sank further in the bed, fiddling with the tips of her gloves. "I feel it, like I normally feel through my magic. The air shifts around him, too, sometimes waves of magic flow out of him, overwhelmingly and then poof. Nothing."

I cringe. Was it bad that I understood nothing? "Scary," I said, propping my head on my hand.

She hit me with a pillow. "Just don't mess with him too much, he is a bit odd."

I blew a breath and leaned on my side. "How is Freja holding amongst the piglet den, is my oar sturdy?"

"No one has called her any demeaning words yet. She has offended two captains and a general so far and made a trade deal with west Koy for timber. You have created a star pupil and obtained another city. Two are on your side now, who's next?"

"I have a few ideas. Pen is inquiring into something for me, but first we deal with the Adriatians in Brisk."

"Heavens," she exclaimed sitting up. "You are defiling the fifteen-year-old."

Cai and Mal had been ready by the door when I made my way for breakfast with father. I had hidden my wounds under a long sleeved emerald dress. A short cape was thrown atop for another layer of lies and my hair was braided to the side to cover the new scar on my neck. Penelope had blushed my cheeks after claiming that I looked like the dead this morning, probably the lack of sleep and the blood loss from yesterday.

"So?" I asked, itching myself under the cape.

"The two Adriatians were faded by Nia to a safehouse in Kirkwall and are with Sam. We sent two decoy bodies for both the couple. And I found this," Cai said, handing me a letter.

The Inn is compromised, see if the princess has any prisoners, do not harm.

The men that attacked us had lied. My father had sent people after me directly after finding out what I had done in Pine Inn. He also did not know Nia had snuck into the Inn to stay the night there waiting for us, fading two decoys and then fading back the two Adriatians to a safe house.

"How did he get the news so quickly? I cannot believe he sent Adriatians. Pretty good actors, too."

We had expected it, but I'd thought a patrol would intercept us, not a whole gang of Adriatians. Father had a flare for dramatic effects.

"He is very subtle in his work," Cai said snidely. "Be careful, Cakes, this was a close one. If he sends someone to inquire about them in Adriata, it will not take long for him to find out you have tricked him. That is if his subtle mannerism doesn't fail him once again."

"He will be too distracted dealing with me, I am not planning a calm next few days."

"I hope not, there would not be a healer good enough to fix you from a state of rest."

I handed him the receipt back. "They lied to me, the guards." Kilian and Mal, both had to have known that the attackers from yesterday had lied.

"They didn't," Cai said, folding the receipt back inside his jacket. "Both came to me and Nia to let us both know the men were compromised and not acting in their own interest."

"What?"

"Kilian stopped his brother, told him and us to let you know only after you'd healed."

"You should have come and told me."

He frowned. "Why?"

"I don't like thinking I've been lied to when I have not been lied to. Next time tell me. I have enough hiding from me, don't you become one, too."

The happy usual four sat in silence when I made my way to my table seat.

Fren huffed a laugh. "What has happened to you?" she asked with a teasing nasally tone and proceeded to survey my withered state with such satisfaction.

"Do not worry, it is not from fucking Elias all night long, that would be another day," I said, fluttering my lashes and giving her a mocking tight-lipped smile. The bleached bitch.

Her eyes and mouth widened, face twisting in a cry. "Father, please."

The man had stopped and rested a hand on his forehead, his eyes on me while his bastard wailed. His jaw tightened enough that the room echoed the gritting of his teeth.

I giggled at her helplessness and the delightful silence of my father. "Now, now, Fren dear, father cannot buy or gift you cock. You got to get out and find one yourself. I doubt Elias will find bedding you an alternative. Also, everyone knows about the Venzors and their lovers. Prepare for batches of bastards and half breeds like yourself to fly left and right," I said motioning my hand back and forth.

I barely held a laugh at her sulked reaction, her eyes were almost popping out of their sockets. Instead, I cringed at the ghastly sight she became. Father again did not speak yet again, instead he rubbed his hand on his forehead enough that I thought the friction would draw blood.

"Do not speak to my sister like that!" Reuben exclaimed, smashing a fist to the table, making the cutlery jiggle.

"Oh hush, Reuben, you can barely handle your own cutlery so do not go flicking a sword at me. Quite the sight you two, the ghastly spirit set to marry a Lord's son to keep the said Lord from revolting, and a wannabe heir whose sharp tongue has only ever been over his own arse. Cheers to that," I said, toasting my goblet in the air.

Interestingly, I was really in the mood today, what had the healer given me? The strain on my tongue was unusually loose.

Moreen looked back and forth between me and father—my oddly silent father. "Snowlin, please, my child, let's have breakfast quietly as all families," she finally interfered after seeing her tensed children ready to pounce at me.

"Moreen, you tend to stick your head in a lot of peacock arses, but stay out of mine," I said, pointing to her hair while I munched on a plum jam toast.

"All done?" father finally asked, his face had heated red and reflected the flame in his eyes. How much alike they were to mine, but how very different they burned.

I stood, taking an apple in my hand before bowing to him. "For now."

"Have someone drop the report of your patrol to Kirkwall to my chambers. I heard you found Adriatians, how did that happen?"

I halted and turned to him, schooling my features down. "I put a reward notice, a private one regarding anyone with information on Adriatians. Call me paranoid, but I do worry for my well being considering their kingdom is tying an agreement with me as a pawn, probably not to their subject's satisfaction. I was right to do so when a group of them attacked us yesterday. You see, I might not be your *Ybris,* but I am still theirs."

"A private notice?"

I scowled innocently. "What? Is there something the matter?"

He waved a hand and nodded. "No, you are right," he said calmly before throwing me an examining look. "Did they hurt you?"

Holding back a laugh, I tried to let my fatigue resurface. "Well, do I look fine to you?" I had to play sheep for the wolf to get close enough to stab a dagger through its ribs.

He sighed. "Make sure to see a healer."

By mid-afternoon, my lids felt heavy with fatigue and lack of sleep, so I headed to my bedroom. My whole body felt sore and in need of rest, but unconsciously I was fighting it away. I rustled around uncomfortably till I tangled in my bed sheets unable to untangle without the help of a dagger.

I had barely fallen to light slumber when I got transported to the dark void of my own head. My dreams were of Thora and Eren again. Father held a sword to their throats this time, laughing as they laid slain beneath his feet, blood pooling around their bodies. They both looked in my direction as if they could really see me.

"Are we dead, Snow?" They said in unison and I jumped out of my dream, sweating and panting.

Throwing a sweater and a cloak, I headed to claim rest somewhere dreams were chased away by the very same presence of them.

Nia and Kilian stood outside my door in grave silence. I startled them more than myself when I suddenly opened it.

Kilian pushed from the wall opposite my door and rushed toward me looking concerned. "Is there something wrong?"

I shook my head, short of an answer that wasn't a lie, and headed down the corridor.

"Snow, wait," Nia called in a half voice, but I did not respond.

I had to go see them before I could convince myself this was all a cruel nightmare. That they were alive still and I was unable to get out of my own head.

"Snow," she repeated, but I did not halt. She then dug her heels. "Snowlin!" Her shout pierced the silent air of the winter garden.

I knew she was worried, but I did not wish to explain myself in front of the silver eyed snake behind me. "All is fine, Nia, just let me be, please."

Before I reached the last turn on the non ending maze, I turned to them. Kilian threw a pair of boots down to the ground and signalled his head for me to wear, I had not noticed I had come without them. "Put those on."

"Both of you wait here, no one comes beyond this point," I ordered firmly, putting the boots on and then pointed towards Kilian. "Especially you."

They both obeyed since their footsteps halted behind me.

I awoke stiff as a log, a pile of snow atop me and my body half frozen. Gently, I pulled my body up, aching at the slightest movement, my feet and fingers completely numb.

Kilian still leaned by a frosted wall and Nia sat on the floor, arms around her knees and half frozen.

It was then I shook my senses completely awake. I had forgotten about them being here all night. Guilt and shame coursed through me. Nia should have dismissed him, and she should have headed for her chambers knowing I would be fine. My father's guards already knew when I came out here and none even dared step in the maze. This whole area was forbidden to be stepped on. I was the only one who ever came here.

"Nia!" I hissed.

She stood unsteady, a hand on her forehead, looking tired and cold. "He would not budge from here and I would most certainly not leave you alone with him," she said, glaring towards Kilian who casually stretched his neck.

"I am under orders not to leave your side. I would have not moved whatever way your friend found to dismiss me."

Steam was about to blow out of my ears. "So if I jumped off a cliff, you would come chasing after me, right? How about we put that to test, shall we?" I spat out angrily.

"I have not come to fan you, but to guard your twisted head." He grabbed my arm, pulling me to him. "This is not a game, princess, like it or not, right now you are precious and greatly hunted. I will not let you run in anyone's trap for the fun of it."

A shudder of pain shot up my spine and limbs, my knees weakened and I toppled to fall. He wrapped an arm around my waist and pulled me up and close to him, tracing the other hand down my arm as if searching for grave wounds.

Nia unsheathed a dagger. "Let her go."

"Are you hurt, where?" he queried calmly without paying mind to my friend. His voice never raised a tone higher than usual. He was annoyingly calm, all the time.

I shook away from his touch and grabbed Nia's arm whose deadly stare was piercing holes in Kilian's head.

"I'd think it would at least made you smile."

He dropped his head back as if to hold onto his calm. "I will make sure to smile next time. For now, get inside before you make the agreement fall apart along with the rest of you."

Snow fell briskly and mantled our vision, but I could see the resembling look Kilian wore, the same my father had once given me. I was meant to serve a purpose; my whole existence was to fulfil a purpose. The only value my life had was that the others gave it. I'd grown used to getting that look, but from him it seemed so unacceptable for some reason.

The warmth of my room felt prickling rather than comforting, my skin almost searing and melting. Kilian nudged the fading fireplace, feeding it kindling while stealing glances at Nia's actions when she peeled my clothes to reveal the greyed flesh of my arm.

He came forward, his eyes on my arm. "I thought Isjordians didn't get affected by the cold?"

"Well, I am not exactly Isjordian."

He took my words with some surprise. He was so quick to remind me of my place, yet he was forgetting. "Get her warmed salt and a cloth," he ordered Nia, taking off his gloves and then jacket.

All muscle and strength, intimidating in all his might, yet Nia rose face to face with him, arms wide while she was shielding me. "You are not touching her, she needs a Medi healer."

He reached close enough to her that she had to look up at him like a ceiling chandelier. "If she loses her arm, you will then send an armless princess instead of a sleep deprived, hungry, fatigued, maddening and crazed one to Adriata. Now move," he ordered, making his way to me.

"Nia," I called and then gave her a nod. "Let him."

She took short glances at me before forcing herself to move away.

I had my other hand on the hilt of one of my daggers, fear had substituted pain. I realised it was fear of him, not losing my arm.

He kneeled before me, helping remove my sweater, leaving me in my exposing nightgown before turning to take my gloves off.

Involuntarily, I pulled my hands back.

His gaze turned to mine, unwavering and cold like a frozen lake. "The gloves, princess, I am not asking." Within a beat, he pulled them off despite my protest. Confused, he looked between me and my bandaged hands before unravelling the white gauze that had soaked and almost frosted to my flesh. He fixated on my palms for a long while, on the skin coated with old and fresh half-moon scars and slashes all over. Unexpectedly, he ran his thumb over them and I instinctively balled them up in fists, pulling them back over my chest.

"My arm," I said, half taken aback and frustrated at him. "You were to do something to it."

Nia handed him the warm cloth and he placed it over my arm before notifying me of his real intention. "I will use my magic."

Nia looked between us wide eyed and ready to refuse on my behalf.

Dread and fear circled around me. I would rather lose my arm than have him do that.

As if he could sense my thoughts, he sighed and narrowed his gall, demanding gaze on me. "I am not taking you back missing a limb. I promised them I would bring you how I found you. Remember? Shining and polished."

Objection stood at the tip of my tongue, yet I gave in and extended my arm to him. He ran a hand over the greyed flesh a few times. His hands were rough, but they were warm and gentle—terribly gentle. I stared confused back and forth at his actions, almost making myself dizzy till I felt something like worms crawling under my skin. The sensation almost made me flinch away, but the greyed flesh began turning to its normal colour.

I traced a finger over my arm half in disbelief that this was not some form of trickery and illusion.

"I moved your blood round to normal circulation, just like how we move objects. It's how we heal some of our wounded and prevent blood from clotting," he explained to clear the confusion that was readable on my face.

"If I was not your pawn, would you have helped me? Would you have helped someone like me?"

There was nothing in the agreement that said missing a limb would prevent it from happening. I could bet a good cheek they'd be most pleased if I returned limbless.

He glanced shortly up at me, shifting on his knees almost uncomfortable. "The truth?"

I rolled my eyes. "No, lie to me, Adriatian."

He continued tracing my skin and quietly said, "I would have not helped you."

"Look at me when you say it." It was my time to demand his confusing truths.

He halted, hesitated, and then slowly looked up at me with that stare of his. "I would have not laid a finger to help you, that arm could have fallen off along with the rest of you, shredded to a thousand pieces and I would have done absolutely nothing, maybe even smiled."

"Lies," I murmured, lost in his glassy telling stare, the ring of cold around them tall and unnerving. Alaric had taught me that truths always softened someone's eyes.

"You told me to lie to you."

I scowled. "It was sarcasm, you absolute fool."

He raised a dark brow then nodded before returning his attention to my arm. "Keep the warm cloth on still, the wound might be gone, but there will be soreness still over the flesh. A warm bath might help," he said lastly, turning to Nia who nodded and headed to do just that.

He pulled my hands down, examining the redness there, gently running his fingers over them before tuning my palms upward and exposing my scars again.

I resisted and fought the urge to close them.

Expressionless, he remained concentrated on his work. Not a word, not a single reaction. Why did it annoy me more than him speaking, his silence was deafening. After he finished, the look he gave me almost made me flinch.

"Don't look at me like that, martyrdom is not my style. Whatever you are contemplating over is only your wrong conclusions."

"I am not looking at you in any way," he answered blankly.

"You, Kilian, have a total of three facial expressions: the angry, the disgusted and this last one which I refuse to take the liberty and call it pity because that is what I despise the most."

He stared at me through pinched features like he was about to solve an enigmatic puzzle. "There is no pity."

"That indeed is the motto of your kind, but I have seen pity enough to easily recognize it."

"You are wrong," he said, standing. He put his jacket back on, turning to me again, running his stare shamelessly all over half naked me. "I'd suggest you stop this extreme sport of testing the most unusual spots to sleep and just settle in your bed, inside where your limbs don't freeze."

How dare he? "And I'd suggest you pull your eyes out, but hey, each to their own."

He dared to huff a scoff shaking his head. "*Dahaara.*"

Had he just cursed me in his wretched tongue?

"The men who attacked us lied to you and you lied to me."

He halted just before reaching the door. "I did."

"Why?"

"Why not? I am your guard, not your henchman."

"Yet you told Cai."

He turned then, all fury. He was a scary man, now he'd become something of fright. "I told him not to tell you till you healed. I figured you cracked this one yourself."

"Flattered, truly," I said, standing. "But you're my guard not my friend, less alone one to make decisions on my behalf."

"They would have not told you anything different. They'd already made peace with their deaths."

"Would you like to know whose bidding they were doing?" I knew he didn't want to hear it, expecting to find out the bitter truth of his people.

"They were there to hurt you, it doesn't matter who they were doing it for."

"Worry not, it wasn't Adriata, but my father."

His dark brows gathered in a scowl. Even doing that he looked deadly handsome. "What?"

"That was why, Kilian darling, you should have told me."

He narrowed his stare utterly confused, possibly considering my words a lie from the doubtful tone of his voice when he asked, "Why would he send someone to hurt you?"

His eyes traced my slow movement towards the room. "Had you not lied to me, perhaps I would have told you." I pushed the straps of my nightgown down and just before it fell off me, he turned around and left.

***

A warm bath indeed had helped with my wound. Just not the one still open in my chest.

"Are we dead, Snow?"

"You are," I said to myself, my dry voice bouncing over the emerald tiled bathroom and over the sweet flower-scented water. "You are, you all are."

Words I had never admitted to myself, an answer that I had always avoided even giving myself. I sank beneath the hot surface of the bath. Image after image of that night flashing in front of my darkened sight.

21

TRUTH AND FROST

KILIAN

FOR THE PAST FEW days, I had just laid in bed tired and ready for rest after my guard shifts, but sleep was hard to come. Everytime I tried to shut my eyes, my head would start spinning the images of her scarred hands and her tear rimmed golden eyes over and over as if wanting to remind me of my own faults. Why had she slept in the garden? Had she lied about the Adriatians sent from her father? Had she done it to test me again? It didn't feel like she'd lied to me.

Penelope, the young red-haired servant, handed me a blue uniform similar to Nia's and Caiden's. "The exact words were: stop parading as walking Adriatian flags."

I examined the navy thin coat and trousers. "So I am to parade as an Isjordian one? Freeze, too?"

"They are magic threaded from wool grown in Koy and then tailored by a Crafter to seal in heat. They will keep you warm better than four layers of coats." She unravelled the rest of the clothing items and handed them to me. "Snowlin does not like attention, especially the one you are giving her. I'd wear them."

"Does that beast have anything she likes?"

Penelope halted and raised her hand to count, "Sun, lavender baths, romance books but the lewd ones, those the castle library had banned a few years ago. She makes me go all over to Tenebrose city library for those," she complained, sulking at the memory and I almost smiled. "She likes that ridiculous song 'Children of the Forest', grapes, loads of grapes, but they have to be firm. She will spit out any soggy fruit, she says they remind her of eyeballs. The colour grey, storms, spinning on her toes till she collapses when she misses the night sky. Is that enough?"

I nodded. "That is plenty, she is just as odd as I thought her to be." I put the white shirt on and I couldn't resist the entertainment and asked, "What are her dislikes?"

Penelope stilled in silence for a few moments before pinching down in concentration. "Well...you for one. She is particularly furious at you at the moment. The other day I found a piece of paper with your name on it and she'd crossed it about a thousand times, almost tearing through it." I bit onto my lip, holding my amusement in while she continued. "Hair pins, meat, and oh gods, fish. Give her fish and she will shiver like I do when I see spiders. Her eyes—"

"Why?" I interrupted abruptly. Clearing my throat I calmly asked, "Why her eyes?"

"They are her fathers, also that brings me to another point. Her major dislike is her father." She tapped a finger to her chin and then jumped in realisation, almost startling me. "Mirrors, she loathes those too."

"Mirrors? What did mirrors do to her?"

"She says something else stares back." She erupted in shivers. "A black shadow, she says. She is indeed odd, she talks about the most ominous things so nonchalantly."

A loud knock sounded on my door, signalling her squadron was ready for dispatch and I turned to the young servant one last time. "When I return, tell me then, all that she dislikes."

She frowned and then shifted nervously on her feet. "She might have my head for this."

"Then I won't be the cause of it. Thank you for the uniform."

She blinked surprised at my words. "You do know I was only joking, right?"

Did I? I would not hold it above the princess to actually behead her.

"Penelope?" I called, bringing her to another halt. "Do you know of a priest called Murdoc?"

I had been curious since that day. I wanted to know if what I'd read had truly been fear.

Her expression dropped severely and she nodded.

"Would you still lose your head if you told me that?"

She shook her head. "He is a priest. Likes to call himself one at least." She took a deep breath before saying, "He used to lock all three of them in the northern tower. My father told me he would...exorcise them. People were terrified of them three, so the king tried to soothe the revolt they had caused by giving them to the priest for at least a day a week. My father was Snowlin's guard so he told me Murdoc used to be particularly...harsh on her. He told people her demon was hard to tame so he kept her there longer, sometimes for nights in a row."

I held my face clean of the shocked reaction my thoughts were cursing. "No one helped her?"

She shrugged. "No one could, many did not want to."

How old must she have been? A child. She had to hurt just like one no matter what she was.

She stood surrounded by soldiers and Mal who had dressed the same as I. The latter shook his head and smiled at my sight. We were in Isjordian clothing, but we did not look the part, any creature with two working eyes could tell the difference.

"Soon she'll make us all her soldiers," he said by way of greeting.

"Her assassins more like it, though she likes doing the murdering part by herself." I searched for her non-present friends before adding, "Mostly."

For a week now we have been travelling on patrol all over south of Isjord. The cities were forts of rock and frost, impenetrable. There were manufacturers and manual workers, but not much to work with considering their lands. Their livestock was boosting, but considering they grew nothing, they had to import hay and feed for them. Fishing, wood, and forgers were their domain, spread wide all along the cities, they were skilled beyond extent. Their craft of steel was on par with ours, they were only lacking the black steel to manufacture first-rate quality weapons. I began to understand part of Silas's desire to propose the agreement, with our help he could fill the empty gaps and make living much easier for his people.

Last night we returned from Arynth. The princess had enjoyed her patrol there, she even stayed longer than her usual walk down city walls and the casual meeting with the lords. Around Lord of Venzor she teased and spoke politics, with the Lady of Grasmere she scowled and offended, with Sebastian she struck in concentration and interest, but with the Lord of Arynth she smiled and laughed, her eyes rounded all warmth and she took in every story and word of his. All I knew of her was her anger, but now that I saw more, I wished I could still only see her anger.

"She still has not spoken to you?"

I shook my head, stealing a glance at her. "Not a word since that day out in the garden. She doesn't even come out of the bedroom at night anymore. I suppose whatever happened worked out well."

"She got you to react to her, twice. It is more of an achievement from her side if you think well about it."

"You know, Mal, you have become less annoying to my ears since coming here. She is making you work for your spot, maybe even challenge you for the pesty throne."

He patted my shoulder all amusement. "Bringing the jokes out of you, I have to congratulate her again. A triple win."

She brought many other things too, but no one would be able to congratulate me for overthinking.

"Stay back, I don't need you dozing off on the horse," she ordered strongly, sliding past me to Memphis.

After a week she spoke to me again. A week of nothing. No offences, nothing.

"No." Her squadron was to patrol in Brisk today and I had seen something unusual flash in her that had not been present for a whole week—eagerness, flaming and eye-glistening eagerness. What was in Brisk that had her up earlier than usual?

"Fucking gods and burning heavens," she muttered to herself.

"Don't be disrespectful."

"My, pardon me. Fucking gods and burning heavens... respectfully," she repeated, raising her smug brows at me in challenge.

"*Dahaara.*"

She halted and turned around again, narrowing her eyes in distaste. "*Klaghne.*" Idiot, she spat back in Calgnan.

"Is it only us three?" Caiden threw an arm around her neck and pointed at me. "Was that one not on night guard, again?"

"He is insistent on coming."

"Another fan of yours," he said and then rubbed the crown of her head. "Don't go flicking those lashes everywhere, you have the Adriatians glued to you now."

She threw an amused glance over to me. "Can't help it, the murderous wiles seem to be the star attracter lately."

He clicked his tongue and pinched her nose playfully. "And Nia?"

She rubbed her nose. "Staying behind, going through some stuff with Sam. She is to attend the meeting this evening as well instead of me. I promised Freja I would not leave her alone."

"We plan to be there till then?" Mal asked and shared a look with me, he had doubted something strange in her as well.

"However long it takes, Mal," Caiden answered for her.

The air as we reached Brisk was warm, even though lands radiated white with thick snow and were situated between mountains and tall hills also frosted over with Krig's blessing.

The princess halted at the gates, speaking to the wall guards before she signalled us to follow after her and onto the city.

Quiet—completely dead quiet, people moved about as silent spirits, they did not look like the typical Isjordians either. Their eyes fixed on us, swells of disdain shadows towards our party. I did not understand their reaction.

We deviated further away from the city toward the north. Houses grew scarce as we were led onto further hollow silence and toward the entrance of a forest thicket. She dismounted in front of a large three floored wooden house, the Isjordian crest above its entrance. It stood lonesome amongst trees and near a thick coniferous forest. Empty looking from the outside, there were no lights, not even a sound.

Caiden and the soldiers drew their swords as if in command.

What was going on? This was not the typical patrol as I had thought.

"Empty?" Caiden asked her and she did not answer.

Tilting her head to observe the premises, she took careful steps to its entrance.

"No," Mal said. "There are people inside. Probably a few."

"Ten," she said pensively, still staring at the building.

I grabbed her hand, pulling her attention. "What are we doing here? You have been patrolling for a week, this is not your usual route."

She shook herself free and Caiden gave me a warning look.

Unsheathing her daggers, she cautiously approached the door, cracking it slightly open before she suddenly rolled to the side of the house wall, avoiding the impact of the door kicking open furiously. A man came from the inside. As soon as he took note of her, he unsheathed his weapon. Black steel, an Adriatian weapon. He swung for her. Quickly, she ducked, leaning back and nailing a foot in his knee before circling round and under him at an impeccable lightness of foot to dig her dagger right behind his neck, piercing right through the front.

The man gasped for air, blood leaking furiously from his mouth and wound. It all happened too quickly for any of us to react.

She pulled the dagger out, wiping the leaking blood on her sleeve.

How did she detect movement to react so quickly?

"There should be ten of them. I want them all captured or dead," she ordered her soldiers who rushed inside the building immediately.

She mouthed something to herself, something resembling a number.

A boom sounded inside the building and glass cracked viciously in the air, hard debris floating above us.

A wave blast of wind pushed the whole debris back, narrowly missing us.

"You idiot," the princess accused her friend.

"A Zephyr?" I asked, absently studying him. I'd never seen one before. In Isjord and right next to her was the last place I ever thought I'd see one.

She gripped my jacket, bringing me close to her. Her fists tight as she demanded, "You will not tell."

"Why would you think I'd do that?"

"You will not tell," she pushed, inching closer and closer. "I need your promise."

"And you have it."

"Say it."

"I promise, princess, I will tell no one. Now let go of me."

She breathed furiously before turning to my brother, surely to repeat the same thing she'd told me, only to be interrupted by Caiden. "He knows."

"What?" we both asked in unison again.

"Since Kirkwall," my brother revealed, raising his hands and taking a step back. "And before you wrinkle my ironed jacket, I also promised not to tell."

He had not told me either.

Stomping sounded from the stairs. "They ran towards the forest, all Aura," her soldiers shouted, and she took off almost immediately before I grabbed her again by the arm.

"There is no point in running after them, they can fade." She'd come to claim her list of Adriatians that Van and Ester had given her, that was why she'd been that eager.

"No, all city walls are laced in craft, no one can fade in or out. They get out those walls and I lose them."

We ran through the thick coniferous snow-covered forest. Several men ahead of us were running away, glancing back at us, murmuring and arguing with one another in Darsan.

The princess, one of them said. They had recognized her.

My magic flickered open, dragging the tree shadows toward them, but they moved quickly, lifting a wall as a shield and causing my shadows to crash with theirs.

Caiden and Mal had separated from us, probably chasing the rest of the Adriatians. Another stupid thing to add to the list of mistakes we'd done in a matter of minutes today. Day grew old quickly in Isjord, the cold was harsh and made it difficult to move fast which will end up consuming more of our energy. If the Adriatians wanted to tackle us and catch the princess, this was the perfect moment.

The group ahead of us split and she shouted over her shoulder to me, "Go after that one."

"I am not leaving you on your own."

"I lose one of them, Kilian, my father will have my head and I really love my head. I will be fine." Her eyes rounded in beseech. "Go...please"

What was I doing? My feet moved away from her as I took one last look at her and parted towards the other side of the forest. There was something in her voice or maybe her plea that lurched guilt in my stomach and made me obey her. I'd seen her in a fight, she was skilled, it would put my restlessness to some quiet till I dealt with the man ahead of me.

Magic creeped from me and slithered on the ground, aiming and catching the man at his feet and bringing him to a halt.

"Henah, you are her guard," he said, wide eyed and panting.

"What are you doing here? Is the Highwall not tall enough for you? Is our kingdom not enough for you?"

His body trembled, fear, longing and pain circled him. "No, not enough. My family starves in Lyra, the unblessed come steal our produce and raid our homes, the last lands I farmed are now under water from the storms that have not stopped for months. Amaris is overloaded in population, the only place my family can sleep is under the stars of Henah. We did what was forced into us—survive."

The man's words fell hard on my ears, hearing that made my body curse with guilt—guilt of not having helped them, of not being able to help them in time before they made such choices.

"You call this survival? She will kill you. Silas will kill you."

He shook his head. "He won't, he is the one that employed us—saved us from the curse of our lands."

"What?"

I began recalling her conversation with Ester back in Kirkwall and it all clicked together. The person they had worked for was Silas. She aimed to stop Silas from using our Aura. Why? Spite? Fear?

Tears rushed down his face and he spoke breathlessly through a cry, "I want you to know that I died for my family, for survival."

He opened his arms wide, his eyes veiled black and dark mist leaked out of him.

"No, no, no!" My warning was too late as he began warping in gusts of gurgling shadows.

I took off before he bursted in a wave of hungry dark clouds. We called it Malefic. It was rare magic that demanded one's life. Forbidden, branded cursed and evil. An Umbra channelled their magic to control shadows, but one could also channel it outside the body, creating shadows that extended and did not need the favours of light to be controlled. Very few—very few who were no longer alive and belonging to hundreds of years ago could manage such a thing. Out of all our Aura, only Obscurs could produce magic—darkness magic, but those were extinct as well, only one bloodline left, the Adriatian King's bloodline. Unlike them, Umbra could only control flow of mana inside oneself, attempting to draw it out could accidentally draw life mana with it, too. But the life spent from the Aura was not the worst risk, the gust of magic floating unmanned and uncontrollable out of him was.

The shadows rushed and chased behind me. I avoided its tentacles wanting to leech onto me and feed onto whatever life I had to fuel their course of magic. Pure chaos, unamenable, uncontrollable. I could only hope his magic was not as strong, the best you could do was wait for it to be dispersed, wasted or absorbed by the earth.

Everywhere was now covered in black mist to the furthest the eye could see and my mind boggled a thousand thoughts. If this had already reached near the princess, it would kill her. I'd have to reach her before it spread further.

"Princess," I called onto the silent air, moving rapidly through the dense forest. Suddenly a clang sounded nearby and I rushed quickly towards the commotion finding her head-to-head with another.

The Malefic mist began surrounding us so I did the only thing I could do, trap us in the middle of it. Lifting a wall of shadows around us, the mist hit the barrier, stopping and spreading around it without reaching us.

I finally turned to the princess again. Two men already dead on the white forest floor and her sword through the last man's chest before he dropped to the ground, dead at the precise strike.

She had stilled for long moments, facing away from me.

"Princess?"

Her knees weakened, collapsing her to the ground, and I ran faster than I'd ever ran before. Her expression frozen, gilded eyes wide open, her breath shallow and stuttering. Pain. That was the look of pain.

I took her face in my hands. She was cold, clammy and paler than usual. "Hey, hey, I am here. I am here. What happened?"

She trembled all over and a tear slid down her cheeks, then another. They almost made me flinch. Her eyes filled with silver could make gods shake. She could not breath, clutching her chest, her mouth gaped open and unable to get air in her lungs.

"One hundred...twelve...thirteen...fourteen," she stuttered out.

"Princess, what happened? Look at me," I demanded, examining her body for injuries.

"It hurts," she whispered breathlessly.

"Where?" I ran my hands all over her, searching for wounds—wounds I couldn't find.

"Everywhere."

I stilled and glanced over the dead man she'd nailed her sword through. "Did that man touch you?"

She nodded in answer and my eyes drew shut in realisation. Empath, he had been an Empath. There was no cure for pain infliction unless an Empath reversed it. Henah, help us.

"We have to find Mal. Let's stand, look at me. I will help you stand," I said, sliding my arms around her.

The moment I managed to raise her body up she collapsed in my arms. Whimpers and small suppressed sobs of agony made their way out of her. A thick violet shadow loomed from around her limp body. The first time I had seen any of her shadows and the emotion was not even belonging to her. Foreign, inflicted. Pure agony—she was in an agony of pain.

"You are not dying on me, let's try again."

I gathered her in my arms, looking around the thick Malefic mist behind the wall of shadows. We would not be able to pierce through it.

She shook her head and sagged onto me. She would not make it.

"I will take it away." Putting her down in my lap, I began taking my gloves off. "The wall around will keep you safe for the night and when that mist dissolves, I need you to run to safety as fast as you can and find my brother to look at you. You will tell him an Empath inflicted you, he will fix it."

I was not an Empath, all I could do was trap it inside me.

"We find Mal together," she managed to whisper strongly between ragged breaths.

"There will be no time."

She shook her head, even though through hurt and pain she had the head of a bull. "No."

"With my life, remember." Placing my hands on her face, a pathway of dark magic floated through me to her. "With my life."

She flung my hands down and shook her head again, pushing and crawling away from me. Digging her hands in the ground, she straightened herself, still shaking like leaves through a spring breeze. "I need a moment," she murmured between sobs.

Her eyes drew tightly shut, swinging herself backward and forward, clutching her hands in fists. And out of the sudden, the trembling slowed till she only shivered. The massive cloud of violet shadows slowly thinned and dispersed. She gasped, her lungs filling with air before erupting in a dry cough.

What had just happened?

"Princess?" I slid down next to her, rubbing her back while her lungs almost gave away.

Her hand gripped my arm tight, helping herself stand straight while she was clutching her chest with the other because of the cough that drew more tears down her cheek. "I'm fine."

I took her face in my hands, examining her, my thumbs fending away stray tears—her eyes were still almost completely black with the faint glimpse of a yellow halo and she was still taking heavy breaths, but no longer gasping for air. "What did you do? How did you do that?" I asked in absolute shock. It was not earthly possible to do what she had just done. Empath infliction placed a mental shield of one emotion, channelling and coursing it endless, till they chose not to. Agony, it would be complete agony of pain, her heart would have stopped from it.

"Do what?" Loose tears still streamed down her cheeks, but she sniffled and ran her gloved hands wiping them away, almost unbothered. Her body limp and beaten up, yet her expression was unwavering, same as her words and tone.

"Escape an Empath's infliction, no one can do that." Even I had broken down and given up in training, not even half an hour through it. Empath infliction was banned in Adriata, no one was allowed to nurture the blessing or train it. The Adriatian court had a special team of two dozen empaths called the Eldritch order, and he was not one of them. This one must have slipped through the cracks, unnoticed and trained away from the eye. One that had gone right under Silas's wing. The princess had been right to worry and inquire through this so persistently.

"He was not a very good Empath then. Now will you unhand me, you're hurting me."

I had not noticed how hard I was holding her, my fingers had left red marks on her face. "How did you do it?"

She barely stood up and went to retrieve her sword from the dead man's body. "I do not know," she answered, her voice monotone.

Lie.

She was probably still suffering the lingering anguish of the infliction and I was being harsh in questioning her this persistently. What answers was I looking for anyway?

Once she settled down, avoiding my suspicious stare, I went to release the men's souls from their bodies.

"From gods we descend, to gods back we ascend. From heaven's we heed, to heavens back we seed," I recited for each in holy prayer and spirits they floated in orbs of light towards the sky, to Cynth.

She stared in wonder through the whole process, curious but refused to let herself ask.

"Was it worth it, putting yourself in danger for precarious odds?" I asked, reliving the thought that she almost died.

She stretched and yawned. "I don't fiddle with odds, just with men. And men have never prevailed over aught in regard to the lengths of danger they present."

I scoffed and shook my head at her thick stubbornness, the confidence she exuded with that answer was impeccably hale for someone who had almost died a few moments ago.

Her long moments of quiet scared me so I asked again, "Are you sure you're alright?"

"I could be better and less cold, fed and in better company." She sighed and sniffled, gathering herself tight. "Damned hells, a lemon cream puff. I'm terribly craving a lemon cream puff."

She was alright, but how was she this calm?

She spun around, noting the wall I'd lifted, poking it with her fingers and blinking surprised once it bounced back on her, still refusing to ask questions her curious glance instigated.

I noted her hair had turned a murky dark burgundy mated to her back. "You are covered in blood," I stated and she startled a step forward when I moved her long hair away from the gushing wound on her back.

She looked back and snorted. "Yes, so it's come to my attention."

I peeled the cut back and revealed a gnarly slash tearing her flesh. "You're hurt."

"No, I usually spurt blood from my back."

Gods, could she not joke for a second. "Take your jacket off, let me see."

"At every opportunity you try to undress me."

A heavy sigh followed by a groan unwillingly left my body, the range of annoyed she had created in me would be historical. "This is not funny, not the slightest."

"I'm stuck with you so I'll take all the entertainment I can find."

"You almost died on me."

She shrugged nonchalantly. "Blessings never come for the wicked."

Her words from that day were still clear in my head. I shook them away before they drove me back to overthinking. "Jacket. Off." I ordered, ignoring her incitements.

Cautiously, she finally pulled her jacket off, then her white shirt, leaving her in a thin almost sheer strappy top in the middle of the freezing forest.

Going around behind her, I untucked my shirt from under my jacket, tearing straps to put over her wound. A thin slash had ripped the sheer blouse right in the middle of her back. Her clothing had not helped at all, the jacket was magic threaded meant to keep you warm, but it was not thick enough to lower the chance of injury.

"I need you to pull this one down, too."

"Can't you just put it on top and call it a day?"

"No, I need to clean it and stop the bleeding." I pulled her face towards me. "Do I need to undress you too?"

She snatched her face away from my hand and blew a heavy breath of annoyance before letting the straps fall down revealing her back while she crossed her hands over her chest.

I froze, not from the gnarly sight of the fresh slash but at old scars that stretched in thin lines and gashes everywhere across her back. My pulse grew fast. Faster. And then almost mad—terribly mad. I could not help but run my fingers over them, hoping that my mind was playing with me and it wasn't hundreds of scars I was seeing on her skin.

She flinched. "What?" she asked, turning her head back to inspect my touch. "Is it that bad? Just put some snow over and be done with it."

"Who has done those to you?" My fingers roamed and curved around every scar. So many of them...so much pain. Her father? Her uncle? Murdoc? My people? Heavens, why? My heart began beating heavy on my ears at each name, drowning every ounce of restraint with rage.

She went still before coldly answering, "You're a soldier, Kilian, I expect you to be familiar with scars. Don't be so disgusted."

"Answer me. Who has done those to you?" Who would dare hurt her? How—

She turned halfway to me, studying my face and her brows furrowed in. "Can't remember, it was too long ago. Now deal with the wound or I'm putting my clothes back on."

Lie.

"How long ago?"

They were thin and thick and twisted, some faded in places and some raised and puckered and rosy. They were not from any injury and they were old. It looked like they were made by a...whip. She had to have been very young—too young. Too cruel. Terribly cruel.

She shifted on the spot she sat. "Heavens, let it go, would you. What is it to you anyway?"

Nothing, it was nothing to me, yet I demanded, "How long ago?"

She groaned frustrated. "Long. Long enough I can't even remember when I got a few of them."

A build-up of primal anger rippled through me as I dared ask, "Your father?"

"My gods, I am freezing and no," she groaned. "He doesn't get his own hands dirty."

"Why?"

"Because I was not shitting magic," she said, hesitating before muttering under her breath, "And a few because of attitude issues."

"He thought he could beat them out of you?"

"He did more than beat, now if you wish to converse with a frozen corpse I suggest enough with the questioning."

I noticed her skin prickle and her breath turning into a heavy white mist. I could not believe my eyes or my ears. How had anyone allowed her to be abused of this sort?

Cautiously, I cleaned her wound, another that would become a scar. She had not healed them, why had she kept all of them? Not even soldiers kept them.

When I put snow atop to moisten the cloth, she hissed and arched her back, the shirt she was holding around her waist lowered to reveal the rest of her back. A dark branch patterned tattoo painted most of her lower back, curving around her hips and her lower stomach.

"A tattoo?"

"What about it?" she asked, straightening and pulling the shirt over it to cover the strange design.

"Unusual, it's either magic or I am recruiting the wrong people as soldiers. I have seen trained grown men and women cry from a small line. You have a back full of them," I said, pulling her shirt down again to have a closer look, refraining myself from running my fingers over them, too. Her fair skin was pristine around the black ink. "Pretty."

She turned to me abruptly. "Pretty? I'd never heard that from men before. It's usually, *'why would you taint your flesh'*, *'aren't the scars not enough to ruin your pretty flesh'* and many of the sort."

What idiot would say that? "You don't have the best decision-making skills, your taste in men is quite the same apparently."

"Correct, but who cares what they say, I don't care much about the talking part. As long as—" She yelped, interrupting herself at the handful of snow I plopped on her back. She sneered and glared at me, but at least it stopped the course of action that sentence was taking.

"Why do you need dark craft carved in your body?" If it was the work of a dark crafter, at this size, it would be no simple magic and one I definitely could not recognize despite all my knowledge on summon magic that they used those for. Summon magic was also much smaller, contained in a halo, usually used from attracting pregnancy to selling your soul to an Eldmoorian Crafter. And if that was the case, she would be mindless and probably chained to a Crafter's tower serving stew and tea to them. It had to be a tattoo, a very good one at that.

She frowned, almost offended. "Did you just automatically assume I can't bear through the pain?"

Fairly accused, I had. "So, what is it then?"

She turned away from me. "Think what you will, don't care enough to give an answer."

"Round these at the front, I need to tie them at the back," I said, giving her two sides of the bandage.

"Scared of breasts?"

"Forgot your severed relationship with respect." I leaned over forward rounding them myself and she startled in surprise as if she had not just dared me herself. Just as I'd thought, she was beautiful head to toe. "I am afraid if you don't want my respect I can't give you anything else since I am not scared of you." She must be used to teasing and not getting a response. Tying the bandage securely, I pulled the straps of her shirt up to her shoulders. "Now I am terrified."

"What?"

I helped her pull the shirt back on. "You have a fine pair of breasts."

She smiled wide, buttoning her jacket. "Second compliment of the day and it's on my breasts. I'll take it, but please don't go soft on me, Kilian."

I wiped her blood away from my hands, cleaning my fingers with snow. "Not to worry, they rather make a man go hard. But your attitude helps maintain the balance."

She then laughed, loud and warm. "Now he offends my attitude."

"That I'll probably never have a compliment for."

She laughed some more and I stared much longer than I'd normally allow myself to stare at someone. I liked her laugh, her smile and the golden irises that washed with gleaming light. My eyes always seeked her out when she laughed. She could still smile. It surprised me. Someone with the life she had could still smile. Was it genuine? She had told me everything felt like nothing. Was this a forced one? Have I ever seen a real one?

"We need to rest," I said, pulling myself out from whatever enchantment she was casting. "The mist will take a while to dissolve. Let us hope the lands here need magic and absorb it quickly. If we are lucky we could move before dawn."

"We will be eaten by wolves in our sleep or worse, we could be killed by your people."

How was getting killed by my people worse than being eaten by wolves? "Your priorities never cease to surprise me, but nothing of the sort will happen." I pointed to the wall around us. "Now let's sleep. If you know what that is."

She let out a sharp whistle that was completely drowned by the wide landscape and dense forest enveloped by the Malefic.

"The morph won't answer, the mist is shadows," I told her. "It looks like smoke but is thick and impenetrable. Memphis would be stuck if she tried to enter and then consumed by it. Alarm her back not to come."

She blinked with worry before letting three short, sharp whistles. "I suppose we can't make a fire?"

"Unless you see anything we can burn around us—no, we can't, princess."

She surveyed around the empty landscape drowned in snow and darkness, before dramatically adding, "Then we freeze."

I'd laid down the dead men's coats on the ground to shield the contact with the cold element. I sat down and unbuttoned my jacket completely, before turning to her. "Come here."

Her eyes shot wide. "What?"

"Body temperature will keep us from freezing. Now, come here."

She staggered back a step. "You are severely mistaken if you believe I will do as much as touch you, let alone let you fondle me to sleep."

"You escaped death thrice today, I will not lose you to the cold. Get up and come here or I will take you myself."

She silently glared at me, refusing to do as told, and just as I was about to stand, she got up and walked to me all battle and resistance.

Cautiously she laid beside me. "Will you not burst in hives from having to touch me?"

"They won't kill me."

She shifted closer. "What if I beguile you?"

"Then you will burst into hives. Whatever sick attraction you have to me you will never fall to it. You only do it to annoy me. Now, arms around me and under the jacket," I instructed, and she did as told.

She frowned. "You're wrong. I want to beguile you. You will be beguiled."

"As you say, Your Highness." I said, pulling her close to me. When her body met mine, perfume of flowers circled us. "Hells, woman, you are frosted," I hissed at the block of ice embracing me.

"You wanted to study my back like a map. How is that my fault?" she grumbled.

"Closer," I ordered, and she shuffled tight in my embrace, her frozen cheek resting on my chest. I buttoned up my jacket, sandwiching us together tight. Like key to a lock, she fit perfectly. She was soft and small, flowery and sweet. Death by a rose, poison and sorbet. Only a woman, a strange woman.

"My wound," she hissed, arching her back.

I noted my arm resting over her back and murmured a curse at my carelessness.

We'd both fallen silent for a long while, it was quiet enough that I heard each blink of her lids. I'd thought she'd be the most uncomfortable, but strangely, she leisurely laid next to me while I'd gone completely still.

"Why do you have those scars in your palms?" I asked, not being able to hold it in any longer.

She took a deep breath. "Maybe lemon drizzle rolls, not a lemon cream puff." She nodded to herself. "Yes, Ken makes the best lemon drizzle rolls."

I blew a cold breath. "You're infuriating."

"And very hungry." Her head raised toward the skies. "Heavens, this Adriatian and all his limbs for a lemon drizzle roll."

I bit my lip hard enough that it almost drew blood, it was becoming harder and harder to suppress how amused she made me at times. My mind began working at what she had said to me before splitting our ways. If she had let them escape her father would have killed her. Was she working behind his back again? She was in the works of something and I could not exactly pick up what it was.

"Did you know they were working for your father?"

She took a moment before answering, "Yes."

"Since when?"

"Since a while, the family in Kirkwall had been supplying my father Aura from Adriata. He had known about the ex-Lord of Kirkwall, even worked together. A general of his had recruited these men."

She was definitely messing in her fathers business with aim. "You had no intention of killing the family, did you?"

"No." She paused, resting her forehead on my chest. "Not then at least."

"You make horrible threats."

Her fingers began moving over my back. "Only because you know they end up in horrible deaths."

"It is what normally comes after threats."

"So smart," her voice was soft and teasing enough to put shame on Rehana, the Goddess of Temptation.

I grabbed her hands. "Enough with that." Hells. Seven burning hells.

She giggled and shuffled closer, her body fully pressed against mine. "Oh my, you're a man after all."

Vexation cursed through me quicker than blood and I grasped hold of my anger a second too late because I said, "I bet if I push my fingers between your legs, I'll find you equally as woman as I am man." I was not supposed to feed her teases. I was supposed to catch onto her games. I had planned and devised strategies.

She raised her head, oddly she withheld a smile, her eyes lowering over my lips. "Lucky for you I don't place bets with losing odds."

Hells, this woman. "Your confidence is irritating." I didn't know whether she truly had that sick attraction to me or still spun me into her wickedness.

She shuffled against me, her body brushing over mine again. "I can tell. You're very irritated."

I gripped her hips tight and she flinched a little. Had I hurt her? I pushed her the furthest this tight situation allowed us and stretched my neck in an attempt to release some tension. I knew how to make her uncomfortable, too. "Why did you have to chase these men tonight?"

She sighed and halted her hand teases. "Spite. I'm spiteful."

Again her tone was awfully deceiving. "Lies."

"It's a secret."

"Isjord's secret or Your Highness's secret?"

She laughed softly. "I hate it when you call me that, or princess. You sound like my father. So angry."

"Good to know."

"Don't enjoy this too much."

"I'll try." I was trying. I shouldn't be trying. It should be easy, yet I was trying.

"If you wanted to get close and feel my breasts, you should have just said so, I would have let you."

"Sleep, you wild beast," I said, tucking the jester tight and hoping she'd shut her mouth with her jokes before she actually made me laugh.

Her head rose again like a rose bud in spring—a black rose. Beautiful. "Was it not heathen, am I a beast now?"

"What keeps your mouth silent for one heavenly minute?"

"Many things, food, co—"

I brought my hand over her mouth and she dug her teeth in my flesh, making me groan in pain. "Hand was not one of them, arsehole."

"Would you rather I put my cock, you vixen!"

She yawned and ducked her head back on my chest. "Maybe some other time, this vixen is too tired for that much work."

It was then I smiled. Every joke she'd made flashed in memory and I grinned like a fool as I let myself fall for her teases, silently.

"Don't hold me so tight," she whispered heavy with sleep.

"Why?" I asked in panic, removing my hands from her. "Am I hurting you?"

"No, I feel trapped... like in a cage...like I can't run." Her soft voice shivered at the last word. She took a deep breath that turned to a yawn. "Offer to give your life for me one more time and I will pluck your balls and feed them to you."

Run from what? From me?

I felt her grip around me loosen. She had gone to sleep.

I looked down at her peaceful stature, so calm and fragile looking. I'd be afraid to touch, let alone hit her like those that had marked her had. She was a resting thunder, crackling heavy beneath her thin surface of hate and suffering. She held terribly much within, it was terrifying to know what would happen once it rained on us.

I dared move my hand through her silken black hair and down to her pale face. Soft and cold like fresh cool silk—like rays of moonlight hitting the water surface in the clearest of nights. My fingers ran voluntarily tracing the outline of her eyes, her brow, the bridge of her nose and then over her mouth. So human. So alluring.

Entranced, I brushed the scar on her cheek and she flinched just slightly in her sleep. How had she gotten this one?

She dreamed, breathed, bled, hurt, lied, joked like all humans did. Gods, didn't she joke. Gods, didn't she hurt and didn't she bleed awfully. Was this truly the *Ybris*? Was the woman I held, half shivering from the cold her skin could not bear like all other normal humans, was she truly her? Gods, wasn't she dangerous. Gods, hadn't we made her dangerous, had she not been hurt by so many.

I pulled my hand back, dazed by my own thoughts. This was the woman I'd learnt all my life to fear and hate. The woman I'd taught myself to hate. Woman.

Have the decency to call the girl what she is.

"Snowlin," I murmured onto the empty night. "Snow." The sound of her name in my mouth was forbidding and...wrong.

"Shhh, so loud," she murmured asleep, patting my chest.

"Do you want me to die, I can't make it stop."

"Hm? Die...yes, die." And then she was gone again, this time a slight snore accompanied the previous silence.

I smiled to myself for a while before it slowly began dying on my lips. I rested my forehead on her flower scented head. "As you wish, princess, as you wish."

22

Scars and Lies

Snowlin

My neck had frozen stiff. Muscles had cramped so hard that my whole body ached at the slightest movement I made. It took a moment of struggle to open my matted eyes. I groaned, attempting to lift my body up and ended up being smacked back down in place, completely restricted. Was I still dreaming?

I wiggled furiously, trying to shake the restrained feel away, panic seeping in my bones when I heard a groan above me.

"Stop going feral, you are still attached to me," Kilian said, blindly running a hand down my back and unbuttoning his jacket.

The moment the last button snapped open, my body moved away from him, half in panic from a lingering feel of restraint.

"You move like mad when you sleep, you know that? What tongue was that you blabbered away all night long?" He lifted his body up, rubbing his tired eyes, voice deeper and heavy with sleep. "And for someone who thoroughly dislikes me, you got pretty handsy. There was not a spot front or back you have not run with your hands," he said lastly, clicking his tongue and buttoning his jacket shut.

If I didn't feel so cold, the heat of embarrassment would fuel a second sun on Numengarth and burn this realm to ash. "I bet you hated it," I said, balling snow and hitting him with it.

"I was stating facts, not criticising or complaining. The attack was uncalled for." He flickered the white flakes from his hair and threw a studying glance over me. "How is your wound?"

How was my wound? Did he not hear himself a second ago?

"Fine." Not fine, it was pounding and sore. Every time I straightened my back it pierced and stabbed. But it had been part of my salvation, I was thankful for it.

He got on his feet and approached me. Naturally, I backed away once he got too close, but he grabbed onto the front of my jacket holding me still. The brute, how dare he? "That dirty four-letter word does not fool me. Take your jacket off."

"The beguiling worked."

"The wound, heathen."

"No need, we will return to Tenebrose soon."

He reeled me back in place when I moved away from him. "I need to see if you have a fever." He put a hand on my forehead, dragging it down behind my neck and I hissed, shrugging at the contact. He stilled, almost worried. "What is it?"

"Cold hands."

He took me in for a moment before gathering my face in his hands, tilting my head up to him. Was this a habit of his? Did he not know who he was doing it to?

He studied my eyes intently, searching to uncover something. Tension gradually built in his features, probably coming to some realisation. "You lied, didn't you? The pain the Empath inflicted didn't go away. What did you do?" His voice was louder and angrier than usual.

"Nothing."

"Princess!" he demanded sternly. "I can barely see the gold anymore, they are almost black. What did you do?"

Gold? "Good, not keen on my eyes much."

His stare turned threatening and broiling with anger, he neared close enough it felt like we were in Hanai, circled with the stink of spring. He didn't back down, tugging on my jacket tighter and it made my eyes roll back.

I took off my gloves and showed him my palms. There was no need for hiding anymore, he probably already figured out what they were. When the pain behind my back had shifted me to some light consciousness, an idea had struck me. "The pain Empaths inflict is the mental sort, right?" Though it had taken me three times to cover the pain the empath had caused me, it had worked.

He stilled, his gaze never leaving my palms. Grabbing both my wrists, he examined the blood coated half-moon marks atop. "Physical pain doesn't make it go away, only substitutes it."

"It makes it bearable. Nothing hurts much in my body lately."

His face dressed in devastation when he looked up at me. "Snowlin."

He had just called my name for the first time.

I hid the flinch at the full sound of my name in his mouth and cleared my throat. "Ingenious, right?"

He didn't answer, only opened his jacket once more, tearing again onto his white undershirt and leaving him almost bare. For someone so bothered by scars, he had more than I could count. Though his body was made to have hands running to trace those dents of muscle, how could he blame me. I almost made myself dizzy tracing them. I shook my head at the thoughts of wanting to run something else beside my fingers over them.

He seemed to take notice and raised a dark brow full of questions at me. "The fever taking a toll on you?"

I rolled my eyes. "Shut up." Madness at such a young age is concerning, lusting after the sort that called me a beast, sent to hunt me and then killed my family. I had to see a healer once we went back. It seemed I was worse than I thought.

"Now I am concerned, where is the snarky remark full of lush insults? My pride, my vanity, my roots, my belief have not been wounded yet and the day is growing old."

"I've never insulted your vanity," I murmured between gritted teeth. For a second I thought I caught a glimpse of a smile. Fever was really taking a toll on me or perhaps hunger or just...another type of hunger. Hells.

He slowly wrapped my palms and slowly put my gloves back on, gently, as if he could hurt me. He didn't hold long into his curiosity because he asked, "How long have you been covering one pain with the other?"

And just like that, snapped and gone, all thought of him and me in some tangled positions. I was tired of his questions, tired of deflecting them, tired of wanting to answer him and give him all my truths. "I owe you no answer, Kilian. I understand to you I am...a curiosity, but there are boundaries that I don't allow anyone to overstep. Now take us out of here, I want to catch the rest of the Adriatians before heading to Tenebrose."

He gave me a stark look without pushing for an answer like he normally did, but he'd seen too much and I knew he would not let it go.

Did he find satisfaction to see me hurt? Did he like finding out how truly fragile my strength was?

Shielding me with his arm at my side, he cautiously lowered the shadows down, revealing a clear forest. The dark mist from last night had dispersed completely, not a trace behind. Like a curse lifting, it revealed the brightest and bluest of days I'd seen in Isjord. Strange, unnatural.

Letting out two sharp whistles, I searched the sky for Memphis. Not even a few seconds later she descended down before us, crowing and batting her wings loudly. Gusts of black wind surrounded her while she shifted onto a large cat and pranced towards me, nailing me on the ground, licking and growling softly, happy to see me again.

"Missed you, too, Memphis, and no, I won't leave you again. My back is fine, no cause for concern."

Satisfied with my answers, she raised her head and sniffed the air between myself and Kilian. Slowly approaching him, she sniffed his spring air too.

Kilian put a hand over her head to stroke her ears, and my heart lurched forward. She was going to make him Adriatian stew. Flashes of many that had dared even breathe near her, torn apart, limbless and drained of blood crossed my sight.

"Don't," I warned in panic. "She doesn't let anyone touch her but me, she will tear into you like venison."

He blinked blankly towards me, stroking under her neck and over her brow. To my surprise, she indulged in his caress and licked his hands leisurely, softly purring and encouraging him for more. Kilian shot an amused glance at me. "You are like your owner, Memphis, she also purred all over me last night. Would have licked me, too, if I had let her."

"Prick."

He smiled. Fully smiled, eyes and all. And attention dropped to the ground unconsciously, it felt too intimate to see him smile. I'd never seen him smile. He looked different when he smiled. Why did he smile? He never smiled. I dared look again at him and the soft smile he wore while petting Memphis.

She moved away from him and came to nudge my head with hers. "Traitor," I murmured before closing my eyes and letting her show me flashes of her sight. Mal and Cai had caught the last five Adriatians and were waiting afront the city hall. Cai must be out of his mind by now, I expected a full telling off when we met.

Memphis shifted back into a large eagle and I handed her a button from my jacket to notify my troubled friend of my still breathing lungs.

"The two have the rest of the Adriatians, I suppose we can leisurely make our way back now."

He wore a reaction between nonchalance and ire as he straightened his jacket. "You must be pleased."

"Greatly."

My stomach rumbled loud enough that it echoed between trees and Kilian's eyes widened beyond their usual extent. "It makes demands."

"Very funny," I bit, balling my fists in threat at the bastard who had just switched to an unusual joking mood.

We walked back through the dense forest. Surprisingly, the sun peaked between angry clouds and warmed our heads. I took a deep breath, adoring its light and basking in its apricity, the comfort of it like the hand of a lover grazing your back. Sunny days and star gazed nights were a luxury in Isjord, but the sun saluting us was not a friend of Krig but that of goddess Plantae. Brisk once was Hanai, before the greed of Krigborn Kings sought their hunger for avarice.

The edges of a village became visible, meaning we were nearing the city. Roofs of black stone, magic grown onyx that banished cold laid for long miles clustering in neat lines.

"Shall we meet demand first, before meeting the others?" Kilian suggested, pointing to a tavern, and I could not really disagree because my stomach was killing me. If I heard another rumble, I would chew snow.

We entered the hollow large tavern, scarcely filled with people who turned intent towards us. Cold stares and glances, but none dared speak ill of true Isjordians. Brisk was a suffering population, they knew what they had to do to keep their existence. Silence.

Pain struck in my chest remembering my own people that were cowering gods knew where in this realm that took no notice of their endure.

"For heavens' sake, what happened to you, pumpkin?" An old barmaid approached us and studied the beaten sight of us, her eyes resting on my uniform and the two circlets.

"Patrol," I said. No flash of dislike in her eyes, the usual visible dislike people of Brisk had for Isjordians, especially Isjordian militia.

"Did they send you to patrol wolves?" She joked, cocking a fist on her hip. "They have torn right into you. What can I get for you?"

"Food, please, loads of it, no meat." I asked, cringing at the loud grumble my stomach let out.

"Ale?" she asked.

"Yes." I needed numbing and distraction. I wanted to see stars, let my world spin round till I'd collapse.

"No," Kilian spoke in hard order. "Water only."

I threw him an angry glare, but he only blankly stared at me as the barmaid left. A flustering look now. Why did he stare so much? I ate and he stared, I walked and he stared, I spoke and he stared, I did anything and he would just stare. Was I truly such a curiosity?

"No meat?" he asked. "How do you build the muscle for sparing and energy to run that heavy mouth?"

I scoffed at his blatant uncovered offences. "Without putting a dead animal in me. What...what's with the," I asked, moving a hand over my face, "quizzical?"

"So you can excuse murder, but the line is drawn at animal cruelty?"

I shrugged. "The *Ybris* has a different list of morals."

"Or none."

I withheld the tick of annoyance at his fearlessness. "Suit yourself."

He rubbed a hand over his face and I swore he stared right into my brain when he asked, "Don't you find it difficult? To take a life?"

"As hard as it is to breathe."

"Liar."

I scowled. "What?"

"Liar. You wish for me to spell?" he asked without an ounce of change in his cold expression, but I could tell he was amused from my reaction.

How did he know? Sigh. I was letting this bastard rile me up for what? "If you know, why do you ask, or are you bored and on for conversation? If so, I have plenty better to give you."

He leaned back onto the chair, glancing around the tavern. "I like your lies, they are entertaining. How you try to disguise words, actions and yourself—all is severely entertaining. Not to mention the creativity behind them."

"You have me all figured out," I teased and leaned onto the table. "Do you know why I tolerate you, Kilian?"

He repeated my actions, leaning close, almost inches away from my face. "Entertain me."

He was close enough I could tell how thick his lashes were, the small gash from a scratch just under his thick hairline, the day-old stubble beginning to show in his sharp jaw, the very odd shape of his upper lip and the little mole on his right cheek. I could paint him, though how much of his beauty could I replicate in a stick figure?

I cleared my throat, back to my point. "I tolerate you because once you truly have me figure it out, I will get what I want from you."

All eager and challenge, he raised a brow. "Which is?"

"To make you scared of me. True me is far worse than what my lies are."

He seemed surprised at my words. "It bothers you, the fact that you don't scare me?"

I nodded. "The hunt is no fun with a doe, but with a scared doe—exhilarating."

He scoffed. "You're a psychopath."

"A beautiful one," I said, flicking my hair back. "My prey die happy and with a great view."

He cocked his head back, staring me down through darkened rings of silver, mouth parted open just slightly as his tongue pressed against his cheek. He examined me long and slow, from the tip of my hair down to my mouth, shamelessly, before turning to the room.

Handsome idiot. Sigh. The only idiot was I and my ridiculous body starved for attention reacting to him.

"Their common tongue accent is different," he noted, looking about.

"Brisk is on the border with Koy, they share tradition as well. Many speak Kemeri too. Brisk was Hanaian once. My grandfather, may his soul be dragged through the burning hells," I said in holy greeting, and he smiled again, "claimed these lands Isjordian after the Terian war ended. Not wanting to ignite more death and destruction, Hanai gave up first, terrified after what Verglasers did to their lands. Brisk was a peace offering. My grandfather intended to use the lands for produce, they were blessed by Plantae after all, but the moment they were claimed as Isjordian soil, they were covered in snow."

Terian wars. The three long years had been my grandfather's attempt on what my father did to Olympia. Well, sort of. He'd envied Hanai and its productive lands, but they were not an easy kingdom to put down, at least not then. My father's wits unfortunately were not passed on from him. Old papa dearest had a grip on war, tactics and steel, but knew nothing of the spiritual and was very underestimating of it, at least my father was wary of that. Wary, not fearful, still not enough.

"Mandeval law. Lands you claim your own will be blessed like such," he recited deep in thought before lifting his gaze to me. "Your grandfather sounded like a delightful man."

I snorted at the attempt of sarcasm that sounded absolutely flat coming from him. "The only blessing I've had in my life as an Isjordian princess was not having met him. If he'd lived a few more years, he would have taken my father's idea and bred the whole of Olympia with hybrids."

"I thought your father was after the Elding bloodline, your mother's bloodline?"

"Aye, but he never underestimated Olympian Aura, found them all equally strong to the Strikers. My father did though, he wanted only what sparkled. The only sparkly thing the greedy fucker got was my personality," I said, tracing a hand over me and he smiled a third time.

I swallowed the thick frustration down and threw my attention elsewhere, at a tiny scratch on the wall beside me. Interesting scratch. Funny scratch. I ran a finger over it. Oak, maple, or ash wood?

"Your accent strikes me as strange as well. Mal told me you lived in old Olympia. Aren't there travellers and all sorts of foreigners there? Odd you didn't lose your common accent."

Demanding and very observing, isn't he?

Dropping the attention from the show stopping scratch on the wooden wall I deemed oak, I faced him again. "I'm a princess. I can mimic all five accents, speak Kemeri, Borsich, Calgnan, Tahuma, old Ysolt, and make you believe I am all of that, too."

"No Darsan?"

I shook my head. "I used to cry when my tutors would make me learn it. Soon, they gave up altogether. I believe I knew my relationship with it before it even started. But even so, it's an utterly boring, weirdly pronounced blabber. You sort enunciate your words too much."

"It is called language of night. People rely on more senses than just hearing to better understand you. Part of understanding speech is reading lips." His eyes darted to mine and I shifted in my seat. "Darsan is meant to be spoken in the dark, that is why we enunciate words. To help people understand them better without the use of the visual."

"So you enunciate your moans too or just settle for doing the deed in sunlight?" Genuinely curious, sort of bored and wanting to entice him for a reaction.

"You will find out." I blinked slowly and confused. When he noted that I didn't understand his point, he raised a dark brow at me and said, "You are marrying one, remember?"

"Oh," I nodded in realisation. "Yes, yes. I'll let you know of my findings. Step one: bed the king who killed my family. Step two: tell Kilian about my experience. Step three: murder the king."

He smiled a fourth time, widely this time and nodded. "I've always been curious, so thank you."

Joking bastard. My glaring got interrupted by a group of men who made their way onto the table next to ours, chatting, cursing and waving their crude jokes and offensive names at the locals in the air. Hunters, bloody thick-skulled hunters from the sounds of them. Weren't Isjordians just joyous?

"Oy, dark headed girl. Your face must turn a few heads, it turned mine. Shame for that scar," he pointed, gesturing his hips in circles.

Ugh. I turned to him, the thing that annoyed me the most was being catcalled. "Your face must turn a few stomachs, it turned mine, shame for that repulsiveness."

Kilian snorted his drink and erupted in a loud cough.

The man's smile soured down and stood in anger, but Kilian dropped his goblet down loudly on the table and turned a threatening glare on him.

"Leave that one," another man said, calming the air and leaning forward. "I know how to please a woman."

"Please," I enunciated, irked at the thought. "Leave me alone."

Kilian spat his drink and coughed once again.

I got annoyed at him. "Darling, it's supposed to go down your throat, not up your nose."

He raised his eyes to me, silently flickering with something I could not understand. "So I have heard," he said darkly, wiping his face.

The barmaid laid the food down on our table, a smile of excitement swept my face and I rubbed my palms together preparing for the feast.

"*Nairi ma,*" I offered my thanks in Kemeri.

A smile rose on her face. "You are welcome, pumpkin. It is nice to hear an Isjordian recognize what these lands are."

"It is nice to know these lands have not forgotten what they are, winter can frost that into you."

"We try," she said with a sad smile, rubbing her apron. "But our young forget, and if they don't, they are made to."

I recognized that pain—too well. Her home too was filled with invaders and foreigners who soiled and spat over traditions of her own, like the whole lot did to Myrdur.

"This pretty face your lover?" she asked Kilian while refilling our drinks.

"That pretty face wants me dead," he admitted.

She laughed, patting his back and throwing us both an exaggerated wink. "There is always quarrel in love. Nothing that can't be worked around in the bedroom."

"I am afraid it would create more issues there," I said to her and she frowned, glancing at both of us.

Kilian had narrowed his eyes on me, observant as if expecting the worst to come out of my mouth.

"How so, pumpkin?"

I lifted a finger up. "He can't really get it up for me."

His eyes drew shut with annoyance and he calmly called my name a second time today, "Snowlin."

"I am sorry," the barmaid offered, looking at him all pity. "You poor soul, gods bless both your hearts."

I barely held my laugh. "So am I." Mockingly I pouted, turning to him.

"You can laugh now," he said after the barmaid left.

My lips drew in a smile, then to a grin and gradually I began shaking with laughter.

"*Dahaara*," he murmured, shaking his head.

"What does that mean, you called me that the other day as well."

"Should have learnt Darsan," he said, giving me a teasing look. "Maybe it would have helped me get it up for you in the bedroom."

I snorted, spitting my drink forward. My nose burned at the liquid I had inhaled.

He leaned in again and offered a tissue. "It's supposed to go down your throat not up your nose, darling." The deep enunciation on the last word sent a shiver down my spine.

"Funny," I sneered.

He nonchalantly nodded in that stern non giving expression and said, "Thank you."

We finished at the tavern, my stomach heavy and my eyes muggy with sleep even though last night had probably been the longest I had slept in years.

Brisk roared with movement while we headed to city hall where the other two waited for us. I could sense Cai's tension in the air the closer we got.

"Snow," Mal shouted, running in our direction and gathering me up in a hug, spinning us both around. "Cynth, what has happened to you two?"

"I didn't know you could miss me, Mal."

"Cai almost ripped my head out of my body a few dozen times. I might say I've never missed anyone that much in my life. Leash the boy."

"Snowlin," Cai called loudly, practically galloping in my direction, full of berating and worry.

Mal took a few steps back murmuring, "Hells know no fury like a friend who takes hide and seek too seriously."

"Where on the blessed gods have you been? And you send a button? A button?" he repeated loudly, throwing the gold circle down to my feet. "I thought that damn morph had plucked it up from your dead body."

"He first thought it was candy," Mal whispered from behind me and I forced my eyes shut to withhold my amusement.

"Cai—" I began taking a step back from him.

"Oh no, you don't get to do that with me. We talked about this, we were to stay together yet you split. I turned around to see no one behind me."

"We were caught in a Malefic mist and I was with her, remember?" Kilian jumped in my defence, approaching us.

"Ooooh," Mal whispered, "bad idea, bad idea."

Cai straightened, cocking his head back, taking in Kilian almost like he was prey. "You being with her worried me more than that damned mist. Now. Back. Off," he warned, but the Adriatian did not even bat an eyelid.

I went between the two, nudging Kilian to move away. I could not risk Cai starting a tornado in the middle of the city and Kilian snapping his neck at the click of fingers. "It will not happen again, Cai, but we both know what would have happened if they had not been caught by us."

"You should have ended it right at *it will not happen again*. We agreed, you run with your plans, but I would be with you at all times." He cupped my shoulders. "While our feet are in these lands, you are not to be out of sight, understood?"

"Noted," I backed, lifting my hands in surrender and he left towards the soldiers inside the building.

Kilian frowned in my direction.

"What?"

"You got scolded like a child. If he wanted you safe, he should have kept you away from here to start with."

"No one can stop me from doing what I want, not even him and he is family, Kilian, he can scold me all he wants. I had made a promise to him last time and I broke it. He likes to have me under his watch, thinks that I will perish in thin air...like all the rest of our kind and his family. I never want to cause him pain again, yet I did." Saying those words out loud reminded me how selfish I had become. I'd hurt Cai more than anyone would ever know.

"All that matters is that you are safe."

"All that matters to me is that he is okay, yet he is not."

Kilian took me in silence and almost in understanding, too. "He will be."

"I don't wish to interrupt this very intimate stare down you two are doing, but here is an urgent matter," Mal said, bringing our attention to him. "There were Empaths among them, Kil."

"I know, she got inflicted by one," he pointed his head in my direction.

Mal's eyes almost popped out of their sockets. "What?" he asked in disbelief. Approaching, he took my face in his hands, examining me like a potion glass. The brothers shared the habit I see. "Impossible," he said, frowning to his brother before turning to me. "I have not the slightest idea how you were able to contain pain infliction, but I still have to pull it out, it is like a mill wheel rotating at your life mana, will never leave you while you're alive."

"Will it...go into you?"

"No. I am not an...Umbra, my skill set is a bit different. I can float the emotion right back onto the spiritual flow of mana, my magic acts as conductor."

I exhaled a long breath. Did I have to? I could live with this pain too, a new one to add to my collection.

"It will feel like nothing," he assured, and I slowly nodded. He took both my hands in his, his brown eyes veiled black and I suddenly felt my body freeing from the clutching pain since I had been in when the man touched me last night. A sigh of relief that might have sounded like a moan left my body, a bag of weights lifting from my chest and head.

"Mal, what does *dahaara* mean?" I asked, and his brother uncrossed his arms, beginning to speak in objection to deny me the truth.

He blinked surprised for a moment. "Steel tongued. Why?"

I threw Kilian a time saving, not so very polite hand gesture that consisted of my middle finger.

Mal clutched his stomach from laughter. "Has he been calling you that?"

I nodded, irked at his brother. Tongue of steel alright, arsehole with facial expressions of a rock.

Cai kept treating me with silence all the way to Tenebrose. I deserved it. Breaking a promise to him was not the same as breaking a promise to any other.

Soldiers lining the castle corridors stared at us nervously and almost shivering in the shells of their uniforms. My father must have voiced his anger loudly from the looks of it, just as expected.

He awaited for me in his private chambers, hands crossed on the table and a look of a mountain beast in his face. He looked like his head belonged to the wall of taxidermied beast trophies of his kills that stood proudly displayed behind him. Colourful *dralgarths,* enormous bird like creatures with their wings spread wide, *morphs* aghast with their thin long canines out, *mantrals* and their abnormally large antlers thrice that of their resembling unblessed counterpart. And so many more martyrs to the killer king's seek for power. All kills and trophies of his work in Aita and his proud claim of their destruction.

Islands of Aita were heavens on the realm, endless gardens of sun and rainbows, peace and tranquillity. It also was the second land father had destroyed after Olympia. He had captured most animals, killed the rest that had not managed to flee and burnt their sanctuary—the blessed sanctuary god Dyurin had gifted them. Animals captured by him had died shortly after from cold and grief, the rest laid displayed behind him. Had he thought about hanging my grandfather's and two uncle's heads like that after he killed them and destroyed their kingdom?

He tapped a finger on the table. "Where have you been? Your squadron was supposed to have reported back last afternoon." He was a moment away from nailing a dagger in my chest and I was a moment away from vividly visualising him stuffed with cotton.

"Apologies," I offered, and he flinched as if he had heard that word for the first time. The faces behind almost changed expression, too. "While patrolling in Brisk, a group of elderly came to notify us that they had seen Adriatians Aura wielding magic in one of the villages."

He blanched, pupils wide and still, almost resembling his dead companions. For a moment, I stared at his unmoving chest thinking I might get to salt up his corpse sooner than I thought for my own wall of trophies.

"We didn't believe it at first," I continued, "but one of my soldiers suggested that it might have been one of the trespassers Esbern had allowed in, so we went to investigate. It was too late to inquire about the list I handed to you to check the plausibility of that thought so we went blindly to check. They attacked us before we even asked a simple question. My team was forced to chase them down and eliminate all danger. They were killed separately. My soldiers have all written a report of their own."

Putting the forged file down on his table, I backed a few steps away and let him soak on my intricate fib.

"You killed them? You killed them all?"

I frowned on command. Brows were my main actors. "Yes, is there an issue, father? I thought you established the order of first kill for Adriatians?" Playing dumb was tremendously satisfying.

"No, no issue. You did well." His voice had jumped an octave up as his eyes paced restless about the room.

I'd waited more than a week for my turn to patrol there. My hunch could have been wrong, this could have easily revealed most of my plans to him had I been caught. The ledgers from Pine inn noted every little detail and all steps of the Adriatians. Now confusion began blurring and separating lines. The Adriatians were stationed in Brisk and Moregan on the Islines. There were no vandals in Brisk, but there was a passage to Hanai, the biggest passage. Adriatian Aura were recruited by my father under a very secretive general and under a similarly secretive mission near the gates to Hanai. They were there only for one thing—my father either had eyes in Hanai, wanted to take someone out without an imprint or he was after something that they could easily fade back, therefore the demand for their Aura. I'd stumbled upon something. I just didn't know what or how it would be to my advantage.

"The belongings were destroyed after they set off an explosion, but the house has been marked to be investigated, nonetheless," I explained. "I would have stayed, but I had to report back before you alerted the army to find me."

"You did well, I will send out another captain, you can continue with your patrol normally. There would not be much to look at the ruins of trespasser scum."

Oh, but there was, father dearest, so very much to look at. From maps to detailed underground tunnels and sewers of Koy, to guard rotations on the Hanaian border, perfectly proving my doubts. They were set looking for someone, something or perhaps somewhere referenced as 'element' all throughout the coded writing that we managed to salvage. They had been smart to set off the explosion but not lucky. How would they know my friend was a Zephyr who had sucked all the air out of the room causing the fire to put out and salvage all that was in.

"If you have questions you know where to find me, good day then."

"Have lunch with me," he called before I reached the doors. My heart pounded through my chest bone loudly enough he could probably hear it from where he was sitting. What did he want now? Did he doubt it so quickly? I had left no loose strands, unless he could read my mind.

"I have a wound that is killing me," I said, showing him my back. "A Medi healer is already waiting for me in my chambers."

He nodded. "That is alright then, have that tended."

I climbed wearily to my bedroom, half in my victory and the other half in fatigue. The wound was indeed killing me.

"Your head is still on," Kilian stated while accompanying me to my bedroom.

"Cannot say the same thing about you for long."

"You like my head attached to my body. It won't be going anywhere."

"I can use you in parts too."

"But where would the fun be in that," he said, opening my bedroom door. "You're unwell, remain put for a while or I will be severely tempted to tell your father about your deeds."

"No need to retort to useless threats, darling. I am unwell and I can't die without fulfilling my purpose for living."

Something tightened his features. "Snowlin—"

"Just Snow, Kilian, you're not my father. You sound too angry when you say my full name."

"If you need anything," he offered, retreating a step back. "I will be just out-side...Snow."

I held my amusement in. I liked the sound of my name in his mouth—cold, skin chilling. "What ever could I need you for, Adriatian?"

"Remembering not to lie." Had he heard the conversation with father? I lazily raised my middle finger to him and he smiled as if he'd always smiled at me, like I'd not just seen it for the first time today. "Civil as always. Grace truly becomes you, princess."

Nia came out of my bedroom and pulled me inside before I could jump on the smug prick. "Deal with the defiled fifteen-year-old before defiling the Adriatian," she said before shutting me inside.

Pen was waiting inside with another servant, perched on the bed end bench, holding one another's hands.

"I saw your notes. Well done, Pen." She had just become a very important ear in all my work.

She stood and almost pranced to me. "Thank you. Nia said she will head to the library to go through the tax records of Brogmere. I have someone who is willing to speak as well," she said, beaming in pride at the amount of help she had granted me.

Brogmere. The oar that was most inaccessible to me. I'd been granted patrol every-where beside the port city. The lord never attended meetings, only communicating through envoys and enclosed meetings. It was not only an odd oar, but one I needed on my side and one that possibly had answers for me. Answers regarding the Solaryans.

I smiled at the proud red head. "Brilliant, welcome to my squadron, little soldier."

23

SUN AND FLAME

KILIAN

THE STABLES WERE BEAMING with squadrons of soldiers ready to be dispatched for patrol amongst the cities. And in their midst, stood stubborn miss dark head herself deep in conversation with my brother, not missing a beat to stay away from danger. She had perked up not two days after our return from Brisk. It was the first time I'd seen her since then, she'd not come out of her room at nights and not till the other two had taken over the guard shift. The first night it seemed normal, but on the second I'd begun to think if it was to avoid me. She always peeked her head out to chat with Nia or play a terrible game of chess with Ken. This time I'd not even heard her hum that song she normally hummed before bed.

She noted my approach and threw her head back, groaning loudly. "Leave me alone, good gods."

My eyes narrowed on her forehead. "How did you get that bruise?" This damned woman, banging her bones just about everywhere. Was she not tired of hurting?

Caiden swished past me. "The floor demanded a sacrifice for holding that much ego afloat."

"You fell? How?"

She did not answer, her eyes darting about the stables while a warm flush stained her cheeks. It had to be temperature, she never blushed. Had she hit her head that hard?

"The hazards of having feet," Caiden continued, "Imagine not knowing how to put one after the other. Deadly."

She sneered and threw a vulgar hand gesture at her friend who remained unfazed while mounting his horse.

Nia handed her a small clear flask of liquid which she poured over a small cloth. Placing it over her mouth, she breathed through it a couple of times and then tucked it in her pocket.

I turned to Nia. "Why is she using mud foam, isn't her patrol in Modr?"

"Change of plans, we are riding to Brogmere," she said as we crossed the city walls.

My head spun in anger at the thought that Silas was allowing her to attend duties so far above the city borders with no thought or consideration of danger. Little did he know she was after his trail as well.

The moment we stepped out of the thick forest, loud horse hooves sounded behind us, shaking the cold snow into the air and fogging the figure approaching.

The whole squadron turned, swords drawn out at the emerging sign of danger. We drew back after spotting the Isjordian uniform and then the features of one from the three generals. Samuel, her friend. I'd seen them together countless times.

Worry wore his shadows. "You have no order to question him, Snow, and certainly any more than that. You have an order for patrol in Modr, he will find out you switched rotations. Whatever it is that you doubt, leave it behind. This time you will face your father's wrath like never before. I beg of you, return," he pleaded, panting and breathless.

The princess was my problem, not Silas. This bloodthirsty lunatic was going to bring hers and my end both.

"I am patrolling there with permission, Sam, and you know I never escape the delicious taste of my father's wrath," she said smiling ear to ear, turning to continue riding toward the empty white landscape.

A lunatic and a masochistic lunatic. How had she escaped it—how had she escaped Silas's wrath so many times? Two lords, a bailiff, his recruits and many more, yet she stood alive and unpunished by the cruellest king of all, the one who knew no mercy.

In a few short hours, we reached the grand gates of Brogmere. Soldiers all appeared confused at our arrival. Just as expected, she had not notified anyone of the patrol which we all now knew was not one.

"Point us to your Lord's whereabouts," she ordered the gate soldier, her voice authoritative and demanding, different from the teasing tone she normally used to tempt her way through things. It almost sounded angry, though I could not see any shadows around her. Her empty canvas was contrasted by the full, viscous and trembling shadows of the Brogmere soldiers.

One of them moved forward, bravely batting a turndown. "It is Captain Grehr who patrols our city, Captain. We are not allowed to permit anyone else in."

She threw down a piece of paper. "This says otherwise, and it's not Captain, it's Your Highness. Point me to your Lord, now."

She'd used her title, there was something inside there she wanted, and from her darkened expression, it appeared to be a life.

The soldiers shared glances between each other, hesitation and a fear of reprisal circled their heads. Strangely and differently from most, they feared obeying rather than disobeying her. Finally, they gave in after some leg shaking glares from the vixen princess herself.

I exchanged knowing glances with my brother and readied a hand on our hilts, both of our senses stringing in tension at the air filled with malice, hunger, greed, pain and filth. Something thick hovered in the air—something between listlessness and air of salty death. Brogmere did not resemble any other Isjordian city we'd visited. Streets lingered with limbless beggars, hungry wolves worn out and half rabid, cheek sunken children with craned arms, torn makeshift clothes and matted yellow hair. The shops, tents and houses were torpid and lacking the richness of the Isjordian cornucopia.

"What is it? Did you feel something?" Nia asked worriedly—the question directed towards us, my brother and I.

Had she seen our exchange? Had she felt what we had?

The princess turned at her words and looked between us and Nia in confusion, as if she knew something.

"*Fovoch*," Mal muttered, still examining the men.

"Fear," I explained.

"They were frightened, just surprisingly not from you," Mal added, giving the princess a charming grin.

"Adriatians and their sensitive arses," she said, turning towards the large tavern where the soldier had pointed to the location of their lord.

Mal and the rest were laughing at her words, but Nia was still staring emptily at the Brogmere soldiers who still wore distress. A knowing look on her face. She had gone stiller than a tree, her chest unmoving and concerning.

"Nia," I called, placing my hand in her arm.

She gasped and charged towards the rest of the group as if nothing had happened. Something was strange, she often seemed detached from her environment.

Her soldiers positioned outside by the tavern doors, not a smart move considering the tavern stretched with massive armed sailors drunk to their heads who stopped and threw looks of disgust and rage towards our group.

"Stay here and enjoy," the princess said, walking towards the main table where a wild-eyed long-haired man sat toasting on ale, two women perched in his lap and both scared to their heads.

Nia slapped down on a seat, flicking a book open. Followed by Caiden who munched on a selection of nuts while keeping his eyes on the princess.

Had we come on a field trip, what were they doing?

I moved to follow her and the latter put a hand on my shoulder prompting a halt on my step. "We sit and wait. You don't want to be in front of her when she is this angry," he said, motioning his head to the chair next to him.

She did not look angry or anything else at that. Not more than she looked amused and at ease, but I had never been able to read any shadows from her and her expressions usually were crafted to hide what she was truly feeling, she was extremely versed at that.

"Is that why she does that thing with her head? The tilt?" my brother asked, examining her.

What tilt?

"Tilt of the head she is angry, but only to the left. Right means she is thinking. Eyebrow up when she is amused, frown and pursed lips when she is hungry, though her stomach will let you know sooner. And that silly wide smile when she hates something," Caiden explained calmly. "Gods, I hate that one."

"Hands behind her back when she has something over you," Nia pointed without lifting her attention from the pages, and the two friends of the princess smacked their palms, laughing. "Might as well know, so you can stay clear of pissing her off. Though I highly doubt it, your faces alone succeed in that."

It concerned me how they would let her do this, behave and prance around danger. However mighty she was, danger and risk never spared anyone. Whatever she was about to do, it would require either someone's blood or head at another's dissatisfaction—at the dissatisfaction of her father.

"Are the two of you morally mute? You find all that she does acceptable? Letting her run around and make decisions as if god—as if untouchable by one as well?" I asked the two amused faces in front of me.

"When you know her as we do, you begin to think she might as well be," Nia said, lifting her gaze toward Snow. "Is it truly moral muteness if you have also seen what those she punishes think, what they have done to her and many others? Is there truly such a thing as morality, don't you find it awfully distorted particularly by those of your like?" she questioned, now turning to me.

It was hard for me to admit but her reasons were somewhat valid. All the conflict had sent a piercing headache across my temples. I turned my attention to the one who had just stood right under the net of blood hungry fishermen.

"At least help her, if not, I will."

"She won't allow us."

"Why?"

"Long story."

I leaned in on the table. "Paraphrase. Unless you intend to help her, then do not let me hold you up, feel free to do so."

Nia let out a long sigh and glanced over to Caiden, almost looking for approval before she began to explain, "Six years ago we had a group of Vrammetheni bandits on the loose on Fernfoss, raiding Myrdur for relics. She is particularly sensitive when it comes to Myrdur so the next day she fetched her sword and left to deal with them. She agreed to let me tag along and we told Cai nothing. They were not the unblessed, but a bunch of Eldmoorian scavengers raiding the place for bones of Olympian Aura for summoning and what other god cursed magic they wanted to concoct. We walked straight into a nightmare veil. She'd seen worse in her nights so it didn't affect her, but I almost died inside my own head. She had to kill thirteen Crafters with only a sword before she could carry me out all the way down to Fernfoss. It took her a full night to get me to a Crafter and a whole week to remove the veil residue. A thousand and one promises later and here we are. She is cocky, but not a fool. If she thinks she can't handle it, she won't go for it. My foolishness, my punishment she says."

I understood her, surprisingly, but not in a way that would have me obey her orders like her friends were. "If she expects you to care about her wishes for your safety, then you should expect her to validate yours for hers."

"She does," she said, pointing to Caiden whose eyes had stuck tight on her, his hands flat on the table. "But from a distance, it was what she made us promise. He can squeeze air out of everyone's lungs in this room. Snow said that you know."

I studied the Zephyr. "Are there many left like you?"

He leaned back and gave me a once over. "Intending to collect the hefty price for my handsome head?"

"Cai," Nia called sternly.

He tilted his head in my direction, wearing a cold smirk, "Joking." Yet he wasn't dressed in any shadows of amusement.

"Well, well, well," the princess said, crossing her hands behind her back as she faced the drunk lord.

She stood like she had him just where she wanted, trapped in her claws—like Nia had pointed. But when I studied the surroundings, it looked like we were in a quite difficult stance.

"Told you," Nia murmured and lifted her shoulders in a cheery shrug.

Snow said loudly, "How is it, dear Lord, that you sit here so lavishly when your city—well my father's city is starving. You drown in riches, yet none have gone to the people, not to mention none to the Isjordian treasure?"

He clicked his tongue, wearing a full grin, eyes wide almost as if he just had a delicious meal served to him. "So you are the little princess everyone is raging about, quite the pretty whore you are. I could free you a seat in my lap and maybe tonight I could have you sit on my cock," he said like he was addressing just anyone, no regard for her status and no fear of repercussions.

His words drew fire from me and I shot up, three hands pulling me back down.

The lord motioned to one of his men who headed to grab her, and my breath grew rapidly, magic of shadows sizzling and growing around me, preparing to shield her.

Snowlin shook her head, displeased. "Not my answer and a very, very wrong one."

In a flashing moment her sword was in her hand, slicing the man's arm. She spun and dug her sword through his chest. Quicker than I could call my magic, quicker than what I'd seen anyone move before.

Cracking and stretching her neck, she smiled and waved at us gleefully as two men charged forward towards her. She sheathed her sword back and took her two daggers in her hand, swinging them playfully.

A man lifted an axe to attack her and my hands braced the hilt of my weapon again.

Swiftly dodging under his arm, she stabbed him behind his neck. Her other dagger flying straight to another's forehead and the other already bloodied dagger towards another. She unsheathed her elegant sword once more, prompting it atop her shoulder like a bat, and jumped on top of a table. Steel clunking from all sides and men after men toppled dead in front of her. This little woman was a titan, a trained assassin and a blood hungry vixen. Her face had drenched in the dead men's blood, she was unscathed, untouchable, a terrifyingly beautiful sight to behold. Her movements were gracious, different from any used by Isjordian or Adriatian soldiers. Footsteps light like petals dropping in the spring wind. Her use of strength was minimal, her manner of fight was all tactical veering, evading and precision for instant death strikes.

She jumped from the table, rounding her legs towards a man's neck, twisting and toppling him to the ground before digging her sword behind his back.

The lord's eyes had turned an angry shade of wild as he called to his men and a giant came towards her. She ran in his direction and swiftly slid under between his legs, her sword angling to anchor right on his back knee.

"Good knee?" she asked, standing. Her steel met two more men before she turned to the giant and beheaded him. "I suppose you might have needed that to decide."

She didn't even flinch when the decapitated head rolled towards the lord's feet.

Death seeped in the air. My senses clouded, the bitter taste of ash in my mouth and a crippling shiver over my skin.

Mal rested a hand on my shoulder. "Shut them, Kil."

I couldn't, not like he was able.

"Are we ready to answer now? I am not as kind as to offer a third chance," she called, stretching her back.

The lord stumbled to his feet, half drunk and half in fear when she politely motioned him towards our table. But he did as told.

Her daggers clanked on the table, blood splattering all over while she perched on her seat next to the lord. The dark hair had matted and turned a shining dark ruby in blood, her face masked from it and her eyes—the amber fires shined brightly, standing out like yellow diamonds. I could not even believe the thoughts that were crossing through my mind at her entrancing sight.

"If you kill me, Solarya will not be happy, your father will not be happy. I have granted him endless deals, trades and secrets he will not want to lose," the lord half threatened in an attempt to plead for his life. But I knew what was brewing in the princess's head and there was no plan to leave him alive.

She threw her head back laughing before giving him an amused smirk. "Why, will they send more shipments of insides and fish heads?"

As I had thought, Solarya and Isjord were growing distant and cold. The sun kingdom had always been quick to dislike the spiritual kingdoms, especially Adriata—their satisfaction was evident when the Highwall was established. The kingdom of day and that of the night had always been under feud since the early days of our gods. They seem to have taken our agreement not very lightly. Solarya was an enemy I did not want, but this was Isjord's mess to deal with.

"How did you smuggle Solaryans into Isjord and why are they raiding north?" She asked, tapping her fingers on the table, already bored of the situation.

"What?" The lord feigned confusion and she rolled her eyes, bringing her sword to his throat.

"It-It was not me, princess. I know of their arrival, but they did not go through Brogmere lands. And I have no information on the attacks. None, except that I knew they came through Casmere and were very persistent in entering Isjord. Discreetly. A merchant, a Solaryan merchant, granted them transport," he confessed, lifting his hands in surrender.

There were Solaryans attacking Isjord? "He is being truthful," I spoke after examining his shadows.

She leaned back, assessing my words before asking him again, "Who is this merchant?"

"He owns a spice shop by the northern bay of Casmere."

Nia clicked her book shut and stood towards the exit without a word.

"And the mercenaries? What are they seeking?" Snow pushed.

The lord shook his head. "No one would speak a word."

She narrowed her eyes at him. "Your spy for my father's information? Who do you have inside the Sun court that he keeps scum like you as lord?"

He remained silent, refusing to give that up and Snow slightly poked his neck drawing blood. "Fine, fine. Queen Cora is a distant second cousin of mine, her fourth son, prince Otis and I...we are close."

"Inner court information?" she asked, worry sinking in her posture.

He hesitated again and she moved the sword closer to his neck. "Yes, yes! Mostly and especially that."

"My aunt is married to their second son, why is he in need of you when he has eyes there?"

"The second son and her were banished to Whitebridge island after an argument among the court regarding this, they have not set foot in Theros for about a year now maybe."

Snow tilted her head. "I've never known Magnus and Cora for petty. Greedy sure, but to find slight in just an agreement, never. After all, they didn't even draw a breath of objection when they let my father marry my mother and slay my kin. I doubt my marriage has any play. So tell me, what does?"

He shook his head. "Their court has been stirring for a while now because of Silas, before the agreement, everyone except Cora and Magnus do not seem to know the reason."

"And what do you think?"

"Well, it could be anything." The lord shrugged unsurely, yet full of knowing. "From the mistreatment of your aunt to hefty pricing Solarya has on products. The dart could land anywhere on the board, but I'd say your father has something they want."

"Why?"

He pushed her sword with a finger, leaning on the table and whispering, "Solarya has sent patrols further down Seer sea and is striking down on Isjordian troops. You surely are aware the vandals are no vandals, but mercenaries. Do you know how much gold those beasts feed on to do your bidding? Only a king could feed their bellies. Simple, they are looking to keep your father under control."

Was he instigating the sun rulers had sent the mercenaries themselves?

"Proceed," she ordered calmly, leaning back.

"Your father sends two of my ships to Vrammethen a week, but about five or six moons ago they came and went back with no goods but with soldiers, few of them had brought back ivory around their necks and wrists."

She narrowed her gold irises, immediately grasping his point. "Seraphim."

"Correct, they'd gone to the fallen kingdom. Otis informs me that the Sun court had dispatched a general to Seraphim about the same time as your father, that is where Malena got two of her ships lost to Solarya, caught right between the Seer channel."

"What is in Seraphim?" she asked.

"Nothing," I interrupted. "Monks, ruins, wild life, nothing worth of any interest."

"Scarlett Aura? Are there still fire wilders there?" Caiden asked.

"Few—few that will not use their magic, they have sworn to it after their fall," I answered.

Seraphim had fallen more than four centuries ago, one of the first blessed kingdoms to have perished. Again because of a greedy ruler, this time their own. Their eagerness for more had not been for riches and power, but for the undoable—the heavens. First king to dare to reach and search for them, to take a seat amongst gods. It was said that Adan, God of Fire, had sent one of his guardians to burn the lands he had graced with his blessings.

The lord shook a finger between us. "You both are missing my point. There is something two kingdoms are after on that island."

"Gold?" Mal asked.

The lord shrugged. "Could possibly."

Snow scoffed in disapproval. "No, it's too pathetic for my father to look for it, we all know his motto."

"Gold comes to us," Caiden answered.

"Who would know better about this?" the princess asked, looking ran out of patience.

"The mercenaries, of course."

Snow turned to me, almost asking for confirmation and I gave her a nod. The man was being truthful.

"Are you suggesting that a princess chases criminals without her father's permission?" Mal sternly called out the lord.

"I would not dare," he almost jumped, arms up in surrender. "Simply putting it out there."

My brother raised a doubtful brow. "You have betrayed her father by telling her all of this."

He gazed bewildered between us. "Surely you would not tell him."

She dropped her head back and yawned. "Pin him, Cai."

Without a second between her words, he nailed two daggers through the lord's hands, pinning him to the table.

His screams and curses bursted endlessly through the echoing room.

I could not understand, she had gotten her answers and managed to frighten him enough to sober his senses, why was she looking to kill him?

She neared down to him, all evident distaste. "I can't charge you for being a drunk whoremonger and an arrogant snout who has sold his own family for scraps. What I can do is serve your lunacy and fucked up brains a taste of your own flames. I heard you have a particular sport that you practise. I thought you might like to try some of it yourself," she said with a growing wicked smile.

I would have been shocked at the cruel actions that she was taking, but he seemed to have some of them coming and deserving.

I shook my head at the thought. Was the salty air frying my head? How was anyone deserving of death?

He shook with pain, fear, and anger. "You dirt bloodied Olympian whore!"

We all left the tavern, more a graveyard than a tavern. Her expression had turned completely detached compared to her usual smugness.

Seconds later, a loud boom danced behind us, rolling between the houses and over the angry sea. Ships swaying in their berths at the impact, croaks of displeasure from their sails.

The whole tavern had erupted in flames, terrifying screams came from the burning men on the inside and those of the lord.

"Why did you have to kill him?" I questioned, somewhat unsure and taken back at her exaggerated form of punishment.

He was not just anyone, he was a lord. Part of her father's court, his informant and spy as well. This already had taken a very difficult direction for her. These actions would not escape easily, why was she looking to be punished by her father?

"I didn't want him alive," she responded casually.

I huffed out a tired breath, she truly wore me out. "I don't even know why I asked."

She halted, her head turning to me. Blood had coated her completely, a fog of molten ire streaming the rings of gold. "Yes, why did you? Why do I have a feeling you always expect me to have a really rooted reason for my actions? Don't waste your time trying, I truly am just twisted."

"Liar." Something was up, I could even make it from the way she stood.

She groaned and ignored me.

We headed to leave the city to return to Tenebrose after directing Caiden to appoint a soldier head of Brogmere to take the position of the burning lord, similar to what she'd done in Kirkwall.

Heavy silence rolled between our group as we left the city walls.

"I want to come with you," a small voice called loudly, running behind us. A girl no more than ten followed behind, her hair and clothing wild. "The lord was my father. I...want to thank you, please let me come with you." She bowed through an anxious tremble, almost fainting. "P-please?"

Pain, it clouded all over her, physical and emotional, she was dressed in it. A fragile, small child bathed in enormous clouds of pain.

To my surprise the princess said nothing. Her features were schooled in an unusual sternness for her. Had she not found out what she had hoped, was this her disappointed look? But she quietly hoisted the little girl on her horse. Was she a price for her, was she to torture the little girl for information as well?

Prove me wrong, I somehow wanted to say.

Silently we made our way through the woods, the little girl looking at all of us and shifting in her seat relentlessly till Snow held her tight and told her not to move.

We stopped to feed the horses, eat and rest. The princess had washed the blood off her face and looked excruciatingly beautiful despite her tired, bloodied and matted form. Even the little girl seemed entranced by her presence, staring at her endlessly since we had stopped to rest.

Snow stopped eating, annoyed. "Speak, child. Words. Use them."

The little girl perked up in her seat, gleaming with canary happiness. "I love your scar, miss, it's beautiful. You are beautiful with it."

She strangely gave her a sweet smile. "Well, it certainly took you less time than it did for me to learn to love it, child."

"Lara. I am Lara," the little girl said.

"Lara," she repeated and smiled brighter.

Such a genuine human form she wore, it had me completely enveloped and staring perhaps harder than I should.

"You could have healed it, Medi healers can remove them." Lara stopped, interrupting herself. Hesitation. Fear. "My father, he used to heal my burns completely before he did them again. They have never left not one scar, look." She rolled her sleeves up and my stomach dropped to the cold ground. "Could you have not healed it?"

A shudder of vile fever cursed my body. *Taste of your flames.* I looked at Snow who ate her meal lazily, her attention floating over the ground.

"Some scars go deeper than skin. Some are just wounds and never become scars though they might look like scars, that is why they can't be removed. They might still hurt even if they are out of sight. Sometimes they are better off staying so we know to take care of it," she said and glanced over at Nia who had seemed to have swallowed Lara's words hard in her throat.

"Yours, are they healed within?" Lara batted her lashes curiously.

Snowlin's eyes never left Nia, worry washed all over them. "My wound is still in the mend, but the scar won't heal, it never will even if I wish it to."

"Why won't it heal? Did bad people do it, did you kill them for it?" Lara asked in a breath, half jumping from her seat and making the soldiers chuckle.

"It won't, it was done with a special weapon, one that even its graze kills."

I went still. Her reaction that day when we returned from Kirkwall upon seeing my sword, how terrified she had looked. My eyes drew shut at the memory of me running my fingers through it, through the scar that had been made by Adriata.

"Adriatian steel, my father tried every healer in the kingdom, they said I had been lucky to survive it let alone heal it. And as for the rest, yes, I killed the bad people that did it," she continued, putting the food away.

My eyes lowered to the ground, not bearing to look at her. The guilt washed over my skin, a heavy pain of bricks weighed on my chest. She must have been about the little girl's age when she had to endure all that had happened to her. Men thrice her size would have died from only a scratch made from such a blade. The black steel was magically grown and forged, mined from mountain Aldrich where the first King of Adriata had been buried, an Obscur Aura, a wielder of darkness. Upon his death, his grand Aura had dressed the rock, metal and even the air around it. The metal was darkness born and shadow forged, deadly. Meant to be used in battles of evil, yet they had tried to kill a little girl with it, scarring her permanently, inside and out.

"Will you teach me please? I want to be like you, a warrior," Lara asked.

Snow motioned for her to approach, and quickly Lara stood before her. Removing a scabbard from her thigh, she placed it around Lara's waist. "A gift with a promise to never remove it from its scabbard till I have taught you how to use it. I don't want you losing a perfectly good hand."

Her young eyes glistened as she ran her small fingers over the scabbard and bejewelled hilt. "Have you named it?"

"No, only my sword has a name. I'll leave it for you to name your blade."

Lara peaked at the silver beauty resting behind Snow. "What is the name of the sword?"

Snow unsheathed the extravagant blade, hovering her palm over it almost melancholically before clutching the hilt tight, some pain behind that embrace. "Lin. My brother named it after me, it was his before."

Eren Jonah Krigborn, fallen heir of Isjord. The blade of the Winter Prince, named after his sister. I'd think it odd, but I'd heard of someone once before to give their blade their sister's name.

Lara's eyes shone. "Could I name her Lin, the dagger?"

The princess smiled and nodded. "Now go by the stream and clean your face, we are going to a very pompous castle. They tend to look wildly at people with even a smitten of dust on them. I wouldn't want them to find you a curiosity. Nia, help her wash up," she said towards her friend who stood and directed the girl by the stream.

My eyes had stuck to her actions, the gentleness and gracefulness of those words had taken me by terrible surprise.

"The forge is going to stop supplying you with steel if you are going to gift them to every helpless child you save," Caiden interrupted. "At least keep a spare stash that are not made of fine steel. Name it *'the perfect gift for children'* stash."

"I'll keep it next to my *'perfect gifts for an egotistical idiot'* stash," she said, throwing a middle finger to him. She sheathed her brother's sword back and said to me, "You will carve another scar in my face if you keep staring at me like that, Adriatian."

I had been looking at her for a long while, mostly unconsciously.

"Heavenly beautiful, not just beautiful like the girl said," I confessed, no restraint in my words and she stilled. "A murderous, angry, blood thirsty, vengeful heavenly being, but one nonetheless." Words that I meant, but I wasn't sure whether they were intended to be spoken loudly.

She stared at me, confused. The air filled with that of a battle thick and a giggling Mal stood to leave followed by a similarly amused Caiden—amusement at my expense.

There was something wrong, her attention dropped down and she didn't even glance at me or respond. I expected her to laugh, joke about what I had said and even tease me. Yet she said nothing, not even looked at me.

"The realm turned upside down and sideways to hells already?" she asked too calmly for her, taking a small sip from a water flask.

"I thought you were beautiful the first moment I laid eyes on you."

She laughed shortly, unamused. "I think I know which moral way this is going. Facades, right? Truest evil hides in the pretties and purest of things. Caelus liber. Not certain which chapter though. I was terribly busy learning to become a murderer. But don't you live vicariously through your beliefs, Adriatian?"

She was wrong, like many other times. But a lot held me from correcting her. I didn't have to, yet I wanted to.

"What happened to calling me Kilian?"

"What happened to calling me the contortion of the unnatural?"

Dahaara indeed. "I never said the contortion is ugly and it happens to almost have a soft spot for children."

"I've heard they taste foul. You know, from fellow *Ybrises*," she said, waving her now lone dagger in the air, and I could not help but smile.

"Which taste best then?"

She glanced at me shortly. "I'd say six and something feet, Adriatian male, silver eyes that of a snake with a penchant for annoying *Ybrises*. But he can't be beguiled."

I liked that she never hid her attraction to me, but didn't enjoy it so much anymore, not when it made me react. "Is that why you can't see me in the eye, because they remind you of a snake?"

"Perhaps," she quietly said, carving shapes with her blade in the snowy ground. "Perhaps I don't want to look at you at all, perhaps I don't enjoy staring at snakes. Or perhaps I like staring at snakes, but I don't want to enjoy it anymore."

I rested my head back on the tree stump, just looking at her. "Freed another bird today, which forest will you take her to?"

"Tenebrose, to honour my promise."

"You hate to see suffering."

Her stare turned hard as if I'd offended her. "Paint me weak, Adriatian, that makes for the finest of snares."

"It only paints you human, not weak."

She smiled mirthlessly. "Yet your sort saw everything but that."

She stood and took off towards the horses, leaving me to process her words—words that I found bitter truths in. She was making me doubt myself and I did not enjoy that, not when you are taught to operate with a certain code of morality. Were ends beginning to justify wretched means? Had eye for an eye, life for a life become the definition of just? It had never managed to convince me before, how was she managing to spell me onto sympathy? Had I let myself get too close to her?

PART III
DAY DREAM

24

BRUISES AND CHAOS

SNOWLIN

I DID NOT LAND an inch of sleep all night, pacing back and forth the room, thinking. But not of my father's reaction. My mind had been on the Adriatian who healed my hands days ago, the one who almost gave his life in exchange for mine, the one who had kept me warm, the one who had helped me, the one who called me beautiful.

I could not stand pacing by my room anymore, and thinking made me terribly hungry, so I decided to get out—the room, my own head.

Mal and Cai stood by the door. I told them I was hungry and that I would head for the kitchen on my own. Both had strongly refused and were now sitting across the table from me and watching me drink my milk, arms crossed over their chest and stern. They looked like they were about to scold me.

"What...what?" I asked both of them, annoyed at their silence and endless staring.

"Nothing, just watching a heavenly being gulp on milk, it's not an everyday sight I get to witness," Cai teased with an expressionless calm.

Mal laughed and I threw grapes furiously at them both. When had they become so friendly with each other, and when had the Adriatians grown so loose around me?

"You think this is funny, too?" I asked Mal.

He shook his head and said, "Hilarious."

I pointed at both in threat. "I will have both of your heads."

"It would be an honour. One does not get to be beheaded by a heavenly being every day," Mal's turn to tease, making both of them laugh again.

"How do you see what others are feeling, Mal?"

Both turned silent and at my attention. I wanted to know if they knew what was going through my head. That left me an exposed book. Had Kilian known my truth after he had asked me all those questions in Brisk? Had that been why he had said those words in the forest, had he seen how I was feeling and how vulnerable I had felt at the little girl's words and those of mine. I was also curious to know if that was how Nia knew how I felt.

"Empaths and a very few Umbra...like Kil, see colourful shadows around others when we channel our magic. They usually circle around their heads if it is a mental emotion like fear or hesitation, lower for others like love and anxiousness, and even lower for lust and arousal," he added slyly.

That had to be why the elemental kingdoms disliked the spiritual ones, they read what they could not control. Emotions were often one's biggest weakness, a weakness that betrayed you in front of an Adriatian.

"What am I feeling now?" I asked to test his theory.

"Well, that will be a problem. I do not know, I cannot read yours," he added, and I scowled in surprise. Did it take some type of key to open, was it based only on strong emotions?

"Neither can my brother," he continued and then turned to Cai. "He is tired, amused and concerned. But when I turn to you there is nothing, empty."

Was this a trick to confuse me, or had I truly been able to mask my emotions unconsciously to them. But that theory proved wrong. I knew Nia could sense me and my emotions—vaguely, but she had managed.

"Is that normal, not be able to read someone's shadows?"

"No, I've never seen one without shadows before."

"Another Adriatian has seen my emotion, how would that be possible?" I asked, confused knowing Nia had, several times in fact.

He shrugged. "If you have established a close bond with that Adriatian they would not need to see your shadows to know what you feel, sometimes they would just be able to. Sometimes one can unconsciously feel emotion like a taste in their mouth or a smell, sometimes a brush against the skin. Stronger emotions like death, love, I can also feel them, sort of like a breeze," he explained clearing my confusion. "This other Adriatian is Nia, isn't it?"

Both Cai and I turned to him. I had just exposed her for my own profit to the people who had sold her body, her mind, her soul and almost her life away. I felt guilt stab me in my stomach.

"You are not to tell her you know, or anyone else if you want to live," Cai threatened quietly before I could, fiddling with a fork, spaced out and deep into the same thoughts that troubled me.

Nia's origin was what she hated the most about herself, it was the past she was fighting away to forget. Her blood was highborn Adriatian, her mother had been a nursemaid for her step siblings in her father's household and had Nia out of wedlock with the master, a councillor in the Moon court. She raised Nia like livestock, torturing and beating her endlessly for her own demise. And when she had needed money, she'd worked her to death and then finally sold her to a slave owner who had bought her illegally over the border to Fernfoss village where Alaric and I had found her. What doesn't kill you certainly can injure you, and wounds last and hurt longer than death. It had taken us days to make her eat, let alone speak. She would not approach Cai and Alaric for months after she had come to live with us.

She had the strength to move forward, the one that many lacked. She had not sought out to avenge her past, only to forget it. It took courage to let go, but with a charging price of closure—though her closure had been the ability to forget.

"I knew since the Kirkwall trials," Mal said, surprising both Cai and I once more. "I am a more perceptive Empath. Kil only confirmed it yesterday when she had felt the soldiers as we had."

They both had known before and had not said anything. If my father were to know he had single handedly let an Adriatian attend his meetings and into secret Isjordian affairs, he would issue an order to kill her the moment he would find out.

I began to speak but he interrupted me.

"I know, Snow. When we said we would come to protect you, it was for all of you, including the ones you consider family. If Nia wants to hold her origin back, it would be for reasons I would never doubt. And she is completely in her right to choose and do so."

I nodded, grateful for his words, words of comfort I would have never expected myself to be hearing from an Adriatian, but for Nia's sake I had made my peace with them.

"What else can an Empath like you do, except read others?" There were stories—terrifying stories of how Empaths could inflict so much pain your heart would stop in a matter of seconds.

Mal's eyes darted about the room before he leaned into the table. "Trained Aura can inflict emotion on others, all sorts. It is forbidden by law in Adriata to practise such magic now, the late king took the decision."

I almost felt my heartbeat lighten with relief. It didn't feel like a lie, though he had no reason to tell me the truth, but I sensed hesitation. "But?"

He cleared his throat. "But we still have special military units, all under control and evaluated. Our king would not allow things to get out of control."

My lungs unconsciously demanded more air. "I would not call it entirely successful, would we now?" One had not only escaped but worked for my father.

"I know every face in that squadron, he must have been self-taught."

Did it matter?

I examined him. "You are one of them." Kilian had said we needed to find him and the other day he was able to absorb infliction without issue, different from how his brother prepared himself. His words that night still prickled my skin.

"Yes…I am actually their Commander," he hesitantly admitted, and my heart skipped a few paces. "I—"

"I am not scared of you, no need for reassurance." My words very loosely matched my truth. I had heard of people dying from Empath inflicted pain without a single injury to their body—they were terrifying. Probably the most terrifying one sat across from me.

"For a heavenly being you are not all that graceful when you eat," he said with a grin, pointing to my face stuffed with bread.

"You should see her when she sleeps," Cai joined and they both laughed away.

They were never going to let this go. I was almost sure Kilian had done it on purpose for others to tease me. They continued endlessly teasing me till the day grew new and I had let them, it had melted a wall of ice around me for a reason still unclear.

When we reached my bedroom, Nia and Kilian waited by the door, looking in absolute shock at us. Kilian's eyes travelled down at my light attire, probably wondering whether I had spent the night in the garden again.

"The friendly three celebrating something?" Nia asked, crossing her arms.

"Yes," Mal answered with a half smile. "Celebrating that she made it out of that meal without choking."

I threw him a glare. "Do you regrow a head, Mal?"

"He is Adriatian," Cai said, stepping in. "You believe they do regrow heads."

"I'll carve a scar in yours."

"And I'd still be beautiful." He threw me a wink before wrapping an arm over Mal's neck and retreating with a salute. "The happy one is all yours. We have survived the night, might gods help you survive the day."

The other two had both crossed their arms alike and shook their heads at both their antics.

I kissed Nia's cheek, avoided Kilian's gaze and slid to my room. My back met the door hard, before I dropped to the floor. Why was I avoiding him? He should be avoiding me.

I got ready very lazily. Without a wink of sleep and travel fatigue my whole body ached from throbbing pulses of exhaust. I wore my most scandalous attire yet. If I were to be yelled at by my father, it would be in style. And if I were to be killed, the red fabric would merge with the blood. My spirit outfit would be splendid, the mid-world would be knocked off their socks.

Pen had brought a bright red strapless dress, tight at the waist and bloating feet away behind me. My bust was severely exposed, any wrong moment and I would be flashing my father more than my grin. A sheer red floaty cape pinned by a ruby jewelled pin at the front loosely concealed my scar. She insisted I put my hair up and I let her arrange it in a contraption of pins behind my head. I spotted a small thinly jewelled gold crown and decided to wear it. She'd jumped up and down from happiness and clapped loudly when she took a last look at me.

"Wait, wait," she demanded, adjusting the sheer cape to cover me better.

"Be done, you insufferable little carrot."

She tugged at the hem of it, frowning at me with panic. "Be still, you impatient aubergine. Your father will have my head if you flash every wolf of Isjord."

I shrugged, drinking in the sight of me. "Some would not mind."

She scoffed. "Yes, maybe the Adriatian one outside."

I peered down at her. "What?"

"He stares at you like there is nothing else to stare at."

"I am a curiosity."

"Yes, that too. He keeps asking me what you like and don't like. The other day he asked me about Murdoc, how did he even know about him?"

I grabbed her wrist. "You did not tell him anything," I prayed more than asked. "Did you?"

Her eyes lowered with guilt. "I might have told him something."

"Pen," I groaned. "Pray father kills me for I will kill you little mouthy vegetable."

"He seems to want to know about you," she argued as if that justified her loose tongue.

"He is my enemy," I almost yelled. "Lurking for weakness. What if he wished to use Murdoc against me?" Gods, had he been asking around about me? Diving onto my past, exploring my fears? I had willingly given them to him. What on seven hells was I doing letting him in closer to me?

Nia first struck at my sight, her mouth gaped like a dying fish before she proceeded to laugh herself to death and tears. Her deep brown coils springing over her shoulders back and forth shaking along her in amusement. "You will not die today, you maniac."

"I might," I said, straightening myself. "Just wish to look fabulous doing it."

Kilian on the other hand took the whole lot of me slowly and then stared lost into my eyes.

"Like what you see?" I teased.

"Anyone with working eyes would," he admitted shamelessly and Nia snorted, covering her mouth.

Avoiding his eye rolling comment, I marched down the corridors proudly at the reactions.

Elias had halted before the dining chamber doors and let out a low whistle at my sight. "A princess all right, you look like a queen, one good enough to eat," he shamelessly flirted though his bride to be was only a door away.

"I am a queen, my dear, one to become very soon. Please move out of my way before you taint my good spirits, I am already in some shit," I said, passing by him.

"I heard," he murmured, entering after me. "Just be careful, he has been in a foul mood lately. He has had to call several meetings with Moregan and only gods know why. He was not pleased about that. I don't want you on the receiving end of it. Go easy today, my raven."

He was always in a foul mood when it came to me, nothing new. I smiled knowing I'd frustrated my father. "Do you know something about Seraphim? Why has Isjord sent his troops there?"

His features leathered down to stern and he threw around a cautious look before warning me, "Don't. Enough of it now. Let it go."

"So there is something. And the Adriatians in Brisk, you of course know of those, too."

"Snowlin—"

I went past him. "Still not using that debt you owe me."

The dining chambers were quiet when I had entered, bowed and sat next to my father. Face his wrath all right, he was quiet as a starved mouse. Moreen and her half breeds on the other hand looked like they just swallowed a sour fruit, only uncle complimented me halfway through breakfast.

After the meal, father dismissed the rest, leaving me alone with him. I knew what I had coming.

"Do I take this as an act of defiance or have you truly gone crazed?" he asked in such a venomous tone it pimpled my skin and sent a shudder all over me.

"Come now, father, the dress is not that bad."

He shut his eyes, his knuckles turned white when he banged his fist by the table loud enough to deafen a mouse. "Snowlin! I thought myself proud of you afront others, every city speaks highly of you, my court finally begins accepting you and then you go and do this? You go and defy me? Again?" he shouted, loud enough my right ear had gone numb.

Pathetic lies and condescending words intended to goad or subdue me, I did not care, but they enraged me more than anything and I had no desire to drag this further now.

"He was useless now to you, father, do not act all concerned about this. He had not paid a tax in years and his," I stopped myself for a breath, "no, your people were left starved and abused by him. He had not left a single woman in the city, your city, unmarked both physically and mentally. He was abusing his power. Ships and ships of Isjordian goods were still found leaving his ports to Solarya whilst you were getting rotten insides by the dozen. He had knowledge about vandals raiding Isjordian villages, your villages, yet he had not disclosed a single word. Is he not your subject? Is that not treason? Now, father, tell me exactly the reason for this anger. Because I took matters into my own hands or because I killed your beloved Solaryan Spy along with his services?" I spat word after word with such hate and spite. My father would never miss an entire city dying off, he was who he was because he was ruthless to his subordinates. He had to have known what happened in Brogmere, but he chose not to do anything only to obtain petty information and deals, one he was putting before his people.

He stood and struck me hard across my face. My jaw flew open, my head thumping at the drumming sound ringing in my ears and my face tingled painfully. I drew my eyes shut when bile rose to my throat at the remembrance of all the times he'd done it before—my head echoing repeatedly in memory.

"Bow and abide to me, child, you do not want to taste my worst," he shouted in threat, his hand shook, eager to strike me again.

I wiped the blood seeping from the cut on my lip and straightened. "But I have. I have tasted your worst, it stands right before your eyes. I am your worst. Why do you refuse to face the consequences of your actions, your worst actions? This, all of this and me are because of you. So bear or burn with it. But I bow to no one, father, especially not to my enemy," I shouted back, meeting the pace of his tone, my lungs flailing at the sharp cold air sizzling against my boiling blood.

I could not tell whether the crackling was that of the ice climbing over air or of his tight gritting jaw. "You do not want to call me your enemy."

Laughter howled from the depth of me. "Or what? What worse could you already do that I have not gone through."

He banged his fist down the wooden table, sending ice all over it before it snapped in half. "Snowlin, my daughter, you have no idea what stands in front of you. I have made you smart yet your foolishness reeks."

"It seems a damn right compliment coming from the donkey carrying a traitorous lord and another monstrous one. One allowing killers in and the other raping, torturing, burning women and little children, your people, Isjordians!"

His mouth peeled back, baring his teeth to me, the vibrating tension of his anger seeping through his magic as walls began lacing with ice. "Do you think I didn't know?"

I snorted amused at his blatant confession. "Oh no, of course you did, silly me. I shouldn't have expected rabbits to grow in your serpent den, not with the cobra king himself in charge. But what would the Winter court think of your little pets and of their actions?" A lord who had not paid a single silver dar to the crown, a spy and an abusing prick in charge of one of the largest cities in Isjord. They certainly would have more than words to say. Especially when Celdric, the soldier I'd left in charge, sends enough gold from Brogmere this week alone to feed the whole of Isjord for a year, then we will see what they will really say. Who will they sing praises to?

"You threaten me?" The whole room began coating in ice. It was not to threaten me, his magic was leaking out of control.

"Should you feel threatened by what I said?"

The temperature had dropped, lower than it was outside, my breath fogged with white mist, yet I was calmer than a fish in water. His acts of wrath were more familiar than he thought. Did he not realise it was of this I was trained against—fearing, bowing and submitting? Did he not know he starved fear out of me and that he fed me ire, valour, wrath, and guts?

"This kingdom has thrived under my rule, even gods will bow to me one day. Your little words and actions annoy me, but they have never bothered me. You have no power beyond that of your title, beyond what I allow you," he snapped.

I clapped my hands, slowly retreating back to exit. "Well, that is just brilliant, glad your poor fragile mentality remains unbothered. Now, I am doing the job that I won myself and will do so till the day I step out of Isjord. If it annoys you and ruins your little devious plans it is not at my behalf, but at your incapable one. Know one last thing, I do not tolerate scum, whoever they are." I halted, making a last turn to him. "And if you think about hurting or punishing anyone I care about, remember that I know where you and your toys sleep."

"I could have you flogged for only that last threat alone."

I threw my hands open wide. "Eat your fill, father, I don't starve my enemies out of vigour, they have to be plenty vile to satisfy my hunger."

And like that my third oar had been broken then replenished and now compromised. All whilst I'd survived him.

We had been carrying the whole conversation in shouts, my throat burned from tendrils of fragile wordy courage I'd fended myself with. I was not afraid, but it was not fear that crumpled my courage, it was memories. My palms had stopped trembling, finally bending to my thoughts. I was not afraid, but he had reminded me of those times when I had been. Memories and their imprint were scarier than any monster.

Nia and Kilian had not said anything when they'd seen me rub my red cheek, the bloodied cut on my lip and the bruise forming on my jaw. I knew they had heard everything said between my father and I. Ice had covered the corridors all over so they knew how much I angered him. Though the consequence for it came at an easy price compared to what would have been done to me years ago.

I headed outside, limbs and eyelids half closed from fatigue and the cold whispering winter wind of the gardens—all was so revoking to my past. I had been hit by my father countless times before when I was younger, but before it had been to beat me into submission, this one was of anger, rage.

"Amerie is being moved today to her new residence, I promised we would accompany her since she is still scared of our soldiers," Nia spoke softly, pulling me back from my endless and absent wondering.

"You will go, send her my apologies for not coming."

"I will go get Cai then," she offered.

I reached for her arm, stopping her. "No, I will be fine. No need to disturb him. I kept him and Mal up with no rest all night. You go to Amerie. I will stay with this one" I said, pointing towards Kilian. "If someone will kill me, it's definitely not him."

She stared madly between me and him who seemed to be taken as aback as her.

"Nia, please," I pleaded, seeing she was about to protest.

She sighed. "Fine." Before she left, she turned and pointed at him. "If you do hypothetically kill her, keep her hair. It would be such a shame."

"I'll keep the hair," he said blankly, and I could swear Nia flinched and truly doubted whether to leave or not.

She called for Penelope to meet me at the gardens just as I had asked her, with a pillow, blanket and a thick cloak. My little servant didn't even ask what I needed them for, she was already familiarised with my habits.

"Let me heal your bruises," Kilian spoke as he followed me about the garden.

"Not this one, I want to have this one." He had bruised my favourite cheek, but I wanted to wear it proudly, the mark of my father's anger. A reminder as much as for myself as for him, that it would take more than a bruise to bring me down.

"The forehead one then," he offered. "Clumsiness should not be something one takes pride in."

I halted and turned to him, pulling my hair behind my ear to reveal the bruise hidden there. "I was not clumsy, just...thinking." Embarrassing moment I wish to forget. Maybe that was why he was not scared of me, even my limbs were traitors who disobeyed.

"Think sitting next time." He neared, scent of citrus flowers with him, he smelled delicious, like lemon dessert. His fingers grazed my brow and I sucked in a breath at the contact, it felt like something between electric storms and the warm touch of morning rays of sun, both rough yet very gentle.

I felt the crawling sensation under my skin for a few moments and then a long moment of stillness. Confused, I looked at him, his fingers still resting atop my skin and he looked down at me...worried. "What?"

"When I swore to protect you, it included against him as well. Next time he touches you," he shook his head interrupting himself, "there will be no next time."

"What, you will kill the King of Isjord?" I asked playfully, but it was still what he had implied.

He stood so near I could see a vein tighten in his neck. "If you ask me I will, and if you tell me those marks on your back are truly done by him, too, I will do it right now." His fingers slid down my face and over my jaw, sending a shiver down my spine.

His words fell hard on my ears. If I asked him he would kill my father? Why would he tell such crazy and heavy lies? Was it an attempt to console me after seeing me hurt? He was here to protect my physicality, not to caress my emotions. But I saw his silver eyes, no starlight shone there anymore, his tensed dimple had appeared, it felt as if he was being truthful.

"For now I just need you to stay very still right here while I sleep," I said, batting my lashes lazily, hungry for sleep and moving away from him.

"You will only stay for a few hours. I need a princess, not a block of ice."

"But of course, Your Majesty, your order is my command," I teased, giving him a mocking bow with an impish smile.

His eyes closed with annoyance at my behaviour, he was so stuck up that teasing him was easy. Cocking his head back, he gave me an examining look that had my toes curl. "Red is your colour, princess."

"Is it?" I asked, looking down on my attire. "I suppose so, this one makes my breasts look good too."

"Yes, but they looked better with nothing on."

I raised my eyes up at him only to find his expressionless features sterner than ever. "Well," I said with a shrug. "There is nothing under."

He stilled and his mouth parted slightly open as if to say something before his gaze travelled down my attire.

"Staring won't burn my dress off, darling."

He shrugged a wide shoulder. "Asking might."

Shameless smug idiot who'd learnt to frustrate me back. "Good joke."

"Am I joking?" he asked, staring at me like he was about to solve a puzzle. "Then you should laugh."

Somehow...I laughed.

"There," he said quietly, staring at me with a soft stare. "Smiling again."

And then as if on cue, my smile dropped. What was happening?

"Why are you avoiding me?" he asked, bringing me to another halt. "After Brisk, even in Brogmere you would not look at me for longer than a few seconds."

There was no shame in the truth, not that it would matter to him anyway. "Because you weird me out. I can't seem to keep my tongue back to your answers, I can't seem to lie to you, yet I don't wish to tell you my truths either."

"Don't avoid me, I won't ask without your permission."

It was now a game of push and pull, this was nothing. "Missing me, Kilian?"

"Yes, I missed how you say my name the most."

It was nothing, he was only playing with me. "I suppose even the contortion of the unnatural has some flair."

"Very, the beast is funny, too."

Another smile creeped in my face. "Good night."

"Can I ask?" he called again. "Why do you sleep in there?"

He asked. No one asked.

Searching for my weakness. Looking to invoke my fears. He is still my hunter. Hesitation hovered all around the air, but somehow my body turned to him again. "My head, it goes absolutely quiet in there," I confessed before I left towards the centre of the maze. I owed him no explanation, yet I gave him one—again.

Nestling in the middle of my siblings' resting place, I fell into such a lovely hard slumber. This place to me was the pure absence of madness.

25

RED AND HER

KILIAN

IT HAD BEEN HOURS since I threatened to kill her father, to which she had laughed and said nothing. The same long hours since she had laid asleep on the frozen snowy ground. Had she thought it a joke? Did she not know I rarely joked, especially about the sort?

"Princess?" I called behind the maze wall, but no response came. She had made me promise not to cross to her. *Especially you*. Especially *I* was not to cross it. What was she trying to hide? Was it my presence that could taint the only place she ever felt calm?

"Snow, it has been hours, we have to get you inside," I shouted loud enough even the wall guards must have heard me, but she did not respond and I was growing anxious. "Come out, woman. If you are playing with me and trying to get me to lose my head I assure you, I can give you five thousand other ways for you to entertain yourself better, so come out."

After the third time, I decided to go after her. I would deal with her anger, it had never been an issue with me before.

It first struck my limbs to a halt and then my chest filled with an unintelligible hurt. She laid on the snowy ground in the middle of three resting places. My breathing tightened while I took in the mad woman sprawled between the graves, an arm over one of them. *Serene Krigborn* it read—her mother. It did not take long to realise who the other two belonged. She slept soundlessly, almost too comfortably, her cheeks red from the cold and she slightly shivered—but she seemed happy, the happiest.

I flicked my hand in the air and moved the snow on top of her with my magic. Quiet—she said her head went quiet in here. How much she must have loved them. How much she still did.

She looked so calm, so frail and so magnificent. I lowered to my heels to study her in this unusual form. I had to wake her up, but I did not want to. For a small forever, I stayed and admired and contemplated her. I'd never seen a storm so calm, yet so thunderous and pained.

She stretched like a napping cat, ready to shift awake, and I went back behind the wall, flicking my hand in the air to drag snow over my steps. If she knew I'd seen her, she'd push me away again, avoid me.

After a few minutes, she came half asleep from behind the wall. Her crown had shifted sideways and she clutched the pillow and blanket tight to suppress her shivering.

I clenched my jaw shut to prevent letting out a laugh. She studied me for a second, her eyes oddly fell to my chin and then she headed without any words towards the castle. Odd never began covering her.

The little murderous vixen had turned to a human woman in flashing moments in front of me and I did not know which was mightier or scarier.

I followed her to the library, a bored look accompanying her surveying eyes. The room filled with officials who had turned to stare at her all the same, and I could not blame them. When she had come out this morning I had stumbled back at the sight of her, her sheer beauty radiated, how she wore her poise, how her eyes of yellow crystal had shone like torches, her strong presence that of a warrior who had been through more than just war but through pain, heartbreak and darkness. It had taken me long enough to realise that beyond everything she was headstrong, powerful, thoughtful and deeply caring for those she loved.

She guided us through the library and sat us at a corner table, grabbing a book and lazily flipping through it till a known figure headed in our direction. He was tall, slender, his skin a rich dark brown and his hair greyed all over. It was the general I had seen around Snow, the one who'd warned her about Brogmere.

She jumped from her seat and hung her arms around his neck, giving him a tight warm hug. I had not seen her this affectionate before with anyone except Nia and Caiden.

He eyed her bruise with concern and then threw a suspicious gaze towards me. "I see your two friends have finally left your sight. Getting awfully confident, are we now?" he said with a strong tone, partially aiming it at me—his shadows cast distrust the more he looked at me.

"I can have all the lives of everyone in this castle, Sam, before most of them have a chance to whisper my name. Having skills like mine does wonders to your self-confidence," she said playfully, making the general laugh.

It was no laughing matter, she actually could.

He glanced over at me before turning to the princess again. "That was a very close one. Twice now, Snow, twice," he enunciated. "Too many opportunities I have let you brush danger." He let out a sigh and rubbed his jaw in frustration. "The two Adriatians, they had given correct information. My soldiers traced a few Adriatians and found your doubts to be true, your father has been forming a Auran squadron. I truly wish you'd be convinced when I tell you that this is only precaution."

I had the same guess as him. Larg had told me Silas collected Aura of all sorts. But why did it worry miss dark head?

She folded her arms. "If your attempts to portray my father as an innocent hoarder of Aura had not been torn to shreds by his own action, I could believe what you just said."

He shut his eyes tight. "I am afraid he will get a hunch of this pretty soon, especially after what you did in Brisk, let this go now."

"Tempted," she said boredly. "But bear with me, Sam. You know my senses have never betrayed me."

What did she fear?

Samuel peered at me. "You were supposed to be her leash. Tie her up and hold her still and safe."

"Believe me, I share the disappointment," I said. "But as for the safe part, I reassure you with no doubt that no harm will come her way."

"I am right here," she grumbled, annoyed. "Sam, could you have Van and Ester returned to their borders?"

He stared at her, blinking confused. "Returned?"

She nodded. "I promised them, but they have a warning and a lengthy criminal record in Isjord, they are banned from ever entering these lands."

She had been truthful. I held myself still from turning wide eyed to her.

The general nodded, still seeming somewhat hesitant to what Snow had said. "I have no news on the Isline villages. Your father has taken complete matter to the new general Moregan, all the matters to the Solaryan vandals are passed to her and kept highly secretive, they even moved the party to a separate camp away from the castle," Samuel informed the princess, looking around us nervously, his shadows dressed with fear.

She leaned in. "Where about?"

"No, I warned you before about Moregan. I'm not sending you straight to flogging or worse. And with my own hands at that," the general expressed, and I sighed in relief.

"Fine." Her foot wiggled under the table nervously. "The burned Lord mentioned that the vandals have been passing through to Isjord from Casmere. I am very unfamiliar with that area and I would go myself if my father had not gone rabid from what I did to his beloved swine," she said. "Would you be able to note anything strange there for me?"

I understood the hunt on the Adriatian trespassers, especially after finding out few were working with her father, but why was she looking into the Solaryan vandals with this much curiosity, for what reason was she so interested in these attacks?

Samuel narrowed his eyes onto the table and rubbed a hand on his stubbly chin. "I will find ground and reason as soon as I can, and will head there."

"He also mentioned that my father has sent troops to Seraphim. He is after something Solarya is after, too."

Samuel struck with surprise. "I have not heard that before. Seraphim, are you sure?"

She nodded and his gaze traced back down to the table, now in pinched concentration. What was she concocting I could not form altogether?

"Sam, is Elias in Moregan's team?" she asked slyly. That had to be the captain that Mal told about, the one who flirted with her continuously. He had gotten on her bad side and earned a punishment that my brother had been too busy laughing to tell me.

"I know what you are thinking, Snow, he likes you, but he would not betray Isjord for nothing. He is as stubborn as his father. Venzors are not to be dealt with," he warned.

"Trust me Sam, I will have him like an open book before I enter his bed."

I turned at her words and she cocked a brow up at me. "Why the surprise, Kilian, I want my fun before I marry your miserable toad of a king."

I did not know why I was surprised at her words. She was about to enter a loveless marriage to someone she hated, she just didn't know how much of a toad the king truly was, and I could not blame her for her choices of entertainment.

Samuel laughed. "You do know ways to a man's heart, Snow, but don't know if you can find it around this one."

"The only way to a man's heart is with a dagger, but I know the way to their head."

"An axe?" I asked.

She frowned, but the general howled with laughter.

Fully turning to me, she cocked an elbow up on the chair rest. "Didn't take me an axe to get to yours, did it now?"

I mimicked her action. "Correct, it was poor manners, bruteness, love of danger, recklessness and many more as such. Might as well have driven an axe through my head, it would have hurt less."

She sneered, smacking the book she held down on the table. "It's never off my list, don't fret."

Gods, wasn't she gorgeous when she was angry?

"I'd take those words to their importance, boy, last time she came asking for luke-warm advice on how to pluck out an eye ended up with her plucking out her uncle's eye," Samuel warned, standing up.

I never have underestimated her, would not begin doing it now. But now I knew to differentiate her threats. "So I have heard."

Her and the general exchanged goodbyes and words of caution. Just after he left, she fiddled endlessly around with her book, looking like she was brewing something.

"Exactly how much of a miserable toad is your king?" she finally asked. Such innocent words. She was fiercer and more dangerous than a dozen soldiers, yet she framed that sentence so cautiously.

It had been long since I had laughed to this extent, shaking and almost tearing up. "He is entertaining, just not the kind you might enjoy," I said, still smiling at her question and she was looking at me with such odd eyes—the oddest. Round and full, so shiny and lively. Had they always been like that?

"Well, that is a shame. If he was good looking I might have let him fuck m—"

"Snow, heavens, please," I interrupted her before she could finish.

Her smile wore down and she gave me a look of distaste. "I like you ordering more than I like you pleading, do not change on my behalf. I wouldn't want the Adriatians to think I have trained their dogs."

That was all it took to have her overthink and crucify her own thoughts, for her to lift that shield up once again. "You are to be my queen," I said, "I might as well be yours."

"You can always continue your plan to assassinate me after the deal has been struck."

I rubbed the bridge of my nose frustrated. This woman. "But why, can't you see I am growing so very fond of you?"

"Even if you are truly fond of me, I am sure others will not hesitate." I turned again at her words and she raised a brow at me. "Come on now, you know what your people think of me, do not act so surprised. They once wanted to kill me, what will stop them this time and now I am to be served to them on a silver platter and right to their mouths. The prophecy lives and so do I, Mal has told me about it."

Adriatians could think whatever they want, she was an Isjordian princess and soon their queen. They will have to deal and live with it, especially when so much was at stake, when they were at stake...when she was at stake. "They will first have to pass my blade and the king's. No harm will come to you in Adriata or anywhere else, the prophecy has already proven itself wrong more than once."

There was a pause, just like it had been in the gardens earlier when I'd threatened to kill her father. She doubted me. "No, darling, I will not let you kill your own for me, whatever my worth is to you and your kingdom. They will pass through mine first, you know the thrill it gives me to do that," she said pensively, lost in her ever-thinking mill that rotated with so little trust in her head.

For once I was glad she was able to protect herself the way she could, but it also scared me. She was more than dangerous, she schemed and plotted. To top it all, fiery vengefulness fuelled her hate towards all of Adriata and especially toward the king, it almost felt like she had everyone where she wanted them to be, not the opposite.

"Could I ask for one truth?"

She studied me for a moment, before nodding, though still somewhat hesitant.

"The lord, why did you kill him?"

"I didn't lie to you," she said, dropping her head on the chair rest and smiling widely. "I truly didn't want him alive."

A half-truth is not a truth either. "Beyond that."

She stilled and her amused features dropped. "Pen, I had her ask around the servant quarters for information relating to anyone that could help a Solaryan find entry in Isjord. You know castle walls have ears, they might have heard something. All had one answer: that pig I roasted." She halted for a breath and I laughed, her round eyes not missing a beat to return, but she continued, "Apparently, a few years back my father had appointed him Lord of Brogmere, the only foreign ruler of a city. That was doubtful as it was, yet he was a poor piss drunk Solaryan bastard highborn without a grain of wits or experience, not a scholar, not even a soldier. Little to no surprise, I knew he was the nephew of Queen Cora of Solarya. Having gotten on the bad side of the royals, they exiled him away sometime ago. Think, someone that close to the royal family of Solarya, just how many connections and secrets did he have, and who could put good use to them?"

"Your father."

"Yes, but a Solaryan is still a Solaryan, sworn oath under the sun, eye of Cyra, to each other's loyalty. A patriot with such liberties and support in Isjord, who would profit from that?"

"The Solaryans."

"Star pupil you are," she praised, wearing a smirk. The vandal attacks—she knew the lord had information.

"So you thought him to be a double spy? But he didn't have much to go around either."

"He had enough, he was only a businessman. All he did was trade one favour for another. The shop owner in Casmere was his acquaintance. Nia checked his tabs, they had done business together and still were. The ships that had left illegally towards Solarya after my father closed trades mostly had his products being shipped and sold."

"You are saying he lied, but it was not what I saw."

"He withheld the truth, not lied. He helped the merchant bring Solaryans into

Isjord through his port check, but the ship actually docked in Casmere without being ransacked by Isjordian patrols. The Lord played both sides, profited from both sides considering the gold we found in his safes. Still told us about the merchant, just not the whole truth. I didn't need the whole truth anyway."

How long had she been planning this?

"You are impressed, admit it," she pushed, studying my dazzled expression.

"Maybe I am, the beast is witty, too."

She seemed quite satisfied with my answer as she smiled again. What she had stumbled upon troubled me immensely. Her father's spy on the Sun court connected to Prince Otis, second to the throne, right on the table of secrets of Solarya. Silas could have known everything, from royal treasure archives to ways to attack the kingdom easily. Had he planned any attack, a breach, was it still in his plans? Was that why Solaryan mercenaries were raiding villages in Isjord and why the dead lord believed they'd been sent by Magnus?

"And about his particular indiscretions, how did you find out?"

She laced her gloved fingers together, absently looking down at the,. "Pen brought me a servant who had worked in his court and Nia did research on his city."

"You wanted to use them as ground for his kill, didn't you? Not to put doubt on your intentions to interrogate him."

"Yes, it was good ground with the court, not to have their feathers too erect about killing one of their own. But I truly did not want him alive either. He was not going to escape his end even if it played nothing with them. The servant girl told me things I wish I had the ability to unhear before she showed me her scars, burn marks everywhere underneath her clothing—everywhere except her face and hands." She swallowed as if tasting the memory again. "Then she confessed the rest, how four of his bastard-born had died merely toddlers upon his sick hobbies." She blew out a heavy breath. "I can't say that was not one of the most satisfying lives I have taken."

Murder was not my first choice of punishment, but I could have not agreed with her more on this one. "You wear it well, the consequence to your actions," I said, moving my thumb over the cut on her lip and then her bruise. She raised her somewhat shocked face to me, that stare turning all warm, soft, gold and feather thorns. "Your bravery frustrates me, but it is admirable."

The whole castle heard them this morning. Nia had physically restrained me from breaking toward the dining chambers after I heard Silas hit her. Then I allowed myself to smile after her every retreat. How could she make mighty Silas appear so small? Her shaken sight, the bruise, the cut—all had triggered something in me. I hated seeing her hurt.

A small smile rose on her lips. "Father dearest has a slightly different phrasing for that. How can someone expect a saint by raising a death bringer is beyond me."

Right. She was her and I was me. I pulled my thumb away from her bruise and she inventively followed it with her eyes. "Why are you trying to work this out? Isn't this his problem to deal with? Every ruler faces such small issues almost all of the time."

"That's what worries me most, he doesn't cause or allow small issues. Small issues have no part in his court. You view the top of the iceberg and your ship sinks from what is underneath."

I blinked. "Iceberg?"

She laughed, hard, clutching her stomach tightly. The sound coming out of her was radiant, like clouds when they parted for scarce rays of sun, like the smell of a rose after rain—deeply intoxicating. My brows rose full of questions at her amusement. What did I say?

"My point was," she said, still smiling. "He never acts on such miniscule stand of action. He is a peacock, grand and flashy. Pay mind to small details and you will stumble on his true plans."

"You fear he is planning something?"

"No, not fear. Doubt. Shouldn't everyone be aware of him by this point?" She was correct, underestimation was a bad habit, especially when it came to Silas.

"That day when we returned from Kirkwall, why did you let them send the bodies back?"

She leaned back, fiddling with her book again, attention detached from her surroundings. "You said one truth."

"So you admit that you lied that day as well. And you ask me why I try to see past your actions as something else."

My words seemed to have taken her aback because she turned to stare at me wide eyed. "Why do you try?"

"I asked first."

"I asked back."

Because she confused me, because she made me dizzy with questionable words and even stranger actions. Because it bothered me, not being able to categorise someone as I had been taught. Fine line between right and wrong Nia had said, but to me there was never such a thing. One was either wrong or right. "Because I want to understand you."

"They didn't send you to understand me," she responded, a frown beginning to form in her forehead.

"Why would that be so wrong, to have someone understand you?"

"Letting on to your truths is like bleeding in front of a shark," she said monotonal. Words that left half-sturdy from her. "You already have learned too much of my weaknesses, and let's not forget who you are to me."

Yet her truths were like moonflowers, they took a certain darkness to open, but once in bloom they stunned and they mystified me. If anything, they had become my weakness.

"Who am I to you, Snow?"

"My nightmare."

Her words settled the shield of air between us once again. It had always been there. Maybe it had been stirred for a moment, but it didn't take to see to know that air was always there, just like her past. Two truths: a sincere one and a heart-breaking one. I reminded her of nightmares and she reminded me of the moon. We both saw one another in the dark, but why was she beginning to glow in mine?

We left the library at her angry growls directed at her stomach that had not stopped rumbling till she forced her way towards the kitchens. She'd removed the red cape, unbound her dark hair, the crown now rolled around her wrist and I carried her red slippers while she sprawled barefooted in one of the servants' benches. She waited for her stew impatiently, chewing on the empty spoon. Ken was never surprised at her presence at the servants dining halls as per usual, he greeted her and promised to quickly cook her favourite food. She was so very odd to me, she looked so normal when she slept and ate that I had forgotten who I was looking at. It became even harder to believe when she stuffed her face so tight with food that she could barely breathe, and when she swallowed, a tear dropped to her cheek.

"Am I funny to look at?" she asked, dropping her spoon loudly on the table. Appearing almost upset.

"Why do you ask?"

She frowned and pointed to my face. "This is the most internally amused I have seen you since we have met."

"It's not amusement."

She stared at me doubtfully before resuming her eating. "A chunk of wood is more giving," she murmured, glancing annoyed at me. I almost laughed again, earning another glare from her. Adorable. She was adorable in this form.

"You suppose this Elias has the information you are looking for?"

She stopped chewing and raised her eyes to me, cheeks swollen with food. "Yes, that Elias is Elias Venzor, son of Lord of Venzor."

A lord's son? Had what I'd gathered actually been true, was she truly attempting a coup on her father? Yet the question I asked did not match the one I wanted to ask. "A lover?"

She finally swallowed, her tongue sweeping over her lips. "Not the word I'd use." Tapping her stomach gleefully, she leaned back. "Kilian, what else is there in Seraphim, tell me."

I took a seat across from her. "*Please* is the word you were looking for."

She extended a hand over my arm, her fingers tracing lines and circles as she slowly rose from her side of the table. My eyes fought hard not to admire all of her form. Leaning close to me, she fluttered her lashes, her locks spilling over my shoulder, the scent of flowers in my air. "Pretty please," her voice was but a purr as she spoke in ear. "You prick."

The beast was indeed funny—too funny. Usually it was hard to smile, but she made it hard not to smile. I didn't fight it, I was amused. "Very convincing, but I am not Elias. No need to try so hard, words would have sufficed."

Her eyes fell to my mouth, proving indeed that she needn't try any harder, she had me right there. "Forgot that my face is enough for you." She shot a glance below to between my legs before wiggling her brows playfully at me.

Hells. The hells was going on with me.

I sighed, crossing my arms and ignoring the tightening of my body. "Seraphim? It might take me a while to remember now that I think about it."

She raised her hands in surrender and sat back in her chair, flicking a hand in the air for me to continue.

"Their last king was a known collector. Jewels, animals, books, herbs, potions, relics, and all sorts. He was a scholar with a desire for knowledge and connection with the spiritual, always hungry to discover more, that was the reason for their rise and fall, too. He wanted too much and what he could not have—pathway to the gods. People still have the misconception that Seraphim belonged to the elementals, but they were blessed by a spiritual god, Adan. Their city, Hayes, was the carrier of the first flame, it still remains burning there to this day, it is called the first blessing. They were the first city to be gifted the Aura of a god—the city that brought fire to the world. It symbolises more than just the element. Fire is warmth, therefore they could manipulate kindness and the seasons as well by warming or cooling the earth."

"Hells, Kilian," she said wide eyed, interrupting me. "What did you swallow, *'Dardanes thousand steps to history'* or *'Numen liber to after the ascending'*?"

Rubbing the bridge of my nose, I sighed. "You were not listening,"

"Continue, I like it when you talk history to me," she said, waving her hand again and leaning into the chair, a smile hitched on her face.

Dizzy—it made me dizzy.

"My point was," I said, clearing my throat. "Your father could want that, the flame of Hayes, to warm his lands. Not only physically."

"Cold is god blessed, cannot be melted."

"It is, but so is the flame, they come both from the heavens."

A beam of interest radiated in her eyes before she scowled in thought to herself. "Why would Solarya want it, too?"

"To have some leverage over your father, to make him dependent on their trade, revenge for the agreement. The list can go on and on."

And like that the interest faded. "You have little faith in the Solaryans, they are not so petty."

"Why do you think he is after something else?"

She crossed her arms and her tongue brushed over the cut on her lip as she pensively held the silence, looking unsure if she wanted me to know or not.

"Three Lords, Snow," I said, and her attention snapped to me. "What are you attempting?" I knew what she was attempting. Lords on her side, intercepting and ruining her father's plans, digging for friction between kingdoms that she could leverage to lure court against Silas. She wanted Isjord. To destroy or to rule I could not comprehend.

"What does it look like to you?"

"Reckless," I said. "What do you intend to do once every Lord is on your side? Take Isjord?" The question sounded ridiculous spoken out loud.

She shrugged. "Perhaps. Will you stop me?"

"If it affects the agreement I will."

She pouted and shook her head. "It won't."

"Your revenge?"

"No, a blood bargain."

I frowned. "What blood bargain?" No one entered those death traps anymore no matter the price, the fragility of that magic was too costly if not fulfilled to its most extent detail of request.

She raised a brow. "You honestly thought my father would have me agree to marrying the man I've sworn to kill? Come now, darling, I thought you would have already known I'm not the most obedient character out there. I made a bargain, Kilian. One I cannot lose. This agreement for Myrdur."

Of course there had been an exchange. I'd wondered too what had her convinced, considering she could have not only escaped but refused to. But a blood bargain? The more I thought about it, the more I understood. She felt responsible for Myrdur, Nia had said it before. For her to enter that bargain meant that Myrdur was beyond precious to her.

"So, you will honour the agreement, receive Myrdur, marry the Night King and what next? Overthrow your father?"

"Oh, no, not overthrow," she said, leaning on the table again. "Snatch Isjord from his hands. Stab his favourite child."

"Destroy Isjord?"

She threw me a wink. "Right there."

"Snow—"

She let out a sigh, leaning back on the chair. "Of course, Kilian *style* I will get the moral lecture of it."

"There was no moral lecture, but the concern of danger you are dragging yourself to."

"I have you, don't I?" She wiggled her fingers in the air. "Lifting shadow walls, telling liars, figuring out truths, offering your life for me, the moral support of your pretty face."

I resisted the urge to fall for the trap she set to forgo the conversation by stating a truth. "I have hurt you more than I have protected you."

She shook her head. "You have not hurt me. I have to feel to hurt."

"Hate is a strong emotion."

"Yes, but it is not a hurting one. More of the nurturing sort, don't you recon?" she teased, slyly giving me a wink.

"Is that why you have emptied yourself of any, because you don't wish to hurt?"

Annoyed I'd forgone every snare, she leaned back in her rest. "I have not emptied anything. They just...left me."

Left her. Forced or willingly?

She swallowed, eyes bobbing back and forth to me and then around the room. "You are staring, enough of it."

"Am I being denied to look at you?"

"Yes," her voice was meek, somewhere between uncertainty and unwillingness of the mouth to obey the brain.

I smiled. "I don't think I have heard you this torn before."

Her lip ticked up in a sneer. "You are so smug sometimes I could swear there are two of you in that body of yours."

"I am sure you would not mind."

Her mouth parted open a few times, but she seemed to have run out of words. After moments of silence and staring, she narrowed her stare in thin slits. "You really think I'll drop my dress if you keep staring at me, don't you?"

I guffawed, dropping my head back. "I think I only need to ask."

She threw a spoon at me. "I don't like this new found mouth of yours."

I caught it mid-air and set it back on the table. "I am sure you would not mind it on yours."

"Seven sweet hot hells of Celesteel," she said, wide eyed.

"My, but why?" I asked in a similar teasing tone she used. "Frustrating to be teased on and on?"

She flung a hand in the air composedly. "Point made."

I nodded. "Good."

She studied me for a moment. "Why do you smile at me? Laugh at my jokes?"

"Now she denies me smiles."

"You know what I mean. Why did you give in? I am sure the Kilian of that first day we met would never tolerate his gaze lingering over me for a moment, and this one is openly flirting with me."

"I am flirting with you?" I was flirting with her.

"What do you call this?"

"Two adults, sincere adults." And flirting.

"Is that what we are? Sincere?"

"You think I am lying?"

She shook her head. "No, you are forcing yourself to tell the truth. That is worse than lies. I am who I am and you know very well. You hate that part of me along with the whole existence of me. You hate when I kill, you hate that I think about killing, you hate my purpose, you hate...the whole of me. It doesn't matter if you feel attracted to me, most are, but you are Adriatian and I am your monster. Yet here you sit there having a light conversation with the one you hate."

She was wrong again. "I don't hate you."

"I think you are forgetting to hate me. I think you have built an image of me in your head and you keep pushing that above all I have done and all I will do. I will tell you, it is a grave mistake."

"Cakes," Caiden called, striding in with Mal down the room.

"Sleep inside," I said, standing to leave.

"Don't forget, Kilian."

I turned to her. "That your revenge won't grow cold?"

"That I am a hateable monster that will end you. Above all that you have seen beneath me, it's still that monster."

Yet I saw all but that.

26

PAST AND PRESENT
KILIAN

FOR DAYS SHE HAD barely left her room, circling back and forth the library, gardens and the kitchen quarters, looking heavily bored and itching to leave the castle grounds. I had been thankful for the few days of peace and indulged in her frustration. Mal on the other hand seemed to enjoy her company. I had seen them chatting and playing around several times in the winter gardens, she had even taught him a few tricks with her daggers which he endlessly practised around our chambers to my annoyance.

Nia and I were the guard for the night. Snow had been asleep when Nia last checked, finally able to do so after parading around the castle like a dead spirit without a blink of rest.

"At least she is not sleeping in the garden," she murmured to herself.

"At least then she was doing some sleeping," I said and she gave me a smile.

"She is not always like that, you know. This place has turned us all twisted, her the most," Nia admitted, hovering by the large windows. "It is not easy to come to a place that reminds you of how you lost your soul and have people that caused that continuously circle around you." Her gaze turned cold and her face stern as she studied me, her shadows had always been the same unchanging vengeance and pain surrounding her at all times. I knew she felt those emotions strongly when she looked at me and Mal, her anger was towards our kind as well. "What cruel irony that she is about to end in the den of another just as worst," she added, shaking her head.

"It is." And it was cruel.

A frown gathered on her brow. "Malik is simple, but I can never understand you, Kilian, do you want to strangle or comfort her?"

"Most of the time, strangle her." There was no reason to hide what I thought, she could read me like an open book.

She smiled widely, breaking her stern expression. "That makes two of us." Her antics were not restricted only to the people she disliked. Though I knew her antics with her friend were always playful and heart-warming. I liked knowing she had people who cared around her.

"Are you not going to ask? I know you know and so does your brother," she said.

"If you had wanted it to be known I am sure you would have told us yourself. I am not going to ask something you clearly didn't want in the open."

"No, I don't," she admitted, "but thank you for not revealing it, though you know the consequences if you had. Snow would have had such a sweet time torturing you to your demise." She laughed at her words, but that was no laughing matter, I knew she would have had a great time torturing me.

"Your magic seems to be different from mine, it looks untrained and unused."

"It is," she responded deep in thought. "I can feel others through myself, mostly Snow. Their emotions become mine for a short moment, but I cannot see any shadows like my mother used to."

They were not just untrained, they were suppressed. Carrying another's emotion was dangerous and came with great risks on the Aura's behalf. Many that suppressed magic could trap an emotion into them forever. The intensity would be unbearable. Many had driven themselves to death either by the continuous happiness that had bursted their heart or sadness so deep that had broken it.

"I am not sure if you know, but that carries some danger. If you would allow me, I could help you train it to some extent so that it won't present risk," I offered, but she looked unsure and frightened at my words.

Hesitation hovered over her thickly, "I still don't trust you."

"I am not asking you to trust me. It appears my kind has done a fine enough job in losing that from you too."

"They have done more than that." Dark grey clouds poured from her chest as her expression turned sullen and fearful. What had happened to her?

"The best we can do sometimes is to move forward."

She frowned. "Don't preach that to Snow, she will have your head."

"I already did and she drove a dagger through her shoulder, that *dahaara* runs on madness."

Her mouth parted open and she threw a worried glance toward the princess's bedroom door. "Please tell me you haven't called her that? She will show you truly just how made of steel her tongue is."

"You speak the Darsan tongue?"

"Bits that I can remember. Before I left Adriata I used to work in a wool house, the older ladies only communicated in Darsan, I picked it up pretty quick, but so can Snow if you annoy her enough. Don't tempt her."

"I wouldn't dream of it." I shook my head at the thought of what course of crazed action she could take just to annoy me and Nia smiled as if reading my thoughts. "Why did you leave Adriata, if that is not wrong of me to ask?"

Her head lowered, shadows griming to mimic her grave expression. For a moment I thought she would not answer me before she said, "I was sold to an Adriatian slave trader who sold me to a Vrammetheni traveller in Fernfoss, old Olympia." She stopped and took off her gloves, revealing a metallic structure resembling bones extending from both her cut wrists. "On our way to Fernfoss a girl fell sick and I tended to her for several days. One morning she became quite ill, I could feel the ring of her pain everywhere on me, it was almost deafening. Somehow I had extracted that emotion from her onto me. The traveller thought I was an Empath after witnessing that, so he cut both my hands to prevent me from inflicting pain on him."

Speechless—she had left me completely speechless. What must she have gone through? In this time and day slavers still roamed Adriata right under our nose. We had allowed that to be done to Nia, she was right to hate us the way she did.

She attempted to straighten. "It is fine though, they feel like my own, it's Crafter metal, blood crafted to fit me. Snow bargained for it and it is rare apparently." She attempted to give me a short smile, but her eyes didn't let her, betraying her sadness rooted in pain and fiendish memory. "They don't hurt or anything."

"Nia, I…I am very sorry. Truly and deeply." An apology that would never meet the end or even the beginning of her suffering. What she'd been through I couldn't begin to grasp what to feel or do.

She slowly put both her gloves back on. "I have moved past that, Kilian, can't entirely tell you it still doesn't haunt me, but there is no one without scars from their wounds. Snow wears them as a reminder, Cai gets over them and I bury them to forget. I suppose it shows how strong one is."

"One's strength is not measured from their worst, don't let it still define you."

She frowned again, but this time a smile stretched across her face. "Again, I beg of you, do not tell that to Snow."

Again, I would not dream of it though I'd never want anything more than to see her shoulders relieve from the weight of what she was juggling. However, she was too headstrong, using those corrosive weights to level and ground her, it terrified me to know what would happen once she took those off, once unleashed.

"Did you have family back in Adriata?"

"Relatives, not family. It doesn't even get close to what I have now. They were from Lyra. I am bastard born, but I did have a father, a mother and," she stopped, for a long while, "a sister, too."

"Do they know what happened?"

She let out something between a laugh and a sigh. "It was my mother who sold me, my father who felt relief for saving his marriage and the sister who lost a toy."

Air burned my lungs. "Give me names, Nia," I demanded. "And I swear an oath on Cynth—"

She rested a hand on my arm. "I bury to forget, remember?" Taking a deep breath she nodded and said, "We will not tell her about my training….at least for now."

"She will understand." I knew Snow would not disagree, knew she'd respect her friend's wishes.

She lowered her head, pensive and already regretful. "She might, but not without upsetting her."

After a whole ten days of sitting, waiting, countless sleepless nights by the library studying gods know what and impatiently prancing around, Snow had called all four of us to the stables. She wore a deep emerald dress, thicker compared to the ones she wore around the castle. Her hair was in an unusual braid and a fur lined brown cloak was thrown over her shoulders to keep her warm. Her attire was not for any of her missions, she never rode in anything except her uniform. She jollily chatted away, her smile bright and her guard loose. After what she'd said to me that day I'd tried to keep my distance, keep words to myself, deny myself glances of her. It seemed she was doing the same and somehow I loathed it.

Talk to me first, come to me first, joke to me and make me laugh again. Those words repeated all the time, but they were unheard pleas just as they were unspoken.

Damned be all. I reached a hand to stroke Memphis and she struck still, taking in my presence. "Trying to see if killing in a dress is equally as easy?"

A shy small smile tugged at the corners of her lips. "Tried, tested and approved, it is as easy."

"I have no doubts."

Caiden approached and pulled on her braid, making her yelp. "She has never killed in a dress before, if she intends to get near blood it's usually done in trousers."

"You don't know that," she grumbled, fixing her hair.

He threw an arm across her neck before turning to me. "Once, there had been a fight in a tavern, but she refused to help part it or even get near it till she unlaced her dress, carefully folded it atop a chair and took three men down in her shift, half naked."

She frowned. "It was a shame—"

"Shame to get the silk dirty, blood is notoriously difficult to get off," he finished her sentence and she gaped at him. He gave her a serpentine smile and they exchanged a look before he flicked her forehead, making her stumble a step back. "Get on the horse, people actually sleep, Cakes, Amerie has a child. She can't cater your royal arse at midnight."

"The two of you are close." My words were a strong statement more than a question. There was something between the two of them, but not in a lovers sort of way. Caiden's shadows read strong in her presence, but it was a discoloured mix of care and love, too entwined to tell.

"Jealous?" Her features lit with amusement.

I ran my fingers on her forehead, over the red spot Caiden had inflicted. I should have cut his fingers for that. "Curious, little beast, just curious." I was learning to let lies slip so easily out of me. Interesting.

She raised a brow and then let out a sigh almost in disappointment. "No need to be anyway, not of him at least. He thinks it is funny to tease me like that, it's the only reason why he does it."

I removed my fingers from her skin, but not from running them down her face first, watching her slightly shiver. "It sounds like you want it to be more than that." Did she have feelings for him beyond friendship? Did it bother me?

She rubbed her forehead where I'd touched a second ago. "Now, now, Kilian, it doesn't suit you, darling."

That word again—she used it almost knowing what it did to me. "Funny ways you find to avoid answering me."

Her face drew back to soft lines. "Cai and I are only friends and that is what we will always be, but we did try to be more than that...once. Well, maybe more than once in that one time."

I gave Memphis another stroke. "Why did you settle on only friends?"

"I was young, easily charmed and he was...Cai, charm incarnate."

"You two are alike in a sense. I'd think you'd get along fine together, he cares about you more than many care about themselves."

The corners of her mouth pulled up. "Trying to set us up again? Am I not marrying your king, what would the *Obscur Asteri* say about his guard playing matchmaker for his future wife?"

I grimaced a little and she laughed. That sun-coloured laugh. "Don't call him that."

Her hand extended next to mine as both of us stroked Memphis side by side. "Heard he cracked the skies and almost summoned night in the middle of day. My guardian said it shone black stars in the blue heaven of Nubil and afront Cyra for a week. Sounds like a scary man with a deserving scary name."

"He was a boy with scary powers, that is all. Now a man with useless ones." The lone Obscur could only learn the craft on his own. The magic had leaked out of control and almost summoned night in the middle of day. The black stars had been cracks of night peeking through blankets of day. Only a boy with no control of his powers, but people adored another being to fear, humans were born for submission.

"Careful how you speak about my future husband," she exclaimed, feigning authority and a straight face.

I fashioned a bow. "Apologies...my queen."

She bit her lip, her face red with wanting to laugh, but she held onto the act and cleared her throat. "Forgiven." And then she laughed. "You know, coming from your mouth, *my queen* doesn't sound so bad." She wiggled her brows up. "Imagine it on those night times. Or was it day?"

I gave her a look and patted Memphis one last time before leaving toward my horse. I was indeed beguiled. "Stop flirting with me."

"But I am your queen," she grumbled all play, and I smiled to myself.

The city was quiet in the evening, the sounds were muffled and contained within the households. The air casually broke from the howls of wolves, a common sound we had heard in Isjord. She directed us down towards an array of black cobbled labyrinth paths till we almost reached the outskirts where the height of the city wall could be seen only by craning your neck. We stopped in front of a small wooden house between a bakery and a closed flowery. A sweet spot that fitted too wildly with the grey fort of Isjord.

She lightly knocked on the door and the young pregnant Adriatian from the trials came into view, throwing herself over Snow. "I have been waiting for you," she said cheerfully, showing us in.

I did not understand what was happening. Had the cold frosted my brain? Was this not the woman that had cursed her to gods and heavens?

"My apologies, Amerie," the princess offered.

Mal stepped toward Amerie, his eyes circling around her. "Are you well?" he asked, carefully assessing her.

The young woman nodded and smiled, motioning for us to enter her home.

The house was simple and spacious, furniture was arranged lightly in the dining room, beiges and browns. It was warm, filled with the smell of sweet baking's, spices and mistletoe. A family home.

Amerie beamed with joy. "You came."

"I thought you might like to see a familiar face. Well, two handsome familiar faces," Snow said, sitting down and reaching for the biscuits displayed on the table. "That was Nia and I, the rest of the entourage was to scare the wolves."

Mal scowled. "Stray from wounding my handsomeness, princess."

She silently laughed, munching on biscuits. "It cannot be wounded any more than it already is."

He flicked his tongue at her and she back at him.

Caiden gave Amerie a hug. "Have you lost weight? The food is a drastic change in here, but to lose a whole pillow of a stomach? Very strange."

She giggled and made for the doors of another room. "My fat sleeps in her crib."

When she came back, a sleeping baby rested in her hands and she joyfully brought it for us to see. Nia held the little baby girl first after the three of us made a pass on the request. Amerie had not named her yet.

"Would you like to hold her?" Amerie finally asked Snow who'd been too busy chewing biscuits to pay attention.

Startled, she coughed her mouth stuffed with ginger biscuits and blinked back her moist eyes before nodding and cautiously taking her gloves off, revealing the small palms adorned in cuts and slashes.

"Have you peppered it?" Nia asked playfully. "She likes them peppered first, it helps with indigestion."

Snow gave us all a look when we chuckled silently from amusement. The baby shifted on her arms and her eyes widened in worry towards us. "There is something the matter, it moved," she said panicked, and the room shook again with laughter, almost waking the sleeping baby.

"Yes, Cakes, they do that a lot," Caiden teased.

"You should see what she does to her nappies," Amerie added.

"What does she do to them?" Snow asked, blinking confused and none of us held it in.

Her slender pale fingers traced the baby's features in wonder, the baby's little hand wrapped around her finger. "*Coghna, neh coghna.*" *Small, so small,* she whispered in Calgnan.

I saw it again, a second time, her gentle, calm and hypnotising sight that paled all gardens of flowers out of colour. I'd glued a stare onto her, on how that little being had seized her better than any trained soldier or assassin. I'd walked another trap of hers when coming here tonight. Not only had I relented to the bite of its sharp metallic jaw of tenderness, but the steel weight of that genuine smile.

"Don't, Kil," Mal warned in a murmur. "Don't begin convincing yourself that she will show this side when it comes to us."

"I am not."

"Then what are you doing?"

"Staring," I said. "Only staring."

"Well, stare any longer and you might see her brains, cut it out."

Snow played with the little baby's arm and I tried my best to follow my brother's advice by glueing my stare to the floor.

"She is trying to teach her sword fighting," said Nia.

Caiden shook his head. "I think it's waltzing."

"Did you come to recruit my daughter?" Amerie joined in while she lit all the candles in the room.

Snow smiled and tucked the baby's arm back in the blanket. "Possibly, but she has weak throws. I'd go for a scholar with this one."

Caiden handed Nia five silver dar. "Told you," the latter exclaimed, pocketing her victory.

"It was waltzing," said Snow.

Annoyed, Nia handed ten silver dar back to Caiden.

Amerie sat down with us. She appeared nervous for the first time around Snow, lacing and unlacing her finger, wanting to say something. "I have thought of a name, but I wanted your opinion on it, more like permission,"

Snow said, "You need not my permission, I am not a priestess, but I am curious about the name."

Amerie looked around us uncomfortably and shifted slightly in her seat. "I would like to name her Serene."

Nia and Caiden were looking at her like a madwoman. Snow stiffened for a split moment but then continued playing with the baby's little hair. It was her mother's name, her dead mothers name, the mother Adriatians had killed. The mother Amerie's people had killed.

"Amerie, I don't think—" Nia began, almost stuttering her words out.

"Serene it is then," Snow interrupted without separating her eyes from the small creature.

The rest of the visit had been mostly in silence except the light conversation Nia and Amerie exchanged with each other about her new house and the baby's needs—needs that Snow had fulfilled beyond what she'd promised when exiling her to Isjord.

We stood to leave after the baby woke up and needed feeding. Before we left I approached Amerie. "Is everything well, how are you settling in these lands? If there is anything you need."

"I am more than well," she interrupted, but I could see that her words only half meant what she felt. "I miss my husband and little Serene needs her father, but I will soon make peace with it, no need for worry. This was for the best, I know. I trust her, it was for the better," she added lastly with a wistful smile.

I finally understood it—the reason why Snow had exiled her here, alone.

She walked along the castle corridors in all the terrible silence she'd been coated from before. Amerie's decision had affected her more than what she'd expressed. Nia fiddled nervously at my side with her cloak, trying several times to step forward and say something, but each time she had held back.

Just as Snow opened the door to enter her bedroom, I grabbed onto her cold wrist. For a moment she did not turn, but didn't push me away either. And when she did turn to me, I wished she hadn't. Her face wore a wistful withered expression. I searched for them—I searched for the lively burning eyes of hers, yet I only found deep shadows of a faded sun. They weren't warm, they weren't cold, only an in-between sorrowful.

"Rest well," I said, lost at anything else to say, lost at words I'd gathered to ask before. *Are you alright? Please be alright. It is all alright, it will be all alright. Don't be anything but alright. Don't hurt, it will be...alright. Don't hurt. Please not you, not ever.*

"I will. Good night." She might have murmured or whispered the words, somewhere in the weak middle. Her cold hand slipped from my grip and over my own warm one. I felt the lingering touch she brushed over, the kiss of calamity and then...I cursed all cruel gods and guardians that watched as my heart rolled, sunk and drowned, lifted and swelled, longed and searched...for her. What was I doing? When did I become so selfish and unreasonable?

"Probably too stuffed from all those ginger biscuits she had," Nia joked to break gloom in the air.

I settled beside her. "She brought Amerie here afraid of what they were going to do to her in Adriata since she was carrying a mixed blood child. She thought if the two were together the child would suffer, that they would do the same thing they had done to her. That is why Snow separated them to different kingdoms where no one knew who they were, a new start."

Nia nodded and looked over her friend's door, behind where she was probably looming restless. Her shadows fluttered with a silent truth. "Yes."

"Why is she looking to take Isjord?"

Nia froze. "You know?"

I nodded. "Does she not understand Silas will catch onto what she is doing, that many will hurt in the process—her ,too. Heavens, her more than anyone."

She swallowed, her stare dropping to the floor. "She does not care."

"But you do, Caiden does."

"We are here because we do."

"Then you agree to her plans." Her shadows didn't.

"I understand what you mean, the killing, I feel it, too. What it does to those that die and what it does to her, but it is her solace. I cannot deny her solace even though I have wanted to." She faced me. "Do not tell her that, she cannot know."

"What have they done to her, Nia?"

She exhaled heavily. "Alaric, our guardian, used to describe it in a way for me and Cai to understand what she went through during her panic. When you try to forge steel into a weapon and it won't take shape, you break and melt it all over again, don't you? It was impossible to make her a weapon, but they still broke and melted her a thousand times. Sometimes just for the fun of it."

27

BARGAINS AND MONSTERS

SNOWLIN

THE CASTLE CORRIDORS HAD gone completely dark inside, barely able to see where my feet were stepping. A soft woman's voice called in my direction and I followed till it grew so loud my feet tingled above the ground and my heart thumped at its echo. I was surrounded by it, continuously shouting and yelling my name. I made my body move forward till I reached the back of the winter gardens. The sky was lit in thunder and lightning, thorns and leaves blew in swirls of air, bushes swayed as sails in a livid sea, and my mother stood at the middle of it. Her long dark hair waved at the touch of wind and her eyes had turned the colour of the void and lifeless. Blood pooled beneath her feet and coated her white gown and face. Tears streamed down my own endlessly. The muted screams crawling out of my mouth assaulted my throat till it ached and throbbed as wounds of nails. I could not move toward her and she could not hear me.

"*Run, Snow,*" she called to me, her voice carried by the wind, "*as quick as lightning, as quick as Nubil. Do not turn, do not stop and do not fear. Run till all you hear is nothing, till all you see is nothing, till you are so alone your thoughts echo in your ears. Promise me, Snow, you will run and you will live, promise me.*"

Her last words to me, the last words my mother had made me promise to oblige. I ran and ran, just like she had told me, as they burned the castle, as they killed her, Thora and Eren. I ran and ran, till my feet bled, till my skin cracked from the cold, till my wound had festered, till it took my father days to find me tucked deep in the woods.

"*Serene, Serene, I will call her Serene,*" another voice repeated in the air and I crouched to my knees, hugging myself tightly.

Shouts and screams, orders and death circled me. "*Kill the queen, kill her children.*" Tears sprawled out of my eyes at hearing those words again and the shiver was no longer a shiver, but a tremble that ached. Day turned to night, blue turned to black. Wind, storms, and frost blew as I hid and lived.

"*Snow, Snow.*" Alaric's arms had rounded me, and I knew then, that home had found me, that I was safe. "*I have got you, kid. I will always have you. Forgive me, forgive me.*"

Strong arms enveloped me, not Alaric's. Scent of citrus flowers brought warmth of spring, shaking me awake. Kilian cradled me in his chest, swaying us back and forth. I never let anyone touch me in a comforting way. I was taught that I didn't need it and shouldn't need it, but I leaned in nonetheless.

I blinked the fog of tears away and searched for his features. "Kilian?"

His hand smoothed through my hair, silent reassurance of caress and soft touches.

"You are okay. Nia has gone to call Caiden. He will help, he can help. She said he knows what to do. I don't know what to do." Desperation climbed his words, and worry swept his features. "What do I do, Snow?"

It warped. Reality warped, too, and I could not see him clearly anymore. "Kilian?"

He moved my hair back, searching for my eyes. "Yes?"

Which had been a nightmare? The one I kept revisiting every night or the soothing caress of the man...the man I'd sworn to hate and unleash my revenge upon, the one that hated me, the one who held me tighter than anyone had ever held me before. The longer I stared at his vivid starlight gaze, the more his features warped onto the ones belonging to the man that had reached me that night to take my life.

I shook myself free and ran. Sprinting past corridors, past guards, past servants and headed towards the garden till I stood in front of them—what remained of the ones I had loved harder than gods and heavens, harder than I had ever loved myself. I stared at them, my breath ragged, my chest flaring from the running and the bite of cold wind. My bare feet stung at the sensation of snow, an attestation of reality.

Be a dream. Be a dream. A silent moment, and then another, and my prayers had not been heard.

"You are so silent, mother, you don't answer me anymore, but," I swallowed the well of emotion down, "but I still hear your voice. Could you not hold me, too? Let me feel your arms around me. Could you have not held me then, couldn't you have let me come with you? I hate promises, they are made to be broken yet I cannot break yours. You cursed me with life, one I didn't want and then made me hold tight into it." A cry coiled between my words. "I hate it here."

Static changed around me. Air turned dense with a sharp metallic tinge leaking out of memory. A blizzard took off across the lands, veiling all sight while skies thundered. As if still dreaming, the place felt so unreal and foreign. I wished upon heavens for all this to have been but a dream, wished so hard and prayed so hard my lids were sore from the pressure. My whole body trembled, but not from the cold, from the hollow feeling that had lodged on my chest.

"Cakes," Cai called breathlessly, and I heard three others behind me as well as him.

This was not a dream after all, I hoped at least this part had been. Embarrassment held me still from turning and seeing their faces. The faces who probably would pin me down as a mad woman. "I made you all promise to not come in here, did I not?" I shouted, half to mask my compromising situation.

"If you had not ran like you saw a dead spirit in the middle of the night, in your nightgown and barefooted at that, out of castle grounds, maybe, just maybe, princess, we would have not been forced to take such drastic actions as to break a promise made to you," Kilian's angry voice broke the static that was forming in the air. His voice had taken a shade of concern as well, he must have thought his pawn had gone rabid when he had seen me. The thought made me cringe with embarrassment.

"He is right, Snow. We thought something was wrong," Nia spoke, and I finally turned in disbelief at her words. She gave me a knowing look and nodded slightly to confirm what I was thinking—she must have felt me again.

Malik lifted his hand in the air, the snow coating, soaking and prickling my skin dropped away and Kilian removed his jacket, throwing it over my shoulders. It smelled sweet like tangerines and sour like lemon flowers, he smelled like spring.

"Don't run from me like that. Ever," he murmured, only for me to hear.

My heart stammered loudly under my chest from the way those words brushed softly over me. I didn't like being ordered, but it felt like an order I had to obey. "You reminded me," I confessed, perhaps too unrestrained. "Reminded me of him."

He froze, refusing to stare at me.

"Of the man who scarred me that night. I ran from him, not you."

His fingers halted over the collar of the jacket, brushing my skin just slightly. "Do I often remind you of him? Lie to me and I will know."

I swallowed hard and whispered, "Yes...no. Maybe. Though not often, but you should. You're one of them, I should be aware of you, loathe your very existence, not bear your presence. Truly, I should...but I don't, not always at least."

His thumb gently grazed my cheek. My eyes briefly fluttered shut at the touch. "I can work with that."

There was something wrong with me and the way he was looking at me. There was something wrong with me and the way he shared the same breath as I. We were in the middle of the garden, putting a show in front of everyone so I slid past him and walked to leave.

The two Adriatian brothers had halted and stared towards the graves.

"Let us all go now," Cai ordered, almost sensing their hesitation.

"We want to pay our respect first," Mal said.

My eyes shot wide, my mouth twisted to a snarl and I grabbed onto Kilian's arm. How dare they taint their resting places, the people who caused their deaths wanted to pay them respect? If this was not the most sacred place to me I would've howled with laughter at their words. "You will do no such thing," I said, and his calm silver gaze slid over my fiery one.

Nia's hand rested on my shoulder, "I would like to do the same." Nia was my sister, she was my family, more than anyone else she knew how I had suffered at the hand of their kind. Why was she doing this, had I allowed her to get too close to these bastards, had she turned on me, did she have this little regard for my feelings?

The static returned and clouds thundered again. I was truly convinced now this was not a dream but a nightmare, one of the worst kind. Betrayal, hurt, disbelief coated all senses.

"Nia, enough with this madness," Cai called from the back, worriedly extending his arm towards her. "Come."

Her face drew in with apology and her sweet hazel eyes glazed. "It can help them, they can. Adriatians are connected the most to the spiritual and the heavens, they can help them and," she stopped and took a deep breath, "and you, Snow, they can help you. It doesn't have to be this hard to sleep, eat, breathe, or mutter the name of your mother. You don't have to suffer because you think you need to be punished—that is not punishment, it is torture."

Disbelief, I shook my head in disbelief at her ridiculous words. "Oh no, dear, they will not help anyone and certainly not me. What makes you think I want their spirits gone," I admitted to her. "I want them here, even if I am to drag them around for years to come, they will be present to witness my wrath unleashed, my vengeance and hunger satiated. I want pain and I want anger and I want torture." I was inches away from her face. Inches away from blasting.

Her expression dropped to disappointment and she shook her head slightly in denial. "Please, you do not mean that," she pleaded softly, but the damage had already been done, she had already hurt me.

A laugh crawled up my throat, my subconscious refused to let this go. "You thought I would pull away, didn't you? That I would regret my plans. Didn't you?" my shouts pierced the air, and she flinched back.

Her eyes dropped down to the floor, full of the truths she had not revealed to me. She really had thought about it. All these years and she had said...nothing. "Every step you take in that direction, it feels like I am losing you," she murmured, gathering herself tight.

"Nia, I've lost myself long ago."

"Not like this. You are not your anger and revenge and what has happened to you. You are so much more and so beautiful and so kind, and I've known that person for so little, but I love that person and you have taken her away from me."

"I am nothing—beyond that I am nothing. They keep me alive. I am alive because of them."

"That doesn't mean you are living."

"I have no desire for that and you knew that well. Now, since you seem so connected to your roots lately, you could just tell me what am I feeling? What do my shadows say about all of this, since you've failed to understand my words before." I didn't mean to reveal her to the Adriatians, but my judgement was in flames of hurt. I regret those words the second they left my mouth.

"Nothing, Snow, you feel nothing."

Nia's hard words took me back a bit, she had always known what I felt. *Nothing*, she said, yet my breath hurt at how tight my chest welled in what I felt. Wasn't it so frustrating to tell someone how you felt torn by a thousand blades, yet they would never truly understand?

"Take the rest of the Adriatian dogs and leave, all of you. Now," I ordered coldly and full of spite.

She waited a while, expression wide in hope that I still had time to take them back. Finally given up, she left.

"I cannot bark it for you two," I said towards the Adriatians.

Kilian turned to Mal and nodded, prompting him to leave, but he stood behind. Just silently looking at me. I never knew what went in his stupid head, his features were as giving as a white canvas. "I meant that for you as well, Kilian, I am in no mood for your games. Go, it's an order."

He neared, guiding my arms through the sleeves of his jacket thrown over my shoulders. "You seem to have no problem doing so with your friends, those you call your family. But you do not order me, princess, you never will. You run that mouth so loosely and so hurtfully. Just because you are angry does not mean you can treat even those surrounding you like they are deserving of your anger." His calm features were flaring in a new sort of ire that I had never seen upon them. He tugged the sides of the jacket tight before beginning to button them one by one. "She is worried seeing you every night suffer the way you do. Just because you like to self-destruct does not mean others enjoy watching you do so."

How dare he? "You speak as though you care, has she softened your little barbarian heart?" I asked, approaching him close enough that I had to til my head back to look at him. My finger touched his chest in threat, pointing to his heart. Terribly loud, his heart was beating in paces of war hooves. First Nia protects this bastard and goes against all that I stand for, all I thought she as well stood for. Then he recites those venomous words with such grace to protect her as well. Had Nia been so concerned for my well-being she would have told, consulted and made known to me how she was feeling. I did not read minds and she had never been one to keep these sorts of things from me, but she chose the least appropriate moment not only to reveal my fears in front of them, but to spread mud on top of my family's memory.

"You have such odd ways of turning the situation to your liking, even if she had, as you say, it doesn't change the truth, the one you are finding hard to swallow," he spat, gently pulling my locks from under the jacket over my shoulder. "The truth that you are confused about your choices, that the second you allow yourself to see past your anger you forget them. As if...as if you can forget them. You are afraid of forgetting and letting them go, holding onto this as an excuse, holding onto pain as an excuse."

I had allowed his words to hit me and they hurt me as if he had truly punctured me with his steel. He did not know me, why was I allowing this bastard to take such powerful swings at me? "You know nothing, Kilian, nothing." My voice broke to my disbelief. I swallowed that choking feeling behind my throat. Even the one who I thought as my sister knew nothing, everyone knew nothing, gods and heavens knew nothing.

His eyes slightly softened, silver sparkles halting. "I know one thing, Snow, she cares for you. And whatever she did, she did for you and you need to stop whatever is broiling in that head of yours and just feel it rather than think it. Things sometimes are as simple as heard. Do not complicate them by rolling your anger and emotions on top. Do not become them," he said. His words sounded like a plea. They almost sounded like a prayer.

"I will do what I please."

"How long can you fight these nightmares for, how long can you torture yourself fighting them?"

"You'd rather I succumb to them?" I shouted, my jaw tight from anger. "I bet you'd love to take back a broken, weeping, fragile little princess. She would be so much easier to tame, torture and kill."

He moved quickly, cupping my face, his eyes piercing through mine. His fingers tangled between my hair and he dropped his forehead to mine for a swift second, breathing fast and so, so furiously. "There will be no need to tame, torture and kill you, it seems you're doing a perfect job of that yourself."

"Good for you then. How happy you must be."

He swallowed, tension circling his features, he was almost panting, his face not inches away from mine. I couldn't not read him. I wanted to read him. "Miserable, Snow, it makes me miserable. So I suppose good for you, how happy must it make you. At least now you might feel a bit of happiness however grim, unearthly and strange it is. Because you will find every reason in this realm to deny yourself real happiness, because you are too scared it might make you forget your revenge. But, Snow, love, pick your sacrifices wisely. Revenge is a bargain, you might be willing to trade your soul for it, but you also have people that love you and they don't see the shattering or the pieces because they still make the whole you. They love you—love you however you are. You told me is it worth living as such, but I want to ask you something else. Are you ready to lose them for it?"

He had silenced me for a while before I gathered all the voice I had left to ask, "This your plea for me to give up?"

He moved his thumb over my eyes to remove the snowflakes coating my lashes. "This is my plea for you to pick your bargains, that pretty little soul of yours might be worth more than you're selling. Broken can be mended in a thousand beautiful ways."

I scowled. "I'm not a vase, Kilian."

His lips twitched into a smile. "No, you're a stunning, witty murderous vase." For a split moment, his eyes darted down to my lips and I sucked in a sharp breath. That simple look chanted a storm inside me, but it was short lived because he moved away from me, letting me go. Not a second later he took note of my feet and turned ten shades of mad.

He rubbed his face and groaned. "Ridiculous woman, how many times do I have to tell you to wear shoes."

I blinked wildly at his loud anger and then down at my frozen bare feet. Within unnoticeable moments he was holding me up in his arms. A yelp escaped me at the sudden action. "Put me down, you burly fool, let me go."

I wiggled and wiggled, but he only held me tighter. "Your feet are half frozen, and as I said, I do not enjoy your self-destructing ways."

I looked down at my feet that had almost turned grey, almost the colour of a corpse. I tried to wiggle them to life, but they were completely numb.

The sun was slowly rising over the cloudy horizon and castle corridors were buzzing with servants who stopped astounded when we passed through.

I buried my head in his chest from the severe embarrassment. "Let me go or I swear to the heavens you will regret it."

"If I put you down on the floor and you cannot stand without tumbling, I will carry you over my shoulder for the rest of our stay here, everywhere we go. And that, princess, is a promise," he warned.

I slapped his shoulder repeatedly and when he did not budge, I pinched him hard enough that he groaned in pain, finally letting me down. The moment my feet touched the ground they turned to mush and ached like pins and needles were being pushed in my flesh. That almost sent me landing face down on the floor had Kilian not warped an arm around my waist and hoisted me up and over his shoulder, like a sack of flour.

"Convinced, you vixen?" he asked, slapping my bottom. "Or shall I put you down so you can crawl there? I'd love to see you on your knees and especially crawl to me, but not of that sort and you would be wearing less than a nightgown."

I felt a flush creep up my ears and cheeks. Did...had...did he slap my bottom? I was too stunned to even comprehend the rest of his words. I hit his shoulder a couple of times in protest, not knowing what to say or do with myself. He'd silenced me dry.

Probably noting that realisation himself, he chuckled—a dark warm sound, his whole body shaking with amusement. "If I had known it only took a bit of manhandling to get you to abide, I would've tried it sooner."

It wasn't the manhandling.

I wiggled and slapped his back several more times. "That's how you want me, tamed like a mare?"

"I want you so many other ways, but not tamed. I like you feisty. It appears I have a thing for vixens. And you don't have to be like this all the time, woman, rest once in a while, pull those claws back, not everyone giving you a hug has a dagger pointed on your back."

"You first, but you might not be alive to see my point."

He rumbled with laughter once more and I swear no man had ever made me flutter and shiver like he had done that moment.

"Prepare the bath, Penelope, as hot as you can get it," he ordered my gobsmacked little red head when we entered my chambers.

"Oh my, are you to bathe me, too?" I asked with a snide tone while he lowered and sat me at the edge of my bed.

Pen still stared aghast between the two of us before running towards the bathing chambers.

He rolled his sleeves and lowered to kneel in front of me. "Just say the words, princess."

My eyes rolled back at his reply. "I quite enjoy this. You, on your knees."

"I'd be better between yours." I hit him with all my fury, but he only chuckled. How dare he tease me like that? "Get a good look, I haven't done much kneeling in my lifetime," he said, tapping a hand over his left knee. "Bad knee. Tripped over a cliff when I chased Mal down after he ran from home. Couldn't walk for three months. Now it sends a sharp pain up my spine and creaks every time I kneel. This cold doesn't help it either."

I didn't know why I found it funny to see him in this human light, but I held my smile in, he looked serious about it.

He prodded my feet before rubbing his palms over them. "Do you have any feel?"

I shook my head. They no longer felt mine, only hot and foreign, but then right at this moment everything felt hot and foreign. My reacting body, the climbing smile, the organ that should be remaining silent at the moment that many called a heart. My skin crawled like worms for a moment and then sigh after sigh of relief left me when I was able to wiggle my toes freely.

"Why did you have to chase Mal down? Why did he run from home?"

He shifted onto his right leg, resting my foot on his shoulder while he ran more magic over my skin. "Mal is a gifted Aura, but Empaths have the hardest training. You often fear and doubt your own emotion, begin to think that what you feel is false or compromised. Sometimes one shuts their magic completely because at times one would become unaware and channel emotion, foreign emotions—others' emotion. Empaths are taught all of them from the start, like the alphabet, then...they practise it." He interrupted himself to examine my attention. "They are not like most Aura, the training is done on other people. One of the most salvaged emotions an Eldritch soldier learns to weaponize is pain and fear, but to know how to inflict them on a weaponizable level, you have to know them to their fullest."

"What?" I asked, my mouth gaping.

"Eldritch soldiers would be strapped to bounds and be taught pain, shown fear. I reckon you might be able to connect how. My brother is not just another Empath, he is...rather gifted and was taught the hardest, a lot was expected of him. To him, the practice was the worst part. So he ran. Mal would rather eat mud for a lifetime than harm a fly. Funny enough now he leads perhaps the most dangerous unit in the whole of Numengarth. I had to find him first, otherwise the next time he would be in bounds would not be to train him."

"Did he not have a choice?"

He looked up to me. "Did you have a choice?"

"But I was created, it was my purpose."

"In my father's head so was Mal. Someone living with a purpose. The curse of those born mighty."

"And you...did he do anything to you?"

He smiled, so very softly. "He didn't have to, I obeyed."

"To all that?" The words didn't hide my shock.

He nodded. "And more."

"Are you not angry at him? Your father?"

"Once, perhaps. Maybe I still am. I just chose not to acknowledge it because even as a half-arsed Empath I know resentment is one heavy emotion to bear." He looked up and threw me a joshing wink. "Back me up, you would know better."

I pushed my foot to his shoulder, almost knocking him back to the ground and the fool chuckled.

He tickled my sole, making me flinch. "Good to know some feel returned to your body." His hand moved over my foot and then up my calf, and I withheld a gasp at the lightness of his touch. His knuckles brushed the inside of my leg and almost up my thigh. He stopped moving and I stopped breathing. It was too quiet, enough to hear my banging heartbeat flutter around the room. "Sometimes I find it hard to believe that there is actually a human under this skin."

Sometimes even I found that hard to believe. "Even monsters bleed and hurt."

He frowned at my words. "You are no monster, Snow."

"So many conflicts you have to solve, Adriatian. Make up your mind, am I or am I not?" I laid back in bed, staring at the wide beige ceiling. "One minute you lash me with a whip, then you smooth a hand over my welts to lessen the pain. If you want to hurt me just do it, no need for the aftercare."

"You need a bit of truth to put you in place, but then I realise that others choose to avoid the truth because it hurts you. And I don't like seeing you hurt."

On cue at such revelation, I rose from where I laid, frowning along my thoughts. "Why the sweet words?"

"What do you want to hear from me, Snow, tell me?"

"That you are scared of me, terrified enough that you wish to get in my good graces."

He smiled, his eyes did too, and it made my skin prickle. I reached for a pillow and smacked him with it. "Don't smile, you fool."

"I am terrified of you, woman."

"Good. Great. Brilliant," I exclaimed, raising my hands to the ceiling.

"Terrified of when you look at me like that." He gently slapped my soles, making me flinch in surprise. "Next time put on shoes then run," he said pointing to me before leaving.

My head turned examining the room left and right, trying to grasp if my head imagined all of it. He left me there blinking myself to confusion and I muttered about a thousand curses, and threw about another thousand vulgar hand gestures behind the closed doors.

I blinked rapidly. How did I look at him?

"Pen," I shouted, chucking the pillow metres away, and she popped from the bathing chambers. "How am I looking at you?" Did I have a particular look I gave people? Like a stinky eye? Were my expressions that telling?

She stood stupefied of thought. "Are you...hungry?"

I paced rapidly toward her, bringing my face close to hers. "Yes, that too, but anything that could perhaps...terrify you?" I shifted my eyes around attempting to recreate the look I'd given him.

"You, uhm, are terrifying when you're hungry," she added, cautiously moving away from me.

What had he meant? I stood before the large dresser mirror for the comfort of an answer, yet I faced an uncomfortable reflection, one that had grown darker and larger, no longer sombre and uncontained, one leaking out of control.

Alone, I'd felt terribly alone. How could I not be. I'd distanced just about everyone after that day, but mostly him. Him I could not even bear to glance without wanting to look at all day. Worst part was the constant state of fervour he'd put me in.

Pen came panting inside the bathroom. "Sharp smile is back. Elias and his whole team has returned," she informed me in a breath before dropping to the ground, tired from the run.

I half patted my hair dry before quickly sliding into a sapphire sleek long sleeved dress that clung so tightly you could see all the outline of my breast and curves. I should have worn something under, but I had no time. He could be called to Venzor and I'd lose my chance. Barely snapping all buttons shut I rushed out with a screaming, flustered Penelope running behind me.

She clutched my arm, eyes livid on my body so visible under the thin dress. "Go back, go back. I will be hanged if anyone sees you like this."

"Die an honourable death and let me go."

"Where is she going?" I heard Cai ask Pen while the three chased behind me.

"To my death," the red head wailed before reaching my pace again. "You have to wear something else or your father will have my head."

"You will not be beheaded, Pen, don't be ridiculous, they are just breasts. Elias will make way for some other form of entertainment if I am not first to greet him." Just as I crossed a corridor corner, I came to face Kilian and Nia coming in my direction.

"Elias?" Cai called half mad behind me. "Why are you meeting him?"

"Because I want to," I said, moving past the other two who had frozen still and looked ridiculously surprised.

Nia made to move forward and say something, her mouth gaped open at my wondrous sight, but I continued past, ignoring them both.

Pen quickly fell right to my step once again. "You might as well go naked. I can see everything from the top of the mountain."

"Do not challenge me."

"Snowlin, you ragged princess, stop right now. No one can see you like that," she called breathlessly, Mal and Cai trailing behind her as well. "Tell her," she pleaded toward all four of them.

What a gathering. From four disrespectful fools to five all in one little corridor. I could almost laugh, had I not repeated what had happened that morning over one thousand times already. Every detail I remembered brought me a step closer to rage, especially with him, the silver eyed snake.

"Be careful, Penelope, she could have your tongue and then feed it to you," a strong male called playfully from the other side of the corridor.

"Elias," I greeted with a saccharine voice, making him smile. Just who I wanted to see.

"I have missed you too, my raven." I noticed his eyes travel down my body and I straightened my back slightly. I was terribly cold, the water from my hair had soaked the silk fabric that clung to all curves of my body, but I wanted him to see everything. He was mine now. I moved swiftly and wrapped my arms around his neck, pulling him into a hug. He seemed surprised at first, but then he placed his hands on my waist, drawing me closer. That was not the slightest bit awkward.

"Should I bring you a cloak, Snow?" Pen questioned carefully behind my back.

"But why? It is so very warm in the castle today," I replied, turning towards them, moving the hair covering my front, back. Her eyes widened at my gesture and I could not contain a smile. The rest looked like they were not breathing, staring at Elias and I. I liked them better like that, silence was a good look on them.

I patted Elias's chest. "It is my turn to ask for a moment alone, you owe me one too many."

He kissed my knuckles. "You have my time and attention completely, you need not ask. Never."

I linked my arm to his and followed him into a waiting chamber. Cai and Mal stood back, barely convinced not to follow me inside after threats of nudity and a lot of dagger wielding.

Elias sat in a large settee, tracing my lines again and then he met my gaze so gently I almost felt sorry for what I was doing.

I waltzed slowly towards the settee and sat closely to him. "You were gone for too long, Elias. Why is my father dragging you away from the castle?" I asked, playing with the lapel of his jacket. "Away from everyone."

He grabbed my gloved hand, lacing it with his and planted a kiss on top of it. Different from his smug character and sly personality, he had always been very gentle with me. I did not know if I liked it or not, being treated like a little delicate flower had never been to my liking before. "Believe me, Snowlin, if I could I would not leave."

"But the Solaryans are getting worse now I suppose, let alone being dealt with only by such a small team," I tested without hesitation. When I told Sam I would get him to speak before I enter his bed it had not been a lie. I folded a leg under me on the settee, dragging the fabric of my dress up, exposing my other leg completely which expectedly was enough to drag his attention.

"Yes, it is harder," he said absently, eyes still there. "Moregan is also not as giving as Samuel either."

I nodded in understanding. "Such a shame the attacks are so far up north, all that travel must not be easy either. Odd they have centred in the Islines and nowhere else?"

He frowned slightly at my words. "What are you doing?"

I pushed it too quickly I suppose. I stood and sat myself in his lap and kissed him. Obliging, he wrapped his hands around me to meet my demand. I broke the kiss and pulled back. "Making conversation, Elias, we have not spoken in ages. What did you want me to ask? How your father's migraine is?" I teased and he laughed.

"What made you change your mind?"

"Does my previous statement have to change? It's so very vapid around here, and my new tails are not making it easier for me. Could it not be just for fun?"

"Fun it is, though my own previous statements do not change," he added before grabbing and pulling me for another kiss. A deep mess of lips and tongue meeting each other continuously till I felt him get hard against me.

I pulled away from him. There was something wrong with me. It took me a small moment to realise the fervour was very particular, not for him and for another.

His eyes stewed with frustration and need. "Is there something wrong?"

"I have to meet Sam shortly, this and you, it will have to wait." Not entirely true, Sam and I had hours before our meeting. I just wanted it to stop.

He sighed, but nodded. "I will return tomorrow evening again."

I halted. "That quickly? Aren't you with Moregan up North?"

He nodded, "Yes and…no. Somewhere closer…only to exchange information then…I will probably get new orders." The war camps. The one Sam had not wanted to tell me about. I knew Elias was inside my father's dirty work.

I waited in the library to meet Sam who had just returned from Casmere after verifying troops, checking on their training and inspecting the new royal forgery weapons at the sea line city. He had found a way after all to do as I had asked him. Though there was much to think, I could not concentrate, my head jumped in a thousand ponds and leaped like a frog between my plans to grip Winter court to the unusualness of my father's behaviour to Nia and then stopping right at him again—Kilian. A thousand conclusions poured out, heating every strand of thought till I was left hitting my head with a book.

"Osmosis doesn't work like that, you have to actually read it," Cai called from where he sat across from me. His silent words danced around me, unsaid and frustrating. He wore the usual look he gave every time Nia or Alaric sent him to bring me back to my senses. Surprisingly, it always worked, he knew a way in. "How are you letting that jester behave around you like that?"

I slammed the book down and crossed my arms. "I have come to the decision that the jester is handsome, likes me and is blessed with some delicious assets. Would you like for me to continue explaining why? My list is so very long, dear, and I won't spare all the nooks and crannies of his graces," I said, giving him a smile and leaning on the table. "Why so surprised? You've never been so surprised before, you know he is not my first jester ride."

"He is the Isjordian kind."

"I am Isjordian, too."

He shook his head. "You're no such thing."

"You can deny it as many times you like, but a truth need not be spoken or accepted to be a truth."

"What is the matter, I've never seen you like this?"

Alone. It felt terrible to feel alone. Nia had made me doubt the closest comfort I had to not feeling alone. It had made me push away not only her, but everyone, even Cai. "No, neither have I. Have you been telling Mal all of my secrets too? Anything I should be aware of, or are you planning on just backstabbing and walking away?"

He shook his head and laughed with faded amusement. "This is not about what she did, is it?" He leaned on the table, his face mere inches from me, skimming for reaction. "It is about what she didn't tell you. It is because you don't want her to be against what you want."

He read my truth, but I still refused to give in. "You are wrong."

"Many times I am. But when it comes to you? Never."

I groaned, slouching on my seat. "Everyone seems to have a thing about knowing me so well."

He took a silver foiled candy out from his pocket and threw it to me. Damned sweets that were terribly hard to find. How did he always have them? "Speak it and I will pay you more."

Salted caramel candy. My mouth salivated while unravelling the sweet. I'd asked bakers to replicate the taste several times with no luck. "I cannot give up. I am also doubting myself about giving up because continuing means upsetting maybe even...losing Nia. I cannot lose another sister."

He threw me another one that quickly ended up in my mouth. "What about you, Cakes? I want to know what you want, not what they would have wanted or what Nia, or anyone else for that matter."

"You know what I want, it has never not once changed." I chewed on the tough caramel and turned to him again. "What do you want, Cai?" Did I not know him, too? Did we have such a vague friendship as to not know the first thing about their desires?

"For it all to end, the fear that creeps up every now and then that we might again lose to your father."

I sighed, relieved. I knew he needed comfort, one I did not know how to give, so I said the only thing that always felt comforting to him. "I will kill him."

"I know." He threw me another piece of candy. "You see, I never doubt you. Maybe I should considering the ledgers of history we two have, but somehow I never do."

Always—he'd given me that promise—the promise to always be there. "Did you know that Nia wanted me to give up?"

"Yes," he admitted, standing and throwing another candy to me before masking behind shadows of the library. "Long time ago."

I knew, yet why did it hurt to hear? I pushed up from my chair. "Where do you get the candy?" Silence. "Cai?" More silence. "I'll pay you."

I only heard faint laughter that didn't belong to my friend. "Heard you, Mal. Go on, be an accomplice, betray me, your queen."

Then I heard two sets of chuckling men somewhere behind the long rows of bookshelves, feeding on my frustration.

Two long hours had passed alone with silence. "Sam," I waved him down when he entered the library.

He settled down and without hesitation spoke, "The merchant, I have found him, and he was not only that." He handed me a letter. Official order from the Sun court sealed with King Magnus's name.

I flipped through the cerulean paper and the orders written in Tahuma. "He works for Magnus?"

Sam nodded. "A few days from now a new delivery is to be sent from Theros. My informant is the merchant's apprentice. His father and I were on the same order back in Whitebridge where our orphanage was. He says the merchant is taking his chances now that you have appointed Celdric on duty. I need you to let the ship through quietly. Once it docks in Casmere I will follow the mercenaries towards the Islines."

Hells. "He'd been right. King Magnus truly has sent the mercenaries."

"It was hard for me to believe too. Snow, I know Magnus well, he'd have to be truly provoked to act to this degree against your father." Sam seemed distressed and tired, had I overworked him on this case?

"I will send word to Celdric. Thank you, Sam."

"Both of you, stay behind. I am going to Elias," I said, coming out of my room and straightening my cloak that hid very little below.

Pen had stood her ground not to assist me in any form in seducing a betrothed man and so I'd settled on the best next and found myself a thin thigh length gossamer slip that hid just enough with intricate stitching in all delicate areas. It had taken me too long to sort out where anything was and I was already late. He'd leave at dawn and I only had a few hours left. Elias was slowly starting to loosen around me, and shortly he'd received duty from Moregan to be sent up north for a week with his team, therefore I wished to prepare ground before his leave. He'd tell me, I was sure of it. If not, I'd use my owed debt. Right now though, however many times I tried to convince myself otherwise, I was doing it for myself too. Forgetting the silver eyed snake was difficult, while he'd slipped me out of his mind and attention easily, not even struggling to avoid me like I did to avoid him. So again, I took the next best advice in dealing with matters of men with the help of an old courtesan of a pleasure house in Fernfoss. *Get in the bed of another.* This had never happened to me before—overthinking a man. Actually...thinking a man at all. When one had no mother, a guardian who took four hours to explain bees and caves, a friend who had betrayed me and another who'd laugh at my issues, it didn't seem the next best thing, it was the best thing. So I took the advice. It had to bring me of this unprecedented haze or I'd officially claim myself deranged.

"No," Kilian said strongly. Now he spoke? Days of barely even glancing at me and this is it? No?

"Yes," I said, adjusting my braid. "It was not up for discussion."

He shook his head. "Leaving you alone is not up for discussion either, especially with him."

What did *especially him* mean? My lips pulled to a sneer. "My, do join us in bed."

He drew close, his teeth gritting and that strong twitch etched in his jaw. "Fine."

I knew he'd give in so I gave him a short smile. "Fine."

"I'll be chaperone, not my fancy watching you being fucked but it comes with the job I suppose."

I almost bared my teeth at him. "You absolute arsehole."

He crossed his arms tight and nodded courtly. "You are welcome. Saved you from two minutes of work. The hassle of undressing, washing and dressing all spared."

My mouth dropped open and I could see Nia barely holding her amusement, which only angered me further.

He tilted his head to the side. "Send word for the idiot, you are not going."

"What?"

"Still want me to take a seat and watch," he asked coldly.

"Fine."

"Fine," he repeated, almost amused before nodding.

"Come then," I said with a shrug and his expression dropped. "Come watch. Not my fancy being watched, but I'll grant you the show you will never have yourself."

I strutted past the corridor with him shortly chasing behind. Had he not learnt that I was shameless?

"This is not funny," he bit out, following behind me.

"You will learn soon enough that I don't joke this sort of way."

I knocked on Elias's door and not even a second later it pulled open. The blond stud stood half naked, his eyes darting between me and Kilian. His smile and excitement faltered the more he looked at my guard.

"I don't have all night, Elias," I said, pushing myself in.

"Don't worry," Kilian called, following me inside before propping in a chair on the corner. "He won't keep you that long."

Elias was now more confused than ever when he asked, "What is going on?"

"He insists on staying to keep watch of danger."

Elias frowned. "What danger?"

"You," I said, taking my cloak off. Kilian's eyes travelled down my body as the cloak slipped down and pooled to my feet, leaving me in the thin short slip. The room was dark with little flickering candlelight, but I was sure even the dark couldn't hide how little I wore. He quickly turned his gaze to the large window and rubbed a tight hand over his chin all angry, his chest rising and falling fast.

"I need a minute with her alone, leave us for a moment," Elias demanded of Kilian.

On the contrary, my unruly guard only leaned back in his chair, crossing an ankle over a knee before saying, "And I demand an audience with Fader himself. Flash the heavens your Venzor smile and maybe they will throw a ladder down."

My mouth parted open and Elias narrowed his eyes on my unusually rude guard before turning to pull my cloak up. Cupping my shoulders, he let out a sigh of disappointment. "I don't want to do this for the spite of someone else."

"It's not for spite," I lied, and my glance caught Kilian's smirk. How the hells did he know when I lied? Why was I letting him taunt me?

Elias rested a hand on my cheek and then quickly retracted it. He'd never had an issue touching me before. If anything he had an issue detaching from me. "Snowlin, we don't have to do this."

I should have pushed, kicked Kilian out and forced myself through it but I didn't.

Elias was not one I'd try to cheat out of a confession, it was never people like him I'd have to persuade, perhaps that was why it was harder to get what I wanted with force. Sigh. When had *I* grown a conscience?

"Another time," I said, gathering my cloak back around.

"Snowlin—"

"Another time, Elias. I didn't know you'd give up this soon." Lifting on my tiptoes, I planted a kiss on his cheek and strutted out of the room. Not only had my plans been destroyed and probably diminished some connection with Elias, but he'd also angered me. He knew all along I'd never go with it, he knew that Elias would not go with it either.

"You will pay for this," I threatened.

He didn't speak.

"You absolute prick."

Silence.

"Vexing Adriatian piece of work." When he didn't answer a third time, I halted and spun round to him.

"He has feelings for you," he said.

I stilled and then swallowed the bile that almost made me sick. "He doesn't."

"He does." A frown gathered between his brows. "Does it bother you?" he asked, studying my features. "It bothers you. Why should it?" He made a whole monologue while I remained stuck in the shell of my regret. He was so certain in his assumptions and I hated that they were correct assumptions.

"Elias is kind, sweet and gentle. I don't wish to give him heartbreak."

"You don't feel anything for him, why should you care?"

"Of course," I snorted. "My black heart can't possibly."

He frowned. "Do you have to be so swaggeringly ironic all the time?"

"Swaggeringly ironic?" I asked, reaching close to him yet keeping my distance. "Could you not be an insufferable gods' arse wipe, barbaric piece of a stern bastard?"

"When your high and mighty, disrespectful, vainglorious self gets off that high horse."

I took off my slipper and threw it to him like all calm and collected people did in a moment of rage. "I will when you take that stick out of your arse, you delusional, infuriating, giant piece of flesh whose brain only operates on two lines of the sacred liber."

He huffed a dark laugh. "At least I haven't made my anger my whole personality."

"I might be against showing emotion, not using it, mister 'my whole personality revolves around my hate for the *Ybris.*' But oh wait, do I hate her? Oh, I hate her, but let's call her beautiful, speak pretty words to her and then think about fucking her when I can't stand the sight let alone the touch of her. But hey, again, I still hate her!'" I yelled the words out, leaving myself panting, pulse roaring in my ears.

"Get yourself to sleep, Snow, now."

"You are not my father, Kilian, nor my friend, nor my lover. You are no one to me. And every day, every moment, your very existence and your sort fuels all the hate I can possibly feel so no need to try this hard to get on my bad side." I glared at him in silence.

He didn't speak, only stared at me.

Tell me you hate me, too, I wanted to say but I didn't want him to hate me.

"Get to sleep, I can't see you like this."

"Like what?"

"Tired, reckless...breaking."

I felt my breath shiver. "I am not...breaking. Don't do that, don't make me look weak. I am not weak."

"No, you are not," he said, picking up my slipper and kneeling to lift my foot up and put my slipper on. His fingers gently slipped up my calf and I sucked in a breath, that flutter returning to my stomach. "Everything breaks, Snow, even steel."

Be angry at him, damn it. "I thought I was a vase."

He withheld a smile and stood, barely inches away from me. "Definitely not one made of clay." His eyes hovered all around my face, mostly over my lips. "Don't see him anymore."

"Who?"

He shut his eyes, almost to suppress his anger before saying, "Elias."

"I need him."

He shook his head. "No, no you don't."

No, I didn't. What I needed was him and what I wanted was him, and what I thought of was him, and what I loathed most was wanting, needing and thinking of him. I took a moment, scrutinising the reverie I'd casted. "Why should I not see him, Kilian?"

"Because."

I laughed tiredly and cocked my head back to lock onto his tall, towering gaze. What did I expect to hear? "I will see whoever I want, fuck whoever I want. Any objections?"

His stare looked like he had a lot to say, but he only stepped forward, reaching almost chest to chest with me and I took a few steps back. He chased me till my back met the door and then leaned in close, his face hovering over mine. Shadows veiled his face, hiding his stare but I felt it all over me. "None. Do as you please."

His words brushed past my lips, my knees weakened and I almost fell backward when he clicked the door behind me open.

His arm went around my waist, holding me from falling backward. He held me for a while. He didn't move and neither did I. His thumb moved in circles over my skin, shivers dancing underneath. "You're in my arms, but once again for all the wrong reasons."

I hoped he'd not noted the pulse drumming loud against my chest bone or the way my lungs wanted to inhale him. "I cannot be in your arms for any other reason."

"No...no you can't be." He raised a hand close to my face, but stopped short before pulling away and letting go altogether. "Go to sleep."

I sucked a tight inhale as the feel of him left me. "It is not that easy."

"I know. Try and if you can't—" he stopped himself.

"Come to you?"

Again, he rested his forehead on mind briefly, his nose nudging mine. "It's just another wrong reason for you to come to me. Don't think of it as anything else, just come."

If it only were that easy. "Good night." I halted one more time and turned around to him. "Why won't you ever say good night to me?"

"Because all nights are good."

"Ah." I blinked in realisation. "Your blessing."

He nodded. "Our blessing."

I gave him a nod and made to enter, stopping only when he said, "Good night, Snow."

It was just that easy to make me forget who he was and what I was, and want him again. Foolishly and inconsiderately want him.

28

WAR AND TRUTHS

KILIAN

NIA AND SNOW HAD not been speaking for days now. She had left the castle borders with only Caiden and Mal, both who had described her to be in a chirpy mood despite all that had happened. She was not backing down to apologise to Nia, nor was she giving her the time to explain or even apologise herself.

Why should I not see him, Kilian? To me it was simply because. To her it would be absolute madness had I uttered those three words. It hurts me.

Elias courted her several times during his stay in the castle, not hiding any affection towards each other. Attempts to avoid them together were futile. She was making sure everyone saw what she was doing. I tried to shake the image of the two away from torturing me any further and focused on the sad soul before me.

Nia sat across the dining table lost of all expression, growing in weariness. I had not known she had been able to feel Snow's emotions before the night when she ran madly towards the gardens. Nia had clutched her chest, foreign panic overtaking her shadows. She had not been able to breath until I'd made the connection and broken in the sleeping princess's room, waking her from the nightmare that Nia had accidentally dove inside of. Her sight had been too painful to bear that it had taken me a while to muster courage and actually look at her. After she awoke and ran, Nia held me back and told me what had happened to her every night, that she had had these nightmares since her family died. Along with Mal, we both had agreed to help part the souls that clung to her toward heavens where they should be resting—the souls that Snow held chained to herself. We expected her to react badly, but I'd never thought she would turn her anger on Nia. It felt my fault—perhaps it was only my fault.

"She will never forgive me, you know," Nia said, lacing her gloved hands together.

She would. Beyond everything Snow cared enough to feel upset and angry by her actions. I knew she cared for Nia more than she cared for herself. She and Caiden were often her first worries, the first she'd catch a glance after passing danger, the only she cared to know if they'd ate, slept or rested, the only she turned to see if they were still by her and safe, the first she'd look for when she was happy.

She sighed. "I was desperate, seeing her like that not only that night but for years, it's hard. Difficult times asked for difficult measures, I knew she was not going to like what I suggested, and I did expect her reaction, but I thought she was going to back down for the sake of her loved ones, for the sake of me."

"Give her time. Let her think of her wrongs and your intentions. She is not a child and plenty smart."

She shook her head. "It won't help, she won't allow it to help. It's a reminder to not let her forget what her aim is. What she said that day, she is not one to lie, she will oblige to it. Wrath, vengeance and all," her voice faded with every word, not wanting to believe what she'd said herself.

We stood in silence and understanding for a while, separating our own thoughts till Caiden appeared behind her. His shadows displeased and an angry dark colour. Hues of distrust, disappointment and worry not only painting his emotion but his features, too.

"Leave us, Nia," he ordered coldly, his hooded stare all deadly.

She stood facing him, pushing her chin up with challenge. "No, I won't. You have known her longer than I have, you knew how much she suffered, yet that day when you could have helped you backed away."

"You are right, I did back away. For years I have chased her around that mad forest, I have cradled her during nights when I thought she was going to scream her lungs away, on days when I thought I had lost her to her own mind. When she wouldn't speak, eat and even when she had forgotten to breathe, Nia. But then she was a child, now she is a woman, a warrior. I do not dictate, command or make decisions for her because I respect her. I would rather still be there to nurse and cradle her then not be there at all. I would suggest, rather than what you did, to find her before you lose that chance. Now leave us," he ordered. His words were biting but dressed in so much truth. He felt every word he said, he had immense love for her, a different strong love, one that would shake mountains. Nia was her warmth, but Caiden was her shield, not only from danger but anything that aimed to hurt her the slightest, sometimes even the truth. However, they had never shielded her from herself. They both seem to forget that Snow was her own evil, her own hurt. She felt alive around him because he was distracting in an irreverent way, similar to her. But how many rainy days would it take for a shallow burial to return to the surface?

Nia, touched by his words, obeyed, and left us alone.

"I will keep this short and understandable enough for a barbarian to understand," he spat, full of spite. "You might have gotten in Nia's mind, but it will take you to go through mine to get to Snow. I assure you, it will not be a pleasant journey. If you try to do even slightly more than the duty you were given by your wretched king, I will send them a piece of you week by week wrapped with your insides. Was I clear enough?"

"I will do whatever she will allow me to do. You spoke such grand words of not deciding for her, yet here you are doing the same."

"It was a suggestion, merely a suggestion. The rest, however, was a threat. One that I think should be embedded deep in your soft head," he spat, pointing a finger to his head before turning to leave.

All I could think was her, all I could dream was her and we never dreamed. Adriatians never dreamed yet I dreamed of her. Her smile, her piercing gold gaze, her words, her terrible life, her scars, her strength, her revenge, her—she was all my head thought about, refusing to let me concentrate on anything else.

I pulled myself out of the cold bath. I finally had peace and quiet, yet I wanted the noise. Only her noise.

Henah and the dark sky. I startled upon entering my room, pulling the nearest item of clothing over my bare chest.

"I'm no shy blushing maiden, Kilian, no need for that," Snow said, leaning back onto the dresser. Her eyes darted to the towel wrapped around my waist and a clean smirk rose on her lips. "No need for that either."

"How did you get in?"

"Mal is a sweetheart."

He would be hung by his ears once I saw his face. Throwing the cloth away, I grabbed the towel behind her, the gold shimmering irises following me intently. "What do you want, or was the Captain not to your satisfaction and you have come for a show?" I said, pulling my trousers up.

She bit her lower lip and her eyes travelled down my chest again. Hells, this woman. Hells, my dissipating self-control. "It is you and me today," she said, pushing herself from the dresser, the sage silk dress she wore shifted with her. "We are heading out of the castle grounds."

"Why? Where is Nia?" Let her not have punished her friend. Gods, what was this woman doing? Let Nia be well.

She moved around my chambers, glancing at the furniture and the odd decor, her finger tracing a line along the walls. The look of a hunter etched on her features, one that played with their prey. She was playing with me. "The sweet backstabber is excused from her duties till further notice."

"Did you have to do that?"

She halted and innocently cocked a brow up at me. "Do what?"

"Spew more venom at one of the few who actually seems to love you? Aren't those few to spare that you spend your chances so loosely, or does a viper need no companions?" I didn't like the words that came out of my mouth, but it felt easy to dislike her right now and I feared for Nia.

"I don't know, you tell me, you're kin to them, correct?" she asked with a snide smile, batting her lashes all force of battle. A battle where I'd fallen, she'd already won the war without lifting a sword.

She looked at me with such distaste, blinking slowly and never losing my gaze. Now I wanted to strangle her and not the good kind. The air was becoming heavy, almost choking. There was no breeze in the room, but her dark hair floated lightly around her. Such an alluring creature. Just why—why on gods did she turn her facade on so many times and why did she do it even to hurt those that cared for her?

"You intend to have a staring contest with me?" I asked again after her loud silence.

"You would win, you love staring at me after all," she said, approaching and parting my knees open till she stood between them. Her thin gloved fingers gripped my chin, pulling my head up to meet her gaze. "Don't be mad at me for things you do not understand."

Hells again, this woman. My fingers curled into tight fists, forbidding myself from rounding them around her. Forbidding myself from running them all over her. "Don't touch me, Snow." Don't touch me or you might regret what I will do next. When I have you pinned down to the bed, my mouth over yours, my hands all over your body and you screaming my name. When I break all promises I've made to myself. Step over every border that keeps me still and have you. That is what I wanted to say. Instead, it had come out as that. As if I didn't crave for her every moment of the day and all night.

She dropped her hand away from me. "I sometimes forget who you are and what I am. How forbidding and repulsive my touch is to you."

"Go," I managed to gather. "I will meet you outside." I was never mad at her. I'd always been mad at myself.

"You look like a wet puppy," she said, ruffling my hair before making for the door. "Do not make me wait."

My hands fell over my face and I breathed out a heavy exhale, and some relief that I'd not lost restraint.

She stood by the door, thankfully wrapped in a warm furry cloak, her eyes lost about in the distance, there was no more sharpness in them, only lassitude.

"Tell me that is your reconsideration face."

She shortly glanced at me. "It is my *'what I should snack on when we return'* face."

"Did you not eat?"

"I don't like eating alone," she said, pushing from the wall towards the dark castle corridors.

"You should have asked Nia then."

She halted and turned all fury to me. "Shut up."

"Why?" I asked nearing face to face with her. "Just why do you use all that head and all that wit for things so gruesome and painful and terrible, but cannot see a friend who cares and treat her almost as your enemy. She is suffering, Snow."

"Why," she almost shouted back. "Why can you know my anger, but never understand my pain? Any of you, all of you."

My feet almost stumbled a step back at those words and the silver rimming her eyes. I was wrong, wasn't I? I was wrong again about her. There was something else and she was right. Had I overlooked what she felt? Had I forgotten how torn she must have been after we left Amerie? Had I forgotten just how much she truly hated us?

She dragged us silently through the castle walls and then city walls, telling the guards she could not sleep and was wanting to clear her mind. She reassured them she was guarded and would return swiftly. By the time we rode out of the woods, I was completely confused where we were heading except that we were riding north.

"Where are you dragging us to?" I asked as we dove deeper inside the empty dark lands after abandoning Sable Abyss. She had not even opened her mouth to breathe, let alone speak the whole journey we had taken.

"Patience, I see, is another virtue you lack."

She was now really playing and walking in a thin strand of it. Why was she being this secretive?

She dismounted and I followed after her, walking cautiously through the forest, and as I had thought, she was indeed plotting something. A camp grew large in front of us, concealed by towering coniferous giants. Isjordian flags topped the roofs and soldiers loomed all around it, pacing towards endless duties. My mind jumped around confused between each tent that was raised for miles. She had found it, the camp General Moregan hid, the one Samuel told her about. I should have known she was not letting that go. It stretched for miles, heavy clank of hammers beating metal, stomps of soldiers, shards of Verglaser ice blast hovering above in the air. Silas had erected an enormous war camp, who were they preparing to fight with such artillery?

"What are we doing here? You swore not to come. You promised Samuel you would not."

Her head swung round, taking in the camp. "I recall saying *fine* and that is not a promise. Sam was worried he would do the honour of having me punished, but I will do that myself."

A masochist, the thrill danger gave this woman was concerning.

I rubbed my temples to relieve some of the beaming headache. "How does Your Highness intend to enter there?" Samuel had been right to not want her here, soldiers and Verglasers circled around endlessly, uncountable and on strong guard.

"Fade me inside that one," she said, pointing to a large tent in the campsite.

She had gone fully mad. I was to sneak her inside a war camp belonging to her own father, who I knew would be more than happy to exert his punishment for her if she got caught.

"No," I responded sharply. I was not hers to toy with, let alone order.

She narrowed her eyes to thin slits. "Fade me in or I will walk towards that camp with a scarf and a hood covering my face, leaving their imagination to play and their duties take over. I know you would like to see an arrow pierce my heart, but after a moon and a half from now, right?" she provoked, standing up from behind the bush we were hiding.

My head began making calculations on how to take her down, tie her and take her back home. As if reading my thoughts she shook her head and pointed to a growling Memphis.

"Gods, you awful woman," I groaned in my hands that concealed my furious face.

She scoffed. "Given up on offending me in Darsan?"

"No, I truly wanted you to understand the offence this time." I was to single-handedly take her right to hearth of danger, the one that I'd sworn to protect her against.

I stood and grabbed her hand and she flinched on my hold. I wondered if I had hurt her, had her palms not healed or had she dug new wounds?

I faded us both behind the tent where I didn't spot any soldiers circling around.

She was cringing and holding her head. Fading was not easy. "Gods, how do you do this so often without collapsing?"

"Practice." I vomited my guts out for two years when I was first learning, but it was the easiest part of my magic that I grasped. Flow of spiritual mana was endless and infinite, harder to channel than the portioned life mana the elementals had. Our magic required the most training and the longest to harvest fruit from. To the elementals it came easy as second skin, they only had to call it out of them. While I had to drag pieces out of an ever-flowing mist, sometimes too overwhelming and at others not enough.

We waited till the voices inside left and entered the large tent. Inside there were several tables and large maps sprawled atop them. Maps of not only Isjord but of all the other kingdoms. Except Adriata I noted.

She circled around them and I stood guard beside her to fade us out at the sight of danger. "Seraphim, hells he was right," she murmured to herself, tracing a finger over ink. "He has map of Hayes and sent an order to dispatch two new ships there." Her face changed, a scowl wore her brows and her eyes narrowed taking in the details of the maps. "Hanai," she counted, pulling maps one after the other. "Myrdur, Solarya, Eldmoor, Vrammethen. He doesn't have this much strength to pull into all of them."

She turned to me. A narrowed expression dipped in her face in accusation. "Adriata is helping him, isn't it? Is that why the only map missing is yours? You are helping my father in whatever madness he is contemplating."

I shook my head at her baseless claim. "Adriata is doing no such thing, careful now with pointing fingers."

She radiated with anger, almost glowing in it. "Tell me, I want to hear it from you. What are you helping him with?"

"Produce, spices, living stock and few others of the same, lands to work free of tax, short pathway towards Vrammethen and a few other movement deals," I explained. "It's an agreement, Snow, not a joined act of war."

"In exchange?"

"The wall to be removed, us to continue and tie new trade deals with other kingdoms, free movement. That was the major intention of it, to no longer be trapped and I don't mean only Highwall."

"Elaborate."

"I don't have to do such a thing."

"Elaborate, Kilian," she shouted, almost shaking. No need for shadows to know the ire haloing around her. "Don't play games with me."

I rubbed a hand over my eyes, taking in a deep breath. "We need it, desperately. Adriata is crumbling, slowly at first and then these last past months even worse. Sea of the Dark is not keeping eudemons at bay anymore, they are lured into our cities. Our lands have grown colder, harsher, wetter, produce is destroyed, animals drowned, villages emptied and Adriatians are fleeing from all sides, some even to Vrammethen. And...the unblessed are somehow sprouting like wildfire. Your father offered this agreement about two or so years ago, very persistently, it was only recently we were forced to accept when every route we took to deflect these events took us nowhere but to him."

She smirked and then gradually chuckled, not because she didn't believe me, she was satisfied. "It goes around, doesn't it? Like a wheel of misfortune. How so very poetic."

"There is nothing poetic about thousands of lives in danger and lost."

She threw a hand in the air. "Misery makes for the best of rhymes. Die, cry, oh my." Her eyes darted about the room. "The term—what was the term that you would not agree on? What was the term that had you convinced?"

She knew, yet I didn't want her to hear it from me. "You," I revealed half-heartedly.

"Of course. What did my father offer in the beginning?"

"Your half-sister."

She nodded slowly, a rueful smile etching and fading in her lips. "Fren would probably be more to your king's liking than I would, no one likes to tame a horse if you can simply buy a trained pony, but I suppose he has greater plans than to tame me."

Staying angry with her was unbearable and I had pretended long enough to convince myself that it was without success. I gathered her cold face in my hands and she finally opened her eyes. Limp, everything had gone limp, from her limbs to her gaze. "It was not the king who asked for you, it was the council, and no one will hurt you. Do not fear him, you are a thousand ways stronger and scarier than him."

"It is all because of me, it has always been so, Kilian. You might need that agreement, but you need me dead more."

I shook my head. "That will not happen, ever."

"Did they send you here to kill me?"

I could not hide my shock. She had truly thought I'd come to Isjord to hurt her. "I came here myself, Snow. I was the one who proposed to come here, to keep you safe, and I have failed more than I'd like to remember, but it was what I swore and what I will swear with my life. Now, till the day I die, I will protect you. Accept my truth," I said, lightly brushing my finger over her lip and she shivered.

"Why did the council want me?"

I did not want her to hear it, but she had too, it was a truth she deserved to know. "From fear that your father might still have his grand plans for you. The old bats would give you a thousand and one reasons more. To have you tested again, keep you away from your father, try and have the prophecy erased with your presence."

"Why did the king allow it? Even with all that he can't possibly agree to this, to marry me."

I combed my fingers through her hair, how soft she was. "He...he was young when he came to power and they had created a big enough grouping of their own, so when time comes to vote on matters, they drown the majority. In Adriata even the king needs permission to act on a grand scale of action. Adriata doesn't have lords, we have Moon court and Night court. One is the council and the other is the king and his private advisers, both take decisions in unison."

She blinked surprised. "For everything?"

I nodded. "For everything."

"Well that is ridiculous, he could substitute them all. And is that even a king if he has very little power over decisions? And is this really a grand scale decision?" she asked, almost in a breath making herself cough.

I gave her a smile. "He is trying to bring new minds onto the council, few are already starting to make somewhat of a change. The council has been in order for several decades—the people, generals, captains and many more have grown fond of them, they trust them. It is difficult to get rid of them without causing commotion. But as you said before, he is a toad of a king, the council doesn't like him very much, so he sometimes gets to have his way despite what they say. Also, yes, it is a very grand scale of action. You are to be queen of Adriata. You are to be my queen." *Mine.*

She flinched and winced slightly at the last part. It was no longer a playful joke. She truly would be my queen. "Why is your map not here?" she asked.

"They would not be able to use it even if they tried. I believe you might be familiar to what we call *alaar*, mist of magic or *zgahna* in Calgnan." I explained. "The trespassers, have you ever wondered why they always pass in pairs or with a guide?"

"For...the conversation?"

I smiled again. "If a true Adriatian is not with you when you cross river Nyx, the *alaar* will get you lost, some driven out of their heads and many more dead. It is a precaution—all the maps. We too have mapping of Isjord and other kingdoms, there is nothing to worry about."

"You don't know my father."

"I know his strength. Isjord is powerful, but not stupid, look at that," I motioned over the maps laying on the table. "That is beyond ridicule. Moriko of Hanai, Magnus of Solarya, hells even the Grand Maiden will not sit and tolerate another attack. They will take it as an act of war against the continent."

"What about my dear betrothed?"

"What about that idiot?"

She bit her smile down. "Will he not rage?"

"Yes, but contrary to the others he has not stopped being cautious and against your father."

She'd calmed, I saw it in her steady rising chest. She pulled both my hands down. "Don't do that unless you intend to kiss me. It gives me some terrible dirty thoughts."

"I will keep it in mind." I said, taking a step back. It gave me the same dirty thoughts. "Anything else I should be wary of?"

"Yes," she said quietly, rampaging through the pile of documents beside the maps. "Keep clothes on at all times. Seeing you naked once had me bothered enough."

"Let me know if you need a hand."

She shuffled through some paper. "It is fine, some is in old Ysolt, code I think."

"Not with that."

Without even turning, she hit me with a carved black horse paperweight. "*Klaghne.*"

I caught it mid-air before hitting me. Her obsession with throwing objects at me was concerning, but adorable. Hovering over her, I set the paperweight back down to where it was. "I can read old Ysolt if you need that sort of hand as well."

She blinked madly. "How?"

"Perhaps I thought I could impress an Isjordian princess?"

"Funny." She exhaled loudly, muttering something in Calgnan under her breath.

"That pile over there." Suddenly she paused, something had pulled her satisfaction. She read and re-read it till I heard voices approaching us.

I took the documents from her, putting them down how they were before grabbing her and fading us out in the forest again.

The little vixen sprawled in the snowy ground, arms crossed and staring towards nothing, pinched with deep concentration. I extended a hand to help her stand, drawing her attention back to reality. She stared at it and then up to me before she slapped it away and stood up on her own. "If I give you my hand, you will take my whole arm. Everyone seems a lot into taking more than I give lately," she said, brushing snow from her clothes.

"Is that why you have been so evidently upset with Nia, because she took more than Your Highness allowed?"

She inched so close to me that I had to look down to meet her fiery yellow flames. "Why I have been so upset, Kilian, was that despite all, despite everything, she relied on and confided in you of all people. With not only my secrets, but," she stopped, probably contemplating whether she wanted me to know. "My weaknesses and fears, which I had given her because I love her, because I trusted her to care enough to keep them to herself. What she asked of you did not upset me. What upset me was how she underestimated my feelings and therefore me, without even taking the first step to open up to me."

Hurt—she was hurt by Nia, not just angry with her as I thought. I did not like seeing her hurt. I moved my hand to tuck a floating piece of hair covering her eye, but retreated, aware I should not be doing it. Why was it so hard to keep my hands off her? "Speak with her, even though she did just what you said, she never meant to. It was something else that drove her to, as you say, 'backstab you'. Silence has never been a good means of reconciliation because there is no communication and where there is no communication there is misunderstanding and injured hearts."

"Well, don't you have the right words at disposable," she murmured, crossing her arms indignantly. "I will, just not now. I do not want my angry mouth taking over my upset head and worsening the situation. Angry me is usually the vilest in the room. Last person I wish to be vile is Nia. I am not...good with people, it will take me some time." She took one heavy breath and ran a hand through her hair, combing it in frustration.

This is why she was avoiding her, to not say things she did not mean and not hurt Nia? She was letting her feelings stew to calm before she did. How frustrating it was not knowing and fighting to uncover her truth, being able to read emotion had done more damage than good. I had forgotten to read others without my magic.

"Snowlin Edlynne Krigborn." Her head snapped up at me and she blinked fast. "How are you so odd?"

She put a hand over her chest. "My pardon, the full name caught me by surprise. Do you think you could summon me to command like some eudemon? I'm an *Ybris*, darling, not Golgotha's creature."

Her joke made me throw my head back in laughter.

"How did you know my middle name?"

"I know about you more than you think." She raised her brows in question, so I took the challenge. "Edlynne is your grandmother's name, last Queen of Olympia. Also named after Edlynne the third guardian of Caelum, the Warden of Dawn, the upper heaven of Nubil. The name is also passed down from generations, it is your mother's middle name, too. Olympians believed the guardian descended at dawn and visited women of the kingdom to train them; it is the origin of *Skye* warriors, a legendary squadron of highly trained Olympian female warriors. The first *Skye* is your ancestor, she carried the name down and now you have it." I knew much more. Enough that I could write a book about her. No, I could write a book about those eyes alone. One full of poems about her lips and how soft I imagined them to be.

Her mouth parted open. "I am the odd one?"

"Yes," I said, moving the wind billowed hair out of her eyes. "Very odd. The oddest."

"What date was I born?" she asked, narrowing her eyes on me.

"Summer, first of August. Heard you were quite the fat baby, couldn't open those eyes till two weeks old," I revealed, tugging her cheek. I'd read her birth certificate and a midwife diary trailing an hour-to-hour observation of hers till she'd been a week old. She'd been concerned throughout for her—this little baby had been too lazy to blink.

She frowned, slapping my hand away and rapidly asked in a breath, "My childhood friend, my first lover, what is my favourite food, my favourite book?"

"Your sister, you had no other friends. I believe the second one is Caiden, mushroom anything, and 'Fire of Flesh' by that dubious Vrammetheni author. You have read it so many times it is falling apart. Spare the poor book."

"Marianne Hawthorne," she said, blinking wide eyed at me. "She is not dubious and your second guess was incorrect."

"Correct me."

Her mouth parted open just slightly. "His name was Miles, Cai's friend."

I nodded. "Miles, Caiden's friend. Did you love him?"

She snorted and blasted into laughter. "I was sixteen."

Was that supposed to have some correlation? "My parents fell in love when they were children."

Waving a hand in the air, she dismissed my point. "Your turn."

I frowned and narrowed my eyes at her, but there was no resistance no matter how much I tried. I wanted to give in to her. With lacking conviction I said, "There were no turns."

She stepped close to me, her hands gripping my jacket like she always did. The dominance in her eyes utmost adorable. "I said, it is your turn. Childhood friend, first lover, favourite food, favourite book."

My eyes dropped to her hands. How I liked when she did that, except that it made me want to lower myself and cover her mouth with mine.

She made a little sound of realisation and opened her palms, making to move away only stopped by my hands over her small wrists. She stilled and I placed them over my chest again. "I was a loner, too, so Mal was my only friend. A girl called May was my first lover. I could eat lemon cake for the rest of my life. And lastly, a poetry book by an Olympian writer called *Zeulen*."

She cleared her throat, her fingers stretching awkwardly over my chest. "So this May, did you love her?"

"No." I'd never been that lucky, my heart had rejected all whom I'd thought to be love.

She bit her lip and nodded. "Lemon cake, it suits you."

Suited me? "How so?"

"Sour and sweet."

I could not help my smile. "Am I sweet now?"

"Your words are, but I'll let you know of your taste, too. You know, when I get my chance," she said, slowly retracting her hands. Her soft skin rubbed against mine, creating such a friction that I felt nothing but her, no cold, no wind, no breath, nothing but her. I'd been so doused in her touch that I'd paid no heed to what she said. The words slowly registering. The tension in my body registering too, with the need for her to take that taste. I shook my head, clearing of all inappropriate thoughts. It bothered me, how often I thought of her, thought of her like this. She was her in all her vengefulness and I was me in all my fault and unworthiness.

"Killian, could you tell me something?" she asked quietly, hesitating to continue, her eyes darting far away.

"Why hesitate, Snow, tell me." *Tell me everything, tell me all, spare nothing, rely on me, lean on me...trust me*—I wanted to tell her that, but again, I was me and she was her.

She swallowed and nodded, her hands gathering in fist at her side. "Why did Nia say I am empty, do you really see nothing?" She put a palm to her chest. "Am I really empty? It doesn't feel like it, though it does at the same time. I don't really understand it."

At her words, my whole body turned unconsciously rigid knowing Nia's words had been weighing on her.

It had not taken me long to realise that the rainbow wheel of her emotions was spinning so fast that her shadows now appeared completely blank, empty and tucked away. That had been why we could never tell any apart, she could not control or cease the fury of her emotions enough for us to see, but she most definitely felt them. Nothingness could feel heavy. And heaviness often felt like nothingness. Once you are used to the weight, it starts bearing no issue.

"Snow, you are allowed to feel empty, full or both. Sometimes the brightness of the moon hides the darkness behind it and sometimes that darkness is so strong that it takes all the stars and candle light on this realm to keep it afloat and not drown in it. It doesn't matter what we can or cannot see in you, only what you allow yourself to be. The moon is still the moon even in darkness or light."

She stood quiet, lost in thoughts and with a sigh she snapped to the usual her. "Mal is right, you and your pretty words."

"Nia is right, you and your sharp tongue, a true vixen indeed," I said, shaking my head.

Her face turned stern, a sneer lifting in the corners of her mouth. "I still very much hate you."

I didn't want her to hate me, but asking her of that would be robbing a wish, unattainable. "Terribly shocking."

She rolled her eyes at my response and gathered her cloak tighter. "Let's go before this cold freezes my body and you freezes my will to live," she said, mounting Memphis.

"As you say, *dahaara*."

She groaned, murmured and mouthed about dozens of curses in Calgnan as she often did before urging Memphis forward.

29

ROSES AND THORNS

SNOWLIN

ADRIATA WAS NOT HELPING Isjord, not with an army at least. I had believed him somehow—I believed what he said and it had brought me a piece of peace. Everything he said brought a sense of serenity.

Father had located troops all over the border cities and that they were now not only dealing with the Solaryans. He had requested immediate dispatch of a unit to travel to Hanai under discretion to retrieve or depose the soldiers caught prisoner trespassing Hanai. For a reason that was not stated anywhere. Whatever the reason, he was willing to go as far as to have his own soldiers executed before they were able to speak or be tortured by the Hanaians. I also had figured where exactly Elias had gone. He was north, but the Hanaian north.

Sleep soaked and transported me to my mother's chambers. Utter dark, tall shadows and light white mist hovered to blanket my surroundings—the same surroundings I'd almost buried in memory. The windows were blown open, bringing in heavy wind and black snow that coated the white marble floor a shade of screaming dark. My mother stood before me, draped in the white dress she wore the solstice from twelve years ago. When I stepped toward her, I felt my feet soak in viscous wetness. Blood pooled all around us, it flowed out of my mother. Her hair blew back and I stumbled to the ground, drawing my eyes shut at the terrifying sight of her bloodied features, leaking of the crimson fluid.

Snow, little snowflake, come see me.

My mother's voice jerked me awake. Cold creeps had raised at the realness and closeness of the sound, as if she had been standing by me. I looked around, studying the unchanging and unmoving surroundings, ultimately making myself laugh. So I was losing it. I was many things, a mad woman was not going to be one of them, yet I gathered my robe around and headed out of my room.

Kilian leaned back by the wall opposite with his arms crossed, he blinked unbothered and almost expectant to my actions. I suppose it was a habit of mine and he was picking on them very well. A flush of embarrassment heated and creeped towards my ears. The other night I had revealed more than what I had ever thought I would tell to an Adriatian, more than I would tell anyone at that. His words, however, had managed to lift a heavy weight from my head and soothed some distraught blankets of thought. I contemplated if I really had done that to myself, emptied my soul and that I was a wandering, breathing and living spirit that felt nothing. The words he had used had left me in enough of an awe. I had not known what to say, although I knew what I wanted to do at that moment—grab his ridiculous handsome face and kiss him till air left his lungs. But though I wanted him, he only thought of wanting me.

"The gardens, mountains, forest or by the sea. Where will you drag me today?" he asked, lazily pushing himself from the wall.

As much as I wanted to indulge and humour him back enough that he would pull his hair out, today was not the day—today was a bad day. Well, night.

"Down a few corridors, prick," I said, charging ahead.

"Are you alright?"

I hated those words. Alright, not alright, was there really such a state? "Mhm."

"You don't look alright."

Why would he not let it go? "What do you think, waking from one nightmare and finding another right at your doorstep?" I only wanted him to understand that I craved quiet, the one my head was denying. That I was tormented and that the thoughts about him tormented me more, but instead...I injured him.

"Snow—"

"And it speaks at that."

He went silent after my harsh words. I would have gone silent, too. My anger took charge and aimed straight—straight at someone I didn't want to aim it at.

I imagined myself making this way a thousand times since returning to Isjord, though my heart had commanded my feet stock-still every single time I'd even neared this side of the castle. It terrified me to surround myself with her presence. If I felt her too alive in memory, I'd long for her till heartache. The wooden doors of her bedroom stood solid and unmoving before me and my hands refused command to open them, so I stood there for several minutes, fighting that inner battle of thoughts a few couple of times before I managed to lift my hand to the cold golden handle.

"Do not come in," I said, and he halted without question, probably already aware whose chambers I'd entered.

The large doors creaked around the hollow room and corridors from the unusual movement. My chest expanded wide enough that I had to lift a hand to clutch away the pressure. I remembered myself running around the marbled floor, jumping atop the large fluffed bed, sitting by her vanity trying every crown and jewellery, dancing around corners of the chamber in her dresses that drowned my small limbs. I remembered my every movement and her every laugh, the caress in her features when she looked at me, the softness in her olive eyes and the gentleness of their invisible touch smoothing over me. Her humming was still eerily reminiscent in my ears, and it prickled the hair on my neck.

The white marble was smooth under me, each touch of my soles sent jolt after jolt of memory in my head, happy memories that were now translated to the most painful ache. Memories were the cruellest form of torture.

I kneeled before her bed and felt the smoothness of it once more, but my hands met thorns that scraped deep in wounds that were still open and leaking. Roses—she always smelled of roses, everything smelled of it still, but its sweet scent had variegated with the metallic stink of blood which brought a sickening feel to my throat. I held my stomach tight, standing to escape the nauseating feel that had coated sweat beads across my temples and sent tremors down my hands.

Voices and heavy steps sounded outside the windows, pulling my attention. It was the middle of the night, why were people marching around the castle at this hour for?

I moved towards the arched window, cracking the pane open just slightly. Below, two long lines of Verglaser soldiers beaming in white marched ahead, carrying a wooden chest between them. They were led by a lean hooded figure towards the old castle quarters of my father's Dark Crafter. Those chambers had been shut down when I was very young—when my father executed the last Crafter for treason and conspiracy with the leader of Eldmoor, the 102nd Grand Maiden, Urinthia. He thought the Crafter had been communicating court secrets to the spiritual kingdom. Shortly after, he had cut ties with Eldmoor and banned all craft in Isjord. There had been fear of war between the two kingdoms. Well, at least the one my father wanted to rage, but Eldmoor had not replicated or even indulged in my father's wishes to create a rift that could end up just in that. The Eldmoorians did not care for war, lands, glory, and gold, to them magic was everything. So, swiftly, the Crafters had avoided war and my father all together, no one heard from them, not that they cared. To them, anyone that was not Eldmoorian was of very little interest. So why had father opened the part of the castle that should have been shut for years, and what was he taking there?

I tilted my head and narrowed my eyes at the Cark Crafter's court, waiting and searching the premises until I noticed a red hued transparent layer flickering in and out of sight—a Crafter's veil? A protection barrier made of dark magic, doubtfully one I could trespass. He had reopened the quarters? But there was still a ban on dark craft in Isjord.

I turned to Kilian who stood still by the door, his features had shaped worrisomely as if he knew what was brewing in my head. "I need you to come here," I called, signalling him with my hand.

He uncrossed his arms and stared at me hesitantly. Before he could question, tire me out and make me lose my golden opportunity, I urged him by fanning my hand impatiently.

Taking careful steps towards my mother's room, he approached me. "How will you use me today?"

I pointed down the window. "Lower me down there, with your shadows or whatever."

He examined the soldiers marching down the castle grounds before his jaw tensed and flexed from anger. "No," he answered abruptly in Kilian style.

I gripped his arm, pulling him to me. Despite the frustrating closeness, I managed to gather my words. "Put me down or I will actually take my chances and jump. You can still use me with broken limbs, right?"

His head dropped back in surrender. "Do you have a vault of threats stashed away for each occasion?"

A smile of satisfaction graced my features. "I have a few other methods as well besides threats. However, we'd be stuck here and I would miss the soldiers" I said, patting my palm on his chest before turning towards the window again, trying not to lose sight of the secretive bunch.

"You live to exasperate me," he groaned, annoyed, wrapping an arm around my waist. His body almost melted to mine. I even felt the tendons of muscle stretch over my own. One moment we were up in the air, and the next we were swiftly landing down on the cold ground. Shoes, again I'd left them in my room. If he saw, I'd earn another mouthful. Unknowingly, I had gripped his arm tight enough to cut circulation and I flinched away from him.

"Clawing away like a vixen, too." He gently shook his arm as if I really hurt him.

"For what I said before—" The apology froze and stuck on my tongue.

"You said nothing," he spoke, interrupting me, "nothing that wasn't true."

Nightmare, you are my nightmare. Except that I wasn't sure if he was.

I said nothing and charged ahead towards the Verglaser soldiers. Strangely, their boots and part of their white uniforms were dipped in mud. You could not see the ground in Isjord let alone step on mud. Silently trailing after them I caught sight of a wooden chest they were carrying. A Crafter's halo seal was carved on the lid to fend away whoever wanted to reach inside it, but that was not what had caught my attention. It was the Solaryan sun crest and metal ridges decorating it that struck me as odd. What had the Solaryans sent my father that he had to gather a squadron of Aura and enlist a Dark Crafter to protect it. Had the sun islanders not halted all deals with my father, was it another threat?

Just as I took another step closer behind them, a bright luminescent shield halo popped in front of me, seven runes of seven hells spun round fuelling it with magic. Kilian swiftly grabbed my arm, pulling me back from hitting the surface. I would have become ash at the touch of it.

He gathered me close, the scent of magic surrounding him. One moment it was there and then waned, like the faint light of fireflies. "Fuck, I cannot fade us away," he said.

"Well, sweet manners, language," I scolded playfully.

"So not the time for jokes."

"Not the time for fear either, Kilian darling." Did he forget I was these people's princess and this was technically my home and I was not exactly sneaking around?

His eyes dropped to me, cast with dark shadows. "Don't do that to me, woman, not now, not when I can't enjoy it."

His words threw my pulse in a gallop and I stared at him long and hard. I didn't dare ask, I didn't dare say anything—I had nothing to say.

He pulled onto my arm and almost onto his embrace, as if he was thinking of using his body for a shield. The soldiers halted ahead of us, parting for the hooded figure to pass through. The craft shield dispersed and the disguised figure pulled the hood down to reveal their face.

"Your father did mention you were back and still curious as ever," a soft woman's voice said. One I'd heard many times before.

What the inappropriate word Kilian said a second ago was going on? Dead or still dreaming? Melanthe, my father's dead Crafter, stood before me grinning and breathing. The same as I remembered her from years ago, short unnaturally bright wine-red hair that fell to her chin, her almost pearlescent skin glowed as if moonlight reflected it, her eyes the same washed sage, except now a pale rosy scar stretched on her neck contrasting across her skin and another one on her forehead. She was alive? How had she escaped death and why had father allowed her back? Was she sneaking in? But there were Isjordian soldiers around her and no one escaped unseen under my father's eye, especially on the castle grounds. That only meant he had enlisted her in whatever his dirty works were, once again I suppose.

"I see even death fears the wicked or is my mind playing games from staying too long in this graveyard of a land and you are truly dead because you definitely were last time I saw you." I said, surveying the sight of her.

Her shoulders shook with laughter and she raised a delicate hand to her mouth, demurely hiding her smile. More gnarly slashes and marks stretched across her hands, deep and almost tearing onto the bone. What on Nubil's heaven had happened to her and how the heavens was she alive? I remember her head dangling onto the rope and her softened limbs surrendered while her soul parted from her body.

"Go, little girl, you should not be playing on this side of the castle anyway," she huffed, flinging her hand towards me as if I were a dog.

"I fear the one who should be playing with dead spirits on the otherworld has no say on what I do. What are you doing here, Melanthe?" I pushed.

Her face turned unforgiving. The red head did take offence very bitterly. I remember her pride took most of her character, if a dead woman could even have one. "I am afraid it's private court issues, little princess, now leave before I make your father aware of your whereabouts."

I erupted in giggles. "As terrifying as that might sound to many, go ahead, do that. I want a glance inside that pretty little chest first," I said, taking a step forward. Kilian's hand was still wrapped tight around my wrist, not letting go of me. I slid my arm up, joining our palms together. If he wanted to hold me it didn't have to hurt my poor wrists. I bit my lip and cringed remembering I wore no gloves and all my marks were rubbing onto his strangely warm hands.

Melanthe balled her fists and crossed them forward, her magic floating in red beams from her hands. "I have an order to use it on anyone and there was no 'spare the princess' rule when your father asked me of that," she spat with threat.

I took the dare and stepped forward. She could not possibly be allowed to hurt me.

Proving me wrong, she sent a bolt of red towards me. Before it hit us, I felt the scent of magic sizzling in the air, releasing, coating and prickling my skin as Kilian lifted a black wall of mist and catching the first hit, enshrouding us inside. The clash sent wind shaking, our surroundings and snow shifted violently in the air. He had channelled so much magic I had felt its tentacles blanket all around us too. Not just shadows, something else, too. It was warm around us all of a sudden. I could not understand it.

He heaved, breathing in loud concerning paces. "Silas has laced this whole place in craft, I will not be able to do more than simple magic. Our magic is not trained to be fuelled by life force. Let us go back, this is not worth your life." In command to his magic fatigue, the wall of mist dispersed and revealed a grinning Melanthe.

Simple? That was simple magic? I've had my fair share from the taste of magic and

Aura, no one had ever emitted that much magic that it had leaked onto the air.

She clapped sombrely. A look of disgust etched in her unforgiving expression. "I heard about your Adriatian guards. He must be powerful given that I have inked this place corner by corner in craft." She drew her attention to him, taking him in for a moment before grinning even wider. "Is that a prime bloodline I smell? I wonder how long he will be able to hold out, it will be my entertainment for tonight." Her fists began glowing red again. Her magic began to pull the hair of my neck up, or was it Kilian's? Still, it was one that sent my senses vibrating in alert.

Sigh. I had to retreat, this was going to be impossible anyway even if we could take Melanthe down, there were Verglasers behind her and I was unarmed, not to mention the seal atop the chest that I would never be able to break or breach through. It had the imprint of her magic, one broken only by her. My courage became my stupidity today, I pushed knowing this battle was at my loss. At least now I knew whatever my father was cooking needed magic—Crafter magic—and that worried me aplenty.

I could not hide the frown of disappointment at today's events while I took a few steps back on retreat.

"Thank the heavens for taking my side just this once," Kilian murmured and reached for my hand again, the feel of his warmth somewhat comforting.

Melanthe straightened and pulled her magic down, smiling satisfied. "Just as I thought," she saluted, waving her hand in the air.

Had this been another moment, I would have pierced a burn through her chest before she could utter a word or draw a sliver of magic.

Her eyes fluttered for a second and then narrowed on me. She tilted her head to study me and she said, "You stink of a Dark Crafter's magic, one very familiar as well."

My steps halted at her assessment. "Maybe you are sniffing your own stink, cows usually eat where they shit so they forget their own smell, and you are most definitely one stenchy cow." Nerves were thumping on my temples and sweat coated my palms as I backed away and pulled Kilian with me.

I could feel his questions and curiosity beside me, though I didn't dare turn.

"Are you alright?" he asked, startling me in surprise. Not the question I expected from him, but my welfare was more important than his curiosity I suppose. My worth to his kind was more important.

I pulled my hand away, his eyes intently following it while I tucked it behind my back. "Why would I not be?"

"Crafters are terrifying, some of their magic can be vile. It works first as a scare defence technique by creeping in your thoughts to put fear there, enough for you to lower your guards for their attacks and then have you ready to easily fall under whatever they cast."

I gathered myself tight, feeling the brisk air through the thin layers of my clothes. "You know quite a lot for just a guard and is every one of you this powerful to resist magic suppression from a Crafter's veil? A prime she said. I didn't know there were so many primes to spare?" I asked, trying to wash my own curiosity. A prime was hard to stumble upon in this day and age. I was one and odd one, both bloodlines I derived from, Krigborn and Skygard, were primes in their respective. In Isjord there were probably only a handful left, all old and carefully tucked to preserve the last remnants of pure magic. This one was part of that rare group.

He took off his jacket and threw it over my shoulders, tucking me tightly. At the touch of his scent I grew hungry again. Maybe for him. "Did you think Adriata would send just anyone to protect you? And why on bright round Cynth would you be so curious as to know what load of rubbish would have been on that chest, enough that you would challenge a Dark Crafter and a whole two dozen Verglasers unarmed and in your nightgown at that?"

His frustrated voice made me smile. "Don't underestimate a woman in a nightgown. The more undressed I am, the more distracting I can be. I am distracting enough even dressed for you," I teased, throwing him a wink to stab his fragile, soft, and easily provoked mind.

He pulled my hair over the jacket. "I give up, you truly are impossible."

"I prefer irresistible," I said, pulling my arms through the large sleeves of the jacket, still warm from him. "Though heavenly is still fine by me."

A corner of his lip pulled up. Pretty—he was pretty. "You probably enjoyed that, didn't you?"

"I did. Call me that again any time you please."

"Does it not give you terribly dirty thoughts?"

"Point on, but you did offer me a hand."

He cast me a glance, he meant it as a warning but it only gave me dirtier thoughts.

He halted before we entered the castle, his eyes had taken that shade of worry again. "Shall I take you to your mother, we can grab blankets from the servant chambers. There is still time for you to rest."

I didn't know why his words took me by surprise. I had told him before that their resting place was my place of calm. He knew I had slept there before. All of the sudden it felt embarrassing. "I can't sleep."

"My magic could help you," he offered.

Annoyed, I faced him. "And that, Kilian, would be over my corpse." Though that night he had helped me just fine without it, I'd slept like a babe. All he needed to do was gather me in his arms and I'd be drooling in no time.

"Go to Nia, she helps you sleep sometimes, right?"

Bastard. Was this his idea of bringing people to reconcile? I put a finger on his chest in threat. "Don't push it. Though someone else could. If Elias was here, I bet he could do more than put me to sleep."

His brows smoothed to stern lines, his jaw tensed and stretched a few times, and the grand act of the play made a show—his chin dimple. "Ah, yes, that face again," I teased, hovering and pointing my finger in circles over his face. The new face I had seen him wear lately.

He grabbed onto my hand and leaned in so very close to me that spring bloomed that night in the middle of the winter gardens. "There is plenty of muscled flesh with no wits about the castle, it will be the exact same as being with him, help yourself to any," he answered nonchalantly, but I could swear his voice had gone a tone darker and a shade jealous. Why did everyone have a bone to pick with Elias, what had the poor man done to him?

I laughed at his comment, did it need wits to get what I wanted? A moment of pleasure, release, a moment out of this whole mess my father was concocting. And I'd done worse in my choices, Elias was a blossom in comparison.

"But you see," I taunted, lowering my voice. "He has wits—witty ways of using his flesh."

"Gods, spare me." Letting go of me, he rubbed his eyes intensively, given up at my wicked ways.

I laughed jollily, it amused me, all of his reactions and comments to my remarks, they always have. He never surrendered to them, as if he could duel my steel with a wooden sword, but I liked his attempts as much as I did when they failed.

He turned to me with his static ungiving face. How on gods could I not find a hint of what he thought? "That," he said quietly. "Do that more often. That truly makes you irresistible."

I sucked in a sharp breath and held it. "Entertain me some more then."

He let out a short laugh, staring at me under dark eyelids. "If my frustration and demise was not your entertainment, I would have indulged in that request."

We both remained silent for the rest of the walk to my chambers, my body had stiffened awkwardly after that comment whilst he had not even blinked after the rubbish he had spewed out.

"Would you be able to answer me without judgement?" I asked, hoping to find an answer about the thing that had been bothering me endless and today more even.

He nodded silently.

"Is it normal for me to hear my mother's voice, not memories or conversation from before, but as if actually speaking to me. Now—presently?" I proceeded cautiously. If someone knew about the spiritual it had to be the Adriatians. I heard her voice several times, not even in nightmares, but casually throughout the day—while I ate, walked, fought, in many peculiar moments, and it had drawn me back.

"Is that what brought you to her room tonight?"

I nodded.

"Sometimes, when someone passes, just as many spirits hold grudges and anger, many hold regret and fear for those they have left behind. Your mother could be looking after you from the Mid-world as her spirit has been trapped there till she is released to the heavens. You are not mad, stop thinking that."

"How did you—" I asked, staring at him in surprise without finishing my sentence.

"You have no shadows, but you have learnt to wear your emotions in your features. If you look into them long enough you can even read them in sentences." Kilian was so very odd. At moments he held back and fired through his silver eyes, at other times it felt as if his tap had been laced in oil and words and thoughts spewed out with no restrain. But as I thought it over, maybe he was just an idiot, words that seemed to affect me probably meant nothing to him.

"Well you must have been staring at me endless to know them in such detail."

"That is all you got from what I said?" he retorted in disbelief.

"Why do you try to read me, Kilian?" I questioned, curious why he always wanted to draw my truth out, especially moments when I had wanted it hidden.

"You are a strange puzzle, one I can't seem to solve."

No, he was very wrong, I was fairly simple and completely plain. "Don't try, I can't even piece them together myself, credit partially to your kind. They truly knew how to shatter someone and then toss those pieces in holes I can't even dig out."

"Snow, I—" Those annoying, frustrating words and expressions of plead and forgiveness that made me sick.

"So you are sorry? What will it do to me? If it had happened to you would it be something you could forgive?" I pushed, turning to fully face him. I felt my electric ire take over as my chest expanded, lit aflame. "So you are sorry? How many others are not, how many still want me dead, how many others have hunted me as if they have not already killed me once." I was lost out of breath, having almost shouted those heavy sentences of truth at him. He didn't dare ask for forgiveness, especially in the name of all. Even if the whole of Adriata and their king kneeled in front of me I would not hesitate to burn them all. He did not dare deny the truth, that they still would do the exact same thing all over again, unapologetically—that they still would kill me at their first chance. I knew how they saw me. It was the same way he himself had seen me when he had come to Isjord. The remembrance of that stare still sent cold shudders down my spine, like staring at a wild beast, and somehow worse.

I rubbed my hands over my face, remembering who I was facing. "I brew in a very insatiable rage, it may or may not ever disperse, but I know it will always be at the expense of your kind. You are my enemy, you will forever be." Why had I let myself grow loose and warm around my enemy? My mother must be weeping tears of blood and thorns at my behaviour.

He stared at me for a long while silently, unwavering, skin shivering and heart jolting. "I know," he admitted quietly.

Did he know that I was the one forgetting? "Do you really? Are you underestimating me? I have done so many wrongs and I will continue to do worse. Do you understand that I am your villain?"

"Well, my sweet villain, have a restful night."

"Don't joke," I bit out.

"I am not joking, I never joke. Do your worst, Snow, I am ready for it."

"Given up so soon, no more pleas, lectures, morals and sweet words to make me realise what a terrible person I am?" I didn't want him to give up. I needed him to fight me, surrender under my fright, crumble by my vengeance. I mean to spare no one—I didn't mean to spare him, why did I wish to spare him, an Adriatian?

"No more."

"Why?"

"Because."

"That is not an answer."

"What do you want to hear, Snow?"

"Enough with that ridiculous answer, you aggravating bastard," I almost shouted. "Why is it always what I want to hear and not what you think? I never know what you think—I have no idea what you think, ever. Do you hate me a little, a lot, maybe less sometimes and more at others? Answer me properly so I know. I want to know."

"You will not like the answer."

Seething in frustration, I tried to contain the grit of my teeth, the strength of my fists ready to wound me, soothe me. "I am tired—so very tired and I don't need you on top of all of this. Get out of my head." A plea, maybe a prayer, I needed him out of my thoughts before he became one of them.

He raised his hand to me, his knuckles brushing the side of my cheek. "Why am I in your head?"

I swallowed the pressure behind my throat and said, "You will not like that answer."

He rested his palm at the small back of my neck and I could not think straight. "Because you hate me?"

"Yes, deeply, badly...desperately. I desperately want to hate you," I admitted, shocking myself more than him. I didn't hate him, that was the issue. I could not believe I just realised that. How could I not hate him, he was—he was...what was he? Why did I have to make a list to justify what he was? He was Adriatian. When I swore to destroy them, I had no intention on sparing anyone, no intention on sparing Kilian or Mal or Amerie or anyone, why would I want to spare them in the first place?

"There," he said. "Overthinking again. If one thing requires that much processing, you are thinking it wrong."

"What the hells do you know, Kil?" It had slipped out of me, freed out of my tongue. Probably muscle memory from the considerable number of times I'd spoken and repeated that name to myself, perhaps at times for hours to no end.

He smiled, eyes alight, too. "There, see how easy it was to make me happy?"

Heat spread all through me. "Don't say things like that."

He reached to move a strand of my hair out of the way like he usually did—too often, often enough that I thought about it excessively. "I don't like this," he said. "You, torn."

You tear me. You are tearing me. "You should not like this. Me, ready to find a reason to tear you, because I will. Don't get close, Adriatian, you will burn."

"Such lovely flames." He swept a hungry look over me, closing a step so near that I only breathed him. "If they could only sleep and rest and eat properly, they would burn brighter."

"Enough," I said, too meekly. Breath caught inside my rib cage.

"Why?" His voice was feverish and I felt his gaze trail over my skin till it puckered as if he had been touching me. "You want to burn me anyway."

"Enough," I repeated, my voice this time was almost a whisper.

"Don't fade, Snow," he said, tracing a finger along my jaw and over my lip. "Don't fade or I will think I am frost. Don't fade or I will think you cannot burn me and step closer. And if I am frost, I don't want to douse you. So burn bright and burn me away."

Heavens, seven hells, nine guardians of Nubil, gods of Ithicea, bloody Numengarth and all the damned insufficient air in this corridor. I was drowning. Deluging in his stare, presence and his words. Saturated and fading. What was I doing? Why was I growing lighter? Why was I sullying the memory of my beloved?

A shiver crept at my own thoughts. Bile raising, revolting on my throat. "Enough," I said loudly, almost panting in realisation.

He smiled and retreated a few steps back. "There she is. Now I am back to being timber."

He was always timber, but there was another fire he'd ignited.

"Those pretty words," I said, retreating to my bedroom. "They will one day become the death of you, and your death the pleasure of me. Don't crave my temptation, mercy is not what I am known for."

He smiled again. "Sleep, pretty liar."

30

ENEMIES AND ALLIES

KILIAN

ENEMY. IT WAS A title I had deserved, but why did my head not want to accept it, especially now.

Kil. I had enjoyed that more than I should have. A smile rose on my lips, absently directed to myself remembering her reaction from my words. I couldn't keep it in, she always paid no mind to my words, but yesterday I'd seen that flash in her eyes when she'd said my name. Thoughts plagued my head and slowed my limbs as I put on my clothes.

The sun had sunk down. The grey clouds helped the evening appear darker sooner and enveloped the white crusted lands with a vain fog. Silent lightning intercepted the grey darkness and it had become wonted these past few days—the constant storm. I wondered why it never drew upon us, all the thunder. Why did it only hover above, unreleased?

Mal entered the room as I was about to put my jacket on. He plopped on his bed, shadows of exhaustion hovering him. "She is by the training pits."

I blinked confused at him. "At this hour?"

He let out a loud sight. "She has been there since Cai and I took over this morning."

"All day?"

"All day, nonstop. The mana of a titan that woman has. Reminds me of a certain bastard we called a father."

The irresponsible man-children looking after her were drawing short sticks of my anger quite often lately. "And you didn't care to drag her for a rest or a meal?" I said, kicking his leg to pass by. Him and Caiden should have not been arranged together to guard Snow, they were like one another, childish and indulging in Snow's antics—dangerous antics even. For Mal, these were repeated patterns of actions—how many times I had covered for those damned actions of his. I admired at the same time loathed the way he perceived life.

He scoffed at my words. "Do you think we didn't try? Do we know the same princess? Cai said it's muscle memory for her. Same as it is for us. We would not eat for days, too, Kil, forgotten on the training courts till we had perfectly executed what father expected of us," he said, sitting himself up.

"It was how he was raised, too. It is something I can never blame him for, wanting to raise us to be strong and able enough to handle ourselves in the position we are."

"I would call it something else, brother, something on the lines of child abuse."

"Blame whose son you are not how he raised you. It is not wrong what he tried to make of us and he achieved it well. If I were you," I said, throwing him a pillow. "I'd be a little less partial to the hate you created for our father." I'd never try to justify our father and his actions, never what he did to Mal, but it was inevitable, the path we were to follow would eventually lead us to the lesson of being strong and undefeated. I was just grateful we didn't have to learn it in a way that would have us lose to it. Standing from a fall was harder than being taught you could fall. He had me—Mal always had me and I'd never let him out of my sight, I'd protect him with all I had—the best I had.

"Would you say the same for what was done to her? You never seem partial to the hate she has for hers and ours was not far worse."

I laughed. "Are you comparing Silas to our father?"

"Answer me, brother, don't duck your response." He chucked the pillow back at me. "Why are you not partial to what was done to her? I have heard you almost every night since that day from the funeral, mumble and toss at how he treated her."

He had not tried to teach her, he'd tried to break her and piece her into an unfeeling marred being of pain and rage which he would have ultimately used to his advantage. "You are trying to get somewhere you will never get, Mal," I said, knowing what chain of thought he was trying to attach me to.

He grinned. "Am I? Denial, has it come with old age?" He observed me for a few moments and a sly smirk rose in his face.

Attempting to avoid his knowing eyes, I concentrated on putting my boots on. "Not the slightest idea what you are on about, but I've never been one to want to break your heart and tell you of your wild imagination. I even let you believe for eight years that the Spring Oak of Sidra doesn't really visit children on the equinox to leave them the first fruit of the season." Mal was quite devastated in the eighth year of his life when he found Driada leaving cherries on his window sill instead of *Verob* the Oak.

He laughed, probably reliving the memory. "They suit you brother," he said, motioning his hand in circles around me and towards my shadows. "Or are those my imagination, too? *Verob* the Oak I never saw, but those," he paused and clicked his tongue, "are hard to miss."

I tightened my scabbards and threw him a warning look before I left toward the pits.

I heard the clanging of swords, heavy breaths and grunts of the unfortunate soul taking on Snow. Before I reached her, Nia's figure came to sight, standing behind a pillar and observing her friend from a distance, hidden. This was not right, I wanted to tell her what Snow had said but that was her truth, not mine. I felt for Nia, but I had faith Snow would make the move to reach her friend.

"She will come around," I offered, planting my hand on her shoulder. Her face wore a grim expression, but she nodded.

"The other night we saw a Dark Crafter, presumably her father's work. They were transporting a chest of some sort with a Solaryan crest. A woman, tall, short red hair, two marks—one across her forehead and the other to her neck. Anything you have seen during meetings?" I asked her, curious from the night before. From what I heard, Snow had presumed her dead, what was her business back in Silas's court and why was it concerning Snow?

Nia took a moment to assess my question and shook her head. "No, I haven't. I will look into it," she assured before leaving.

The training pits were countless, stretching further than the eye could trace but only one was lit up by torches—the only one from where sound came.

Caiden stood up from the benches after taking notice of me, dark shadows had formed under his eyes. "I don't care if you have to drag or knock her unconscious, get her to rest," he said breathlessly, walking past me.

Lara, the little girl from Brogmere, sat by the benches as well, tracing every move of hers. Snow had kept her word, even training Lara a few times herself, the rest it had been left to us. The little one was a quick learner and very eager.

"I can't believe she has kept you here all day. Go rest, Lara, is past bedtime for you. Stop by the dining chambers first for a meal," I ordered, ruffling her yellow head.

She smiled and nodded. "I begged her to let me stay, I just love watching her."

So did I.

Just as she left, I turned to the reckless princess. She must be overthinking and brewing on what she saw yesterday. I knew talking with Nia would have helped soothe her worries, but she was still not giving up.

"Still angry, *dahaara*?" I called, assessing the sight of her. Amazing or terrifying, I tried to juggle the two words to describe her, only to end up settling on both. There was never just one word to describe her.

She halted her movement and turned to me. Gods I was doomed, completely doomed. Beads of sweat coated her porcelain skin and matted the dark hair to her forehead and neck like climbing black wisteria. She had shed down to her tight trousers that cinched to her thighs and a vest that had completely melted to her skin. Lean muscle and curves, she was like a feline. She moved a bandaged hand up to tuck a bunch of hair behind her ear, giving me a way to fully immerse into her striking eyes. Thank the heavens for those concentration practice sessions that I had gone through during my training, otherwise I would have blankly stared at her raw beauty till she would have laughed herself to death. Nothing would have satisfied her more than my gawking.

"Working on it," she said, turning to the soldier in front of her. She stomped on his knee with her heel before she jumped up and spun in a high kick that sent him flying back down to the ground.

"Need help? Who better than I to unleash your anger and I did offer to teach where to point the sharp end of a dagger," I said, hoisting myself up to the pit and shedding my jacket.

Her eyes roamed all over me, halting to my arms as I folded my sleeves. She looked at me just the same as she looked at food, full of relish and hunger. How I wished it didn't tempt me to do the same. "For a moment I thought my ears had betrayed me, you do joke on purpose besides to offend me. Fascinating," she teased, leaning to rest onto the pit's wooden borders.

"And you joke too much."

She narrowed her eyes on me, pushing herself from where she rested, gesturing a hand for me to approach. She didn't hesitate to throw her foot in the air towards my thigh where it met my hand, tricking me before she spun into the air as if invisible wings carried her up and her other foot hit my shoulder, making me stumble back from impact. We pushed and pulled several times, she was exquisite, but I could see she was tired. Her fist flew forward and I grabbed it into my hand. It made me laugh, the size of her hand to mine looked adorable, but I appeared to have angered her as she twisted under my arm before her heel met the back of my knee that threw me kneeling to the ground. I attempted to turn, but she rounded her legs around my waist, twisting me down flat to the ground. She straddled my waist, a hand over my throat and another holding a dagger to my pulse.

She blew a flyway of hair, brows narrowing on me with puzzlement. "You let me."

"I didn't." A lie, I did. She might have eventually managed to put me down, but she had been out here exhausting herself from the brink of morning, with no rest and no food. The quicker this ended, the quicker I could get food in her empty stomach.

"Why did I enjoy it better when this was the other way around?" she said, a sly smirk wearing her pretty lips. "I like your hands better over my throat, maybe further down too and your mouth—" Her gaze darted over my lips, staying there. "Everywhere."

But that was all it was. A want. A like and a want, nothing beyond to act on. She was drunk in her fatigue and I held her—the one who made me drunk with her sound, her sight, and her smile. But two intoxicated truths made for a burning hangover. To act on it she would retch regret and I would bleed longing.

"Enough, this is your burnout talk."

She giggled, her breaths tired. "It might be, what else should I say? What do you want to hear while my tongue is all loose? Here you have me all sincere."

"Nothing," I said. "Nothing that you cannot tell me usually. I won't force them out of you anymore." I wanted the truths of her soul, not jagged confessions of the stomach.

"Aren't you so righteous?" She lowered her lips to hover just above mine and I hope she hadn't taken notice of my furious lungs and the strain of my hands digging on the ground.

I grabbed onto her, flipping us over and her under me before I'd let my will slip away and my need slide in. She yelped and laughed. Lifting her dagger up again, she traced a line along my jaw. Brush of unfelt pain, she was like the dagger holding, always brushing me so close to pain. If I dared to feel her closer, I'd bleed.

She rested it atop my chin. "Hello, handsome."

"Hello, gorgeous." I pushed strands of black away from her eyes before running my thumb to straighten her brow. "Let's get you up."

Yet she had stilled, unmoving, eyes lost and dazed as if she was spelled. Nothing like her, nothing I'd seen before. Her dagger was still moving along my jaw and I gripped her wrist to make her stop. She gasped and I felt the tip graze my skin. A drop of my blood dripped in her cheek and it rolled over her skin like a sinful tear. She shut her eyes tight, as if the sight of it terrified her and threw her dagger away. When she forced them open again, she gripped my face, examining the cut intently.

"It is fine, Snow," I said, wiping the red stains from her cheek.

Next thing I know, she pulled my face down to her mouth. Warm full lips resting atop the cut, her tongue gently sweeping atop and she gently sucked on the cut. After planting a soft small peck atop, she pushed me back. All my senses lost at the feel of her lips on my skin, a spear of heat cursed my body and I felt myself strain in my trousers.

She licked her lip. "You do taste sweet, too." Heavens. A temptress, she had become my temptress and I—I was still her enemy.

My lungs demanded more air, my body demanded her and I could not hold it in anymore. Tilting her face where I wanted it to be, I lowered my lips to hers, stopping short once I felt her body stiffen. Her breath matched mine while she stilled under me, like thunder at halt, gurgling storms beneath. I wanted to be inside that storm, to taste her rain, feel the hail, let my skin dance around the lightning. But this was an august shower, forced and unnatural. A thunder of scorching panic.

She gripped my shirt when I pulled away. "Why?"

I gathered all the scrap of will left in me to admit what she wouldn't. "You'd hate it—you'd hate it terribly."

Something I could not read flashed in her eyes and dimmed her expression. Regret, realisation? "Yes," she whispered. "Yes, I'd hate it. Terribly...tremendously hate it." She blinked slow and lost, staring at me, and I finally moved away, her words weighing against my chest till it almost hurt. I knew that truth, why did it strike me as strange to hear it aloud?

"Another round," she demanded, straightening herself as if none of that had happened, as if I'd imagined those moments. But I still felt her touch, scent, her gaze on me, reminder how I'd take burning days and chilly nights of lifetimes to forget. If one could forget her.

I stood and grabbed onto her wrist, pulling the dagger from her hand and sheathing it down her thigh. Her tired eyes followed my movements intently and without words. Sign of her fatigue, no words, no retorts, no maddening flirts.

"Ken, the cook, I had him ready your favourite stew." I pulled her out of the pit. To my surprise and luck she didn't pull away or reject, but she shook her arm free and followed beside me while we made our way to the dining chambers. My head still fogged with what had just happened a moment ago, the feel of her lips on my skin. Hers seemed empty of everything. For the first time since I'd met her she was not thinking at all.

Ken laid down a hot steaming meal to which Snow took and pleasurably licked her lips in anticipation before digging through it as if she had been starved for months.

"Snow!" She had stuffed her face so tight and ate so quickly that she had coughed a few dozen times. Before it amused me, now it had gotten concerning. This was a habit—a bad one. "Just who is chasing you?" I asked, shaking my head at her wondrous sight.

She stopped chewing, her cheeks were swollen with the amount of food, resembling a squirrel collecting nuts for winter. She lowered her eyes, straightened and slowly continued. She finished two rounds of food before one could have three spoonful's.

"The way you spar, it's not a style I have seen before," I said to her, somewhat impressed and curious. The way her body moved, the lean muscle almost feline, the light steps that of a dancer. Sparring was strength, tactics, bulk built favoured, yet she could swiftly put down someone twice her size with impeccable speed and minimal effort. The soldiers spoke how she'd gained her position, by taking down a general. That wouldn't have come easy.

She leaned back on the chair, lazily rubbing a hand over her pleased belly. "My guardian, Alaric Drava, he was my mother's friend and an Olympian general. He taught me. It is a fighting technique brought down by Zephyrs called Peregrine. I am not as good as a Zephyr would be, like Cai. They would use wind magic to swift them up in the air. I have to rely on gravity, agility and muscle." I knew it was one I had never seen before. Had the man been the one to look after her when her father tucked her away following the attack?

"Alaric, he is the one that raised you?" I asked, curious about her life before she came back to Isjord. Alaric Drava, even I knew the man, everyone did—the famous Olympian general.

She looked up at me, mischievousness written all over her gold eyes. "Why, are you looking to kill him, too?"

"Snow!" She chuckled at my frustration and I shook my head. "You called me Alaric that day."

She stilled and quickly retorted, avoiding my point as usually, "Well, one can't really see while they sleep. I am an *Ybris,* not a bat."

I folded my arms. How I loved her logic. "Bats sleep with their eyes closed."

She rolled her pretty eyes. "You get my point, Adriatian."

I pursed my lips and shook my head. "No, not really."

A smile rose up her face that I almost unconsciously traced with my own.

"My turn now," she said, leaning forward in all her eagerness. "Let's say I have a skilled fighter and a handsome Umbra, how can the two break through a Crafter's veil? Ah, and possibly unnoticed as well."

She spun my patience in circles, to the point that tension was building in my neck. I stretched back and forth to release the pressure from the exasperation. "No," I answered strongly and pointlessly because I knew what would come next.

Her features dropped. "Fine, just the skilled fighter I suppose," she said, standing up. Gods, she was going to kill me.

I followed swiftly behind her. "What is of this importance that you have to get in there?" The building quarter where we had been that night neared, ominous and threatening. If blocks of rocks could be threatening.

"I will answer that the second we find out."

We halted before the large dark building doors. There was no Crafter's veil shielding it anymore, the whole area was lifeless and empty, as if there truly had been no life here. She reached forward, cracking the door open, the sound of the rusty hinges combined with the heaviness of the wood grew consonant about the vacant surroundings. Releasing my magic, I dispersed the shadows, leaving only faint light from outside to brighten the empty chambers. There was no one and nothing in it, completely empty.

She hovered about the room, her features drawn in disbelief. "You said I am not mad, did we or did we not see them coming here that night?" She groaned, frustrated, taking in the unexpectedly empty surroundings.

I examined the empty space, filled in cobwebs and reeking of death. "She must have known you would try to come back and warned your father. Whatever they were hiding they wanted it to remain as such—hidden. What is it, Snow, what do you fear he is hiding?"

She let out a heavy breath. "Nothing I will like. Do you sense anything strange here?"

I expanded my magic further, despite it feeding on my life energy. I surveyed the room once again and stilled. Had she felt it as well? Patches of an unnatural luminescent green shadow lurked here and there about the room, the whole area was buzzing heavily in craft magic and something else—unearthly. "They have practised here. Not just any craft. Strong craft. I cannot tell what sort it is. Portallers, Potioners, Summoners or Medians, whatever it was it has left a heavy print of it."

She squatted down, cupping her face in her hands and soaking deep into thought. Why was it so important to her what her father did? She had gone out of her way to find out about the Solaryan vandals, enlisted Samuel and was now hunting down her father's Dark Crafter. It was bothering her more than enough. In the beginning I had thought she intended to find more to elevate herself in court, but none of this made sense.

A shuffling sound came from behind us and I reached for my sword. Memphis came inside swiftly, growling in my direction before nestling around her bonded companion who had crouched on the floor. She looked up at me, examining my weapon. "What happened to your black steel?"

"A gift from Caiden, much lighter and just as deadly. I like this better," I said, sheathing it back. Her eyes felt as if they could unravel my truth, perhaps they did.

"Trace Melanthe," she ordered the animal. Memphis stood, waltzing around, her lean muscle gliding with elegance while she took in the scent of its surroundings. Growling loudly in the air, she shifted around black smoke into a raven before flying out towards the skies.

"How did you bond with her?"

"Looking to kill her, too?" she teased, inspecting the dust on the ground.

"Does it hurt to just answer me for once?"

Her giggles were a symphony around the empty quarters, making my skin prickle as if it had been traced with silk. "No, it's just more entertaining," she said, leaning back onto her hands. "Six years ago she got really sick. Memphis was born in the lands of Aita, before as everyone knows, my father burnt."

Silas's famous second claim of his killer king title.

"They said her kind grew heartsick quickly, but it took her a few years after. She would not shift, not eat or move, so I stayed with her, not eating, not moving as well. One day she woke me by pulling me to the kitchen. Alaric swore my loud stomach had scared her."

"He might have had a point."

She threw me a glare. "As I was saying, she wanted me to eat, but I refused to do so till she would do the same."

"Why? To trick her?"

She sneered, throwing a pebble at me. "Because it broke my heart. Is that what you want me to say?"

"I want you to tell the truth, now I got it, so continue."

Snow blinked annoyed at me, but went on, "She ate with me, walked, ran, slept and then finally shifted again. One night I dreamt of a land I had never seen before. Magnificent wouldn't begin to describe it. It looked like what I imagined the heavens were. I was in her head and seeing memories of her lands. Memphis showed and spoke to me. She told me of her life and offered her soul to me, so I offered her mine and that was it. Bright lights, internal warmth all of that ride. Now I can see, feel and sense everything she can, and unfortunately she can do the same for me."

"Not unfortunately, she wouldn't have done that if she thought like that. Morphs are beyond intelligent, she picked you because of what you are." Dyurin blessed animals were connected to the spiritual, they felt through that rather than actions or words.

"You might as well have just called her dumb," she murmured, glancing around.

We waited in silence as the morph rapidly flew back in, landing in front of Snow. She pulled her forehead away from the animals, her face dressed with worry.

"What is the matter?"

"Not a trace of her scent anywhere within long miles from the castle. How can she disappear? No, how can the whole of what has been here disappear within a night?"

"We will find out. I will help you. For now let's leave this place. I know you can feel it as well, it creeps of darkness and death." I reached a hand down to her.

She stared lost about the room before taking my hand. I didn't want to let go of her, I held her palm tight in my own savouring her unusual touch, it felt as if the hearth of heat had gathered between them.

"Do you feel this danger would require us to hold hands?" she asked playfully, and I looked down where I held her. She wore no gloves today, had she forgotten? She also no longer flinched from me when I turned her hand over, running my fingers over her palm.

"How can they even hold a sword when they are so...small?"

She scowled. "Not everyone is six foot and extra, and I seem to handle myself just fine as they are."

"Four," I said, and she blinked in confusion. "The extra."

"Ah. You must have been a tree in your past life."

"There is no such thing as a past life."

"To the unblessed there is, perhaps I wish to pursue their way of living, they seem happy. A different, nonjudgmental sort of happiness."

"You're blessed."

"Correction," she said. "I am cursed."

I felt a frown bunch in my brows. "Snow."

"Darling, the world hates, fears and wants to either use me or kill me. Those I love are either dead or in danger, my worth nothing or precious and that is depending again on whether one wants to use me or kill me. Do you truly reckon unicorns and sirens from your prophecy sprinkled spirit dust over my crib?"

My teeth scraped my bottom lip, suppressing a smile and an entire laugh. "Wolf, dragon and thunderbird."

"Yes, yes," she said, waving her hand in the air. "Beasts of the same sort."

"You are not cursed."

"I certainly am something, but not blessed. Do you prefer I keep the contortion of the unnatural metaphor?"

I gripped her jaw with a hand, tilting her head to me and her eyes shot wide. "You do hold onto things pretty tightly. You want me to beg and apologise on my knees for calling you that? Tell me and I'll get on my knees for you again."

A smile grew over her pretty lips and I gently brushed my thumb over them. "Yes, but not on your knees, otherwise I'll want you between mine."

Yes, I'd probably want to do that, too. I leaned over to her ear. "Forgive me?"

She shivered. "Alright."

I faced her full of doubt. "Alright?"

She nodded. "Yes, alright. Want me to spell?"

"You let go of that pretty quickly." Even I had not forgiven myself for all I'd said and done to her. Perhaps I'd never forgive myself.

"That comment only inflated my ego, it did not offend me. I let it go the moment you said it then. I just wanted to see if you would really ask for it. Ask for an apology."

"You know I would."

"I knew," she said, confidently. "But it's different to hear it. I like hearing your thoughts."

I thought she hated my thoughts. I let go of her face and she ran her fingers over her jaw. "I've never been into this before, but you have my vote."

"Is that all you think about?"

"Come now," she purred. "Don't you? It's not like we can act on it. What will a little thinking do?"

"At times." That little thinking did a lot, more than it should.

"Night times?"

I sighed, rubbing my eyes, this frustration of mine was slowly turning something on the lines of arousal. "You tire me."

"And you bore me." Her hands met my chest and she eagerly blinked up at me from her shorter stature. "So? Only at night time or is there some sort of rule for your sort?"

"You have some interesting conceptions on my people and our traditions."

Her eyes narrowed for a moment. "So it is not only at night?"

I cupped her shoulders and pushed her a step back before I lost all sense propriety. "No, not only at night."

She approached me again. "What sort of thinking?"

I took another step back. "What is it that you want to hear?"

She fluttered those eyelashes. "How do you think of me? Silencing my mouth or making me scream."

Fuck. "Hells," I said, blowing a heavy exhale, my head dropping back. "Enough, Snow." I hated that she hated the thought of me touching her, it was all I wanted to do. I hated how my body reacted to her despite knowing she hated being touched by me.

"Ask Krig, why are you asking me? I don't control the skies, I am not the cloud dove of storms."

I laughed along with her. "I love your humour."

Her smile dropped. "Am I overthinking again?"

I nodded. "Yes." No, maybe she wasn't.

We headed to her chambers. I had been up only for a few hours, but she had days of no sleep, not to mention all the energy she spent today. Rest needed her at this point.

"Do you plan on sleeping tonight? You have not had a break in days."

She nodded. "Yes, I am heading to Venzor tomorrow," she revealed while confusion coated my head. Venzor? What was in Venzor? Did it matter, she would have me worry again.

"Any reason in particular?" One with yellow hair and no manners? Gods, tell me that was not why she was dragging herself all the way to another city just to see him. She had not left for patrols or any other duty outside Tenebrose city walls, yet she was heading to Venzor for him. It made my blood simmer, frustration creeping over my skin.

Her eyes dipped to my chin. "I suppose we will see," she said, throwing me a wink before entering her chambers. "Don't miss me too much."

I pulled onto her wrist and she turned to me again. "You have not said my name today. Say my name."

She stood still for a moment, assessing the madness I'd just spoken out loud. She reached close to me, her hands as always playing with the lapels of my jacket. Holding onto them she got on her toes and reached over my ear to whisper, "Prick."

I still enjoyed that more than I should because I laughed.

She gently touched the pad of a gloveless finger where her dagger had grazed me earlier. "Good night, Kilian."

I held onto her wrist, pulling her to me again. "Not like that. Like you did yesterday. Call me like I am yours."

She was silent for a moment and I could feel the quick hum of her pulse grow even quicker. "Good night...Kil."

A spell. My name in her mouth was a spell with such power. I took a deep breath, attempting to ground some sense back in my body. "Yes, like that." I counted to five and I let her go, moving away. "Good night, Snow."

Her eyes darted lost about the corridor, not meeting mine, and she backed toward her room. I read the regret, fear and confusion, and then later mine accompanied hers along. The doors shut, but there wasn't going to be any sleep for her, she had seen too much today, probably brew and stew on what she had found out. There was not going to be any calm for me either, overthinking her infatuation with that Isjordian brooding yellow head. This was going to drive me insane. If I saw him ogling her like dessert I would scoop his eyes out and would definitely cut those hands to the wrists if they lingered over her waist as if he was petting a cat.

31

Silver and Him

Snowlin

You would hate it—you would hate it terribly, he had said. Was it wrong that I wouldn't?

I erupted in a shudder every time I remembered last night. *Call me like I am yours.* I didn't know I could, I didn't know my need for him had been that obvious that night. I never knew how it was to want someone and not be able to have them, I didn't know how it was or how it felt to have someone like they were mine. I never had someone who was mine. Gods, his touch—had he not let me go, I would have never let him go. He had moved away and regretted what he'd said, I read it all over him. He always hesitated. Was it hard to forget what I was? I shook my head and crouched down to the ground before letting out a frustrated groan. Insanity at such a young age was concerning.

Murky skies were desolate from all light made for a thick blanket of darkness despite the hours of morning, so very typical Isjord—where night was night and day was just...a grey night. Sam and I were to meet by the stables before he headed to Casmere with pretence of the fleet check, readying it for the frozen surface sea waters. Celdric had notified us that the illegal ship had successfully crossed Brogmere Bay and would dock there today where Sam would be waiting. He hoped to find someone who could actually answer a question properly without puzzles, missing pieces and loads of enigma. The unknown annoyed me, I was already being left out of too much, this was now the borderline.

"Please tell me you really did wake up early and not spent the night staring at either the sky or your ceiling?" Sam called as he and his team entered the stables, readying to head north.

He opened his arms first, already accustomed to my habit of hugging him. "I slept. I have somewhere to be as well."

"Please stay out of trouble till I return," he pleaded, giving my hands a squeeze. Why did everyone jump to the ultimate conclusion that every step I took led me to trouble?

"You know I can't make you a promise I will not keep."

"Don't make me hold my heart in my hands."

I offered him a smile. "Bear with me for a little while longer. When this ends, Sam, come with me. You and Alaric can give each other another chance and I can have you near me forever," I offered. I could not leave someone I care this much behind, not again—not anymore.

I saw and read the care in his eyes. "I will—I will come with you and let's both learn how to live. Together," he said, planting a kiss on both my hands. "Be safe now."

He'd make me happy, but he'd make Alaric happier. I, of course, will take all honours and praises for playing matchmaker of the realms.

Solaryans, the soldiers in Myrdur, the agreement, spies in Hanai and a dead kingdom entangled and wedged between my plan to take Winter court made for a great headache. But now I had a dead witch to juggle in the mess, and that headache had turned to perpetual overthinking fatigue. No trace, not even a single smudge of her scent anywhere near castle grounds, Tenebrose and long miles away from it. All of her presence was either a fiction of my imagination, which Kilian keeps swearing it wasn't, or the red-haired-presumed-dead witch had veiled her presence. Nothing fell under the trace of Memphis, a Dyurin blessed with the sharpest senses. If I tried to not put much meaning to it, all the reasons justifying her presence that meant nothing suddenly had become reasons why I should fear her. Crafters were not to be messed with, Melanthe even more. Melanthe was destined to be the next Grand Maiden before Urinthia succeeded and took the role from her hands.

"What are you thinking that has parted your love for food and pinched your concentration this early in the morning?" Kilian asked, annoying me first thing.

I squeezed my eyes tight in concertation and slowly turned to face him, sitting by my side on the breakfast table. "Do I really like it better from behind or is it because I don't find most attractive enough to have them on top facing me?"

He dropped his spoon and rubbed his hands over his face in frustration. "Cynth, spare me."

Why, what? I found that really funny. The other three facing me were shaking in laughter. Didn't he say he loved my humour?

"Don't taunt him, Snow, he hasn't seen the front or the back of anyone in a few months," Mal said.

Kilian glared death threats to his snickering amused brother, he looked too tired to hold onto his composure.

"Issues with the little one?" I asked, pointing down at him. Definitely a tease, I knew he had no issues, let alone little.

He shut his eyes tight, dropping his head forward. "I am going to kill you, Mal." He lifted his hand to punish his brother and I rested mine atop before he could. He turned to me as if a spirit had nudged him, as if I had burnt him.

"Spare him, compensation for being the first to annoy me this morning. I didn't presume you a man with a fragile ego to be annoyed by this."

"He isn't," Mal called in his defence. "Just raised with a stick up his arse. He was father's golden boy, raised, fed and trained to be a soldier. My attitude and especially yours is out of the protocol, it annoys him."

Why did Mal have a predilection in thinking of his brother as a puppeteered wooden doll when even I thought him a soft summer cloud?

I cleared my throat, turning to my meal once again. "We are heading to Venzor."

"What's in Venzor?" Cai asked.

"A witch, well, two if you count my grandmother."

I could swear a smile rose on the silver eyed snake at my explanation. What was he playing in his head that made him smile? I had not said anything funny enough to have mister sternness here grin so wide. Ridiculous man, probably brewing on whatever sick thoughts of his or making another perfectly revised speech to lecture me again sometime today.

My friend studied me under a suspicious stare, crossing his arms and looking like the perfect posture of doubt. "You hate the hag, and what witch?"

Hate was an understatement. I had a list with her name which I intended to cross with a feather tip dipped red with her blood. "Melanthe, father's Crafter, the one me and Kilian saw from that night had a little sister. If my memory holds strong, she was under the service of my grandmother as a Potioner. The hag loved her and her beauty contraptions. I bet my black heart she still has her."

Everyone let out gasps of understanding at my plan. Kilian instead sighed loudly, leaning back onto his chair and looking like he needed a long rest. This close to the arrangement, my actions probably seemed too risky for him to allow me in the way of danger—risk the agreement. This was probably why he had foregone rest and had decided to come with us.

"What if she refuses to help? They are sisters after all," Mal questioned rightfully.

"Oh no, dear, no one says no to me. Ask your brother, three times he has done my bidding without a word."

He did not replicate, only stared me down through tired lids and unwavering silver halos—it worried me somehow.

"Where does your father think we are heading?" Mal asked and my head snapped away from Kilian, but not disturbing my line of torturous thoughts.

"Brogmere, Cai found Lara's grandmother and she is willing to take her in. From there we will deviate to Venzor," I explained.

"I will ready the horses," Mal announced and they all stood heading towards the stables.

The room slowly emptied one after the other till it was only I, Kilian and Ken pondering about and checking how well his celery porridge had gone down.

"Stay back," I said, tightening my thigh scabbard, unable to look at him. "You look exhausted."

"No."

I rolled my eyes at his stern reply. "Fine, drop dead if you must."

He grabbed onto my wrist before I made to leave. "You didn't sleep last night. You said you would. What is troubling you? It seems you have this settled so it must be something else." My eyes travelled down to where he was holding me, to where his thumb made circles over my skin, sending shivers down my back and tingles over my stomach.

"How...how did you know I was not asleep?"

"You were not snoring."

I bit my lip and raised my fist at him in threat, but he only smiled.

"Your shadows were restless. I can trace their movement like a sixth sense."

"It's nothing," I lied, and his thumb stopped moving.

He nodded and pulled his hand away. It was not nothing, there was too much circling around me. I'd traced every step since returning to Isjord. Tracked, backtracked and repeated them twice before I'd settled in bed, eyes wide while my head took turns spinning from fatigue.

"Why do you do that?" At my question his attention turned to me again. "Why do you pull away from me?"

He stood, hooking a finger to hold my chin. His thumb brushed my skin gently, a lullaby of touch, and it ran again, my heart—it galloped. "Because you hate it. Terribly."

I swallowed and finally said, "Only because you do."

His dark brows pulled in a frown and his hand dropped. "I hate it because you do."

"I don't hate it." Too late, it was now out there. I would not regret it. Maybe not now or maybe never, I did not know.

"Neither do I."

My confidence picked so I demanded, "Then don't pull away." I took his hand and guided it under my chin like he'd held me a moment ago.

A light smile rose in his lips, his fingers skimming and exploring my face. "Then I won't pull away."

"Well...then we are settled."

He nodded. "We are." He studied me for a moment and then his hand moved to rest above my chest. "Why does this one say otherwise?"

"Because it's stupid, I never trust my heart." I dragged his hand to my head. "See, this one is silent as it should be."

He smiled and gradually laughed, shaking with amusement. He fluffed the crown of my head and tapped my nose with his finger. "It is too quiet. You will have to tell me to know and understand you. You have no shadows and I have no wits about what others feel without use of magic." This ridiculous man and his ridiculous words that did things to my body.

"I will and right now it is telling you to stay back. I don't like worrying."

A smirk carried his features. "You worry about me?"

"Pardon, I meant annoying me," I retreated too meekly for my usual behaviour, and his eyes narrowed, detecting my lie.

"Hm, is that so?" he said, flinging the lapel of my jacket to one side and revealing the skin of my collar. He ran a finger there, circles and stars, torturously slow and I almost gasped. Pulse shifted my breath and heat pooled below my stomach from that sensitive touch and that damned sensitive gaze. "Your annoyance doesn't compare to my worrying. If I don't have you in my sight I'll go mad—mad from worrying."

I inhaled deeply between frustration and mild arousal. "Stay back, you know I won't do anything to endanger the agreement."

His hands slid to cup the back of my head, conviction shone behind his silver irises. "Damned be the agreement, I need you to be well and I know something is not right."

Perhaps not...mild? "How do you know?"

His hands slid down to my neck. He traced lines with his fingers severely slow on the sensitive area. "Would you believe me if I told you I just do?"

My eyes drew shut at the touch—there was too much happening in me that I couldn't concentrate. Blessed heavens, I'd forgotten to answer so I nodded.

"Snow," Mal called, returning to the dining chambers before stopping short, taking note of us and raising his brows. "Did...I interrupt something?"

"Whatever do you mean?" I asked, tidying my jacket that Kilian had almost peeled off my body.

Kilian stretched his neck and walked past Mal. "Yes, what do you mean, brother," he said, tapping his shoulder with a palm before leaving Mal half hallucinating in his own head.

The younger brother rubbed his shoulder with a wince. "Crescent moon, might his poor victims never experience the strength of his phalanges."

I walked past him, planting a hand on his shoulder the same. "Crescent moon, aren't his lovers blessed?" I threw him a wink and left.

I had decided to let Nia accompany us there. I wanted to approach her, but my tongue had tied on each occasion. Forgiveness was one of those things that I had not asked very often, it felt foreign to me. I could not stand seeing how upset Nia was. I had really hurt her, but until I calmed my own hurt I knew I would not be able to muster the words *forgive me*. I hated my pride, my issues with anger and my distrust, but at the same time they had become so familiar with me to the point it was difficult to put them aside. I had never learnt to apologise, perhaps this was the time.

Venzor was a short ride through Sable Abyss from Tenebrose, but I had taken the long road through Brogmere to avoid having my father track me. Lara would finally find home. We'd left her under a safe oath of care, a bunch of golden dar for her expenses and a promise to recruit her once a warrior. I could not say it felt good to part with her, the ride afterward seemed empty. I hated goodbyes.

Cerelia, my grandmother, had lived with us in Tenebrose, but moved after the attack to her home city. As Queen Dowager, she had helped my mother in her duties so that she could be present raising us considering how my father had loaded her like a work mare. I had created respect for the woman, she had taken her son's side at all times, but in the shadows she'd always supported my mother. She was born of high blood, last child of the Lord of Venzor before Elias's father ascended to take the surname and the title. Her and Moreen had never gotten along and had always thought of her son's choice in taking a consort dislikeable—let alone when she had found out the squid he had chosen amongst many pearls. Whilst she'd butted with the crone, she appeared to respect my mother. The night of the attack had been when my thoughts and like for her burned to ashes. Evil lies in caves, but this one had laid hidden under pillars that held mountains. All the games she had spun my mother round, making it seem as if my father and Moreen had done it, all the ways she had humiliated, stepped and played her made me shake with rage.

The surge of remembrance of all those times, dressed in the crackling of the fire and the smell of burning flesh of that night made me shut my eyes and pull my head down with a wince. My eyes had coated in black specks, my breathing rapid. Gods, not now. I barely managed to pull Memphis to a halt. Dismounting and taking off behind bushes to empty my stomach raw. This was why I never had breakfast.

Don't run, please don't run. Don't take off, gods, please keep me still. I remained kneeling on the ground, gathering my breathing and my shaking limbs.

Four shadows had halted behind the bush, but there was no time to feel embarrassment as another round pulsed from me. I stood up, dragging my sleeve to wipe the sweat coating my temples and forehead. I wished to have kept my eyes down and not met the four pairs of heavy stares pointed on me because now I was embarrassed enough that a flush felt creeping on my face and ears.

Kilian reached into his pocket and approached me.

"Ah, of course you fold an embroidered handkerchief in your pocket. Adorable. Does it have your initials?" He startled me still and silent when he gripped my jaw with one hand and with the other he wiped my mouth with the piece of neatly folded cloth. I had just emptied my gut, but filthy thoughts filled my head. Now, if he could only dip a bit lower and press his plump arse lips to mine that would be genial. I shut my eyes and let out a long sigh, what was wrong with me? Completely in my defence, the fault was his. How could anyone look, behave, speak and think like him? Just why did it have to be someone from the wretched side of the Highwall. So I was twisted after all. Anyone, I could put my eyes on anyone and have them, but did it have to be this one? There was another truth in wanting him. I wanted to have him. It was no longer about need, it was about satiating that need.

Cai handed me a bottle of water and I cringed, shaking my head and pushing it away.

"Drink or I will make you," Kilian ordered, grabbing the bottle from him.

I tilted my head to him in the position he had held it a few moments ago. "Oh yes, I'll take option two." And just like that my mind had mixed with my line of thought.

He scoffed. "Ridiculous woman, drink," he ordered sternly, wrapping my hand around the bottle before he leaned over to my ear slightly. "Provoke me some more and I might use my grip to hold your pretty face still for something else and make your tongue of steel turn to butter. Enough provoking me—enough provoking me in public."

I spat the water forward and hit my chest repeatedly with my hand, my lungs erupting in coughing fits. Sweet gods. I ran my sleeve over my mouth. "I don't know why you think I would be opposed to that."

He suppressed a smile and threw me a side look that made me shiver. "Enough with the flirts and that hair thing."

"What hair thing?" I batted my lashes, running my fingers through my hair and dragging my locks to one side.

He sighed. "I give up with you."

"But no," I sulked. "Play with me, Adriatian, I'm bored."

He shook his head and huffed a soft laugh as we silently walked back to the horses. "What made you sick?" he asked.

"My head," I confessed with no restraint.

He halted, fully turning to me. "One of us could go, we can retreat. You don't have to go there. If she won't cooperate I will make her cooperate. Stay."

"I owe her a visit in substitute for her funeral that I won't attend."

His brows pinched together and I begged gods he wouldn't bring back face number three. "Is it that bad?"

I snorted. "The mother serpent is up to par with my father and your king."

His features wavered and a gut lurching feel tightened my stomach. "Snow," he spoke in what I would call a soft winter breeze, soft, cold but not chilling.

I felt myself tense, automatically reacting to that reaction. "Don't pull that one, Kilian. I told you I hate it, out of all, you and your kind don't get to give that to me," I spat, pointing at his face.

He straightened, temples flaring and that tense dimple in show. He was angry—angry at me. "I told you that it is not pity."

"Tell me then, what is that ridiculous face I cannot stand?"

He shook his head, his hands rustling the back of his hair before he dropped them down and turned to leave me there with no answer and more frustrated than before.

Adriatians did not deserve to give me pity, him the most—I hated his pity the most.

"You are quick to judge him while I've known him for a lifetime and still rely on using my magic to understand even fragments of him," Mal said silently from my side, he had heard us argue. "His facial range expands from stern to extremely stern and the in-between is very limited. He doesn't open up or let anyone open him up. The closest to that I have seen is with you."

I turned to the younger brother, somewhat surprised and overthinking again. "Why? Because I will rage out of his head?"

Mal smiled, shaking his head. "No, but that's Kilian's truth to give. All I am trying to say is that whatever makes you so upset with him is your own assumptions, not the truth. Kilian is difficult in many ways, but I've recently learnt that it takes a certain emotion to get him to change."

I scoffed. "Anger?" That's how I got most people to react to me. Kilian did not need me to anger him, my existence alone did that. He'd always refrained himself from acting on it, I could bet he would very much like to.

"You will have to ask him."

32

WITCHES AND BLOOD
KILIAN

WE REACHED INSIDE VENZOR. But before approaching the open coast line of Seer sea, we turned and rode between a narrow black stoned street similar to Sable Abyss, all surrounded by walls of tall century-old conifers. After a little less than a mile, we reached a stone fence imitating those around the cities. Four guards stood affront, but not in Isjordian soldier uniforms. A large grey stoned house laid in the middle of the tall wall fencing, surrounded by statues of guardians, possibly from Krig's realm, Hodr.

My eyes had settled unmoving on the dark-haired princess whose thoughts of coming here had sent her sick. That exterior she put up always held well, but a wall built with uneven stones is the easiest to fall out. Even falling apart she tried to hold herself to the might of heavens. Those hidden marks behind what she had been through, the flicker of her eyes, how she dug in her palms, when she shivered, the nightmares, sleeping out between her family's resting place, all of them gave it away. You had to be blind not to see her suffering. She had already been broken before my people even approached her, she'd known hurt and pain since a child and then drowned in it twelve years ago.

The air inside the manor was filled with tobacco smoke and musk, walls were severely decorated—overly decorated but dimly lit and lifeless. A young servant directed us to the main room, a large conservatory overlooking the coast. A woman who didn't look beyond her fifties stood by the large lace curtained windows, white hair pinned and pulled back, she was propped in an Isjordian attire of olive-coloured ruffles and a large skirted dress that took most of where she stood. She remained still despite our presence, holding a cigarette and puffing smoke onto the air. The presence of a late queen was there still.

"Hello, Cerelia," Snow greeted with a tight cold voice I had very rarely heard her speak in. She had the traits of a teaser. It was how she played people in her trap and how she hid her truths. Did she feel as if she had entered someone else's? Caiden and Nia had reassured us about a thousand times, but I felt myself reach for my sword.

She patted the cigarette butt in a golden tray before turning to us. "You used to call me nana, what happened to that?" she questioned, studying her granddaughter. When her eyes rested on Snow's face, her smile faltered and she pulled her gaze away as if the sight of her was painful.

Snow straightened herself slightly, pulling her fists tight. I wanted to run to her, to hold her hands, to smooth over the dents she was about to leave again.

Cerelia let out a short cold laugh, but it didn't meet her eyes. "You are still upset I see."

My eyes glistened black allowing her shadows to flickered in sight. Muted tones of fear, regret and guilt.

At Snow's silence, she threw glances at us and slowly moved to pour herself a drink before sitting down. "I have heard of your marriage with the spiritual king," she expressed with a sigh of disappointment, but not disapproval. "I had not expected your father to do that, I have to admit."

Snow's head dropped forward while she chuckled under her breath. "My, but why? He is your son after all. Like calls to like, right?"

Cerelia straightened, her face falling to stern lines of unyieldingness. Her shadows fluttered around in a mixed array of all emotion, a strange cocktail—one stirred with fear. "I was a dowager queen and I had a decision to make, Snowlin. A choice between saving what could not be saved or preserving the line of our royals. It was my duty, I could not spare to lose them all, the least I could do for my son, for his kingdom, was save them."

"They weren't royals. While directing soldiers to save the two half breeds you let Thora and Eren die," Snow revealed, crossing her arms back and seizing her prey. "For that I hold no king responsible, neither father nor the Adriatian. I hold *you* solely responsible for their deaths, you owe me what cannot be owed."

She half stood from her chair, almost aghast upon Snow's accusations. "The hall had set aflame beyond what could be saved, screams had stopped long before any guard reached there."

"You heard me beg, you heard me cry, you heard me plead and crawl to you. All that time you could have used, but weren't you good with all the pretending. Could have fooled me had I not seen and heard what I did." Snow picked a vase, studying it intently, almost as if to distract her from the murderous flow of the ire she radiated. "What was it again? Ah, 'I will not have Olympian breeds on the throne, save the upper hall first, our better chance to preserve Isjord'. You used to call me sharp-wits when I was younger. My, weren't you right?"

We all turned our attention to her grandmother who slowly cowered in her faults. Faults that had possibly cost Snow her soul. To know that they had burnt, to know that they died while they could have lived, to know that they had died while she had not been able to save them. It had cost her the restlessness of her nights, the ache of her feel.

Cerelia swallowed her guilt. "Thora and Eren were dead the moment that blast sounded. Whatever you heard me say, they were dead. Thora and Eren had been dead," she repeated, her voice rising and shaking.

"Do not dare say their names," Snow bit in anger, throwing the glass vase she held across the room. Crystals floated in the air and her grandmother flinched hard. "We will never know, will we? If they had been dead or not, like no one found out all the damn load you truly did behind my mother's back all while playing nice to her. But let's not dive through that, shall we not, dear nana? One doesn't have enough lives to pay those debts."

The older woman sat back down, refusing to meet her granddaughter's eyes. "I suppose you have come to collect it?"

"You will live to pay it. I don't give easy deaths to those that owe me lives."

The old queen sank further down her seat, tracing her granddaughter's predatory movement about the room with the corner of her cowed gaze.

"Melanthe's sister, father's Crafter, the wine red haired witchling, she still serves you?"

She studied Snow, looking confused and trying to assess the odd request. "You lived, child, try and hold onto that life. Whatever you are trying to meddle with will be dangerous. I know Silas, he won't spare you. Let him be and for your fate pray to the gods and send them to the heavens," she said in a plea that the princess definitely took for a threat.

Snow halted, her fingers stopping atop the wooden table swirling dust in circles before she raised her head to her grandmother. "Gods do not care and heavens might go light themselves aflame. Do you think I fear your son? When you live my life you fear nothing." She approached, leaning down to her head level and tracing a finger over her grandmother's face. "Every wicked was once a saint, but one born wicked can never become a saint, so save your new found belief blether for one who gives a fuck. Now, will someone call the one I am seeking or shall I fetch her myself?" Spite in each biting word.

"You have changed, girl, truly."

Snow scoffed, moving away from her. "What did you expect when you cook sour poison? A sugar tart? Now, send for what I need. Precious little house you got, would be a shame to wreck," she subtly threatened, wiping a layer of dust from a painting.

Why did I let myself get entertained from this? Her belligerence was sophisticated, to those in her clutches it was skin creeping, to me it was the most attractive thing I'd witnessed. I liked that side of her, feisty but with such poise and composure. People forgot the prettiest roses had the sharpest thorns, but this rose had a sharp dagger inside her, too. Even at the least favourable situations she had held herself high, her battle of wits was unchallengeable, likewise her fighting.

Her grandmother sat silently huffing smoke till a red-haired girl in servant clothes showed. Her pale skin had greyed and hued in colours of fatigue and violence. Shoulders hunched forward, she cautiously entered the room, throwing assessing glances to all of us before striking stunned at Snow. The Crafter's poise that her kind always wore had vanished from her halo, leaving her with a servant's robe of humility. Isjordians and their vices of feeling above just every other kind truly made for a morbid culture.

"Privacy, Cerelia. Whatever poison I will order from her I don't want father dearest knowing," Snow threw at her and she stood to exit in all her pique.

The Eldmoorian raised her head, a fearful look in her face before she stuttered out, "I...I don't make poisons."

Snow scoffed. "Anyone can make poison, dear, in different ways. I will teach you how to make mine." She traced her grandmother's steps as she left the room before turning to her again. "I need your blood, nothing more. It is not you I need, it's your sister."

The young Crafter raised her chin all challenge. "My sister is dead," she spurted out courageously. Her shadows of fear masking the rest, she was smart and aware that there were Umbra around her, a skilled Crafter despite the young age and what had been done to her.

Snow turned to me. "Did sweet Melanthe look dead that night?"

The sister paled and swallowed when I shook my head in answer.

"Don't play with me, witchling. I know you can feel each other through tugs of magic.I have read all about your neat tricks. Now, blood and preferably an explanation on how she is alive."

The girl retreated back. "I cannot betray her, it would be as betraying the king. She serves him and if he doesn't want you to see her that means something."

Snow stood annoyed, unsheathing her dagger and the girl called two gusts of magic to her fingers. My own magic floated round us, blanketing around Snow and grabbed onto whatever shadows stood amongst us to pull in protection.

The girl suddenly clutched her chest and gasped for air, her magic faded and no longer a threat. Caiden's fist extended forward toward the Crafter, his magic restraining air from her lungs. "Speak, witchling, she might like to play with you, but my patience runs dry pretty easily. Shall I turn your lungs to dust or let Isjordians have their way with you? King Silas could have sneaked in a Crafter, but it's still illegal here. Isjordians are suckers for tradition, burned at stake, was it not, or drowned by the Seer sea?"

"You heard him. The pretty face or a place of your choice?" Snow asked and the girl nodded fearfully, still unable to breath.

Caiden pulled back and she began coughing, her eyes wide and her face red as she examined the Zephyr. She lifted her arm and Snow dragged the tip of her dagger over her skin, drawing blood and dipping a white cloth in it before folding it neatly and handing it over to Nia.

"How is she alive?" Caiden questioned.

The girl hesitated before glancing over at Snow who had sat cleaning her dagger. "She has told me very little and we have not met more than discreetly. The Caligo mark was on her, two horns of guardian Keres of the soul gates, meaning she had reached the Otherworld, even entered it. I know it sounds mad. She died, but she also did not come from the dead. Mel said something had saved her, dragged her from death, literally. I don't know what that meant," the girl hastily explained, her eyes bouncing in fear about the room.

Her explanation was either a blatant lie, either told by her sister to fend us off or an evil truth that was about to make this situation a bit more complicated. For someone to be dragged from Caligo onto the living realm was nearly impossible, complicated, and dangerous. But just as impossible, there was always a little chance of possible. Why exactly on Silas's court? If it was enough to bother Snow, it bothered me, too.

"Lower your magic," I called. "If you speak the truth, why are you masking it for us to see?"

Snow glanced shortly at me before flicking her dagger in threat to the Crafter again. Slowly, a gust of colour swirled around the Crafter, revealing the truths and more she'd hid. She was in pain and she was in half. The other half of her was missing. She'd sold her soul.

I gave Snow a nod, she had not lied.

"Where is Melanthe now?"

She shook her head. "I don't know. Last I met her, your father had ordered her to the *azul hela*." Seraphim, fire lands.

"Why is she needed there?"

She shrugged unknowingly. "I don't know, there is not much for us to do there anyway, the further we are from Eldmoor the more our magic fades, we have to be near Celesteel's gates in Asra to draw mana from Caligo and wield a good amount of it. That much further away her magic would be as faded as in Vrammethen, inexistent."

Snow turned to me, her expression drawn in question and I nodded to confirm that the Crafter spoke the truth.

"This remains between us," Snow said, standing and ready to leave. "I do not wish to hunt or harm your sibling, only to track her hiding spot. You let anyone know what we did, well I suppose threats are unnecessary as I will come kill you myself. You made me a nightmare cure, a horror elixir, blood threaded to my nightmares if anyone asks about the scar, clear?"

Nia neared, handing her a cloth to wrap her wound before giving the girl a coin pouch. "Fifty gold dar for your services."

The girl nodded and tucked the coins under her dress.

Snow halted her step before reaching the doors to exit. "Is she holding you here against your wish?"

"Not-not exactly," the girl answered and Snow faced her once again. "After the king killed Melanthe, Lady Cerelia and I struck a deal for my life. A life threaded oath, unbreakable till death." Heavens, she'd sold her soul to live, yet was she truly living?

Snow let out a long exhale. "The bruises, why for? She already has you under full obedience."

She raised her hand carefully trying to mask the large dark violet mark on her jaw. "It is not her."

"The other servants?"

The girl nodded and we all heard the crunch of Snow's tight leather gloves gathering in a fist. "You will be free very soon. Once you are, head to the centre of Venzor to a man named Goran, he owns a printing shop down by the southern bay, tell him you were sent by me, he will know how to help."

The girl's eyes turned hopeful. "Why-why would you help me?"

"Why not, the old bitch will die anyway. Shame to have a Delcour witch chained, shame to have such a powerful bloodline end."

Delcour? Was she the 101st Grand Maiden's daughter?

We left Cerelia's house, all of us had been pacing long steps behind a very jittery dark haired someone. We'd stopped for rest shortly after and all of us stood gathered in silence staring holes onto the tavern table. Caiden had gone to order drinks and food for the soldiers and us as we sat by the far corner of the large tavern in Brogmere, where she'd made us deviate to distract her father from our trace.

Snow's face rested troubled on her hands, biting her lip in concentration, she nudged my leg. "I can't understand a thing from the spirituals, every time one speaks all I hear is tales and fables. Eldmoorians give me the creeps," she said, shuddering. "Now, which one of you can explain it simply for me to understand what a whole load of rubbish she just said."

"Eat and I'll tell you all, not a word before." Her hands were trembling. It was not from fear and not from cold, she just had no food in her system.

She threw a glare at her food and then me, rejection at the tip of her tongue, so I leaned back and raised a brow in challenge, one she knew not to take.

"The otherworld is another realm," I explained as she began putting mouthfuls of stew in her mouth. "Celesteel's heaven is not a spirit pane like the Mid-world. When an Eldmoorian dies, they head either to his heavens or to his hells like the rest of the rotten spirits. To be precise, they don't exactly die, only get transported to that realm, into a physical body as well. Dark Crafters can open portals to Caligo, if the young sister is to be presumed correct, someone from outside would be needed to have reached for her, and found Melanthe inside Caligo. But we are not talking elemental conjuring, that magic it is almost impossible...both Crafters would need to be wielders of immense magic."

That was the only way in and out of Caligo, the only realm reachable still—to Eldmoorian people only. You could no longer find a full-fledged Crafter within a village, let alone two. Not to mention that it would require insane amounts of magic to be wielded, runes, ancient text and many more magical elements that were rare to find in Numen. A whole circle of impossible tasks. I wanted to fear Silas just as she was, but after leaving Venzor, I wasn't so sure even Silas knew what he was doing. What she had told us now truly did sound as Snow said, a whole load of tales and fables. I had a faint idea what she was spinning in her head.

She chewed quicker, almost in a hurry, trying to say something and ended up coughing and almost choking. I rubbed her back trying to soothe it away. "Eat slowly, woman, I don't want to lose sleep over another thing because of you."

Mal coughed, too. "What did you say now?"

"Eat, Mal, or do I need to feed you like I did till you were six because you didn't exactly know how to hold and dip a spoon."

Nia and Snow were clutching their stomachs while my brother reddened.

He scowled. "Was that necessary?"

"Would you like me to tell the fork story next?"

He blew a vexed breath and continued to his food. The fork story was a winner. He had a tine stuck right between the gap of his front teeth for a whole two days. I held back a smile. Mal was an adorable child, but terribly clumsy.

"As I was telling you," I said, putting a second dish before Snow. "We are taking her words too seriously."

Snow gulped on some water before shaking her head. "Not really. Melanthe is the daughter of Valas Delcour, the 101st Grand Maiden. She was to take her place as well, so that answers that. But who would bring her back and why? What boggles me completely is why would she come back to my father. And don't say lovers, Cai, or I will let your corpse be eaten by Memphis," she threatened her smirking friend who had just settled down.

He threw her a wink and stole a fried potato from her plate.

"Hey, my food," she grumbled, devastated at the loss of her favourite vegetable.

"What would your father want with a Dark Crafter as well? Didn't you mention he banned craft in Isjord?" Mal asked.

"Yes, I must have been about ten or so, shortly after Urinthia came in succession. Father made a big show and even made us attend her accession. Apparently some court information was being traded between Melanthe and her. Father was displeased at best," she said, lost in internal perusal. "What looms inside Caligo? Can my father get hold of Celesteel's monsters, those spoken in the sacraments? I have read about some of them, they are scarier than what a hybrid Aura would have been. He could be looking for them or maybe he is trying to create the ones from the Ater battles."

There it went, what had bothered her all this time.

Anyone else could be puzzled about her concerns, but I was not just someone. "Snow, no god, guardian, plant or creature can pass through those portals to our realm. Obitus law—god given law, they will disperse to dust the moment their feet step on our realm. The 97th Maiden took all of her craft to hells. Even if anyone tried it, that is now banned and hunted. Adriata has trained Canes, Aitan sniffer dogs from after the Ater battles. If a Canes gets a trace of that practice they will tear apart whoever. We have them at Highwall as well. Even Memphis would have been affected by their presence. Whatever you are worried about, it won't happen and it is not what he is planning. Even though you said fuck the gods a moment ago, little heathen, they still see, believe it or not."

She frowned. "But—"

"There are no buts, not possible."

Mal stepped in, nodding in reassurance to the words Snow was finding hard to believe. "Celesteel is a god with brooding pride, he would not let be played by whatever king in this lowly realm, not again, not ever."

"So my theory stands, the lover," Caiden added and Snow moved quickly, chasing him in circles around the tavern.

"Could it be simply for protection?" Nia asked after Snow returned, panting from having nailed Caiden in the ground.

"With all that is going on with us, Isjordian revolts to the deal and now the Solaryans, he could need it. Castle grounds are under her protection and we saw the craft veil when we left the walls. That chest could have been a threat or magic, therefore the protection. Glares are powerful, they can store their magic in objects and spaces," I clarified. The whole of Tenebrose and all other cities in Isjord were coated in dark craft. That was what they were best at, isolating magic, transforming or nullifying it. And right at this moment, I stood with Silas in needing the extent of protection he had placed.

Mal nodded in agreement. "We used to have training with Glares when we were foot soldiers, some of their blast power can go several feet. A good Crafter would definitely help in containing those."

Nia did not seem to believe that either, her shadows still disturbed. "It could be, but this is Silas we are talking about. Why drag a whole dead woman from the Otherworld when any Crafter would have done just fine?"

Caiden sighed and Snow threw him a glaring warning not to joke. "I suppose any

Crafter would not even suffice for him. He had to have the best, that is supposing he did drag her from the dead. Anyone thought this could have been planned and we actually got lied to?"

Nia lifted the blooded cloth in the air. "I suppose we will find out. I will procure a Crafter when we get back."

"In Isjord?" Mal asked.

Caiden nodded. "There is plenty hiding away, just like the one today,"

"How would a half spiritual and half elemental hybrid compare to me?" Snow asked again, seething in worry beside me.

"I believe Isjordians and their mother's pants have learnt he won't repeat that wasted idea again. It will not work," her friend replied. And quite truthfully, I agreed.

She leaned in all eagerness. "Adriata, Hanai, Seraphim, Solarya. Don't you recognize a pattern? What if he is looking to acquire a bunch of them, maybe he is using the Crafter to sort them out like a batch of the best Aura to produce hybrids. Maybe he thinks a battalion of them is better than what three powerful ones would have been?"

"Come now, Cakes, their prophecy would have read about the ant nest of destruction or the beehive of power, not about the dragon birds of storms and frost."

Did these two share a head? They most definitely shared the same stomach for jokes.

"It was luck and careful choosing when he plucked your mother for his plans," Mal revealed what many did not know. "Most *Ybrises* don't live past their tenth birthday. Once an Aura reaches the age to bloom their blessing, it consumes them and that is when they are most dangerous. Tell me, how many *Ybrises* have you heard come into existence in your time?"

"Three. Me, Thora and Eren."

I reached for her hand under the table and laced it together with mine. Her grip tightened and then she placed both of our hands on her lap. She traced another hand almost up my arm and it got terribly hot all of the sudden.

"Have you ever asked yourself why?" my brother asked.

She frowned. "No one dares."

My brother shook his head. "No one can. Many unions have happened in the past however unholy and cursed they are labelled. What makes your father and mother different from others and what have you got more specific than most?"

"They were prime Aura, she originates from two primes," Nia said wide eyed in realisation. "How did we not know of this?"

Caiden threw an arm over his friend's neck. "Because, sweet Nia, we have never once before looked at Snow and thought: we are friends with an *Ybris,* let me do my research."

"Speak for yourself," Snow murmured under her breath.

Caiden, surprised, turned to Nia and she raised her hands in surrender. "I was purely curious."

Snow held back a smile. "She read somewhere that I'd grow fur under my soles and kept staring at my feet for weeks."

"It was good research. Youi Terra is one of the most renewed toxicologists in Dardanes," the stunned friend countered, almost offended. "He'd done his due diligence."

"I believe Youi was great once in his time, his new research just as folly as his knowledge on how to live a life. The man rarely saw sunshine, let alone an *Ybris*," I spoke. No one had been able to study a hybrid Aura. Not many would have dared either.

Nia smiled wide. "You know him?"

"Doesn't everyone?" The man was a legend.

Mal cleared his throat and murmured, "Show-offs."

"So you are saying Snow survived only because she is deriving from two prime Aura?" Nia asked again.

I nodded. "Though her humanity is still something none, alive or dead, can explain."

Her grip loosened from mine and I rubbed my thumb over her knuckles in apology. I hadn't meant it like that.

Mal must have noted the shift in my shadows because he changed the topic. "Are you sure the girl won't run to your father? Worse. Your grandmother could notify him that you not only went to Venzor, but asked for the Crafter's sister. He will connect the dots."

I feared the same, though this time I would not stand for her to fall under Silas's punishment again, because he might as well be king of the realm and still I would rip his heart out before he even laid an angry eye on her.

"She won't," Snow said. "Twelve years ago I made her a promise, one of death. She should be happy I haven't gone today to collect it."

"Was that why she was drowning in fear, enough that I couldn't make out her shadows?" Mal asked.

Snow's smile rose wickedly. "I am a scary person," she teased, flicking a bunch of hair behind her back.

All four of us scoffed in an unplanned unison that made her straighten her features in surprise before a sneer rose in her pretty lips. Her favourite reaction. A vixen—no, a hellcat, the feral stare of a hellcat. If I was not aware she was terrifying, I would think she was adorable. Utterly adorable.

I ran my thumb in circles over her thigh and she flinched a little, pulling her legs close together before giving me a look of frustration.

"Now what? We have the vandals, the Adriatians, two fallen kingdoms and now a Crafter all round your father. Who do we chase first?" Caiden asked after gulping down on his ale. "No plan?"

She shifted in her seat as my touch moved higher up. "There is a plan," she replied quietly, not in her usual confidence. Her fingers curled around my wrist, but I didn't know whether it was prompt to stop or continue.

"Ah, there is a plan," Caiden retorted with a yawn. "Like there was a plan when we went to retrieve your sword out of that lake with that funny name full of flesh eating merfolk and you said: swim. Or like there was a plan when you dragged us to that firebird layer for a gilded feather to gift Alaric and you said: run. Yes, grand, excellent plans."

She frowned while the rest of us laughed. "We are alive, aren't we, because of those plans, too. Unless you have one I suggest you appreciate mine."

"I might have one."

Nia giggled a little. "Heavens we are all doomed, Cai has a plan. Flirt and charm?"

"Better than yours, compassion and salads."

She scowled. "For the millionth time, they are herbs, you fool, not lettuce."

He bowed all tease. "Apologies, compassion and grass."

I leaned in over Snow. "Are you always this partial to their bickering?"

"Wait a little while longer, this will get very entertaining."

"Flirt, charm, compassion and grass, in that order or it doesn't matter?" Mal chimed in and both the bickering two turned to him almost murderously.

I leaned over to Snow again. "Yes, this is about to get very entertaining. Do join in, I'd kill to see who would win."

"Who has your vote?"

I slipped my hand out of hers and rested it between her thighs, palming her flesh, marking it with my touch. "You, of course. I don't think I've met anyone with a sharper tongue than yours, *dahaara*."

"No, Mal," she said, leaning in enthusiastically and almost flinching again when I ran my hand higher up her thigh and then between her legs, my fingers tracing the seam of her trousers. I wanted to know what my touch did to her, to tear that layer of cloth and dip my fingers in her and then taste her—fuck, I wanted to taste her. She gasped a little, swallowed and then continued while her hips moved just slightly along my fingers. "There is an order depending on what we are dealing with is allergic to a man-child and smugness incarnate or nonchalance and empathy. But now that I think about it, we could just send you, Mal. You tick all the boxes."

My brother gaped slightly stunned. "Now I understand why Kil calls you *dahaara*."

Her hand went over mine, her thumb smoothing over my skin while I moved over her. "Kil calls me many things."

I smiled at the sound of my name.

"She has a nickname back home, too," Caiden said, and Snow's eyes shot wide.

I moved quickly, holding a hand tight above her mouth while she slapped me viciously. "Go on." I wanted to hear this one.

"The Moody Crude. They even have a song for her."

I turned to her, cocking a brow up. "I don't feel special anymore, I thought you had that dirty mouth only for me."

I finally let her go and she gasped before calling upon a million curses for both her friend and I. "That crude enough for you?" she asked, panting.

I plucked a hair stuck to her lip. "Who on Numen has taught you those?" I wanted to kiss that dirty mouth. I wanted to taste those words on my tongue, all of her words, and then I wanted her to taste me.

"She hung out with lumberjacks, fishermen, farmers and all sorts of the finest gentlemen. They made for the finest gentle woman," Caiden explained.

"You taught me most," Snow accused.

"No, no," her friend said, shaking a finger. "You heard them out of me, I didn't teach them to you."

"The one thousand quotes of the best philosopher in Dardanes," Nia said, toasting her drink, and Snow laughed.

"Have you always been this close?" I asked, and then put my hand over Snow's mouth again. "No, I don't wish to kill them, too."

Caiden stared between the two of us, confused, and explained, "Yes, I was probably the first face she saw after leaving Isjord."

"You were," Snow answered.

"And she was the first face I saw after waking from a nightmare. When she brought me out of that basement," Nia continued, "and then the first to cry for me, the first to ever take care of me, the first to look after me, the first to hug me, kiss me, call me her sister, the first to laugh with me and make me laugh. The first to go above and beyond for me, the first to almost get killed for me, the first to make me feel whole again. The first to give up something precious for me." Her eyes brimmed with tears. "To give up her mother's pendant to the Crafter for the metal of my hands, undoubtedly, as if you didn't lose a piece of your soul that day. To sacrifice for me because I was loved just the same."

"Nia—" Caiden warned, looking between the two friends who refused to look at one another.

Nia sniffled a little. "I even remember the first words she said to me, the first words I'd heard from another human being in days. I have you. And she had me."

Snow stood and exited the tavern, a storm of misunderstanding hovering between the two. Snow was not angry, she was touched and hurt that was why she had run out, to avoid showing just that. So I stood and left after her.

"She doesn't like being disturbed when she is like this. If she goes for your heart I won't stop her," Caiden warned.

"I will wave a fish in front of her nose, it ought to buy me some time to run for my life."

She walked slowly and absently toward the stables. "Go away, Kilian."

I smiled. "How did you know it was me?"

"The only one who would dare tempt my fury is you. Nia knows and so does Cai and Mal, but you never learn. You always come and give me words and pity, and—" She crouched down, her hands over her head. "The damned pity."

"I won't give you anything that you don't want, so stand."

She stood and turned to me. "What have you come to tell me?"

"Nothing, I've come not to leave you alone."

"I like being alone."

"No, you don't. You hate being alone, silence and the dark."

"Oh, don't you know me so well."

"I do." My hands again, demanding to touch and feel her. I cupped her face. But now I knew that she did not hate it. "I also know you don't know how to apologise."

She sneered. "Well, how do I apologise?"

"Nia," I started. "Forgive me for entering a state of exulansis and blaming you for not understanding me when I don't even tell you anything. When I suffer and pretend I don't. Forgive me for not letting you help me. Forgive me for letting fatigue, two minutes of sleep, the cold, the Adriatians and my wounds that never heal clog every thought of mine and then for speaking unmeant words to hurt you. Forgive me for

I knew your intentions were good, but chose to hang on my spite and hide my pain instead of the truth. Forgive me for I didn't not know how to aim my anger, reveal my hurt and let go of my doubt. "

A frown drew on her brows, but instead of berating me she only said, "Could you put that down in writing? I didn't quite remember it word by word. Maybe I could have it sent to her as a letter."

I squeezed her cheeks between my hands and she became the prettiest gold eyed blowfish. "Ridiculous woman."

"Ridiculous man," she said, pulling my hands down and rubbing her cheeks. She paced around for a few moments, her breath misting white from the cold air. Then a feigned smile pulled on her lips, her eyes glazing with unshed tears. "Why am I so wrong? Like I'm made of ten different things and the messiest way possible. I cannot let go, love, fear, care, apologise." She stopped and faced me for an answer. "Why am I so wrong?"

I hated how she thought. Hated how she thought that the wrong was her. "You are not wrong."

She tilted her head back. "And you are not listening to me, Kilian."

"And you are not believing me."

"Why should I?"

I nodded. "You are right, you shouldn't. But I want you to. I want you, the one I have wronged, to believe me, trust me, confide in me. Tell me, Snow, why am I so wrong? I cannot want that, but I do. So desperately." I wanted her so desperately that I was willing to kneel in front of every god there was and sell any part of my soul to erase...to erase...time.

Her mouth opened and closed a few times with no answer.

"See, everyone is made of wrong and made wrong. We all are. One bad step as a child can leave you limping, a light shone too bright can leave you hazy, a bad word can leave you hurting, a hit can wound and scar. We brush life so viciously and life caresses us back so sharply that we mould ourselves in the worst of shapes, and then atop of it all we heat to a barbed solid by scrutinising ourselves for faults that may not even be ours." How long it had taken me to realise that myself. I hated that I'd realised that too late. I was one who'd made her feel that way.

She blinked slowly at my too long tangle of the short truth: it was okay to be wrong, made wrong and made of wrong. "Am I a vase again?"

"The prettiest." So, so pretty.

She swallowed, her hands gathering and flexing uncomfortably at her sides. "What should one do when they feel like this?"

"Feels like what?"

She glared at me. "You know."

"Speak it." I wanted her to acknowledge how she felt, voice it to reality and then realise she did feel.

She attempted to speak several times, struggling to find the words and then I saw the desperation she dove into when she couldn't figure it out. I saw doubt seep in her, the stammering paces of her breaths and the panic of not knowing.

"Hug," I said quickly before I'd lose her to it. "A hug is comforting."

She opened her arms wide. "Hug me then."

I gathered my arms around her, pulling her body close to mine, making sure not to hold her too tight. She was in my arms and for the first time perhaps not for all the wrong reasons. I held her and she held me, fiercely, as if someone were to tear me off her.

Her head buried in my chest and she took a deep breath. "How do you smell so good? Like those soaps that smell delicious enough you want to eat them." She inhaled me, almost vitally. "I know why they call it the forbidden fruit. You want it but cannot have it without consequence."

I wanted to enjoy this moment and those words, indulge and enjoy her. Yet my heart caved. "I have a feeling we're not discussing about the enchanted berries of Ithicea."

She laughed heartily. "They'd never tempt me as much as you have."

"You tempt me, too, more than the enchanted berries," I said, daring to rest my head on hers. "I have held you before, but you have not allowed me, it was not done by choice. This would be the first time. Could I ask for something else?" Selfish was not the word to describe me. Greedy bastard came somewhat close.

Her head rose up to me, her small features curious as she nodded.

My thumb went over her brow. "Could I kiss you just there?" I felt her heart over my own beating at the pace of a war drum, realising a moment too late that my request had been odd and she felt awkward, repulsed, disturbed and much more by the thought.

"I'd let you kiss me elsewhere, too, but till you make that request I'll grant you this one."

I stared at her, long and hard. The unexpected words she uttered, how terribly fast they made my blood rush. Sucking in a deep breath I leaned and pressed my lips over her warm skin. I could not explain how it felt, that touch. It would be like explaining satiety to the hungry, prosaic and scant.

She sighed. "You know I want you, Kilian, and I have no shame to admit I have wanted you perhaps since the first time I saw you. You are too handsome and tempting and smart for your own good."

"I want you too, Snow." More than how she wanted me. More than how she could ever want me.

"So to be clear, was that only at night?"

I laughed. "You damned woman and those jokes of yours that have me think of you every second of the day."

"Ah," she murmured. "So it is at daytime now as well."

"All the time. All the fucking time."

She raised her head again, still sticking tightly to me and blinked surprised. "What do we do?"

We. It was the both of us now, not just me. "I would give in, but at a price that I don't wish to pay. What I hardly built with you. I got close to you and you'd push me away, taking this and overthinking it till you'd blank me out." I ran my thumb over her eyes and down her nose. "I want the madness, the feisty, the angry, the jokes. Gods, I don't think I can bear without hearing those lewd, lewd jokes of yours."

"How do I stop thinking about this?"

I halted my finger over her lips, thinking about everything else besides not thinking about this. "Step one, enough reading that dubious book. Enough with page forty."

She blinked wide eyed and I noted the blush heating her cheeks. "Have you read it?"

I shrugged. "Got me curious. Then it got me extremely disturbed after page twenty." Miss Hawthorne had a wild imagination.

Her mouth parted open. "Those little comments? Were they yours? I had hid the book between the shelves so it must have been you." She gaped in realisation and then flushed entirely red. "Hells."

"Yes, I tried to guide you out of her madness." She laughed hard and I narrowed my eyes on her. "It is all lies." And I was serious.

She frowned. "It is not, how would you know?"

"I cannot possibly ever put you in that position and do what she claimed her lover to have done." Not denying I had not tried to imagine.

"I thought we were making a list of ways to stop thinking about it and now all I am thinking is you putting me in every position possible or impossible."

I sighed, my arms tightening around her. I needed this woman with every grain of my fibre, but I needed her to be well above everything. Well and near me. Her solution in solving what had her overthink was to erase. "Friends?"

She blinked wildly. "Me and you? Friends?"

"It sounded more ridiculous after I said it out loud. A treaty? Me and you, how we were before this conversation?"

"Deal."

"Deal," I said, sealing another kiss on her brow and she almost melted in my embrace.

"Will you in all honesty not ask?" she demanded strongly, almost upset.

"Ask what?"

"To kiss me elsewhere."

"The treaty—"

"Not yet in effect. It is when I say it is."

I bit my lip, suppressing my smile. She raised a brow and tapped her foot loudly.

"Permission?" I asked, grazing my thumb over her lips.

She groaned. "You righteous fool. Hells, I imagine there is a need for a ritual for you Adriatians. What about when you fuck, do you demand a human sacrifice? The blood of a lamb? Henah herself as a witness?"

I laughed hard, harder than I'd laughed before. It might have been at her frustration or her joke or both. I cupped her face, lowering mine to hers. When I nudged my nose to hers, her eyes drew shut. Then I tasted her impatience in the air...and something else. The way she swallowed, how tightly her lids pressed, the nervous patter of her fingers on her leg. Maybe she had lied to me? Maybe she hated it, terribly. I'd hate to think she was forcing herself through this.

"Call it to effect, Snow," I said, half-heartedly. "If I kiss you, I will never be able to stop. You already hate this enough as it is, don't give yourself a reason to hate me anymore than this." Perhaps it was what she wanted—to find reason and hate me. She'd admitted to struggling to hate me, this would do the trick.

She hates you either way, and will hate you even more later. Taste her, have her, feel her, kiss her. I wanted to be greedy as my insides demanded, but it was no longer only about hate.

"Kilian—" I was right, I felt it in her shivering voice. "It is not that."

I shook my head. "Don't make me one of your conquests, please."

She raised her hands to my face. "You're not." Her voice was small and defeated. "You're not."

Fuck, I wanted her. Damned hells and guardians I wanted her badly, but I didn't want her hurt or upset or forcing herself or hating me anymore than she already did. "Call it, whatever it is," I urged, fighting against all instinct of my body demanding for her. "Call it or I will not know how to tear my body from yours. Please."

She tightened her embrace around me, her head burying deep in my chest. "Just be my friend then."

33

FRIENDS AND LOVERS
SNOWLIN

AFTER OUR RETURN FROM Venzor we had separated quietly, heavy on what we might have found out. We could now track Melanthe, but we needed a Crafter and that was my next plan. My father had banned all craft in Isjord, he probably knew of all those in hiding too, so I had to go somewhere he could not find out what I needed, and some place where his Crafter could not to scent the veil of a blood trace craft under her nose, wherever she was.

I wrote to Albius, who I had been frequently exchanging communications and keeping a good relationship with, notifying him I was going to travel to his city as I had no duties to attend to at the moment and was looking to leave the Tenebrose walls. He was a polite and quiet man, he had shown the most respect to me out of all the lords, as well as responding the least drastically to my not so agreeable actions. He had been the only lord to show up to my father's meeting after I had roasted the pig of Brogmere.

I also loved hearing his stories so I was looking forward to the trip. He remembered so much of Eren, so much that I myself had forgotten and I loved hearing him speak about him. Albius had not refused each time I'd asked him to describe my brother detail by detail, over and over again till I had fallen asleep at the image his words had painted. He had told me Eren was everything he expected a future king to be, his wits and skills, despite my brother's young age, had beyond impressed him.

A knock sounded at the door. The list of those fearless to visit me so early in the day was extremely small, but I was curious to meet the brave one so I slid out of bed and threw a gown over my night slip.

"Good morning, Snowlin," the crinkled crone said, entering my room. She looked all the same feathered peacock I had left her to be after I stopped attending my father's happy family breakfast routine. Her lurid yellow dress washed her out severely and I wondered if stomach sickness was the look she was after. If it was, an applause to her, she had well achieved it.

"My, my, my, Moreen, don't you look," I said, my eyes tracing her top to bottom, "sickly?"

She had always been unreasonably jealous of my mother, despite knowing my father never loved my mother as he loved her. Moreen looked frail and soft, but she was a twisted maniac. How many smart ways she had found to torture my poor mother. Once she had ordered my mother's servants to sprinkle her bath with thyme, to which my mother had a severe reaction, forcing her to rest sick in bed for weeks only so she could attend the solstice ball along with my father instead of her. Moreen had paraded in that ball so proudly and happily alongside him, I could swear she'd shone like a torch. She still held her nose so high and mighty. How did she even think to breathe around me when I knew what she had done—when I knew her darkest of secrets that even my father was not aware of. How was she so courageous to bring her throat so near my hands, her heart so near my dagger and her puffed up confidence near my blood hungry one. However, it was not her time yet. I wouldn't want for her to pass easily through the sift of my anger which right now was honed to kill.

She faltered a little. "I see you are not coming to attend breakfast anymore. Your father has been most upset about it. I wanted to come to invite you to join us today. No matter if he has wronged you he is still your father and loves you so," she said, and I could not hold it any longer.

I howled in laughter, one so deep I had to hold my stomach from aching, tears already wetting my face. This was so very entertaining, it made my morning brighter—it truly did. The old peacock really dared to come directly to me and thought she could be the one to convince me to return, to obey my father with such wrong words, such wrong lies. I knew what she was planning. She had earned my father's affections like everyone else—she was just another link in his court. Moreen had always bargained her way to people's trust with empty and decorated words, making herself appear as if she were the one to convince them to turn to his side in the first place. She wanted me to return so she could get credit for it from my father and appear as the pure little saint everyone thought she was. For her to take such dramatic actions would have to mean father was truly starting to lose whatever affection he had for her.

Her face finally betrayed her in front of me, eyes widening with some fear at my amusement. "Oh dear, thank you for that. Will you pass a message from me to my father? I did not know he missed me to this extent."

"Of course, whatever you wish I will pass it on, my child."

A shiver crept down my spine and I almost brought another Moreen in the room from my throat. "Yes, well," I said, opening the door, motioning for her to exit, "tell him I said I will return to breakfast."

Her eyes and mouth drew back in satisfaction.

"I will return when he is able to fit an apple up his loving arse. Also be a dear and notify him that I am leaving for Arynth," I added with a kind smile and nod to her. If I had a smidge of talent, I would have painted the shocked view of Moreen all over the castle walls. Such a shame this masterpiece had to be lost at the uselessness of my skills.

After Moreen left, Mal and Cai shook with laughter, which I didn't know whether was directed at me or the old peacock, but my amusement different from theirs was now almost non-existent, she had done a perfect job at annoying me.

"Are we really going to Arynth?" Mal asked.

I nodded, entering my room. "Ready everyone by the stables. I have a Crafter waiting for us."

"That was quick."

"I'm a woman of many talents, Mal."

He suppressed a smile. "Yes. Yes, I have noted. Not many get to have Kilian riled up, frustrated and restless. Not many get to have him at all, he is a very reserved sort of bastard."

I bit back my question, once and then twice before turning round and asking, "Who is May?"

His smile faltered and he blinked wide in confusion for a moment. "She is...was a friend of ours."

A frown began narrowing my brows. "Was? No longer is?"

"She is dead."

Everyone had gathered by the stables reading to head south. Steeds huffed white mist from their large nostrils and shook in agitation ready for journey. Nia was amongst my soldiers just as I had instructed, the privacy of Arynth would give me some opportunity to attempt my chance with her.

I glanced shortly over at Kilian and looked away as he was about to turn to me, pretending to brush Memphis though her fur was pristine. *Don't come over. Don't come over because I will say something stupid.*

"What is with the rested, the shy and why on heavens have you never had your hair up before? You're stunning," he said as a way of greeting.

I bit my lip at the compliment and slowly turned to him. "I slept. Am not shy, perhaps...befuddled. And I could not be bothered to comb it so up it was. Also, thank you," I tried to offer nonchalantly, and he slowly began smiling. That endearing and maddening smile he always gave me.

He cocked a brow up. "Befuddled?"

I shrugged. "For lack of a better word to describe how very confusing this is."

He nodded and began moving backward, his eyes never leaving me. "Befuddled it is." *Don't say it. Don't say it. Don't make a fool of yourself.* "Did you lie to me, Kilian?"

His steps halted and he wore an expression I'd never seen before. Fear, worry and something else.

I cleared my stupid throat. "I thought I could read you like you read me, but it appears you can easily lie to me."

"How so?"

Still not too late to retreat, yet in contradiction to my inner confidence, my very sharp mouth spoke, "May, did you love her?"

Mal had told me of their friendship. They had known each other since they were children. He told me that if Kilian had been open to someone, it had been with her. She had been the last person he'd had a relationship with, everyone after had only been passing pleasure. She had to have meant something to him and he had to have loved her. Not long after they'd chosen to get together, she'd passed away from illness. Mal said he'd not seen heartbreak, but a sadness he'd never seen before. I could not even imagine him being sad.

His head dropped, lips pursing back from anger. "I'm going to hang that busybody by his tongue." He approached me once again. "I didn't lie to you, Snow. Her story, mine, ours, is somewhat...for a lack of a better word, bad. And also ten long years ago. But I didn't lie to you. I was not in love with her. I loved her, but not in a way lovers do. I don't—" He stopped himself and his expression melted. "I don't think I've loved a woman before, loved in a way lovers do."

"So you did not lie to me?" *Really, Snow? Was that what really bothered you?*

He shook his head, and then narrowed his eyes on me. "Why did this matter?"

Yes, Snow, why did this matter? I had not thought about him asking back, no one dared demand of me before.

"Did you ask Mal or did he tell you?" he pushed.

"Ask," I confessed.

He blinked confused. "Why?"

I clapped my hands together, eager to let this go now. "The horses are ready and Albius would worry if we got there late," I said, and then made to march away before he grabbed me and faded us behind the stables. The sudden movement and stink of magic made me dizzy, and I almost collapsed in his arms.

"Tell me," he demanded, holding my face with one hand while the other held me to him.

I rolled my eyes. "Are we really doing this again, Kil darling? I thought we had put this behind our backs."

His mouth was so close to mine when he said, "Not fooling me, princess. As much as my name in that mouth of yours makes me dizzy, my answer is more important."

Sweet hells, his mind shattering and stomach fluttering confessions. I shrugged surely. "I know nothing of you."

"Why do you want to know?"

"Are we not friends?" I knew he had read through my lie and there was no escaping it—the embarrassment.

He raised a brow in challenge. "Are we now? And the first woman I have bedded was the best conversation approach to this blooming friendship?"

"I asked him many other things as well."

His smirk was taunting. "Is that so? What exactly, the first time I shaved?"

Smug bastard. I cleared my throat. "He said if I tickle you behind your ears, you'd roll twice for me." The second after I said it, I took off in a run as many other brave people did.

He faded right behind me and wrapped an arm around my waist, lifting me up and burying his face on that spot between my neck and shoulder. His mouth was soft on my skin as he left a gentle trail of kisses all the way up to my face. Sweet hells. "Jealous?" he whispered in my ear, his lips lingering to brush the sensitive shell and my knees almost gave away. "Now, now, Snow, it doesn't suit you, love."

"Let me go, you giant piece of Adriatian flesh." Translation to Snowlin tongue: don't let me go.

As he spoke my language with perfection, he wrapped my hair around his free hand, gently tugging my head back to him. "Now I know why I like the hair up." He bit my bare neck softly and I lost all perception. "And don't worry, I like jealous you."

"Are you two rabbits?" Mal called from behind, startling me. Kilian did not let me go, the man only held me tighter. "Thank heavens they sent me to find you."

"I am going to pierce you through and through, brother," Kilian threatened all cold and darkness. That gravel in his voice vibrated all around me and I pulled my thighs closer together, trying to relieve the smallest bit of snapping tension.

Blessed be my dark heart that no one could read my shadows.

Mal flinched and uncrossed his arms. "What did I do now? And for sacred heavens, let go of her," he said, looking around as if someone finding out about us could incite a war.

Kilian planted a long kiss on my cheek and my eyes drew shut at the feel of his full lips, the heat, the touch, the strange caress. He let me go. Damned Mal.

The younger brother stared between the two of us. "How did this come to be?"

"What did?" Kilian asked all composed while straightening himself.

Mal narrowed an examining glare on him. "This. The two of you."

"I can't possibly grasp what you are on about," I said, fixing the tail of hair that Kilian had twisted around his hand a second ago.

Kilian planted a hand on his shoulder, grasping it tight enough to make Mal grimace. "Yes, what are you on about? Tell me since you love telling plenty."

The younger brother moved away from an almost murderous Kilian and pointed at the two of us. "I liked you better when you fought."

I shrugged. "We fight, don't we, darling?"

Kilian nodded. "Yes, love, we do."

The endearment made my toes curl.

"The two of you are mad and maddening," the younger brother accused, shaking his head and signalling for us to follow him.

I waited for Kilian, but he motioned a hand for me to head first. "I enjoy the view from behind."

The way he admitted to things so blankly and unphased really bothered me because here I was absolutely rattled. "You play a dangerous game."

The shadows in his face grew dark. "It's not as if I can lose. I don't have what would hurt the most to lose."

Ignoring the crawling paranoia to take those words more than what they probably were, I teased, "Sanity?"

He bit his lip, almost suppressing a smile. "That too."

The journey had mostly gone quietly, except the casual chatter between the soldier, Mal and Cai, the rest remained in their own bubbles of silence, including him. Winter was finally viciously taking over Isjord and had it not been for the main passage roads, it would have taken us days to arrive in Arynth.

"Snow, it is so very nice to have you back," Albius greeted while we arrived at his outskirt mansion.

I dropped from Memphis to give the old man a hug who laughed jollily. "Thank you for expecting us on such short notice."

He offered me a warm, eye sparkling smile. "Consider this your home, you are welcome at any time."

He greeted my entourage and directed us towards his house where we had stayed the other times I had visited. The house was massive, but decorated very simply in muted whites and beiges, there was not a woman's touch in the house. Albius's wife had died years ago from sickness. Surprisingly, I remembered her. She was very much like him in many senses.

After setting our belongings to our assigned rooms, I headed with the lord for a walk. He made a promise to show me the city and I did not hesitate to accept. We walked and spoke for hours regarding our pasts. He told me a handful of his wonderful stories which were like sweets to my ears. Finally, when I noticed a slight limp to his leg, I had sent him to head for rest which he accepted after I'd promised to continue our conversations at another moment.

I was roaming around the city, admiring its warmth and peace when Nia appeared before me. I knew it was the time to either put what had happened behind us or forever hold our...*my* grudge.

She was the first to speak. "You do not want this as much as I don't, Snow, and it is not like you can ignore me forever. I want you to know I have never been more apologetic about what I did, for suggesting what I had that day, it was very insensitive—"

"You know very well that was not why I reacted the way I did, Nia, and it was most certainly not that," I said, interrupting her. This was already going in the direction I did not want it to go. Was she that unaware of how she had hurt me, what truly had done it?

"Tell me, please," she pleaded, approaching me.

"Tell you, just like you told the Adriatians my truths or how you didn't tell me yours?" I asked. If she had the intentions Kilian had told me, she certainly had never made me aware of those before, let alone how she had contracted a plan to aid them.

"Snow, at that moment I did not consider what or who they were, I just knew they could help you. But I realised that I was wrong for doing so, and I am still very, very sorry," she said, grabbing my hands to hold them in hers.

I think this was the time to let this go, no matter what I thought, I loved Nia and I could also no longer see her affected by my words and situation.

"Forgive me, Nia, for a lot I have said to you, too."

She threw herself towards me, hugging me tightly. It was not something we did often, but maybe we should. Basking in its comfort brought some sense of serenity.

Slowly letting go, a grim expression wore her face. "There is something else I have been hiding. I knew you would not agree to it, but now I understand it was wrong to hide it from you." Whatever it was, she had prepared herself for a bad reaction from me. "I have been training my magic with them."

The revelation left me slightly shocked, not because I was against it or because she hid it from me. "I thought you did not wish to learn."

"I thought so, too."

The nervous fiddle of her pupils, the chew of her lips, the curled fist on her lap told me more than she ever had. "Please, Nia, tell me you have not declined to learn because of me? Please," I begged and hoped I'd not become a villain to her as well. "Please tell me I have not become something for you to fear."

She swallowed hard. Her eyes rested above the cold ground, answering more than words ever could.

I felt my face twist in a brief cry. "Why?"

"It would hurt you. I still remember your reaction from when I told you the first time what I was. I didn't want you to hate me again."

"Nia, I could never hate you, never. It will never matter to me because you are my sister. I care about you, all sides of you. I never chose to like only the part of you that isn't Adriatian."

"I was afraid," she said, swallowing a wavering cry. "She...she would hate me because of it—because of the magic I possessed. I thought it would be the same again." Her sister, her true sister who'd taunted her for inheriting her father's magic which she herself had not. It wasn't her mother who abused her endlessly, not the father who spat over her worth or the man who tore her limbs, it was her sister, the evil she feared most. Her words still whispered with the wind, everything and everyone reminded Nia of her.

"Nia," I said, cupping her face. "I am not her, but I will be the one to kill her, your father and your mother and both of their bloodlines to the root."

Her expression turned woeful, two hot tears sprawling from her hazel eyes while admitting it for the first time to me, "I don't want them dead."

"Then I won't kill them," I said, wiping her tears away. "That is all I want you to do, tell me. Apparently there is something with miscommunication and some injured hearts." I flung a hand in the air, already forgetting his words. "Never mind."

She nodded and rounded herself around me. "A hug to warm the soul," she murmured, her face buried between my hair.

"A kind word to soothe the mind," I finished. The two sentences Alaric had made us remember time after time. They could heal the world he had said. Two simple effortless actions. I was happy that she grew away from her past, accepting and moving on, not letting it affect her life. I adored her so much for it, for her strength and will. She deserved all the sweet this life could offer.

The sky had turned completely dark and for the first time in Isjordian land I could see patches of star adorned skies. Nia had left for dinner, but I stayed behind to marvel at the entrancing magic of the dancing sparkles, already fed with guilt. They dazzled, radiant. It felt as if they were the only normal thing in my life at the moment, their glimmering stillness had enchanted my troubles away for a few moments. That and the vanilla cream bun Nia had brought as a peace offering.

"You will love the ones in Adriata, they shine brighter and lay as far as your eye can take." Kilian startled me and I almost choked on the last bite of my food. He had kept Nia's training a secret from me all this time.

A vein in my temple tensed in anger at his sight. "You lying bastard," I said, hitting his chest but he did not budge.

Grabbing onto my wrist, he pulled my glove off, catching me by surprise when he pressed his lips over my palm in the softest kiss anyone had ever given me. Sweet gods. "You went from calling me a snake, a dog, a barbarian to a lying bastard. I know you can do better than that now," he said in a flat cold voice, but I could sense the teasing tone along with the teasing words.

I'd ran out of words and my heart was running out of my chest. Pulling my hand away, I put my glove back and threw him a threatening glare.

"What are you upset about, Snow? Tell me, don't stare it into me." He brushed a thumb over the top of my lip before bringing it to his mouth to suck the cream that had been stuck there from the bun.

Nubil's air that was not meeting my lungs. "Nia," I said, clearing my throat. "When were you to tell me you are training her?"

He licked his upper lip as if savouring the taste. "It was not for me to tell, but I am glad you have your friend back. Maybe now you will stop bossing me around," he said, running a thumb over my brow. His fingers slipped to my chin and he tilted my gaze to him. "Tell me, whatever that you are overthinking, tell me all. Speak to me, woman, senseless words if you wish, just speak to me. I fear your silence."

I blinked taken aback for a few seconds. "Thank you. Thank you for helping her, it means a lot to her. It means a lot to me, too. You have no idea how difficult that was for her, yet she let you teach her."

"I know, she has told me."

"She did? All of it?" I asked, and he nodded. Nia trusted him. Nia trusted no one. "That look again," I sighed. "I am glad it is not only I who gets that terrible pity of yours."

Something flashed in his eyes, he seemed mad. Grabbing my wrist, he pulled both of us to sit down on a bench. Silence and many impatient taps of his foot graved the situation more than I'd planned it to be.

"It was not pity," he said, leaning onto his knees.

My fists gathered unconsciously at the tension. "What is it?"

He shook his head. "You will hate the answer—you will hate it."

"Please." He stilled at the word and his gaze turned to meet mine again. "I hate everything, it won't make a difference."

He exhaled loudly and leaned back on the bench. "Pain, I feel pain every time I see you in pain."

I could not hide my shock at that revelation. "You were right, I hate it," I said, and his head dropped. "It was not what I wanted you to feel from me. I want to make you smile, maybe even laugh if I can see the dancing starlight in your silver eyes."

His head rose gradually, the look in his face almost made me flinch. "You said they reminded you of a snake."

"A silver eyed snake," I corrected, and he smiled just slightly. "But I never said I hated them. How can a creature not be relished because of its nature? And it happens that this particular snake's venom is sweet words."

He stared at me so endearingly it had sent a deep flush all around me, I prickled and hissed in heat everywhere because of him. Taking his arm, I slid myself close to him and draped it over my neck so I could lean my head on his shoulder. How terrible was I for seeking the comfort of him? I settled to overthink it later. Right now I only wished to feel between clouds and under stars.

He gathered me close and I snuggled closer, shamelessly. "Do tell me your stamina has not weakened this early in life. Hold me tighter, you weak Adriatian."

He chuckled silently. "You said not to hold you tight. You don't like it."

I raised my head to him. "What?"

"In Brisk, you said holding you tight makes you feel like in a cage, like you can't run."

My mouth parted open, and I meekly said, "I did not."

He held my chin, tilting my gaze up while his own hovered over my lips. "You did, you said many more things that night too."

My eyes shot wide. "Like what?"

"That I have a nice behind, that was after you groped me."

I stood stupefied of embarrassment. Had I really?

He threw his head back and laughed, making me a thousand red shades of frustrated. "Are you embarrassed, little beast?"

"Severely." I admitted. "Kil, is this alright? Us doing this?" I'd often wondered what he thought about doing whatever that was that we were doing. I thought he hated me or maybe he still did? Maybe we were both...mildly needy, but we agreed to not act on it, so what did this mean? Also, there stood the fact that I was marrying his king.

He groaned at the back of his throat, inhaling over my hair before planting a kiss atop my head. "Say it again, my name."

"Answer my question first."

"Yes, were we not friends?"

"I don't think friends get all hot and bothered by the way I say their name."

He laughed, hard. "A different sort of friend. We are an unusual pair, nonetheless. Fulfil my request now."

I took off my glove and reached for his hand resting on my arm, lacing them together. "How are you warm all the time, Kil?"

He had gone silent, so I dared look up at him. It was almost terrifying being met with such warm liquid silver staring like he stared at nothing else.

"Enough with that." The words had come out but a whisper, my voice dimmed by the terrible heavy feeling resting over my chest.

"Snow, brother," Mal called loudly in the cold air.

I made to move away but he only held me tighter.

"Sweet crescent moon," the younger brother murmured in realisation before backing away. "Continue—do continue. I will meet Larg myself."

Kilian's attention went to him. "Larg has sent for us?"

"He found out from the wall guards we were in Arynth and sent a note for us. It's about Stregor."

I tensed at the sound of that name.

Kilian exhaled deeply and let go of me completely. "Forgive me, Snow. I am afraid this could be important."

Where he had held and touched me felt cold, almost turning a lingering frost. "Of course," I said, and then turned to Mal. "Give Larg my greetings."

I made to leave, but I was reeled in place and right back on his hold. "Good night," he said.

I blinked, surprised. "Good night."

Yet he didn't let me go. Confused, I looked between him and where he held me and surprisingly he raised a brow. "You forgot to add something to that goodnight."

"Good night, Kil."

He smiled, and then barely, just barely let me go.

Mal crossed his arms, shaking his head at me and his brother. "You two have a lot of explaining to do."

I tapped a finger to my temple. "All here Mal. All a hallucination. Right, darling?"

"Correct, love," Kilian added, smiling.

I had apologised to Albius and not joined them for dinner last night. I was too busy arranging my plans in Arynth and overthinking about stabbing my gut over and over for letting myself get carried away with Kilian. More than a dozen times I had peeked outside my door to see if he had returned and each time I had met a dubious Cai.

I arrived for breakfast bleary eyed and almost swaying on my feet. I had never been a morning person before because I indulged in my sleep, and now because I could not sleep. Usually mornings were when I started feeling the most weary and dizzy from lack of thereof.

Albius and Kilian were in a deep discussion with one another. He had such a wise demure and strong posture, it almost looked like he belonged between scholars not holding a sword.

"Two old men chatting, nothing unusual, the room is safe," Mal said from behind me.

"He hears that and you will scream like an old lady."

He scowled. "Bring back my partner in crime. It's no fun teasing him all on my own."

I patted his shoulder. "You have Cai, let him have this one."

Greeting the lord with a kiss on his cheek that made him rumble in sweet laughter, I took my seat next to the older brother.

"Snow," Albius called, standing. "I am afraid duties await for me, but enjoy breakfast. Would you meet me in the viceroy quarter in the city centre this afternoon? There is a matter I wish to discuss with you."

I nodded. "I will meet you there."

"Slept well?" Kilian asked, reading a piece of paper deep in concentration.

"Sleep is for the dead." Hungry, I turned to pile food on my plate.

He folded the paper and put it in his pocket before facing me. "Why won't you let me help you?"

"How?"

"With my magic of course."

"Ah."

"*Ah*, what?" he repeated, staring confused at me. I didn't reply, only stared back shamelessly till his mouth gaped open in realisation of the direction of my thoughts. "I doubt that would get you to sleep, Snow. It's never a short ride with me, neither sweet. Maybe you are too used to the Venzorian. I bet his hooves tire out in seconds."

My fingers curled and I squirmed on the seat, I could only pray that the action was not too obvious.

Cutlery dropped loudly from my left and we both turned to Mal.

"You two—" he began.

I placed a hand on his arm. "Hearing things, too? Kil, darling, you should honestly consider checking your brother's well-being. I am getting concerned."

"Of course, love, I'll take him to a healer right after."

"I am mad, yes, do take me to a healer," he said, waving a fork in the air before murmuring, "you two are driving me mad anyway."

"What was the matter with Larg and that man?' I asked Kilian.

"Stregor," he answered somewhat sternly, putting more food on my plate. "An idiot who plays mighty with a gilded feather. I cannot complain, however, I was one of them who gilded his feathers. He is one of them, one who uses gods' ambiguous ways to do his bidding."

He remembered my words. "Give a donkey too much attention and it will think it's a horse. Don't pay mind, darling."

He smoothed jam over the bread I'd buttered before handing it back to me. "If I asked you to call me that every time?"

I took a bite. "Depends, what do I win from it?"

He wiped the corners of my lips with his thumb before bringing it to his mouth. "Depends, what does my beast want?"

I coughed. "Am I yours now?"

He filled me a glass of water. "Are you not?"

I took a few sips. "You are very versed in deflecting my questions."

"And you're still stubborn enough not to answer me first."

"You live to exasperate me."

"The tables have turned," he said, leaning back on the chair and throwing an arm over my backrest, his fingers weaving through my long locks.

"Sweet round heaven of Cynth," Mal muttered from my side.

"Tired?" Kilian asked, tucking a bunch of hair behind my ear, his thumb gently stroking my cheek, aiding to the fatigue.

I nodded. "Very."

"Let me help you. I cannot see you like this."

I couldn't let magic get to my head, no matter whose it was—I couldn't. "You know the only way."

He turned stern—more than the usual. "If I fuck you, it won't be to put you to sleep, woman."

I giggled weakly, whatever it would be for I just wanted him to. Tired, I slouched back in my chair, munching lazily on a toast and indulging in the soft caress of his hands when I felt the air grow light. Fragrant with scent of tangerines and lemon flowers probably from mister spring sat next to me. Involuntarily, my lids gave up and I was thrown in the dark void of sleep.

Fog grew out of the winter gardens of the castle, slowly creeping along the ground above the trees and through the sky surrounding me—all I could see was its grey shadows.

I searched around, but I was alone.

"Snow," a small, sweet voice called before me. A little girl with dark hair and the deepest emerald eyes stood in front of me, dressed in a little blue dress with frills and lots of layers. Thora, it was her, my little sister.

"Thora...Thora, what are you doing here?" I cried, tears streamed from my sore eyes and I moved towards to hug her, but she disappeared. I screamed her name and ran through the gardens looking for her till I was facing their resting places. She stood there, with a rose in her hand over our mothers grave which was pooling and leaking blood all over the garden and over Thora.

"Why is my name on that one, Snow?" my little sister asked. *"Am I dead?"*

My throat swelled with emotion and I did not hold back my cries as I nodded towards her, my whole body hurt at seeing her, at hearing her—my little sister.

"But I am not dead," she said, scowling. *"I am alive, look at me,"* she continued, waving her hand towards me and within flashing seconds she vanished into smoke and the world around me sucked itself into nothing and empty darkness.

I awoke back in the dining room, Nia and Cai were now sitting across us, chatting with Mal. No one had paid any mind to me, thank the blessed heavens for sparing me the embarrassment. When I leaned to reach a cup of water, I noticed my hand under the table clutching Kilian's. I stared down in confusion at our interlaced fingers, his thumb gently smoothing over my hand as if in reassurance. For a while I held it there till I noted the blood and jerked it away, free from him. Gods, I'd clawed his hand hard enough to draw beads of blood.

I'd hurt him.

I wanted to apologise, to ask if I'd hurt him, yet my mind still circled the odd terrifying dream and the hollow feel of my head after being dragged from it.

After breakfast, I headed towards Arynth centre with Nia and Kilian behind me. I had yet to apologise to him or even look in his direction. We went past the busy main roads towards the training courts of the Isjordian soldiers, and as I had expected and planned, amongst them stood the one and only Elias. His returning itinerary came through in Arynth. I had him in this small city to my advantage, away from castle distractions and fresh with information from Hanai.

"Elias?" I called with such a perfect surprise that I shocked myself. He looked tired and worn out, probably at the long travel he had gone through in such a short time. Elias had to be one of my fathers most trusted confidants and probably had intentions of keeping him as such by betrothing him to that sea urchin.

"My raven," he responded, shocked. "What are you doing here?" He examined our surroundings and the two behind me.

"I want to ask the same. How are you not up north? Have you lied to me?" I asked, my voice turning upset and I pulled myself away from him, feigning disbelief the best I could. Sigh. I would punish myself later with endless thoughts of my evilness to Elias's kind soul.

He looked terrified. "No...no, Snowlin, I have not lied. I can explain to you, just...just not now." His attention fluttered around us again. He wanted to be in private.

I turned towards Nia and Kilian whose eyes had darkened and almost pierced a hole through Elias's head. He had stilled, both looking taken back, probably their gears had just started shifting over my initial plans for the trip to here.

"I will be fine now. I am with Elias. You are free to wander till I return," I said, waving my hand to them both, hoping they would just oblige. Kilian tensed and made to move forward in objection, but Nia stopped him.

I nodded in thanks and understanding and linked my arm to Elias, planting a kiss on his cheek before heading towards the guest house he was staying at.

I surveyed the sage green room, decorated in the gold and dark wood Isjordian furniture of the most extravagant shapes. Stopping by the bed, I sat at its edge, facing him. "What else? Is your hair fake as well and your affection towards me the lie I had originally detected it to be?"

He half kneeled in front of me, holding my hands and anxiously shifting them around. "None of that part has ever been a lie, and you know better than to say that." He hesitated for a swift moment, but continued, "I did come from the north, just not our side of the north. Your father had sent us to retrieve our people from Koy in Hanai."

I already knew that. "Hanai? Isjordians in Hanai, for what reason would they need you to retrieve them, Elias, what are these fables? You think I'm a fool?" My voice angrier and my face crowned by a deep frown that was starting to give me a headache. The role of the usual jester was easier to play than that of the slighted princess.

Elias stood, hands on his hips as he circled distressed about the room. For a second I thought all my work had been for nothing, until he sat in bed next to me and said, "Your father sent to retrieve a relic from them and they were caught in the attempt."

My father had infiltrated Hanai for an object? Risking his soldiers' lives was one thing, but risking their exposure was another. If Hanai knew Isjordians were behind it, there would be troops marching their lands, Queen Moriko of Hanai was not the forgiving kind. I suppose that was the reason he had asked for immediate dispatch of Elias's team to retrieve them. It took a moment and then it clicked, the Adriatian Aura in Brisk. They had been working toward this mission, the 'element' they were to retrieve, was it this relic?

"A relic, is this all for a relic?" I raised my brows at him. The part that disturbed me the most. What of this object was so important? Why did my father have his eyes on it and how did Hanai come upon it? Elias was either lying to get out of this or my father had truly lost his already fragile mind.

He let out a deep sigh. "Yes, according to your father it is one of great importance to Isjord. We were told it used to belong to us, bestowed to us from our god Krig and stolen centuries ago before being located just recently in Hanai."

I did not understand. I grew up studying and reading history books all my childhood in preparation for my place as princess and never came across such an object, let alone one that belonged to Isjord. Isjord was a very plain kingdom compared to the rest, their connection and adoration to their god and heavens was already towards faltering, their temples closed years before I was born and their only sacred book, Eirlys liber, despite being extremely thin, included only overly repeated and hyperbolic phrases that boasted their god Krig. He had a scarce number of heavenly guardians, all which I could easily recall by name, his realm was plain like ours and certainly nothing about a relic resembling what Elias described. The mention of such an object did not skew my brain as much as the true reason why my father was looking for it. But I knew it was not to bring back their adoration to their god. This did not appear as the normal grand scheme of my father, but from him I expected everything. Whatever this object was, it had me already scared.

"Why would he need that?"

"According to him our lands are wilting because of our fading belief, we don't pray to Krig or for Hodr anymore. He believes if we bring it back it could stimulate belief to recuperate whatever has been lost."

I mentally snorted at that explanation. No, I cackled at it. A manipulator and the manipulated, both in symmetry. Silas was the master of it. Still, a major applause, he had fooled Elias and probably many more.

"And Solarya, Seraphim, the soldiers in Myrdur?"

"Snowlin—"

"Come now, I am not a fool."

"I only know of Hanai. I had no idea of Myrdur and only recently I found out about Seraphim when that witch returned from there a couple of weeks ago. And it is nothing grave to have missions outside our borders."

"When did Melanthe come back?"

"About two years ago."

It struck me then. The deal with Adriata. Kilian said Isjord had proposed it two years ago. The soldiers in Myrdur, they too had only shown about seven or eight seasons ago. The buzzing, the calling, the mist broiling in agitation. *Zgahna* calling to me. Was my father behind all? Had he orchestrated everything with purpose?

"You surely must remember, Elias, her hanging, she was dead."

"Yes, I know, a friend of mine, another captain, he is of Hecan descent, he believes she was reincarnated from Caligo. Just about a few months before her return, a squadron was sent down to Asra and you can only imagine what for."

"And you didn't bother to suspect or doubt why he brought a witch from the dead? Why is he hunting a damned relic? Why is your rot stepping on my mother's lands? Why are you an inch away from war with Solarya or why is he scavenging a five-hundred-year dead kingdom? So many premonitions and questions and yet you obeyed, undoubtful."

"You understand how it feels to be caught between my father and yours. I was like you," he said before dropping his guard, surrendered. "I still am like you, a pawn and a weapon. Do you think I wish to marry Fren, obey commands I cannot understand? I just chose a side to run away from the other, and believe me, either were ideal by any means but now, Snowlin, now I don't have to tear myself apart for it. My choice granted me no freedom, but it did grant me purpose. I serve your father and Isjord, there is no place for me to doubt."

"You are right. I sometimes forget how it feels to be leverage, not human. I did not mean to accuse you of anything."

He took my hands in his. "Tell me you are not planning anything mad, please tell me you are not going to inquire any further than this. I told you to satisfy your curiosity not to send you on a goose chase. If you get harmed by this I will never forgive myself."

"I came back, Elias, you forget. I returned when I could have run away and he would have never found me."

Astounded, he let go of me. "Snowlin—"

"I returned to get what belongs to me. Myrdur, Isjord and payback."

His eyes drew closed at my words. "You don't know what you are up against. You don't know how mad those words sound."

"And you don't know me. No one knows me and if you knew, you would think I'm absolutely deranged, not mad."

Elias laid back in his bed, tired, frustrated and probably regretting having told me this much already. He need not worry, I planned to keep this information more confidential than he had.

"It was never meant with us, was it?" he called half lost from where he was laying. I sensed his desperation and my chest felt a bit heavy, but I knew what I was getting into when I convinced myself to drag him into my plans. Perhaps I was growing a conscience because it felt terribly wrong.

"If that night had not happened twelve years ago, it might have somehow been different, but no, it never felt that it was," I added with a sigh. "I've actually never had a thing for blonds."

He laughed groggily. "I had fair warning from Thora."

"What?"

He chuckled to himself, almost in memory. "I came once after the ball when we met, asking for you. Your little sister gave me a look, one of resentful judgement. *Not with a head like yours, you won't,* she said to me."

I laid alongside him, giggling myself to tears, woeful tears. "Tell me more." And he did. For long hours, he could recall more of her than I ever could. How could I have forgotten her?

The shadow of dusk settled in from the large arched windows like an old spirit and I felt the lingering longing for the sight of someone. So I stood to satiate the hunger before I'd start to crave. Hunger once known could become a growing beast that would be hard to feed.

"Goodbye, Elias," I whispered to him sleeping beside me. Tired from being milked out of memory by me.

"Goodbye, Snowlin," he said when I reached the doors.

34

Spring and Them

Kilian

I HAD BEEN PACING back and forth for an hour now. The sight of them repeated on my head in a loop with purpose to affect me. It bothered me beyond what I could control. She had the right to do whatever she wanted, to toy or even like him beyond her plans, it was her right. For hours I had tried to embed these thoughts in my head, that my reaction was wrong, that I had no reason to feel this gnawing on my insides, that she was not mine.

"You will wear your soles and brains out at this point, Kilian," Nia said, dragging my attention back to my surroundings. She was always so calm that it bothered me. Should she not be worried about leaving that Isjordian fool with Snow. Or was it the opposite?

"She cannot dismiss us like that, no matter her intentions and infatuations with him. He is her father's soldier and a lusting idiot," I finally blurted out, sending her in giggles.

"What is it that you worry about, that he will kill her or bed her?" Her shadows danced in amusement. Again, I did not know what I was worrying about either. Nia had taken enough of a response already. Her grin grew wider when I did not answer and she pointed her finger around me, over my shadows. "Instead of taunting one another, teasing and flirting and then back to fighting from all the frustration you are causing each other—put an end to it and tell her. The truth, Kilian."

My head dropped at the remembrance of the promise I'd made myself—to never tell her. "Nia, I...I can't."

I couldn't tell her that she drove me mad when she ate at the speed of wind and worried me when she walked barefooted most of the time. That she made me laugh when she rampaged the library in the hopes of finding a romantic book, then complained for hours to Pen at the ridiculous cliches she had read. That she soothed me when she hummed the same melody of that folk song every night, readying for sleep. That she made me flush in heat when she spun in front of me every morning to show me her dress. That she annoyed me when she insisted her moves were right when she played chess with Mal and Ken despite them not making sense. That it puzzled me how she scratched and wiggled in frustration at her dresses, but still wore them as if they had come with her. That she impressed me at how the sight of cod terrified her but monsters far scarier were her playthings. That it surprised me how she stole glances over her friends as if she wanted to know if they were alright when she was suffering all the same. That her smile made me smile, that her pain made me hurt, that I was beginning to match our breaths every time we saw each other and that my guilt had opened a hole on my chest every time I had seen beyond her actions. How could I tell her that I had to dig my feet on the ground from running and gathering her in my arms at every moment of the day. How could I tell her that I was scared of losing her when I could not have her. How could I tell her...forgive me for I am the one you hate the most, but you make me feel like no one has ever made me feel before—to forgive me for I was so selfish to forget who I was. How could I tell her that I didn't deserve her, but I wanted her nonetheless.

"Kilian, trust me. What is worse, never telling her or her knowing? Tell her," Nia called me out of my thoughts, planting a hand on my arm.

"Tell me what? Are you two plotting how to deceive me again?" Snow's nectarine voice filled the room. She leaned against the door frame, arms crossed and wearing a satisfied grin. I almost let out a sigh of relief at her return.

Nia chucked a russet velvet pillow at her. "I should have been doubtful when you insisted on coming to Arynth instead of Kirkwall despite the Crafter being nearer there. A warning would have been nice. Do you have any idea how stupid I must have looked when I saw Elias and heard you squeal in that ridiculous tone? Which by the way was very well done," Nia said and they both laughed.

Her plans had surprised us both. But the trip to Arynth had finally gotten to fix their relationship, for that I was grateful.

"Two birds, one stone," Snow said proudly, throwing the pillow back. "Nia, would you see how the process with the Crafter is going, I need a moment with him."

"Do it," Nia whispered, going past me before leaving.

"Did you get what you needed from Elias?" I asked before I realised my mouth had betrayed me. I did not care what had happened with him, yet I became a fool by my own doing.

"I did, and if you would like to know, it was done just like how I had promised."

"Snow, I did not mean," I closed my eyes, angry at my own words. "I didn't mean it like that, forgive me."

Her eyes softened and a pleased smile grew on her lips. "You knew my plans and methods. You have to make peace with them however they unfolded." Pacing around in circles and squares about the waiting room, she finally took a seat by the fireplace. "I am sorry for this morning, at breakfast. I did not realise I'd held you, let alone that tight...to hurt you." She stood again toward me and took my hand between hers, examining the small scratches atop.

"You do not need to apologise, Snow, because I was the one that held you not the other way around."

She frowned, somewhat confused. "What? Why did you?"

When she faded away to sleep, for a split second I felt darkness surrounding her. Not emotion, just pure darkness, pure nightmares and terror. The sheer size of ache, fear and pain measuring that of a battle, even Mal who sat away had felt it.

"When I touched you, I drew you out from what you were feeling by emptying your emotional state into me." Which had resulted in my stomach retching all its contents after breakfast. I drew the panic, fear, pain, frustration and longing out of her. I felt all that she had felt when she drifted away to sleep, but in a more physical form.

"Why would you do that?" She was angry and upset, her voice almost broke. "I was seeing her and you brought me out, you made her disappear."

"You were drowning in what you were feeling, whoever or whatever you were seeing, I could not lose you in it."

Her eyes set aflame and she took a step back from me. "That is for me to decide, you understand, for me to decide! If I get lost, hurt or go mad. Only for me to decide."

"Do you understand how hard it is to watch you decide and become like that? I told you I will not stand by and watch you self-destruct."

"That seems to be your problem, Kilian, not mine."

"It is, but you see, little princess, it is only for now. I will drag and take you out every time I even remotely feel you drown yourself in those sick emotions and then I will make it your problem as well," my voice was cold, I had not meant for it to be, not to her.

She looked furious. "Why...why do you care or act like you do?"

You know why, Snow, you know, I wanted to say. "I do not need to explain myself to you."

She came closer and closer to me. The warmth of her body spread towards mine. I wanted to move my hands to tuck her hair, to run my fingers over her skin, over her lips. I wanted to trace every bit of her. My skin burned at the thought and the desire to act on my thoughts. I had wanted to strangle her, she had been the cause of my worry, anger and frustration. She was dangerous, vengeful, angry, a vixen. How many times had I chanted those very words to get her out of my head?

Her eyes roamed over my face before meeting my own. "Do not play games with me. My importance to your king must be tremendous by the look of it, isn't it?" A wicked smirk stretched on her face, looking to incite me. "Holding something else from me?"

"Think what you want if it helps that ice shield of hate, anger and vengeance of yours stay intact."

"Don't chastise, answer me," she spat, her palm hitting my chest. "Answer me and tell me this is all nothing, tell me that this is all but—but," she continued, taking a step closer, "but nothing." Her whole body shaking with anger, she hit again and again, and I stood there silently holding my truth, knowing I could not lie and tell her what she wanted to hear.

Her head dropped and her chest heaved, panting, half breathless and half rageful. "Fight back," she said, hitting me again. "Fight me back like you always did, hate me like you always did."

How could I, when she was the only person I wanted to protect, the only one who I would fight the whole world for.

"I can't and I think you already know why," I answered, instinct taking over to hold her face, resting my forehead on hers. To feel her, inhale her. "Here it comes, Snow, all that I'd promised not to say. Here it all comes."

She stilled under me, her chest flailing in and out of breath.

"It is hard, so hard not to think about you so I dare and let myself. I think about you when I look at you, when I eat, walk, talk, think. Hells, I even dream about you. You've plagued my days and my nights with daydreams—terrifying daydreams of smiles I can never fully have as mine, of eyes that I cannot stare to all my life, lips that I cannot make mine, a head that once I'm in I don't want to get out, of words and jokes that I could hear for eternity and never get tired. I think about you. I think about you now. I think about you always. My thoughts are only of you, my hunger is only for you and it is starving me to insanity. It is more than the need to claim you, it is the need to have you, all of you. Your silent head and your loud heart, I want them both. I want all, mostly and especially all."

A slight tremble permeated her limbs, and she blew a heavy breath. "I think I'm in trouble too, what do I do?" Her eyes rose to mine, filled silver with regret, doubt and fear. "My thoughts are only of you as well. That day I was...afraid that I felt for you...and I do. I think I do." She took my hand and placed it over her chest. "Why can't you read me, see my shadows? I can't read myself. I don't even know myself. Read me, Kil. Read and tell me what it is."

My heart stilled, then somersaulted in my chest at the unexpected reaction and words. She felt like I did? She felt for me? "Snow—"

She rested her fingers over my lips to stop me. "How is it so hard to breathe when I am with you, yet you have become like air that fills my lungs. What should I do? I cannot want you, yet you are what I want the most. So here it goes, the words I'd promised not to say." She took a deep stuttering breath. "Where do words go once we've said them? Do we forget them, do I live regretting them or wishing I'd said more, do we pretend we never said them in the first place?"

I kissed her palm. "What do you want, my heart?"

Her eyes drew shut. "I want to hear more, I want to hear you more. Call me that again."

"Come to me, my love. Do not push me away. Let me hold you, let me hold you like this, even if for a while, even if it is for a short while. For however long you want." I wanted her to allow me more than just that, I wanted her to allow me in her whole world, I wanted to see her skies and land, I wanted to understand her better, know her better.

A smile rose on her lips and she put her thumb in the middle of my chin, stroking so gently till it sent my body slumbering with peace. "Do you know how long I've been wanting to do that? It drives me mad. Do you know how many times I've gone mad because of it? This damned, damned dimple."

My body released from the tension and shook with laughter at her unexpected words. At the same beat, her eyes rounded and stared at me with that odd unexplainable expression.

"I have lost count," I said, lacing my fingers through her silken black hair. "Of times when you look at me like that." I liked it when she did, it was a look she had only ever given me.

She gave me a berating scowl. "Don't laugh like a madman then."

I understood then, the trigger for her odd eyes and my thoughts began searching for the first time when she'd looked at me like that. "Is it that strange, to hear me laugh?"

"Rare, not strange. Enough that it makes me want that sound for myself only, to lock it in a soundbox and let it soothe me to sleep every night," she said, tracing the centre of my jacket.

Her words felt dreamlike. What god was messing with my mind to play me like this? This was my torture. I groaned, pulling her closer, drunk in her presence, her face a thin page away from mine. "What are you doing to me, woman?"

"You started it," she whispered over my mouth.

"If I get to see you give me those eyes again I might never stop and laugh myself to death," I said, half smiling, I was immensely pleased.

She narrowed her eyes in slits and hit my chest with her palm so I took my chance, grabbing her wrists and pulling her into a hug. A little hesitantly, she too warped her arms around me. She was tall but compared to me much smaller, her head rested just above my chest and I rested mine on top of hers, planting a kiss on the crown.

"I forbid you," she murmured. "You cannot smile at anyone that is not me."

"It's all yours. I am all yours."

"All mine," she repeated, taking a deep breath. "I have never had someone all mine before."

We stood there for a while, to me it seemed like a small eternity. Her hands slid under my jacket, exploring every corner of me. "You remind me of spring, you smell like it as well," she murmured between us, and I laughed again. I did not know how anyone smelled of a season, but I was satisfied with her comment nonetheless.

"Kilian?"

"Yes?"

"Do you plan on assassinating me by means of suffocating? Would you be a darling and attempt another day? I have to meet with Albius in a few moments." She did not break our hug despite her words. Her fingers were still lazily drawing circles over my back.

"Keep doing that and you will make the Lord wait a while. A long while."

Her head hit my chest and she groaned, annoyed. "Don't say ridiculous things like that unless you intend to do it, you fool. You always take me to that edge only for me to jump myself. It's no fun on your own. And no, I don't need a hand, I have two."

I smiled and with strained will, I unwrapped myself from her, kissing my way down her forehead, eyes and almost all over her face. I could not get enough of her. She inhaled deeply as if I had really been suffocating her. Her face had received a rosy blush, golden eyes darting around the room not meeting mine.

"At me, Snow, I want you to look at me."

She raised her sparkly yellow gaze to me again. "This is severely embarrassing so spare me a few moments," she said, nestling close to me again.

"Being with me?"

She frowned, looking somehow hurt at my words. "No, telling you that I want to be with you."

"Because of who I am?" Again it looked as if I had hurt her by reminding.

She shook her head. "Because of what you mean to me."

"What do I mean to you? I want to hear it." *Nightmare.* That word pulsed heavy in my head.

Her fingers traced gently over my face, as if she was too scared to touch me.

"Spring—you are spring to me."

That was all it took to shake me wholly. "What changed?"

Her sigh was heavy and trembling. "I cannot give you the answer you are looking for."

"Snow," I asked, tilting her chin to me. "Do I still remind you of what I reminded you that day?"

Silence, yet it was all I needed to know. I stepped back from her. "How can you bear to do this? To let me hold you, touch you." I could not imagine the battle of thoughts in her head, her confliction readable through her eyes.

She grabbed onto my hands, placing them over her face again. "Because for moments I allow myself to forget and because other times you make me forget. Because I know it will end, it has to end, it is destined to end, and it makes me want to cherish you more than push you away despite whatever my head uses to push me away from you."

"Snow, I have to tell you—"

Her hand fell over my mouth. "You have pushed me away for a reason, too, but I don't want to hear it, not now. Maybe I will never have to. I know I will not change, you know I will not change. My purpose has never changed and it will never change. Tell me that you know. Tell me that you understand that I will do what I have to do."

I nodded. "I know." I did know, more than knew, yet I'd become selfish without thinking of her.

"You will hate me so, so badly. You might as well already hate me or still hate me. But would it be wrong to want you, for a while? Can it just be me and you, no realm, no past and present. Can I not just have you, a piece of you, whatever piece you choose."

The words warmed and then blistered my heart. "You always had the whole of me. It can be whatever you want, Snow, but I will never hate you." Not when she would hate me first.

"I will not hold onto that promise, Kil, I cannot."

"Go," I said, giving her one last tight embrace. "We will talk about this later again. You have time to think if you want to pull those words away. I'll pretend I have never heard them if you choose to and cherish them forever within."

Her head dropped in surrender. iIt took her a long moment before she straightened and nodded.

We'd agreed to a lie wedged between a cruel truth. It didn't exactly make us liars, only authors of an end written before its start. Perhaps we were liars, authors were the cruellest romancers with a penchant for the cruellest ends. This end had tangles, she'd hurt more than I.

35

WARS AND QUEENS
SNOWLIN

A SMILE STOOD SHAMELESSLY hitched on my lips. I tried every method in the book from thinking of puppies and lone abandoned baby birds to subdue it before meeting with Albius. My chest was pulsing out of my skin and that untameable ache I had for him had hitched higher up my throat as if still hungry for him. Maybe even more than before. I should regret it, yet I couldn't. It should start feeling wrong, but it wasn't, and it didn't. He would forget it if I told him so, but I didn't want him to forget it, only wanted him to profess more. I'd never felt this before. And now I wanted to be showered in it.

Nia arrived shortly after me and we both sat in the meeting room waiting for Albius.

"So?" she pretended to ask calmly, but the corner of my eye caught the smile she also was trying hard to suppress.

I glanced over the window overlooking the city outside, hoping to sneak a glance of him. "I have not the slightest idea what you wish for me to answer that question with?"

She shrugged. "I'll ask him then."

I snapped at her. "You conniving quisling."

Albius arrived, interrupting us. He sat across the room, his expression flashing a thousand signs of hesitation and worry before he abruptly stood, swallowed hard and strutted towards the exit. "I will return shortly," he announced before leaving the room. Had he not gathered us to speak?

I motioned to stand after him, but stopped when footsteps approached me from behind. Nia drew her dagger and we both turned to the sound of the intruder. While I was deep in thoughts, overtaken by what had happened today, I had entered a trap, one set by someone I had already settled too much trust in. It was expected when I calculated my friendship with him, but I had wished hard it had only been paranoia.

A tall, slender woman came into view. Her eyes were one of the darkest brown, that of wet soil, her hair was dark, straight, cut sharply just above her chin. Her features were youthful and sharp, she was elegantly beautiful and impeccably stoic. Dressed in a tight plain deep emerald cotton dress that loosely came to the floor with a flowery rose sash tied afront falling down almost the length of the dress, she looked like someone I'd once met before long ago. A different long time ago.

"We meet again, Snowlin Krigborn, but now you don't come below my chin. My name is Moriko Uzumi, Queen of Hanai," she introduced. Her voice was strong and elegant, very suited to her exterior.

The Queen of Hanai was in front of me in Isjordian lands. Had Lord of Arynth betrayed my father or me? I did not wish to jump to conclusions that confused me further, this was either a deception raised by the lord and my father, or the Queen of Hanai truly had wanted to meet me. A few reasons came to mind, including the soldiers my father had snuck in her kingdom to steal from her. Had she already found out who was behind them? What did it have to do with me?

"Queen?" Nia asked, bewildered. "Like the one that...holds a crown?"

Moriko lifted a brow at my stuttering stunned friend who was having a hard time processing her presence. "Yes...that one. And you are?"

Nia straightened, pulling her chin up. "Helenia Drava." She bowed her head slightly. "Her...friend."

I almost snorted. Helenia? She hated her full name, only Alaric called her that.

She swivelled a look on Nia before narrowing her eyes in question. "Drava? Are you perhaps the Olympian general's daughter?"

"His adopted daughter, he has given me his surname. How do you know of him?"

She nodded, her sleek bobbed hair shifting forward. "We served side by side in the Ater battles. The Olympian encampments were stationed in Aru. Zephyrs and king Jonah with his Elding children, her two uncles," she said, pointing to me, "they were first in line in battle. They also lost the most. Your father is a tough man, one I deeply respect."

War stories, peaceful stories, legends, happy memories—Alaric recalled them with so much pain and bitterness that he would bail in the middle without ever finishing. I had been told very little from the one who'd been the closest to my family, who remembered the most.

Nia swept a quick look over her. "Sixty years ago?"

"I am much older than I look." A prime Aura like her probably would look like that even at five hundred years of age.

"Well," I said, interrupting the reminiscence. "Your Majesty, you have gone to great lengths to corner me in this meeting, recruiting the Lord and all. Please do not hesitate on my behalf."

She took a seat across me, enthroned in her halo of might, the chair almost transforming into a dais. "Albius has been a good friend of mine for years. I have expressed the wish to meet with you for a long time now and only gave me that chance when he had studied you well enough to decide if you would go running to your father or not with information I am about to give you. He likes you dearly and deems you of great character," she lowered her gaze, studying me, "such an odd trait given you are Silas's offspring."

"What a great honour to be deemed as such," I said somewhat bitterly. "It appears the Lord has misjudged me greatly, dear. My great character comes from my mother, but I am still my father's daughter and therefore loyal to him and Isjord." Wanting to mark myself as a traitor was not on my list of accomplishments, but I knew a lot of people would find deep satisfaction for me to earn that title and I knew a lot of people who would stage all this for me to actually become one.

Her face was still expressionless, not betraying her of any emotion. She was known to be a great queen, her people adored her and she ruled with poised practices that her lands had never been more productive and flourishing. She had been a general in her predecessor's court. Hatori, the eldest king to live and perhaps wisest in Dardanes, had trusted her well enough to pass his throne to her instead of his own children. Moriko was a tactician and ruled over her land as one, too, carefully placing laws and regulations that benefited her kingdom and its people Well enough to bring it to ancient glory. My mother would call her an equation, she ruled to bring exact answers. She was a woman of war, yet she ruled with peace in mind.

"Do you know the easiest way to stop a war?" she suddenly asked, and I did the only thing I could do: shrug in question. "To prevent it. War is ruthless, many die and many more lose more than just their lives. I deem you smart despite whose side you take, to help me prevent it."

I raised a brow at her. "You have me well confused, Your Majesty, I see no war. And just what makes you think I have any ability to prevent this non-existent war?" How had I been enveloped in so many fables that drove most of my attention from a deranged ruler that now was becoming two, and right out of my true goals.

She leaned back. "I am sure you are aware of the growing tension between Solarya and Isjord, and your father believes me to be a fool not to notice his troops preparing at our borders and the spies he sent to infiltrate my court. The deal he is to make with Adriata, have you ever thought what he is to win from it?"

She knew about the Solaryans and about the soldiers my father had sent to her kingdom. Elias either lied to me or my father's intentions were truly to take that rare object and the queen had not known about it. Well, my father had succeeded in keeping their intentions a secret if that was the truth. It would have bothered me before, her suggestion that my father was to rage war on them with the help of Adriata, but I believed Kilian, he had not lied to me.

"What makes you think war is his intention?"

"Hasn't it always been his only intention?" she asked, her brows raising in question while she traced a hand in the air over me to make her point.

I rolled my eyes, court games did tire me. Language of rulers was not one I spoke with patience. "Concrete answers, Autumn Queen, you came here to gain my graces or lose them?"

She smiled, cocking her head to the side wearing the confidence of a ruler. "My spies have been after your father the day your brother was born," she explained. "I am sure you are aware of the Adriatians under his services. Brisk is still Hanai whoever's border they belong to. Ibe Brisk is also another acquaintance of mine, one very close to your fathers business. The attackers who quartered you on your return from Brogmere—they were your father's."

My expression dropped at her revelation. I should have known. I should have doubted. The direct order, how he had acted and pretended. It all had been an act as I had doubted. But why? To keep me from my duty?

She took note of my silence and continued. "Esbern Kirkwall was his closest ally despite what he made it look like in court. He was his Adriatian spy, the ex-Lord was from Sitara, son of an old priest there, one with prime knowledge of Henah's blessed."

"And she killed him," Nia said absently.

And I had indeed killed him, well done me.

The queen nodded at my friend. "Indeed, that she did. She did much more than just that. She ruined a large part of his plans. There are now no eyes in Adriata and no more shadow recruits. It was smart to organise the fiasco. But it also seems that he is not the best judge of your character."

I shook my head from the puzzling directions and leaned forward. "How does this have to do with anything?"

"The shadow blessed recruits, they were not only inside my court. My spies have seen them in Solarya, Vrammethen and...Myrdur," she gave lastly. "They were not there for you, your father had kept your hiding plenty of a secret. They would fade and take coordinates as well as this," she said, rolling an engraved emerald quartz stone over to us.

I studied the Crafter's halo marked atop, the unfamiliar pattern and strange runes, the ring of familiar magic being emitted. "What of this?"

"A tracking craft. They were trying to locate someone, something, somewhere. It could be anything." She then threw five others, naming each place she had found them, "The one on your hand was found in Myrdur, Theros, Aru, Heca, Comnhall and the last one in Hayes, Seraphim." Six kingdoms, missing only Adriata.

Nia examined them, looking just as confused as I before reaching for a piece of paper and tracing the patterns and runes atop. "We can ask our Crafter what they exactly are," she murmured close to me.

Moriko noted the exchange and only smiled before saying, "What I meant by mentioning Adriata was not to include them as partners in your father's plans, it was to state that you are being used to get to them. The only kingdom he has no access to freely search for whatever he is searching is Adriata. Once that chess piece is in his game then he will act."

Melanthe, that is why she had returned, my father had after all enlisted her purposefully. I took one of the stones, running my fingers to trace the halo and I felt it, the bitter and sweet scent of mint and death. Melanthe's magic. Realisation came heavy. The soldiers and Verglasers in Myrdur were they being directed by the tracking halos? They were indeed looking for something. "What is it you propose, you certainly have come here more than to tell me a few tales?" Panic began crawling to surface at the thought that this was beginning to make too much sense and none at all at the same time.

She laced her hands and leaned forward on the table. "They are not tales and you are well aware, otherwise you would have stood and left the moment I spoke. Join me, refuse the Adriatian deal to begin with and then join my army. I have heard plenty of your skill and this comes all with a promise of safe living for you and your generations to come," she finally added, and I guffawed.

No, my father did not take her for a fool, she was a fool. If my father was to rage war he would have found another deal with Adriata nonetheless. If war was to come I was not going to hide away to my benefactor's underarms scared, I'd be at its front, cutting heads.

"You must have known I would not agree to any of this madness, yet you chose to cross to Isjord and try to convince me to do so. How very odd, my dear." Amusement had now left my body completely. "But you will get what you came here for, I promise to side with you if truly my father is to rage war. Till I know those are his intentions, I will not take any of the ridiculous actions you mentioned." I was not to be bargained like the last sweet at the solstice banquet. Albius must have surely made her aware that was not how I played my games and certainly not this three-player chess game. If she had come to seek my support then that she had, but on my terms. The Ianuris agreement had to be fulfilled, I would not abandon Myrdur in the hands of my father, not again.

She narrowed her stare, assessing me. "Albius was right in his observations. Though I would not say strong headed as he did, more like...stubborn." Sighing, she nodded in agreement. "Very well then."

"I also need a favour from you," I demanded.

She laughed and leaned back, assessing me once more. "A bargain. Very Isjordian of you."

Ignoring her words, I continued, "You mentioned Lord of Brisk and you are acquainted."

"Yes...yes, I did. Ibe used to be Captain of one of the battalions I directed during my time as general."

"I want him pledged on my side." Nia nudged my foot in warning the second the words left my mouth, my little toe now a fallen soldier.

Moriko's brows rose and so did her smirk. "A coup? On Silas? What about your loyalty to him?" she marked sarcastically, almost dismissive of my plans.

"Those were your words not mine, I am not planning to overthrow my father, differently from you I don't underestimate him. What I am looking to overthrow is Isjord."

Her expression faltered when my seriousness didn't drop, slowly her eyes went wide in realisation that I was not joking. "I came to you to end a war, not to start another one."

My turn to laugh. "Again, you misunderstand me, Your Majesty, there will be no war." Only destruction.

"How will you end perhaps the strongest kingdom in Dardanes?"

Was she mocking me? She clearly thought my allegiance to her would make an impact on this war she spoke of, why would my own not? "From within," I revealed, and Nia stomped hard on my foot, my whole carpals lining in mourning now. Maybe she was right, it did seem unsmart to reveal my intentions, but she needed me and hated my father. Ignoring the pain, I wiggled my foot away from her reach. "A whole sea cannot drown a ship, but a tiny hole can slowly fill it with water till it's too late to realise they are drowning."

Nia covered her eyes with a hand, and murmured silently. "Sails and anchors, here we go again."

Moriko stared confused at the both of us. "I do not understand."

I offered her a smile. "I only need Lord of Brisk to pledge on my side, not for you to understand."

She scoffed. "Has anyone told you that you are too rude for the title you hold, princess?"

"Yes, plenty. Yet politeness isn't what granted me this deal."

Moriko turned to Nia. "Is she always this rude?"

"Does the wind blow?" my friend asked in all seriousness, and Moriko smiled at the oddly shy Nia.

"Very well then," the Autumn Queen said. "You have your bargain, Lord of Brisk will pledge on your side as long as you hold your side of it."

"As I told you, I have my mother's character. Many others tell me I also have my grandfather Jonah's bargaining skills and his truth in promise."

"And her guardian's stabby character," Nia warned bravely. "In case you do not hold to hers and betray the trust she has bestowed you by asking for this favour."

I glanced at my friend and the sudden oddness to her character.

Moriko nodded. "Well warned, miss Helenia."

We sat there taking in all the information for a long while—long enough that I had not noticed it was growing dark outside.

"Do you think she lied?" Nia asked nervously.

"I don't know, what does *miss Helenia* think?" She reddened at my words and my mouth drew open from surprise. "Someone has been impressed."

She slapped my shoulder and stood quickly. "Don't be ridiculous."

I was being ridiculous? "Will you run to the Crafter? I want to know if those patterns are truly tracing halos. I recognized the scent of Melanthe's magic in the quartzes. I think Moriko Uzumi was right."

"If you want to have alone time with Kil darling, just ask."

I pinched her nose. "The Crafter, miss Helenia." She turned red again. "Odd," I said with a rising smirk. "I didn't know queens stroked your fancy."

"I didn't know enemies stroked yours."

I flicked my hand in the air. "You know I have done worse."

"Actually, I don't think you have done better." She put a hand over her mouth to hide a giggle while waving me a little goodbye with the other. "Say hi for me to Kil darling."

In a similar fashion to how I solved all my problems, I shoved two middle fingers up in the air.

Once I was left to the sound of my head, I drowned in worry. My plans have shifted more than I'd like to count, it was becoming hard to keep focus on taking over Isjord when my father was spinning all sorts in the background. The worst part was that all seemed to be all over the place and loosely linked to each other, but all related to one. There was fear of war. One that looked to be initiated by my father...again. To do what, expand lands, resources and a handful of working forces? Oddly, that was all that my father probably needed.

"Snow," Albius called, coming from behind me. He had disappointed me the most, but for him to break my trust meant that he also feared war. Meeting Moriko should have been a choice made by me. If anyone had grabbed notice of our meeting or if Moriko's intentions had not been sincere, Albius could have put me in serious danger.

"I just want to know," I said, interrupting myself to swallow the pressure rising behind my throat. "Were all your stories true or did you need me this much that you made them up?"

His head lowered to the ground, pensive and guilty. "All, word by word, true and deeply meant," he responded, pursing his lips back apologetically.

I did not like to be caught by surprise, and worse, to be used. It reminded me of my purpose, that of a weapon. "Then I believe we still have our alliance."

"It was a blood promise, you will always have me at your side."

I nodded. Albius had not needed to be compromised, an oar who had leaped to faith in my intentions to be good. One who had perpetually doubted my father and his perpetual plans of mass destruction. The lord had tied his allegiance to me deeper, sworn an oath of blood and magic, one that if he broke would demand his life as payment.

"I will leave tomorrow morning," I announced, standing to leave. "I also cannot join you tonight for dinner, you will have to continue with your stories on another visit I suppose."

It had gone completely dark, clouds were so thick they were gurgling above each other for space. Not a trace of the stars from last night but lightning that flashed, cracking between them silently and violently. The blinking white light reflected over the glossy onyx roofs of the city that silently rested in the warmth and comfort of their home. The quiet of night and winter was only broken by the noise of unsure skies, sound of lighting and thunder—a hair-raising symphony. Epiphanic. To my ears it was a calming chaos. Eye of a storm hovered above me. I wondered if it saw all trouble.

Kilian sat by a bench in front of the lord's house, his head had dropped in surrender to the spiralling thoughts he'd dived into. The only starlight I wanted to see was that of his, but even his eyes stood between troubled storms. I knew his troubling storm.

I gathered all strength in my voice. I wanted him to know I meant what I'd say next. "I don't regret them, Kil, do you?"

His silver gaze rose to me. "Never."

"I'm going to hurt you."

He stood, stalking careful paces to me. "I deserve it."

My feet meekly moved forward. "I cannot spare you."

"I cannot be spared."

I reached closer, my steps quickening. "I will lose you."

"You will be grateful."

"And you will lose me."

He shook his head. The stream of glitter and chips of silver still sent the most shimmering flutter over my stomach. "I have already lost you, I'm losing you now."

I swallowed the pain back to my chest. "This is a disaster."

He gave me a lachrymose smile, it still lit up his whole features. "It is, but one of the sweetest kinds."

"Once I step in Adriata, once I wed your king, I will not look at you the same and you won't look at me at all. It will be our end. We are running on stolen time, once it ends, this will end, too."

"We might be thieves, my love, but we won't be ungrateful ones."

I smiled at his words. "I still want you."

"I never stopped wanting you."

My steps were as large as his and I practically leapt in his arms. He held me tight, my forehead pressed to his while he slowly spun us round. We shared a breath, a heartbeat, one touch—an aching and needing touch. It didn't feel like flames, it felt like the first break of light through the greyest of clouds, soft feathers and mist. His nose nudged mine and I anticipated that joining, his lips on mine, his taste and need...for too long. Both of us did and yet none leaned in for that first contact. Never before had I hesitated, never had I doubted, backed away or reconsidered. Never had I wanted one person of this sort, body and soul, all flesh and all blood. Yet for the first time, I hesitated and then gave up to the odds of chaos that kiss would have enkindled.

Kilian's eyes dropped shut and he gently shook his head. "I cannot do it, my heart. It will kill me if I get to taste you and not be able to do it for my entire life. I'll go mad, slowly and tortuously."

My chest swelled and I suddenly couldn't breathe anymore. "And I will go mad if I never do. I'll go mad anyway."

"Forgive me," was all he said as he held me there for a lost eternity.

I cupped his face and raised his gaze to mine, devastation wearing all their colour. "I have someone who is all mine and I cannot even make him mine," I said, my smile tremulous and crooked.

"Forgive me," he repeated. The pain that gaze cursed, it almost branded my skin like fire.

"Why is this so hard? Why does it have to be you? The first time I wish to belong to someone, why does it have to be with someone who cannot have me?" I blew a long breath, and yet my chest felt even heavier, the new breath was even harder to take. "This is all your fault."

He laughed softly and I bit my lip at that sound that almost shattered me whole. "And I have never been more guilty in my life, but for this...I'd pay for a thousand lifetimes."

"You and your pretty words. Those hateful pretty words."

"Liar," he said, kissing the bridge of my nose. "You like my pretty words."

He could drain air out of your lungs staring at you alone, the closeness of our bodies was a drug that had me desperate for more. I didn't like his pretty words, I loved them. I took a deep inhale. "Does this mean we will not get to sacrifice a human either, or ask for Henah to be our witness?"

He threw his head back and howled with laughter, harder than I'd ever heard him laugh before. I wanted to eat him and that laugh alive.

I gripped his jaw, hovering my lips just above his. "I would have devoured you."

"You already have." He grazed his lips over mine just a little, barely a touch, but it was enough to make me gasp.

My pulse shifted from the desire to claim him and I cried out a little whine. "I want you inside me and out and everywhere."

He ran a hand down my spine, that tease truly unravelled me fully. His lips pulled to a smile, probably knowing what he did to me. "If you still need that hand, do let me know."

I slapped his shoulder repeatedly. "Put me down before I damn you and your righteousness."

He held me tighter. "Do we have a deal? I have you like this till then, no pushing away now that you know my feelings for you."

"You and your bloody deals," I groaned, and he laughed again. I would not push him away, especially now that I knew how he felt for me. After a few moments of processing and his doe eyes softened in a plea, I kissed his maddening chin and said, "Deal."

He slapped my bottom and put me down before reaching to lace his fingers with mine. "Bed."

"Oh, yes, the ground here is fine, too, though."

His large body shook from silent chuckles. "You need to sleep."

"Can do, right after."

He ran his free hand over his eyes and gave me a look. "You are making it hard."

"Good, it has to be, otherwise I'd worry."

He no longer held it in, his laughter travelled almost all over Arynth. I loved that sound, my body did, too. After he was almost in tears from laughter, he gathered me close and kissed my brow. "Be good now."

I stuck my bottom lip out at him. "But I am good. So good, Kil." I fluttered my lashes in innocence. "Care to find out?"

He bit his lip tight. "That is the last I will say or you will ruin me." Before I could utter another word, he covered my mouth with his large hand and with the other he picked me up in his arms like a little child and made toward the house.

He delivered me to my bedroom door and then slowly retreated away from me. He'd made it to the end of the corridor thrice before returning, and ultimately by the fourth time he'd truly left. I stood at the door in a daze, savouring the electric sensation his voice sent down my spine, the warmth and feel of his lips on my skin. The image of them over my own sending a hot flush pooling on my stomach, until my anger started boiling in buckets. I muttered curses from heavens to this realm for the bastard that had taunted and pulled my strings to madness, only to leave me empty. Twice, no, three times he had left me like a gawking idiot, and I had let him. What was becoming of me? A fool—I had become a helpless fool. Why had I not kissed him myself? Bloody heavens, I had now even agreed to a deal of doing none of that. I'd become a saint. Maybe I should join a monastery, shave my head and let cobwebs dangle between my legs. Nia will be proud of me at least. Oh hells, Nia. She would never let this go.

I startled to a halt once she popped her head out of my bathroom chambers, grinning like a cat.

"Do not, I warn you," I threatened.

She hopped jollily on my bed and propped her head on a hand. "Tell me all, tell me why you are not keeping the whole of Arynth awake riding him to daylight."

I frowned at her oddness. "Since when doesn't it bother you, to discuss about that?"

"Since now, I like you with him. So?"

"We made a deal."

Her smile dropped. "A what now?"

"We agreed to not do that or even...kiss."

There was a moment of silence and then she cackled so loud that the room almost began to shake. "Heavens and he got you to agree? You?" she emphasised in a loud shock.

"Yes. He was right. I think I'd not be able to forget him and then I'd crave him like mad. The less we know of that need, the less we will miss one another. We both know the fate of this."

Nia stared at me for a while and then gradually smiled again before laying back wide armed and lost in a dreamy ponder as she stared at the ceiling. "This is what's written in books looks like? I thought I'd never see you like this."

"Nia," I said, taking a deep breath. "I am not...I'm not in love with him."

She frowned and then stood completely. "But—"

"I am not." A chant more to convince myself than her. "I am not afraid, just...happy." I realised I was happy. How could I be happy? I feared happiness. I feared it because every time I felt the emotion, I lost it to pain, to my father, to the Night King. I lost it to the world where someone like me was born only deserving of hate.

She frowned. "Love is happiness, love is not fear."

"No...no, it's not fear, it's worse."

"Ma, do you love father?" I had asked absently as my ten-year-old self had rested a hand on my unfeeling chest, noting it did nothing for the man who had sired me.

"Yes," she had said almost regretfully. *"I do."*

"How does it feel? How would I know I love someone?"

She'd thought about it for a moment and then gathered me on her lap. *"It feels like fear, but it is not fear. It makes your heart beat fast enough you cannot separate each pulse. You feel dizzy, lightheaded and your limbs turn weak, yet it holds you strong in anticipation and palpitation, half wanting to run from it and the other half to face and run in its embrace. Often we mistake and blame it for fear, because fear is easier. You get over fear, but that emotion is not fleeting, it's branding, often hurtful, too often overwhelming that we forget the hurt and at other times just simply delightful and airy and fulfilling. But never just one thing, waves and rocks, bricks and glass. It is a war, my snowflake, the hardest one someone can fight. You win and it can leave you feeling like you have lost it. You lose it and you rarely feel like ever winning again."*

Part IV
Lucid Dream

36

PROMISES AND LIES

SNOWLIN

WE LEFT EARLY IN the morning for Tenebrose. I left a letter behind, thanking Albius for his welcoming and all he had done for us. We journeyed quietly through Sable Abyss despite the overflowing snow that coated the lands, almost swallowing the trees as well. Nia had stolen glances between myself and Kilian till she had giggled herself to tears. A few death threats and slaps later and thankfully she had stopped, only continuously clicking her tongue at both of us. Not bearing it anymore, I glanced at Kilian and the bastard dared to throw me a wink. I knew him to be many shades of stern and stuck up, but this was a new one from him—shameless.

My mood started slowly shifting for the worst when we reached Tenebrose city gates. I noticed the air turning into a thick static that I had not felt before this heavy. Something was wrong. The guards looked grim and did not pay mind to us as we crossed through to the castle. Like the *zgahna* warning, it struck me. A sense beyond sense, somewhere between magic and human awareness. A prickle of skin and a lurch of worms in your stomach, an omen signalling that something was not right, that something had happened. The hair on my neck rose in awareness while my heart drummed heavily against the chest bone.

"Snow, no!" Cai shouted a moment too late.

I rode ahead furiously, each pace closer to the castle sent shudder after shudder chasing the feeling down. Dismounting Memphis, I ran towards the castle, towards my father. My feet touched the ground so rapidly that they almost lifted me afloat into the air. I felt the ground warning me under my feet, a whisper of the earth carrying malice. Bypassing the guards, I pushed the door open to face the snickering serpent.

"What have you done, you monster, tell me!" I shouted loud enough to echo over the thunder raging outside. I knew it the moment a grin stretched wide in his face that whatever he had done, I would be the one to suffer its repercussions. I will finally kill him, going to dig my dagger so deep in his skull it would reach his throat.

Two guards approached me from behind, ready for any movement I might make.

"Not yet, my rose, I have not done anything just yet," he said, letting out a rumble of laughter, the disgusting noise I hated so deeply. "I see you have not relaxed at all despite your journey to Arynth," he continued, standing to approach me. "But it appears the warmth of the south has melted that ice shard mouth. You are unusually quiet."

"Don't mess with me, father, I think I have proven enough to you that I am not only words and spite. If you even think of any madness, strap yourself in for a joy ride." *He could not hurt me, he cannot hurt me. He could not hurt me, he hasn't hurt me.*

"You never learn, do you?" he asked, waving a hand to his guards.

Time stilled for a fraction of a moment. It was then I realised he could hurt me and he had hurt me. I could barely make out his face, bruised and bloodied, all four limbs chained as the Bruma Commander pushed him forward into the room. His right foot limped, blood dragged behind him and dripped from wrists and ankles. With each drop, a thump of my heartbeat sunk and rolled and bled and then faltered.

Sam.

Not Sam.

Panic took over and radiated burning my insides, pushing up a cry on my throat and a tremble over my limbs. Not him, heavens, not him, not Sam.

Father titled his head to him. "The shining General came galloping down the corridors for my head, that is just before I found out what he had done in Casmere with his spy. When my father bought this human soil, I did warn him about Solaryan nature and the undying oaths to their goddess. As I had thought, he'd gone crawling back with information to the Sun court."

Renick laughed, eyes gleaming with pride. "He tried, but we sank the ship not a mile before it left the bay. Then I caught this worm." He spat at Sam and my blood simmered.

Father sighed and stood, making paces around his dais. "Opposing me is one thing. Betraying me is quite the other. I waited for your return, otherwise his head would have greeted you at the entrance. I want you to see what happens to those that betray me, you along with all the others in my court." He signalled the sentries behind me and the room filled with familiar and unfamiliar faces of lords, captains and generals.

My eyes never left his sunken one's. I met no fear in there—the fear was only mine.

Renick nudged him with his foot. "Any last words, General?"

Sam straightened despite the tremble of his limbs and stared right into me, fearless and headstrong. "You were right, Snowlin Edlynne Skygard, and you will take him down in my honour." He swallowed and a tear slid down his cheek as he repeated in Calgnan, "You will take him down and rise from his cold ashes, build this kingdom and free the realm of his plague." It was then I stopped breathing. "You will wage no destruction, honour my request. Give peace with no fear."

I shook my head.

No.

No.

My father signalled Renick. I felt it then—what I had forgotten to feel in a while, the fright of losing someone you love. Air thickened and reeked of malice. I made one step forward, my hand slipping to the hilt of my dagger and at the second step I took air was drained out of my lungs. Cai's steps chased mine from behind me, his magic sealing my breath and denying me of it. Then I felt Nia, the light touch of her magic gripping my shadows, attempting to nail me to a halt.

At the third heavy constricted step I took, Samuel shook his head. "No. Don't. Live...live to carry out my honour, not for revenge."

A sword pierced his chest and life fled from him.

Time forgot its pace, it went too quick and too slow. Magic, shadows and air held me from collapsing, held me from shouting and screaming and blasting in the waves of what I felt. Held by Cai and Nia, held by nothing of mine.

Sam. Not Sam. The cry and plea choked on my throat.

My world silenced, grew younger, warped and I felt myself shift in the form of that child years ago.

"Stand girl," my father had ordered in a leering stare that scathed all courage. *"A weapon does not feel, it doesn't weep and it doesn't scream or rage or fight or think. You are mine to wield, a shell whose heart beats for me to command, you cannot take it, you cannot bend it, only I can. Now stand, wipe those ridiculous tears away. Would you bleed before a shark? Will you waver in front of your prey?"*

I'd cried for the first time—I'd disappointed him for the first time that day after Renick had beat Eren to unconsciousness, so hard he had not woken for a week. I had begged and crawled at him, tears of blood and pain had burned deep while I had pleaded for him to stop. I still felt them, marked on my skin, burning still. A reminder of never feeling again.

And I would not weep, or scream, or rage, or fight, or think, but I would also never be his to wield or please and obey. He had ripped part of my soul today and I wondered if it was the last one I'd been left with.

Sam. Not Sam.

We were supposed to live, Sam, and now I killed you.

He killed you because of me.

37

Sky and Thunder

Kilian

MAGIC BEAMED AROUND ME, floating out of Nia and Caiden in her direction to hold her still while Samuel bled under her father's feet. Her friend, the man who adored her, who helped and laughed with her, the one she had called her family now laid lifeless in front of her. The man who had looked at her with nothing but love and admiration, the one who had cared and feared for her, was dead.

"Was this supposed to hurt?" she asked coldly, before her scornful laugh broke the silent echo of the panic-stricken Winter court. "Pathetic. Even for you, father, this is so very pathetic. Shall I show you what really hurts?"

I flinched at her tone, the fleeting of the Snow I'd grown to know replaced by this. I knew she felt, I knew she hurt, yet she almost convinced me that she did not.

He halted, facing her, studying and seizing before dismissing the room from the audience. "You would have been magnificent in my hands, child, mighty even. With that heart and your languid for compassion you were perfect. Your powerlessness was such a misfortune. And to my chagrin, you became a perfect thorn in my heel." Contempt at her silence, his lip stretched to a smirk, his shadows swirling with pure satisfaction. "Thankfully, soon you will be the Night King's to deal with."

She took a step closer to him, the string of magic holding her broken out of Nia's touch. Just as quickly, my brother's shadows lengthened to her, his grip tighter, more powerful than Nia's and she halted at the command. "I'm a dagger, father, right between your ribs. I make you ache at every move, each breath harder than the other and you twist just slightly more than the steel allows, I pierce your heart."

"Brave words for someone so unhurt," he provoked.

"I love it when you elicit me, I get to show you just the monster you have raised. You never once got to see what you forged. You would be proud."

He glowered at her, the stare of a hunter. "I had not heard that name in a while, Skygard. But you are no Skygard, my bud, you are Krigborn till heavens fall."

"I am Krigborn, my name will be marked all over it for I will scrap this bloodline till the very root of it with your bones, papa."

"Try, you can try," he challenged, but he finally took some degree of caution in her threat, his shadows betrayed that truth he so well hid. "That is all you can do, try and gloat and threaten, petty threats and petty words, empty and meaningless just like your worth."

He stared at her with such languid hate. I had forgotten how she was raised. I realised that side of her had always been provoked, she was never the monster. She was only a weapon.

He left, gleefully gloating in his victory.

A grin wore the Bruma Commander's face as he strutted head high and satisfied past her. Her hand extended lifelessly and met his chest. The sound of the contact was a dark echo accompanied by his cackling dark laughter. "You always do this after your losses, scavenge for consolation in threats, you piss Olympian whore."

The words drew fire from me, chest tightening in ire, yet I did not move. Not for a moment did this feel his ground like it felt hers.

Her attention never left Samuel's lifeless body, or Nia's movement as she shut his eyes closed for the last time. "Do I?" her voice, dark, deep and cold.

"My whip and you got personal more times than I could remember, I know you to your nub."

I finally made forward, an unbearable burn flaring inside of me, he would die for what he had done to her.

Caiden's hand on my shoulder brought me to a halt. He slowly shook his head. "She has this—has for a while. Now it's the time."

I didn't know what he meant, I did not understand till Snow spoke, "Tell me, how did your wife and son die?"

His smile began faltering, attention pinched with agitation while taking in her revelation. His head slowly turned to her, something between confusion and fear read there till I opened my senses to read gales and gales of unending terror and distraught.

"Tell me, Renick," she continued, "how did you find Jens and Sigrid in your home above Morrow grove in Casmere, the little sweet cottage by the northern bay?"

I felt myself hold a breath, anticipation and disbelief holding it hostage at the same time. Casmere—we had been once in the bay city. Brief words of her conversation with Caiden flew around my ears. What had she done?

Her gaze turned to meet his, a grin spread wide and vile in her face and he paled, his breathing growing deeper and features drawn in. "No...no!" he shouted, shaking his head.

Her head dropped back, laughter of success taking over and filling every nook and corner of the open hall. She shook and shivered, not from amusement but at the broiling heat I saw boiling beneath her skin lit irate. "Oh yes, yes. And take credit I beg of you. I did it just like you taught me, oh great master," she said fashioning a bow.

"Cannot be."

She pulled closer to him, her hand never leaving his chest. "Look at me, Renick. Look at me and see the last face they saw before their souls parted their bleeding bodies."

Her revenge was here, and it was cold and unremorseful.

He gasped for air and made to move away, but she dug her palm in a fist over his heart. "Tell me, how did you find them? Bleeding, in pieces over the walls? Which parts of theirs did you find first? Did you ask yourself which soul had you forced to murder your family because of your actions? It must have taken you a while because there are so many."

For a few moments all I knew of her felt a dream—a daydream I'd built. If I had not seen her eyes at that moment it would have truly felt as that, but I saw the flashes of armour she wore cracking.

"I did it how you used to say," she pushed. "One whip for a fragment of soul, name their fears each time it meets their skin. It is how it breaks someone. It's how you tried to break me."

My body moved, my chest flaring with fire with each breath I took. I'd suck the life out of this man who had marked her. Mal and Caiden both wrapped their arms around me, holding me back. "You interrupt her now and she will lose her composure, let her win her own battle," her friend warned, pushing me back.

She glanced over her shoulder at me shortly before facing Renick again. "I did it the same, but the only fear I mentioned was my name, the only fear they had was me and now the only fear you will know is me."

A loud growl escaped his throat as he reached his hands over her throat, squeezing tight. "I will kill you."

My feet ached to move, my magic flared to be used, my fists tightened to strike, yet I didn't move.

She cackled loudly. "Then who will remember where dear Fiona is, your pretty little daughter? My soldiers picked her up a few weeks back now, still distraught at her family's death. The sweet thing has her mother's face."

"She is still alive?" His eyes shot wide and he pulled back from her, shaking his head as she stretched and rubbed her throat. His hand fell over his chest and he crouched down, falling to his knees.

"Not yet dead, more like it." She drew nearer and nearer, her steps predatory and calculated.

Caiden stood and cautiously traced her pace, reaching his hands up, a breeze lifting with scent of airy magic. "No, no, Cakes. Come now, leave him, we are to leave him alive. Don't make me do it, I know you hate when I make you faint." He meant to stop her. He knew there was no stopping her.

She halted at her friend's warning and bent down close to the commander. "What will I use her for, Renick? You taught me to use my pawns meticulously or kill them if they become dead weight."

His face twisted in a snarl. "You cannot kill her."

She snorted. "Is that so now, on what basis? Pity? But no, you beat that out of me, remember? Care, compassion, any feeling in general, that too," she said and snapped her fingers, "all out of my system, just like you wanted it. Proud?"

I shook my head. I could not believe what that man had done to her—all that had been done to her.

He paled, tears streamed down his face as he stared at her wide eyed, pleading. "What do you want?"

"I want it all, but from you I want allegiance."

Allegiance? Even now she would not drop her revenge.

"No, no, I will not betray my king."

"I never asked, I don't need to ask. I have Fiona, but I'll take what you cherish the most, your king's trust. A little bird whistled to me about a little drug and about your little students. Does father know that you dose them on mirkroot and do they know mirkroot kills you. Slowly, but it kills you."

"Not slow," Nia called strongly, sat by Sam. "Quick and painfully, it only takes a few doses after your third for your body to ingest it at the speed of a heartbeat. Then the fourth will go straight to your head and you will die a very explosive death. Burma halls stank of it on the first whiff, your Verglasers will fall within a year."

She'd been planning this for a long while, this truly was her battle.

"Did you hear that?" Snow gasped mockingly. "They will fall within a year. I have not the slightest idea how you were to cover that up, but now father will know it was because of you. Your dear king will be your end." She clapped in his face. "Beautiful tragedy. I'd pay good coin to read about this."

He shook his head. "I beg of you."

Her grin spread wide. "Did I not tell you, Renick? That you will one day be at my mercy. I hold onto my words, very tightly. You will pledge for me and you owe me one more favour for Sam's life."

He swallowed and then nodded between strong dark notes of disapproval. "I will."

"Blood oath."

He shot up. "What?"

"You will give me a blood oath, Nick dear. I don't trust my own heartbeat, what makes you think I trust a python?" She took off her glove and extended a hand to him. "You will pledge your life. I vow blood, flesh and bone, ash and soil," she recited, and magic floated around her, lifting her hair in waves. "You, Renick Salazar, will pledge to my allegiance, and I, Snowlin Krigborn, will keep my word."

He shook his head, but she leaned and took his hand, squeezing it tight. He repeated, "I, Renick Salazar, vow blood, flesh and bone, ash and soil, to plead your allegiance, and you, Snowlin Krigborn, will keep your word." There was a small gleam under their sleeves where the magical bargain would have made a mark.

Blood oaths were purer in darkness than dark itself. The more you tied to yourself, the more your soul grained to pieces. How many had she signed already?

She peeled her sleeve back to reveal a line of tattoos wrapped around her arm amongst a few others. She examined the oath with relish. "Who would have thought all those lessons would come to such help. Shoo, Renick, back to your hole," she flung with her hand and the commander rapidly exited the room.

Her arsenal had grown, she was close to her plans by large paces, they were no longer just steps though. Today there had been a cost and no longer just at her expense. Sam had been killed.

Slowly, she took small steps toward Samuel's lifeless body, lain in blood. Her knees gave away before him and she raised a trembling hand, reaching over his cold face. "Sam, Sam. Oh Sam, what have they done to you." Her voice shook, the chant of his name was a prayer and a plea. The armour she wore flaked to a carcass and she peeled out of it, baring her soul in the open once again. "Open your eyes, Sam, I am here now. I won't make you hold your heart in your hands anymore. I will give up. I will give it all up for you, Sam. Just open your eyes...please."

Her head dropped forward and she took a deep heavy stuttering breath. "You promised me, you promised. You promised to come with me. You promised to be close to me," she murmured in breathless paces. A single tear rolled down her cheek and my heart ached hard.

"Forgive me," she whispered, raising a trembling hand to stroke his face. "Forgive me, Sam, for putting you in danger. Forgive me for not protecting you. I couldn't protect you either." Her head fell resting in his chest, long moments as she silently mourned him. "I can't feel your heart anymore."

The realisation in her voice broke me—it tore me throughout. Through the hopelessness and the dusk of helplessness, I did only what I could do, let my shadows around her, gathering tight. Magic and warmth seeped through me and onto her as she stood there cold and coldening, strength devoured. She didn't let him go, did not move until day grew to night, until the clouds grew to thunder and until limbs grew numb. She would not part with him, she would not let us touch him or even get nearby.

"She does not seem strange," Penelope said, coming out of Snow's room. "She keeps humming that terrible song again and again and murmuring to Memphis endlessly in Calgnan, otherwise she is just her normal self," she explained. Her lips pursed back in hesitation and she threw an unsure glance towards Nia.

"Pen, it is okay, tell us," Nia pushed.

The young servant fiddled with her apron nervously. "You know those black marks in her back, they have somehow shifted, not their normal shape. What are they? I have never asked her, but I have always been curious."

Nia halted her endless circling at her words and cast a long look to Caiden.

Snow's tattoo had shifted. So it was a dark craft after all.

"It is just a tattoo, Pen, and don't be silly, they cannot shift around, you must be mistaken," Nia answered, but I saw a speck of lie in her shadows. She was getting better at hiding, but I had seen enough. Nia had told me that Snow had seen a Crafter before to remove her nightmares, but to them that was a simple trick, not one that required to be marked by them. Had it been what Melanthe detected on her, the scent of magic from another Dark Crafter?

"But I swear, they—"

"That is enough, Pen," Caiden interrupted sternly. He knew of them as well, but I did not question further and neither did Mal, we could not care what they were, just wanting to know she was well.

"Samuel, he came and saw me while you were away, the night you left for Arynth, he had just returned from Casmere," Penelope revealed, and the two friends crowded over her.

"What? Why did he come to you?" Caiden asked hurriedly.

"He...he gave me a letter for her. He had this look in his eyes, something was wrong—very wrong. He kept repeating that something was terribly wrong, like he'd seen the dead or...worse. My mother thought he'd gone mad, that the frost got to his Solaryan head. But I told her, Solaryans are not bothered by the cold either—"

Caiden grabbed her shoulders, startling her. "What letter? What was wrong? Speak."

"Cai, enough," Nia warned. "Come, Pen, try remembering all he said and did, please."

Penelope had fallen into a pit of overwhelm within herself and struggled to gather words to speak. "He didn't say much more, but the next morning after delivering the letter to me he had returned to Casmere and then...when he returned again, he'd gone fully mad. The servants said he killed twenty soldiers to get past the king, he tried to kill her father."

"Heavens," Nia murmured, covering her mouth in shock.

Cai shook his head. "That is not the Samuel I know."

"Why would he do something that mad?" my brother asked. "To kill Silas? What was he thinking and why?"

Pen rubbed her arms. "He...the servants think he was under craft."

I put a hand on her shoulder and her distressed attention rose to me. "Why would they think that? It doesn't look like an assumption from what I can tell from your shadows. You seem more certain than what you're saying."

She looked nervously around the corridors. "I...I am part Eldmoorian. My father was a Crafter." Her eyes shot wide between Mal and I. "But I am not a *Ybris*." She waved her hands down. "I don't think I am a Crafter either and my mother is din-Aura. I just felt...felt a veil masking Samuel's halo. You have heard what Samuel Raşar is, he is a legendary Glare whose powers failed him before twenty soldiers. He has killed mountain beasts and monsters and eudemons, but when he returned from the north, he was a shell of fear."

Fear. That was a Crafter's biggest power over others. They knew to creep in and search for them, and then push till they surfaced above all. He must have been under a craft veil. Veil of fear.

The redhead had stunned the two of us, however Caiden and Nia remained unimpressed. She took notice of it, too. "You don't seem surprised."

"We knew, Pen," Caiden revealed. "Snow does too. Your father was Alaric's friend."

She gaped in shock. "You did not tell me."

Was he the one who'd imprinted magic onto Snow? I shared a knowing look with my brother, but the two of us retreated from asking. Right now I did not care for any of it.

"Do you think it was Melanthe's magic she felt over Samuel?" I asked. Had they caught onto Snow's plans?

Nia crouched to the floor. "Could have been."

"What was in the letter?" Mal asked. "The one he gave you for Snow."

All of our attention went to the young servant once again. She shook her head in apology. "I don't know. Only she's read it."

"Did she start humming before or after opening it?" Caiden asked as if it was supposed to make some sort of sense.

She blinked confused and focused on the floor as she tried to recall. "After...after, I think."

The two friends exchanged a look before Nia took off, almost running down the corridor.

I didn't care what was on that letter or when she hummed or anything. I wanted to see her, hold her.

She had not come out all night, neither had we heard any noise come from inside her room. Nia stood continuously on standby, staring endlessly towards her room, waiting for any signal of emotion from Snow, waiting for the smallest reason to burst in her room, impatiently wanting to know how she was.

Despite the continuous thundering and the snow storm playing outside, the sun had finally started to brighten the new day behind clouds and Snow burst the doors of her room open, startling all of us to our feet. Dressed in one of her blue silk gowns, hair propped away from her face, with a tight-lipped smile adorning her face, she looked unphased. "Are the corridors that comfortable, why are all four of you camping out here?" she asked in her usual playful tone.

I was worried before, but now I was terrified of this exterior she was putting on. Her strong facade had rounded as her armour, becoming skin again.

"I am heading for breakfast, not war, dears, only one of you comes with me," she said and strode down the corridors. She had not joined her father for any meal since that day weeks ago. He had not broken her, but I did not fear that as much as I feared what she planned for him.

"I will go with her," I said, buttoning myself up and following after.

Caiden grabbed onto my arm before I left. "She is planning something, do not interfere unless you see her getting close to him. If she does, stop her. Her. Not him," he enunciated.

I nodded and fell right into her step.

She halted before the dining chambers and turned to face me. "You come in with me."

Before she could move toward the chambers, I pulled her tightly in my embrace, holding her and bathing in her presence. Her small hands smoothed over my back as my need for her grew tighter in my chest and all over my body.

"My love, my love. I am so sorry. So very sorry," I said, soaking as much of her as I could, my lips pressing to her head, neck and shoulder. How could anyone miss someone this much?

"It is okay."

"Mourn him, please, I beg of you, enough of this. Enough of this terrifying silence. Just mourn him, the one you cared for and loved and called family, please."

"Close your eyes, Kil," she almost whispered. "Today I am that monster again. It's dark around me."

I could not stop her. I had no right to do so. The only thing I could offer was to keep her safe. "I will be right beside you. I will not let anyone hurt you."

"They can only try, for they will find there is not much worse they can do."

She unravelled from me, giving me a short smile that never met those eyes that had now turned ice cold. It hurt me more to see her like this than anything else.

She had never let any of us enter with her before. Had I not known her the way I did, I would have thought she was scared.

Her father sat along with four others, a satisfied smirk on his face. Had he enjoyed his general's death that much or was his daughter's suffering he was feasting on?

I took a spot in the corner of the room along with two Isjordian soldiers, all tense as I was, ready as if expecting a battle to emerge from within the room.

She bowed and sat to his side.

"Your presence pleases me, my bud, I did not know I had to go through such great lengths to acquire it. Rest assured, I now know for future reference," he said half laughing.

My chest heaved from anger, but she gave him a pleasant smile. Upon it, her father's shadows halted, became grimmer and frustrated. Not the reaction he had expected. Now I understood her behaviour, she would not give her father the satisfaction.

"Oh, but no, father, I only came because dear Moreen deeply begged for me to return. She mentioned something along the lines of a loving arse. Wait, how was it now again, crone?" she asked, turning to the older woman sitting opposite her. The soldiers next to me giggled, silently shaking their heads.

"Do not speak to my mother like that," Reuben exclaimed. His shadows were all shades of anger, all intertwined with fear—he was terrified of Snow.

"Hush, half breed, you are to speak when permitted. Go fetch a bone or wag your tail at a guard. Moreen, as we were saying," Snow silenced him and turned to her prey again.

Her father did not seem to mind the banter, he did not interrupt either, only stared at her, probably trying to gather how she did not look an inch affected by what he had done. Snow looked like she knew what they all felt and played around with those emotions. She was in control, not the other way around. Even her father was wrapped around her despite what he had done. I could see it in her stance, this was her battle ground and they were all trapped in it.

The consort did not answer for a little while. "How was the Lord of Arynth, Snowlin? Did you leave him well?" she asked, avoiding the question. Similar to the rest she felt terrified of Snow, but she showed it the most and very plainly.

"Very well, I left him plump as an apple." She took a bite from an apple and Moreen choked on her drink. "He was not the only one I left well in Arynth though, your half breed's betrothed was there, too, deliciously plump as well," she said with a smirk.

I had missed the fact that her half-sister was betrothed to Elias.

"Elias was there as well? Did you meet with him, why?" the young blonde woman asked all angst.

Snow looked satisfied with their reaction. Licking her upper lip, she threw a wink at her, making the half-sister pale and her forehead crinkle with worried wrinkles.

"Father, how do you allow this?" the blonde girl pleaded half crying, but her father did not answer.

Snow teased her back with a mocking pout and the half sister began tearing up under a tissue.

This was the princess everyone knew, the one the Adriatians had seen and the one her father wanted to break to his will. I knew the princess and I knew Snow. They were the same and different at the same time. In Brogmere she had been both, in here she was the princess, with Caiden and Nia she was always Snow. I wanted to know who she had been with me. Because I wanted the whole of her, not the pieces that she chose to show.

"I was not aware you had grown so close with the Captain," her uncle said, sharing a look of suspicion with Silas.

"Close is one thing, uncle dearest, I prefer other words. Those like—"

Her father's loud fist hit the table, interrupting her. "Have respect for your sister, Snowlin."

She threw her head back laughing. "My sister is dead and bold of you to assume I care to respect any on this table," Snow calmly added, munching on a mouthful of grapes. She was such a wondrous sight when she ate. "And dead is the respect for the half breed, which by the way, how have you been feeling lately, dear? All well?" she questioned with a terrifying amused grin towards her.

They all looked at each other, worried and panicking, making Snow laugh.

Caiden was right, she had planned something.

Her half-sister's breathing suddenly went rapid and she turned to her mother for help. Cough took her chance for air. She stood up, terrified, blood now beginning to drip from her nose. Her mother screamed and Rueben unsheathed his sword towards Snow in threat who took much amusement in the pointless action—the man could barely hold up the steel.

She had poisoned her.

I did not move, didn't even think about interrupting.

Let her fight her own battles.

"What have you done?" Reuben shouted, waving his sword closer to her.

The consort barely managed to her feet, tears blanketing her hollow sea blue eyes. "I beg of you, undo what you did."

Snow laid back in her chair, grinning ear to ear. "That one was for Thora's broken ribs, you insufferable mellow bitch," she said, toasting a goblet in the air to her half-sister. Revenge, she was out for it. But this didn't feel like the empty of her tipping point, her cup had just filled.

"Everyone out, except you," her father said calmly to her before turning to the panicking three. "Take Fren to a healer, now."

Snow's amusement grew. Just as they were about to head out, Reuben fell to the floor and their mother screamed harder. Screeches of devastation and panic filling the room with shadows of anguish.

"And that one was for continuously breaking Eren's spirit, you insufferable wimp," Snow said, toasting again.

Silas stood, vibrating from rage. "What have you done?" his words echoed loudly, rolling further down the corridor and even making the doors rattle.

"The promised joy ride!" she exclaimed, standing to face him.

My body steeled, ready to pounce in front of her at the notice of Silas's murderous shadows of malice.

He moved to strike her, but she quickly grabbed onto his wrist before he could.

I flinched, barely holding myself still. The witch had dressed the castle in her craft, but I could still yield parts of magic. Widening my shadows till they reached under Silas, I held the trap ready in case he thought of any other trick. Snow had this and I had her.

He was panting, everyone had left besides us and the soldiers. Ice began forming along the walls in their direction and my heart grew in fear for her.

"You fed me violence, father, swallow when I feed you repercussions. Don't choke on crumbs of consequence, I've got a whole feast prepared for you."

"How dare you!"

"You see, I have come to realise that I am, after all, just the same as you," she spat, and the ice halted as if by command—just not his. "Did your little soft head think you could mess with me? Whatever you have done to me is what I have allowed, this one was out of my calculations. But rest assured, you will receive the same coin for it. I know you care more for your underwear than those half breeds, but I do enjoy seeing you like this, it fills me with such pleasure."

"I am going to send you to Adriata in ribbons, alive enough to marry their king. I do not care if you die the next second."

She laughed and tightened her grip on his wrist, hard enough her black gloves had turned white around her knuckles. "Then I will do just what I aimed, let dear Fren and Reuben die. One that is your heir and the other you intend to use to keep Ivar Venzor in your clutches. Everyone knows just how much he likes your little dais." She stopped and got closer to him. "He would be a good king don't you think, father?"

"Do not threaten me, child!" he shouted.

"Oh no threat, I don't do threats, but do you know of the little delicious poison I just used?" she provoked, raising a brow. "Well, you couldn't have known, I paid the Dark Crafter enough to feed a city. Blood craft poison. It's actually very easy to find the antidote, you just have to figure whose blood it was. A little hint of kindness, it was not mine or anyone you know, which I of course will give you once I have married into Adriata, away from you. The little red-haired witch you've sent to Seraphim might help to prove the theory, so be my guest."

I had never seen Silas' shadows like now, they filled the entire room black in fury deeper than the colour of nothing. She did not deserve them, he had done enough on his part to deserve what she served to him. The ice coating thickly the walls cracked and blasted in small shards.

Satisfied in her victory, she let him and turned to exit the dining chambers, her steps halting at the crackling dark laugh echoing from Silas in flagitious gales of ire.

"You will bend, Snowlin Krigborn, one day you will bend. Wherever you are I will make sure to break every last bit of you, to melt and forge you into steel that I will wield to my desire. You will do my bidding till the day you leave this realm. I will be your end." A vile promise made to his own daughter whose features had turned the shape of hurt before sternness took place once again.

"You cannot bend what has been forged in the fire of courage, wrath and inhumanity fed by you. You made me unwieldable with your own hands, sharpened my edges thin to become this. So I dare you, father, to try and do so. I want to see your hands bleed deep trying to wield me. I want to watch you bleed every time you hold me and use me, because I am no simple weapon, I am double edged," Snow challenged.

His hand lifted toward her. "I will if I get to see you subdued."

Swiftly I faded between them, freezing his shadows in place along with him. "You touch her one more time, Adriata will send their part of the deal in shreds, and I will tear you to ribbons right here, right in front of her," I threatened.

Guards behind me unsheathed their swords and Verglasers took position to protect their king.

Lifting a wall of shadows around, I trapped us together inside. My limbs trembled at the feel of life feeding my magic. The craft veil around the castle had cut the flow of spiritual mana. I had rarely relied on my life mana before, except from training, never to this degree.

"Do you understand what you have just done, Adriatian? A foreign guard, holding me under magic and threatening me? How do you dare?" Silas shouted wide eyed at my actions.

"Just like that. Play nice, Silas, don't make me test your might. It's more fragile than many think. Take a look. One thought separates me from horns blaring to announce your death."

He laughed roughly before a sneer lifted in his face. "I will have you hung, your ashes spread over hers."

His daughter was right, he did rely on threats to hide shame. "Brave words for a king who signed a treaty of peace with two guards which he allowed himself into this kingdom. No harm shall come to them while they protect the princess from whatever harm comes her way. Your words, not mine. Break it and let's see if you will have that agreement after all. Or any after that. With any kingdom at all." I knew he was very persistent on this deal, he had tried for years and insisted on all sorts of arrangements, his words were empty.

Lowering my shadows, I moved back and he signalled his guards to lower their weapons. Snow had frozen still, staring blankly at me.

"Well then, aren't you efficient in protecting my daughter. But do that again and no treaty shall hold me back," Silas added, taking a seat again and finishing his breakfast as though nothing had happened.

"She is no daughter of yours, but she is to be my queen. Threaten her again and no Highwall will keep Adriata away from you."

He scoffed with disregard at my words, and I felt the tip of Snow's fingers grazing my back just lightly, prompting me to retreat, so I did as asked.

His promise rung loud on my ears and heavy on my bones. I'd never felt such power and damage from words. She was all mighty, but she was still just human made of flesh and bones. It was not easy to hurt her, but it was easy to injure her enough to make her suffer.

She walked the castle walls silently and slowly, her shoulders and back were moving up and down rapidly, guided by her hard breaths. Her fingers coiled into a fist, blue gloves starting to run ruby dark. I followed behind, too afraid to hold and grab her, it felt like she would melt away if I did.

She stumbled and fell to her knees, her hands shaking and her breaths furious. Lifting a blood coated hand signalling not to help, she tried to stand herself up.

I could no longer help it seeing her like that. Despite her protest, I wrapped my arms around her waist and hoisted her up, feeling her whole body trembling and her bursting heartbeat pound everywhere. One moment. I'd give her a moment and then I'd panic and run to a healer. Burying my head on her neck, I held her for minutes long. Was I comforting her or me? I did not want to lose her to herself, the princess was also Snow, and right now both of them were slipping away from me.

I soaked in her flowery scent and warmth till she took a final deep breath and stopped trembling. "You are an idiot," she bit out with force, making me smile.

"I am, but you have stolen my heart, so now I am *your* idiot."

"He could have had you killed there."

If it only was that easy to kill me. "And I would have died head high protecting you."

She turned, her brows narrowed and angry before slapping me across my face, and then jumping to wrap her arms around my neck.

"Say ridiculous things like that one more time and I swear, Kilian whatever your surname is, I will end you."

"You said you would cut up my balls and feed them to me."

"No, I need you to have those for a while longer. Maybe I might actually get you to use them." Her lips grazed the shell of my ear causing shivers to erupt at the back of my neck. Pulling back just a little, she planted about a dozen pecks on my cheek.

Never knew hearts ever felt that much warmth, I learnt it only today.

"Come, my little kitten," I said, slapping her bottom and putting her down. "Let's tend your hands first, you can purr and lick me all you want afterward."

She sighed and unravelled from me. "And I'm a cat now."

"I will call for a healer," I said when we entered her room.

"No, don't. I am fine." Her voice was schooled to strength and coldness, but she was not fine. Fine, was the dirtiest four-letter word starting with an F and that was beating the word fair and fail, and another one Snow liked to use.

"Nia then, or Penelope," Anyone being there was enough, enough not to leave her alone and slip to her self-destructive ways.

"No, all is fine, do not call either of them. I just need a bit of rest."

I did not insist anymore and left.

38

Spring and Promises

Snowlin

I HAD WORKED THE plan all night to distract myself from giving in to my overflowing emotions.

Alaric had sneaked vials of blood craft poison before I left for Isjord.

You will never know when you could need them, just do not use them on your father. I will not use my blood to heal that one bastard, he had said, placing the vials in my satchel.

But someone else had used it. Memphis was not only my guardian creature, but one of my best spies. She had dropped the poison onto their clothing this morning, it did not need to be ingested and that was why it came with its price and rarity. Alaric was one well connected man, he knew almost every Dark Crafter in Eldmoor—and the only few who were willing to bear the cost of blood craft.

I reached under my pillow again as I had continuously done for the past couple of days. His last words to me, delivered by Pen the morning after his death. The cerulean coloured envelope smelled of the sea and salt, lingering with Sam's presence. I felt my throat clog, my eyes welling hot, but I refused to cry. Not now. When I would avenge his death, then I would be allowed to cry. I did not deserve to mourn him.

A thin silver chain with a small white sun stone fell out.

"I picked this from a Solaryan merchant, it reminded me of you. Wear it when being alive feels right and when there is no hate corrupting your heart. Let's head out on a spring morning to see the first light. The stone glistens at the touch of sunrise." – Sam.

Oh, Sam. But I've lost you.

My breath stuttered, clutching his gift and I swallowed down on that cry. Sunrises were now my new curse, part of new nightmares. Sam was dead, his memories were now my torture. He was dead, gone, because of...me. What if it will never feel right, Sam? How many battles would I have to fight and how many more would I lose? My heart could never be uncorrupted by hate, my bleeding palms were proof of it.

He threatened to bend and break me despite all he had already done. It was not enough for him, he wanted more, he was hungry for it, for my pain. He might as well have already bent and broken me, but I also intended to keep to my words to make him bleed. For the love of irony, the only hands that were bleeding were my own.

I peeled my gloves gently to not let them rub with the wounds and headed towards the bathroom sink to wash them. The warm water more than soothed the skin, it dug on my wounds, giving a stabbing sensation. I had been so immersed in the pain from the wounds that I'd not noticed Kilian standing beside me and I startled out of my skin.

He held a salve bottle and white gauze in his hands and raised a brow. "I knocked."

I blinked back surprise. "You did?"

"Would you like me to go knock again?"

I gave him a push and he went behind me, his body pressing to mine as he washed my bloodied hands gently over the sink, delicately tracing his thumb over the fresh wounds to clean them. He kissed the back of my head and guided me to a stool so he could apply salve and wrap my palms in the gauze. Being nursed was another thing I disliked, but I would dig new wounds for him to wrap all over again. I studied his features so carefully and closely while he was busy tending my hands. If my hands had not been wrapped in a thousand layers of cloth, I would have traced my fingers along his tall nose, his dark eyebrows and his thick lips.

He smoothed lines on top of my bandaged palms and threw me a pained gaze. "It is difficult to feel all of that and hold it without any means of release. I cannot tell you to control or stop it, but can I help you find a way out of hurting the one I care about?"

His words sent a hot flush across my cheeks.

It hurt when I did it, but it hurt less than what I felt, and that temporary physical pain dragged me out of the deeper emotional one. I have been doing it for so long that I have forgotten how to stop. "It is difficult sometimes to ground myself and not act on what I feel, and Kil, I feel so much, too much, that no one would be alive in this kingdom if I did release them," I admitted.

His hand smoothed over the side of my head. "We will find a way to prevent you from committing genocide," he said, making me laugh. "And to keep you from hurting you. There are enough who want to do just that, it feels unfair for you to be your own evil on top of everything. Pain cannot override pain, Snow, let's find something else that does."

He was right. I straightened myself and my features, weakness was not a good look on me. I did not like showing that side to anyone, especially the one in front of me. "Mal is—"

Knowing my line of thought, he interrupted me, "Stubborn woman, stop fighting me away with those methods. I know you enough to see through them."

He stood, drawing me a bath, sprinkling questionably all sorts of salts and scents inside all while stealing glances of confirmation toward me.

"I am not a tea bag," I said, lifting my severely wrapped hands. "With these on, the best I can get out of my hands is to beat you." He had taken it too far by wrapping them like inch deep war wounds, such a dramatic Adriatian. Mal was right, he did make a lot of fuss.

I took a step back when he removed his jacket and started folding the sleeves of his tight white tunic. He took soft paces towards me, teasing me with a smirk. "I am not cruel, my love, as to leave you to struggle as such."

I shook my head. "First time you will see me naked won't be to be scrubbed clean, that I won't allow." I wanted him to join me in a bath, not give me one like a wounded child.

He unbuttoned his collar and gave me one of them teasing looks. "How should I see you naked for the first time?"

I blew a breath. "Red lace and possibly under you, over you, on top you, riding you. You get my point."

He laughed and shut his eyes for a brief moment. "There, I saw you naked in red lace, over, under and on top of me. Now, do you need to be striped as well?" he teased, playing with strands of my hair, curling them around his fingers.

I crossed my arms tight over my chest in resistance and he grinned like a fool. "Pardon my rudeness, love," he said, leaning in over my shoulder and reaching to unbutton my dress. "I should have offered, given your poor condition."

"Smug bastard," I murmured, and he laughed over the skin of my neck. Once the last button snapped open, he ran his fingers over my spine before peeling it from my skin without losing my gaze—even as the dress dropped pooling to my feet, leaving me naked. But then again, the bandages hid my hands plenty for someone to be called mildly clothed.

"You can look. I told you I am no shy blushing maiden."

He grazed a finger over my temple. "I think the most undressed I have seen you has been with words." He glanced between us and over my body shortly. "Though I have to admit, I had been wrong to think that was the best naked I've seen."

I slapped his shoulder and he laughed. I could no longer hide the effects of that sound over my skin, the prickling and the changed pace of heartbeat shifting my chest. All I could think of was his body over mine, his lips over mine. I wanted him to have me, however he wanted.

"Kil?"

"Yes?" he answered absently, staring all over me with savouring relish.

"If I bathe in cold water, you will eat snow out of my spoon for a week."

"Shivering threat," he said, tracing a finger over my arm and realising I was indeed shivering. Worry swept his features in seconds. "I didn't mean to get you to prickle from the cold, let's get you in."

"It's not the cold, it's you," I said shamelessly.

He halted his movement and stared at me so wondrously his irises shimmered like sun glitter over the clearest of waters.

"Enough with the staring."

He gripped my face with a hand, pressing his forehead on mine. "Enough making my heart beat madly."

I was naked, extremely bothered, wet and an inch away from stripping him naked to give me more than a bath. Except there was that little agreement. So I inhaled deep, as deep as I could, to tuck the frustration down and cleared my throat. "My, uhm, my bath."

He rubbed his palms over my arms, moving away. "Now you are cold."

"No, still you."

He smiled and bit his lip, pointing to the bath.

My arms hung on the sides of the bath to keep my wrapped hands dry, my head had propped back at the rest, the warmth of water always relaxed me thoroughly. Kilian took a stool and sat next to me, slowly running his hands with soap on my hair, his fingers massaging my scalp so delicately that my eyes rolled up from pleasure.

"Fuck, your hands are heavenly. Have you considered a change in profession?"

"To massage women's heads? No, but I'll take consideration after your suggestion."

I spun in his direction, soap bubbles floated around from force. "Women? What women? Woman, me, singular."

"Ah," he taunted, all low tones and dark chuckles, popping bubbles on my cheek. "Jealous?"

"Let me be, it won't be for long."

I saw the shift in his pulse and the wither in his expression. "What about after? Will you not be jealous then? I know I will."

"Love her, Kil," I barely murmured out. "Make sure whoever will be after me—make sure to love her. I don't wish to be jealous of a passing desire. Make my jealousy worth having."

"How can you ask that of me when you are so warm in my heart? Imagine me with someone else when even I can't."

I had no answer for him, only words that would have him debate with me.

He rinsed my hair and sat silently beside me, staring. More like gazing like one gazed at stars.

I leaned forward, resting my arms on my knees, so close to him that spring blossomed again a third time today. "Maybe, just maybe, one day you might actually stare me to death, you Adriatian bastard."

He smiled that maddening smile. If he was not going to stare me to death he would smile me to it. He traced the scar on my face with his thumb, its presence had not bothered me but somehow it felt heavy when he slowly dragged his fingers along the sides of it. "I cannot help it, only seeing you scarcely during the day is not nearly enough. I want to take in as much detail as I can. It feels like every time I get to hold you—you might melt away like snow out of my touch, away from me."

"The reason I melt, my spring, it's that you are too warm," I said, nudging his nose with mine. "But never away from you."

"You undo me, woman," he breathed over my lips. "When you speak your mind, you undo me." He slid his hand to my neck, his thumb tracing the rest of my scar and my skin pebbled at the touch of his rough fingers, a gasp escaping my lips. My rapid heartbeat shifted the bath water slightly when his hand moved slowly further down to my breasts. "My weakness," he said, the top of his fingers grazing my nipple and then traced the rest of the breast curve before his head dipped down to suck on the hardened centre. His tongue teased my flesh and he murmured, "Who would have thought these made my knees weak more than any monster or fear."

"I-I thought we said none of this. Not that I'm complaining."

"There is no need for kissing or for my cock to be inside you to please you, woman," he murmured between kisses he trailed along my neck while his hand palmed and kneaded my breast.

I lifted a bandaged hand to cover my moan, but he pulled it down. "I want to hear you, that would be for my side of the pleasure."

His fingers played with my aching breasts, but once his mouth took their place, his hand moved further down over my stomach, down my hip and thigh before snaking back up to my lower stomach and drawing lazy circles and lines. A map of teases.

"Kilian, gods," I moaned or begged, perhaps even prayed.

In answer, his hand lowered to my centre and I flinched at the contact. My limbs spread to surrender to the rippling pleasure building all over my body, my breath its servant. Fingers circled excruciatingly slowly over my sensitive skin and I moaned and writhed.

His other hand gripped my chin to force me meet his gaze that had veiled with shadows, before his head dipped lower sucking on my breast, making me hiss in pleasure. "I don't think I'll ever forget this, your sound," he murmured over my puckered skin.

I bit my lower lip to control my breath. Wrapping my arms over his neck, I rested my head on his shoulder. He kissed the top of my head, the shell of my ear, nipping gently and then my shoulder. Vibrations of warmth chilled my skin.

"Did you know I can preserve an emotion inside me?"

"As much... as I like...the lesson," I breathed out in pants while he licked the column of my neck, "save it for when you are not about to teach me another."

He laughed over my lips, planting a kiss just at their edge and I felt the electricity of that kiss everywhere. "What I meant to say was, that it would be useful. You know, at night times."

I cried a bit in frustration. "Fuck you."

"Ladies first," he said, sinking a digit deep inside me. His thumb teasing that throbbing spot, drawing circles while he thrusted in and out of me. I bit his shoulder trying to muffle out my moan, slow and deep he continued pumping them and then adding a second finger inside.

Not enough, barely enough. It was him I wanted inside me.

"Fuck, Snow, you would have taken me so well." His lips curved lightly in a smile over my ear, knowing what every word did to me. "You would have taken me so, so well."

His movement became harder and rougher, his other hand over my shoulder and caressing my back. He held me in his arms as I was slowly falling apart, shattering in my pleasure. He torturously ran his lips over the skin of my shoulder and then my ear as he whispered words that sent me to oblivion.

My hand fell to his arm, muscles strung hard on my grip as I moved my hips to match the motion of his hands. "Shit, Kil."

"That's it, ride my fingers, love." His lips twitched to a smile over my neck before he bit my skin softly. "Tasty, so tasty. I could bet you're as sweet as nectarines." He kissed the aching spot and I gasped, air met my lungs too fast and not nearly enough.

I could feel the tension build in my core, wanting release as he continued thrusting tortuously inside me. I moaned over and over, till I was left calling down on all gods and their heavens in between.

"My name, I want to hear you moan my name when I make you come."

"Kil...Kilian."

"Good girl. Like that."

I wrapped my arms tight around him as pleasure built inside me and released, sending sparks flying in my sight. "Oh, gods!" Panting out of breath, I rested my head on his shoulder. He held me there, his fingers gently stroking my back, his mouth leaving soft pecks over my shoulder, murmuring whispers of teases and gentle words of caress till my breathing grew back to normal.

He kissed my ear and whispered, "I believe heavens owe me some thanks, it appears I've guided you back to the path of gods."

I slapped his shoulder, moving away from him. "I hate you."

"Yeah?" He laughed and laughed, till it echoed so far up my ears it was the only thing I could remember. His laughter was just as springy as him. I wanted it only for myself, for no one else to hear it but me. To bloom my seasons of gloom to light and warmth.

"I want you," I blurted, half still over my head at what had happened. His teases were to blame, all I could think about was him buried deep in me.

His hand gripped the small of my neck and he rested his forehead on mine—darkened eyes and raging breath. "And you have no idea how much I want you. I want to hear you moan my name with something else of mine inside you. I want to taste you, I want your pretty cunt in my face until I am breathless. And you would be begging more than gods. I would have not taken you slow and sweet, Snow. I would have marked and fucked you till you would never have forgotten who you belonged to." Every part of me curled and tingled at that. The vibration of his frustrated goran against my neck sent prickling jolts all over me, the warm feeling building on my lower stomach again. "To my torture, it can't happen and you know it."

I groaned, dropping my head back. "I curse the gods for the moment I agreed to those words."

"No, you don't, my heart, you will thank them."

"Promises are meant to be broken."

He scowled. "Not mine. If I ever have you it will be with you knowing all of me, not just who you have seen here. I am not one to profit from a situation and I want no regrets if I make you mine."

He didn't know that for all I cared he had already made me his, since that day in Arynth. "So much protocol, heavens," I said, moving away from him and dipping further in the water.

"I will not fuck you for the sake of it. If I do, it will be because you are mine."

I am yours, gods be damned.

He inhaled deeply and stood, kissing the top of my head before grabbing a towel and motioning for me to stand. He wrapped it under my arms and hoisted me out from the bath as if I was made of feathers not heavy bones. Lowering me down gently, he removed the towel to dry my body, leaving me completely naked in front of him. He dried my back and then my front, kissing my breasts as he went further down my stomach, planting another one there, another on my sex and one on each of my thighs.

His hands roamed around my midriff where the scars of my back peeked through.

"Do they still bother you?" I asked.

He sighed, resting his forehead on my belly. "They have never bothered me, the bastard that has done them does."

I held him there, lacing my fingers through his hair. "He will suffer for them."

"I heard what you did to him, to his family."

"See what I'm capable of doing. How capable I make myself to be hated."

"You know I don't like that, but I also am not you and not one to judge." He kissed my stomach one more time and stood facing me. "And not one who would have let that animal breathe after what I heard that day."

I had forgotten he was there. Some embarrassment creeped to my ears all of a sudden. After I'd seen Cai and Mal hold him back, I had wanted to swallow myself. I hated what he'd heard.

His finger circled the scar on my shoulder from the time in Kirkwall. "Why do you not heal them?"

A wave of disappointment washed over me. "You hate them that much?" Were they that ugly?

He sighed, shaking his head. "I cannot love what reminds me of your pain."

Relief. I kissed his hand. "They are my strength, too."

He kissed my brow in return. "You are strong, my love, here," he said, pointing to my heart and then to my head, "and there. Don't remind yourself how you crawled to survive, but how you rose from that survival. Bear the triumphs of your victory, not of those that aimed to bring you down."

I tugged his jacket till he was pressed to me. His honey mouth was torturous. "Enough, I am yours already. Enough enchanting me, you prick."

He smiled gradually, teasing my lips with his thumb. "Are you smitten with me, miss dark head?"

I frowned. He called me all there was in the dictionary. "Terribly, mister smart arse." Leaning against him, I reached and cupped his behind. "Correction, mister tight arse."

"Heavens and seven hells," he groaned, dropping his head back. "Give me patience no man has ever asked before."

"Heavens and seven hells," I said as he did, "let him fall for my enchantment."

"You wicked woman," he accused, dabbing the towel violently to my hair.

"Tie this, please," I asked, fiddling about with the robe tie, my hands impaled in bandages. Could swear he had done this on purpose.

"Better not. It looks better like that anyway," he pointed, tilting his head to my open gown and I hit him with a brush.

"You have no right to this, remember all the shit you sang for me a moment ago?"

He laughed and tied my robe severely slowly and loosely, until I hit him again.

It was growing dark outside. Kilian had positioned himself in a corner of my room watching me brush my hair, looking tired and worn out. He had stayed guard for almost two nights without sleep and helped me bury Samuel. I had not attended the funeral they had organised, I did not deserve to be there. When I went, it would be with the blood of those that caused his death in my hands, with the blood of my father spread across my sword in his honour. And then I would plead for Samuels forgiveness and send him to the heavens he deserves to rest at. With Samuels death in my hands, my plate had become overbearingly hard to balance. I had so much to do, to dig out of my father's well of lies and secrets, yet here I was, almost two weeks away from being sent off to Adriata without a grain of any information on his plans. To make matters worse, I was infatuated with a man who was not just any man and certainly not my husband to be. The same idiot who was about to turn himself into the living dead because he wanted to stare at me for eternity. Not a usual stare, one that had raised my temperature enough that I was sweating. This was very frustrating.

"Nubil's heaven, leave or fuck me, otherwise cut that."

He did not even bat an eyelid at my frustration, except the gradual growing smirk in his ridiculously handsome face. "So impatient and so needy, my *dahaara*. I hope you stay like that. It gets me really hard."

I did not like the tease or whatever game he was trying to play to test my patience. Little did he know I was shameless. I would make that first move myself, strip and rip him apart, promise or no promise. "Prick, your left hand shall be very jealous of your right these next few weeks then."

"I'm ambidextrous, love, that means you will be jealous of both my hands."

I turned round and threw about a hundred combs and pins at him till I was left panting and him laughing his tight arse out.

After several attempts to persuade Kilian to rest, he had given up when Mal and Nia showed up and dragged him out to his chambers. He had stared longingly as though we were not to see each other for lifetimes when he had been taken out, the ridiculous man.

Just as the half dead spirit left, Pen came to bring me the dress Moreen had picked for the Solstice ball. The one I'd completely forgotten was only a day away. An event that I hated, one carried only to insult the memory of my family. Tomorrow would be the thirteenth anniversary of their deaths, yet my father danced around chandeliers and stuffed his stomach with candy while others served him exalt.

"Well," Pen said in a grimace, while both of us studied the contraption the crone picked for me to wear. "At least it's not a funny yellow or green."

Layers of white lace, tule, almost a skirt that seemed like five, trumpet sleeves that widened about two feet, a neckline climbing up almost to the jaw that could make nuns and monks appear immodest. Now that I saw it in more vivid detail, I'd take a green or a yellow dress with no questions.

"Pen, swear me an oath to tear it, burn it and then have a royal painter paint a middle finger with the ashes for Moreen as my farewell gift."

She blinked, almost stunned for a moment. "Framed...or just the canvas?"

"Whatever suits your relish."

"What will you wear?" she asked, taking the insulting dress down from the hanger. "If you will go naked, please let me salute my mother before my hanging."

"Severely tempted. However, have you come over my mother's wedding dress in her chambers?" It was an Olympian dress, one of the most beautiful one's ever seen. A plain white silk ball gown coming in a tight shape around the torso and dropping to thick layers and skirts of hidden tule, and the long sleeves were cropped from the bust, exposing the shoulders like wings of star spirits. I would always make mother try it on for me to admire its beauty and hers with it.

"Yes, I often take it out to admire it. The white silk is blazing. It would look fantastic on you, good thinking," she said, before leaving for the garment.

When she returned she was jumping around happily at her find. The dress had not been damaged, but I was about to alter it slightly.

Pen had almost cried at my request but had done as told, nonetheless.

The whole morning the castle vibrated in movement and buzzed with preparations of the ball celebration, as per usual my father would have put all the riches he owed to prepare for it. He liked boasting greatly about his thirty years as a ruler to everyone, particularly foreign emissaries. The Solstice ball, an unnecessary holiday to welcome the coming winter. Before, the season was a blessing from their god, but seeing it had become more a burden to their lands compared to advantage, more and more had chosen to forsake the celebration, thinking winter a curse rather than a blessing. The royals kept the tradition more as a celebration of their rule than anything spiritual. The concept was not even the worst part of it. Everyone was to be dressed in white to symbolise the snow and ate white sweets and danced around a white adorned conifer tree for a whole night.

Cai entered my room dressed in an all-white uniform, which judging from his face he did not enjoy as much as I was. "Pen made us all dress like dead spirits. She should applaud herself for the job, I look dashing nonetheless," he exclaimed, spinning around. He did look dashing and handsome.

"You are a peacock, you know?"

"A handsome one." He studied me for a moment. "You look better, how is the heart?"

I could not answer, but my silence seemed to have offered him my reply.

"Soon we will go home. A couple more weeks, Cakes, and this will all be over. The Lords are falling into line one by one, once you bound the bargain with Silas, we move to Adriata. Isjord will stew in their end and Adriata will soon prepare for theirs."

I offered him a smile and a nod before heading onto my dressing chambers, though now a stone weighed inside my heart. Penelope coiled my hair to the back of my head and placed a gold crown adorned in red rubies atop my head as well as a matching set of large earrings. They were my mother's wedding crown and jewellery.

I looked complete already, but the red rubied jewellery and crown were not the main attraction—my mother's dress fitted me to perfection. I took Pen's word that I looked something beyond beautiful and then pulled the long gloves over my arms to conceal several blood oaths I'd made.

Cai gawked like a dead fish and I rolled my eyes. "Collect your eyes, you will need them for a while longer."

"You look beautiful, Cakes, you always do."

We both headed towards the winter garden. The other three were to wait for me at the entrance of the ball room because I wanted to see my mother, Eren and Thora first.

Cai collected three red roses for me which I used to replace the old ones already there. Another year, another solstice that I had spent speaking into the nothingness and now to their graves. My heart wept and continued to pierce hard, but was unsure what exactly it was feeling. Anger, love and vengefulness were tangled in such a bunch. Right now I was everything but empty, quite the opposite, my vessel filled to such a level it was not only tipping, it was flooding my surroundings. Before they could take over, I had to shut them down.

Every year I allowed myself to make a wish on this day. "One last time, gods and heavens, please let this all be a nightmare, let me wake up in their arms and with their voices around me. Please," I pleaded hard before them.

And as every year, gods and heavens forbid that wish tonight, too.

39

SOLSTICE AND SWEETS

KILIAN

ANXIOUSNESS HAD NOT FLED my body since being told about this ridiculous ball. One more place for her to be surrounded by danger—one more place for her to become dangerous and provoke her father again. If one asked me, I'd keep the both of us in her room till the day of the agreement, till when she would bid us goodbye.

"Should one of us go and look for her? She should have been here a while ago now," Mal said, pacing back and forth the corridor.

We were to meet Snow and Caiden at the hall entrance, but they were taking longer than what was planned. Both of them were capable enough to fend the whole castle so my anxiousness was not severe despite Mal's words. But I did regret not staying with her before and letting Caiden take a shift to escort her to us. I'd considered breaking that promise, too, when she had sat calmly brushing her black silken hair, severely tempting me to gather her in my arms and make her moan my name louder and harder till the new day grew.

"She will come," Nia said, looking out the massive windows in wonder, rays of sadness circling around her chest. "It is the anniversary of their deaths today, she has gone to visit them first."

I gathered my face in my hands, angry at myself. How had I forgotten. The winter solstice was the day that Isjord was attacked and her family killed, thirteen years from today. Along with the death of Samuel, she was still mourning theirs.

Nia stood and smiled towards the corridor, drawing our attention as well.

Snow came into view, dressed in a black gown, a ruby crown atop her head. She looked astonishing, truly like a queen. Her beauty shone beyond that, radiating as strong of a warrior as she did a queen, her eyes were sad but covered with bright sunlight beams. They were like the sun. To me they were the sun.

"Now I feel like a fool, I thought the dressing requirements were white?" Mal grumbled, and they all laughed.

"I thought that was a regular thing for you, Mal?" Nia asked.

My brother blinked confused. "What is?"

"Feeling like a fool."

"Very funny, Nia, next time I might tell you to fade in the middle of the ocean."

"Now, now, children," Caiden called, throwing his arms around both their necks. "Inside we get, I don't want my face to go to waste another moment."

"I will only have one of you trail me. I am not the mother wolf to lead all of you with me," Snow said.

I stepped forward and everyone agreed for me to stay close guard with her.

Only the two of us were left in the corridor, waiting to enter the celebrations, but my feet did not move. And I stood there, admiring all of her instead, the crown, the red lips, down to the last fray of the black dress.

She moved to me and tapped my nose as I had done before to her. "My spring," she said, playfully bowing her head. "You look dashing in white."

"My heart," I responded, leaning in and planting a kiss on her neck and then another on her shoulder. I loved hearing her gasp under my touch. "Black is your colour, too. Naked, however, was better."

Her smile dropped. "Shall we forfeit my attendance? I did not feel like joining anyway. I was thinking of a smaller celebration with only me, you and less clothes. Preferably in different locations and several positions."

Her joke made me rumble with laughter. I grazed a thumb over her fiery red lips, how I wanted to smudge that colour. "You will not break me, love. I'm a soldier, trained to not fall into traps, especially such easy ones as your pretty self." My hands moved over her hair. "*Maa maroh maalya omorya,*"

A scowl formed in her brows. "What new nickname have you graced me with?"

I traced the dip between her brows, her angry expression always made me smile. "My black haired beauty."

She smoothed a hand over her head. "I have been told it's rather ominous for a hair colour."

I ran my hand over her arm. "Rather magnificent to my eyes." She had no idea.

She studied me intently, her features dropped and her hand fell down to her side as if my words did not settle well with her. "I warn you, don't fall for me, Kil. Your heart is too pretty to break, darling." There was no teasing in her voice, but their seriousness did not bother me, nor did the warning.

It was too late. It had always been late, the moment I stepped in Isjord, the moment I had seen her at the trials, maybe...maybe even long before that. So long before that.

"It's yours, do what you will with it. Do what you will with me if I break yours, I deserve your worst."

She wore a short smile that didn't last, not even a heartbeat. "Already thinking of getting on the wrong side of me?"

"I have always been on the wrong side of you. I fear I still am, my love. Fate is cruel, so very cruel."

She took a small step back and swallowed hard, not wanting to meet my eyes. "I set this recipe for disaster. I shouldn't have encouraged this any further."

I closed our distance, cupping her face. "If you hadn't, it would have killed me, to never know what this feels, what lo—"

Her hand covered my mouth, stopping me from finishing my sentence. "Don't, please. Don't say that. I can't hear it," she pleaded, shaking her head. Exhaling a long stuttering heavy breath, her face twisted shortly in a slight cry before taking a shaky inhale and lifting her gaze up to me again. "Can it not just be this sometime longer, for what we have left? I don't want my head to spin those words and avoid you. I want you near me as much as I can have you." She swallowed hard and whispered, "Before...before I lose you."

Lose you. I would lose her too. "Whatever you want, my love." I was a beggar at the mercy of cruel fate.

She rested her head on my chest, tugging me in a tight embrace, so tight her fingers dug into my back. I felt the battle with herself going in her head. Fate was indeed cruel, crueller than she would ever imagine. We both stayed like that for a while, a very long while. Endorsed completely in our presence and scattered thoughts, barely taking notice of Mal approaching us.

"Yes, brother?" I asked, and Snow raised her head from my chest in the direction of my brother.

He studied both of us, his attention lingering over me most as sadness flashed in his own shadows, probably reading over my troubled ones. "Your father is getting fidgety. Cai says it's ringworms, but his shadows say it's because of you."

The three of us laughed at his joke, but Snow remained still tightly attached to me.

"You two planning to stick to each other like that all night? Should have stayed in your bedroom."

My miss scowled. "No use, he refuses to sleep with me or even kiss me for that matter. Made me agree to a deal. Had I let him, he would have asked to have it in writing and signed."

"Forgive him. His sense of righteousness is second skin."

I sighed at their remarks. "I stand right here, you know?"

"Is it only me or is his frustration severely pleasurable?" she said, ignoring me.

"Discovered the biggest gift of nature, I see," Mal answered and she raised a hand to smack palms with my brother.

As I had expected, every head in the blinding white hall turned when she marched to its centre, her attire stood out, but it was her presence that had all their attention. Crystals hung from all over the ceiling in the shapes of snowflakes. White dust floated in the air, resembling snow—all magic and illusions, nothing real. And all in white, guests from overfitted the hall and parted as Snow passed through to the white dais centred in the middle of the celebrations, resembling a citadel. Many bowed and greeted her as she went to face the dais where her father was sitting, dressed all in white like the rest of the attendees. His consort, Moreen, and his two other children were missing from his side, still affected by the blood craft poison Snow had used.

"Father," she greeted, bowing before him.

Silas's eyes drew wide, almost in horror at her sight. She only wore a black dress not murdered a village of younglings. Her father had his dramatic ways, after all he was the Isjordian ill-famed king.

"Is that—" he started struggling for words.

"Mother's wedding dress? Indeed, your memory works better than I had thought," Snow answered.

My eyes jumped to her, almost resembling in surprise to her father's.

Silas's shadows engorged from anger and pulsed with a flicker of hurt that I had not seen before in him. "What have you done to it?" he demanded, almost maimed of memory—memory of his wife.

"Only dyed it the colour it should have originally been, had she known she was entering her death-trap when she married you," she answered, making her way to the seat next to her father's.

He had found her words as biting as I did as there was no other feeling circling him but hurt now. Snow had really managed to wound her father after all. She seemed to think her father did not care for her or anyone, but I had witnessed him go through emotions she had not felt or seen from him. He did a good job at hiding them. Sometimes they hid so far behind his dominating feelings of anger, resentment, boredom and frustration, that they were often no more than a minute speck. So he had truly loved his queen.

"Where is your pretty witch, father? Call her out, bring her from the dead again, you have already done it once," Snow provoked without missing a beat.

"I have warned you too many times, haven't I? Keep your head out of my business."

Snow clicked her tongue. "How can I when your business is so tasty."

"The aftertaste will be bitter, young rose," he threatened, a tone away from shouting.

"Then I will chase it with some honey." She turned to him in her seat. "How did you do it, how did you bring her from the Otherworld? Your friends from the burning hells helped?"

Her father's face twisted with a snarl, chest rising heavily in anger. "Yes," he answered sternly, ruining Snow's indulgence strike.

"Blimey, introduce me. I have a few I need to bring back from there. Sweet grandpapa is first. He is probably rolling in his grave from your time on the throne, old snake would die a second time from shock," she exclaimed.

Their conversation, thank the gods, was cut in half when Elias and his father stood to greet the king and the princess. Ice had formed under our feet. I didn't know if I could have jumped between them in time or if I even could considering how many soldiers were surrounding him all of a sudden—all of their eyes on me alone.

"Your Majesty." The flashy Lord of Venzor bowed alongside Elias. "My congratulations regarding the celebration and congratulations to your marriage, princess."

Elias did not lift his eyes to meet Snow's, his shadows showed he was hurt and angry. She had not told me how the two had ended things between them, I only knew it had ended with his broken heart.

"Thank you, Ivar," Silas greeted back all displeasure.

The puffed up lord lifted a yellow brow. "I expect to be convinced greatly from this union, hopefully the benefits outweigh the horrors your daughter and so many of your people experienced."

"You will," Silas offered sternly. "Isjord will, too. It is my kingdom. I would do nothing to harm my life's work and blood inheritance."

"Of course," he retreated carefully. "You are right."

"Balls and arrogance make you a man, not right, Ivar," Snow said, and all of the attention turned to her. "He is a king, that makes him the most wrong of all. I'd wait a tad bit longer to give congratulations."

He glanced between both her and Silas, not knowing whom to fear more, his shadows jumping around in array. "I expect everything will go smoothly, Your Highness."

She chuckled shortly. "You expect a lot. Just pray my father holds his promises well. Or don't, both would be to your benefit, would it not?"

Her father abruptly turned to her and murmured tightly under his breath, "Snowlin Krigborn, I warn you for the last of times."

The two Venzorian stepped back and scattered along as another made forward.

"Your Majesty," an older woman greeted next in line, before half-heartedly turning to Snow. "Your Highness."

Snow leaned back in her seat wearing a wicked grin, as if entertainment was just brought to her on a platter. "Malena Grasmere, which guardian hound of Caligo's hells we owe the pleasure for letting you out again?"

I almost laughed, barely holding it in as I lowered my head to hide the amusement. Her father had turned to her wide eyed and it was pointless to describe how very angry and displeased he was with her.

She smiled shortly at Snow with masked humour. "I see your teasing behaviour remains, credit to the Olympian blood in you, they were jesters at best."

Snow to their surprise giggled at the very offensive jab. "Krig's frosted testicles, aren't you petty, Malena. Which one was it again? The Olympian that broke that tiny little nut of a heart? Oh yes, Alaric Drava. Grudges are gnawing, but you would know better, wouldn't you? You have only lived like what, two centuries already?"

Speechless and hurt, she glowered in distaste at her before turning to her king. "Silas, I purposefully came to ask for a moment. There is trouble in Grasmere. Few of our ships have not returned from their last expeditions."

He shifted in his seat, carefully stealing a glance at his daughter before turning to his court member. "I will meet you at the meeting chambers after the celebrations, Malena, nothing to be concerned about."

Distress dressed her. "There were fifteen ships this time, Silas, the third time in a month. Steel, machinery and not to mention hundreds of soldiers gone, two of them were to be received from Vrammethen," she pushed, now concern washing over her like a wave.

Silas threw another glance to his daughter and stood to leave along with Malena.

Had the rift with Solarya deepened to this extent?

"Do not leave, I will be back shortly," he warned her.

Her face had warmed with some amusement, strange satisfaction in her amber eyes. "Would not miss having you back for the world, father. Go chase your ships." She leaned forward again towards the lady, mischievousness written all over her features. "Give the Otherworld my salutes when the hounds of Keres pick you back."

Her father cleared his throat and threw her a glare before descending to the severely offended lady.

Once they were gone, curiosity took over and I lowered to my knees next to her and asked, "Your guardian and her were together?"

She snorted and shook her head. "No, she chased him round in circles the moment he had stepped in Isjord, very persistent that woman was. When Alaric had told her he preferred other men's company, she had said, and I quote: I can work with that."

I shook with laughter alongside her, a genuine sound so easily distinguishable to my ears.

Lord after lord stood there and greeted her. Most to my surprise wore respect, others a fear that did not resemble fright and others a hate rooted beyond dislike, somewhere between resent and wanting to rip her heart out. Isjord was strange in a sense, they did not fear or dislike her for what she was made to be, they disliked her from where she came. Why was pettiness so overruling over their lives? But then again, pettiness and greed were wed at the dawn of others' success.

A long while later, a sternly disturbed face and shadowed Silas returned to his seat.

Had the riff between them and Solarya gotten that intense as to take it to war?

"Trouble in the frozen heavens?" Snow asked, almost pleased.

"None of your concern."

She chuckled. "Nope, not one of my concerns. The concern is all yours." She propped an elbow at the side of her seat holding her head up, half a blink away from fading to sleep. Her eyes rolled every time someone came to the front of the dais. She was bored to death and I did not have to read her shadows to know that either.

Lord of Arynth came to give his own greeting and Snow finally perked up again. She looked a bit taken aback this time though, different from how I had always seen her with him.

"You have organised a stunning celebration, my king, but yet the centre of everyone's astonishment is your beautiful daughter. I congratulate you, nonetheless," Albius said. He did not look scared of his king though his comment did not exactly compliment him. Albius and Snow were more than friendly, they were allies, one of many she'd surely recruited on her side, but differently, he seemed not to have taken much convincing to join her side. I wondered if she truly were to use the cards she held in her hand. Would she do it once on the throne—once my queen? Had she not sworn to destroy us just the same?

"Both products of mine, so I will take your congratulations," Silas spoke proudly.

My mind was pleading with itself for Snow not to say anything that would aggravate him, but came to realise gods and heavens seemed to have lost their liking toward me when she laughed hard enough that the music faded and the whole room turned to her attention, murmuring amongst each other about the princess.

She cleared her throat. "Please, continue, do not stop on my behalf. Just enjoying this circus greatly that is all," she said, still laughing. "With so many clowns in one room one can only laugh, right?"

Both the lord and her father were taken aback from her comment. What pulled my attention were the shadows of the lord that were still stitched to one another with apology and guilt.

"Please visit Arynth after your marriage, Snow, you will be missed dearly," he said to her before saying his goodbyes, but she did not answer. It looked like something had happened between them, nothing else explained her cold reaction.

We'd left earlier than expected from Arynth last time. Had something happened?

I lowered to her again. "What is wrong, love? I thought you had taken a liking to him."

"I still like him, Kil, he just showed to be one of the same pack after all." Disappointment—her voice was laced in disappointment.

Groups and groups of attendees came to greet for hours long, so Snow stood and headed to leave.

"We are not finished," her father said.

"You are not, Moreen and the half breeds would have not been, but I am. Do enjoy having your pride caressed. Even gods find it hard to wash the blood of murder out of their hands, maybe this will soothe all the gnawing. Compensation for when you burn at the hells of Caligo," she said, going down the stairs.

"I don't plan on going there any time soon."

"All the mightiest kings die, check the grave of your father, all the bird shit there should give your reality a check."

He laughed roughly. "You won't get to see me like that, I will make sure of it. I will bury you before my hair grows white."

Her father's words creeped over me, the hate and vileness of them was skin crawling.

"Such certainty," Snow mused, grinning. "Since I don't do threats, I will issue a small warning, gratis for the one who sired me. If you want to hold to that statement, I'd sleep with both eyes wide. You should be happy your frustration pleases me more than your death. Imagine if I had spilled that little poison in your clothing. It would have been one heck of a show. And, father dearest, you would not want to live with my spirit haunting you to madness." She toasted her goblet to him and descended down the stairs.

Snow had plainly threatened him, she reminded him what he was—human. His eyes slipped to me and his frustration grew twofold. We left behind dark and thick shadows of anger, enough that the whole room ceiling was starting to fill with them.

Casually, as if her father had not just spewed the vilest form of hate, she headed to the food tables and filled her cheeks and arms with food. Her attention to the room as she munched on some white powdered soft sweets, studying those in attendance and swaying slightly to the music.

"Quite the sight," I said.

"It is, you should have seen the ones when I was younger. They were so much grander though. Perhaps Isjord is faltering after all," she said, almost choking on her food.

"I was talking about you, my little glutton," I murmured close to her ear.

She stopped, swallowed, and wiped her face with her glove like a little child. "I will join the dancing, maybe you will find me doing that prettier than me eating," she sneered, and threw the rest of the sweets to me.

An obvious misunderstanding, I found her pretty doing anything, especially when she ate.

Linking arms with Freja, they both jumped around at the cheery jig till they were panting and tired and sagging onto one another, no longer taking steps, only swaying in place to the jumpy music.

"She grows very uneasy during these nights. I still have no idea how I did not find her running through a forest today," Caiden said, approaching and grabbing food from behind me. "Pinch me, she is even dancing."

"Why does she do that?" I asked. He had never been close with me, but I still asked.

"That night she lived because her mother told her to run, she has not stopped ever since, her words are Snow's trigger," he admitted. "Once it was only a couple times a week, then everything began triggering her. A memory, maybe a mention of your kind or black steel. Then it became worse, sometimes she'd lock herself in her room, not standing the sight of the moon. She was not robbed out of life, like her siblings and her mother were, she was robbed out of living. Trapped, only able to run." He turned to face me. "She still is, otherwise she would not be here today waiting to marry your king."

I hated myself for forgetting so easily who I was and what my people had done when she was branded by the memory.

"Do not underestimate what she holds within, my family suffered the same at the hands of her father and had she not been here, he would already be dead. No one will be able to hold her when she meets your king, Kilian. You have not seen her plans for him," Caiden added before leaving.

He was right, just because Snow had changed around me and Mal it did not mean what she felt for Adriata or its king was gone—her revenge was not gone, it was what kept her away from me, why she didn't want to hear my words.

I'd been so lost in my head and in Caiden's words that Snow had slipped away from my sight. Panic creeped all through me as I rampaged between the crowds, the corners of the halls and the food tables. I could not lose her, not now, not like this. Long minutes passed searching, my heart chasing with worry while I looked for her everywhere. And right before I headed to alert the others, I noticed the floating balcony curtain and her figure flashing behind it. My heart was near to stopping. A second longer and it would have stopped.

"You still wish to kill me? I thought we had changed our stances?" I asked, still panting from worry, but she only looked at me in surprise when I ran toward the large balcony where she stood and gathered her in my arms, making sure she was real and that my mind had not betrayed my sick heart. "Do not leave like that, Snow."

She lifted on her toes to kiss my chin again. Such an innocent gesture that left me utterly impaled. After burying her head in my chest, she quietly said, "I just needed to leave there, the air was growing suffocating."

The air was not suffocating, she was jittery, as if wanting to take off in a sprint, like she wanted to run away and far. This would be the thirteenth year of her nightmares and here she was, almost reliving it again, another solstice night and with Adriatians all-round her, one even holding her in his arms.

I held her.

I was holding her.

Realisation struck me and I let her go, pulling away.

She frowned and moved quicker than I did, grabbing my jacket and dragging me back to her while she wrapped her arms tightly around my waist. "I didn't say move away, you Adriatian bastard, did I?" she murmured between us.

I planted a kiss on the top of her flower-scented head and at that moment it really struck me how I would lose her. The feel of her hair, the paces of her breaths, the exact gold of her irises, the precise sound of her words, the vibration of her laugh...there was too much to remember and I had so little time.

"Dance with me," she said, extending a hand. "I wish to tick this off the list of all I've done with you."

I laced my hand with hers and tugged her against me as we swayed to the soft melody leaking from inside the celebrations. She raised her head all angry at me. "Which woman taught you to dance?"

I kissed her brow. "My step-mother. Now which man taught you to dance?"

Her head laid against my collar. "My brother. I'd step on his feet and he'd sway me around all day."

"You miss him."

She swallowed hard, her eyes dropping to the ground. "Terribly. Do you think they will ever forgive me? For living while they died."

I couldn't help the shake of my voice when I said, "There is nothing to forgive you for, you did nothing wrong." Her thinking it was her fault hurt me worse than a wound.

"I did nothing, that is exactly what I did wrong."

My eyes fell closed at the truth of what she felt. "You were a child and you lived, if anything your loved ones would be proud you survived."

"If I had not been the one to run, maybe Thora or Eren would be here. It would have been better, they would have known what to do, they were always better than me. I should have been the one to die."

They broke me—her thoughts broke me. "Don't. I beg of you. Don't think like that."

"I can't even remember any of them," she whispered. "Their faces are either a blur or...burned. Some faint memories I have are of their worst days and some others I am convinced that they are made up because they seem so happy. We were never happy and I might have made that up. That day in Arynth, I was really upset and almost mourning her again because when I saw her, I saw her the same as she'd once been, no fog or blur or blood. I never felt happier and devastated at the same time."

How little of her pain I understood. "Forgive me."

She raised her head. "Don't. If I'd seen her a bit longer, I would have hated to wake. I would have not wanted to wake up."

"They were the luckiest to be loved as you loved them."

"They were all I had, Kil. At the end of the day, despite all that went on, I still had my sister snake up in bed with me, my brother kiss my brow goodnight, my mother tending to my pain. I woke for them and when they were gone, I wanted to be gone with them. Instead she bound me to a promise of a life—a life I did not want. Even though I am not alone, I feel alone. I feel worse than alone because now I have to keep all my senses aware that I might lose more. I have Nia, Alaric, Cai and...so much more and," she took a deep breath, "you, I have to lose you and Mal, that ridiculous idiot with good hair."

I halted our step. "Thank you."

Her brows rose slowly. "For what?"

"For caring, for telling me all of your thoughts, for opening up to me, for letting me hold you, for letting me hold your heart. Thank you."

"I don't like this," she whispered, catching on a breath. "It feels like farewell. I don't want to be reminded of it. I have you for so little. The last thing I wish to think about is goodbye."

I rested my forehead on hers. "I don't deserve you, Snow. This selfishness, this greed, the want...it will send me right to hells."

"You will be doing me a kindness not to leave me out there all on my own."

She snorted first and then I followed before we were both sent in laughing fits.

"End tonight. Rest. You won the battle today," I said.

She nodded and I faded the two of us to her bedroom.

She tried to steady herself when we stood in the middle of her bedroom. "How can you do that? Nia said she can barely feel any magic in her because of the veils Melanthe has put up."

"I am a prime and a soldier who has trained since before I bloomed my blessing." I went around and lit a few candles around the room for light like she always did. She hated the dark and I hated that I was the dark. "If you need anything, I will be right outside."

"I need you," she said, bringing me to a halt. She pointed innocently to her hair. "My pins. Help...please."

Was it the flutter of those teasing lashes or the way she swayed or perhaps the look she'd given me or how she bit the side of her lip, but I was close to begging gods to spare me and take me. All of her was mine, yet I couldn't have her. I took her hand and she guided us to her dresser with a large silver mirror. She perched right on my lap and I hissed at the contact. "Wicked woman."

"Whatever do you mean?" She took off her long gloves slowly, several black bands of oaths beneath. It struck me in the chest each time I saw a band, but I refrained from saying anything.

I took off her crown, setting it on the dresser and then her heavy earrings while all she did was stare at me. She was so painfully beautiful that I could not concentrate. I began removing her diamond pins one after the other and her black silky hair spilled over her shoulder, making my work torturous. I ran my fingers through her hair in an attempt to straighten it and her eyes drew shut.

"Done."

She puckered her fiery red mouth. "The lips, too."

I blew a long breath while staring at the soft flesh. "Evil woman."

She smiled and reached over the table for a cloth. I felt her flinch and then freeze still facing the mirror. I knew it was one of the things she hated. "What do you see me as, Kil?"

I realised it was not mirrors she hated, but what they reflected. And then I hated why she saw what she saw. "You are all I see. I cannot compare you to anything else."

Her eyes were lost in her reflection. "I see dark...and terror."

I didn't want her to see herself as what she thought others saw or what others forced her to be. Pulling her round to face me, I gently tried to wipe the red from her lips even though I liked the colour on her. "No one is but light, my love, it would be such a vain world of bright."

"I still don't want you to see me like that."

"I live to see you like that," I said, moving her hair to the back to kiss her shoulder. "You're the night sky I am so desperate to paint. A deep cave I'd cower to safety. A shadow of shelter in scorching summer. Smoke of lames that never tasted warmer. The most beautiful dark." It was darkness that made shine, not light.

She bloomed a sunny smile and it made me melt. "Never before have I wanted a man's lips to speak pretty words to me more than kiss me."

I moved a strand of hair back. "Never before have I wanted to see those lips curl in such a beautiful smile more than kiss them."

She sighed. "I still want to kiss you more."

I smiled. "Me too."

"It was for dramatic affect."

I nodded. "It was."

"We were being romantic."

I pressed my lips just outside the corner of hers and she gasped. "We were."

Her chest rose furiously. "It wasn't awkward at all."

"Not one bit." I ran my finger over her neck and shoulders. "How will you torture me next?"

"My dress," she said, standing. "Since you love undressing me."

I drew out a long frustrated exhale. "Horrible woman."

I began unlacing the back and slowly it peeled off her body, pooling at her feet. She remained in the thinnest, shortest slip my eyes had ever seen. It hid nothing, if anything, it accentuated her chest and their hardened centre needing for my touch. Too lost there to pay mind, she sat back on my lap and I began growing dizzy. "Fuck."

"That is a bad word, darling." Her fingers stretched to explore my chest and then up to my neck. Leaning over my ear she whispered, "I thought I could feel something hard down there."

I dug my hands on her hips to stop her from squirming over my cock. "Cruel woman."

She threw her arms around my neck and pressed her forehead to mine. "I am, but you're a cruel man, too."

I rounded her tight in my embrace, pressed against my chest till we breathed in the same loud pace. My hands trailing all over her. I wanted to remember every curve and dip. "I would have devoured you."

She smiled and kissed the bridge of my nose. "You already have."

40

Wars and Allies

Snowlin

Dressed back into my uniform, I made my way to the usual weekly meetings. Witnessing his face unravel at my plans was my indulgence for the day. Father tried his mightiest to keep me away from the meetings, but Nia had been there to represent me all every single time without missing a single piece of information. Today he would finally get to see me again and his loving arse might finally fill with joy.

"King Magnus has sent the mercenaries. The Brogmerian Lord was correct and now I fear more than before. If Magnus had to resort to this solution, it means something is wrong, terribly wrong. What they were looking for remains in a temple up north, in the village Sodart. I have left towards the north of the village along with the mercenaries to enter the temple to find what your father is hiding. You were right to fear. If I do not return, go north, your answers are north."- Sam.

The lords got over the surprise of my presence fairly sooner than thought and propping myself back on the chair and my feet on the meeting table, I drew a large smile for them. Celdric, Sebastian, Albius and Freja amongst them, Malena missing. The horned eudemon finally left my father's side.

Alex Casmere approached me and bowed. "Your Highness, I suppose we owe you gratitude for what you did in Brogmere. I was not the slightest aware how many trades the previous lord had stopped and the criminal activity he was letting skid past to us."

A smirk rose on the corners of my mouth and I nodded. "You're most welcome. It is what any other good Isjordian would do to protect its people and lands."

He measured my words. He, too, had been deceived by the ex-Lord of Brogmere—made a fool. Isjordians did not enjoy being made fools. This one particular fool was Renick's brother and my extra favour. The oath still burned fresh on my arm. Oar number five laid down at my request while his brother seethed in his loss, quenched in fear of me, both under blood oath, both hanging by thin strands of my mercy.

"Modr, too," Freja said, throwing me a wink. "Isjordians are people of value and morals and to allow such creature upon our own was a mistake us as a council should have prevented. We owe people of Brogmere and you an apology." She bowed slightly, a small smile spreading across her face. Power suited her, the best accessory to her new confidence. Freja had played the part along with Sebastian as offended by my behaviour to not show partiality that would have prompted suspicion.

"So does Brisk," the lord said. Oar number six bought on debt from my unusual friendship with the Autumn Queen—he too was now on my side.

"Us as well. We are most grateful," Ivar Venzor nodded with a smirk.

Elias noted the interactions looking somewhat confused until his eyes flickered with some sudden realisation.

Father entered, his eyes staggering back and forth the room when he noticed my presence. He cleared his throat in an attempt to warn me of my unmannerly posture. Tortures came to many kinds, to my father disrespect and defiance were the cruellest one. I saw his frustration at not getting a reaction from me. He killed Sam in thought of enraging me, he'd killed someone I loved only to torture me, and he'd achieved it. He just didn't know it.

"My team heads to the Islines in less than an hour so shall we wrap this one quickly?" I asked, breaking their important and interesting discussion on the fine quality of fish caught in Venzor these past weeks.

Every head, lord, general, captain, scholar and priest, snapped toward me, including *his*. Dear father had kept me from dealing with the Solaryan vandals and the raiding for a reason Samuel revealed before his dying moments. After all, there were indeed direct intentions to keep me particularly away from them. Judging from the severe difference in reactions the meeting room attendees gave me, more than half were definitely not aware of what their king was planning. Sam had chased my father's footsteps, and I had chased Melanthe's. Her craft pattern had traced over one specific location. Islines. Particularly a tiny village near a temple called Sodart. Big surprise, right? The two were after all somehow connected and I was a short trip away from getting my answers.

I was no Adriatian Empath, but I knew how to test a room. And as expected, their reactions were like black ink on white canvas, extremely giving. Very few knew—very few that were not lords as well. The tyrant was into his secrets. Or was it fear of refusal and defiance from Winter court?

"That is not for discussion. General Moregan is already dealing with them, you will not leave for the Islines and that is an order," father said calmly, almost unbothered. Though I could bet he was thickly considering stabbing me to death.

"My, my, since when does anyone decline well needed help? The Solaryans are growing in masses and you can only spare so many soldiers from your east war fort's, father. Surely Moregan is in some need of help?" Hiding from him was no longer any concern of mine. I wanted him to know his secrets were only *partially* secrets now, the game was out in the open and it was his turn to move.

His eyes widened, half confusion and realisation, and jaw tightened so tight the whole room heard the crack and grinding of his teeth, exquisite. Right under my foot, let me go or let me reveal. "I see you are well informed," he said calmly, tapping a finger on the table. "Very well, you can attend the vandals, but another Captain will escort you with their team as well as that is too much of a danger to take so close to your wedding," he continued, looking uncomfortably between all the faces in the room. Not as planned, but I would still get to go with his blessings. Asking him was only a courtesy of mine and a test to his reaction. I would have gone, nonetheless. He must be sure I won't find answers. Little did he know he had only intrigued me further.

"I will escort her," Elias interrupted. "After she returns to Tenebrose I will head to Moregan's camp, it was on my route either way."

My father agreed and without further comments, I stood to exit not wanting to delay this any further. I was also not very fond of spending my nights in the Islines. Isjordians had terrifying tales of a snow creature that ate your spleens and livers. Eren had sworn for months to us he had seen one during his travels with father. We had not believed him, but he had never been one to lie— always too honest for his own good.

"How did you know of the war forts?" Elias finally said, breaking the silence while we headed for the stables.

"Just as I knew of the Solaryans, Seraphim, the Adriatians and much more. I have my sources."

"Did I serve as one of them?" he asked coldly.

Had he realised it just now, or since Arynth?

"What if you did?" His eyes faltered and I realised that was a bad blow on my side, he looked hurt. "But it was never just that and you know that well, so enough acting hurt. You are a friend, Elias, one I really appreciate, so be honoured. It's very rare." Elias was nothing like his father. I'd done my research well before deciding the route I'd taken with Venzor. Elias would do good once he took his father's position. I had faith in him and that was why I had grown such a like for him. When you live amongst demons, you learn to recognize a saint.

"You truly are trying to stop him," he said, glancing around cautiously. "Truly take him down from the throne and truly take Isjord."

"Will you run to him with that information?"

He took a moment. "No, I owe you a debt."

"It is not because of that you're not running to him with what I told you and you know it, Elias, Captain of the fifth guard, soldier with no kills. You cherish life, that is why you won't." It was rare, one like him was truly rare.

He stood taken aback by my words. "How do you plan on stopping him?"

"With wits, persistence and an army."

"Adriata's?"

"We shall find out. I want to know though, would you be on my side if that were to happen?" Venzor did not support my father and never had. A city as influential as Venzor would give me the greatest leverage considering Grasmere was yet not entirely under my foot.

He frowned at my proposal. "Snowlin, I am Isjordian, I—"

"There is no choice in life or death, you are either for the living or with my father," I interrupted.

He ran his fingers through his hair all distress. "You will need many on your side."

"I don't need to get anyone on my side. I am the side. Everyone else is just simply making smart decisions."

"Would it mean something to you if I chose life?"

"Yes, it would mean that I was not wrong about you. It would mean that your debt to me is paid."

His eyes hardened at my words and he carefully took note of all my seriousness before he bowed his head slightly. "Then you have my pledge."

My smile grew gleefully and I nodded in thanks. And just like that, my seventh oar would soon be resting on its thole, ready to be stirred at my order.

He headed to gather his team and prepare for the journey, letting me sift my thoughts and begin to regret accepting to have him be the escort. My brain was already in a thunder, I did not need a tornado in there as well. The first face my eyes focused on in the large stables was Kilian's, who had narrowed his ones on Elias. That maddening dimple on full display, such a giving trait that did him no favour to hide his anger.

"Good news or the least good one?" I teased the three surprised idiots and my angry silver eyed snake. "Well, you have no choice but to hear both. We have the blessings for the journey, but he is to come with us along with his men," I explained, pointing towards Elias. "Shall we? You have all the way to the Islines to marvel at him."

Kilian walked over to me as everyone gathered their bearings for the journey. I was mad at the fool, very mad. His hand rested on the hollow of my neck and he pulled me into his warm embrace. His mouth brushed the shell of my ear, a shiver travelling down my spine. "Hello, my sweet villain," he whispered softly.

I rolled my eyes. "Hello, soon to be eunuch."

He cocked his head back and chuckled darkly, shaking and amused. Had I stared a bit longer at the extension of his neck or at that jaw that could cut through air, I would have drooled all over myself and him. I bit my lip, swallowed hard and made to sulkily walk away, but his firm hand gripped my wrist, spinning me in place like a needle and straight onto his chest for another embrace. His hands teased every inch of my back and I melted onto him—all resistance gone. I knew then why cats had domesticated. He could domesticate me all he wanted if it meant to be caressed like the sort.

"Don't be mad, my little beast. If I stayed last night there would be no morning and no other day for that matter."

I reached down, slapping his perfect arse viciously. "Don't speak like that, you deceiving sadist bastard. You turn me on and then expect me to stew in my own frustration?"

He tilted his head so endearingly, looking down at me so softly I almost collapsed in his arms. I would have, almost, had he nodded and said, "Yes."

A sneer twisted in my face. "Well then, maybe I'll visit Elias. He is very eager and never expects that of me."

His grip loosened and he pulled an inch away, those grey eyes darkly lowered as he examined me.

"What?" I asked, batting my lashes guilelessly.

"Well done, I think you have achieved to make me jealous for the first time in my life."

A smile crept on my face. "Is that so? Then that makes it even. I am no longer mad," I said, patting his chest and strutting away, making sure to sway my hips slightly more than usual. I knew it was a job well done when he blew a frustrated breath that turned to a low groan.

Winter had become unbearably rough, snow climbed in feet tall walls along the main Isjordian road officials used, making us feel trapped as the only visible routes were that ahead and the one we were leaving behind. Everyone had gone completely still, especially our team. Even my men were tensing around those of Elias, as if they could not trust their own comrades.

We arrived at Sodart, the furthest Isline village that rested the closest to the other Krigborn territory. The small gathering of houses stood right by the slope of the mountains, massive, unwelcoming giants of frost and magic. It radiated that core magic that no longer surrounded Isjord—primal magic. The Isliners were said to still possess the raw magic of our ancestors, yet they never had dared or even craved for more power or to rule over Isjord. Quietly, they'd settled in the roughest small patch of land that was offered to them more out of pettiness than thought, and they'd thrived within their own. I wondered if they knew of my father, the kingdom killer. If they knew of me, the beast of legends. Their belief was rawer, too, no sacred books, no tales of other gods, just sheer adoration and devotion to Krieg. *Khôl, mon vâl Khôl, Krig.* God, only one god, Krig.

The whole atmosphere had changed from my last visit, the wooden houses were lifeless and emptied. Wind whistled loudly between them when a few elderly Isjordians crossed by us, their faces drowned with grimness. These people were suffering at the hands of Solaryans, but at the expense of their own king's doing.

My attention turned to the elderly sitting outside a grand half collapsed temple just across the main square of the village, hidden by the large conifers and the mountain rocks. They had lowered to their knees, murmuring prayers silently, their eyes tightly closed. Considering how unpractised faith was here, they looked like the only few of worshippers left in the whole of Isjord. A thin grey book clutched between their hands, book of Eirlys, the thinnest holy script on the realm. What did these people pray to? Hodr was just another snow crusted waste land and Krig...well, he was another smug story all together.

"*Ner Krig't khôlda, zel Hodr khôlin,*" I greeted in old Ysolt, approaching them in holy sign.

"*Ner Krig't khôlda, druval ât wâlkya da,*" they all greeted back in unison towards me, looking terrified, the fingers they held in holy sign trembling.

"I am Captain Snow, inspecting for the vandal attacks. Do you have any given on what they might be looking for? These villages are your ground, you know them better than anyone."

They hesitated, taking a moment to absorb my words. An elderly woman stood and grabbed my hands to cradle them to her own, she looked older than time, probably even older than time itself if she was an old Aura. "We do not know, but they raid the temples worse than they raid our homes. Whatever they are looking for is to be found in them. We never enter any, they are laced with strong craft magic as old as a thousand generations to protect portals, objects and blessings left from our gods. Most are random objects, only a value to us believers, none that would matter to anyone else," she explained, patting my arm gently before leaving.

No one could enter them. Was this why the villages were continuously attacked, because they could not get in? Their acts were fresh so it meant they still had not found a way in—my father, too, had not found a way. It looked as if attacking the rest of the village was only a ploy to mask their true actions.

Now the question was why is Melathe's magic stench reeking in patches particularly here? Memphis had ingested a potion by our Crafter who had worked out a way to trace Melanthe's craft pattern. Immediately, my morph had flown here and above the temple directed by the potion, her sight had shown hovering red mist all around the village and spectacular traces of her craft practised right here, by the temple. The Crafter we visited on our journey in Arynth had also told us that Melanthe was a known Potioner and Summoner back in Eldmoor. It brought me back to the conversation we had in Brogmere with Kilian and Mal, but what would she summon here, what would a gate and elixir do to help her with my father's cause? Breaking another Crafter's veil was impossible whatever skillset you bagged, especially when this one's owner was probably long dead—not considering the wielding power elder Crafters used to have. Melanthe was practically an ant heavy lifting a bull. Was it why father had brought her back from Caligo, to help him procure whatever this temple hid? But then, how were Seraphim, Myrdur, Hanai and Solarya even related to this?

I ran my fingers over the faded rock carvings at the entrance of the moss and omen filled temple. I felt the old language engraved there lift in the air and almost whisper the words at the back of my neck like the breeze of a cave, hollow, echoing and hissing.

Khôl gval, gral, glârda. Khôl zul. Âr rhakili re wah, Khôl balka. Âr rhakili re zúl, âr rhakili re khar wô âra din rhakili re khur.

"What does it say?" Cai asked, crouching down next to me.

"God came, left, remained. God gifted. Be aware of what god banished. Be aware of gifts, be aware of her who was not aware of him." A shudder went through my body as I repeated them aloud. "Cai—"

"It's the same passage written on the road to Valda Acme." Valda Acme was the highest point of the Volants. Just about where the Isjordian soldiers were found heading towards.

"The veil around the temple affected Sam, it drove him mad...it wasn't Melanthe who'd done it, but—"

"You made him a promise. Go," he finished for me before standing.

"Thank you, Cai."

"Always."

"I will enter alone, no one else," I said to the grand crowd pacing behind me like goose younglings. My madness, my blame. I was not going to carry their lives in my guilt as well.

"That will not happen, anything but that. No one enters temples, they are all rounded and guarded by Dark Crafter magic," Kilian pleaded worriedly, approaching me. The one who always dared to take doubt or challenge my decisions.

"There is nothing in them anyway, my raven," Elias said, coming between me and Kilian, the latter frowned so deep that a canyon formed between his brows.

"I will decide that for myself, Elias. Unless you know something I don't." He stood there surveying me and then his soldiers for a moment before nodding and moving back. It was signal enough that he did indeed know something more, but we had watch spying on us. That was why my father had insisted someone accompany me. To spy on me.

"If I don't come in sixty heartbeats you send for me," I said to the stern cold face of spring.

"With how fast it is beating right now, sixty heartbeats won't even be before you take that first step. Can I plead you into changing your mind?" he asked in that soft, irresistible stare, resting a palm on one of my cheeks, but I shook my head. Surrendered, he closed his eyes and let out a deep sigh. "I terribly want to stop you. I will come with then."

"There is no stopping me and if something happens to me I know you will be right here to come get me." Everyone was looking towards us, including a bewildered Elias. I did not care. I never had this—this felt good. I wanted the world to know that I deserve to feel this.

"You don't come back in sixty heartbeats, we tear that thing down," Cai called as he, Nia and Mal approached, their swords drawn at ready. It was a temple, not a monster's den. Their steel was as useless as a fork when you got served soup.

Nia gave me a nod of reassurance. "You don't come back in sixty heartbeats, we tear the whole of this land down."

Mal glanced between us all as if waiting for him to say something, too. "You don't come back in sixty heartbeats," he said, pensive. "Well...just return in those sixty heartbeats. Those look like some tough walls and I'm quite partial to less work is the best work."

I smiled at the younger brother and he threw me a wink as I backed into the unknown.

The temple was dark. Taking a torch fixed at the entrance, I made my way in towards its dim halls. Walls were covered in drawn figures of battles, monsters, and at the centre wall, the statue figures of our gods stood still and grand. Father of all gods, Fader, at its centre.

As I moved past them, the air shifted warmer and my torch blew off, leaving me in complete darkness. Panic. Utter panic settled in me. Navigating blindly ahead, my fingers grew warmer as if I was approaching a flame, and then a small spark lit in front of me. Moving toward the flickering light, I stumbled and fell to a cold wet floor. I yelped at the impact and noticed my whole body soaked as well. The light grew bigger and brighter till it slowly lit the grand room little by little. I stood to marvel at the grotesquely drawn walls and not moments later water began to rise to my ankles. No, not water, something thicker. The razor-sharp metallic smell of blood hit me before I looked down at my clothes. My breath lost and my mouth gaped open at the horror rising now to my knees. The floor and my body all drenched in crimson red thick blood, leaking everywhere, streaming and filling the room.

I drew my attention away and towards the drawings on the ceiling. There was something in its centre. A white haired woman with wings and something I could not make out from the dim light stood at its middle, along with what looked like a kneeling man's figure surrounded by chains and a circle of moon phases. Dozens of other drawings of maps, unrecognisable creatures and weapons spread to each corner. Old Ysolt letters lined in circles around her and I spun on my toes to form the sentences while blood crawled up my body.

Har wô dorla, har wô baŭl, har wô sâ. She who defied, she who betrayed, she who pays. *Sor zir ŭ dâ sverga, sor zir arê ŭ khila.* Eight chains to the land, eight chains from the skies. *Sor sŭl ndar har eto. Sor sŭl garta rô sat har arê eto.* Eight souls part her living. Eight souls guarded to keep her from living.

Who was *her*?

Squinting tight, I tried to refocus on the ceiling painting with no avail. The blood leaking onto the room had reached to my neck, nearly overtaking me. I forced myself to swim forward in the thick, skin creeping liquid until a familiar voice echoed twisted and strange words about the room—the echo wore my mother's voice.

It's dark Crafters' magic, this is not real, I repeated to myself over and over, moving to exit the pool of blood. Then I heard Eren, moments later Thora, both pleading for me to save them, to not abandon them again.

My entire surroundings turned to that night, bloodied bodies lying lifeless ahead of me. Flashes of black Adriatian steel sending sparks clanked and hurdled around me. It smelled the same as that night and I tasted black smoke coating my tongue. Thunder and fire crackled, snow and soot dropped around me, coating my charred white dress as my mother's words from that night repeated again and again. I had frozen still, claws of fear and sharp talons of darkness dug deep in my mind. My whole body trembled as everything around me was blurred by tears.

"Stop, please, stop," I pleaded to them, making myself move forward. The voices and screams of my loved ones grew louder and disturbing, they anchored and aimed to stop me and drown me under—under their call and under the blood.

My hands fell over my neck and my lungs swallowed the last bit of air. I drowned between blood, my tortured memories of that night and sorrow. *It was the Crafter's veil. It is the Crafter's veil.* I tried to repeat those thoughts over and over, but I could not breathe let alone move.

Run, Snow. Run, my snowflake. I heard her voice again. It was not the Crafter's veil. I knew it, I could feel it whisper in my ear as it always did—not like the call of a memory at the back of my head like craft veil did.

I grabbed onto the string of feel, pulling onto it and forcing my feet to take a step forward and then another.

By the time I managed to leave the blood-filled room, my chest rose furiously, panting and gasping for air. Before I could collect myself and prepare to enter again, a sharp pain hit the back of my head, sending black flecks to my sight. A blurred figure stood in front of me, and I toppled to the cold marbled floor, the world spinning and thumping into darkness.

Snowlin, Snow? My little snowflake, wake up. They are waiting. My mother's soft melodic voice echoed again in my buzzing heavy head and I snapped awake. The back of head and my neck were completely taken over by a dull sharp pain, my ears whizzing sharply like the noise of glass scratching metal.

I shook my head and cracked open my throbbing sore eyes, pins and needles blurring light and shape. More than a dozen masked men stood before me, cramped inside a massive wooden walled room. A man sat on the table a few feet away, playing around with my sword and daggers, my brother's sword and...Sam's daggers.

"She has awakened. You did not hit her that hard after all," one of the men said in Tahuma to the others who laughed all together. They were not just any men, they were Solaryans.

How had they managed to get me out of the temple without the others noticing? Considering how long I had been inside it, the others should have already been in there. Right now I was praying they hadn't entered to face what I did.

"We have great plans for you, little sweet princess, we hope your father is more loving than he looks because our price will be high," the one that seemed to be their leader spoke.

I shifted my bound wrists round to loosen some of the pressure they had put on my skin. "He is not. Though you are wasting his time and yours, you're not wasting mine. I am exactly where I wanted to be," my voice was hoarse and breathy, the attempt to clear my throat only hurt. "What are you looking for in Isjord?" I questioned. However, I didn't plan on staying here forever.

All the men laughed themselves to tears and none answered me. Instead a fist met my cheek, sending me further back the room wall and my head in thundering pain.

I spat blood in front of me and clicked my jaw back in place. "Losing those chances of getting out of here alive. Tell me now or they will level to zero," I threatened, straightening myself, but they all laughed again and a leg kicked my shoulder hard, toppling me to the floor. I heard the click of my shoulder dislocating and felt the stab of it all over down my spine untill was breathless from the radiating sharpness and dullness of the pain.

"Last chance, gentlemen, what are you looking for?" I asked, panting, almost gasping for air.

This time they did not laugh, they looked angry at my persistence. One that had slouched down to the wall beside me carving a piece of wood with my dagger answered, "A piece of the weapon your father will use to ultimately kill us all, little princess. You can ask him better when you return to him in exchange for it. He stole ours, it's only fair we steal his."

Piece? What weapon needed pieces? I then guffawed, my head lolling back and forth from amusement. Getting back on my father? What was this, a game of tag? Had the poor Sun King already fried his brains under the heat of Cyra?

Their leader threw a kick on my stomach. "Shut that fucking mouth or I will, you *leşa*."

I had managed to back away but not enough to avoid all its impact as my organs shifted from the force of the blow. "What weapon?" I asked fully in Tahuma. "This *bitch* is curious."

"One of the worst, a divine one," the man who'd answered me before explained.

I blinked annoyed. "There is no such thing as a divine weapon, never has been. Gods bore no weapons but peace and prosperity. The only divine gift is that of spirituality. Forbidden are the gifts that gift greed to humans, forbidden is the divine ruling above one and many. No god shall gift weapons or war," I recited from the Caelus liber. "And if there was such a thing, why did he need to get it from you or Seraphim?"

He dropped his poor attempt at a wooden sculpture. "It might not be a weapon, but to your father even a lump of hair is. And I said, piece, princess, piece. There are eight of them."

I rolled my eyes. "Can someone elaborate or are you trying to spare your voice, is that why you eat your vowels?"

One of the men brought eight fingers forward, crutching down in front of me, his dark gaze rimmed with ire. "One in his lands, one he stole from us, the others elsewhere. And together they make one. That good enough for your half animal head?"

Eight souls part her living. Eight souls guarded to keep her from living. The words flew around me almost alive.

The men laughed all together and I fashioned one following them. "Adorable that you need fingers to count."

The leader growled, his fist glowing bright and he charged toward me with lost patience. "Blind or a mute, what shall I make you, *Ybris* child?" he said, lowering to his knees, eyes alight with the malice of a killer—death stare of a mercenary.

Father had stolen from them and they were looking to steal back from him. If my father had already obtained the piece they would not be looking for it, which meant father did not have it either. Probably locked in one of these temples. What were these objects, magic or just random objects everyone was taking their proportions out of control? This pattern was unusual, the probability that I should be terrified that my father was indeed planning something big ran very high. But one thing I was sure of. If my father was to be asked for it in exchange for me, he would not do it. The thought of it had me giggling like a madwoman in front of the Solaryan mercenaries.

The ties behind my back melted and I stood, kicking the man in his knee before he reached to grab me. The moment he stumbled forward, I twisted his neck and he limped dead on the ground.

The rest of the men stood and approached wide eyed, unsheathing their weapons.

I now knew what I had to do. It had been what Sam had wanted me to do. But first, I needed to know what the truth was—the full truth. For that, I had to keep being a pawn in this drawn out game of falseness.

"It was the last time, just as I promised."
And the room lit bright—brighter than the sun.

41

Dreams and Nondeamers

Kilian

She had vanished right in front of me. I had let her enter that temple and let her disappear all while she was only a few feet away from me. It had been hours of us entering the temple one by one, facing its living horrors as we searched for another living horror, but there had been no sign of her. My mind had gone dark, my body numb and I was lost. I was lost and she was gone.

"She is fine," Nia said, dropping to the ground breathless after coming out of the temple. She looked shaken, more than the others. The Crafter's veil was strong and it had never let us further than the door of the main temple room, facing us all with some of our darkest fears which constantly kept us away from even coming close to the middle of the temple.

But she was not fine. Snow could not have just vanished out of thin air. We rampaged the insides and all exits of the temple, but found out nothing. Had whatever was beyond that veil taken her to gods knew where? I rubbed my head hard to get such thoughts far away. I only had hope, I could not lose that as well.

"Kilian, she is fine. Now stop pacing about, you are giving me a headache," Nia said, grabbing my arm to pull my attention to her. "She will be very offended if she knew you underestimate her capabilities like this. Trust me, I know her."

"Let her be well and I will face whatever wrath she will unleash upon me."

Her hazel eyes softened over my worried ones and she gave me an understanding nod before turning towards the entry of the temple, waiting for Caiden and Mal to come out.

"I will send word to her father," Elias said, approaching us.

Nia shot up from where she was sitting. "You do such a thing and I will send you dead to yours."

He assessed her in disbelief before turning to me. "Should you not be afraid, isn't she the key to your kingdom's freedom? Should you not be panicking and running around looking for her, aren't you her guard? Weren't you sent here for that? Does your king know you haven't protected her at all?" His words were stabbing and dipped in anger.

I stood facing him. "I am afraid. Afraid of losing the woman of my heart, should your salt dried brain understand. Snow is a grown woman, stronger than you and the rest of your little soldiers. I cannot chain her, I cannot make her do something she doesn't want to do, and I am looking for her. Unless you know a secret that we don't, Captain? Aren't you on the General's team, the one dealing with the vandals? Tell me, does your princess know that you haven't protected her at all to guard whatever secret of her father's?"

He retreated back a step as his shadows dressed with puzzlement, frustration, disappointment and a line of heartbreak. "Do you love her?" he asked, averting his eyes to the ground.

"Your ears will not hear that before hers do. Now move and hold your mouth shut. Look for her, don't make her life harder."

Panting, two figures came from the temple. "She is not in there, I am sure of it," Mal said, plopping to the ground, tired. "My magic can't read her, but my senses don't catch any human presence in there at all."

Elias's eyes darted between us, hesitating to form words for whatever he wanted to say. "There are other exits to the temple, some get you out to the forest or by the edge of Islines, and some to other temples in the other Krigborn line territory," he revealed, and his soldiers all gave him a cold look. "They are connected by tunnels."

I nodded in gratitude at him. She could have followed one of those routes. I didn't know if I should thank the heavens or worry that it would be more difficult to find her.

"The morph, do you think she can trace Snow? This could last for hours or even days. Memphis could trace her bond down in moments," Mal threw the question none of us had even thought about.

Nia and Caiden's eyes grew wide in realisation and they immediately turned towards the forest, letting out two sharp whistles. There was no response even though they both tried several times to call Memphis.

"The damned thing only answers to Snow," Caiden cursed, kicking a rock in the air.

I whistled twice like Snow did. Grave silence followed until a roar sent trees shaking in the air. Our heads turned to the sound erupting from the forest and a sigh of relief washed over us. Memphis elegantly made her way to me, growling and nearly biting my head off.

I fluffed her mane and ordered, "Take us to her."

Caiden pulled my shoulder. "Why is she taking orders from you?"

"She could have responded to anyone's call ad is it truly time to argue this?" I pushed his hand off me and mounted my horse, following the morph's directions towards the forest near the Island mountains.

Elias's team remained by the temple in case our instincts were wrong and the morph had gone mad at the disappearance of her owner. Miles and miles of forest lands were left behind as we passed through conifers and inches of snow following the black animal. Tree folk, elder ash trees and snow flies startled into hiding, clearing the road ahead of us.

Please let her be well, gods and heavens let her live, do not take her away from me, do not take her. Prayers that repeated over and over in my head, almost echoing in them. The skies were furious, mountains echoed loudly while thunder cracked between them and around us. It felt as if the sky had come to the ground, the land and forest vibrated as if hit by lightning though none had struck land. Large flocks of winter birds flew above us, one after the other towards the opposite of where we were heading.

Fear.

I felt fear.

I should have begged for her not to enter that damned temple, for me to at least go with her. Let her be alive and that would be the last time I let her out of my sight even if I had to sow her to myself.

Memphis began to slow her pace when a large wooden cabin came to view a mile ahead from us. Thumping in anxiety, I furiously rode forward at a speed that almost sent my horse flying, the others chasing right behind me. Few men were running out of it in our direction so we all slid down from our horses and unsheathed our blades as they approached. Their features ghastly and wide as if they had faced an ancient mountain beast. They appeared tired, worn out as our blades met their flesh easily. Whatever they had run from had been their battle.

A bright light beamed from inside the cabin, radiating a wave. Glares. There were Aura trapped in there with her. Fear had never seized my bones as it had now, primal fear—one sort I'd never experienced before, raw and gnawing.

The closer we got to the woodhouse, the more a red figure began to focus into our view. She came from inside it, soaked red in blood head to toe, her eyes shone like dull sunlight beams. Carrying her sword over her shoulder, she lazily descended down the woodhouse's stairs. Alive.

She almost did not look human, her movement unnatural as she sat comfortably on a step. "A little late, aren't we?" she calmly teased, a smirk rising on her lips.

I ran, gathering her bloodied body to my chest. "Hells, woman. Hells."

She flinched and reached for her shoulder between us. Panicked at what I had done, I moved away, but she grabbed me back, not letting me go. "Don't ever push away from me."

"What happened, Snow, I thought...I thought—" I could not even finish my words. What had I thought? "You are hurt," I continued, examining her.

She did not look at me. Her face lost toward the nothingness of the forest ahead.

Caiden came from inside the woodhouse and shot a long troubled look at her, his eyes wide, studying her blood painted face before they dropped to her weapon.

"What is it?" I asked.

"It doesn't matter," he responded before throwing a flaming torch inside the room and blowing a swirl of wind around it, setting the woodhouse erupting in flames within moments. He had seen something to make him this distressed. For now it did not matter, what mattered is that she lives and that I had her beating heart in my arms.

"Make sure no one says anything to my father about this," she said to Nia who gave her a confirming nod. "His loving arse will defecate itself to death from concern if he finds out."

Her playful words made everyone relax and laugh. She was looking to ease everyone's grim expressions at her condition.

"Your humour remains intact despite all, for that I am glad of," I said, lifting her to my horse.

She threw me a wink. "Always."

I let out a tired laugh, my energy had been spent worrying that my whole body had become foreign. My head rested on her thigh and she caressed the top of it gently, her tender fingers alone could calm a storm. "Fucking gods, woman, you have taught me fear today."

"And to swear, apparently. What have I done to my prim guard?"

"Ruined me, that's what you have done." Gathering my strength, I managed to hoist my body up on the horse behind her. "You are to never leave my sight from now, do not force me to tie you to myself," I ordered, shifting her closer to my body, aware not to hurt her shoulder.

She snuggled in my chest leisurely as if it was moulded for her particularly. "My, my, you went from me calling you a dog to you making me one."

"More like I am yours." That is how I felt, she had me wrapped so tight around her finger I was all hers to have how she wanted.

"Mine alright," she said quietly.

"You on the other hand still seem to be a certain someone's feathered bird."

She laughed loudly, making everyone turn to us. "Darling?" she asked, playfully sniffing around. "Is that jealousy I smell? Ah, never mind, it was the rotting stink of blood." It was my turn to laugh and make everyone turn to look at us in wonder. The two giggling mad creatures, one covered in blood and the other in worry.

I gripped her hips, pulling her close to me and she let out a little yelp, her hand resting on top of mine as she laced them together. Every little touch felt so whole.

"Please tell me none of it is yours."

"Not a drop," her answer was no more than a murmur. Whatever had happened there?

After silence fell amongst us again, impatiently I asked her, "It was the Solaryans, right? I saw a Glare." I did not want to pressure her, but I was still concerned.

She shifted around my arms to make herself comfortable. "It was them."

"What did they want with you?"

Her hesitation and tensing told me everything already—she didn't want me to know. "Nothing," she lied, her voice monotone. "I only stumbled on their way."

What was she trying to hide from me?

Evening arrived in a blink. Half the day had been spent travelling and the rest panicking, searching for Snow. When we met with Elias's team at the temple, where we had left them waiting in case she came back from out of there, they had looked with absolute horror at the gory sight of Snow. She had lied to them, explaining that the temple had a secret passage that sent her towards the forest where she met the Solaryan vandals who had travelled through them from the forest to the villages as well. She explained that she had fought and killed all of them since they had refused to give information and had not attempted to settle down grounds with her, attacking her almost immediately. Her story was used as more than just a back cover.

Everyone agreed and settled to spend the night in the Isline village, down one of the respite taverns that was still functioning. Caiden, Mal and I were to share a chamber due to the tight accommodation situation, and Snow with Nia. Most of the soldiers and Elias had chosen the night guard duty, he was to stay another day in the village after we left in the morning as he was to head to the general's camp. We were also still unaware of the Solaryan vandal numbers and we did not want to risk it. Out of everything, my brain was still trying to understand Snow's reasons to lie to me. It was not paranoia, I knew she had found something out.

Between the loud chatter and laughter of Caiden and Mal, my thoughts separated like grain, their distraction served well to annoy me. My father raised me as a soldier, amongst war and training camps where I slept, ate, trained and spent most of my youth and the rest of my adult years. Their behaviour unconsciously bothered me, I was not used to it. Mal on the other hand had never bothered to oblige to our father's wishes, he did not have to. After all, our father already had created his perfect soldier. Mal always challenged him, lived carelessly and freely enjoying both of the worlds he was living in. He fought and trained like a soldier, but he was also a young man who played, courted beautiful women, laughed and enjoyed life—-to him this was normal.

"You will raise whatever beast graves in these mountains if you do not stop rumbling and shouting," I said. It was almost the middle of the night and they had to stop at some point. That point I decided was now.

"Sensitive patience and ears, Kil, have always been the worst trait of yours," Mal joked and I threw my hand in the air, my shadows hitting him in the chest.

"Still, very low blow, brother," he said breathlessly, clutching his chest, but it did not stop Caiden and him from laughing.

By morning, my ears had already been buzzing from them, but I had still managed to sleep a few hours despite it all. Nia and Snow were by the horse stables with the rest of the soldiers already waiting for us.

My feet froze when Snow turned to me, her arm was tied in a white cloth hung around her neck, her throat was tied in more bandage all around and a massive dark violet bruise spread all over her left cheek. Yesterday she had been so covered in blood that the extent of her injuries had been hidden—she'd hid them from me.

She raised a palm to me. "Before you fuss around, it looks worse than it actually is. Can I ask if you can make this one go away? This is my good side," she said playfully, pointing to her bruised left cheek.

Her glowing suns tired and rounded with shadows of fatigue. "Did she not sleep, Nia?"

"Nope," her friend answered.

I sighed. "I understand you won't let me help you, but at least let her, you stubborn woman."

She picked on her lips nervously. "I told you, I'll let you help me."

"And I told you, that would not work."

Mal cleared his throat and both of our attention turned to him and the other two intently following our conversation. "The arguing has not stopped, I see," my brother said, somewhat amused.

"You don't know the half of it," Nia said, leaning on a wooden fence.

Ignoring their stares, I concentrated my magic in her cheek where my hand was resting, but my eyes never left hers. It took me merely seconds to bring colour back to her skin and soon there was almost no trace of the gruesome bruise.

"Where else?" I asked as she seemed to want to say something.

She looked around and motioned for everyone to wait outside the stables. "Again, do not make a fuss. I have had it much worse, this doesn't bother me," she said, slowly unbuttoning her jacket, putting it away before lifting her white shirt. Another massive bruise forming between her stomach and her waist. What had they done to her?

My chest was beaming with fury, my hand rubbed my cheek over and over from gnawing frustration. "You should have let one of the fuckers for me to kill."

"It's fine."

"It is not, my love, you got hurt under my watch. I let this happen to you. Had I insisted and come along—"

"Brave of you to assume," she teased, lacing her fingers through my hair. "That I'd let you."

She flinched a little when I rested a palm on top of her bruise and again, it took me a while to understand she'd broken a rib. How did she hide it so well, all that pain? Why did she hide it from me, too?

"Don't sulk, Kil," she said, smoothing her thumb over my forehead. "Wrinkles don't suit you."

"Don't give me reason to sulk, woman."

"Already on your knees for her?" Nia asked, smiling as she walked towards us.

I planted a long kiss on Snow's stomach before pulling her shirt down and her jacket over her shoulders, careful not to hurt her. "Further down if she would ask me. I would go further down."

"Heavens spare me," she pleaded, making Snow laugh.

I took a deep breath and decided on my next words for a moment. If she was still afraid and untrusting to open up to me about what had happened, I would take the first step towards the truth. One that I did not intentionally want to keep away from her, especially at this point.

"Snow, I have been wanting to tell you something for some time now—a long time," I started, and her smile slowly faded, worry shading the gold. I was not ready, but I had to tell her.

"Whatever that is, it can wait. Everyone is ready to leave this frozen nightmare," Nia interrupted as the others started coming in.

Snow rose on her toes and kissed my chin again. I loved the feel of her lips on my skin, I wanted to press my own over their rosiness till they bruised. "So do I, but I suppose later it is then," she said, angling her head towards Nia.

What was that she wanted to tell me, was it about what she had kept from me the other day? Had she changed her mind?

Before parting to head for Isjord capitol, Elias and Snow stopped to say their farewells. He would not return from his duties before she left for Adriata, so this was the last time they would see each other before she married the king. And Elias was not taking this very well. He had not let her go from his embrace for long minutes.

I moved to rip his arms apart from her, but Nia stopped me. Like a jealous child, my feet dug in the ground to keep myself still from launching forward.

Nia threw me a look. "They are friends and allies, nothing more."

"I never got to thank you for what you said in Arynth," I said, turning to her. "Thank you, Nia."

"You have nothing to thank me for. I just wanted you to know that is the way with Snow, she will never take that first step to apologise or confessing or letting go. She is not stubborn, it is just who she is and how she was taught. With her you have to take those steps. I also want you to know that for the first time she has already prepared herself to lose someone. Question is, have you?"

"I don't think I will ever prepare myself for that."

"You have to, Kilian Henrik Castemont, you have to."

My head snapped to her and she nodded before heading toward the horses.

Snow had only randomly left her room the past few days to visit the gardens and the dining chambers to feed. Only two days left from our journey to Adriata and she was growing anxious as I was.

Except Nia and Penelope, she had not spoken more than just greeting words to the rest of us. She'd also stopped attending her father's meetings which were now frequented again by Nia. She was plainly avoiding our meeting which bothered and unsettled me—she was growing distant from me before we even left for Adriata. This heavy air between us was my torture.

I reached the kitchens where Ken stood surrounded with preparations of dinner and before I could wave him down for attention, he took note of me. "Is she not with you today?" he asked, surveying around.

I shook my head. "She is not coming out of her bedroom. I have come to take something for her."

He perked and threw a look at the pot boiling behind him. "It will be ready in a second, it is her favourite. Chestnut mushroom stew."

"Gods, she will choke herself getting that down." She loved mushrooms.

The old man laughed and took off his specks, folding them in his breast pocket. "I suppose she picked that as a habit."

"What do you mean?"

He let out a heavy sigh. "The king used to make her work down here with us everyday but Sundays. She took care of the living stock, killing, skinning and chopping the meat for us. Servants only have a couple of minutes of feeding time so she ate as quickly as she could, more than what everyone had. She left early for training so she missed breakfast and she would not eat dinner because it made her sick after she'd killed animals of all sorts all day long. That meal and those few minutes was all she had. It stuck with her, unfortunately."

I felt my features tremble and waver, and my eyes drew shut at the image he had just described. She rarely ate breakfast, never ate dinner. She didn't eat meat and fish terrified her. All of that—all that was done to her. What had they done to the other half of my soul? What had they done to that little girl, that tortured girl who could still smile today?

I knocked on her door and entered the room, heavy hearted and drowned in an unusual ache. She laid back in her bed while staring at the white ceiling completely lost in thought before taking note of my presence and turning to blink rapidly towards me when I laid the tray of food before her.

"You cannot do this forever, you will have to see me at some point," I said, taking a seat on her bed.

"I was not avoiding you as much as I was rotting in my own head." She got on her knees and lifted the spoon to her mouth. The moment she tasted the food, she sighed at the taste. Cautiously, she glanced toward me as she slowly took bite after bite and my heart sank.

"Eat how you like, my heart." The words barely left me without breaking. "I love watching you eat, however you do it."

She blinked surprised for a moment and then asked, "Tell me about it, about you, about your city." She did know very little about me compared to how much I knew about her.

"Mal is right about everything he has told you about me and how I was raised. My father was not a kind or a gentle man, but he had also lived through war. He was a soldier and he made one out of me as well." However I looked was never even nearly close to how I felt, my exterior and words never betrayed me. I had willed them in place to survive strong situations my training had prepared me for, but I had adapted too much into it that my whole persona had dressed in it.

"Is he not alive?"

"No, he passed from illness when I was younger."

She halted her chewing. "And your mother?"

"My mother was a strong woman from what I have heard at least, she passed as well when I was no more than five," I confessed and she dropped her spoon, her eyes locked in my gaze. One thing we both would somewhat relate to, losing your mother was never easy despite when and how you did.

"Forgive me for never asking."

"It is not something I usually enjoy sharing." I never spoke about her. The memory was heavy, but the longing was heavier. "My city," I said, raising a hand to trace her face. "It pains me to say this to you, but it is a paradise of warmth, sunlight, flowers, bright round moons and clear star glazed skies." She would have loved it if her eyes had not been blanked by the hate she had for its people.

She put a finger on my chin. "Like you, your city is like you, at least what you remind me of," she said, and my chest rose furiously.

My heart commanded me to her, but my body was frozen still. I wanted to put my lips on her plump ones, to trace every inch of her body with them. To make her mine over and over till we both grew hoarse. A promise—I'd made that promise for the both of us no matter how tempting it was to break right now.

She smiled as if she knew what she was doing to me.

"Don't tempt me, little beast," I said, when she began tracing my jaw with her finger excruciatingly slow.

"It is not my fault you are easily tempted." Her hands slipped to my jacket, pulling me closer to her. Our faces were not even an inch away as she studied me with a soft smile. Her eyes dropped to my lips, and just as my urge to commit to both of our thoughts was about to take over, she nudged my nose with hers and diverted to trace small warm pecks along my jaw and down my neck. My limbs weakened at her touch. She was right, I was easily tempted and absolutely aching for her. My will was of gods. While I held still, my lungs were running out of air to breathe under the flame of her soft lips and the warmth of her breath hovering my skin. She reached over my ear, lips gently smoothing over there. "Mal is right, you are made of rock."

I stretched my neck, the pressure keeping me still was giving me a headache. "Part of me feels like it, especially now and a few other times when you are around."

She glanced down between us for a moment, driving me mad. "There are ways without kissing or for you to be inside of me to please you."

Fuck. "Snow, I will not put my cock in lips I have not kissed yet." She frowned and began to speak when I interrupted, "Certainly not on your hands either to taint scars that were dug because of me."

Almost all days going to sleep, I had laid thinking of her wanting to release the state of need and want she'd put me in. I imagined myself inside of her, those rosy lips around me, her moans around the room, her hips riding me as she had ridden my fingers that day, but I'd never let myself do it. She was not only the object of my desires, she was my desire and I'd treat her as much.

She groaned and tilted her head back all frustration. "You are the only man who has ever made it this difficult for himself."

"I am a fool, but a fool who does not want to hurt you."

"For someone who has already been inside of me, you speak on very rough blurry lines," she complained, blowing a heavy breath.

"That was an appetiser, my *dahaara*."

She rolled her pretty eyes at me and groaned angrily once more. Kissing two of her fingers, she put them to my lips. "I don't want to regret not having given you one."

I pulled her hand again and kissed every inch of it. "There is so much I regret too, Snow, unforgivable things."

"Is it because of your king? Or because I am still the *Ybris*?" Her eyes shot wide. "For the love of heavens, tell me you don't have a wife with a child on her hip waiting for you there?"

Her last guess made me erupt with laughter, but her eyes narrowed on me in slits as if truly doubting that to be true. "No wife, no child, no lover. It's not you, my heart, the one who is being selfish in this it's always been me—"

The bedroom doors flew open and Pen marched inside nonchalantly, several dresses draped in her arms.

Snow sighed and pushed up from the bed. "Pen, for the love of Nubil, knock! What if you had entered to see us both naked and in compromising positions?" she exclaimed loudly. My dramatic dark head, not shifted from her ways, not one bit.

Pen lifted her chin up. "Well, I have seen you naked and should most certainly not be expecting to find him naked in your room, let alone in said compromising positions. Should I now, you ragged princess?" she huffed, moving towards the dressing chambers.

Snow groaned in her hands. "This girl draws fire from me."

"Don't get frustrated, you have basically made her a second you. You are to blame."

She laid back on me. "She has agreed to come with me."

"I had a feeling," I admitted. They had grown very close and comfortable with one another. Penelope saw Snow as an older sister figure so it was expected she would go with her. I also doubted she would let any Adriatian servant touch her even, let alone dress her.

"Stay," she asked. "Stay tonight, just hold me or even stand at a corner if you don't want to be near me. Or just...hold me better, please."

I began unbuttoning my jacket and her eyes lit alight as she attempted to suppress a smile. She pulled the cover back and I got in, rounding her in my embrace. "You will be good, my little beast, or I'll go get Nia to be our chaperone."

She frowned. "She would be a terrible chaperone."

"Then Malik and Caiden."

"Every girl's dream."

I reached down, smacking her bottom and she yelped. "I will kill them both if you say anything of the sort again."

"I didn't finish my sentence," she said, planting a kiss on my neck. "This girl's dream is already in this bed. I wished it could last longer, this girl enjoys this dream."

I kissed her brow, gathering her tight around me. "This boy's dream is in this bed, too, but this boy will perhaps never wake from it."

She went silent beside me, her head buried at the nook of my shoulder. It did feel like a dream, holding her. I wanted to hold her for eternity. Wake to her in my arms, fall asleep with her still buried there. Her silk skin brushing mine, her small touch vibrating on every inch of my skin. How could someone want another like this?

Penelope came back to the room and threw us a dubious look. "I still have that letter with your name on it crossed so many times that it almost resembles one of those curse callings Crafters do on sand."

Snow stiffened in my arms and slowly rolled her eyes up at me. "I don't have the slightest idea what she is on about."

I shook with laughter. It had made me laugh back then, too.

"But you did." her little friend insisted.

"Pen!" Snow shouted, drawing her eyes tightly shut. "Leave or I will feed you your own liver."

After giving the order, she snuggly glued herself to me. Her hands had slid under my shirt and roamed over my stomach, relentlessly tracing two lines that pointed down my hardened cock. "You would be a lot more comfortable naked."

I laced my fingers through her hair, smoothing a touch over and over how she liked it. "I would be. You would not."

Her hands began sliding lower down and I grabbed her mid crime. "Not there, little miss."

She went still for a long beat, then her head slowly rose to me. "Little miss?"

I kissed her nose. "You are not that big of a miss."

Her mouth parted open while she blinked confused. Dazed by thoughts, she just stared lost for a little while before ducking back to my chest. "So loud," she yawned. "Always so loud."

She made it loud. For her it beat so loud, only for her.

"I thought you remembered," I said, resting my forehead on hers. "I thought you remembered, my little miss, all of my promises and my lies."

She'd fallen asleep. She slept—she had slept while I drowned in sorrow without even grieving. This boy really didn't want to wake from this dream.

PART V
AWAKE

42

Kings and Pawns

Snowlin

I had fallen asleep in his arms and woken up to him gone, a note left by his pillow.

"My heart, Mal called for me to meet with your father. I will see you again soon." – *Your Kilian.*

My Kilian. The dream I was going to leave behind in Isjord. The dream I was about to give up, the one I had lucidly touched and then admired from afar.

The room that had become my temporary home was now emptied, the life Pen had once given to it was now gone. I felt as empty as the room looked, the captain's uniform was folded on top of my bed, no longer mine to wear. Pen had dressed me in black breeches and a long dark violet jacket resting just below my knees, sown with silver threaded birds, trees and flowers everywhere. Very repulsive to my taste, but did not have any energy to protest. She had tried to dress me in the colours of Adriata, going on and on about how I should give a good first impression to my soon to be husband.

The brand of the new blood oath wrapped around my wrist still burned every time I glanced at it, but the pain had a smile stretching wide across my face. Myrdur would soon be mine.

I vow blood, flesh and bone, ash, and soil, what was once mine is now yours, from now till heavens, once the seal of marriage between the Night King and you, Princess of Winter, is forged.

My father had given his vow as I had given mine along with the bargain to marry the king of Adriata. *I vow blood, flesh and bone, ash, and soil, what was once yours will be mine, from now till heavens, once the seal of marriage between the Night King and I, Princess of Winter, is forged.* With that vow and promise to honour the bargain, I had bid my forever farewell to my father.

I pushed my sleeve back, eight more oaths there. Soon Isjord would be mine, too.

To ruin.

Here it came—my retaliation. Isjord hung by a thread, six lords on my side, Malena out of the picture, Venzor in my alliance, Renick in my clutches and my last gift—my last gift was yet to be gifted. Despotism was always a king's greatest weakness. A pawn can chase small steps to elevation, but the only thing a king can do is side step here and there till caught in a corner. Here comes the chase.

The corridors felt different, colder, gloomier and eerier, as if life was taken away from them. The swift breeze had started to resemble the presence of relentless dead spirits haunting the halls as I made my way across them one last time towards another one who owed me.

"It suits you, Moreen. Pain. You should wear it more often."

She stood paled and thinned between two beds in the infirmary, Fren and Reuben sleeping restfully atop them. Three in one strike, three souls in my mercy—but I had no mercy. Three souls that were to die.

Her eyes were veiled red. "You turned worse than your father after all." Her anger was fatigued, it didn't please me, I wanted more, I wanted her fury.

"But they are alive. See? Still breathing. Mine are dead, taken away from me primarily because of father and then...you," I revealed, clicking my tongue at her.

She knew what she had done that night. But she had not seen me witness it. She had not seen me when she had guided the Adriatian soldiers down to where my mother was—she had not seen me sprint to warn her in the winter gardens. She had not seen me remember her face alight with eager and vile amusement at my mother's demise. Crone dearest had been working with them, but I still had doubts if she was the one who had sent and had brought them through the city walls. The documents Nia had found in her vault did not indicate anything of the sort, except that she had reassured them entrance to the castle and guaranteeing them her cooperation. What I had done after Sam's death had not been for my father, it had been for her and for her half breeds. What I was about to do now was for my father.

"Does your king know what you did that night? Does he know how the Adriatians knew so well where to enter the castle and where to look for us?" I asked, approaching to see that surprised reaction in her face better.

"How did...how did you know?" she stuttered, shooting up from her seat.

My eyes fell to her trembling hands and I smiled. "The question is, how are you paying for it, dear, not that."

She took a small step back in horror, the stool knocked over and rolled loudly on the ground. "I didn't know it was Serene," she argued, shaking her head. "I thought you were there! She'd come to find you. You should have been there instead of her!"

Years and years of waiting for this, then months and months of her parading in front of me as if I was a wounded child and her a saint to acknowledge it, and I had let her—let her think she could toy with me as she had let herself think with my mother who was now dead because of her help.

I chuckled. "Come now, you could have done better than that."

She knew I read through her lie and there was no hiding. "You cannot kill me, your father—"

I raised a palm to stop her. "My father will do nothing. You are already dead as your children will be very soon. I've delivered father a gift. Your documents and communications with the Adriatians that Alaric had extracted from your chambers years ago and more we found during my stay here. All waiting for him to be read. How disappointing I will not be here to witness." A wild grin stretched across my face while my heart welled in joy. This made me so very happy, happier than digging a dagger to her heart, having my father do it. "Your final nail in the coffin will be from your very lover, and your children's from mine. This should go down in the sacraments, the perfect tragedy written by fates. Devised by Snowlin Krigborn. Inspired and played by you."

"I didn't mean to have Serene killed. Silas will understand," she cried out and then leached on my arm. Dread had paled her face and she sobbed, "You promised the antidote for them, to your father."

I shook her off and she staggered to the ground. "No, I did not promise such a thing to anyone. I make no promises to the wicked. Happy grave digging."

Moreen screamed, roared, pleaded and cried behind me as I once had because of her. People hurt you and act surprised when you hurt them back. Another face I had to cross out of my nightmares—another face amongst the non ending that had wronged me. Another step and another brick to my retaliation.

Yesterday I left my goodbyes with them. With a painful heart, I had left them again, and soon I would also let go of them. For their spirits to rest.

Hold on a little while longer, please, I had asked and hoped they didn't hate me as much as I hated myself for doing what I was doing to them—for holding them hostage in a world that had no wanted them.

Father was not coming to Adriata, but uncle Aryan was.Though it appeared he'd yet to give me goodbye because he intercepted me in the corridor, causing me to halt midway. His face, attitude and confidence showed he had achieved what he had wanted—to get rid of me and get to Adriata. He was immensely satisfied and was almost soaring in victory. But fly too close to the sun and you have your wings burnt.

I bowed. "Father."

He laughed, his swivelling leery stare could inject all inferiority on someone, but I wasn't just someone. "So after all you did yield to me. I thought I might have to drag you to Adriata, tied and leashed. All that revolt and for what? Nothing? Daring to defy me, hovering around my business and threatening me, was that really all for nothing?"

My death would probably taste sweet to him, my demise cloying. It always seemed that his best meal had always been my suffering. Was I really his child? I hated how such thoughts still managed to clog my throat. "You hate me." Not a question, and the first time I had admitted that out loud.

Spite wore his eyes. "Everyone hates their biggest mistakes."

I straightened. What he made me feel was heavy, but Alaric had spent years helping me carve muscles to bear the load of his hate. "My parting gift is already in your chambers."

"Always so high headed," he continued, bringing me to another halt. "When will you realise the world under your feet is ash and silence. Is it my fault for raising you to be so much and aim so high when you're so little and sit so low? Did I raise you to believe a kingdom could bend to you and that they could adore the abomination that you are?"

"As much as you taught yourself the same."

"And I am king."

"You are, maybe eternal but not immortal. And do you know, father, what they say when the king is dead?" My brows sketched up. "Long live the queen."

He began laughing roughly and a grin stretched wide on his wicked mouth. "You will be no queen."

"No. No, I'll never be." He was right, I *will* not be queen. "I am ruin and therefore

I will ruin you."

"Good luck, my rose."

"It doesn't take luck to melt ice. Just fire."

"You were to be my heir," he called again, and I halted once more. The deception of rue in his voice willed me still though I didn't wish to hear what he meant to use to trick me into loss. "I chose you. I thought you should know. Even Eren had given up the moment you were born. I'd never imagined my son to be born weak and caring. You never broke, never tore, barely felt, you were my perfect choice. Had I some more years before that attack, I would have shaped you into a ruler. You would have been mighty."

"I could not rule your kingdom, father," I said, my voice fading on the echo of the corridors. "This was always his. Your only heir."

Our caravan had grown massive and new faces circled all around me though father had permissioned my soldiers to serve and escort me one last time. Isjordians lined the streets as we crossed though to the gates, their expressions weary, cold and afraid. They had to be, Adriata would soon loom freely around the continent once again.

Uncle rode ahead leading the group. Nia, Cai and Mal all around me, but Kilian was not seen amongst our large travelling arrangements.

"Mal, what of your brother?" I was slightly worried. Our conversation from last time had been cut at the start. I still had something to ask of him and he had also wanted to say something to me back in the Islines.

"He will be riding at the back. You know he worries a lot during these times, important times."

Panic rose to my throat and I tasted regret. I had not said my goodbye. I had not seen him one last time. I shouldn't have slept, I should have milked that night and just stared at him till I was sure I couldn't forget him.

"You are being odd and so is that fool, what is happening?"

Mal's brows slowly rose. "Nothing...nothing is happening, but I am glad you two are inseparable now."

When the air grew warm and light, I realised that we'd approached south. So soon. Too soon because our caravan had direct orders not to stop for rest anywhere along the lands of Isjord, let alone Adriata.

My eyes rolled back when uncle started riding towards me, my batin was in no condition to stand his banter. I was already jittery and angsty enough without his vile words which I was sure he was going to give plenty judging the slyness his features had taken.

"I was the one who took your mother from Olympia, now I am sending you off. It feels almost prophetic, don't you think, sweet niece?" he asked all so jollily. "Not quite sure about Adriata, but Olympia was magnificent. To my luck I got to see it before it perished."

"It still is, and you mean before you made it perish," I responded coldly.

"You mean what is still left of it. You do not understand, girl, that kingdom with that power should have not existed among our own, it was not natural. Everyone had grown uneasy around them and were living in fear. What if a cruel king had taken over and ordered all of our extinction. Believe me, they had the power to do that. Your uncles were not Jonah, they were young and full of desire for power," he added with a fading amusement.

I knew he did not like talking about Olympia, Alaric had told me he was terrified of them. My uncle Leren, who was to take the throne of Olympia, had been wise and fair. Alaric would say that my brother had taken every inch of his personality. He would have been a great ruler just like my grandfather Jonah was, like many before him had been. The only one uneasy had been my power-hungry father, no one else. Olympia had always been passive in wars, that was why their kind had been happy and blooming with immense power. Their relationships with the other kingdoms was almost non-existent, they barely left their borders, their god had blessed them with lands beyond productive, mountains to mine and living stock to boast. They had been artisans and forgers, extremely skilled manual workers—a kingdom completed. Till my father wanted it all for himself and ended up with nothing.

"My, my, it reminds me of a particular someone. It feels almost prophetic, doesn't it, sweet uncle?" I replied with a snide tone, and his amusement had now faded to nothing but displeasure.

Uncle had always been second player in every game of the kingdom, he had always come second. He was also a royal just like my father and aunt Eleonor, but he had little to silly power over Isjord. However, despite everything, he was always an avid supporter of my father. They had a good age difference so he saw my father more as a father than a brother. Also, given how absent my grandfather had been painted in their lives, their bond had grown closer. They both equally despised the dead old serpent.

He also had hated my mother more than all the rest, his support for Moreen and her half breeds had been evident at all times, but his dislike for my mother had not been similar to the masses. His eyes always told on him. How he watched her from a distance, how he traced her every feature, how he disliked me and my siblings. Alaric told me my mother had been promised to him instead of my father, a deal arranged by threats of war, forced to be threaded to prevent it. My grandfather had accepted as had my mother, both had been willing to spare their people the pain of war. Their betrothal would have been blessed by all kingdoms and by gods, an Aura and a human. They had met several times before my father brilliantly revealed his true orchestrated plan to steal uncle's bride as his. I saw it every time, Aryan hated my mother because he had been in love with her since the moment they had met, his eyes longing but filled with fury, one misdirected at her, one that should have been for my father.

Despite all this, the man gave me the creeps, something about him was more rotten than the rest, it was as if he would wither flowers with his touch. His energy had always been dark and wrong. Him I distrusted most out of all. Another cursed version of my father, another monster of his doing.

The Highwall grew tall and long ahead, the gruesome giant was as fierce as the first time I had seen it. Kilian was still silent at the back of our caravan and my concern was growing rapidly. The back of my neck throbbed with a dull pain at how many times it had turned to look for him, back and forth.

"He is fine, you can't start to miss him this soon, you would be in for torture if you do," Nia said, putting a hand on my shoulder, pulling me back to reality.

I did miss him and it was unusual for him to be this far from my sight, he never let me out of his and...my goodbye. Would I not get my goodbye?

"Snow," Nia called half-heartedly. "I found something else between Moreen's safe."

I blinked in anticipation as she handed me a stack of lavender envelopes, the crest of Adriata stamped atop. "What are they?"

"Letters to you, from...their king. From the Night King."

My heart began furiously palpitating in anger, revulsion and dark memory. "Why are you giving them to me?" I said, handing them back to her.

"They were addressed to you. I think you should read them."

Panic was seeping to the surface. "Nia, it won't change anything."

"I know, I just want you to learn a piece of his truth."

"Have you read them?"

"I am sorry, I did not know what they were. I opened one and then before I knew it I had read them all."

"Why had he written to me?"

"It was directly after the attack, for three years after and the last one was from five years ago."

I looked at the stack of strange letters and felt the hate I'd somehow let slip away fall back into place. "I don't want them, throw them away."

"Snow—"

"Throw them away or I will." I didn't want them. I didn't want his words—his disgusting words. How dare he write to me? Apology, threat or whatever else he had dared and addressed to me, I didn't care for it. I loathed it. Another sign of his apathy, another sign how he underestimated what he'd done to me.

The Highwall's Zone of Peace grew in sight. My heart had grown numb the closer we'd neared and I held my breath when the loud black steel cracked open on both sides. Adriatian land laid ahead of us as we finally crossed through to the warm sunlight that pierced their skies. My world felt like it was fading and my head became light. But before I could lose my consciousness, I let air enter my body once again, panting and breathless I took in my surroundings. Every limb and thought of mine trembled when the Adriatian salted air carried my hair in waves, when their blazing sun grazed my skin with heat.

My lungs expanded without their volition and took regular paces of air, calming the stream of panic in my body. My attention turned to Cai who gave me a slight nod and mouthed, "Breathe."

A group of Adriatian soldiers approached us in greeting, few ones I had previously met. Larg and Nesrin, all there as well.

"Greetings, welcome back, Malik. Princess, welcome to Adriata. I'd like to formally introduce myself, I am Larg Orbrow, General of Highwall and a member of Night court."

So the king would have heard of my good character from him first hand.

"Well, Larg Orbrow, aren't you lucky? You will now have me all yours and no longer to share with Isjord."

He laughed deeply. "We are, believe me, we are."

Was my head that tired or did I truly not get what he meant? "It still isn't too late to introduce me to your godson."

He laughed again. "You are marrying him, Your Highness."

It was then I lost my expression and he pursed his lips almost in apology, taking notice of his mistake before backing away and letting us pass through.

Adriata was just how Kilian had described it. Warm, green and full of life, one that Isjord missed greatly. How hard must he and Mal have had it to live in that cold wasteland coming from here.

A great massive dark watered river floated along the wide scenery, white thick whispering mist hovered all around us while we crossed it through a tall well-built stone bridge. I stopped and slid from Memphis to adore its view and study the strange mist Kilian had described as *alaar*, their own version of *zgahna*.

"Get back on the horse, girl," uncle shouted from the front, and soldiers surrounded me in seconds.

My eyes were lost to the black silken water of the river to pay attention to them. The mist cleared, revealing the picture hidden below. Silver and gold flakes lit from inside it, shining through the thick black blanket of water. Night sky in a stream. Small water spirits floated inside furiously, but stopped to gaze back at me from under it.

They broke the water barrier and jumped all around me, their little transparent wings sputtering glitter all over us while they chanted in a melodic voice, *"Princess, princess is no princess. Eyes of gold, heart of steel. So ever beautiful, so ever unfortunate,"* they whispered, floating around me. Strangely they spoke words I'd never heard from them. *"It makes him happy. Your smile makes him so happy,"* they continued in unison, circling above my head. *"It makes him sad, too. So sad his heart bleeds. Both your hearts will bleed."*

I felt my heart swallow itself at their words and immediately my gaze began searching for him, relentlessly.

A hand landed on my shoulder, pulling my attention. "River Nyx, blessed by our goddess for us to have night skies around even in Cyra's light," Mal explained, motioning his head for me to mount Memphis again. "I will bring you here first thing after the wedding. I'll take you everywhere you wish to go."

I stood a few more moments to take in what laid in front of me, lost at the thought that I'd marry the king of Adriata.

The forest we went past was smaller than Soren, but judging from the trees growing taller than most, it was much older. Small sand-coloured stoned houses were built scarcely till they gradually grew clustered and the city came into view.

"Amaris," Mal explained, riding beside me. "Built on the hill where Henah stepped for the first time in Adriata. The ground under grows glowing crystals of pure magic, they feed our mana and our crops. Mostly everything mimics the night sky in Adriata. The crown of trees we left behind glows under the full moon, the songbirds resting on top of them don't fly, they sort of fade like us and leave a trail of light behind—at night they look like falling stars. It is a change from Isjord, isn't it?"

"It is." I knew why they wanted to protect it so viciously, to think of losing such beauty I would grow claws as well.

The whole city beamed a warm white and gold, houses and buildings climbed towards and all around a large hill, fluttering violet flags with the Adriatian crescent moon crest resting on top of each. An enormous castle filled the middle of the city, resembling a climbing citadel. The further up the hill we went, the clearer the wide sea horizon stretched ahead. Blue clashed with white, the ground reflecting the day summer sky of Adriata. The salty breeze floated along the cobbled streets and the stone houses which were all dressed in climber plants and flowers, decorated in hues of violets, blues and lilacs. Flower folk glistened under the sun, joyously travelling from bud to bud, something from a daydream. The streets began growing lively, people halted and all stared in surprise at us, children waved and chased behind. Whispers, gasps and a few cries filled the air around us and I shuddered. I wanted to run, to sprint away, to cover my ears. I wanted to blast in waves, to disappear.

The people that hated my mother, that hated all of us, that killed them, almost killed me. The ones that scarred me, not only physically but whole, body, mind and soul. I ached all over in remembrance. My hands tightened in fists, almost digging in my palm until I felt a hand rest upon mine.

"Shall we ride quicker ahead?" Mal spoke gently and laced his hand with mine before I got a chance to dig new wounds.

My body steadied from the unconscious shaking. Gathering control of my limbs, I nodded to him and all four of us rode ahead despite my uncle's loud protest. We rode speedily ahead till the castle grounds grew into sight. It truly looked like a heaven of warmth, sunlight and flowers, all three were everywhere as colours of all sorts sprouted from bushes scattered all over. The castle walls were draped and trapped from blooming violet wisterias. A heaven indeed.

Mal directed us all down the castle corridors to our rooms till tomorrow, but my mind could no longer concentrate on taking in my surroundings. Kilian was still not here, he had not followed us when we took off from the rest of the group.

Nia and Cai stood stiffly perched on two chairs facing a balcony that overlooked a field of white roses stretched out to a cliff. I could not even sit down. The beige, gold and white tones of the room were making me dizzy.

A knock sounded by my door, and somehow my heart began thundering in hope that it might be him, that I might get to say goodbye.

Without caution that it could be someone who could hurt me I swung it open. "Kil—"

Mal leaned in the frame, almost devouring the whole of it, and smirked. "No, tis only I, the better brother."

The evening dawned on us beautifully, a silken fabric of purples, oranges and reds wrapped Amaris like I'd rarely seen before. It seemed like a vague dream, one you'd once dreamt years ago but still remembered. Winter gardens of Tenebrose paled in comparison to those of Amaris. Rows and rows of rainbow ribbons, perfume of summer and glare of sunset made for the most melancholic dusk before death.

The shadows chased behind full of life, deeper and darker while Mal guided us through the maze of scents, full of butterflies and flower folk, a heaven on land.

We halted at the edge of a garden and so did my breath at the dark beauty laying in front of me.

"These are his favourite," he said, as I twirled around in fascination at the black roses blooming around me bigger in size than a tea plate. My mouth and eyes widened from astonishment, senses prickling and pimpling from the sweetest smell of the flowers that resembled something between honey and fruit.

I traced the outlines of their petals and the smell of sugary pollen filled my lungs. "Have I scared him away, Mal, why is he not here to show me them himself?" I could no longer keep my questions in. It was not like Kilian to be this distant. I needed him today and he was not there. I still felt his hands over my spine soothing me to sleep, his lips on my brow as he planted peck after peck or the sound of his laugh every time I'd complained of my frustration. The lack of his presence around me left a trail of cold and prints of longing. My goodbye...unsaid.

Mal picked a white carnation and weaved it through my hair. "Nothing like that, Snow, you just need to believe him, he will come to you."

"What was he like when he was young? List me all his lovers."

He laughed and swung a rose, hitting my face. "Let's sit. This will be a long one."

We both sat by a garden bench, my hands carrying flowers Mal had picked for me, their aroma entrancing, almost glamouring me to mellowness, a perfumy distraction.

"Kil is considerate though he plays to be very bad at it. My mother was not treated very well by our father. He loved Kilian's mother and after she passed, he was tied to a political marriage with mine not even months later after he'd buried her. Everyone had a thing about disrespecting and mistreating my mother, more so our father. Everyone but Kilian. He was cold, very cold. I thought he hated her, too, but he'd watch her knit and sow every evening. Day after the other, he sat with her just staring at her till he came with his own sewing case and learned it side by side with her. They barely spoke, but it made my mother happy, she was the happiest in the afternoons she spent with him."

I took a deep breath, trying to expand the tightening of my chest. "The embroidered handkerchiefs he carries, were they done by him?"

"No, they were done by my mother. He would do hers and she would do his." He reached into his pocket and gave me a handkerchief with his mother's initials atop. *D.C,* sewn in sage green with a little daisy on the side.

I smiled widely, running my hand over the stitching, imagining Kilian's hands over it. "Would you mind if I kept it?"

He smiled. "I have more if you would like."

"I would want to have them all and all of him, and it would never be enough. For now a piece will do," I said, tucking the cloth tightly between my hands. "More, tell me more."

He took a deep breath and leaned back on the bench. "He's also...caring, almost too caring. Every time I put myself in trouble or caused trouble he always took responsibility for them," he said somewhat painfully. "Once a fat butcher beat a child for stealing a liver for his starving family and I thought it funny to uncage all his living stock and set it free." He stopped to laugh at the memory. "Three large cows and loads of sheep, not a small stock at that. He had complained to our father the right next hour. But righteous Kil had taken all the blame and silenced me by promising not to tell otherwise. He took twenty lashes in each hand from our father when he was barely a teen boy. My father was not lenient on us, never was, especially to him, but he got to training and lessons the next day, took care of his wounds and cleaned them till they healed. He acted as if nothing had happened. He is almost hateable if you think about it."

"He is," I said, my voice almost a whisper. Did I like hearing about him? Did I like torturing myself by knowing more of him only to lose him? Silence fell between us, almost too grave. "And the lovers?" I asked, hoping to liven the mood.

Mal laughed. "I would be dead before I could mutter even the first name."

"Ah, so there have been several," I teased, in fact half jealous. Now I really wanted to know all of their names. "I hoped with the personality and emotional range of a rock he would have found that difficult."

Mal's laugh rolled over all around the garden before he turned to me. "It is hard to know what he really feels, do not judge what you see. I read his shadows almost every time because I cannot understand him without. They are filled with so much colour, more than you could imagine. When he sees you," he interrupted himself, shaking his head, "it would be difficult to even paint what they turn when he sees you."

I shivered hearing that, it was either the flowers making it hard for me to breathe or my lungs had forgotten how to inhale—his words had me almost panting. "He didn't come with us, did he?"

"Forgive me, we didn't mean to lie, but he had to return last night with duties to report back. With the agreement so close, he had to."

"Why didn't he tell me, I didn't even get to say goodbye." The word goodbye shattered on my lips.

"He thought you would panic if he was not there, so he made me promise to tell you he was watching you."

Did he know how I felt? He could not read my shadows to understand and I had never told him truly just how he makes my heart tremble and falter at his sight, how his presence masked the rest of the world away, how nothing mattered anymore. I hated and feared that deeply because I still loved my family more than anything. My world had now come crashing and the choice I was going to make would send it shattering even harder. It pained me to think and admit to it, but it was still them. My choice was always them—my family. They overrode everything else. It didn't matter if it would hurt him, that I was about to hurt him.

My fingers tugged on the folded handkerchief—a piece of him. Tomorrow I would marry the king of Adriata. Tomorrow I would end us.

The three of us.

43

STARS AND NIGHTS

SNOWLIN

IT STILL STARED AT me. The black fog of my sight still stared at me. Today it was darker and hungrier than ever. It needed feeding, it needed satiating, or it would devour me. But this beast fed on carnage—it was the mist of who I was meant to be.

Pen stood behind me, devoured in a daze as she examined the white painting of me.

The dress was simple. A bright white that contrasted my dark hair perfectly. It flared in soft layers of tulle and scarcely stitched with rose embroidery. Today there was nothing to hide, so I bared my scars openly, the dress stopping shortly above my bust, nothing to cover the straight slash that ended just down my shoulder.

"Well done, Pen. I look like a bride."

She tidied the sides of my hairdo, pinning all sorts of jingles at the back. I'd refused to wear a veil so she'd convinced me on the pins.

"Are you not afraid?" she asked, holding in a cry.

"Yes," I said, tracing a finger over the rose embroidery on the skirt of the dress. "He is my fear." I was terrified. If one could ever fall in a pit of suffocation without light, four crashing walls slowly tightening around, air sliming with scent of sulphur and death, a crawl of scales over every inch of skin, then it would slightly resemble how it felt to be under my bones right now. But what was fear but another emotion. A controllable one and one I'd escaped once, twice and a thousand times, even that inflicted. Fear was chains, and I'd broken out of those too. I would have to break out of these sooner or later, same as I'd done with my father's.

"You don't have to do this," she blabbered, pacing around me nervously. "Kill him, I mean. Maybe not now, you will be surrounded with soldiers and Empaths and Umbra and...and he is an Obscur." She gasped loudly, putting a hand over her mouth in sudden realisation. "He can...he will kill you without even seeing light."

"He can only try, Pen. Remember, I am never alone."

She frowned. "But you dismissed Nia and Cai. Where on Hodr have you sent them off to, especially today?"

I stood from the dresser and threw a glance over the balcony framing a grey morning full of unloaded thunder. "I was talking about me. I have me and perhaps the greatest weapon of all."

"This is such a terrible time to be speaking in cipher."

A knock sounded by the door and the little red head's paces of breath grew heavy, sending her in a fit of panic and she clutched her chest tight.

"Believe it or not, it was not a cipher." I cupped her shoulders. "You do not move, once Nia returns, you will leave with her." I handed her one of my daggers. "In case you need to be brave one more time today."

The last time perhaps. Once I'd kill the Night King, there would be nothing in Adriata but ruin.

She held my wrist, not letting me go, emerald eyes filled with beads of silver. "Promise you will come back for it."

"You have my promise, little carrot." A promise this time I intended to hold and attain.

The heavy doors creaked open and light footsteps chased inside the room. I expected a squadron of Aura to drag me out to him, perhaps a tasteful lashing, a public stoning, maybe a quick beheading for dramatic effect of crowd pleasing, but they sent a lone woman. Perhaps she was to do all three of those? A garroter in a dress, nothing more tasteful than that.

"With gods' blessings, might their heavens welcome us," she greeted me with a white smile. Streaks of grey stretched towards her bound hair, the lilac cotton gown she wore floated lightly as she approached me. Demure features of a gentle woman. But then even I could trick a wolf into a snare.

I studied the thin diamond jewelled crown set atop her head, the black diamonds almost made me second guess my sight. They warped within, like hovering black mist contained in a glass.

She bowed her head gently, a glowing smile etched in her lips while her eyes swept over me more in adoration than anything. "Pleasure to finally be acquainted, Your Highness, my name is Driada. The king has given me the pleasure to walk you to him."

Pleasure? She dared talk to me this lightly? I stared at her for a long while till her smile began faltering. "Lead the way," I said, finally bored out of whatever trickery this was.

She extended a hand, taking mine and draping it through her elbow, leading us out of the white and gold castle corridors filled with the scent of roses and painted colourful glass that reflected the gentle morning light of the hidden summer sun. She directed us through a large garden, different from the one Mal had taken me a day ago. A grand maze of colour and greenery, open and stretching as wide as ten fields of corn. That was not what made it different. Strangely, flower folk, spirits, enchanted birds, bees and butterflies sounded heavy in the air, gurgling without fear. Magical creatures never laid within ground of humans, never on soil grown where steps of humans laid more than ten paces and ten moments. They were bound by their god as such to lay protected. How?

"This is his garden," the woman spoke as if she'd heard my thoughts. "No one is allowed here but him, and now me and you. The creatures reside safely here."

I almost scoffed. Did the Night King have a hobby? Murder by day and gardening by night?

"Do all his servants wear crowns?"

She chuckled softly, lifting a lace gloved hand to hide her soft smile. "No, this servant is his mother."

"I thought he was an orphan." He was a child king, crowned at only fourteen years of age. The Obscur Asteri had built his fame since barely a child.

"He was and now he isn't."

"Where are his executioners, I also saw you not bring shackles, why am I not being dragged there?"

She let out a heavy exhale before cracking open a small metallic gate that led to a straight corridor of white roses. "Quite the impression you have gathered on my son. He is rather cutthroat, cold, maybe sometimes dim-witted and so ungentle with his words, but not one to shackle a woman he is to make a wife, let alone one that is to save his kingdom."

"He should have not killed my family, maybe then he would not have to save his kingdom."

"It is not that he had a choice—"

I giggled mirthlessly, too tired to be amused by this. "We all have a choice. I make many right now. Do not kill the woman who raised that monster, do not obliterate everything in the vicinity of this flowery hell, do not tie knots and stitches with all Adriatian guts. See how many choices I have? All so very tempting, yet here I am, holding you, marrying the king whose life will bleed from these hands and saving this kingdom of the wicked."

We halted and she gave me a look of uncertainty, making to say something, but unable to.

A noise outside the castle premises grew heavy. Synchronised steps, shouts of orders rang in the air, but they were not there for me. The squadrons of soldiers were moving away from the vicinity and outwards.

"Nothing to worry," she said, resting a hand on mine. "The trouble is far from us."

I slid my arm off from her and continued forward. "I don't worry, the trouble is where it needs to be."

We walked silently along the guided path while buzzing flower folk and sun spirits began irritating my senses—there was too much noise in and out of my head. A giant temple resembling a crescent moon grew in sight, white and blazing with belief of the wicked. Violet wisteria cradled the columns affront, curtain of scents and lovely sight. Closed buds of moonflower laid all around, an attempt at mimicking the night sky—again.

Several sentries all draped in sun-soaking black leather, silver hilts and black steel were all posted around the entrances and many others tucked away further in the distance.

A frown bunched between my confused brows. Had Adriata run out of guards? "It is quiet," I noted, soaking in the panic of silence.

"The king has ordered for only you two to be present. He doesn't normally keep much guard or protection. To summon darkness is to summon death."

"Trust me, no one knows better than I do."

She blanched, almost devastated. "Let us...make haste," she said quietly and then suddenly halted, clutching her chest from the dry cough that erupted out of her lungs, almost claiming her out of all air. She wheezed between hard breaths and blood splattered on her hand as she searched the pockets of her gown frantically.

"Pardon me," she said, as I helped her find a handkerchief in her pocket and wiped the blood around her mouth.

"You are ill," I said, noting that the blood was not only blood, but black fluid signalling death.

She shook her head, attempting to flash a sweet smile, but a cough overtook her once again. "Pardon me."

I rubbed her back and chest. "Your damned son should have not tasked you when you are this ill."

"Because I am this ill he asked me, granted me a long wish of mine, to meet you like I met Serene."

I staggered a step back at the mention of her name. "You knew her?"

She nodded. "My father was a Lyran merchant trading saltwater pearls with Myrdur and we would often be invited at the house Skygard, your mother was fond of her jewellery. You are every bit her, it is almost a gift to have seen you before—"A cough interrupted her again. "Before this claims me."

Tears warmed my eyes. "You knew her from before? Before Isjord?"

She gave me a wry smile and nodded. "Even your voice is hers," she said, reaching for my face.

I moved away from her creeping touch. "You let them kill her. You did nothing while they killed her."

She halted, pulling her hand away. "For that I will repent till wherever gods chose to take me.I will pay for doing nothing."

"You could have stopped your son."

"It was not him who needed stopping, my *asteri.*"

"Tell me," I grit out, my tone dipped in fury. "Tell me how many lives besides that killer's do I have to claim." One, five or five hundred million, I intended to take each and every one of them.

The doors of the temple drew open behind me. A loud creak and careful steps of what resembled my fear made toward me and my body refused to turn.

"Just mine," an all too familiar voice called.

I froze at how that fear turned to strange comfort in a matter of seconds. My brain was betraying me, it had to be. Yet my sight didn't, catching the queen's handkerchief on the floor.

Two initials engraved at its corner.

D.C.

An empty moment passed. Then two. Like the world had stopped on its hinges and stood quiet. A breath stuck on my chest, taking my lungs prisoner. I shook my head from disbelief. It had to be a mad nightmare. It had to. Yet when pain struck my palms I didn't wake, only slumbered further into reality.

I was awake.

Slowly I turned around and he stood there, the presence of a king, draped in black, a crown of might and black diamonds on top of his head. *The Obscur Asteri.* The Night King. My true nightmare. All this time the King of Adriata had trailed me, surveyed, touched, embraced, kissed me. He had comforted me, known my truths, tried to know my pain and I had let him...the one who had caused it. The king of the people who had killed my family. The one that could have prevented what happened to them, the one who made plans and sat through decisions to kill thousands, the one who I was almost...almost nothing.

His stare didn't waver. His stare bore no regret. His stare remained the same silver one and I hated it. "Only my life, Snow," he repeated. "No one else's."

I felt and I didn't. I was human and I wasn't. Yet every part of my soul tore when I inspected the features of the man I'd sworn to kill. When I looked at him with the sweetest care as if he were my world. I saw the man who robbed me of light like I saw a treasure.

Forcing my steps forward, I walked towards the temple. My features straightened. My hatred weakened. My venom sugared. The only bit of strength I could gather to speak hate to the one who had softened me came from a place of care. "I have a bargain to fill and you have an agreement to sign. Let us get it over with," I said, strutting inside the temple and past him, loathing my own shell for faltering. My feet barely carried the weight of pain that struck me like the bite of a viper, quick, rapid and deadly poisoning.

"Snow, let us—" He reached for me and I backed away, slipping from him.

Snow?

Snow?

Laughter stuttered out of me, my body shaking, just not with amusement. "You know, K—" I cleared my throat. "You have taught me something I'd forgotten. That no matter how hurt I am, I can always hurt a little more. You won, Your Majesty, beating my father at his own game. You won over me in every human way. But I am not human, so now I will win over you in every inhuman way."

"Snow," he called, reaching for me again.

I did not stop.

"Snow, stop for a moment and let us speak," he called strongly, and when I took no notice, gusts of black darkness lifted a wall afront me. It withered the wisteria around, birds flew in gusts, screeching almost in anguish and even his own guards flinched. This had been what I'd felt that night when he'd fought Melanthe. He'd suppressed this all along.

All the signs in front of me. When did I become so inattentive?

I did not stop.

I could not stop.

"I said let us speak," he shouted, echoing around the hollow temple, and I flinched this time. He no longer was him, the one I was so unafraid to trust. He was him, my fear—my only fear.

I turned round to the one I'd once submitted to. The nightmare warping around and behind him. He wore the mask of death. The thief of light. A sneer quirked in my shivering lips and I grit my teeth. "I will not kill you before that agreement, so let us get this over and done with because I am not even close to holding myself back right now. I will kill you and then me, and I will not die, king of the damned, before I harvest all life out of this land!"

He reached for my arm and I flinched back away from him, rubbing away the feel of his skin on mine. My skin searing where he'd grazed. "Don't touch me."

Given up, he only stared in a frozen state as I backed further in the holy room.

The altar stood between darkness and magic grazed skies that flickered pretend starlight above us, the only source of light. White petals laid all over where I would sign my death.

I took my place before the oddly young priest blending among the darkness in his velvet black robes, clutching Astrum liber between his visibly shivering hands that took a tremble at my sight.

Moments later, he stood beside me, his warmth wrapping around my skin, the scent of spring yet with him and luring my senses to deception.

"Welcome, child of Henah," the priest greeted his king, waving an incense of sage before him.

Turning to me, the mist wavered from the stick in directionless patterns because of his shaking hands. "Welcome, child of...Krieg."

"Nubil, too," I spoke, and he swallowed thickly, making me chuckle. "Make it quick, I grow horns at strike of midday and might ebb them right in your eyes."

He staggered a step back, his stare aghast as it bounced to glance at his king who let out a deep sigh and said, "Continue, Atlas, she is only poking fun."

"Oh, you would know, wouldn't you, darling?" I asked snidely, almost chewing my teeth, holding all the venom I'd savoured for him back. I smirked at young Atlas. "No one else wanted to do it, did they? Wed a monster to their most beloved killer. You look but a boy, did they force you?"

"N-No," he stuttered. "Uhm, Kil, I mean, His Majesty, asked me to. He thought you'd be more comfortable. And I am not a boy, I am sixteen."

"Ah, he thought I'd be comfortable," I said, nodding to myself. "If he wanted to accommodate my wishes he should have slit his own throat this morning and made my job easier."

"Continue, Atlas," he prompted the boy sternly. "I have a lot to discuss with her, don't take my time."

Discuss? How dare he?

The young priest raised a hand to the heavens. "W-With Henah's blessings we have gathered in this day of peace, day of reunion, day that marks the end of hostility, animosity, separation and fear," he recited, almost stuttering through his words. "H-Hope brightens like morning sun, better days gather in our future. Due to the nature of this union we will not ask the heavens for a blessing, but we ask of them of understanding. T-This...uhm, marriage shall only be of this soil, your souls will not be parting together as one to the heavens." He threw a bunch of flower petals over us and cleared his throat. "With Henah's blessings."

"With her blessing," I whispered, smiling at Atlas. "Might death of all you befall upon this marriage."

His Majesty took a deep breath beside me and nodded to the terrified priest to continue. "S-Soil of life blesses, you will water one another's lives to reap the bloom of this hearth's flowers. T-To live and prosper."

My jaw was about to snap in half from how tight I'd clenched my teeth. "I will burn you and I will burn your lands. I will be fire," I muttered between my teeth. "All will be dust, all the ashes of men fed to your younglings."

The priest halted and...the king sighed once more. "It is fine, Atlas, continue so I get to hear these words in private. I like her speaking dirty only to me."

I scoffed and tightened my fists, nails digging and breaking my skin.

"To become one another's. Two pieces of one, to become a whole," Atlas said, crossing his hands back and forth.

My tongue bled, mouth filling with the taste of blood when I said, "And they will become my toys, I will butcher one each day, spread their limbs, organ by organ while their lungs still breathe. I will keep them alive as I etch their guts."

Atlas swallowed thickly, but continued without prompt this time, "To merge and forge a union of marriage."

"And then I will carve your very soul out and fest till there is no soul of yours left."

"You already have my soul," the king spoke calmly, "and carved it out as yours."

I breathed heavily, but continued. "Only then, when I have made you watch your own doing befall upon your people, I will kill you."

"You have already killed me."

"Not enough," the words came out barely a harsh whisper. "It will never be enough."

The priest handed the rings, surprisingly not dropping them from his trembling hands that shook the box. Two twin silver halos, a crescent moon carved on top the both of them.

Facing him, I dared meet his gaze. Devastation wore his terribly beautiful face as he stared at me like he stared at his world. He raised a hand, looking for mine and gently slid the cold ring on my finger. The silver metal was heavy with the feel of him.

I was his and he was mine in all the ways we shouldn't be.

"Your hand," I said, pulling mine from his. "Let's see exactly where I will cut off."

He extended his strong hand and I slid the ring on quickly, not wanting to submit to the terrible feeling of wanting to hold it, to lace my finger through his, to seek the comfort of them—wanting them to hold me.

Atlas crossed the sage smoke over us. "With the sacred steel of Lyra, I seal you bonded to matrimony. You are now one another's to joy, to sadness, to live."

The seal of my blood oath on my wrist burned and sunk under my skin. It was done, he was bound to me and I to him, for till death do us apart. Till I did us apart.

"Your Majesties." Atlas kneeled before the two of us. "My king, my queen."

I snorted and then cackled loud enough it enveloped all the large hall. "Out," I said quietly, but the priest blinked surprised, so I repeated a second time shouting, "Out!"

My name was soft when he spoke it, "Snow—"

I stared at the ring on my finger, turning around and refusing to look at him. "Did I really downplay the pain caused by you this much or did you put the matter on your hands to disregard it?"

"I did not disregard it, my love."

"You did!" I shouted, patting my aching chest. "You did. Otherwise why did the King of Night...why did you even think of breathing near me, let alone cheating your way into me."

"There is much I have to tell you, but I never intended to, my heart, to deceive you.

But this. This, I couldn't stop from happening, even if I tried. You have had me as yours since perhaps the beginning of it all." He took a step to me, cupping my shoulders to turn me to facing him again. My skin erupted in shivers where he held me, not those of fear or cold, not those of repulsiveness either, but because of him and how he made my heart pulse. He raised my chin and when I lowered my eyes, still refusing to look at him, he pressed his forehead to mine and I drowned once again in his inhale, every piece of me refusing to move away. His fingers were soft on my face. "I've been dying slowly day by day and I'd never known this and how this feels. Now...now, my Snow, I die a little less. I began dying a little less when you smile and when you make me smile. When I held you I held my stars. I had been in the dark and never known. You are my stars. *Maa asteri*," he whispered, nudging my nose with his. "One doesn't get to stumble upon them, not in a thousand lifetimes, yet I did. Call it fate. Call it a twisted fate, but I did."

"Fate?" I asked, my voice a fraction from breaking. I pushed away from his touch, scratching the searing feel of him red raw from my arms, enough to draw blood—the pain numbing whatever I was feeling.

"Don't, please," he pleaded, drawing his eyes shut.

"Let's call it fate, but don't you find it strange, Your Majesty, how one moment your heart burns and burns and suddenly in a flicker of a mere ember it turns completely to ice? So there...there goes your fate. Our fate was meant to burn and hurt, it is written in blood and sealed in death. You knew and yet you ignored it and my feelings." I felt blood leaking down my arms, soaking my white gloves. "You disgust me, repulse me. Seeing you breathe so close to me I wish I could choke on this very air."

His silver gaze withered at every step I took away from him. My heart had not turned exactly to ice, it had turned to a razor flame of frost, one so sharp that it could carve your very bones. "All of this must have been so very entertaining for you. Well at least I hope it would have been because what comes after this won't be all so pleasant."

"I know you, Snow, do not push me away like this, not without hearing me first," he said, trying to close the distance between us, but I moved further back. With each step of mine, his chest rose faster and hope fleeted from his expression.

"You know absolutely nothing," I spat without hesitation. I didn't care for his explanation. "You never did, had you known even the slightest, you would have not even thought of even looking at me."

I was not going to let his words break me, I would not allow it, he had already shattered me to pieces—pieces that for years I have not been able to collect, they were still missing, probably never to be found.

I unsheathed the dagger hidden between the layers of my skirt and pressed it to his neck. He did not flinch, not even waver, only stared at me like he always did, like I was his whole world, like there was nothing else to see, like he only saw me beneath what most saw.

A tear slid from my eye and I trembled in front of him, weightless and unwilling to finish what I'd waited twelve years to do. He'd done it, truly won his way out of me killing him.

He reached for my face, wiping a tear away with his thumb. "Don't cry, my love, do it with a smile."

"Be afraid," I barely managed to utter between stuttering breaths. "Be afraid."

"I am afraid." His knuckles grazed my cheek ever so softly. "How can I not be afraid when I am losing you."

"Enough," I said, covering my ears and turning away from him.

His arms wrapped around me, his body melting to mine. "Do what you came here to do, but listen to me first."

I didn't want to hear it. I wanted to hear none of his reasons. "Let me go!" I thrashed as furiously as my weakened will allowed me to, yet not enough to push him off me.

He rested his forehead at the side of my head, his warm air over my skin turning every limb of mine languid and I stopped moving. "Forgive me one last time for what I am about to say." His hands smoothed over me, caressing my skin, as he whispered the next words so gently they had sprung around scents of care and colour of want. "You have turned this realm upside down and sideways right into the hottest of hells, Snow."

"Enough, enough, enough." I said, shaking my head. A plea more than a demand.

"I'm in love with you, so in love with you. To keep you, I kept quiet so selfishly." At his words my whole body reverberated with pain and fear of the worst kind. "I want you to know that even if it is wrong, even if I do not deserve to do so, even if you won't allow me, even when...I lose you—I want you to know that I am utterly and completely in love with you. Even though it hurts to know that you will slip away from me, that these feelings will die with me. I want you to know that despite everything, despite all, I love you and always will."

He buried his head between my hair. I could feel the speeded paces of his breaths, the want in the tightness of his embrace, how he shook holding me. "You taught me how to feel, you taught me love, but you didn't teach me goodbye. So I waited and said nothing because I knew that you would teach me that now. Forgive me for not saying anything and forgive me for not regretting having loved you."

I broke myself free and turned to him. Grabbing onto the lapels of his jacket, I rose to my toes and pressed my lips into his.

Touch of cold darkness against the smooth moon, a dark so bright it shone. The contact broke me and a whimper left my throat. Every inch of me burned and ached and felt electric at the warm feel of him on me, at the touch of his hands over my skin, the flutter of his breath, the scent of season enveloping me. I understood then what he'd meant that day—I understood that I, too, would have to live knowing this and never having it again.

I held him and he held me. I burned as if being in flames was being alive. His hands gripped my face and he sank the kiss deeper, obliging to my demand. His fingers spanned over my neck, the other bringing my body closer to press it against his hard one. I was never anyone's, but at this moment I was his. His finger curled between my hair, my own tight around him, almost afraid he'd part from me. Moans escaped me only to be drowned by his, and I swallowed them deep till they vibrated low in my stomach, stirring my desire and desperate ache for him. It felt as if sky had touched land, epiphanic and longing as he devoured me and I salvaged him for as long as what had been left from his Snow remained from fading. It was when my breaths ached and the cry in my throat welled beyond containment that I pulled away, biting his lip softly, each fibre of my being demanding to relish him more. It was how I'd imagined and so much more, overwhelming and strange, it made my heart hurt.

I would break him, but I realised a moment too late that I would break me just the same.

He sucked in a breath of pain, the sound of steel parting flesh broke the silence and then the heavy air filled with metallic stink of blood.

"Such pretty words. Had I a heart, it would have been yours," I whispered over his lips, twisting the dagger in his flesh. "Ah, yes, you ripped that away twelve years ago. Soon I will have yours with all its roots, King of Adriata." I pulled back away in a voice that was no longer mine, a step that would hunt him and an unforgiving gaze that would soon see his pain. "Expect and be aware, I have great plans for you."

My dagger had embedded in his shoulder, yet he did not flinch or remove it. A silver thread of a tear slid from his eye and I tore my gaze away, making for the doors before I could no longer hold it in.

The skies welcomed me ghastly, spinning, lightless and tempest brewing. Behind me doors heavily creaked shut as all the ones in my heart did. Finally tears streamed down my face and I let silenced small whimpers and cries escape my mouth as I no longer was able to suppress them. The overwhelming wave of emotion that had not drowned me since when my family died rolled all over me again. The feeling of loss was heavy and I clutched my chest tight, fear cursing every corner of it—illogical, unconscious fear. My fingers grazed my lips, afraid, as if I would wipe away his presence there.

I love you.

The words rang loud in my ears, my heart taking stab after stab, it wavered and then it stilled, sending me in an agony of hurt as I cried the well and swell of it all out, the sound drowned by my palm and heavy mourning skies. I was happy and then I wasn't.

He could not be mine because happiness never knew me, refused to know me. He could never be mine for I was sentenced to hate him. He could not be mine for he was never mine, never to be mine and never meant to be. And I was lost, now to never be anyone's, to never be his. For I'd sold each part of me on the premise of retaliation for those who had me for a bit, for too little and far too short, for a while and never long enough. For those I loved and never said I did till they were gone, the one's he'd taken away from me. The irony of fates, the irony of gods, the one I had vowed to kill was the one my heart vowed to protect.

"Snow!" His footsteps left the temple directed towards me and he called in the air again, searching, "Snow...please. Please, come back to me. Come to me, Snow. Come to me however you want. Hurt me, hit me, battle me, hate me, stab me all you want. Do it all, but do it all close to me. Do what you came here to do. Don't...don't go soft on me, my love."

I bit on the smile and the stuttering laugh that left me full of heavy tears. I wiped the fog of tears away with my palm and blood smeared across my face, air tasting of salt and steel.

Rage, pain and unshed tears fogged my sight, missing the two blurred Isjordian soldiers slowly approaching me, malice intended with every step they took towards me.

Within flashing seconds, a cloth was over my mouth. A dull pain rang behind my back and before the world spun, one of them grabbed and hoisted me onto their arms.

Then the pure nothingness of the void, again.

The heartache gone with it.

Snow, my mother's voice called, jerking me awake. *It is time.*

Why was this becoming a habit of mine? Next time, if anyone wanted my attention or wanted to tie and bargain me to anyone, they need only ask. I would happily oblige to avoid the razor-sharp pain in my skull and the whizzing sound drumming along my ears and head, all of that good stuff.

We were close to the sea apparently. The wind breezed furiously around me, coating my lips with a salty taste, the waves crashed against the rocks like sharp lightning cracks, the bashing noise accompanied by the only other sound of seagulls. At sea. But not far from land.

When I gathered to open my eyes, my surroundings felt beyond foreign. I laid on a cold stone floor, my hands bound tied behind my back. Someone liked bondage more than many by the looks of the intricate knots my fingers grazed. Metal bars separated the grey stony room between me and another dark figure sat in front of me on their other side, arms and legs crossed, quietly observing.

Dragging my body up, I managed to stand upright and lean on the wall. A tower, I noted. One face of the wall completely ruined and open, facing an angry sea and rocks almost hundred feet below us.

"You are a busy man, dear uncle, whatever it is that you want to say or do, please do not hesitate on my behalf," I said with a raspy voice, smiling like a madwoman. The amount of backstabbing today was on a legendary scale, quite the crowd of haters I have gathered. My, my, wasn't I popular.

He stood solemnly staring hate at me, his eye betraying nothing but vileness. "For years I had to stand your mother's presence around me, then you and your siblings came along and that dolour doubled, tripled then quadrupled. The spawn of her betrayal looming and growing into princes and princesses that one day would inherit the graced lands of Isjord. How did you think that made me feel, niece?" he said, squatting in front of me. Eye glowing in a washed out creeping blue.

His dramatics made me roll my eyes. "For the love of Caelum, spare me pissing pity talk. Dear, dear uncle, don't you think your anger was a tad bunch misdirected?" I spat. "She did not leave you, she was stolen from you."

He leaned in, lips peeling into a snarl. "Your mother had the choice to refuse his request, but she chose him, not me."

"How about I take you to that other land, maybe you can take this up with her yourself," I threatened, tugging on my bounds hard, making him flinch. Whatever had happened, my mother was dead, and him talking like this about her felt as if her memory was being tainted.

He examined me and smirked, standing to pace about the room. "Do you know how difficult it is to kill three royal children and a queen?"

I straightened at his words.

"I could have made my work easier if I had just killed her before she had Eren, but my loving brother had been so taken with her that he never let her out of his sight. I'd never thought Silas could love, but whatever that bitch had done to him soon would fade. But then, just when I was about to give up," he said, slapping his palms together, "a bright solution came. So eager, aren't they, the Adriatians? Something about a terrible prophecy of wolves, dragons and thunderbirds, was it not? One moment they received my letter, the next they attacked. How could anyone doubt my confirmation? I, the Prince of Winter, a liar?"

My eyes drew closed from the fiery anguish that dug through my heart and pierced every bone. I could not hide the cry twisting on my face. His words, they stabbed me deep—deep on my still open wound, and I bled as I had never before. He had been the one to tell the Adriatians. He was the reason. He was the one. I could not think. I rocked myself back and forth, shaking with pain and fury. It felt as if I mourned them for the first time. He was why they were dead.

He sighed. "You three served no purpose to Silas anyway, after Eren and you didn't bloom any blessing it was pointless to wait for Thora, he also had Fren and Reuben. Whatever happened did not affect him whatsoever, but the damned lords and other kingdoms almost overthrew him over that damn wall and then he was forced to agree in the end, putting his plans to a halt, unfortunately. Till he thought of the agreement. The lords would fall for it, they knew we needed what Adriata could offer, trades became costly, our Aura weakening till we invested most of our coin in guard and maintenance for those damned walls. But the barbarians refused and then came you—till they asked for you," he said almost laughing. "The salvation."

Snow, my snowflake, open your eyes, look and listen. My mother's sweet voice circled like a breeze about my ears and my eyes flew open. Even gone she still watched over me.

"What about me?" I asked, but I already knew, and he had already said enough. As Moriko had said, my father's way into Adriata was me.

"You, sweet niece, you are his key to this damned wall, into this damned kingdom," he answered, flinging his hands in the air in exclamation. Clicking his tongue and shaking his head, he continued, "But the troublesome little wench you are, almost lost him that as well. You even forced him to stage that fiasco of bandits to kidnap and keep you locked away and out of his plans till the deal. But he learned then that you were not only words after all."

Moriko had been correct.

"A smart girl, weren't you, but you did not count the extras. Silas knew of your alliance with the General, he knew it was useless to trail you, that you were far from knowing any of his plans. But poor Samuel, he had connections. If you had found out, you'd have ran, hid, perhaps even warned someone. Samuel did come very close and I dare say found out enough to know what was going on. Very unsmart on his behalf, it earned him death after all."

My father trailed Samuel because of me, because I was using him for information. He had died because of me. I could not stand it anymore. Everything that had happened was my father's doing, the evil was him from the whole beginning, without him would not be the destruction of Olympia, the Adriatian attack, the thousand Isjordians dead, my mother's, Eren's, Thora's, Samuel's deaths and so many more.

"First he stole from Solarya, then Hanai and Seraphim. Now Adriata. What is next, Eldmoor? I do not understand what it is that he wants? War?" I questioned with a half voice.

"No, the point is to get all of them without extensive war, there is an easy way now. You finally were useful to him, congratulations, niece," he laughed and clapped towards me.

"He is a fool to think he can march in all of them freely."

"But he will, there will be nothing for him to march freely into. A clean slate, free empty land for him to create and expand Isjord, the only kingdom."

My father was thinking of wiping out populations of millions to empty land, had he gone mad finally? I laughed. "The old fool is losing his mind after all, has that sweet red headed witch been spinning tales in his ear again?"

He stood and faced me behind the metal bars again, the viscous blue eye glared beams of threat onto me. He was so near I could squeeze the light out of his life in seconds, but I was up for conversation. "Years and years ago when gods blessed our lands do you remember what God of all Gods, Fader, bestowed as his gift upon us all?" he questioned.

Were both brothers losing their minds alike, and this one had kidnapped me to tell old tales of gods? All this fussing was based on children's stories of gifts and blessings? My mighty father was basing his war theories on this? Krig would wipe his shame with mud knowing his blessings were rolling over the brain of mice. Cyra, too, to find her people catering to my father's brain twiddling ways of fear propaganda that worked better than any war.

"Fader, my niece, once had a lover called Aurora. The mighty Guardian of the old White Flame, she who guarded the balance of realms and the chain of peace, mighty powerful amongst her sort if not the most powerful. However, one day his most beloved lover betrayed him and fell for an earthly creature that roamed our realm during those times, as all wenches seem to do. Fader was flaming in fury, betrayed and hurt he chained his lover and bestowed her services to this realm—to the realm she had betrayed him for. He gifted the realm a sceptre called Aurora's *Virga* or the *Octa Virga*. A divine relic that imprisoned her within. When great evil or danger was to invade or erupt amongst us, we were to summon and use her to our will in defending Numengarth," he explained as he circled about the room, and I was now beyond confused.

Octa Virga? Guardian Aurora of the White Flame? This story had never been in any of the sacred books I have read, or any history books. Was this his plan of torturing me, reading me tales till I begged for mercy? It was working until my tired brain began scattering around every piece of information available and my eyes widened in realisation. What the Solaryans had told me, the winged woman at the centre of the temple and the object that had been too difficult to see—she had been her and the object her sceptre. The drawings around it flashed uncontrollably in front of me, the weapons and the maps.

She who defied, she who betrayed, she who pays. Eight chains to the land, eight chains from the skies. Eight souls part her living. Eight souls guarded to keep her from living.

Pieces. He was looking for the pieces of the sceptre. The divine weapon was the sceptre. The tracking stone halos Moriko had found, they were they used to track them? That meant the soldiers in Myrdur were after the Olympian piece? Adriata, the one kingdom they had no access to. The agreement. Everything connected too well—too terrifyingly well.

"Such power. To have the guardian for one man to yield was far more dangerous than any other danger that was already roaming our realms," he continued, running a hand over his pale beard. "Rulers grew hungry for its power, as did many others who saw this opportunity as useful against their contenders. Five hundred years ago, King Kegan of Seraphim took the sceptre and invoked the guardian to open the heavens for him. He lost control of the guardian and she ended up wiping out Seraphim and almost destroying the whole of our continent. Because of this, the sceptre broke into fragments, divided amongst kingdoms for safekeeping. If the threat gods feared came, they would all gather in unison against it and use the *Octa Virga*. Then many knew, now not even rulers have the slightest idea what lies dormant in their lands—the most powerful creature that could roam our realm."

This was not all tales after all. The fire guardian who had destroyed Seraphim had never been named and from what he had said, Aurora was Guardian of the White Flame, easily mistaken as one from the lands of Adan. Had history been written wrong or to conceal her?

"Soon all that power will be ours to wield. With the sceptre, the guardian will be willed to do our bidding, erase all life amongst other kingdoms. Isjord will expand beyond the continent, beyond the blessed lands and all of it will be ours," he finally unravelled all that had been sowing all around me.

"What makes you think you won't end up like Seraphim, destroyed along with the continent you intend to take?"

He scoffed all distaste. "Kegan was a drunk. A worthless king with ambition taller than his height. The only thing good that came from his head was to use the guardian for his purposes, but even that failed. Your father is mighty, girl. You haven't seen a fraction of what he is capable of. I saw him wipe grand Olympia within a night. He is a god and he will soon reach them, too."

Solarya had known my father's intentions, that is why they had interrupted the trade, that was why they were looking around the temples, they were searching for the other piece. Melanthe, she had sealed the Solaryan chest with her seal, the sceptre piece must have been in it, she was in this as well. Had it been why father had invoked her death?

"How many do you have?" I asked, praying to gods and heavens once again to let it not be true, for all this to be a lie. I prayed that they had not allowed the worst creature in the whole realm to get access to even a fragment of it.

"We have now you to thank for the third one, my soldiers have already infiltrated their city searching their damned lands and castle for it, as well as a whole army waiting for my signal to attack their lands. They were once a strong kingdom, but now easy prey. Your father has promised me their lands for me to rule. I plan to be a very generous king."

My features drew wide at his revelation. "If you attack them, you will make it very difficult to do the whole wiping out plan without war. The rest of the kingdoms will not stand by and watch Isjord raid their neighbouring kingdom as if their own," I stated. How big my father's plans had been, how I had underestimated him.

"No, they might not. But again to our advantage we have you."

"What?"

He tilted his head all disparage. "Isjord cannot stand by while their princess were to be killed by the Adriatians minutes after getting married, can we now?"

Opening the iron prison door, he pulled me to my feet.

They had told everyone I was dead to rage war against Adriata. Very smart. So this was their plan all along, my death. But I had two of theirs in my hands, if my uncle was not interested, my father would be.

"Reuben and Fren's antidote is Alaric, isn't it?" he asked, and my eyes widened in horror, he knew. He clicked his tongue at me. "That Olympian scum knew just about everyone so it was not that hard to guess, sweet niece, and judging from your reaction, I have guessed correctly as well. Worry not, he will follow right behind you to the Otherworld, my men are already looking for him in Fernfoss."

I could not help but laugh. The sound rolled over the stone wall, almost drowning out the sound of the sea. "My, my, who will inherit Isjord now? Soon they will both be very dead."

He sneered and grabbed my arm tightly. "Your little games do not work with me."

No, dear uncle, believe me, this was no game. The half breeds were dead by my decree.

He unsheathed a dagger and in a flashing moment, my side pierced and throbbed a dull pain. The man who had tried to kill me twelve years ago had now succeeded, he had won, and I had let him win.

I looked down between us at the dagger stabbing my flesh inches deep. My knees gave out and I fell to the floor, blood streaming rapidly out of me and all over my white dress, dripping slowly to the floor. I'd make such a ghastly spirit with this outfit. Gods, don't let this be my Otherworld look.

He dragged me up once more and stood me before the missing wall. Below us, white foamed waves crashed violently under the cliff where the tower was sitting. Death was waiting for me all force.

"Any last words?" he sneered in my ear.

"Signe oşh toc etter sben ys zguh," I whispered, and pulled back with a smile that made him blanche.

His face wrinkled from a scowl. "What did you just say?"

His grip loosened and I stepped back to the edge of the cliff. Bowing, I flashed him a wide grin and said, "Thank you for your cooperation, dear uncle. You're an impeccable story teller, loved the attention to detail."

His expression widened, following me intently as I pushed myself off the cliff until my body broke the cold lucid barrier of water.

The seas and skies boiled above and below as the cold waters surrounded and devoured me. A mist of crimson gathered around my body like roses in bloom. A rose scented with death.

It felt peaceful, death felt too peaceful for my liking. Maybe I was the one who didn't want death. I passed it, ignored it and then made fun of it for not taking me, for not being able to take me. It was chaos I craved, never peace.

The world went white, and my lungs filled no longer with air, my sight no longer with light, my senses no longer with life.

One hundred fifty.

44

MOON AND DARKNESS

KILIAN

SHE RAN AWAY FROM me. I hurt her and she ran away from me. She ran away from me before I could tell her of a promise and a lie. A truth and a forgotten one. I'd gone to see her, to figure her out and find back the girl I'd met long before all tangled to a mess. I'd prepared to take all the blame. I'd prepared for her to hate me. I'd thought hating her would make it easy for me to face that end, but how could I hate her? I tried. I tried so hard. I tried to shut my faults and my people's faults and blame her, then guilt her with so much wrong. I'd tried all the wrong to make right. How I was so selfish?

We looked everywhere and could not find her anywhere, as if she'd evaporated from the face of the realm. Castle grounds were all cleared for searching, the whole city dispersed with soldiers looking for her there. My fear grew, my concentration already faltered from worry. Had my people gotten hold of her, had they wanted to kill her again after all? No, that would not happen, I would never allow it.

Caiden broke into the meeting chamber and charged furiously toward me, his fist landing heavily on my stomach. "If anything has happened to her, to gods and blessed heavens I swear, you damned idiot, I will kill you if it is the last thing I do," he shouted, and all my guards tensed before I waved them down to retreat.

If anything has happened to her there would be nothing for him to kill.

Mal stood between us. "Nothing has or will happen to her, and be aware, we might be friends but he is a king. How about you try and stay alive to actually look for her?"

Caiden madly laughed. "Friends? I should have killed you both when I had the chance. It is not like her to hesitate, you know. No matter what you thought you had with her, she never would betray her family. You have not the slightest idea why you were spared," he spat before turning to leave.

He halted and turned to his quiet friend resting between shadows of worry. "You knew, didn't you?" She did not answer and that was enough truth for him. "I will not stop her this time, neither will I get between you two to mend this...what you call a friendship."

She laced her fingers, dropping her head in surrender and plainly lied to her friend, "She would have killed him if she knew before the arrangement got sealed."

He only scoffed and shook his head, almost as if he'd read through her lie.

"That day, before we left the Islines, you were about to tell her, weren't you?" Nia asked, throwing a lost stare at the ground.

"Nia, I had not meant for this to happen, to hurt her. You knew who I was and you didn't tell her because you also knew...that I love her," I said, feeling air tighten in my lungs at every word.

"I stopped you."

"Why?"

"Because I thought I knew Snow better than anyone. Because I thought she would back down and know your truth, the one you had written in those letters. But she didn't. She didn't love you the same as you love her or read those letters or consider that you love her or consider your truth, and I was wrong again."

There was the truth, the one I didn't wish to hear either. "Had she received them? Had she read them?"

Nia shook her head. "The consort had kept them after they'd been delivered. They were not even opened."

"You...read them?"

"Yes, you know now why I didn't say anything. But after this, I wish I had. I underestimated her feelings again. I was wrong and now my only wish is I had not let her this far so as to get more hurt from you."

Hope seeped away from me as I said, "I will let her go, for her to stop hurting, I will let her go. Just let her be well."

"You are an idiot, Kilian Henrik Castemont, a damned idiot," she added before fading out.

A day and a half later, we had searched Adriata inch by inch with no use. Now it felt like the erupting pain of my head and heart would finally do its bidding and take me. Never—I would never forgive myself if something had happened to her. I was now allowing myself to think that she might be truly hurt. Gathering my face in my hands, I tried to push the maddening thoughts away, far away. She was Snow, nothing could contain her enough to hurt her, not anymore at least. Her strength and skills outdid many, she would have never allowed to be subdued and become someone's prey, prisoner or victim.

"She has left with her own devices," my aunt countered. "This is an issue Silas will have to solve, the agreement will hold, we will hold onto it for Adriata. You married and she is queen, the agreement is fulfilled."

"Will we?" Stregor called. "The *Ybris* could still follow her father's plans, maybe there was something to his plans, like Kilian warned."

I studied the smug satisfaction in his features and then the rest of the room. Few were dizzy with panic, then some were confused, a couple distraught and then him...satisfied. In Arynth, Larg had sent word that his spies had caught a glimpse of Stregor speaking with several priests that were to be selected for our ceremony. He'd laced and bribed them to forge paperwork that would ultimately kill Snow when she'd signed and not been able to fulfil her bargain. I'd quietly chosen Atlas, changed guards for Driada and the wedding halls for my personal temple last minute and behind everyone's back. Stregor quietly lost, but now that I thought it better, had he?

I leaned back in my seat, seizing him. "Isn't it strange, Stregor, how your wishes come true? Right after the wedding at that."

He wore no offence, he was proud instead. "Are you accusing me of something, son?"

"Your Majesty to you, councillor, I am no son of yours."

His features flared as did his shadows, but he knew to subdue them before me in time. "If not by me, she would have gotten what she deserves."

Magic leaked out of me, clouds and gales of black death warped and enveloped the room, leaking and crawling around every limb of his. Darkness howled, it echoed the sound of storms, it craved light and spread over it, devouring till the whole room was left in gloom.

"You have touched—no, have you even breathed near her," I threatened, "I will destroy you to the root of your bloodline."

His eyes grew wide, sweat beading on his brow as tentacles of my magic surrounded and twirled around him. Darkness hissed at the touch of his skin and he let out a scream of anguish. Darkness burned, hotter than any flame. It burned all sense of light, all sense of life, it was death itself.

"Kilian, enough," my aunt called, standing from her seat.

I turned to her, my magic twirling around her next. "Haven't you become good at giving orders, head councillor. Sit down before I tear your soul out and then your heart."

She swallowed and took her seat, and I pulled my magic away from Stregor, the room still hovering with murk. "Answer me, Stregor, did you do it? Answer and I will bury you with your limbs still intact."

"I have not!" he shouted, rubbing the blackened skin the imprint of my magic had left there.

"Leave," I called, leaning back on my chair. "All of you." Not once had anything tempted me to the degree I'd had to rely on my magic to threaten my council.

One by one they stood, but Stregor halted before his feet met the doorstep. "This is the thing about evil, Henrik, it invites the pure, lures light and defiles nature. You were only a man, too, after all, and you as well fell for that trap."

Mal was right again, he was an odd one to speak sense of evil and just. "Tell me, Stregor, how many have you caught on that same trap yourself?"

"I am no evil."

"No, you are just a man, too, one led by it."

The meeting room echoed from the deafening silence, even my pulse had stilled since she went missing yesterday. Darkness blanketing around me, invisible hands of comfort attempted to gather me tightly. They had been my succour since I was a child, but now even they could not soothe the worry in my heart.

Driada laid a hand on my arm in comfort, but my body rejected it. "She is alright, son, you told me she is strong and skilled. I have faith and so should you."

Mal erupted in, panting and eyes widened in horror. I read so much in there, fear, shock, overwhelm and deep sadness.

No, nothing has happened to her, nothing. Despite trying to convince myself, I could no longer breathe or see, my whole body numb. "Please, Mal, do not—" I begged. Not being able to hold myself up, I collapsed to my knees. My world was robbed out of its light.

"They found her, the Isjordians. Dead on our shores," my brother said.

Two hot tears streamed down my numb face. She could not be dead, no. I refused to believe that. This could not be happening. God and heavens, do not let this be true, do not take the woman I love away from me, do not take her.

I felt Driada embrace me as I rocked myself in disbelief. She was gone. "Please, son," she cried out, holding me while she sobbed.

She couldn't be gone, no, no, she was not gone. It was all a lie, a cruel evil lie. "It is not true, she is not dead. I want to see her, this is all a lie," I shouted, trembling. I stood to march out of the corridors, to look for her. They could not lie to me like this, they could not take her away from me like this. My knees gave up and I fell to the floor again. Mal's words faded to nothing in the background as I stood once again. I will kill and burn all that lied to me, all that dared to deceive me like this. The last time I had seen Snow, I had hurt her. She had found out my lies, the same lies that had turned her to a creature of ice. She could not leave me. I still had the eternity to beg for her forgiveness, she would have to see me beg for my mistakes. I was going to give that to her. She had to be here, alive, she could not leave, not like this.

"Brother," Mal called, gripping my arm. "She is gone."

My chest sunk and sunk at his words and my head shook in so much disbelief. I felt my eyes well up and melt. "She is not. I will find her. I can find her," I protested, my voice breaking at the thought of my very words.

"Please, listen to me, please" Driada pleaded as I crumbled.

Tightening my fists, I hit the stone wall over and over and over uncontrollably, till blood gushed out, coating the wall and the ground crimson. My heart bled and crushed a thousand pieces and my soul began tearing. I felt my magic leak out, power that scourged souls. The corridor clouded black and then Driada screamed at the horror it spread.

Mal's hand rested on the back of my head and then the world went blank into darkness, opening back to the emptiness of reality. I felt hollow, empty.

The moment I scrambled to my feet, my fist met his jaw. "How dare you?" I said, as another one flew, painting his face red in my blood. "How dare you take it away?"

Driada stepped between us, she didn't need to, I had given up to the nothingness.

"I had to, I cannot let you drown yourself to breaking point. I need you, your people need you, you are still king." I let go of my brother before collapsing to the ground. He spat blood on the ground. "Isjordians are marching towards our lands," he revealed. "She had been marked by our people. They are taking this as treason."

Marked. Dead. Those words dragged claws through my heart. It could not be. "Let them, we might as well deserve it," I said, my voice empty as I dropped to the floor. My body had stopped shaking but my heart would never anymore, tears streamed down my face still despite the hollow vessel that I felt now.

"Kil, please. We all have lost her, not just you," he said, grabbing my shoulders. "But you are king, this is your duty, your kingdom to protect. We rot out the evil within later, now we fight for our lands and our blessings."

He was wrong, no one in this kingdom deserved my protection. My heart had died and all my strength had been taken from the pain I had felt before Mal took it away, but the sooner the Isjordians were gone, the sooner I could burn this city out of the fanatics that had killed half of my soul, that had let half of me dead.

When you learn of forced grief, tell me then what would you do.

You were right, my love. Terribly right.

Havoc and pure chaos circled and sounded all over Adriata as troops drew in lines toward the Highwall where Isjord had already begun breaching through. I had come to the temple where I'd last seen her, where I had hurt her again, where I'd wed her.

My head fogged, heart beating at a pace of wanting to stop and give up. Flashes after flashes of her laugh, voice and scent lingered all over, as if I ran a hand through the air I could feel her once again. Fingers grazed my lips where she lingered so tenderly before clutching my chest where she'd claimed its warmth. I'd died a half death. It beat not to live, only to keep me alive.

What mad god was feasting on this chaos, what mad heavens stood watch over her death? What mad gods planned these madly entangled twists of fate? How did I let her die?

My knees gave away and I fell on the ground. Pain, anger, love lingering, spinning and twisting around me till my eyes drowned once again. It would be less painful if I could tear my heart out than have it beat inside me one more minute without her here. My palms beat at my chest continuously, as if they could subdue the pain. Promise—I had made a promise to hurt those that had hurt her. I felt the need for retaliation, I felt what she had felt, I felt how she had brewed in this gnawing feeling for years and I broke, again.

"Laugh. Laugh, please. Laugh and tell me you're okay, that this is all a nightmare. Laugh and tell me all this was a game of yours. You're cruel, my love, so be cruel, please. Be cruel, not heartless." I hit my aching chest with a fist. "You are not there anymore, how does it still beat?"

I might have screamed or roared or cried, but whatever sound left my chest did not soothe my ache. Hot metal seared my insides.

I stared at the ring on my finger. I stared at another pain I'd given her. I stared at how I lost her. "In the next life, my heart, and all of the next ones I will find you and I will beg for forgiveness, as long as I get to see you again."

Barely hoisting my body to stand, I straightened, bidding goodbye to her presence when my eye caught over the dark ground at her bouquet from that day still standing there, wrapped in white. She walked to me holding it, my bride, my wife. The white memory of her sight fogged my eyes with tears and my breath with restraint.

I ran my finger over the delicate small flowers. Lilies—lily of the valley, the whole bouquet made of them. I stared at them for a long while. I stared at the strange flowers for longer than I should have. The smell of them was strong, perfumy and...familiar. Lifting to scent them, all sorts of memories lingered before me. My hand loosened unconsciously dropping them to the ground. The drop an echo of disbelief and confusion. I took a step back and then another as I remembered. Lilies, her perfume, the sweet light scent of flowers over her, she had always smelled of them. Her humming sounded around me and my eyes grew wide in realisation.

Little lambs with sunken hearts harvested the white flower with their smarts. Forbidden the taste of such delights,mother had warned countless times. Nimble as spirits and quick to almost no limits. The sap of the poisonous beauty a hundred deaths had as its duty. For that night the dark death bringer blight celebrated akin every other night. Unaware of the sweet sap that lingered their blight they feasted on the poisoned night. Death they swallowed with every bite while little white lambs laid fading as light.

She had hummed that song, 'Children of the forest' every night. Poison—a tale of blood payment, the ultimate tale of revenge. According to the tale, the children had survived the attack of western enemies, hid in the forests, and poisoned their beloved's killers with...lily of the valley.

The flowers that had grown in Sitara, Sidra and Lyra after each attack, they really were warnings.

Her words, she had never hidden them, and I'd known and not understood, my answers had been right in front of me all the time.

My hands fell over my head, dizzy and light from realisation. It had begun, her revenge had begun. How? Gods, how—how had she done it?

45

CHECK AND MATE

SNOWLIN

BIG BAD WOLF HIDING *behind the tree. Big bad wolf almost swallowed me. Little Snow small as a deer. Little Snow battled the fear.* The honey soft voice hummed around the hollow room.

"You know, my snowflake, this once you were brave, but danger does not find you the same way twice. The big bad wolf might have run away from you, but he will return and this time it will be prepared for whatever trick you did to him. The castle walls are to keep you safe, the forest is too large and dangerous for my little Snow," my mother had said, wrapping a bandage to my foot after having tripped in a tree branch running away.

"Mother, I am always brave. I want to be the big bad wolf, then they will have to run away from me," I had responded in a snarl, poorly imitating a feral cat at best and making her laugh. The sweetest melody to my ears, a sound so pure that made falling snow tremble and melt mid-air.

She had wished hard that I had become the white sheep that never stood out from the crowd, that I fit in as she had not, that I never let danger even approach me, let alone touch me. She'd become afraid of wanting to do anything more than survive. Living was asking for too much.

But my path had always been that of the big bad wolf after all, though never carved by myself. The daughter of a rose and a serpent, a mess made of venom, blood, thorns and sweet scents is not made for vanity as a rose is never made for plucking, though many wish for the taste of prickling pain.

My palm began cooling over the wound on my side, a thin coat of ice forming on top, sealing it in place and making the bleeding stop.

I marched up the enormous obsidian bridge alongside Memphis, drenched head to toe in seawater, wearing my torn wedding dress that had turned almost brown from blood and salt. Though I'd thought I'd make my return as a spirit, I was very much alive.

Thunder clapped loudly alongside, echoing around the terrifying enormous black castle rising between heavy rocks and mountains that fluttered in and out of sight from the heavy lightning striking my surroundings endlessly. A symphony of deafening silence and thunder mixed in the air. And I was its conductor. Blue flamed torches danced feverishly atop the pillars lining the bridge that directed to the dark giant towering among and between clouds. Soldiers scattered alongside it, all dressed in grey leather armour, hoods drawn over their heads and their faces concealed, solemnly still, a hand over their hilts, blending seamlessly between the grey mist of sky. We were high enough that the air tasted sweet and tangy with electricity.

A familiar tall figure approached in my direction, coming from inside the obsidian castle walls. Eyes darker than his surroundings, a grey beard adorning his stern rough and scarred face, his grey hair shaved on both sides and arranged in a bun on top of his head, exactly the vanity concerned man I had left him four moons ago.

You see, there are many great villains in everyone's story, but none is greater than the one these villains have created themself. If there is one thing I have learnt in my many years of torment from my physical and emotional demons, is you either fight, side with your nightmares or you become a nastier one.

Signe osh toc etter sben ys zguh. We will rise between sky and clouds.

I rose from worse.

Alaric fell to his knee and the guards behind followed in motion one after the other, echoing like dominoes. His scarred face twisted in a welcoming smile. "With Nubil's blessing, to Caelum heaven. Welcome back, my queen, how was your holiday in Isjord?" he asked playfully, studying the gnarly sight of me, somewhat expectant of it.

"With Nubil's blessing, might it welcome us. It went fabulous, Alaric, perfectly fabulous," I answered, giving him one of my satisfied grins.

Nightmares were everywhere around me, but I, Snowlin Edlynne Skygard, daughter of Serene Edlynne Skygard, heir and queen of Olympia, was the vilest of them all. I was no princess and I could be no queen for I was already one. One of the many faces of Khryn, the Goddess of Deceit, was the past, and I wore mine as she had. But my, wasn't she right. Indeed, one's older self is already the perfect lie—the mask of weakness as she had called it.

"Isjordians have always been poor at dressing, but what on five heavens of Nubil are you wearing?"

"It was rather nice," I said, smoothing the scarps of fabric that now resembled a dish cloth. "Lysander's daughter picked it for me."

"Penelope?" Alaric asked in bewilderment. "How is she?"

"On her way here."

He laughed. "A reunion. Thought you'd fall for your father's trap and only bring me his head. This is much better."

The thick warm static air of Olympia had been what I missed most, it sent my blood racing and dancing with such thrill, almost electric.

I did not retch and ache in that frozen wasteland for nothing, especially having to conceal so much of me. I got what I needed—answers—which my uncle had so generously handed me in mere minutes after I had spent months searching for them to no avail.

When he rode with us to Adriata I finally knew I had not spent my opportunity there for nothing, they were heading for something—something bigger than I had originally doubted. Nia had trailed him for weeks prior to secret meetings and gatherings. She had insisted he was indeed hiding something and somehow had convinced me to chase the danger. He had met general Moregan and the ex-Lord of Brogmere almost every day, and afterward, he'd seen Melanthe twice. Quite the interesting crew, right? The very same one that had spun my father's plans all together, the same one I had been doubting all separately without making connection. I had always regarded him as a useless game piece. It was not like me to underestimate people, but this time they almost caught me off guard.

The walls of the castle shimmered as the candle light hit their sleek surface, my hand softly grazing them, remembering what I had been missing for months—home. My home, my kingdom. Blue flame torches lit the grand corridors and massive obsidian chandeliers suspended heavy from the ceiling lit in candlelight. White gossamer drapes hung over the large arched windows, fluttering at the soft becalling wind of the mountains as the capital of Olympia, Taren, grew along the tall face of mountains, down the abyss and valleys between the rocky giants. My chest boosted in pride at seeing the city broiling alive in front of me.

The kingdom of Olympia stretched all along the Isliot peninsula, separated by a dozen of tribes. They lived amongst sea lines, forests, villages, mountains and every other crook of space along it. A secluded population that did not deal with their neighbouring kingdoms nor did they need to, they already had everything. Myrdur, the old city of Olympia, laid from the edge of Volant mountains to where Fernfoss village was built now, that was not nearly half of the Olympian population, but my father did not know that. No one from outside knew that. They only knew nothing survived, lived or breathed behind *zgahna*, the cursed mist of the Volant's.

The night of the attack, few of those residing in Myrdur had retreated secretly towards the deep caves and tunnels that ran hidden among the line of Volant mountains and escaped.

The mist was magic, protective magic left by my ancestors, the elder Skygards, veiling our presence. Veiling the tribes of Olympia while they lost the largest one, Myrdur—the one of my origin.

Whilst the whole continent learnt of their perishing, Olympia built from within, deep in the centre of the highest and toughest mountains of the Volant lines. My mother, their last living royal blood, married to the King of Isjord. With the help of Alaric and all tribe leaders of Olympia, she had managed to establish a new council from afar and formed the new kingdom from the foundations of the eldest city of our kind. New Olympia began to build where our ancestors had settled first, hidden deep between mountains, sky, clouds and mist.

After the Adriatian attack, when my father exiled me to live away from Isjord, Alaric had taken me to Olympia, trained and taught me for years. The day of my sixteenth birthday, the twelve tribe leaders had crowned me, the last remaining royal blooded Olympian, heir by birth and by right, their queen. Taking the position from Alaric who had acted as reagent for eighteen years by my mother's decree.

My father had failed to destroy Olympia as he had planned and thought. We had faced difficulties in the early years, but the kingdom was flourishing and the population beyond count, strength and power.

Not to put down all the hard work he had so viciously fought for, father had not failed completely just very badly. And the Adriatians had not been completely wrong after all to fear his plans of raising weapons of destruction. The one to ruin my father's plans, however, had never been Adriata. It was my mother, Eren, Thora and me.

"Notify queen Moriko of my father's plan to steal pieces of Aurora's sceptre from their lands and send our soldiers to help protect them if it comes to it."

As I had promised, my support was hers now, just as hers was mine. After our meeting, I had sent Alaric to Hanai, who had informed the queen of my true position. A risk I'd taken with too much faith in Moriko and one that had served me best.

He stood surprised at my words till he seemed to process what was going on. I explained in detail everything my uncle had mentioned and revealed about it, including my father's plans to use the guardian as he'd wished to use me. The sceptre of Aurora was never mentioned anywhere, from what my uncle had described it did not take much to realise why, yet my father had grabbed a whiff of it.

"He is getting his mass destruction weapon one way or another, isn't he?" he asked, lost in shock.

I sighed from the same realisation and took my gloves off to reveal the seal on my wrist standing at the bottom of eight other bargains I'd made with each lord and Renick Salazar to pledge their allegiance.

His eyes went wide and mouth parted open to speak, but words had frozen from him as he only murmured, "Myrdur?" His eyes traced the ancient language runes spelling out the name of the city that curved around my wrist like a bracelet.

I nodded. "My blood oath. Myrdur is mine, it will be Olympia once again, soon."

He frowned. "Your father will know you are alive the second he tries to enter and the land doesn't allow him."

"The land will allow him because I will allow him, until we longer need to hide that is."

He smiled again. "Myrdur will be Olympia. Myrdur will be Olympia again." It was just as unbelievable repeated out loud.

"How many of their ships have we salvaged?" I asked, making my way towards my room.

"Thirty-two, all stocked north in Drava in my father's port. Did he have doubts?"

"With their current situation with Solarya, none."

"When you said we would not have to build ships, I didn't think we would steal them. Witty, but concerning."

Our lands were rough and mountainous, it would have taken us months up to years to salvage sturdy wood, build and bring them down to the only suitable location for a port, and that was the furthest up north. Our sealines were high cliffs all over, brilliant in keeping unwanted company from embarking and discovering New Olympia, but impossible to dock our own fleet. To go to war, you needed a fleet. That first day in Grasmere, the brightest idea had hit me. Sturdiest and best timber in the continent the sailors had said, and my father had plenty to spare. No one would take a single doubt, hence all the charades with Solarya. While I'd stolen his ships I'd also taken Malena down, soon Grasmere, too.

"You taught me well, old man."

"Oh no, don't pin that on me," he said somewhat offended and I laughed.

"Call the tribe leaders to meet and ready soldiers for battle, we are heading to Adriata.

Nia and Cai have already been sent there," I said, beginning to strip the blood and sea water drenched dress.

After Memphis had dragged me out of the Adriatian waters, she had flown me here where I had met both Nia and Cai, drowned in mad worry, looking for me after I had gone missing in Adriata. After loosely explaining what had happened, I had asked them to fade to the battle Isjord was going to rage—to aid Kilian. The idiots had both given me some strange looks at the mention of his name, and with the strength of my life I had held my eyes from rolling back.

"Battle? I thought we would not obtain Adriata until after dealing with Silas?"

"My husband is being cornered by Isjord with the pretext of my death and intends to steal his lands. Those are soon to be mine. It is only fair I go and help, isn't it? Well, you know, not exactly help," I said playfully, giving him a smile.

He shook his head at my antics. "Will you not let me in on this plan either?"

"You blabber like an old wife, so no." The whole of Olympia from Volant to Drava had learnt of my plan to return to Isjord. They'd held a whole goodbye ceremony and people had even cried—I hated weeping people.

"I deserve to worry for my kid."

I sighed and threw him a glare. "If I have the council members shed a single tear over their worry for me at my meeting, I will have your bearded head on a skewer." I pointed to him in threat before retreating to my room, only to halt and half turn to him again. "Ah, call the Crafter to the meeting. We need to be quick. I want my king alive. He has particularly angered me and that piece of his sceptre needs to be away from my father's hands."

He gave me a confirming nod. "Shall I send word to our spies there to help out?"

"No, they still have to keep Adriata's battalions as far from each other as possible. I will win this one for them. The plan has changed again, but I still need them at their weakest when we go through there. It appears we have been successful all these months, they are already on the last leg considering what the two guards have told me. They were desperate enough to hold onto my father's agreement."

For almost two years I had begun manipulating Adriata into thinking of their failure. Teams of Zephyrs have been monitoring their skies, bringing heavy winds onto their shores, destroying ships, fishing nets and boats, bringing high tides and heavy storms, making it impossible to use their sea resources.

My team of spies led by my royal spy, Nia, have been directing the unblessed from Vrammethen onto Adriata through countless maps provided by us, handpicking trespassers of my favourite sort—thieves and criminals.

The winged Volantians, a tribe of humans blessed with white feathered wings resembling the guardians of Nubil's heavens, monitored the Sea of the Dark unnoticed, luring in thrice the amount of Golgotha's creatures onto their lands, poisoning the soil and scaring villages onto abandonment.

Nimbus Aura, cloud wielders, would send constant inappropriate conditions of wind, storms and rain to destroy their produce. They would cover the sun for so long, Adriatians had seen frost in their lands for the first time.

Sky was a mirror, but reflections hid more than one thought. The sky saw, the sky hid, the sky was always there. Between clouds and storms, wind and blue, I'd poisoned Adriata. It would be slow, that was how I had planned their end. First I would starve them of food, pride and belief, then I would kill them.

Adriata's blight of misfortune was nigh, I was nigh. And I had been patient enough.

I half entered the door to my room. "I have another agreement for them now and they won't be able to refuse. How can anyone refuse their queen?"

Pawn to the eighth rank.

The queening.

How one learns to like the colour grey

As told by fates

Urinthia Delcour had succeeded her sister, Valas. Eldmoor had finally chosen their new heir after the sudden passing of their previous Grand Maiden.

Urinthia was special, not only because she was one of the most powerful Summoners since after the accession of gods to their heavens, but because she was also a politician, one that intended to bring the secluded and closed lands of Eldmoor closer to the rest of the continent. Red Coven, the house of the Grand Maiden, had organised one of the largest gatherings in centuries. Kings, queens, rulers, princes and princesses, lords, merchants, scholars and everyone from all corners of Numengarth had gathered to celebrate her crowning.

The Prince of Night stared silently between the heavy celebrations. He wondered for how long his father would take to snap and make a show because of the Winter King's attendance. He wondered how long it would take his father to offend him, demonise his hybrid Aura children, how long it would take him to make threats of battle, how long it would take for the room to erupt in gales of night and shards of winter. Instead, he'd seen his father concentrate in conversation with Eren Krigborn, occasionally offer opinions and even lightly laugh at the young heir's jokes. His father and the one he'd demonised the most, the Winter Prince.

"I need the toilet, Kil," Malik grumbled, pulling on his jacket repeatedly as he'd done for the past quarter of an hour.

He extended a hand to his younger brother and broke across the celebrating crowd. "I am not your maid, Mal, you are old enough to go to the toilet yourself," Kilian scolded as he waited for his brother to finish his business.

The younger brother frowned. "My blessing is surfacing, back home is fine, but every time a Crafter approaches me I get scared."

Scared. His father should never hear Mal utter those words. He sighed and attempted to rub the intensity of his headache with a temple rub. "I will keep you out of the room, let us go."

For the past hour he'd sat outside the Red Coven gardens watching his brother patter around, catching and bothering a few flower folk and poke a grand enchanted oak with a stick.

"I have a sister the same age, but she'd rather slice the oak for wood than play with it," a young man's voice called, approaching the bench he sat on.

The Winter Prince neared, sitting beside him, his eyes still on the younger brother.

"Should we trade? My father would love your sister," Kilian offered and they both laughed away.

"Eren Jonah Krigborn," he said, extending a hand.

The Night Prince considered the greet, scorned the desire to introduce himself back and measured the knowledge he had on the hybrid Aura before shaking his hand. "Kilian Henrik Castemont." Should he be more afraid or repulsed? Yet he wasn't. If not, he'd built a strand of respect for the boy who'd impressed his father enough to keep him quiet for most of the night.

"*Anima accissor*," Kilian spoke, surveying the blade attached to Eren's hip. *Soul Killer.*

Eren's eyes shot wide. "You know?"

Kilian nodded. "The ring of magic around it reminds me of my own. I'm an Obscur, my magic scours the soul, not the physical, and so does that sword. We are alike in a sense." *Soul killers.*

"It was forged for an Elding," Eren revealed. "It is supposed to not melt if it is struck by lightning."

Kilian considered how he should feel afraid and take the Winter Prince's words sourly, but he didn't. He was purely curious and enchanted by the silver beauty.

He extended a hand. "Could I?

Eren gave him a smile and unsheathed the elegant blade full with a ring of magic, almost syncing to his own.

The Prince of Night ran his fingers on the top of the elegant blade, over the old Ysolt engraving at the bottom of the hilt that made no sense. "Lin?" he asked, having read the strange name.

Eren nodded. "After my sister."

"Your sister?" he asked almost in surprise, never having heard someone name a sword after one. Most he'd heard were of ancient dragons, name of a father and if one dared perhaps a guardian of heavens, gods were too far, but never a sister.

"Snowlin Edlynne Krigborn, the one other blade mightier than this one."

As being summoned by her brother's subtle praises, screams and laughter travelled along the Grand Maiden's mansion back garden. Raven hair floated almost down to her back, eyes curved onto half-moon smiles matching her lips as she ran around, behind and almost above trees, chased by a black wolf cub. She rolled on the mud, the odd animal licking her scrunched face while she giggled surrendered under.

"Lin," Eren called, taking a step to stand.

She startled a little, the smile fading and revealing honey eyes. "Lands of Caelum," she said, blinking surprised. "What are you doing here, you should be with mother."

She stood and straightened her almost destroyed dress. "And what are you doing here, you should be with father, feather tickling some emissaries ball—"

"Lin!" he interrupted, looking almost embarrassed toward the Night Prince who withheld a smile at the insolence the little princess had almost spoken.

She studied her brother and then smirked. "Oh, I see now."

"See what?" Eren said, sitting back down.

"Finding a little consort to sit next to your throne," she teased.

Kilian coughed his drink, almost choking on it and turned to stare wide eyed at the snarky girl.

"Forgot, you're into blondes," she retorted quickly, snatching her brother's sword from the Night Prince's hands. The blade was almost lightweight on her tiny hands as she manoeuvred it around a few times before handing it back to him. "Shame, truly, you're handsome."

Her shamelessness didn't strike him as much as did her sense of humour for such a young age. "Thank you," he said, reaching for it.

"For the compliment or the sword?" she asked, pulling it back from his reach.

He assessed the ready to go tease her eyes betrayed, so he settled to tell the truth. "Both."

She handed it back to him. "Then you are most welcome...uhm?"

"Kil," he introduced.

She struck still, staring at him for a long, long moment, and he almost thought she'd stopped breathing before she spoke again, "You have the greyest of eyes."

He raised a brow. "Do I owe you a *thank you*, little miss, or a how so?"

She frowned. "Little miss?"

"You're not a big miss."

"A thank you," she said, chin up with authority, almost making him smile again. "They are a great pair of eyes."

"Well, thank you, again," he bowed just slightly.

"Go inside," warned Eren.

She retreated to head back inside, but halted and half-turned to him again. "If you do not grow yellow to please my brother, wait till I am old enough to fancy a brunet."

He raised a brow again. He realised she didn't know who he was. What those words meant. She'd not realised that he took much to heart. She didn't realise that the answer to his next question was more than a promise, it was a brand. "Is it an order?"

"Would you obey if it better was?"

No, he wouldn't. He was heir of Adriata, soon to be king and she was what his kind hated most, what they prayed against and what they wished to watch burn. "Yes."

"Then it's an order."

He noted her irises molten with golden lava, the strength behind her stare. "Then I will obey it."

And he would obey it, he'd look for her.

And he'd keep that promise.

ACKNOWLEDGMENTS

First, to my readers who took the leap of faith and purchased and read this book, thank you. It means more than a lot to someone who has been undermined and made unworthy most of her life to be appreciated in this form, I am forever grateful.

Secondly, I'd like to thank myself for not letting the crimpling fear of never being good enough, to hinder finishing this book.

Thank you Lizzy, my sister, who has been there every single step of the way, from first drafts, to tears, to complaints, to midnight monologues why my book sucks and how shitty of a writer I was, to the end editing hours you've put out to help me polish this book. Thank you, forever and always for being the bests of friends.

Thank you Aneta, my forever friend and perhaps most avid supporter and girl boss, who inflicted me confidence in moments when I've felt my lowest. I cannot wait to have sushi and bitter candy from that shop in Cambridge, with you again.

Thank you, Fantastical ink, for making the cover making process the most exciting part about writing this book, I've often stared at your work just to inspire myself.

Thank you, mum, dad and my brother, Levi, for not only encouragement but the financial support to complete this very expensive project.

And a special thanks goes to those who inspired my villains in these stories that I write and created my own real-life villain story line. Relatives and bullies, might you have the same burning end.

About Author

Wendy Heiss is an indie author debuting with a new adult fantasy trilogy. Winter Gods & Serpents is the first book in The Auran Chronicles, releasing autumn 2021. She has graduated with honours in Forensics Science in the United Kingdom, but literature has been one of her passions since she could manage to read and write. Despite being severely tempted to ride the Agatha Christie route to crime novels, she chose to follow the Tolkien path to fantasy. She forwent fingerprint powder for ball pen ink, inevitably forgoing her parents' hope for a good life and becoming what they always feared...a figuratively starving artist.

Any whom and how, she likes cats, coffee, particularly that cr*p from instant sachets. Claims to despise mafia romance from the pits of her gall bladder but will probably end up writing one herself to try and outwrite the greatest line in history: Are you alright baby girl.

Also, fried sweet potatoes, she can definitely eat some of those without claiming to be allergic to yet another vegetable. On that last note before straying too far from a simple bio, please read her book and more to come.

If you have enjoyed the read, please consider leaving a review on Amazon and Goodreads.

ALSO BY

The Auran Chronicles

Winter Gods & Serpents
Spring Guardians & Songbirds
Season Warriors & Wolves
Autumn Queens & Shadows (October 2023)
Summer Heirs & Fire (Early 2024)

Daughters of Chaos

City of Alabaster (late 2023)

Blue Fairytales

At the end there was you
The last war we ever fought (October 2023)

Dictionary

Ybris-Hybrid Aura, a child of two different Auras.

Eudemon-Creatures of Golgotha, god of demons. They rest in sea of the dark after their realm, Dissiri, fell.

Mid world-A spirit pane, between the living and the heavens. Crowded by trapped, revengeful or fearful souls.

Astrum liber-Holy book of Adriata, believers and followers of goddess Henah.

Caelus liber-Holy book of all gods. A dictate of laws, rules and principles.

Eirlys book-Holy book of Isjord, believers and followers of god Krig.

Hodr-Heaven of god Krig.

Cynth-Heaven of Henah, the moon.

Caligo-Heaven of Celesteel, the other world, realm of the dead and of hells.

Hemera-Heaven of goddess Cyra, the sun.

Mankai-Heaven of goddess Plantae.

Empyrea-Heaven of Adan.

Caelum-Heaven of Nubil

Neith-Heaven of Dyurin

Kemeri-Language of Hanai

Darsan-Language of Adriata

Dahaara- Steel tongued

Borsich-Language of Eldmoor

Calgnan-Language of Olympia

Zgahna-Calgnan for magic mist, sense beyond sense between magic and human awareness.

Alaar-Darsan for magic mist

Tahuma-Language of Solarya

Old Ysolt-Language of Isjord, no longer spoken in mainland winter kingdom. Only used by Isline Krigborn's.

Karndu-Language of Seraphim

Laoghrikrease-Language of the unblessed, spoken main land Vrammethen and Islands of Comnhall

Anima Accisor-Soul Killer